C450774635

KT-579-892

Born in Preston, Patricia Fawcett has lived in various parts of the North including the Lake District. She is married with three grown-up children and runs a creative writing group as well as writing full time.

FAMILY SECRETS

It is Christmas 1988. Meeting her son's girlfriend for the first time, Josie is shocked to discover that Alice is the daughter of Jack Sazzoni. She and Jack once had a fling but she married Ray instead. She has never forgotten Jack and she dreads meeting him once again. After so many years, will they still feel the same? Jack's wife Valerie is also apprehensive about the meeting, uncomfortably aware that Jack married her on the rebound. As Easter approaches, Josie and Ray are invited to the Sazzonis' house — now it is time for family secrets to be revealed.

Books by Patricia Fawcett
Published by The House of Ulverscroft:

SET TO MUSIC
THE ABSENT CHILD
EIGHT DAYS AT THE NEW GRAND
OLIVIA'S GARDEN
THE CUCKOO'S NEST
RETURN TO ROSEMOUNT
EMILY'S WEDDING

PATRICIA FAWCETT

---◆---

FAMILY
SECRETS

Complete and Unabridged

ULVERSCROFT
Leicester

First published in Great Britain in 2007 by
Robert Hale Limited
London

The moral right of the author has been asserted

British Library CIP Data

Fawcett, Patricia
    Family secrets.—Large print ed.—
    Ulverscroft large print series: fiction
    1. First loves—Fiction 2. Family secrets—Fiction
    3. Large type books
    I. Title
    823.9'2 [F]

    ISBN 978–1–84782–057–0

C450774635

Published by
F. A. Thorpe (Publishing)
Anstey, Leicestershire
Set by Words & Graphics Ltd.
Anstey, Leicestershire
Printed and bound in Great Britain by
T. J. International Ltd., Padstow, Cornwall

This book is printed on acid-free paper

*To Jo, in Argentina
with special thanks to
Natasha and Emma for their help*

1

Josie Bailey stuffed the bumper pack of cheap wrapping paper down the side of her supermarket trolley and headed determinedly for the checkout, closely avoiding running down a woman, who was dithering in the wine aisle. Honestly, she thought, as she smiled a brief apology, get your act together. Christmas Eve, with the shop closing shortly, was no time for dithering.

She had attacked this last minute shopping with the precision of a general working out a battle strategy. Providing the powers that be at the supermarket hadn't opted for a complete shift round of stock, which they were irritatingly apt to do from time to time, she was on target this evening for a relatively smooth shop. Not only had she come armed with a list, she had come with a list broken down into aisles. Super efficient, she reckoned, with not one single extra item added, although she had nearly succumbed to the temptation of a chocolate hazelnut gateau.

Impulse buys were off limits tonight.

Josie was working to a strict time schedule. She was allowing herself a further twenty minutes to get out of there and home, otherwise her carefully planned itinerary would be knocked for six. She was very aware that she was not of the natural-talent school of cooking and had to work hard at it to achieve something approaching edible, let alone delicious. She couldn't go wrong with the Christmas dinner this year, not if she followed the timing countdown in her woman's magazine. The only snag was she would have to wake up at seven o'clock in the morning if it was to work. Thirty minutes for this, five for that, and woe betide him if Ray cocked it up. Tonight, she still had the trifle to finish off — Ray was such a baby about a home-made sherry trifle — and there were a couple of presents left to wrap, plus some emergency ones, just in case a neighbour surprised her at the very last minute.

She scanned the checkouts, making a quick and probably foolish decision, weaving her trolley into position at the end of the smallest queue and letting out a huge relieved sigh. The woman in front, mistaking the reason for it, turned and gave her a sympathetic glance.

'Terrible, wasn't it? That thing in Scotland,' she said with an excited gleam in her eye and Josie knew instantly what she was talking about. 'It doesn't bear thinking about. Just before Christmas too. I can't get it out of my head, can you?'

Josie nodded, upset to be reminded of it.

'You don't get on a plane, do you, and expect it to be blown sky high? Nor do you expect a plane to explode right over your house.'

'No, you don't,' Josie said, seeing again the wreckage of that Pan-Am jumbo jet blown apart over Lockerbie. It was one of those news items, like the Kennedy assassination, that stop you dead in your tracks. She and Ray had visited Lockerbie once and she had loved it, wandering round the little streets, enjoying the peace and quiet, the pleasant Scottish accents, the welcoming smiles. Just imagine, there you are wrapping presents, decorating the tree, doing all sorts of normal family things and then an awful noise in the sky and wham. It had hit her hard, bringing tears to her eyes, which was daft seeing that she did not know any of the victims, not personally. It was seeing all those scattered suitcases, coats, Christmas presents and even the seats from the plane just lying there that had done it. People had set off with a purpose, such hopes, so excited to be going home for Christmas or just visiting a new place for the first time. She could see them on the plane, talking, laughing together. She hated things like this. Whenever there was a tragedy of these proportions, she could not disentangle herself from it. She always took it to heart, put herself in the position of the victims and she should know by now that it did no good. Ray had given her a swift cuddle, told her to buck up; that there was nothing they could do and that the victims both in the air and on the ground wouldn't have known what had hit them.

Maybe not.

Josie had just started to put it out of her mind or try to and this damned woman had raked it all up again.

'Mad, isn't it?' the woman carried on, Lockerbie gone from *her* mind. 'All this panic buying. They open again on Tuesday, wouldn't you know? There's no need to get paranoid, is there? Nobody's going to starve. Anybody would think we were in for a six month siege.'

As her trolley was also loaded to kingdom come, that seemed a bit rich but Josie nodded in agreement, in no mood for a chat as she checked her list for the very last time.

Above their heads, a new tune jingled from the loudspeakers and Josie frowned, feeling like killing whoever it was who was in charge of the medley of grotesque seasonal music that had been blaring out since sometime in late October. Corporate policy, she had been told when she complained, and the staff did not like it either but there was nothing they could do.

'I wouldn't mind if it was something religious,' Josie had told the girl who was standing in for the manager, who, it seemed, did not have the guts to face an irate customer. 'Carols or something.'

'We do have carols,' the girl had said, cold-eyed, the-customer-is-always-right philosophy obviously passing her by. ' 'Winter Wonderland', 'Little Donkey'. You can't have been in then.'

'They are not carols.'

'They are.' She was a tough one, standing there with her arms crossed. 'Anyway, nobody else has complained,' she finished with a sniff.

Josie had given up at that point, worried for a second that she was turning into her own mother, who had over the years honed grumbling about anything and everything to a fine art.

Keeping busy by rearranging the items in her trolley, Josie supposed she could have made it easier on herself by taking up Ray's lukewarm offer of help, but she was not letting him anywhere near her list. She was totally focused when it came to lists and he meandered. He would end up buying kids'

5

cereals and tins of baked beans and sausages, things she absolutely did not need or want.

It did not feel like Christmas Eve. She had been awake at seven as usual even though she had the day off and, strictly speaking, could have allowed herself an extra half-hour in bed. It was mystifying why she had to drag herself out any other day and today she had been raring to go as soon as she opened her eyes. She had always loved Christmas, even the lead up to it, if she was honest, and the excitement had been childishly getting to her. The office party had been got through without Kenny Balfour trapping her underneath the mistletoe, and at last she had felt she could allow herself to dream of the wonderful day itself.

After that initial euphoria, it had all gone downhill. Unwisely, she had allowed her hairdresser to coax her into trying both a new colour *and* a new cut. Ray would go spare when he saw it. It was very short, razored, and she had caught a glimpse of herself by the frozen foods counter. It had taken a moment to cotton on to the fact that the woman with the reddish unruly mop on her head was her.

Josie touched her hair self-consciously, willing it to calm itself down a fraction, peering ahead at the same time to check how things were progressing. Oh for heaven's sake, somebody was querying the bill and mutinous grumbles were creeping up the queue. There was no time for this, why didn't they just pay it and sort it out later? This checkout looked like a bad choice, the girl predictably the slowest on the line. Wearing a tinsel halo, with silver wings pinned on to her overall, looking about as angelic as a stripper, she yawned hugely a while later as, having got rid of the troublesome customer, she embarked on the next one. Her name tag declared her to be Charlene, which said it all really.

'Christmas does my head in,' said the woman ahead of her as she shuffled uncomfortably and managed a thin tired smile. Josie had her pegged in an instant. Poor soul. No clothes sense. She was kitted out in a lime-green shell suit in a crinkly material, which did absolutely nothing for her and was so loose that she could have been anything from a size ten to a sixteen. Maybe that was the idea. She had a friendly smile though. 'Have you got people coming?' she asked.

Goodness me, she was not easily put off. 'Just my son and his girlfriend and my sister,' Josie heard herself saying, confident that at least *she* looked her best in a pale blue swing coat.

Owing to yet another dispute at the till, she might be here some time and there was every chance of a lifelong friendship developing between her and the woman in front.

'Have you people coming?' she asked, throwing the question back at her and wondering if she had enough toilet rolls. She had forgotten to check . . .

She listened politely as the woman rattled on, giving a potted family history and becoming so animated as a result that she had to be reminded when her turn came to stop the prattling and start offloading her trolley.

2

Josie lived in the Riverside district of Felston, one of the districts that the town council would prefer not to exist, as the moody residents there caused more trouble than any two of the other districts combined. She lived now in a street about three away from the house she was born in, the one she frequently visited still because her big sister Margaret lived there and, aside from double glazing and fitted kitchens, things had not changed so much in forty odd years.

The council acted as if Riverside really let the side down, although Josie thought they exaggerated the problems and that actually things were improving. However, she had to acknowledge that, if Felston had a Monopoly board then their street, Crook Terrace, would be the equivalent of Old Kent Road, rock-bottom value and the cheapest rents. The houses in their street were generally well looked after and they had got rid of the only bad family recently, a family who hadn't given a pig's snout about the house and garden: four snotty-nosed kids and a mangy dog, and it was good riddance when they'd upped tracks. Crook Terrace sat bang up against the football ground and Saturdays and opposing supporters were something else. When Felston Rovers scored, the house shook with the cheers.

One Sunday morning, Josie had drawn the curtains back and seen what looked like a body lying under the hedge in the front garden. She had sent Ray down to investigate and it had turned out to be a lad from Manchester who had spent the night there, his pals having deserted him. It had been a warm night but, if the lad had had a bit more gumption, he could have been more comfortable in their garden shed, which they never bothered to lock for all it had in it was a lawnmower that had seen better days. They had a bigger than average corner plot but the state of their garden sometimes made her spit with annoyance and she would send Ray out with a spade and a wheelbarrow in the hope that he would suddenly develop an enthusiasm for it. Some hope. He would be out there all afternoon, supplied with endless cups of tea but he did the minimum, leaning on his spade chatting over the fence as often as not. As she was no great shakes in the gardening stakes either, it was no surprise that they struggled.

That Sunday morning, she had made that

poor lad a cup of coffee and a bacon sandwich before sending him on his way with a ten pound note stuffed in his pocket because he didn't look as if he had two pennies to rub together and was barely streetwise, so she worried how he would get home. She had tried to slip him the note secretly, but Ray had spotted her and afterwards he had gone daft, telling her that the lad had her number, a soft touch if ever there was. Never mind. He'd had such beautiful blue eyes, had been about sixteen, somebody's son, and he had touched her heart, reminding her of Matthew when he was that age. Matthew, their boy, had remained a sweet innocent for almost too long but then he was like his dad, a bit lost where the opposite sex was concerned with absolutely no talent for sweet-talk.

Anyway, Riverside was definitely on the up with new people moving in, doing up the houses and moving on, and as soon as the council twigged that, they would be increasing the rates, so it was perhaps as well they were behind the times. Unbeknownst to Ray, she had got the particulars of one of the last remaining flats in an exclusive development by the old docks. If she got the job she was up for, then she was determined they would move, and one of those new flats with no garden to sigh about would be just up their street. They were beautiful and, for what they were, a bargain, but Ray would take some persuading. Her sister Margaret wouldn't mind at all, in fact Margaret would shoo her on her way, happy so long as she was within easy travelling distance, but Ray wouldn't think he was up to it, living in a place like that, not with the sort of people who had snapped them up, executives and all, people with briefcases and posh cars. Ray had no confidence, that was his trouble and she was getting a bit sick of trying to boost it. She'd spent years trying to get him to take one more step up the ladder, but he was ground down in his belief that it was far better if you accepted who you were and didn't try to get too big for your boots.

Just like her mum.

What a load of twaddle. It was Felston Town Council who was getting too big for its boots these days. It was trying, heaven forbid, to be trendy. Moving on. The description 'northern industrial town' made the council shudder with all that it implied and they had appointed a PR man from down south who knew nothing about the town, found the means of giving him a huge salary, and briefed him to drag the town forward as the nineties approached, discarding unpalatable cargo, such as its long industrial heritage, along the way. It drove Josie mad that they tried to sweep all that had gone before under the brand new red carpet at the town hall. Working as she did in the treasurer's office up on the second floor, she knew precisely how much that carpet had cost and it wasn't some off-cut from Felston Carpets Centre either. She knew all about that outfit, too, as Ray had been on their books as a carpet fitter for years.

Miraculously, the magnificent nineteenth-century town hall with its awkward interior still remained, despite a plot to blow it up during the demolition crazy days of the sixties. In fact, to give the council credit, it had been done up recently, been given a face-lift, years of pigeon droppings removed and the stone cleaned. Notwithstanding the rejuvenation of the town hall, the council seemed to have more money than sense and she should know. The town centre had been modernized, paved, with sickly-looking saplings dotted here and there, the attempt at pedestrianization coming to naught, as people still carefully walked either side along what had once been the pavements.

A couple of controversial sculptures were now lodged in the market square, their commissioning and cost to the ratepayer still causing rumbles and grumbles in the letters page of the *Felston Gazette*. Josie had very nearly written a letter herself because, although she seemed in a minority, she liked the damned things. When it came to art, people round here were so provincial. She decided not to pen the letter because she thought her boss might object to her getting involved in a public slanging match and Ray said he didn't want her showing them up. Along with the bulk of Felstonians, he couldn't understand the concept anyway. What the hell were they supposed to be?

'They don't have to be anything,' she had told him, trying to curb her impatience. 'Art can get away with not being anything.'

'What are you talking about?' He had put on his puzzled daft look and, knowing it was hopeless, she had given up at that point. It was true the statues only vaguely resembled people but Ray thought that, if that was the case, then if you looked closely, it didn't look as if they were up to any good.

'It's art, for heaven's sake, Ray,' she had repeated, not knowing whether to laugh or cry at his indignation. 'Not pornography.'

Arriving at the trolley porch, Josie saw, without surprise, that it had started to rain. Well, that figured because it had been on the verge of it all day. It was sleet at that and, pulling up the hood of her coat, she hurried as best she could to the outer reaches of the car park where she had left the car. It was a big old Volvo estate, nice and roomy, and it ran well, but it was a right so-and-so to park. The rain had a cutting edge to it, the easterly wind catching it and swirling it, so that by the time she had dumped the shopping in the boot, she was soaked through.

Flinging the coat in the back seat, she sat there demisting herself and the car before backing out. Traffic was surprisingly light as if everybody had given up, and she had a clear run. Now that the last of the shopping was bought in, she could begin to relax and she was so looking forward to having Matthew back home for a few days.

After he finished his technical theatre course, he had worked briefly as a props boy at the Theatre Royal in Felston and she had liked having him at home, although, a year on, she had had enough. He was no longer an endearingly sheepish sixth-former but a grown-up man and, because Ray wouldn't tell him, she did. She didn't actually throw him out but she did tell him it was high time he moved on and out of the family home. She was fed up with tidying up after him, picking up his laundry, ironing his shirts and so on. She knew she only had herself to blame but it was easier to do it than let it sit there. Anyway, it was time he did it himself. He'd had it too cosy here and, even though he would soon turn a place into a pigsty, it would be his own pigsty not hers. She got her wish with a vengeance, for not only did he move out but he landed on his feet, getting a job as an assistant stage manager at a little theatre up in the Lakes.

Perversely, she missed him and the house seemed empty now and altogether too tidy. The girlfriend he was bringing down for Christmas was called Alice and she was twenty-three, but other than that Josie knew nothing about her. Matthew had been a bit slow on the uptake where girls were concerned and, for a time, she had worried about it, not wanting to arrive at the obvious conclusion. She had never dared say anything to Ray about her concerns because, salt of the earth northerner as he was, he wouldn't have tolerated having a gay son but, in the end, it all turned out fine. Alice was not even Matthew's first girlfriend although, judging from his voice when he talked about her, she might very well be the one that mattered. He had known her since summer and it was about time they met her, otherwise they would start thinking something was wrong with her.

Even so, Josie had been surprised when her casual invitation to bring her along for a few days at Christmas had been accepted. It had never happened to her, this assessment by the potential in-laws, because she had lived in the same street as Ray all her life and known his family nearly as well as her own. Matthew was twenty-five and that seemed young to her to be getting into a serious relationship, although she had some room to talk. She and Ray had married young and, by and large, she supposed she would do it all again and Ray certainly would. Better the devil you know and all that. She had known Ray since they were school kids together and had been singularly unimpressed by him, although, as she seemed to recall, he had gazed at her even then with a rapt expression. Ray didn't say much, never had said much, embarrassed by what he called lovey-dovey stuff but she knew he would be in a pretty pickle without her. As she would, without him. Life was life and it didn't stay a bed of roses for ever.

It wouldn't really bother her too much if Matthew and Alice just moved in together but Ray would not like it. Ray was just a touch stuffy about things like that. You'd think he was the one with the staunch Baptist background.

Not knowing Alice, Josie had bought her a

little gift — a hand cream and body lotion set from Boots, more a stocking present but she didn't want to embarrass her by going over the top. Ignoring Ray and his doubts, she had put the couple in the spare room together, making up the twin beds, after gently probing Matthew for what was expected. They could push the beds together if that's what they wanted and she was sorry she couldn't supply them with a nice double.

'Bloody hell, Josie, your mum would never have done that for us,' Ray had protested. 'Not before we were wed.'

Too true. But then her mum was of an abrasive and unforgiving nature and Josie did not care to be reminded of her. Hetty, nudging eighty-five, was in a nursing home now over in Upper Felston, getting on everybody's nerves. Josie had bought her a new night-dress from BHS for Christmas, which she knew would be sniffed at and tossed aside as every present she had ever bought her had been. She wouldn't care but she had gone to some trouble about it, choosing a colour she thought her mum would like, brushed cotton with long sleeves and a few frills round the neck. Margaret had gone to some trouble, too, buying her some new slippers. She and Margaret would pay mother a duty visit on Boxing Day, although

18

she would not expect Matthew to come along and certainly not Alice. She wouldn't put the girl through that experience for anything for Hetty would very likely give her the third degree, jumping to all sorts of ridiculous conclusions.

Hetty was dangerously unpredictable at the best of times and these days she was likely to go swanning off at a tangent, talking about the past, mixing up past and present like nobody's business. It made visiting her unsettling to say the least, just in case she got on to *that* subject and, if she did take to rambling, then you could guarantee she would start making inappropriate remarks.

Sometimes, Josie felt like throttling her. If ever there was a woman who was adept at ruining the lives of those nearest and supposedly dearest to her, it was Hetty Pritchard. There was just something about her and, when she had been younger and fitter, nobody in their right mind would do anything to go against her wishes, certainly not Josie. It was just as well that Josie had learnt over the years to keep the lid firmly shut on all those feelings of old, of the what-might-have-beens if Hetty hadn't put her foot down.

She saw no reason to acquaint Ray with the facts for some things were best kept in the dark. She saw no reason to acquaint Matthew with the facts either, for it didn't seem fair to have him know that his dad, whom he thought the world of, had been very much her second choice. He came a close second, true, but he wasn't quite the man of her dreams.

3

Earlier that afternoon, Ray Bailey found himself standing outside one of the big stores in town, trying to pluck up the nerve to go in and buy his wife's Christmas present. Josie had the Volvo but he had the use of the big carpet van and, because, as he might have known, there was nowhere to park this afternoon, he had left it sitting there for all the world to see on a double yellow line, half on the pavement at that. It was Christmas Eve, the season of goodwill, and he hoped the spoof 'Carpet fitter on call' card he had left in the van window would raise a smile rather than a parking ticket.

Ray was a big, handsome, dark-haired man with dodgy knees, the result of spending so much of his working time on them. He knew that, sooner or later, he would have to admit to Josie that they were bothering him, the knees, but he didn't want to make a song and dance about them — not yet, not at his relatively young age. Dodgy knees ran in his family and, looking back, carpet fitting had been a bad choice of a job. He should have stuck to plumbing, but plumbing ran in the family as well and, just to be awkward, he had wanted something different.

He felt his right knee twinge but that could be nerves because they were always worse when he was anxious and he had put this off already too many times. It was Christmas Eve and it had reached the stage where it was now or never. It would only take a few minutes to nip in the shop and buy it. Whatever it was. The trouble was he felt out of his depth. Screws, nails, tins of paint, car stuff was no problem but a woman's present . . . bloody hell, Ray, just do it, it can't be that bad.

Squaring his solid shoulders, he walked in through the swing door and found himself ambushed in the perfume section right off. It offended his nostrils, ponging as it did to high heaven, a woman's heaven at that, and he hesitated a minute, fumbling in his pocket for the little bit of paper on which he had noted down the name of the scent on Josie's dressing table. Good thinking that. He had rummaged through her underwear drawer as well and written down sizes, although scent would be easier than knickers. He would die a thousand deaths in the knickers and bras section. He had seriously considered buying her a new electric kettle because the other one was playing up but Matthew had laughed out loud when he'd suggested that on the phone.

'She'll have your guts for garters, Dad,' he warned.

Pity. It would have been a whole lot easier. It was Matthew who had suggested perfume or underwear.

Hell. He had lost the scrap of paper and he couldn't for the life of him remember the name of the scent. Panicking, he stood at the nearest counter looking in amazement at the bottles on display. How many scents were there? There were any number of fancy shaped bottles that made the ladies' eyes light up.

'Can I help you, sir?'

He stared into the well made-up eyes of the girl behind the counter. She was a brunette like Josie but nowhere near as pretty, even though she was young enough to be her daughter. His Josie was some looker, always had been and he worried that, whilst she seemed to be holding her own in the age stakes, he was rapidly going downhill, although, thank God, he still had his hair, another thing that ran in the Bailey family, a nicer trait this time.

'Scent,' he muttered, knowing at once it was a pretty damned fool thing to say. 'For the wife. For Christmas,' he added, feeling daft and awkward as he caught her smile, which verged on patronizing.

'Did you have anything in particular in mind?'

'God, no.' He picked up the nearest one — a prettily shaped bottle that looked as if it contained a urine sample — wanting to get out of here asap. 'This will do.'

She gave him one of those withering female looks. Josie was good at them too. 'If I might make one or two suggestions . . . '

'Go on then. But I'm on double yellow lines outside.'

'Right.' She quickened her pace. 'Vanderbilt is very popular. And Guerlain's Samsara is really lovely. That's new. Then there's Chanel, of course, if you want to push the boat out and Obsession. Does your wife like Obsession? Or Ysatis . . . ' she was getting desperate he could tell, 'and Lou-Lou.'

'That's it.' He pounced on that happily as the name clicked. 'I'll have a big bottle of that.'

It wasn't so simple. There were mysterious choices within the range, which she rattled off in a bored fashion but, wisely, he settled on the most expensive, which turned out to be the smallest bottle. He also resisted the urge to say, 'How much?' when she told him the price. Josie was worth it. Every penny.

Although he could have got a top of the range kettle, one of those new fangled shapes for less than that and thrown in a set of kitchen knives.

The girl, hampered by her extremely long, red painted fingernails, wrapped it for him better than he could ever have managed himself and then, pleased as punch, sticking the little parcel in his pocket he picked up the van, which had miraculously escaped a ticket and drove home. That was a first and it had been a doddle. He had done it. He had been in town, on his own, and bought Josie's Christmas present single-handed. He couldn't pretend it hadn't been a bit of an ordeal and, before he'd gone in the shop, he'd wished for a minute that he had taken up Lynn's offer to get it for him as she usually did. It was kind of her but he sometimes wondered about Lynn and her motives. The chiffon scarf she had bought on his behalf for Josie's birthday had been emerald green, the only colour that he knew Josie did not like. He had never seen it since, so she must have taken it back to the shop and exchanged it. If he didn't know Lynn better, he thought she might have done it deliberately. He couldn't make her out, sometimes it was as if she was jealous of Josie and he couldn't think why. She was an old friend, an old mate, and she was Josie's friend, too, so he couldn't understand it. Lynn had done well for herself and was a chartered accountant now. By rights, it was Josie who should be jealous of her because she hadn't made it, giving up on the exams after a while and settling for a part qualification.

The little present for Josie was upstairs now, in the drawer beside the bed at his side and he would remember to give it to her first thing tomorrow. He couldn't wait to see her face. She was a little cracker, his Josie, his girl. He wouldn't do a Mick, trade her in for a younger model as Mick had done with Lynn, not in a million years.

Mission accomplished.

He sat down in his chair in the lounge, drinking his coffee, thinking with a smile of Josie, thinking, not for the first time, that he was so lucky to have her.

4

Josie had popped in to see Margaret that afternoon, confirming the arrangements for tomorrow, so there was no need to stop off at Percy Street. Driving down Crook Lane, Josie could see the lights, the Blackpool illuminations as Ray called them, before she saw the house. Ray always went crackers with the decorations at Christmas and, whilst it had been nice when Matthew was little, it seemed daft now with just the two of them.

Kenny had laughed his head off when he saw it and, surprising herself, instead of leaping to its defence, she had felt suddenly ashamed of it, the twinkling on and off fairy lights, the 'Season's Greetings' banner, the blown-up Santa Claus and the reindeers — the whole caboodle. Worse, she had felt ashamed of Ray that he should be so boyishly proud of it all.

It had taken him all day to set it up, hanging on the ladder with her directing operations from below. It was an anxious time with all the stretching and twisting, twiddling and fiddling with the electrics, and the delight in his face when he finally switched on and they all sparkled into life was something to behold. Josie, scared to death about him either falling off the ladder or going up in a puff of smoke, had hugged him and, at the time, shared his joy. But then, standing there with Kenny, she had seen it for what it was. This sort of over the top display could only happen down here in Riverside and maybe, behind the façade of admiration, the rest of the street was hanging on to its sides with laughter. When did you see one of those detached houses in Greenfield — Kenny's neck of the woods — done up to the nines like this? Mind you, a lot of those folk were as tight as they come, some of them living on their wits at that, so cost could be a reason.

She knew she had been comparing the two men of late and she ought not to be doing that. That was dangerous. She was married to Ray — they'd celebrated their silver wedding anniversary last year — but she was spending more time these days with her colleague Kenny. Ray was hardly ever at home because, as well as the carpet fitting, he supplemented their income by doing odd jobs, assembling flat-pack furniture, putting up shelves, that sort of thing, so he was often out in the evenings and at weekends too. She didn't know what he did with that extra money because it never seemed to come her way, but she knew he didn't gamble it or spend it on himself. Knowing Ray, he would be shovelling it into a deposit account for a rainy day and there were enough of those in this part of the world.

Apart from gardening, he was handy with his fingers, a plumber by trade, and it was no great hardship for him to be doing these jobs, for sometimes it seemed he was only happy when he had a screwdriver in his hand, but it was beginning to irritate her more and more. They could manage without the extra money he coined in but Ray had a thing about it, needed to earn more than she did although, if she got the promotion, he would be hard pressed to manage that, even if he took on three extra jobs. The promotion, if it happened, would shoot her up not one but two grades and it would make an enormous difference.

Josie rarely saw Kenny out of the office but he had been round here last week on some lame-dog of an excuse, bringing round a sponsor form for some deluded soul in the office who was up for a charity parachute jump. She ended up giving a fiver, adding Ray's name, too, and putting him down for the same because she could never in a month of Sundays jump out of an aircraft, charity or no charity.

'Thanks, Josie.' Kenny slipped the sponsor form back in the pocket of his black leather jacket, clicked his pen and popped that away, looking odd in informal get-up because she only ever saw him in his office suit.

With Ray out, she was taking the opportunity to pamper herself, do her nails and have a leisurely bath and so on. She had just washed her hair — longer and darker last week — and had a towel wrapped round her head when she answered the door. She saw him glance at it, at her make-up free face and her generally tousled appearance, and the look that had passed between them had seemed too intimate somehow and had flustered her, so she hadn't invited him in, just stood there on the step, whilst he jeered at Ray's handiwork with the illuminations.

Shutting the door on him eventually, pleading it was cold which it was, she knew she would have to put a stop to the silly flirting before it got completely out of hand. People, colleagues, were beginning to cast sidelong glances their way and it might get back to Ray. Mind you, she couldn't imagine it having much of an effect on him. He was too knackered with all the work he did and didn't have enough passion these days to get wildly jealous if another man looked at her. The days were long gone when he might have fought a duel on her behalf. He once had, years ago, well not exactly a duel but he had told Jack Sazzoni in no uncertain terms to leave her alone. Jack had seen the look in his eyes and known he meant business. She had rushed over to separate them, fearing the worst, worried that they were actually going to come to blows, but thankfully they had stopped short. Just as well because Ray was considerably bigger and heavier, and Jack would have surely come off worse. Ray had been blazing mad, the first and only time she had ever seen him very nearly out of control and that had upset her, making her wonder what she was letting herself in for. Had her mother ever seen her dad like that before they got married? Had she wondered if he would ever turn that anger on her? And had she dismissed that idea as daft, as she did then? Up close, she had heard Ray spitting out the words inches only from Jack's face.

'She's my girl, Sazzo, and don't you forget it.'

Jack, showing admirable control, holding out his hands in surrender, had stepped back, looking at her all the while.

'Are you, Josie?' he'd asked quietly. 'Are you his girl?'

It could have gone either way at that

31

moment. If she had followed her heart, she would have told him no. But, mindful of the family, her mum, her dad, Margaret, she made the decision that would shape her life for the next twenty-odd years.

'Yes I am,' she'd said.

5

Ray was sitting dozing in his favourite chair, paper spread out at the sports page, gas fire full on, his slippered feet on the sheepskin rug that was gathering bits of glitter that would be a devil to shift. In the corner opposite the television, twinkling lights were draped over the artificial tree. It was covered in baubles and little bits and bobs that Matthew had made when he was little, things she knew she ought to throw away, things she could not bear to throw away. They used to have a proper Christmas tree but, last year, when she was still hoovering bits of it up in July from the deep pile 80/20 carpet that Ray had got at a heavy discount, she said never again.

On the mantelpiece, she had moved the small carriage clock and her collection of little brasses and put holly and other bits of greenery from the garden in their place. The cards were pegged on to silver ribbon but she had put Matthew's special one in pride of place on top of the sideboard. He always remembered, even when there was no girl in his life to prompt him. He remembered her birthday and their wedding anniversary and,

33

sometimes, he remembered to remind his dad. Ray hadn't sent her a card this year but then he seldom did. She had sent him one: 'To my darling husband at Christmas', and it sat there, large as life, accusingly awaiting its partner. Fat chance of that. Ray was blissfully unaware that it bothered her. He had asked what she wanted for Christmas and she had said a surprise would be nice.

'A surprise?' he had echoed in dismay. 'You know me, Josie, I'm no good with surprises.'

Quite. But then she had known when she married him, that there would be precious few surprises. What you saw with Ray was what you got. There were no hidden depths. It hadn't mattered then, for there had been something terribly attractive about him, a rough-hewn look that she liked, a no-nonsense, salt of the earth persona that delighted her, a rough passion that, after Jack's gentle romancing had been exhilarating. Rough but kind-hearted, that was Ray, the sort of man who would not knowingly hurt a fly and would never dream of hurting her and, after her dad and his uncontrollable rages, that mattered a lot.

Now she longed for somebody with a touch of style, the sort of man who was at ease with his feminine side, who wouldn't consider it soft to shed a tear at a poignant moment or present her with a bunch of flowers for no reason. Somebody like Kenny. Kenny dressed well and had clean fingernails but then he wasn't on his hands and knees all day, tugging on carpet and hammering it into place. Kenny was a lazy so-and-so and didn't do a lot round the office but had a clever way of always *seeming* busy. He had breezed in two years earlier taking up the post of chief office clerk, smarter dressed by far and driving a superior car to Mr Walsh, but it was quickly rumoured that he had a wealthy wife, ten years his senior. Enough said.

As to her Christmas present, Ray would do what he always did. Ask their friend Lynn to get her something. Lynn would wrap it as well, beautifully and neatly, although she would get him to sign the little card attached. No wonder he always looked as surprised as she did when she opened it. She hoped Lynn would steer clear of chiffon scarves this time. She knew she didn't like green, especially the emerald variety, and it had ruined her birthday. She would give her the benefit of the doubt. Ever since her husband had gone off, she and Ray had tried their best to offer her some friendly support. Josie had the feeling that Lynn was trying, not always subtly, to tone her down. On a recent shopping trip together, searching for an evening frock for the work do, Lynn had pursed her lips as Josie slipped into a fantastic silvery dress with puffed sleeves and a low-necked bodice. For a moment, looking at herself in the mirror in the changing room she had felt like Princess Di and then Lynn had burst the balloon by saying in that voice of hers. 'Do you really think, Josie, at your age you should be showing so much bare skin?'

She had seen red at that. Lynn could take a running jump. Sometimes it was no surprise that Mick had left her and taken up with a younger woman. Goodness knows how she had tried to fix her up with somebody else but it had been hard enough first time round.

Lynn might think the pair of them were on their last legs at knocking on forty-six, but she didn't. She wasn't going under yet, not for a long while. She had ended up buying the dress just to spite Lynn but, when she got it home, she wasn't sure she liked it anyway and it had never been off the hanger since. She had shrugged and put it down to yet another of her 'shooting herself in the foot' moments.

'That Kenny bloke's been on the phone,' Ray, roused from slumber, called out from the lounge as she set about unloading the shopping. She had peeped in but he hadn't looked up so, thank heavens, he hadn't noticed her hair yet.

'What did *he* want?' she asked, feeling her heart give a little jump. 'I hope it's not a panic about work.'

'What else would it be about?'

What indeed?

The nervous relationship she had with Kenny could be termed sexual harassment, she supposed, but in an odd way she enjoyed the feeling of power she had over him. She could drop him in it any time she chose and she suspected he knew it but it didn't seem to worry him unduly because he didn't think she had it in her to make a fuss.

Maybe he was right However, she was keeping an eye on what was going on elsewhere. The newspapers were full of it, this so-called sexual harassment, and women like her were getting *thousands*. The problem was it was her word against his and she hesitated because mud stuck and, unable to shake off some aspects of her stern upbringing, she minded about her reputation and minded also about what Ray and their son would think. But it was what it would do to Margaret that really mattered the most. She could not risk upsetting her sister. It would make the headlines in the local paper and there would be a picture of the two of them, Kenny looking handsome and innocent and swearing blind he had never touched her.

Could she, a policeman's daughter, put her hand on the Bible, the book she still regarded with reverence, and swear that she hadn't led him on, just the teeniest bit? She'd always been able to catch a man's eye and perhaps it was all getting a bit desperate now as she grew older. She needed to know, as she and Ray dipped ever more into the old married couple mode, that she was still capable of causing a man to catch his breath. But she really didn't feel she could cope with the publicity, so who was she kidding? Kenny could rest easy in his bed next to Dorothy, whom she had met a couple of times. It was a shock meeting Dorothy for she had imagined a dull, older woman, maybe with greying hair, because that was how Kenny talked about her. Dorothy was older, yes, but she was an eye-catching woman. She had perfect make-up, smooth skin and — surprise, surprise — long straight blonde hair caught up into an elegant plaited ponytail. Classy clothes too.

Josie bit her lip, smoothing down her jeans that were tucked into knee-high, tan leather boots. Maybe the jeans were a touch tight round the bum and maybe the neckline of her sweater was a bit low and maybe Lynn, whose dresses would offend nobody, was right. Perhaps it was time she sobered up her image a little before she started looking like mutton dressed as lamb. The trouble was when you were as curvy as she was, you either showed it off or hid it and she had no intention of covering herself up completely. She had not won the 'fantastic knockers' competition that the boys at school had run for nothing. The girls were not supposed to know about that but by heavens they did.

She had no intention either of returning Kenny's call. Whatever it was, it could wait until after Christmas. Nothing could be that urgent and she was fed up with carrying that lot in the office. If the general public knew about the workings or non-workings of that department, they would go to town on it. That was another thing she could blow the lid on if she had a mind to. She did the lot in that department, worked her socks off, and nobody would thank her for it. In any case, just now, she and Kenny were rivals for the deputy job and she felt she had to be on her guard. They were the only internal candidates for the promotion and because the external ones had been a useless bunch, she suspected that it was going to go to Kenny. She hadn't had a good interview and one of the councillors on the panel, keen to flaunt his authority, had asked some awkward questions and got her in a bit of a frazzle. It was annoying because, taking Lynn's advice for once, she had toned herself down for that interview, wearing the navy suit with the padded shoulders and a cream ruffle-necked blouse. She'd gone easy on the make-up and even calmed her hair down. As for jewellery, she had discarded the bracelets she was so fond of and just worn her plain wedding band and her engagement ring.

She hadn't recognized herself when she'd looked in the mirror — Ms Po-Face — and maybe that had something to do with it. It had succeeded in inhibiting her. It was wrong to pretend to be someone you were not. She should have gone for her usual glitz, and stuff what they thought.

She would, she decided, be gracious in defeat, even though it would scupper any ideas of moving house. She suspected that Kenny would get the promotion simply because he was a man. Discrimination of this sort would be hotly denied but it was a fact of life in the town hall and the treasurer, Mr Walsh, was so old-fashioned he might as well come to work dressed in Victorian clothes. He treated the women in the office as if they were about to expire any minute, whereupon he would very likely produce a bottle of smelling salts. The worst scenario would be Kenny getting the deputy job now and then getting the chief job a year on. He would make her life a misery then.

How dare he ring her on Christmas Eve at home? And how dare he buy her a bottle of the perfume she liked best just now — Giorgio Beverly Hills — when they had all agreed to spend no more than a pound on a daft little gift? The perfume had to be a bribe for keeping quiet if ever there was. She grew hot as she thought of the little flirty moments in the staff rest room when the easiest thing was to just laugh it off and push him away. She ought not to have accepted the perfume, that was for sure, but she hadn't been prepared and couldn't come up with a satisfactory reason to hand it back.

An hour later, with the vegetables prepared and the trifle somehow squashed into the overflowing fridge, she relaxed at last opposite Ray. He had finally noticed her hair, raising his eyebrows before saying that it was very nice, looking as convincing as a serial crook up before the court. Ray knew nothing about current fashion, so it didn't worry her too much. To be honest, it was growing on her, the new look, made her look quite perky and she had no intention of following in the footsteps of her mum, who had looked ancient by the time she was in her mid-forties.

Matthew and Alice would be here around

nine o'clock depending on the traffic. It had been touch and go for a while whether they would manage it at all because Matthew was in the middle of the Christmas pantomime season and he had to pull a lot of strings to get a couple of days off. Honestly, the way they worked him! It was like the slave trade. She consoled herself because she knew he loved the job and it was nice to be doing a job you loved. She didn't love her job, sometimes didn't even like it, but it brought in the money. You couldn't blame Ray for not exactly getting over-excited over the carpet fitting either for that could hardly be called a vocation.

She wondered what this girl would be like. It wouldn't matter. If Matthew liked her, loved her even, then that was fine with her. If she took an instant dislike to her, as she was apt to do with some people, then it wouldn't matter. She would put her personal feelings aside and act up for all she was worth. And so would Ray. She would make very sure of that.

She wasn't being the cause of any family friction. No way was she going to be another Hetty.

6

Clutching the jar of luxury mincemeat, Valerie Sazzoni headed for the baskets-only till, surprised and irritated to find there was even a queue there. It was extremely annoying having to do this last-minute shopping when she thought she had every-thing organized. She hadn't even known about the baskets-only till, until somebody had pointed it out. Quite clearly, the notice stated one hand basket only but, unlike some supermarkets apparently, there was no limit on the actual number of items in that basket and she picked up a few grumbles about that. Glancing ahead, it looked as if everybody else had a basket heaped with things, stretching credibility to the limit. It reminded Valerie of those awful carvery restaurants where you helped yourself from a buffet, which some people took as meaning that they could pile their plates with as much food as would sensibly remain on the plate. Sheer greed such as that appalled her.

For a moment, she contemplated going to the front of this queue, smiling sweetly and saying that, as she only had one item and had cash, the exact change in fact, could she possibly skip them all?

No. She thought better of that idea. Everybody looked as harassed as only last-minute Christmas Eve shoppers could look, and about as likely to be flexible with the rules as sheets of steel, so she decided she would simply have to wait her turn. It had taken a surprisingly long time to locate the jar of mincemeat, as she rarely came into supermarkets, which she considered to be perfectly ghastly places. She had no need to visit them anyway, not when she could get such fine foods sent over from the delicatessen. The bulk of her day-to-day shopping for what she considered the boring yet essential stuff was done by her housekeeper, Mrs Parkinson. She was a genteel lady who really ought not to be working for a living but there had been a problem with her late husband's pension and she was really rather hard up and was so grateful to have the little self-contained flat in the annexe. She was a touch above the sort of woman you might expect to be employed as a housekeeper and Valerie thoroughly approved of that.

It worked admirably for both of them. Valerie had come to rely on her more and more and would really miss her over the holidays, but the poor woman was due some time off and she wouldn't exactly be enjoying herself on her visit to the States to see her dying sister. Jack had insisted on paying her fare but then that was Jack. Generous to a fault. His charitable giving verged on the insane. Valerie restricted her personal contributions to charity to two causes and all the begging letters went straight into the bin.

Despite her doubts about the wisdom of paying for Mrs Parkinson's air fare themselves, she would much prefer to be married to a generous man. She had a loose rein with her personal expenditure and he liked her to look good, insisted on it in fact. This Christmas, for the first time in a very long time, there would be just the two of them here at home because Alice was going down to Lancashire to visit her boyfriend's parents for Christmas Day and Boxing Day. They would be back up here for New Year. Even though Alice lived only a short drive away over in the South Lakes, they did not see her as often as Valerie would have wished but then she could hardly expect her to spend her precious leisure time visiting them, and Jack was not in favour of popping over on the off-chance. Dropping in unannounced wasn't fair on Alice, he said, and they had to respect her privacy.

Alice had always been of a private nature,

close to secretive, and Valerie found herself both worried and hopeful of the outcome of this new relationship. She knew Alice was still young and there was lots of time, but she wanted to see her settled. Alice had met this man in the summer, shortly after she moved to her cottage and, even though they had visited her there on a couple of occasions and she had been back here several times, they hadn't yet met him, which was worrying her. Other than being told that his name was Matthew Bailey and that he worked at the Little Gem Theatre, Alice was giving nothing away and Valerie knew from experience that the harder she pressed, the less fruitful the outcome. Alice was a slow starter when it came to boys and, for her age, a touch naïve. She had been too caught up in her dancing as a teenager and that absorption, amounting at one time to an obsession, meant she operated in her personal little capsule and everything else, including boyfriends, was put on hold. She was an unusual looking girl, her father's dark brown eyes a pretty and surprising contrast to the honey blonde hair she had inherited from Valerie.

She was putting them in adjacent bedrooms at New Year in the guest wing of the house, many walls away from her and Jack, so no sounds would travel. Nice and convenient all round. It was really up to them whether or not they made anything of that, for she did not feel able to ask Alice if she was having a sexual relationship with this man. Jack had merely laughed when, fretting about the sleeping arrangements, she commented on it.

'What's the problem?' he asked with a grin, the same infectious smile he had been shooting her way for the last twenty-odd years. 'It's not as if they're teenagers, darling. I would be worried if they *weren't* sleeping together. We were at their age, weren't we?'

'We were *married* at their age,' she told him tartly.

He was right to be unconcerned and she determined that she would adopt a modern attitude if it killed her and turn a blind eye to whatever happened in that direction.

With an impatient sigh, Valerie edged forwards in the queue, feeling out of place in her smart clothes. Why did women think they could abandon all attempts at style directly they entered shops such as these? At least the checkout lady seemed efficient in spite of the Santa Claus hat she was wearing on her brassy blonde, newly-permed hair. With a bit of luck, if she continued to proceed at this rate, she might be home before Jack arrived back. She had left a note in a prominent place but she doubted he would notice it. She could leave a suicide note and he would probably never find it.

There was no longer any danger of that. She had climbed out of the depression. There was a time, after she had lost the last of the babies, that she had thought about it, so bogged down as she was with sadness and despair. That depression had been slow to lift but lift it had, although she felt fragile still when she thought about it. Conceiving Alice had been so easy, the pregnancy and birth perfectly normal and she had just assumed, as had Jack, that it would continue in that vein, that they would have the large family they both craved. Not so. After Alice, after the other baby who lived for a day only, she never had any trouble becoming pregnant again but it was hanging on to the baby thereafter that had been the problem. After she suffered the last miscarriage, the third in as many years, Jack had taken her hand, stroked her hair and said simply 'enough'.

'I love *you*,' he told her as she wiped away her tears. 'And it doesn't matter. It really doesn't matter and I'm not putting you through all this again. We have Alice after all.'

Yes, they had Alice but he did not have his son and Lorenzo never had his grandson, the son and grandson they so wanted, the fine boy who would carry on the family business

— Sazzoni & Son — and no matter how much Jack pretended not to mind, she knew that, with no son to succeed, he would sign the business over to his cousin and wife next year with a very heavy heart. Alice had no interest in the business and they could not force her into it.

The young woman ahead of her turned, frowned, and said something but Valerie pretended not to hear. She was not in the mood for conversation with anyone and particularly not with this Goth-like creature. She had a dead white pan-caked face, black-rimmed eyes and blood red lipstick. She wore black cobweb lace mittens, Valerie noticed with surprise, for they would be rather charming in any other context. She really didn't know how to react to somebody like this, whether to brazen it out and look her in the eye or simply ignore her. It was their parents' fault, she thought, knowing that she would have soon put a stop to it if Alice had shown any of these tendencies.

It was snowing as she came out of the supermarket, proper snow at that, fat frothy flakes, and she acknowledged that the weatherman had been right in saying that they would catch the bulk of the snow before it swept across the rest of the country. This supermarket had to be in one of the prettiest locations and the planning application had been rubber-stamped on the understanding that it was to blend in as far as was possible with the beautiful surroundings.

Valerie could feel the hills around her, if not see them, as she drove carefully out on to the narrow winding road that skirted the lake, the dark deep lake that was almost too beautiful in soft warm daylight but vaguely sinister now. The road surface was icy and she concentrated fiercely, worried that a single lapse of concentration could send her spinning into those gently moving inky depths with not a hope of getting out of them alive.

And all for a jar of mincemeat!

7

The occasional lights of the large houses fronting the lake were welcome and Valerie steered by them, the familiarity of the road losing itself as the snow flurried and dazzled against the windscreen. Bing Crosby might be dreaming of a white Christmas but she was less thrilled. She was a summer person and would really prefer to spend the whole of winter at their villa in the Italian lakes, close to the little village from where the Sazzoni family originated, but they couldn't contemplate doing that, not realistically, until Jack retired. With no money worries, he was intending to retire early at fifty, although she would believe that when it happened.

After so many years, this area in the northern lakes was home and now, when she occasionally visited the town where she was brought up, she felt almost like a stranger. Not quite a stranger for some of it was the same, but enough had changed to make it mostly unrecognizable. The Sazzoni brothers including Marco, Jack's grandfather, had emigrated in 1905 settling in Felston, armed with some capital and a lot of verve, starting first with an ice cream parlour and confectionery business. Valerie knew she ought to be grateful to Felston for providing those long ago opportunities for the family, but she had precious little affection for the place and had long since ceased to visit.

Having successfully demoted Felston to the back of her mind, it wasn't entirely a happy coincidence then that this boyfriend of Alice's originated from there. Unfortunately, after a little gentle probing, she learned that he was from Riverside, which, when she had known it, had been the closest Felston had to a no-go area. Worse, his parents still lived there.

Valerie's Felston address had been much more salubrious, living as she did on the leafy and wide-avenued outskirts, but then her father had been a consultant ophthalmic surgeon at Felston & District General Hospital. Valerie, an only child born late to her parents, had been educated privately at the Catholic school where her mother taught Classics but she had floated through that privileged education and come out of it with poor grades that had sorely disappointed her parents, especially her mother, who had high academic hopes for her.

'The sky's the limit for girls these days,' she told her. 'Look at Maggie Thatcher. Wonderful woman.'

'We can't all be like that,' Valerie said, privately not too upset to be compared unfavourably to her.

'If you'd just applied yourself a little more . . . ' The sigh was deep. 'I don't know what we're going to do with you, although I suppose with your looks you'll land a good man at least. But you should have something to fall back on.'

Oh that. To please them, Valerie had started a course in domestic science with a view to teaching eventually, but then she met Jack and she gave it up before she got the diploma, which succeeded in exasperating her mother all the more.

Shortly after she and Jack were married, his father, expanding the delicatessen side of the business, had entrusted his son with the running of a new enterprise in the Kendal area and she and Jack had quickly taken root there. With a bit of a leg up from both sets of parents, who had tried to outdo each other with lavish gifts to the newlyweds, they bought a brand new but poky house on a small estate but, since then, under their own steam, they had moved three times, ever onwards, outwards and upwards. There were now six Sazzoni prized delicatessens in the Lakes area, some of them with a small coffee and ice-cream shop attached and she and

Jack were settled in the house of her dreams, a house in a prime location beside the lake. Jack split his time between the shops, keeping a close eye on the buying and choosing of the provisions they stocked. Quality uppermost was his motto.

Jack had that keen look about him, ever since she first set eyes on him in the summer of '61 and, although he was caught up at the time with another girl, a short busty brunette, she just knew that he was the one for her. It was just a question of waiting for the right moment and, as soon as the other thing fizzled out as she had guessed it would, she made sure she was there.

It niggled for a while that she was required only in her capacity as a 'good listener' but she was patient and eventually that was rewarded. She had never been entirely certain that Jack wouldn't have dropped her like a ton of bricks if the other girl had changed her mind about ending their relationship, but by then it was too late for she was utterly won over by his charm. They found they had much in common — a love of the same kind of music, books, rather a serious outlook on life and when he proposed, she accepted without a moment's hesitation. Things were made easier because her parents liked Jack and also the verve and enterprise of the

Sazzoni family, so they had been terribly gracious about it all and genuinely thrilled when Alice was born.

Sometimes she wondered if Jack proposing to her had been a throwaway 'see if I care' gesture to that girl of his, the girl that she remembered still. She was not one of their set, so she scarcely knew her and they all thought that Jack was slumming it a little with that girl from Riverside but he wouldn't listen. He had been besotted. Seeing them together had made her heart ache, the way he looked at her mirrored the way she looked at him. Valerie had wondered if they were sleeping together but, surprising maybe to today's youth, things like that were considered private and were rarely talked about, at least not in her set. Maybe the boys discussed it amongst themselves but not in mixed company, and she certainly never discussed that side of things with her girlfriends. All she knew was that, old-fashioned or not, she kept Jack at arm's length until they were married and he maintained later that he had loved her all the more for that.

Valerie was nearly home, that final bend, and she remembered how the house had looked when they first saw it on that fine spring day. Wordsworth had clasped it in a nutshell when he talked of the splendour of a host of golden daffodils for that frankly had swung it for her. The condition of the house itself was a disappointment but that could be remedied. She was a frustrated gardener and the garden, packed with spring flowers, was a joy, its location by the lake an added bonus. She quickly pooh-poohed the idea that the house was too big. What were a few extra rooms? Jack was persuaded.

Jack could always be persuaded.

Valerie turned into the drive at last and the security lights came on showing up the softly descending silent snow as she clicked open the automatic doors of the garage and drove in. The empty space beside her car signified that Jack was still out at the charity auction, but she did not mind because it would give her the chance to unwind after the unexpected dash to the supermarket.

The unmistakeable scent of pine invaded the hall for she had placed the larger of the Christmas trees there, simply decorated because she could not bear — Christmas or not — to have too much froth and fuss. There were so many cards, personal and business, and she had chosen just a few of the special ones to put out, the remainder were in a box out of sight. That Bing Crosby song was lodged in her head and she found herself humming it as she made herself a cup of

56

coffee, opening one of the boxes of chocolate that had been brought from the shop for Christmas — well, it was very nearly Christmas and she hadn't had a chocolate for ages. It was such a bore trying to keep to the same weight she had been in her twenties, but she did, if only because she liked to look good in clothes and was proud of her model height and long, long legs. She was the same height as Jack without heels but he did not mind, liked her to wear heels anyway, which she did. She kept her shoulder-length bobbed hair the same colour it had always been and spent a fortune on discreet make-up and clothes — ah, the clothes. She had any number of elegant dresses and tops in silk and linen, her shape showing them off to their full advantage. She and Jack went to quite a lot of functions and she was confident that she always looked good.

'How do you do it, Valerie?' one of her women friends asked. 'You have such style.'

'Perhaps it's because I'm married to a man who has Italian connections,' she would say with a smile. This was true although the Italian blood was by now greatly diluted, each of the male line marrying an Englishwoman as they had, each of the male line becoming ever more English as a result of his mother's influence. However, that little speck of

Mediterranean root remained, showing up in odd ways. 'Jack takes an interest in what I wear.'

The truth was she worked at it, taking particular care with accessories, that's how she did it, and it certainly was not in the genes if her mother was anything to go by. She had two new outfits for Christmas but this evening she was wearing old favorites, a long burgundy skirt with a soft ivory angora sweater and because the whole effect would be spoilt by the addition of slippers, she was wearing low-heeled comfortable boots.

Jack would expect nothing less of her. She had once made the mistake of going for comfort instead of prettiness in bed and he had — with a smile on his face — accused her of dressing like a bag lady. My goodness, she had taken that to heart. Jack would very likely buy her something silky to wear in bed for Christmas, for she had dropped a few hints, but he was just as likely to surprise her.

Mrs Parkinson had helped her put up the tasteful Christmas decorations and Valerie smiled as she set a match to the ready prepared fire. It was beautifully warm anyway for they had an efficient gas-fired heating system, but the real fire was a nice touch and reminded her of her childhood when she would sit and gaze at the flames and see shapes in them. Within minutes, the flames had caught and she crossed quickly to the wide bay window, drawing the curtains, shutting out the snow and wondering what on earth it would look like tomorrow morning.

She had long since given up trying to do an *Italian* Christmas, knowing that there was no way she could do it properly. Jack's mother had been indisputably English and as Jack often ruefully observed, the rot had set in by then. To do an Italian Christmas, you need first and foremost an Italian Mama. It might well be *la vigilia di Natale* over there but here it was Christmas Eve. It might well have a truly religious meaning over there but here it was largely an excuse for a few days' holiday and, if Jack regretted the almost complete loss of his roots, he only occasionally let it show.

She was preparing a special dinner for the two of them this evening and, after a hectic pre-Christmas social calendar, she was looking forward to a quiet evening in. The television programmes this Christmas Eve were all too predictable, frantically festive, so they would put on some soothing music and relax, go to bed around midnight. Once upon a time, she would dutifully have accompanied Jack and his father to midnight mass but no longer. When Lorenzo died, there was no need for Jack to pretend any more and, with his father laid to rest in the family plot, he dropped religion with a haste that smacked of insensitivity. No consultation. No arguments. No recriminations. Alice, picking up on it, had lapsed too.

Thinking of her daughter reminded Valerie that this would be the very first time she would be away from home at Christmas and it hurt to know that she was pulling away from her. It was only right and proper that she should and she must wait in judgement on this boyfriend. She had spoken to him, just the once, on the telephone and he had sounded nice. He had a pleasant voice with a light northern accent to remind you of his roots, but the thought of Riverside, Felston, would not go away. She had to get a hold on herself and stop being so snobby. Jack hated it and so did she but she couldn't always help it. The way you had been brought up took some shifting and her mother had always been horribly dismissive of people she thought of as lower class.

She listened to the radio, frowning at the update on the weather conditions, which were worsening by the minute. A white Christmas — wonderful of course and didn't everybody secretly long for one — but not until everybody was safely where they were supposed to be, not in the middle of getting there.

Ah, there was Jack at last. She heard the car, the garage door opening and a few minutes later, he was coming in the back door, stamping feet on the mat, telling her what she already knew — that it was snowing heavily and looked set for the night.

The meal was in hand, the champagne chilling, and she warmed her hands a moment over the coals, turning as Jack came through, a bouquet of flowers in his arms.

'For you, sweetheart,' he said, kissing the top of her head. 'Sorry about leaving you on your own this evening. It was a poor turn-out. There wasn't a lot of support so we'll all have to dig deep and make it look decent as it's for the children's hospice.'

'These are lovely . . . thank you, darling.' She admired the flowers, put them aside a minute as she poured them both a drink. 'Have you heard from Mrs Parkinson? I thought she might have rung. Shouldn't she be there by now?'

'She should unless there was a delay. I hope she's OK. She's getting a bit long in the tooth for flying off on her own across the Atlantic. And this thing at Lockerbie will have unnerved her. Just think, it could have been her.'

'But it wasn't,' she said briskly, glancing at him and hoping that he wasn't going to go all emotional on her again. Of course it was a tragedy, a tragedy of dreadful proportion, but they couldn't let it affect them. There was no point in brooding. 'She'll be fine. It won't happen again. Not so soon.'

'Try telling that to a nervous traveller,' he said. 'It's her getting on the connecting plane that worries me most. I wrote it all down for her, step by step.'

'I know you did and she was so grateful. What more could you have done? We could hardly go with her and hold her hand. She'll be fine,' Valerie said. 'I shall miss her.'

She told him later about the plans she was hatching for a little party on New Year's Eve. She had sounded out a few of their friends and, although she intended to keep it fairly low key with at the most twelve guests, she wanted to make it special for Alice and Matthew.

'He's a carpet fitter of all things,' she said, as they lingered over coffee in the dining room. It was at the back of the house, furnished in a light modern style because she disliked both dark wood and antique clutter.

'Who is?' Jack asked, reaching for a chocolate mint.

'Matthew's father. He's a carpet fitter and

his mother works for the treasurer's depart-ment. Something to do with accounts, although I don't think she's a qualified accountant.

'So? There's no problem with that, is there?' Jack had a twinkle in his eye but she sensed a warning there nonetheless. 'Don't go jumping the gun. They're not even engaged. Alice hasn't said anything, has she?'

'Not yet. I just have a feeling. Suppose they announce their engagement over Christmas?'

'That will be great. It's about time and I think she's ready for it, I'm looking forward to having grandchildren.'

Ah, the *bambini* . . . it never went away. Valerie sighed at the look on his face but she wasn't going to bring it all up again, the lost babies that they seldom talked about. She often thought about them herself, thinking of them as the young men they now would be and sometimes, oddly, she could almost feel them beside her. She always shook that feeling off quickly, believing it to be faintly unhealthy to be thinking that way, unwilling to prompt another bout of depression and she certainly never ever mentioned it to Jack.

'I'm a great believer in marrying young before you start having second thoughts,' he said with a smile that faded as he caught her expression. 'You're not worried, are you?'

'It's too soon,' she said. 'And we haven't met him yet. Suppose we don't like him? How will we tell her that?'

'We won't tell her that. What *we* think, my sweet — ' Jack said, crushing the chocolate wrapper before dropping it on his saucer. 'What we think is neither here nor there. We stand back from this one. She's a grown-up. It's her decision. Parents have to learn to stand back.'

She gave a little huff of disbelief, knowing that he was a typical dad and no man would ever be quite good enough for his beloved Alice. The two of them were so close she felt excluded sometimes and it had been like that from the beginning, them against her.

Now, she was being paranoid but she saw that Jack's mood had changed and she was uncomfortable to have reminded him of the circumstances of their getting together. They never spoke of it. What was the point? The girl, that pretty dark-haired girl, who was surely the love of his life, had lived in Riverside, too, all those years ago. The reasons for ending the relationship had never been spelt out to Valerie but she suspected it was to do with religion — hence Jack's dismissal of it — and the girl's parents disapproving of him, maybe because he was part Italian. The girl had married somebody

64

else not long after she finished with Jack, very likely on the rebound or perhaps to prove a point. It had nearly broken Jack and for a long time it hurt that she was only second best.

She was still jealous. After all these years, she was still jealous as hell. And she had never rid herself of the thought that, if that girl reappeared on the scene, Jack would be off without a backward glance.

For a moment, as Valerie loaded the dishwasher, she wondered where Josie was now.

8

The previous summer, on one of the hottest days of the year, Alice Sazzoni moved into Brambles Cottage. It was just as well it was a bright sunny day because she had no time for second thoughts, and buying a house seemed such a grown-up thing to be doing.

The sunshine helped to make the little cottage look at its best, linking arms as it did with an identical one on the one side and a slightly larger, double-fronted one on the other. The stone here was a warm grey, tinged surprisingly with pink. Her cottage did not have roses round the door but instead a ravishing crimson clematis and, growing round the window and joining up with it, a white jasmine. Open the window on a summer's evening, the previous owner had told her, and the scent drifts in. She'd had to take his word for it because it had been early February but she saw now that it was true.

Perfect then. But perfection comes at a price and the bend at the end of Brambles Lane was so tight that the removal van driver had been forced to do a seven- or eight-point turn, coming perilously close to demolishing a great chunk of her neighbour's garden wall until the van was facing backwards and they could unload, blocking the lane and marooning the other residents for the duration of the move. Thank heavens she'd had the foresight to explain beforehand so that they could all move their cars; the last thing she wanted was to antagonize them from the outset. There were only five cottages in all and she wanted to be on the best terms possible with *all* her neighbours.

It was a complete hotchpotch of people, a widow in her eighties, a young couple, two guys, and, in the bigger house next door to her, a middle-aged couple with two teenage boys. As soon as she was settled, she would invite them all round for a house-warming but she would not tell her mother about that or it would turn out to be cringingly formal when all she wanted was a free-for-all with drinks and a few nibbles thrown in. With such an eclectic group, it promised to be interesting if nothing else.

Trying to save on cost, Alice had imagined at first, ridiculously, that she could do the removal job herself with the help of a couple of hefty girlfriends but, having inherited some splendid solid pieces of furniture from her maternal grandmother, antique pieces that had been waiting patiently in store for some time, she knew she could not risk amateur enthusiasm. Her grandmother would never forgive her if the furniture was damaged. She had loved her granny, heaven knows, but been a bit scared of her at the same time.

Feeling useless, not wanting to get in the way as the men struggled with her large terracotta-coloured sofa, she did the one thing she could do, put the kettle on, digging out some sweet biscuits, a bag of sugar, a teaspoon, a carton of slightly off milk, four mugs but no plate. It was just as well her mother wasn't here. Her mother would be better organized and have had a tray handy with several plates and napkins, a sugar bowl and pretty cups and saucers rather than mugs from the market, but then that was her mother. No matter what, standards never slipped. She had never seen her mother looking the worse for wear. Even when she was ill, she would be carefully made-up with her nails done, her hair in its perfect bob. She even managed to do gardening, potentially a very scruffy job, and remain clean and unruffled.

'Where exactly do you want this, love?'

'Oh . . . I'm not sure,' she dithered, squeezing into the sitting-room behind them and thinking about arrangement of furniture, trying to do it quickly as they stood there, poised and expectant. She had to get it right because it would be hell on earth to move again on her own. 'Under the window, please,' she said, aware it would block off the window seat but it seemed the most sensible place to put it. She hadn't even been able to see the window seat when she viewed the house because of the previous person's clutter.

Thank heavens they had got professional cleaners in before they disappeared; everything was pleasantly sparkling. There was a busy-patterned wallpaper but that couldn't be helped. It wasn't such a bad colour and went with the curtains and carpet they had left for her. Spicy shades of rich bronze and burnt orange which, whilst they were not the colours she would have chosen, were easy enough on the eye and would make a good background for her dark wood furniture.

'Under the window it is,' said the foreman, standing back and wiping his brow. He was wearing an olive-green vest with 'I'm the Boss' on the front and 'The buck stops here' on the back. It had damp marks now under the arms and there were beads of sweat on his face. Overweight as he was, she wondered at the wisdom of him doing a job like this, feeling rather concerned on his behalf. She did not want him keeling over from heat exhaustion. Apart from anything else, with the lane blocked, there was no way an emergency vehicle could get anywhere near at the moment.

Gently, they lowered the sofa down and then, with the precision of a fussy housewife, rearranged the large cushions that had slipped. A bee, disentangling itself from the jasmine, buzzed in through the open window, circling them and the room before making an exit through the same window. Sunlight flooded in and it all felt so warm and inviting. When she first viewed it on a cold crisp day, there had been a log fire in the hearth and, looking back, that had clinched it for her. Like her mother, she made quick decisions when it came to where she wanted to live.

'Ready for a cuppa?' Alice smiled at them all and, with sighs of relief all round, they followed her into the little kitchen. It was a neat fit for the four of them but they wrestled round each other in an easy enough fashion and the biscuits quickly disappeared.

'Nice place you've got here,' the one called Eric said, spooning three generous spoonfuls of sugar into his mug. 'Cosy.'

You could say that. Three's a crowd but four of them in the kitchen was close to disaster. Not fancying ending up in an accidental embrace with any of them, Alice carefully retreated with her mug and left them to it, taking a seat on her newly positioned sofa. She supposed they must wonder how she could afford a place like this in this prized spot, a young woman on her own, and the truth was she couldn't or, at least, would never have managed it without a little help from her dad.

'Don't tell your mother,' he had said as he handed over the sizeable cheque that not only secured the deposit but also reduced the mortgage payments to a sensible size.

Dad had been saying much the same thing all her life. They had secrets from mum and it made their relationship special. If, heaven forbid, she had to choose between the two of them, there was no choice. It was her dad's presence she remembered most when she thought about her childhood, which was odd because mother was always at home.

Uncharitably maybe, Alice sometimes wondered what on earth her mother had found to do with all that spare time, for there had been help in the form of a nanny when she was little. Her mother was not very robust and spent a lot of time being 'not very well' and recuperating from various things. Mum was always one step removed or so it seemed to Alice. She was not a hugger, never actually pulling away from an embrace with her daughter but never encouraging it either.

She supposed she had reacted to her mother's aloof elegance by becoming a scruff, never quite recovering from the jeans and baggy tops of her teen years, feeling uncomfortable when dressed up and always being pulled apart by her mother for her clothes sense, or rather her lack of it.

'You're just like your granny,' her mother would say, shaking her head in frustration. 'Look at you. My mother was always a mess. Far too academic for her own good. She never cared what she looked like.'

'Do you want your bed putting up, miss?'

Alice turned round, looked into the kindly eyes of the foreman. 'Yes please,' she said, neglecting to remind him that it was actually on the contract she had signed that they would do that.

'Will do,' he said with a funny half salute. 'I always ask. Thought there might be a Mr Sazzoni coming by later. Sometimes the gents want to do that job themselves.'

'No, I'm on my own,' she said, instantly sorry to have admitted that, but he looked a nice man and she didn't think he would be returning at dead of night to break in and molest her.

A few hours later, the van was empty and the interior of Brambles Cottage was looking like home. The sitting-room had all its furniture. The oak bookcase in the alcove was waiting to receive its books, the lovely old desk had just squeezed into the other alcove, the sofa was looking settled as if it had been there for ever and the new rug was in place. Next door her granny's dining-table and chairs added some grace and class to the dining-room and with the bed, her lovely big bed, safely installed upstairs, she could begin to relax.

Everything else could wait. At least, she was in and everything was in one piece. The men had even unpacked fragile items, as per the contract, and nothing was broken.

'That's your lot then, love.' The foreman handed over the paperwork, which she signed with a flourish. 'We'll be off. Give us a ring when you've unpacked the rest of the boxes and we'll pick them up.' He gave a little cough as his colleagues waved at her and made their way back to the van. 'We hope you'll be very happy in your new home, miss.'

'Thank you,' she said, feeling herself flushing with embarrassment about the tip she suddenly realized they were expecting. How ridiculous not to have thought about that. She gave her hairdresser a tip for goodness' sake and these three had been at it in this heat for hours and hours. 'Hang on a minute,' she said, disappearing in search of her purse. Agonizing over what to give them, she wondered later if she had been generous enough and, worse, if she had distributed it fairly. The foreman had done the lion's share but the driver had managed somehow to get the van up the lane and out again.

Too late. Closing the door on them, ignoring the packing cases that were stacked in the utility room, she could at last take stock. It felt good, if a little daunting, to be here. There had been a problem a few weeks ago with the seller's solicitor and it had seemed at one time that it might all fall through. It was only then, when she thought it might slip through her fingers, that she realized just how much she wanted to live here. It had felt like home from the first moment she stepped through the door. She had seen beyond the mess that the previous owners lived in. Just a bit of tarting up, that's all it needed, and she wasn't frightened of getting her hands dirty.

The garden, 'a delightful cottage garden' according to the agent's details, was over-grown but everything was in place and all it would take, she told herself confidently, was a couple of days weeding and sorting. As it was the height of summer, everything was out, weeds and flowers mixed together in a happy profusion of colour and texture. Her mother with her vivid green fingers was aching to get her hands on it but Alice was discouraging that. She didn't want her mother seeing it in this state and, just to annoy her mum, she might insist on hanging on to some of the prettier weeds. What was a weed after all? She would invite her mum and dad round shortly but not until she was completely unpacked, for she didn't want her mother helping with the sorting.

Making up the bed for later was the first essential. The quilt was a moving-in gift from her parents and it was utterly gorgeous. In soft lilacs and pinks it would be the inspiration of the colour scheme. Thoroughly hot and bothered by now, Alice slipped off her shoes and lay, fully clothed, on top of the bed seeing the lightweight curtains moving softly in a now welcome breeze. There were sounds outside of summer and the country, and she sighed deeply, knowing she had done the right thing coming here.

It was the best of all worlds. Remote enough for her to feel completely cut off but that was just an illusion because the bustle of the village was just at the end of the lane and neighbours within banging-on-the-wall distance. Smack bang in the middle of the area where she did her teaching, it could not have been better placed. Providing her dance and drama contract with the education department was renewed next year, then all would be wonderful. If it wasn't renewed, she would be hard pressed to make ends meet with the money she made from the little private dance group for under-sevens she had set up in the nearby market town. Eventually opening her own dance studio was the aim, giving all sorts of dance tutoring from ballet to tap to ballroom and, with people keen to keep fit, she saw dancing really taking off as a new leisure activity. If it all went wrong and she had to do something else then she could always admit defeat and step into the family business. The trouble was her plans had all gone wrong once before, when she reluctantly but realistically gave up on any hopes of becoming a professional dancer, so she was already on the second option.

New home and a new start, and maybe it was time she took a fresh look at herself and where she was going. Although she had hesitated about moving out of the house she had shared with some girlfriends, the set-up had begun to stifle her and she yearned for her own space.

It had been tempting to do a house-share with Felicity, the one girl she got on with best of all, but in the end it was not a sensible option and, having negotiated the best possible deal on this place, she could just about afford the mortgage on her current meagre salary. It would be tight but she would do her best to survive on her own, convinced that she had accepted the very last so-called gift from her dad. She was twenty-three and it was time she stood on her own two feet, although admittedly it was comforting to know that, if it came to it, her parents would be there to bail her out. Knowing her dad, there would be no questions asked.

Reluctantly, she swung her legs off the bed and went downstairs and, shuddering at the sheer volume of packing cases standing accusingly by, she picked up her car keys, closed the windows and locked the door before going off to buy something to eat. A gold star hamper would no doubt be already on its way from the mail-order section of Sazzoni & Son and although she wouldn't say no to that, the fact was, and this was something she would never admit, she wasn't really into much of the specialized food they stocked, never mind that each item had been lovingly selected by her dad, hand picked or whatever. Even though it made her feel like a traitor, she certainly did not turn her nose up at a simple supermarket, factory-prepared pizza, the very idea of which would have her dad turning cartwheels.

It was a twenty minute drive to a decent supermarket on the edge of the nearest town and she shopped quickly and efficiently, ending up with yet more things to unpack when she reached home. After the hectic day, the heat was beginning to get to her and she wanted most of all to step into a shower to wash away all the day's grime. To her relief, the shower worked, the hot and cold a bit variable but OK and, as she dried herself, she dreamed of what this bathroom would look like when it was done up, when she could afford to have it done up that is.

Hers. All hers.

Wearing just a towelling robe over her knickers, she wandered into the little back garden. It was, as the estate agent had pointed out, so private that, should she wish it, she could sunbathe there naked. He had been an odd man, given her the shivers, and, although she had made no comment, she thought the remark offensive.

He was right though. It was secluded, hemmed in by tall hedging on both sides, which in fact made her feel a touch claustrophobic. Still, she had time to think about it and, enjoying the last of the evening heat, she examined the plants closely, most of them a complete mystery. She must look them up in one of her gardening books before her mother arrived and took charge. She had seen her mum attack what she called an untidy bed in the garden and it was frightening. She hadn't issued an official invitation but she had no doubt they would invite themselves anyway within the next couple of days.

So, tomorrow, she had to dig in and make a start.

She rang her parents' number but there was no reply — out at one of their dos no doubt — so she left a message saying that she was finally in and all was well and thanks for the 'Welcome to your New Home' card.

It took a while to get to sleep. Her bed was the same but the room was different, the window was at the wrong side and there was no Felicity in the next room. An owl hooted and there were strange rustlings outside during the night that woke her. Heart hammering, she sat up in bed until she calmed down, although Felicity's suggestion of having a cricket bat handy came to mind. There were a few sounds from next door though they were indistinct, the walls being incredibly thick, but it was comforting to know people were there if she needed them.

This was home and she had better get used to it.

But, lying alone in the big bed, she wished there was somebody, a warm loving man, to share it with her.

9

The Little Gem Theatre was only ten miles or so as the crow flies from Alice's new home but so difficult to find that it would seem twice the distance. Matthew Bailey liked its remoteness, although it could be a problem for actors and public alike. The number of times he'd had a frantic phone call 'Where the hell are you?' was running well into double figures.

It was worth the effort, worth all the diving and ducking down the narrow lanes and over the little stone bridges, through a ford at one point, and, just when you were about to give up the ghost, what a sense of achievement when there it was in the glade. A perfect little theatre snuggling there, the hills soaring beyond it, a rushing stream somewhere nearby, and, for the public, the three things that came high on the list of must-haves: a decent car park, a coffee shop and good clean loos.

Matthew, although he loved living here in the Lake District, did not intend to stay for ever. This was a stopgap, the opportunity to prove himself. It would look good in a few years on his CV and maybe help him get a job down in London. Here, as assistant stage manager, he was a relatively big cog in a small wheel, part of a solid team of five with some part-timers helping out in front of house. Helen, the general manager, ran the show, a competent fifty-year-old who was grooming him, so she said, for her job when she retired. He was grateful for the confidence she showed in him but kept it under his hat that it was most unlikely that he would still be around in ten years. He dreamed of London or New York, the big time and why not? He was young, fiercely keen and, ever since his mother had taken him to see his first pantomime back home in Felston, he had been hooked on the theatre.

At first he had imagined performing, as an actor, but the inner workings of the theatre, the getting it all together, the behind-the-scenes hullabaloo, had started to appeal more. He loved the excitement, the variety and even the blazing rows and tantrums that resulted from working with such talented and volatile people. He often wondered how his mum, bright and vibrant as she was, could have lumbered herself with a job in such a safe and boring environment as local government where, from what she said, doing very little and achieving even less seemed to be the name of the game. 'Don't quote me,' she had said with a laugh when she said that, 'or I'll be out on my heels.'

'Matthew?' Helen breezed in, fair hair frizzing all round her face, wearing her trademark black leggings and large loose grey smock. 'Have you done last night's show report, darling?'

He handed it over. 'Good audience,' he said. 'And Brett was in fine form. I think he's got over his rocky patch. There were three curtain calls.'

'Thank Christ for that. The last thing we need is the leading man going through a crisis.' She scanned the report. 'Has Claire dressed the set for this evening?'

He nodded, not bothering to add that, to save time, he had swept the stage himself first thing as Claire was having one of her worse than useless days. He had fondly imagined he was finished with his stint as props boy but Claire needed somebody to hold her hand and she couldn't handle anything extraordinary. He could not trust her, that was the top and bottom of it and, unless he checked things meticulously, she was quite capable of forgetting to put a vital prop on stage, leaving the poor actor or actress to turn their talents to improvization. To their credit, they often did that and so smoothly that the audience never realized the problem. Troopers, the lot of them, and he admired them, admired their sheer nerve, for setting foot on that stage was not for the faint-hearted. It gave him goose bumps just standing there as he sometimes did on his own, looking out at the empty seats. It took a special person to confront an audience, to seduce them, to win them over, so maybe it should come as no surprise that so many of the actors he came across were ever so slightly unhinged.

Helen leaned on his desk, knocking over a pile of box office leaflets as she did so, cursing loudly as he rushed round to pick them up. His office was a converted dressing room, dingy, windowless and stuffy. The sickly mustard-coloured carpet had seen better days, trodden by the feet of some well-known names no less, but, even with the help of the wealthy and influential members of Friends of the Little Gem and one or two theatre 'names' who acted as patrons, they couldn't run to new carpets in the back rooms. As for air conditioning that was out of the question and the heat of the last week was building up, turning this box of a room into a little sauna. There was an electric fan but it was so noisy that it was like working with helicopter blades on full power, scattering papers in its slipstream.

Helen tugged at the neck of her smock, loosening it a little. 'Things to do this week. We'll need to fix up a rehearsal room for the murder mystery play,' she told him, consulting her diary as he picked up his. 'There's only six characters in all so they can manage with something small. And we'll need to pull in some children for that *Oliver* production. Can you organize that? The director will be up' — she riffled through the pages — 'the week beginning the twentieth. So we'll need to have the auditions for the babes arranged by then. OK? Can I leave that with you, sweetie?'

Like clothes buyers, they were always thinking a season ahead. For summer read autumn and even winter. And, as Matthew was quickly finding out, things could go badly wrong so there had to be a Plan B and sometimes even a Plan C.

The worst possible scenario was when a name signed up to front a play and then cancelled at the last minute. Shit flew then. People brought back their tickets, wanted their money back, grumbled like hell and you could bet your bottom dollar there would be a mention in the local rag. Funny that, when things were running smoothly as they so often did, not a word would appear, not even when Simon, their marketing guy, sent in the copy himself. Simon reckoned that, even if he strode into the editor's office naked, it would make no difference to her indifference. She would still lose the bloody copy or decide in her infinite wisdom that it wasn't newsworthy enough. It didn't happen often because they didn't often get a big name, not here, not in the back of beyond and more, but Helen kept on trying, appealing to the actor's charitable instincts if nothing else.

Matthew loosened his tie and undid the top button of his pale blue shirt. He had to tread a fine line between too formal and too casual and liked to think he had struck the right balance. The tie could be discarded as and when, but could be quickly added if somebody turned up unexpectedly. Helen might dress like a cleaner herself but she expected the rest of the staff to look reasonably smart, keen on projecting the right image. The colour scheme for the front of house crew was royal blue and yellow, very Swedish flag, but effective with it.

Matthew spent the rest of the morning making phone calls and, by three o'clock, he had arranged a meeting for the next day with some woman he hoped would be able to help him out with the children for *Oliver*. It promised to be a good production with a company they had worked with before, a northern outfit whose director was on the lookout for local kids for the chorus, children who could sing and dance and maybe — if this wasn't asking for the moon — act too. Matthew was doing the initial spadework, but he wasn't pinning too much hope on the kids this woman would produce. In his view, children who could act were rare as dinosaurs' eggs and, in his view also, having children on stage often ruined a serious production. He liked kids, but not on stage. If he were the director, he would be in favour of insinuating them into a play but never actually seeing or hearing them. Of course, even he had to admit that you couldn't get away with that with *Oliver*.

'*Ciao*, Matt!' Claire sidled in, dressed ridiculously in the holiday gear she would be wearing for real in a week's time. God knows how she'd managed to slip past Helen. The buttock-skimming, silky turquoise dress with enormous padded shoulders was surely a beach outfit, the sort of thing you wore over a tiny matching bikini. Having seen Claire in a bikini, having seen her without one come to think of it, Matthew felt his heart pound, instantly annoyed that she could still get to him.

'Good morning, Claire,' he said crisply.

Have you finished? Are we ready to go out there?'

'Yeah. Slight problem.'

'What?'

'You know those cups and saucers? You know when they have tea in the second act?'

'Go on,' he said, fearing the worst.

'I dropped the tray,' she said. 'In the wings. The pieces went everywhere. I've been on my hands and knees. Look.' She held up her hand. 'I cut my finger. Those tiny slivers are lethal. There was blood everywhere and I couldn't find the first-aid kit, and how on earth are you supposed to open those stupid little plasters when you've got blood pouring out? I could have sliced through an artery. I filled in a works accident form. Who do I give it to?'

'Me,' he said quickly, taking a cursory glance at the offending strip of elastoplast. 'Replacements. Have you done that? Replacements for the tea set?' he added, saying the words slowly and clearly as he caught her puzzled expression.

'Do you want me to?'

'Yes, Claire, I do. I do,' he repeated, hearing his voice suddenly, reflecting in a mad moment that it was just as well he was not uttering those words in a church with Claire, a vision in white, at his side. 'Do it now. Get yourself into Kirkley. Four fine china cups and saucers. Matching ones,' he said, rapidly losing patience. 'I've got to check the lighting and sound and the flats on stage. For God's sake, Claire, can't I trust you to do anything right? You're props. You have to keep track. I'm not telepathic.'

'Matt . . . ' She edged nearer, bringing her heady perfume with her. 'Don't talk to me like that. Don't be mean.'

'Mean?' He glanced at her irritably. He didn't have time for the soul-searching she was apt to engage in these days. And he certainly didn't have time for soul searching when they were only three hours and a bit away from a performance.

'I know you're upset, darling,' she said, so close she was very nearly on his lap. She was drenched in the cloying perfume and he knew now what was meant by too much of a good thing. 'But you have to get over it. It's tragic for you but it's not my fault that I fell in love with Paul.'

No. He knew that and he was sorry he had spoken sharply to her but working together was proving to be difficult if not impossible. He had known at the time of their short-lived but boisterous affair that it was insane to mix business with pleasure, but she was very attractive and, for a while, he had genuinely felt a fondness for her, for her sweetness and even for her wide-eyed stupidity. Now her incompetence merely annoyed him. She was useless at the job and it was just as well that she was working her notice before getting shacked up with Paul and moving down south.

'Sorry, Claire,' he said with a slight smile in case she took a huff and walked out right now, leaving them up the stage creek. 'This weather's getting to me. I don't do heatwaves.'

'Don't be miserable,' she said. 'It's gorgeous. We're having a barbecue tonight. Fancy joining us?'

We? Was she referring to the bloody marvellous Paul?

'How can I? I'm working,' he reminded her tartly. He was always working, snatching a few hours off here and there whenever he could, but he had to be on hand for the performance, so that he could do the show report and sort things out if there was an emergency at the last minute.

'All work and no play make a very dull boy,' she said with a smile.

'Do you know a woman called Sazzoni?' he asked, checking in his diary. 'I'm meeting her tomorrow.'

'Sounds foreign.'

'The name does, she doesn't,' he said, remembering the voice. A lovely voice. Middle pitched, easy on the ear. No discernable accent but verging on the posh.

'What does she look like?'

'How would I know? She lives at Penington Bridge. I thought you might know her as it's your neck of the woods? An Alice Sazzoni?'

The name drew no response and he watched, momentarily mesmerized as Claire sashayed out, knowing perfectly well that, if she hadn't left him for Paul, he would have let the whole thing go anyway. So, in a way, she had done him a big favour because he had dreaded being the one to break it off. And now Paul was doing him an even bigger favour by whisking her away.

10

The next day was another scorcher and the constant blue skies were becoming a touch boring. Was there to be no let up? Allowing himself plenty of time, mindful of the holiday traffic, which was at its peak just now, Matthew drove out to Penington Bridge. It was a picturesque place, not much more than a big village, full of hanging baskets and big bright tubs of flourishing flowers. He gave up on the one and only car park, which had a blackboard at the entrance chalked FULL, and he had to drive round three times before eventually squeezing his car into a space by the green.

The place was heaving with hot, sweaty bodies, although they were mostly dressed in cool summery clothes. He had his suit on because it was a business meeting and Helen had watched him leave, peering at him over the top of her glasses, giving him the once-over. On the one occasion he had seen her dressed up, he had barely recognized her — a shocking pink ball gown with peculiar sleeves — hair de-frizzed, make-up carefully applied. He preferred the other Helen

— Cinders before she met her Prince Charming.

Locking the car and glancing at his watch, he saw he was now ten minutes late. Bugger. It was so unprofessional and he hated that. First impressions. He could hear his mum talking earnestly about how important first impressions were.

They were meeting, at Miss Sazzoni's suggestion, in a tea shop which seemed a bit twee for a business consultation but who was he to argue? He had proposed she come over to the theatre but she had knocked that one on the head, sweetly but firmly. That had not gone down well with him because he was up to here with work and, from past experience, if anything was going to happen, it would sure as hell happen when he wasn't around. He knew Helen would take the brunt if something went seriously wrong but he could not help feeling the weight of his own responsibility as ASM. He had been in competition for his job with older, more experienced candidates and he was aware they had taken a chance with him, that Helen in particular had championed him, so he had something to prove.

Miss Sazzoni? Voice notwithstanding, the name conjured up a certain image. Curly dark hair, rosy cheeks and plumpish, he assumed, and because she worked with children, she would be of the jollying-along variety no doubt. The name was exotic, but she was a dance and drama teacher so maybe it was made up to make her sound like that. The last woman they had on their books as a dance contact had retired, so he hoped that this Sazzoni woman would be her replacement. They needed somebody they could rely on, somebody who knew about schedules and deadlines and somebody who would not panic. Some of the staff, particularly Box Office Shirley, were on the verge of panic the whole time although, looking back on the last year, he saw that it had been very successful and that the Little Gem was more than holding its own amongst similar small theatres.

There were only three streets of any significance in Penington Bridge, but a preponderance of antique shops, climbing gear shops, gift shops and cafés. The Market Tea Room was a double-fronted café with frilly curtains and, opening the door, he saw it was full of the sort of olde worlde charm that for some reason irked him. The sort of place where you had to be on your best behaviour, the sort of place his dad would hate for fear of dropping crumbs, the sort of place old ladies frequented and certainly not the place for a guy like him.

There were little circular tables covered with white cloths, tiny pots of fresh flowers, dark spindle-backed chairs and a highly patterned maroon carpet. There was a striped maroon and cream wallpaper below a wide dado and, above it, a particularly awful shade of pink on the uneven walls. The framed pictures of old Penington Bridge showed how little it had changed. It was gloomy, too, or maybe that was because he had stepped inside out of the bright sunlight.

'Mr Bailey?'

He whirled round and returned the enquiring smile the blonde girl in the corner was giving him. Wrong on all counts then. Not dark-haired, not rosy cheeked and definitely not plumpish. She was sitting down so he couldn't be sure of her height but she had a lean look about her with fine features, but it was the big brown eyes that really did it for him. They were the sort of eyes that could turn a grown man's legs to jelly. Add that to the voice and he was well and truly hooked.

'Have you been waiting long, Miss Sazzoni?' he asked for she had a settled look about her and there was a cup of coffee in front of her. 'Please forgive me. The traffic was bad and I couldn't find a parking space. May I get you another coffee?'

'Thank you.'

He sat down opposite her and they exchanged an awkward smile.

Silence. Say something, Matthew, you clown, he told himself fiercely, even if it's only 'what a lovely day'. The fact was he was a bit taken aback by his reaction and hoped to God he wasn't staring like a lovesick teenager. The last time he had been struck dumb by a girl was when Marilyn Rawley joined their sixth-form group but then she had silenced the other boys too.

'I moved house just the other day,' Miss Sazzoni spoke first, as they waited for the coffee to appear. 'My best clothes are still packed away somewhere,' she added, indicating her casual get-up with a rueful smile. 'Otherwise I would have dressed up.'

'Not at all. You look fine,' he said, still hot under his collar and grateful for the small smile she gave him.

He went on to explain how many children they would require for the production plus the back-ups and she took notes.

Could she handle this?

She could.

Did she know of a hall they might hire?

She did. She would make enquiries and get back to him but she was sure there would be no problem.

'Fine.' He gave her an outline of the proposed future programme, indicating where her help might be needed and she made the appropriate notes. She had lovely hands, long slim fingers, no rings but a narrow silver bracelet nestled comfortably round her slender wrist. Right-handed. No polish on her nails but they were cared for and he liked that. A fresh floral scent was drifting his way, barely discernible but there none the less and he liked that too, wanting to get closer, so that he could lift up her lovely fair hair and plant a tiny kiss by her ear.

'Anything else, Mr Bailey?'

'What?' He caught her amused glance, pulled himself together. This was going well, too well, and after the fiasco with Claire and her rambling incompetence, it was refreshing to be dealing with somebody who looked as if she knew what she was doing. If she needed any help, any more information, he told her to call him at the theatre, handing her his business card.

'Leave it with me,' she said, tucking the card away into a small, cream, envelope-type bag, the sort Princess Diana was fond of. Miss Sazzoni, it would seem, travelled light.

'Good.' He settled back in his chair, glancing across the room as a bunch of

American visitors loudly took their seats before requesting pots of English tea and crumpets.

They shared a smile, business concluded.

'Were you an actor?' she asked as they found themselves dallying over the last of the coffee. Matthew wanted to prolong this, wanted to ask her out socially but it was a bit soon and he worried that she might snub him. His chat-up lines were at a minimum and always sounded bloody corny.

'Never,' he said. 'Well, I was in school productions, but I think I knew then it wasn't for me.'

'I wanted to be a dancer,' she said quietly. 'I trained in ballet. I had an audition for the Royal Ballet School, which I was told was an honour in itself but it came to nothing. My sole professional roles were in a couple of musicals in Manchester. I was in the chorus. *Carousel* and *Oklahoma*.'

'They're great musicals,' he said, glancing at her and seeing the disappointment that she was trying her best to hide. 'Didn't it work out then?'

'No. Various reasons. I am rather tall but I think I could have got round that if I had persevered. Perhaps I wasn't hungry enough. Who knows? I did go to an audition for a West End show and I had great hopes for that but . . . ' She shrugged. 'Nothing doing. So I did the next best thing. I did a course in speech and drama and turned to teaching.'

'Lucky for me you did,' he said, anxious to see her smile again. 'Maybe you're best out of it. I've seen what happens behind the scenes. All the bitching. And I'm talking about the men here. All that 'darling' stuff is complete crap . . . sorry, but it is. They're all jealous as hell of each other. Give me admin anytime. It gets the adrenalin going in exactly the same way. There are still deadlines to meet and so on. It's no picnic.'

'I'm sure it's not. Your theatre's got a really good reputation, hasn't it? Not that I've actually been myself.' She grimaced. 'Sorry, I shouldn't say that. I did look at the summer programme but — '

'A bit top heavy,' he conceded, glad she'd pointed out what he had been worrying about. 'We need some comedy to lighten things up. We've got two comedy plays coming up in autumn.'

Walking back to his car, he sensed she wanted to say something but she waited until they were at the car before she said it.

'I know it's very cheeky of me as we've only just met but could I possibly ask a favour?'

'Shoot,' he said cheerfully, thinking that he might well lie down in the middle of the street if she so desired.

'It's the light fitting in my dining-room,' she said. 'I can't work out how to make it stay up. It's one of those things that fit snugly to the ceiling and it's fallen on my head three times already when I've tried. Could you possibly have a look at it? I would ask one of my neighbours but I don't want to start off by looking as if I'm a complete incompetent.' She blushed. 'Sorry. It's OK if you're dashing off but I'm only just round the corner.'

You bet.

'Pity you couldn't ask my dad,' he told her as he finally and not without some considerable effort got the light in place. She could not find her set of steps so he was standing precariously, shoes off, on what was a very nice dining chair. 'He can do this sort of thing standing on his head. He's a marvel round the house. And still my mum complains because he's not much of a gardener.'

'It's the opposite with my parents,' she said. 'Have you time for another cup of coffee?'

He was swimming with coffee, did not even much like coffee, but he grabbed the opportunity to chat a while longer, watching as she rummaged in several cupboards in the kitchen before she found the cups she was looking for. Just for a moment, he thought of telling her about Claire and the sorry episode with the stage china cups but decided not to, as it might look as if he was being critical of a colleague.

'My mum's the gardener in our family and you should see her garden,' Alice went on. 'She does it all herself and it is beautiful. As for my dad — he's not very good at do-it-yourself but mum just calls people in anyway.'

'I like your name,' he said, perching on a high stool at the narrow bench. 'Is it Italian?'

'Oh yes. You know Sazzoni delicatessens?'

'I'm not good with shops,' he admitted. 'But I think I've heard of them.'

'My father owns them,' she said. 'We have Italian connections from way back, but to be honest, I don't feel terribly Italian. My dad does even though he was born in England and had an English mother. We go back from time to time and I speak the language reasonably well, although I wouldn't say I was bilingual. Did you know that it's not as easy as it sounds to make a child bilingual?'

'No I didn't. My parents are both Lancastrians so the question's never arisen,' he said with a grin.

'Last year my parents bought a villa in Italy. It's lovely. It overlooks Lake Como.'

'Very nice,' he muttered, feeling suddenly inadequate.

'So that's him, my dad. That's what he does. What does your father do?' The question hung in the air. It was nothing to do with her what his father did but the moment's irritation passed as he saw that she had not meant to be intrusive but was simply curious to know more about him and his family. He must stop being so sensitive.

'He's a carpet fitter by trade,' he said, looking carefully at her. 'He's very good at it. And he does all sorts of odd jobs too. He's a great bloke.'

She nodded and smiled, and he felt ashamed that he should feel ashamed. It was true. His dad was a great bloke and it was his dad he had to thank for all the encouragement over the years. Given the right opportunities, his dad could have made it to higher things than mere carpet fitting but would he necessarily have wanted that? It seemed to Matthew that, provided you were happy with your lot and didn't start getting dissatisfied with it then it led to a stress-free existence, and his dad was the most laid-back guy he knew.

Alice moved with the grace of a dancer and he just knew as he watched her that he would be doing this — watching her — for a whole lot of years to come. If there was such a thing as love at first sight then that had happened to him when he walked into the Market Tea Room. Maybe he would tell her that someday.

'Must get on,' she said at last, clearing away the cups. 'Sorry to have delayed you and thanks for putting the light up.'

'Give me a call if you're stuck again. I'm not too far away. I have a flat — ' He did not want to call it a bedsit. 'A flat in Kirkley.'

'I like Kirkley. It's a good little market town, isn't it? And very convenient for the theatre.'

'Yes, it's convenient,' he said, knowing as he looked round here that he could never take her there. He didn't say it but he wondered quite how she had afforded this. It was a prime location very close to the centre of Penington Bridge, which was one of the most sought after places in this area. It must have cost a bomb. 'I only have a bedsit,' he said, deciding it was best to be up front about it. 'I hope to get a bigger place sometime but it's the cost.'

'House prices are ridiculous,' she agreed. 'I've had a bit of help with this. Dad was keen for me to get my foot on the rung.'

He got the picture. Her family had money and that could be a serious stumbling block.

He might very well be out of his depth with her. He had always steered clear of girls whom he considered to be out of his league. Daft really, but something of his dad was stuck inside, this fear of stepping over the threshold and trying to be what you were not. Auntie Margaret was much the same, although it was her shyness that did for her. His mum wasn't like that. She wasn't afraid of what his dad nervously called 'mixing'.

'Will you be at the *Oliver* audition?'

'I can be,' he said, determined that he would find some reason to be there.

'See you there then,' Alice said, opening the door and letting in the sounds and smells of the hot sunny day. 'I won't let you down, Mr Bailey.'

'For goodness sake, call me Matthew,' he said quickly. 'Or Matt. Whichever.'

'I like Matthew better,' she said at once. 'And I'm Alice. Just Alice.'

'Just Alice it is,' he repeated, hearing the word roll off his tongue and loving it.

He just had time to nip back to his flat. He needed a quick shower and a change of clothes for this evening. It was the penultimate performance of a play by a new playwright and it was getting good reviews.

His flat was over a florist's but there was a side entrance he used so he never went through the shop. He spent so little time up there that it showed in the general air of neglect. He did his best but he couldn't keep on top of the cleaning and, looking round, he knew his mum would have a fit if she was to see it now. When he had a minute, he would get the Hoover out and give it a going over.

It was just somewhere to doss down. He never cooked. Somebody, a friend of the woman who ran the florist's, did his laundry as there was no washing machine here and it was worth his while to deliver a bag of dirty washing to her and get it back clean a couple of days later.

His flat was a mess and, after seeing what Alice had achieved in just one day, he frowned as he entered. He had never been tidy and he blamed this mess on the fact that there was precious little storage, so his things had to sit either on the floor or at the bottom of a deep basket.

Looking round with fresh eyes, he realized he could never entertain here. Claire had been here but then she was as bad as he was if her own place was anything to go by. Two messy beings together had no hope and in his childhood home, it was always his mum who tidied up after his dad.

He picked up some fish and chips from the chippy down the road and opened a tin of peaches and a tin of custard for dessert. Gourmet meals he did not do but then neither did his mum. She never could be bothered much with cooking and the meals he most remembered from his youth had been made by his grandma. Guiltily, he wondered how she was for he hadn't been to visit her since she had moved to the nursing home. He would not say that they got on that well but then she was an awkward customer and didn't really get on with anybody. For reasons not obvious to him, she did not consider him to be good grandson material and he knew he had disappointed her. She had once told him in that plain-spoken way of hers that she had always wanted a granddaughter, looking at him accusingly as if it was his fault he was a boy. He had told Auntie Margaret about that, not his mum, and she had laughed and said he hadn't to mind because that was what his grandma was like and she didn't mean it.

'People often say things they don't mean, deep down,' she had said, looking at him with that nice smile of hers but, thank God, stopping short of giving him a cuddle and ruffling his hair as she used to.

When the time came and come it would, he wondered what Alice would make of them all, his grandma, his auntie and his mum and dad.

And, perhaps more importantly, what would they make of Alice?

11

Josie's schedule for Christmas Day was in tatters because she had overslept. She had overslept because it had taken her ages to get off last night because her mind had been churning with thoughts of Jack Sazzoni.

It was incredible. She had known even before Matthew had uttered the name. She had known as soon she shook hands with the girl, who was the spit of her mother Valerie. She might well have fainted on the spot but she was made of sterner stuff than that. She was rocked, true, but she did not have the time to ponder on it, not then, because she had so much on her mind, mainly to do with that nerve centre of Christmas: the kitchen. It was just an eating marathon from start to finish. Cooked breakfast to start then the big dinner then the buffet tea and the leftovers would be piling up by then.

'Switch the television off. They've arrived,' she had told Ray the evening before as soon as she heard the car. He had done so, grumbling, but knowing that it stayed off when visitors were in the house. And, although Matthew did not count as a visitor,

Alice certainly did. She did not want Alice to think that they spent their days glued to the damned television, even though, when he wasn't laying carpets, that was precisely what Ray did.

After the introduction, numb from the news, she acted thereafter on automatic pilot. Making them feel at home, providing hot drinks, chatting about everything and nothing, working out almost immediately that Matthew thought the world of this girl. Ray did his best, even though he was a bit shy, and she thought that, all in all, she had managed tolerably well to keep the conversation going. Getting a bit desperate at one point, she had even suggested a board game, and was just about to send Ray off into the loft to locate the old sets of this and that but they had declined, tired from the drive. The weather had been horrible, snow when they set off and now this rain, which looked like it was set in for the night.

Christmas Eve. She remembered the excitement of it when she was little. Sometimes, the best times, her dad was on duty over Christmas and they never saw him but, other times, he was around and, although she never remembered him losing his temper over Christmas, it made for a tension that was not there in his absence.

Tonight, this Christmas Eve, she listened for what seemed hours to the rain pattering for all it was worth against the bedroom window. The damned fairy lights outside the window did not help, flickering on and off all night long. Oh heavens, what a thing to happen. She still could not believe it. Lying in bed beside Ray who was off as soon as his head hit the pillow, she thought about the implications. Memories whirled in a heady mix, back and forth, and as always Jack was there.

★   ★   ★

'Jack Sazzoni's got his eye on you,' Lynn said with a giggle as they waited to be asked to dance. Some people were already on the floor and she and Lynn were doing their best to look as if they couldn't give a bird's feather whether they danced or not. 'I told you he was keen. No, don't look.'

'I'm not looking,' Josie said. She had done the flirting bit already when she had seen him with his friends in the coffee bar they all frequented and she was aware she had caught his attention. Now she had to play it cool for what happened next was entirely up to him. There was a thin dividing line between gently flirting and being thought common.

'These shoes are killing me,' she said, 'My toes are all squashed.'

'So are mine. He's really heavy-footed, that Mick. He kept saying sorry but it's too late then, isn't it? My feet are black and blue.'

'Jack Sazzoni's a good dancer,' she said, for that, in a dance hall full of Felstonian boys like Mick, was something of a rarity. 'I wouldn't mind a dance with him.'

'He's had a few dances already, one with that Penny and one with Valerie whatshername, but he might be saving you for the last waltz,' Lynn said wistfully. Josie gave her a look. Lynn was like this. Full of impossible flights of fancy. She was also having trouble with her hair. Poor Lynn. She had spent all night with rollers in to perfect her 'flick-up' style and it had looked great when they set off but it had drooped by the time they reached the end of Lynn's street and she was not best pleased.

'Will you be going home with Mick if he asks you?'

'Might do. And then you can go home with Jack if he asks you.'

'He's not taking me home,' Josie said. 'He could only take me as far as the football ground. If my dad saw him . . . '

They had never been alone, the two of them, always seeing each other at a respectful distance in the presence of their friends. They thought they were a touch above, that lot he went round with, but Josie was not having any of that. She thought herself every bit as good as them, even though she wouldn't be keen to broadcast in their company that she lived in Riverside. People were so quick to make generalizations, often didn't give you a chance, labelled you straight off. It got on her wick, that sort of thing.

She tried not to look Jack's way because that was such a give-away, but then, as the band returned for the second half of its performance, starting with some upbeat stuff before they switched to their smoochy late-night mood, she saw him pushing his way through the crowd towards her and there he was, standing there in front of her. He was wearing a snappy suit and she was glad now that she was wearing her favourite dress, a good one to twist in, red with its own net petticoat that showed as you danced. She'd done her eyes on the sly over at Lynn's before they arrived and, as he stood there smiling, she gave him the full benefit of her extra lush, super-long lashes.

'You dancing?' was the normal way to do it in Felston, but he asked her properly, holding out his hand as he did so and she warmed instantly to that, smiling and allowing him to draw her gently on to the floor. She caught Lynn's raised eyebrows but ignored her.

And then, as the music soared, she was pulled into his arms.

And that really was that.

★   ★   ★

'Why didn't you tell me she was Jack Sazzoni's daughter?' Josie hissed, drawing Matthew into the kitchen, ostensibly to help her bring the coffee through. 'Talk about knocking the wind out of my sails. You could have said her name was Sazzoni. Why all the mystery?'

'There is no mystery. I thought I had mentioned it and you never asked what her surname was. I didn't think it would matter. How was I to know you knew her dad from way back?' he replied with a puzzled smile, not understanding the significance of all this. 'I knew her family came from Felston originally but it never occurred to me that you might have met him. It's a big town. It didn't seem likely.'

'Why not? Why shouldn't I have met him?' she asked aggressively. 'Was I not good enough for him? Is that what you mean?'

'No, mum. But she did tell me where they used to live and I didn't think you would know anybody from that side of town,' he said.

'The posh side,' she said, unable to keep the bitterness from her voice.

He looked squarely at her. 'Let's be honest. It doesn't matter to me but people like grandma — and dad . . . ' he added with a grimace. 'You know what they're like. Do you know what inverse snobbery is?'

'Of course I do. It's what those two suffer from. I could knock their heads together. Your dad in particular has this inferiority complex. It gets my goat, I keep telling him he's every bit as good as the next man.'

'Exactly. Better than most. What if Alice comes from money? What does it matter? She can't help it Anyway . . . ' he stopped as he saw her face. 'Sorry, but how was I to know you'd had a fling with her dad? It's just a coincidence, that's all.'

'It's an awful coincidence and we didn't have a fling. You ask your Auntie Margaret. She'll tell you. I hate that word, fling,' Josie muttered, placing warm mince pies on a plate and giving them a quick dusting with icing sugar. She poured coffee, the real stuff, from the percolator into a pretty coffee pot that got used about twice a year, and got out the little matching coffee cups that were like doll's china and held about one gulpful.

'What's the matter, Mum?' Matthew's voice was gentle, still not understanding. 'I'm sorry if this has upset you. It's not going to be a problem, is it?'

'It could be. We didn't part on the best of terms if you must know, if it's any of your business,' she went on, furious with him for doing this to her. She was also furious with herself for reacting like this. Talk about making a mountain out of a molehill. Jack Sazzoni would have relegated her to the back of his mind and, by rights, she ought to have done the same. She hadn't a clue why he still lurked there. She had only started to go out with Jack originally because she knew full well her mum would have kittens about it. It was Lynn who had dared her to make a play for him and she *had* done, trying to do it with some degree of subtlety — as subtle as a teenager could be anyway — and it had worked. It had finally worked that night at Bristles. She was like that in her teens, a bit bolshie, maybe she still was. Margaret had tried to warn her off but when did a seventeen-year-old take any notice of her much older sister — twenty years older, in fact — who had never landed a man herself? She knew it wasn't Matthew's fault that Alice was Jack's daughter and it wasn't the girl's fault either, but that didn't make it any easier.

This situation, as she saw it, had the potential for one huge blow-out.

'He was my first proper boyfriend,' she said, popping the bag of icing sugar back in the cupboard and avoiding her son's eye.

'Was he?' Matthew smiled but she could tell he was a touch embarrassed.

'Yes, well, we went out together for about six months and then I finished with him. And that's all there is to it.'

'I see. Why did you dump him?'

'We weren't suited and I'd met your dad,' she said. 'And that's all I'm saying. That's all you need to know and that's all you're getting to know.'

'Like me and Claire, I suppose,' he said with a grin. 'She dumped me and then I met Alice so she did me a good turn.'

'Yes. That's how it is.'

'So you've no need to worry about it, Mum. It happens all the time. You'll probably laugh about it when you do meet him.'

'Am I likely to?' she asked sharply. 'Are you two serious?'

He shrugged but smiled anyway and it was as good an answer as any.

'I don't suppose I'll recognize him these days and he won't remember me either.' She fussed with the cups and the little cream jug, a sudden sharp vision of Jack — aged twenty

— appearing. 'Does Alice take sugar?'

'No.'

'We're right then. I've sugared your dad's already.' She picked up the tray, put it down again. 'Look, Matthew, the fact is her dad really gets up your dad's nose. God knows what will happen when they get together again. They were at each other's throats. I know you can't imagine it, not your dad, but he used to have a temper once he got going. If something really riled him that is.'

'Temper? You're joking. It's a long time ago,' Matthew said, nicking one of the mince pies. 'I hope you're not going to hold it against Alice,' he added, a dangerous glint in his eye that told her she would get nowhere if she did. It also told her, and this gave her a jolt, that she was no longer the number one lady in his life. Alice had already stepped into that role and that was how it should be.

'I wouldn't dream of it,' she said, trying to tell herself to calm down. It wasn't the end of the world and Matthew was right. It was a long time ago.

12

Margaret, as she so often did, was fussing round, helping her get ready. She never went out herself, not to dances anyway, and she took pride in helping Josie make the best of herself.

She stood there, big for a girl, dark-haired and solidly built like their dad, taking out Josie's rollers and handing her the hairpins one by one and, not before time, Josie stuck the last of them into the French pleat, very nearly piercing her head in the process and grimacing. A final touch up with the tail of the comb and there she had it, a fantastic beehive. She reached for the extra-hold cheap hair-spray and lavishly applied it.

They had the radio on and, from its place on the window ledge, the only place where they could get decent reception, Chubby Checker's 'Let's Twist Again' blared out, still in the charts after goodness knows how many weeks. It was too fast a song to be listening to when you were doing something as important as putting the finishing touches to your hair.

'You look smashing, love,' Margaret said, squeezing her shoulders and smiling. 'Go easy on the make-up. You know what he's like.'

Through the mirror they exchanged a sisterly look. They both knew what *he* was like. She had no idea what her dad had done when he was in the police force but she wouldn't have liked to be a criminal and have him facing her. He was a brute and Josie knew their mum put up with the occasional, what she called, 'lashing out' for one reason only. She was terrified of being 'shamed'. Being shamed as a family was the very worst thing that could happen. You could be knocked about rotten, as she often was, you could watch him knock your kids about, you could defend him and make excuses for him but you could never ever be shamed in other people's eyes.

They were never to breathe a word outside the house. And they never did. Bruises could always be explained away. For some reason, Margaret bore the brunt of it. 'Our Margaret's accident prone,' her mother would often say with a sad shake of her head. 'She can trip over a pin, that girl.'

Josie felt guilty to be going out enjoying herself, as she would certainly do, and leaving poor Margaret here at home. But Margaret brought it on herself, and sometimes, uncharitably, Josie wondered if she deliberately acted the martyr. There was no need for Margaret to act like she was some sort of Cinderella. She had a job and some money and she could go out and enjoy herself as well, except it wasn't so easy now she was in her thirties and most of her friends were married ladies. She didn't know why Margaret had taken the decision to put a stop to all thoughts of finding a man and getting married and, more importantly, moving out of here. That wasn't an option, Margaret had told her, for she wouldn't leave Josie here on her own with them.

The general public assumption about Margaret was that she had lost a young man in the war, lost in Singapore, and never got over him. Somehow, that was acceptable. That meant you were looked on with sympathy, understanding. Josie suspected there had never been a young man, that he was just a figment of Margaret's romantic imagination, but that was by the by. Margaret had him in her head and, in an odd way, had almost come to believe he had existed. She had once found a photograph in a drawer in Margaret's bedroom, a photograph of a man she did not know.

'Who is it?' she had asked but she never got a proper answer.

'It's him. Put it back,' Margaret would reply and that was the end of it.

Margaret was plain with slightly bulbous eyes, not at all pretty, but that should be no obstacle. She was nice and thoughtful and had a lovely way with kids. The truth was Margaret had just stopped trying. She was thirty-seven now, which seemed elderly to Josie but she was still young enough to have a baby if she got married and she would be such a lovely mum. She was a nurse, not fully trained, but she worked at the psychiatric hospital just out of town, going there every day on the bus. Josie did not enquire what went on there but she could not help thinking that it did Margaret no good to be working with those sorts of people. She had once said as much but, unusually, Margaret had flared up at that and told her they were lovely folks and they couldn't help it if their minds had got a bit out of skelter. Suitably chastened, not often told off by her sister, Josie had never referred to it again.

Margaret was old enough to be her mum and in many ways, Josie thought more of her than she did their mum. Her mum had got set in her ways, used to having just the one daughter and then she had come along unexpectedly when her mum had turned forty. Margaret had apparently been thrilled to bits but she wasn't sure what her mum's reaction had been. But she could guess.

Coming into the bedroom without knocking — well, it was her mother's room after all, the only one with a decent sized dressing table, her mum waddled over to the window and switched off the radio, coughing and waving the offending whiff of hairspray away as she came over to them.

'Powerful stuff that hair lacquer,' she said. 'It can't do your hair any good. It looks better loose if you ask me. It puts a good two years on you like that. Unless that's the intention?' she asked sharply.

It was, but she had no *intention* of telling her mother that. 'Everybody wears their hair up for the dance,' she said. 'It keeps it neat. And it shows off your earrings.'

She only had three pairs of her own, clip-ons because she hadn't had her ears pierced yet and she had chosen the sparkly ones tonight, the ones that looked like diamonds. At the end of the night, they left ridges in her ears and hurt like mad when she unclipped them, but it was worth a bit of discomfort for the effect.

Her mum sniffed. She was good at disapproving sniffs. 'If you've any thoughts, young lady, of getting serious about Jack

Sazzoni, you can forget it,' she said. 'Your dad won't have it that's for sure. Tell her, our Margaret.'

Margaret frowned. 'She knows what's what, Mum.'

'I'm not serious,' Josie said, catching Margaret's warning glance in the mirror. 'I'm only seventeen.'

'I was serious about your dad at seventeen, more's the pity,' Hetty said, folding her arms below her ample bosom. 'And girls have babies at seventeen so just you watch it. If you bring shame on us, the Lord help me, I'll swing for you. Take heed of Margaret. She's always been a good girl.'

She saw the look her mother and Margaret exchanged in the mirror. She could never fathom why her mother could take such a nasty turn with Margaret from time to time because Margaret was not far short of a saint.

'Margaret never does anything wrong and it's not right that he takes it out on her,' Josie said, seeing her mum's expression tighten and doing what she knew was best. Shutting up.

The happy moment between the two sisters was lost now and Josie eyed her mother warily through the mirror, watching as she picked up the new shoes she had bought for tonight, pale blue pointy-toed shoes with tiny Louis heels. She turned them over noting the price label but making no comment; Josie had a job now at the town hall and was earning money although, by the time she had given her mum something for her 'keep', she didn't have a lot left. The shoes were lower-heeled than usual but that was for Jack's benefit. He was not a lot taller than she was and she liked him to be able to look down at her as they danced. Margaret had given her something towards them but she would not blab about that. Margaret liked her to look nice and it gave her pleasure to help out.

Josie continued to put on her make-up, her hand shaking a little under her mother's steady gaze. She didn't know what her mum meant about being serious. She liked Jack, goodness knows, and he was good fun and perhaps more importantly all the other girls were after him. It was the Italian connection, of course, that made him interesting. All the other boys, Felstonians to the very core, were so hopeless when it came to compliments, but Jack was wonderful, slipping effortlessly into Italian and murmuring soft words. She hadn't a clue what he was actually saying, but she could hazard a guess by the look in his eyes and the Italian language was so beautiful, so musical. Jack was so gentle, not afraid to be courteous. He treated her well, like china, putting his hand in the small of her back to guide her along, helping her to her feet . . . little things like that, little things that made her feel good, like a lady.

'That's more than enough,' her mother said, putting her hand on Josie's shoulder but, unlike Margaret's, her touch was like a clamp. 'Your eyes don't need make-up. And go easy on that scent Your dad's waiting downstairs to check you before you go out and you know what he's like.'

Josie put the tiny bottle of Coty L'Aimant in her bag. She would do her eyes later, round at her friend's, but she must remember to wipe it all off before she came home. Her dad usually stayed up until she got back and, like the policeman he had once been, he could spot illicitly-applied eye shadow and sooty layers of mascara from the depths of his armchair even without his glasses on. She had no finer feelings for him, how could she? She looked at her friends' dads with wonder, saw how proud some of them were of their daughters and that was hard. What had she done to deserve this? What had Margaret done? Had he wanted sons? Was that it? Somewhere, deep in the back of her mind, there was a memory of a big man calling her name, lifting her off her feet and twirling her round and round and she was all of a giggle

. . . What had happened? What had gone wrong?

'So, are you meeting him tonight then?' her mum asked, handing her the little boxy handbag.

'Meeting who?'

'Who do you think? That Jack Sazzoni and don't try to be clever with me, Josie Pritchard,' her mum said, lowering her voice. 'Because if you are then think on to what I've told you. It won't do. It can't come to anything. If it carries on, it'll only end in tears. Your dad won't have no truck with foreigners. And that's a fact.'

'Jack's not a foreigner,' Margaret flushed but still spoke up for her. 'He's as English as we are. He was born here. His mother was born here.'

'That's as maybe. He's got Italian roots and you can't shake your roots off. I knew his father Lorenzo and he was as Italian as they come. His accent was terrible. When I say I knew him . . . ' her mum seemed flustered suddenly, 'I knew of him and I did see him the once. It was during the war and they weren't liked, him and his family. They weren't to be trusted. There was a lot of whispers and it all got a bit nasty and then the men in the family ended up being arrested.'

126

'What for?'

'What do you think for? The Italians were enemy aliens that's why,' her mother said. 'You have no idea what it was like during the war. Has she, Margaret?'

'She wasn't born until it was very nearly over, Mum, how can she know?'

'Where did they go?' Josie asked, slipping one of her earrings in and admiring it, 'when they were arrested.'

'I don't know and I can't say I cared either. Isle of Man I think. After the war, he came back, large as life, no worse for wear, and that business of his blossomed. It didn't seem fair. He had a big opinion of himself, although he ended up big and fat.' She nodded with satisfaction. 'That's what happens to Italian men and women. They start off lovely but they go off. That English girl he married thought she was better than anybody else. She had to turn for him as well. They won't have it any other way, them Catholics. And that's another reason why you're not to get yourself caught up with him.'

She was off. Josie sighed, caught Margaret's sigh, too, but luckily their mum did not. Her mother was an out and out bigot and there was no talking sense into her because she was too far gone and too set in her ways.

'Anyway, you haven't answered me.' Her

127

mother gave her a shrewd glance. 'Are you meeting him?'

'I'm going out to Bristles with Lynn Mason,' Josie said, to shut her up, pleading with Margaret through the mirror not to say anything, even though she knew she would not. Margaret was loyal to the point of insanity. The things Margaret had done to protect her made her feel ashamed. Margaret had taken punishment after punishment from dad to save her skin. If anything went wrong, she always pushed Josie aside and shouldered the blame. It wasn't fair. Margaret wasn't a child any more and she should be standing up to him. They both should.

What she didn't tell her mum was that, after she had called on Lynn, the two of them were meeting up with Jack and a lad whom Lynn was sweet on called Mick. Before they went dancing, they were going out for a quick drink and she and Lynn would probably opt for a Babycham. After that, they would be having a meal in town and, having starved herself all day, she was looking forward to the prawn cocktail and mixed grill she would choose but wished it was just the two of them, her and Jack, because Lynn was very awkward with boys and, as well as that, she had no style and no conversation of interest. She was good with figures, the paper kind, and had a job in an insurance company, but no idea when it came to making the best of her own shape. Very few girls were perfect but you had to play to your good points. Josie knew that. Hadn't she read that sort of thing time and again in her women's magazines? For instance, she had short legs, which did her no favours but an enviable bosom which did.

She sighed again, stepping into the new shoes, taking a last look at her reflection in the long mirror in her mum and dad's bedroom. She had worn the dress before but Jack had never seen it. It was crimplene, straight, sleeveless, blue, a lovely colour that matched her eyes. Jack would notice. He always noticed little things like that and always offered a little compliment. Round here, you practically had to call up the firing squad and have a lad up against the wall before he could manage to utter a compliment. They considered it soft.

'Ray Bailey's mum says as how he's fixed on you,' her mum said, her voice taking on a wheedling note.

'Does she now?'

'She does and don't take that tone. He's a good lad is Ray. He has a good steady job. He'll look after you, will Ray.'

And he'll never hurt you. But she didn't say that.

'He's a big dope,' Josie said, fastening her bracelets. 'He was a big dope at five and he hasn't changed.'

'He has changed.' Her mother's indignation was comical. 'Ask your sister. Margaret likes him well enough.'

'He's a nice enough lad,' Margaret confirmed. 'But he should speak up for himself. That's what I think anyway.'

Hetty's eyes flashed with annoyance. 'You don't know anything, our Margaret. When you're married with a family then I might take some notice of what *you* have to say.'

They both ignored that. Josie was not getting into a conversation about Ray Bailey, big lump that he was. Imagine having to get his mum to speak out for him. Margaret was right. If he hadn't the guts to ask her out himself then he could lump it. Lynn had a fancy for him. Maybe they'd get together?

'Do you like this colour on me?' she asked, seeing her mum's critical eyes on her.

'It's all right,' her mum said abruptly. 'Could be worse.'

And that was as far as the praise went.

It was left to Margaret to give her a little kiss and tell her, her own eyes shining, that she looked very nice.

13

Margaret went back home after the Christmas buffet tea, saying she had to check on Percy, her blue budgerigar. She thought the world of that bird who seemed to rule the roost at that. Percy of Percy Street, it appeared, did not like to be left alone too long and it seemed a shame on Christmas Day. Anyway, she'd bought him a new little toy and she wanted to see how he liked it. And she had her knitting to finish. She was on the last sleeve and then she could get it stitched up.

Josie had glanced at Ray, saw his deadpan expression, and had to stop herself from laughing, but this was her sister and she was deadly serious.

'I'll get your coat then, Margaret,' she said, retrieving it from the peg in the hall. It was her warm winter coat, rust-coloured with a belt, quite nice, but Margaret wore it with clumpy shoes and a pull-on knitted hat that wouldn't have looked out of place on a teapot. At sixty-five, her face was unlined as yet, eyes clear and in some ways she looked better now than she had for a long time. Dad dying and her mother being shipped off to the nursing home, resulting in her being left in peace at last, had worked wonders. She had done her duty by their mother, looked after her for as long as was humanly possible before it became just too much.

'Jack Sazzoni's girl, eh?' Margaret said, as she slipped her coat on. 'Heck, Josie, that could be awkward for you.'

'It will only be awkward if our Matthew's serious about her,' Josie said. 'You know what they're like these days. It could all blow over.'

'I don't think so.' Margaret spoke as if she was an authority on such matters, clamping her hat on her head, covering her greying curls, before pulling on matching wool mittens. She enjoyed her knitting, always had something on the go. 'If I go now, I'll catch that old film I want to watch. And thanks for the dinner, love. It was very nice. That turkey was a treat. Very moist.'

'It wasn't bad, was it?' Josie said, pleased she'd said that because she'd worried herself sick over the blessed bird. How she'd managed to get herself back on track this morning she would never know, but Ray had for once turned up trumps and succeeded in not making too much of a mess of the minor kitchen tasks she set him. She and Margaret gave each other a little hug, saying that they'd see each other tomorrow when they went to see mother. Margaret never wore perfume or make-up, smelt instead of soap and Vosene shampoo.

'Ray, love, she's ready for off,' she called and he came downstairs, his hat from his cracker still on, shrugging into his best overcoat for, after all, it was Christmas. Josie pulled the tissue hat off his head before shoving the pair of them off into the dark night. 'Watch your step,' she called after them, for it was a lot colder and the path was already icing over. Closing the door on them, she could hear Ray starting up a conversation, not that he would get far because Margaret never said much. Somebody had once asked her why she was so quiet and she had remarked, quite tartly for once, that when she had something to say, she would say it.

Ray would walk Margaret home because it was dark and he didn't like her being out on her own in the dark. The damned budgie was just an excuse, Josie knew that, but she didn't argue. Margaret led her own life. She had not made many changes to the little house they had grown up in, although Ray had redecorated it for her from top to bottom and had got her some end of rolls of carpet that he fitted in the back sitting room and the front room that Margaret kept just for show.

'She's a lovely lady, your sister,' Alice said as the door closed on them. 'She was telling me she's retired now but she used to do nursing. I admire people who do that.'

'She's all right, is Margaret,' Josie said, playing it down. If she told her the whole story, Alice would have a blue fit but then you never understood about domestic abuse unless you'd suffered it yourself. She had kept it quiet as her mum wanted. To be honest, she had never been tempted to tell anybody. She did not want people to know. She hadn't even told Ray who would have been astonished because he and dad had always got on quite well together, and he'd looked up to him on account of his getting the medal. The medal sat in a drawer upstairs and she never looked at it. You couldn't get away from the fact that her father had done it, rescued that child from a blazing house with no thoughts of his own safety. It had left him with health problems, for the smoke had got on his chest and that all contributed to his death and so the medal, like it or not, had to stay.

She'd been a bit funny about leaving Matthew with his granddad when he was little but she needn't have worried. Her father was like Jekyll and Hyde. He was kindness

134

itself to the little lad and, because a bond had developed between them, she'd never ever say anything to Matthew about it. Some illusions were best kept intact.

The honest truth was that she had been glad when he died and never felt an ounce of sympathy during his short final illness. He'd never bent to make amends either. If he had, if he'd begged forgiveness at the last, she didn't honestly know what she would have done.

Alice, to her credit, seemed embarrassed to talk about *her* father and the undoubted success he had achieved. The Sazzonis, as Josie was well aware, had gone from strength to strength. There was a branch of their deli in Felston High Street but she never went in, not because she was frightened she might meet Jack because she knew he had moved away long since, but because it was just too pricey and Ray didn't care for fancy stuff, very much a pea and pie man. He liked plain boiled ham, not the fancy Italian cooked meats that Sazzoni & Son stocked, together with so many different kinds of pasta. It would never catch on, that Mediterranean cooking, that olive oil and so on.

Alice had eaten everything put in front of her and that pleased Josie who could not abide faddy eaters. In fact, she was not spoilt

135

in the least and, in any other circumstances, she would have been thrilled that Matthew had picked such a nice uncomplicated girl. She wasn't afraid to muck in with the chores either, which was another point in her favour. One of his previous girlfriends, a girl called Claire whom he had brought home the once, had just sat there and been content to be waited on hand and foot. A real giggler with nothing between her ears and, although Ray had taken to her for obvious reasons, she was glad that it hadn't lasted. There had to be something other than sex in a relationship for it to last, although try telling that to hot-blooded youngsters.

Alice was tall and slender and had the most beautiful corncoloured hair that wouldn't need any help for a while to come. She got all that, her shape and colouring from her mother. She had her fathers deep brown eyes and his way of talking with her hands. Tie her hands behind her back and she would be silent as the grave. Ray was taken with her, she could tell that, although it would take a long time for him to thaw out, to get over his nervousness at meeting a stranger, a young lady at that, who spoke nicely and had a classy look about her. He tried to cover up his nerves by striking up a conversation about his blasted carpets which was about as boring as you could get, and eventually she had to silence him rather abruptly to put an end to it. Who the hell wanted to know about the merits of different types of carpet? Although Alice had gallantly put on a show of interest.

Margaret had not been a lot of help either, managing about ten words in total, but then she was shy in company and Josie could see, rather to her irritation, that she was overawed by Alice. What was wrong with her family?

When Ray got back, Alice offered to help with the washing-up that was piled any old how on the worktop and, to Josie's surprise, Ray promptly escorted her — there was no other word for it — into the kitchen. At least the kitchen would not disappoint. Ray had just put a new one in, a fitted one, all bought in from IKEA, wood effect and very nice. Ray would be hard pressed to know where the washing-up liquid was but he would find it soon enough.

'Your dad likes her,' she said quietly to Matthew when the door had closed behind them. She had made a brief protest about the washing-up, saying they should leave it, but Alice had quietly insisted. 'Nice girl. Looks like her mother as I remember.'

'What's the story behind it all?' Matthew asked, rummaging for his favourite as she passed him the box of Quality Street. 'Don't say Dad went out with her mum?'

'As if!' Josie managed a laugh. 'Valerie was too good for the likes of your dad. Or thought she was anyway,' she added, feeling a moment's indignation on his behalf.

'Is Dad OK?' Matthew asked, voice casual but a hint of anxiety there nonetheless. 'He doesn't seem himself.'

'Doesn't he? How doesn't he seem himself?'

'He seems preoccupied. His job's secure, isn't it?'

'Oh yes. Safe as houses.'

'Well, something's up.'

Surprised, she stared at him. Ray didn't seem any different to her although, come to think of it, she had caught him out just sitting staring into space once or twice lately. She hoped to God he wasn't ill and keeping it from her. Just you wait, after Christmas, she would tackle him about it. If he thought he could get away with not seeing the doctor then he could think again. She'd drag him there if needs must. They had this new young woman doctor at the practice and he was scared stiff of having to see her.

'Your dad's fine,' she replied with a smile. 'Don't worry about him. I'll sort him out. But, getting back to you — ' She checked her voice, looked towards the kitchen where they could hear Alice's cheerful voice amidst the clattering dishes. 'I know it's not something a mum's supposed to ask but just how serious are you about Alice? Come on, you can tell me.'

She had overstepped the mark, she saw at once, saw also from the tight look on his face that she would get nowhere taking the bossy approach. Subtlety had never been her strong point.

'In my day,' she went on, feeling about a hundred years old as she uttered the words. 'Back in the sixties, we generally got engaged at about eighteen, saved up for a deposit for two years then got married. That was the norm round here. It was expected. You had a nice wedding and a honeymoon up in the Lakes or down south. A whole week if you could afford to take that long off. Do you know, Matthew, before we got married, we wanted a house in Long Drive but we couldn't afford it because they wanted £2,300.'

Matthew laughed. 'Time's change,' he said.

'They certainly do.' She smiled with him. 'And then a year on, you had your first child and it was considered nice if you had a boy. A couple of years later, another child and again, it was nice if this time it was a girl. One of each. The ideal family. It was all planned to

139

perfection,' she added with a slight smile. 'Didn't always work out like that of course. Rarely worked out like that. Some had two boys. Or two girls. An extra baby you had not planned. Or just the one sometimes.'

She stopped talking. Josie had known from the moment Matthew had walked in with this girl last night that, for him, this was very much it and, judging from Alice's face, from the way she looked at him, it was the same for her too. There had been no need to ask the question for it was plain for all to see. They were in love. Her boy and his girl. In that case, the only way for her to play it was to be honest. Well, fairly honest.

When she met Jack again and odds were that she would, she would be pleasant and friendly, happy for her son, happy for his daughter. They might mention the past in passing for they could scarcely do otherwise, but plenty of water had passed under the bridge since those far-off days and they were grown-up enough now to deal with it. Ray hadn't realized the significance of the name yet, so smitten by the girl that he had scarcely taken it in. Ray would be fine. He had mellowed a good deal and, after all, he had got his girl, hadn't he?

Valerie would be harder to take. She had not changed. She knew that from one or two things Alice had let slip. She was still the brittle, starched knickers Valerie who, she had heard on the Felston grapevine, had had a tough time with her babies. She was sorry for that, of course, wouldn't wish difficulties like that on her worst enemy. At least, she had managed to produce Alice and that was some achievement.

'You all right, Mum? You look tired.'

'I am tired,' she said. 'It's Christmas and that Lockerbie thing upset me.'

'Yes. It was awful,' Matthew said with feeling. 'But you haven't to let things like that get to you.'

'I know. Your dad says the same but I can't help it.' She smiled at him. She would never say it, not exactly, tell him how much she loved him, how fiercely proud she was of this handsome young man who, once upon a time had been her little boy, but surely he must know it.

She had wanted more babies after him but it hadn't happened and they had never bothered to find out why. Ray would have died of embarrassment in front of the doctor and, to be honest, she wasn't too keen on all the buttering up she would have to do if he had been told he had a low sperm count. It would shatter him, something like that.

So they settled for Matthew.

14

'We'd like to come with you and Auntie Margaret to see Grandma this afternoon,' Matthew said on Boxing Day morning. Josie had done a proper breakfast with all the trimmings and felt now that she couldn't eat another thing for a week. The fridge was still stuffed to capacity and you had to get every damned thing out before you found what you wanted. Eventually, she would have to throw most of it away. But that was the joy of Christmas.

She looked at her son. He had originally said he and Alice would be setting off back to the Lakes directly after breakfast, but it seemed they were hanging on a while. She had not, however, anticipated that they would want to see Hetty. She sighed, trying to hide it, realizing she had been half-expecting this to crop up. Hetty was his grandmother after all and, strange as it might seem, Matthew had some sort of understanding with her, seemed to find something in his grandmother that had slipped by her. Hetty had never been one for the fond grandmother bit, never one for quick cuddles, more on the brusque side with him, so it was hard to credit but there it was.

'I'm not sure that's a good idea, love. She's gone downhill these last six months and she's not looking so well. It will just upset you. It might be best to remember her as she was.'

'No, Mum. I'd like to see her,' Matthew said, adopting his obstinate stance, which told her it was a lost cause. She glanced at Ray hoping for some support but he was engrossed in the *TV Times*, planning his evening's viewing.

'We've bought her a little present,' Alice chipped in. 'It's a lavender gift set. I know it's a bit old-ladyish but I hope she likes it.'

'That's nice of you,' she said, managing a smile. They had bought her a black handbag and a car valeting pack for Ray. Very likely chosen and bought by Alice, so the family tradition would continue. 'She will like that, Alice,' she added, wondering how to put them off when they were so obviously raring to go.

'Good idea,' Ray said, looking up. 'Why don't we all go together. We can make a family trip of it. Get it over with in one go. Mind you, she'll need reminding who you are, Matthew. What have we bought her, Josie?'

'We have bought her a nightdress and we have wrapped it in lovely gold paper,' Josie said, giving Ray a withering look which completely passed him by. Turning aside, she exchanged a small smile with Alice. Alice knew what was what.

They had done the Boxing Day visit, ever since her mum had been in the nursing home. Christmas Day was chock-a-block, matron had told them on the first Christmas, and they liked to stagger the visitors. And with so much happening on the day itself, carols, the excitement of the turkey dinner and a few games, the residents were normally very tired, so a visit next day made more sense.

'All right then, but I'll ring first,' Josie said, stalling for time. 'Just to make sure she's well enough to see us. If she's feeling off then it will be a waste of time. We'll just be standing round like spare dinners. I'll see if this afternoon will be all right.'

She went into the hall. The others disappeared into the lounge where *Only Fools and Horses* was on television and she waited a moment until she was sure they would not disturb her before dialling the number. At that moment, she would have welcomed the news that her mother had passed away peacefully during the night, hating herself for thinking such a terrible thing but it would save any embarrassment and she did not fancy one little bit having to sit in that small room at the nursing home, trying to steer the conversation into safe waters. Hetty was like a time bomb, likely to go off at any second.

Her mother was fine, she was assured, although she had enjoyed her Christmas dinner a little too much yesterday, was suffering from indigestion and was a bit grumpy.

So, what was new?

'We were thinking of coming to see her this afternoon if that's all right?' Josie asked, crossing her fingers as she spoke. She knew she could fib her heart out, tell the others that mother was not well enough to see them but that didn't seem right somehow.

'Hold on. I'll have a quick word,' the nurse said. 'It could be a problem, Mrs Bailey.'

Problem?

There was a roar of laughter from the lounge, Ray's guffaw predominant, and she covered the mouthpiece a moment as if it was inappropriate, listening to the silence at the other end of the phone, waiting for the nurse to come back.

'Mrs Pritchard's in a very odd mood,' the nurse's voice at last, breathless with the hint of a giggle in it. 'She says she will see you and your sister but not Mr Bailey or your son. She requests female company only today. I'm sorry. She's very insistent.'

Josie made a decision. Her mother had never mentioned Jack Sazzoni in twenty-odd years so why should she talk about him today? Josie would take Alice along and introduce her as Alice and that would be that. It was all first names only in that place so there would be nothing odd about it. And, if Hetty did show any signs of talking about him, she would divert her and Margaret would help. She was good at that, little diversions. A box of Mum's favourite fruit jellies would do the trick.

It would have to be a flying visit anyway for Matthew was fretting about getting back to Kirkley. Getting time off at Christmas *and* New Year was unknown in his business but Helen, his boss, had insisted on him taking it this once. Everybody else was in and for Christ's sake did he think he was indispensable? It would mean he would never get Christmas off again, she told him, not whilst he was working for her, so he had better make the most of it.

★ ★ ★

'I haven't told Ray yet that you are Jack's daughter,' Josie said promptly as they set off.

146

Margaret had insisted on making her own way there and she hadn't pressed her. If she wanted to be a martyr to buses, Christmas schedule at that, then so be it. 'It will have to come out though. I'll wait until you've gone. I am right in thinking that Matthew told you about it?'

'Yes.' Alice laughed. 'I couldn't believe it.'

'Neither can I.' Josie sighed. 'It's a big coincidence but there you are. These things happen. It won't matter, not to you and Matthew and I don't suppose we'll be in each other's pockets, not with them living up there and all. We don't get up to the Lakes much. Ray's not one for driving long distances and he hates the motorway. We've only been up to see Matthew once since he's been there and that was because I was beside myself to know what his place was like. Ray made such a fuss. He can't do with packing and holidays. I used to drag him off but he was such a wet week he spoilt my holiday so now we don't bother. What I'm trying to say is that we won't be up to the Lakes much to your mum and dad's. That is . . . ' She paused. 'Sorry, I'm making far too many assumptions here. It's just that you two do look right together. You and Matthew.'

'We get on very well,' Alice said but there was a little caution in her voice and Josie

147

knew she was stepping on thin ice. Stop being so nosey, it was nothing to do with her whichever way it went. It would be more convenient all round for her if it went all ends up and they parted company, but that wasn't fair because she didn't want Matthew to be let down or Alice for that matter. For better or worse, she already liked this girl, was starting to think of her as the daughter she had never had.

'I always feel Boxing Day's a big let-down, don't you?' she said, turning out of Crook Terrace on the way to Upper Felston and the nursing home. 'And it's a complete waste of time planning a proper meal because everybody's too stuffed to enjoy it. Matthew likes his chocolates, doesn't he?'

'He does.' Beside her, Alice laughed. 'He's lucky he doesn't seem to have a weight problem.'

'That creeps up on you. Are you sure you want to do this? I wouldn't have been offended if you'd wanted to stay with Matthew. I hope I haven't dragged you along.'

'No. I didn't want to watch *The Great Escape* and they seem glued to it.'

'You might change your mind by the time you've had a round with my mother,' Josie warned her. 'She might be getting frail but verbally, she's a heavyweight. She can stun

148

you with a word. Speaks her mind. And the annoying thing is I still feel about twelve when I'm with her. Do you feel like that with your mum?'

'Not exactly,' Alice said, relaxing back into her seat. Josie was a good driver, handling the elderly Volvo and the busy traffic with aplomb. 'It's funny you knowing my mum and dad. It's funny, too, that we didn't realize.'

'How would you? Have you told them yet?'

'No. Not over the phone,' she admitted. 'I'll break it gently when I see them at New Year. It seems so strange you and mum knowing each other when you were young. How old was she then?'

'She's a couple of years older than me so that would make her nineteen.' Josie seemed to make a decision as they approached a roundabout, moving quickly into the inner lane and signalling left, with a quick wave of her hand as apology to the driver behind. 'I'll take you round by Bristles,' she said. 'Show you where we used to go dancing. It was where I met your dad. You never lived here, did you? In Felston?'

'No. Mum and Dad moved before I was born. I used to come to visit my grandparents and then . . . ' She fell silent, remembering. 'There was an accident. Granddad had a heart attack at the wheel and crashed the car into a wall and Grandma was injured and died soon afterwards so, after the funerals and everything, we never came back again. There didn't seem any point and I suppose it would have upset my mother.' She wasn't exactly sure about that for her mother had never, as she remembered, shown much emotion when the accident occurred. But then, when *did* her mother show emotion?

'I'm sorry, that was a dreadful thing to happen losing them both at once. I didn't mean to pry. This is it. This is where Bristles was.' Josie pulled up and switched off the engine. 'Over there. It doesn't look much from the outside, does it? Offices now, of course, but believe me, it was a very smart dance hall when we were young. They had a live band and a singer who fancied himself rotten and we loved that. In the interval, they put on records but it wasn't the same.'

'What sort of dancing?' Alice glanced at her, saw the intent expression.

'All kinds. Ballroom and jiving and twisting. That sort of stuff.' Josie shrugged. 'I was never much of a dancer, not like you. I was a bit top-heavy for dancing but your father wasn't bad. A lot better than Ray. He can't dance for toffee. Says it makes him feel a complete twit. But then that's Ray. He blamed his size but that's nothing to do with it. Some big men are very light on their feet. Matthew's quite a bit like him, deep down. Oh I know he's done well for himself and he's ambitious but he's insecure underneath it all.' She stole a glance Alice's way, smiled. 'Sorry. It's not meant as a criticism. And I suppose you've noticed that already?'

'Of course I have. He's very good at his job, you know, but I like it that he's not too full of himself,' Alice told her. 'And it does no harm to be cautious as he is.'

'Will you marry him if he asks you?'

'What?' Alice stared at her. For a moment, it irritated her that Josie — mother of Matthew or not — should ask such a personal question, but then she realized, as she caught something of the anguish in the other woman's face, that she hadn't meant to be rude or nosy.

'Sorry . . . none of my business,' Josie said, flushing with sudden confusion. 'You don't need to answer that.'

'It's OK.' Feeling an unexpected fondness for the older woman, Alice reached over, touched her hand, was relieved when Josie gripped it, surprised when she saw the moist eyes. 'The answer's yes. But I don't know if he will yet. We haven't known each other that long.'

'Huh! That's neither here nor there.'

'I don't think he's looking forward to meeting my mum and dad. Scared that they'll think he's not worthy of me.' She laughed to show that she thought that idea preposterous. 'He's no need to worry. Mum might give him a tough time but Dad will be fine. And frankly, I don't particularly care what my mum thinks.' She withdrew her hand and fiddled a moment with the amber necklace Matthew had bought her for Christmas. It was an expensive gift, one he could not afford, and managed to pale into insignificance the shirt and tie she had bought him.

'Oh, I see.' Josie took a final look at the nondescript building which seemed to hold so many memories and switched on the engine. 'We'd better get ourselves there. It will be afternoon tea and, if we ask nicely, they might bring us a cup of tea and a mince pie.'

'You won't say anything to Matthew, will you?' Alice asked, clicking on her seat belt and seized by sudden doubt. 'I mean, he hasn't proposed and I wouldn't like to think that — '

'Good heavens above, no. It's just between you and me,' Josie said firmly, doing a nifty three-point turn. 'But, just out of curiosity, was it love at first sight?'

Josie was good at listening and by the time they reached the nursing home, stuck for a while in an unexplained traffic jam, Alice had told her pretty much the lot, give or take the details of course. As Alice talked and Josie listened, it occurred to Alice that this woman was much easier to talk to than her own mum. Her mum would have constantly interrupted for one, whilst Josie just let her talk.

The gist of it was that, after their first meeting, followed by the auditions, she had been to the theatre as his guest and then they had managed to grab a few quick lunches and one very special day out together. And before long, they were on kissing terms and then lovers' terms and that was it really. As straightforward as you like. They got on so well, they enjoyed being together and they shared the same interests. In other words, they were friends as well as lovers and that was good because, once the passion evaporated, you needed a friend. And yes, they had talked of living together already, she admitted when Josie gently prompted, but Alice's suggestion of him giving up his bedsit and moving in with her had not been well received. He was proud — Josie laughed at that — holding the view that, like the cavemen of old, he ought to be the one doing the providing of accommodation.

'Stubborn,' Josie commented. 'What did I tell you? He's just like his dad. Or maybe like me. Can I let you into a secret, Alice?'

'Oh yes.' She smiled her way. 'I like secrets.'

'I haven't said anything to Ray because nothing might come of it but I might be up for promotion in the New Year. I don't know what Ray will say if I get it. He won't like it.'

'Why not?'

'Same reason as Matthew wouldn't like it if you were earning more than he was. Daft, isn't it? Marriage is a partnership, love. Or it should be. But Ray doesn't see it that way. I'll have to break it to him gently if I get it. Mind you, chances are I won't.' She pulled sharply into an entrance, driving round the big, old, red-brick house to a small car park at the rear. 'Here we are. Now, before we go in, Alice . . . let me warn you, this will be no picnic.'

'You needn't worry,' Alice told her, feeling nervous now as Josie's nerves transmitted. 'I've had some experience with old people. One of my neighbours, Mrs Osborne, is in her eighties and still going strong. She's a little bit eccentric but we don't know what we'll be like ourselves if we live that long, do we? Anyway, she told me just before Christmas that I should put some weight on. She said I looked like a bag of bones.'

'Hetty might say a lot more than that,' Josie said, biting her lip. 'The thing is, love . . . '

Alice held her breath. Whatever it was, it was taking some shifting. Josie was on the verge of telling her, the very verge. After such a brief acquaintance, she liked Josie. She was flamboyant, a little overdressed, and the cerise fingernails, matching lipstick and none too subtle glitter eye shadow would drive her mother mad but *she* liked her. 'Yes . . . ?' she prompted, catching the agony of the indecision on Josie's face.

Too late. The moment had passed. 'It's nothing. We'd best go in,' Josie said, reaching across for her brand new handbag and looking at her nails as she did so. 'Oh hell, I meant to take this polish off. Mother doesn't like it. Now, sometimes she's asleep when you get there and she doesn't wake up the entire time you're there. So, we shall have to talk amongst ourselves.'

Feeling very nervous by now, Alice followed her inside.

15

At the theatre, Claire's replacement was dug in and doing well, so at least that was something positive on the work front. Claire had gone by the end of August, vanished without trace, the cut-off complete. He remembered that, on her last day, he had taken her out for lunch, just the two of them, worried at the wisdom of it but feeling he needed to do it to draw a line under it all. After all, they had had some good times together and, for a while, they had both sizzled under the impression that their relationship was going to run the course.

'Any regrets?' he'd asked her, seeing her fiddling with the cutlery opposite. It was an upmarket venue, recommended by Helen, and Claire was looking pretty in pink, excited and happy at the prospect of a new life with the love of her life. He hoped for her sake that it would not turn out to be a huge disappointment. He could not see what the hell she saw in this Paul but then when did men ever understand women, and might there just be the tiniest bit of jealousy there?

'Regrets about what?' She smiled. 'I have

none about the job. None at all. Working in the theatre's not all it's cracked up to be. Frankly, it's bored me to death. I shall look for something completely different. Something in publishing, I think.'

He hid a smile, thinking of the chaos she was more than capable of creating there. He ought to send out advance warnings that she was on her way.

'But I do have regrets about you, Matt.' The smile slipped. 'I am genuinely sorry to be leaving you. I'm very worried about you living all alone in that crappy bedsit. You need somebody to look after you. I'm not sure you can cope on your own. Oh, you can cope at work but privately . . . '

He didn't want her thinking of him as some sad, lonely guy pining away without her, so it seemed the right moment to set her straight. He told her something of how he felt about Alice, about the impression she had made on him, about the way their relationship was panning out, about how he would like to take it further, make it permanent even.

'Do it then,' she said firmly.

'We haven't known each other long.'

'Oh come on, Matthew. When did that matter? What are you waiting for? You don't need my permission. But be careful. Rebound affairs rarely work out. She's not me.'

He almost laughed aloud at that. Claire had attached more importance to their liaison than he, clearly imagining that he was heartbroken when he was not. But it would be most ungallant to say such a thing.

'I'll be careful,' he promised. But people in love were seldom that; impulsive, jittery, optimistic maybe but seldom careful.

'Wish me luck,' she said as they exited the restaurant.

He felt a stupid lump in his throat. Maybe it hadn't meant the world to him but she had cornered a small space in his heart and he wondered how long she would stay there. 'All the luck in the world, Claire,' he said as he kissed her goodbye.

And with a final '*ciao*, Matt' she was gone.

★   ★   ★

This year's pantomime *Jack and the Beanstalk* was in full flow, but well-tuned by now and almost running itself. It was a sell out and would get them off to a good start in the New Year. He could take or leave some of the plays but the annual pantomime, whichever one they did, always delighted him and no matter how many times he watched it, he would find himself smiling at the same old terrible jokes, humming the frequently terrible songs.

The stage children were excellent and you could get away with a lot in panto. Alice had done well by him, both with the *Oliver* production and now the pantomime and he marvelled at how she could get these children, some of them very small, to learn the steps of a dance. Christmas being over and having had a couple of days off, he was back to work with a vengeance, putting in extra hours to make up.

'Relax, won't you?' Helen said, coming into his office, carrying two mugs of tea. 'Everything's under control. I like the look of the summer programme, Matthew. I think it's pitched just right. There's only so many serious plays people can take in one go. The Shakespeare season will go down well. And it's a scoop to be doing *A Midsummer Night's Dream* in the middle of June. I wish we could move the whole set outside into the glade — just think how wonderful an open-air production would be?'

'Midges and all.' He pushed his work aside and relaxed with his tea.

'How did your Christmas go, darling?' she asked. 'Did your girlfriend pass the inspection?'

He laughed. 'Hardly that, Helen.'

'Don't you believe it? They can't help it, the old parents. Mine gave me hell I can tell you. In the end, I told them to bugger off the pair of them and John and I sneaked off and just got married. We dragged in two people off the street to act as witnesses. My mother was livid but she couldn't do a thing about it.'

Matthew knew very little about Helen, hadn't even known she was married. She wore no ring and had never, until just now, talked about her husband.

'We're divorced,' she said with a little laugh. 'He turned out to be an absolute pig so perhaps mother was right after all. She never liked him. My point, darling, is that you can't really exist in a vacuum and it is really rather important that you all get along. So — ' She grinned at him. 'How did the inspection go?'

'OK. Or at least . . . it was a shambles to be honest. You'll not believe this, Helen, but it only turns out that my mother and her father had a fling years ago when my mum was seventeen. How weird is that?'

She whistled through her teeth. 'That's very novel. Who dumped whom? That could be crucial.'

'My mum dumped him.'

'Thank Christ for that. That's OK then. No problem. Take it from me, her father will be sweetness on earth when they meet. I take it they are destined to meet?' Her smile reappeared. 'You wear your heart on your sleeve, darling. I'm afraid it's very obvious that you've been on cloud bloody nine ever since you met this girl. It pissed Claire off I can tell you. She wanted you to be heartsick and it peeved her that you weren't.'

'She never said.'

'Well, she wouldn't, would she? You men are hopeless at understanding female logic. So, does he know then? Alice's dad?'

'Not yet.' He pulled a face. 'She's telling them at New Year when we go over. I am still OK for that?'

'Yes. Get yourself off before I change my mind. Are you peeved that things have gone so well in your absence?' she asked cheerily. 'Did you secretly wish that there had been the cock-up of all cock-ups?'

'No,' he said, although maybe he had.

'So, it's your turn now. For the inspection, I mean. Off to meet the prospective in-laws, eh?' Her blue eyes were merry. 'Rather you than me, sweetie.'

He laughed but found the words had hit home.

On New Year's Eve, as they eventually turned into the drive of the Sazzoni's splendid house by the lake, he found, to his great irritation, that he had the most awful stage fright.

16

The food was all ready for the buffet and it would be some time before the guests arrived, so Valerie was taking time out to relax. She needed to conserve some energy for it would be a late night tonight. She was missing Mrs Parkinson because, although she was more than happy attending to the food herself, it had been hard work finding time to get the house up to scratch. Jack had helped in a fashion but she still had to go round checking after him, because men didn't see into corners, round bends, and there was always the chance they would, horror of horrors, forget to put the toilet seat down. It was all very well having three bathrooms but they all needed cleaning and she sniffed her hands anxiously, hoping the disinfectant smell was abating. She had instructed Jack not to use the bathrooms from now on but he had just laughed and told her to stop fussing.

Alice and her young man had arrived earlier in the day and her first impression was very positive. Alice seemed thrilled and Matthew was pleasant and handsome and the wedding photographs — if there was to be a wedding — would look good. She knew she was jumping the gun and there had been no mention of an engagement, but you had to prepare yourself for the eventuality. It would very likely happen someday and it would be nice if they approved of the match. They hadn't had much time for a sit-down and chat but Alice had managed to murmur in passing that she needed to talk about something.

Valerie wished she hadn't said that. From the look on her face, it seemed important, so her maternal mind started working overtime instantly, narrowing it down to three possibilities: Matthew was moving in with her, they were about to announce their engagement or lastly, the most tricky one, she was pregnant and neither of the previous two possibilities were on the cards. Alice had a worried look which might well mean the latter.

The youngsters had gone out for a walk beside the lake. It was cold but fine and she had declined their invitation to join them saying, quite rightly, that she had too much to do. Alice had offered to help but Valerie had said no thanks as, perversely, even though at one point in the afternoon she had wondered if she would ever get the cleaning finished, she was actually rather enjoying the pressure she was putting herself under. She had, she realized guiltily, rather an easy time of it normally. Everything was finished now, on standby, and it all looked wonderful.

She had checked all the rooms that the guests were likely to go into. She had refreshed the Christmas decorations, brought in some new greenery from the garden and even found some more holly with berries on it. There was a log fire blazing in the sitting room and she must remember to pop fresh logs on from time to time. The plan was that, over the course of the evening, they would mill about in the adjoining dining room and probably spill over into the conservatory, the long narrow plant-drenched room that overlooked the back garden. The garden was gently lit in the evening, giving it a new dimension but it was unlikely they would go outside although they would no doubt hear the sound of the New Year fireworks, too far away to hear the church bells. The guests were all old friends, members mostly of the various charitable organizations that Jack and she were part of.

Jack was sorting out the drinks and making sure that there was more than enough of the Deli's produce out on show. He never missed a trick and she felt no guilt at taking a few short cuts, knowing that the little salads and mayonnaise were top class.

She had bathed and changed and was taking a few minutes to sit down, even though she felt stiffly formal in the elegant navy dress. She was wearing the lovely sapphire pendant Jack had given her for Christmas. He was wonderful at surprises and rather good at dropping red-herring type hints so that she had guessed — wrongly — that she had been in line for a new handbag.

'What do you think of Matthew, darling?' she asked as Jack came through. 'I think I like him.'

'I'm not sure yet,' Jack said. 'I haven't talked to him properly. Actors aren't really my scene.'

'He's not an actor,' she said quickly. 'He works in theatre admin.'

'What on earth's that?'

'No idea. You shall have to ask him when you get the chance. It sounds interesting.'

'I did hope we might find time for a game of snooker but it's getting too late for that now.'

'Perhaps tomorrow,' she said, knowing that a game of snooker in the room off the conservatory would be an ideal opportunity for Jack and Matthew to get to know each other a little better.

If Alice was pregnant, then Valerie determined to approach it positively. Babies, *bambini*, were only good news as she well knew and she prayed that her daughter would not experience the difficulties she had. It was time they talked about that. She needed to tell her a few things, should have told her before now.

Jack was looking pretty good tonight. He always dressed well, would dress well even if she wasn't there to help him choose clothes, and tonight she thought he had hit the mood on the head. Smart black trousers, highly polished black shoes, a striped shirt, neck unbuttoned with no tie, and one of his beautifully cut jackets. She hadn't seen Matthew yet in anything other than jeans, but she hoped Alice would persuade him to change for the party. Alice was looking well, thin but no thinner than usual, clear skin and shining eyes. Anybody would think she was in love.

★ ★ ★

Matthew could hardly believe the house. He had suspected it would be something special and he was not disappointed. Alice's mum was a keen gardener and it showed even now in winter, when the grounds were still patchy with the last of the snow. Apart from a holly wreath on the front door, there was no other sign of Christmas.

'Where are the outside decorations?' he asked, grinning at her. 'This all looks much too tasteful.'

She laughed. 'I liked your dad's decorations. Don't knock them. He was very proud of them.'

'I know.' Matthew sighed, following her round to the back porch where they slipped off their boots. As they did so, the inner door opened and a woman stood there.

'Alice . . . there you are at last.'

He would have guessed she was her mother and he watched, awkward now, as they smiled at each other, holding hands briefly but not hugging, before Alice turned and introduced him.

'Hello, Matthew, nice to meet you,' Valerie greeted him with a smile. 'Come on through and get warm. Your father's out,' she said to Alice. 'He's expected back in a minute. But we can have a drink and a chat. Or would you like to take your things up to your rooms first?'

They settled on a drink. He had noted the 'rooms' the plural which was fine by him because the arrangement at his house had been embarrassing. It was thoughtful of his mum to put them together, but he knew his dad hadn't liked it, muttering something about the bed settee in the lounge — how they could have pulled that out for him and given Alice the spare room. He and Alice had ended up with the giggles, lying chastely apart in the twin beds, painfully aware of the thin walls.

This lounge, or living room as Valerie called it, was beautiful, simply furnished and his dad would love the creamy expanse of deep pile carpet. And his mum would approve of the furniture for it was just the sort of thing she would like. Everything top quality and effortlessly stylish. As was Alice's mother. He had formed an impression of her from some of the things his mother had said and he was not far wrong. Starchy was a pretty good description.

She was like Alice, facially, and Alice had inherited her tall slimness but that was far as it went. Alice was much warmer. Valerie Sazzoni had unusual grey-green eyes, cooler than Alice's beautiful brown ones, and he suspected that she would be the sort of woman he might never get to know properly, the sort of woman who kept people at some distance. Glacially beautiful then and he could see what Jack must have seen in her but even so . . . the comparison with his own mother was difficult because she and Valerie were so very different. His mum was like a bubbling volcano, seething with merriment and excitement, and over the years she must have mellowed a little, so what must she have been like at seventeen when she had known Alice's father? Firecracker came to mind.

Frankly, he was glad to get out of the house after they had unpacked. It was, on reflection, too tidy, the off-white sofas just too pristine, the bathrooms sparkling to an inch of their lives. It was like being in a high-class country hotel. He and Alice were in rooms at the far end of the house. It would be all right, Alice had whispered, coming into his room as he unpacked his few belongings, if he slipped into her room last thing. They were miles away from her parents' room and nobody would mind, Alice insisted.

He would. He was not into furtive meanderings at dead of night and with the layout of the rooms so confusing, there was always the possibility that, in a sleepy state, he might take a wrong turning at the end of the corridor and end up in Valerie's. He grimaced at the thought. Good start with his prospective mum-in-law. Jack, whom he had met briefly, looked much more approachable.

★   ★   ★

The cold afternoon air was a shivery contrast to the over-heated interior of the house and, as they walked down the drive, he glanced across at Alice. She looked lovely and he felt his heart give that quick turn that he was beginning to associate with just her. She was bundled up, of course, on account of the weather, but glowing, her softly booted feet making no sound as they crossed the road and took the path down to the lake. The sky was grey, great clumps of cloud, and bits of snow still lay around.

It was quiet today, not a soul in sight, but he liked it at this time of year, could only imagine the bustle of spring and summer.

'Isn't it fabulous here?' she said, jumping ahead of him over the stile so quickly and easily that he had to scramble over it to catch up. Following her, smiling a little at the determined way she was striding out, he debated when to ask the question, the big one, the proposal. They loved each other and he knew that Alice was thinking of marriage and children eventually, so, in a way, the question was superfluous, but it still ought to be posed. Making assumptions was a dangerous game. He didn't necessarily want to fix an exact date but it had to be there, somewhere, sometime, and in the future. He needed to be able to hang on to that.

'I know it's been a funny sort of Christmas at Mum and Dad's,' he began, anxious to get down to it but starting by skirting round it. 'But you did get on with them, didn't you, and I know they both liked you a lot? And, although it's early days with your mum and dad, things seem to be going all right so far.'

She smiled. 'And?'

'And what?'

'Oh come on, Matthew. I always know when you have something on your mind.'

'OK. I think it's time we got a few things straight. Firmed up on one or two things. The question is this.' He took a breath, grinned at her. 'God, this is hard. Ready?'

'Oh go on,' she urged, eyes shining. 'I think I've guessed anyway. I just knew you'd be really corny and do it now, here by the lake. You're right though, it is a romantic spot. The perfect spot really. If I had to choose the spot then this would be it.'

He smiled. If the answer was no, he was nicely placed to jump in the lake and it would be a quick cold end. 'Here goes then. Alice . . . should I get down on my knees?'

'Don't you dare.'

Her smile had faded though, her eyes had dulled and, even before he uttered the words, she was shaking her head. 'Matthew, I'm sorry to put a dampener on things but all this will have to wait a while,' she said, turning away from him abruptly and very nearly losing her balance on an icy bit of path.

'Hey, don't say that.' He caught her, whipped her round to face him, drawing her close. They were in a dip, out of sight and he traced a cold finger down her cold cheek before holding her close and kissing her. It was too cold to dawdle and they smiled as they drew apart and, he rather thought that tonight, scruples or not, he would end up in her room, in her bed.

'I will marry you, you great fool,' she said. 'I love you, you know that. I want to live with you. We're going to do that anyway, aren't we, but marriage is different. I will only marry you if we can sort this thing out. This thing with the parents. I haven't told my mother yet. Nor Dad. I need to know how they're going to react. After all, if we get married then they'll be in-laws, my lot and your lot. Like it or not, they're going to have to face each other.'

He felt a shiver running from his scalp downwards. She had said no, an iffy no but still no. 'It's me and you, darling,' he said quietly. 'I wasn't including them in the proposal.'

'I know that.' Her smile was awkward. 'But like it or not, we're stuck with them. Let's take it slowly. We have no need to rush things. OK?'

'OK,' he said with a rueful smile.

'Tell me, what was it like growing up in Felston?' she asked changing the subject neatly before putting her hand in his as they slowed their pace. Their breath puffed out into the cold air of this last day of the year, the rutted path under their feet still stiff from the overnight frost, the daytime temperature struggling to get above freezing.

'You never think about it much when you're growing up,' he said, accepting that the proposal, such as it had been, was firmly on hold. 'It was just home. I never felt deprived because I didn't live in the country if that's what you're thinking,' he added. 'And I was happy. Money might have been tight, I suppose, but we laughed a lot. Mum wouldn't have anybody miserable around her.'

'I like your mum,' she said, squeezing his hand. 'But this thing with Dad and her is not going to be easy to resolve. I don't know what we're going to do. Don't you see, it's going to bring it all back to both of them. And don't forget my mother either. What's it going to do to her?'

'I don't understand what all the fuss is about' he said. 'So they knew each other once upon a time? So what? They went their separate ways, don't forget that. And your dad married your mum and my mum married my dad . . . and they all lived happily ever after. More or less.'

'There's more to it,' she said unhappily. 'She's not saying. But she was very agitated when we went to see your grandma. Scared I think of her saying something.'

'About what, for God's sake?' he asked, getting fed up with it all. 'You're making this more important than it is, Alice. I wish you wouldn't.'

Her face closed over in that way of hers. 'I'll tell Mum and Dad when we get back,' she said. 'And perhaps it might be best if you're not there.'

★ ★ ★

Valerie felt her heart freeze over. Opposite her, Jack laughed. She searched his face, looking for clues, looking for relief or anticipation but seeing neither.

'Matthew's asked me to marry him,' Alice told them brightly. 'And I really want to say yes but I have to make sure that this is not going to be a problem for you.'

'A problem?' Jack echoed. 'What are you talking about? Of course it's not a problem. The only problem is, are you quite sure yourself? You shouldn't be giving a toss about what we think. What we think doesn't matter. Isn't that so, Valerie?'

She nodded, forcing a smile, but her anxiety remained, a solid lump of something approaching fear. She did not want Jack to meet Josie again. She was worried that it might set everything off again, all the old feelings that he had managed to keep buried all these years. Josie, too, for she could never quite believe that she had just gone off him. There had to be another reason.

But, with Alice marrying Matthew, there was no way she was going to be able to prevent a reunion. They were both looking questioningly at her and she had no option, under the circumstances, but to agree wholeheartedly with her husband.

17

To Josie's relief or irritation — she wasn't sure which — Ray had difficulty remembering Jack Sazzoni.

'Bloody hell,' he said at last as it dawned. 'So, he's her dad, is he? Well I'll be blowed. Imagine that. Cocky little devil, if I recall. Snappy dresser. Wouldn't take no for an answer from you, would he? In the end, I had to tell him to leave you alone or he'd have me to deal with.'

'I do remember,' she told him dryly. 'I was there. I didn't know where to put myself, Ray. You carried on something rotten.'

'That I did. My girl, I said,' Ray announced, looking pleased with himself. 'She's my girl and you can bugger off, Sazzo.'

'You didn't say that,' she said. 'You didn't swear so much in those days.'

'Neither did you.'

'I only swear when I'm agitated. Anyway, we'll have to meet them again,' she said, increasingly flustered at the prospect. 'I don't see how we can avoid it. We're going to have to meet them if Matthew gets married to her. I bet she'll want a big wedding. It will look awful if we don't go.'

'Married? Hang on. Where's that come from? Who said anything about them getting married?'

She clicked her tongue. 'Wasn't it obvious? Matthew's a traditionalist. I know he will be thinking of getting married rather than living together. I'm surprised you didn't notice, Ray. He thinks the sun shines out of her and she's as bad the other way. Even Margaret noticed. They're in love, Ray. Remember that?'

He nodded, flushed. 'Like we were?'

She noted the past tense. 'Yes, like we were. That time when you go all goosepimply just thinking about each other.' She sighed, and for a moment was back there. 'That time when your heart turns over when you hear his voice. That time when you'd give your all just to have him smile at you.'

Ray laughed. 'That's a load of bollocks.'

'Maybe.' She came down to earth, gave him one of her looks. 'It happens to youngsters.'

'It happens to oldsters too, Josie love,' he said.

'Does it?' She hid a smile, seeing he was working up to saying something profound. He had that earnest look.

'Bloody hell, I know I don't say it much

but I still love you, Josie,' he said and she looked up, surprised and more than a bit pleased, knowing how much it had taken to squeeze that out of him.

'Thank you, kind sir,' she said, dropping a kiss on the top of his head. 'And I love you too. We should say it more often.'

'It doesn't mean as much when you say it too often,' he said.

'That's your excuse,' she said, smiling at him but getting the point.

'I like the scent you're wearing,' he said appreciatively and it seemed there was no stopping him now that he had got going. 'Is that the one I bought you?'

She nodded. It wasn't. It was the one Kenny had bought her but Ray wouldn't know the difference. It made her feel guilty though and she turned away quickly, bringing the conversation round again to Jack.

'It's worrying me sick I don't mind saying. The only hope is that memories will be blurred all round. I said some terrible things at the end to him. I had to,' she added, trying to defend her actions to herself. 'It was the only way to get him to leave me alone.'

'Well, I can't remember for sure what he looked like,' Ray said stoutly. 'Nor her. The girl he married. Stuck up piece, wasn't she? Wasn't her dad a doctor?' he asked and she could almost hear his brain ticking over. 'Fair-haired, I think. Tallish. Thin. Oh . . . ' Light dawned. 'She's like her mum, isn't she? Alice?'

'In looks, yes. She's got a nicer nature though. Valerie was always a cold fish. Eyes like pellets. She used to look at me like I was something the cat had dragged in. I could never understand what he saw in her.' She looked at him closely, deciding enough was enough. Time for a change of subject. 'Are you all right in yourself? Matthew said he thought you didn't look well. You're not ill, are you? Because if you are, I'm booking you in at the doctors' after the holiday. They'll be rushed off their feet but I'll get them to squeeze you in. I'll come with you.'

'I'm all right,' he said hastily. 'I don't know where you got that idea from. I'm as fit as a fiddle.'

'Yes, well . . . that carpet fluff must get on your chest after a while. It's time you looked for something else,' she said, fixing him with a warning stare and picking up her handbag, before checking her appearance in the hall mirror. Back to work, first day, and it was always the same after a holiday. You had to drag yourself in and the time would go so slowly, second by second, minute by minute, and by the time it was six o'clock she would be exhausted even though she would probably have done very little actual work.

You had to ease yourself back in gently.

And, after the Christmas she had had . . .

★ ★ ★

It was like a museum, her place of work. It was a big stone building. Cold in winter because the heating system was something else. Stifling in summer because you couldn't get the windows open. It had never been designed to be office accommodation but they managed as best they could. At the treasurer's section, there was a public enquiry desk and a little waiting room, and then the big office and the two smaller private ones for Mr Walsh and the office deputy clerk, whose job was the one up for grabs.

The heels of her boots clicked over the tiles in the big entrance hall from where the red-carpeted staircase rose to the first floor level, splitting in two lovely sweeps to left and right. It was a grand staircase, more suited to beautifully dressed ladies in long evening gowns descending slowly and gracefully, rather than unfit office workers puffing up and down.

They shared the building with the clerk's office and the housing department and a

181

basement full of dusty old records, very likely dating back to the Domesday Book. There was a lift, the old-fashioned variety, slow and trundling, but it gave her the creeps because it had a mind of its own and taking the stairs was healthier — after the over-eating and the chocolates, she needed to lose a few pounds quickly.

At least the visit to her mum on Boxing Day had gone fairly well. Hetty had been in a dozy frame of mind and had more or less ignored Alice. Aside from her mother's comfortable armchair, there weren't enough chairs in the room for three visitors but Alice had perched illegally on the bed leaving her and Margaret the two others. It felt suspiciously like a regal audience with Hetty dispensing small ambiguous smiles, quite clearly not sure who they were, in between bouts of drifting off. They had scoffed the mince pies offered during one of her naps, whispering so as not to disturb her.

Margaret, forewarned, had been on hand with the fruit jellies but they were not required for Jack Sazzoni's name was not mentioned. Just as well, Josie thought as they left, that she hadn't blurted it all out to Alice, as she had very nearly done. She had thought a thing like that would be better coming from her rather than Hetty but she had chickened out at the last.

The magnificent town hall tree, greeted initially with such excitement and anticipation was now sitting forlornly at the base of the stairs, its decorations looking tired. This twelfth night thing was a pain. She had given Ray instructions to take the blessed decorations down at home because, so far as she was concerned, it was all over for another year. The Christmas record at the supermarket had been despatched on its merry way until next year, replaced by flat-voiced staff announcements. The Christmas crackers and chocolate selection boxes were half-price and, for the people who had organization off to a fine art, packs of Christmas cards were heavily reduced.

'Josie! What the hell have you done to your hair? I almost didn't recognize you.'

'Hello, Kenny . . . it will grow again,' she said, uncomfortably aware that she had made a mistake with it. Kenny had a nasty habit of sneaking up and taking you by surprise. 'Did you have a nice Christmas?'

'Quiet,' he said, walking up the stairs with her, making no mention of the phone call on Christmas Eve. She wasn't going to remind him about it for it couldn't have been important. 'We had Dorothy's aunt and uncle up from Surrey. They aren't exactly a bundle of laughs. He's nearly ninety, deaf as a post and she has to have every single quiz programme explained to her over and over again and she still doesn't understand the flaming rules.'

Josie smiled, taking a deep breath at the turn in the stairs. One more flight yet. They had to go past the kitchen and little staff rest room first and, as they passed, she felt Kenny's hand on her waist, as he gently guided her in and clicked the door shut behind them.

'What do you want?' she asked. 'It had better be quick.'

'I've got the job,' he said. 'Old Walsh has told me on the quiet. He pulled me back just before I left on Christmas Eve. He said that, after great deliberation, they were giving me the job but I wasn't to tell anybody until it was official. I tried to ring you. I thought you ought to know. You gave me a run for my money, Josie. The others were non-starters.'

They were in the kitchen, safe enough for it was too early for brew-ups, even in the town hall. She looked at him, startled because she had thought they would have to wait a while yet for the announcement. Normally, it took them for ever and a day to make up their minds.

'Congratulations,' she said after a moment, forcing a smile. Damn it, even accounting for the dodgy interview, she had thought she might have a chance; after all Kenny was the new kid on the block. She had been working here absolutely yonks. She could toss the brochure away now, the one about the flat by the docks. Pity because she'd already started to decorate it in her mind. It had been in a really good spot, walking distance from work, in an area they called up and coming.

'I've been bloody miserable over Christmas,' he said. 'And do you know why? Because I can't get you out of my mind, that's why.'

'No, Kenny. Don't talk like that,' she said, as he reached for her and drew her towards him. 'Please don't.'

'How long have we known each other?'

'A couple of years and what's that got to do with it?' she said, moving so that her back was against the door, so that at least if somebody barged in they would have a minute to regroup. 'Look, Kenny, this is just a bit of fun. You know that. I'm married. You're married. And we have to stop it. This is kid's stuff.'

'Oh Josie . . . ' His hands were on her back, moving low and she wriggled free. She had never meant this to become serious in any way but just the fact that she was thinking about it, about him, considering the possibility of secret meetings was enough. It had become sort of serious, but it was not too late to stop it before she ruined everything. She liked Kenny even though he was generally known as a likeable bastard. He had brought a breath of fresh air into the department since his arrival. He had blown the pants off the stuffy set. He was a bit of a clown but he was good company, intelligent and she knew perfectly well that he would do a lot to get his hands on her. She had known for some time that she was slowly succumbing to his winning ways and not liking it, not liking it that she was beginning to find Ray dull and predictable these days. When had Ray last pinned her in a corner and kissed her just for the sake of it?

Throwing caution temporarily to the wind, she let Kenny kiss her then, in the damned kitchen of the town hall. Just one kiss and then she pulled free before it got completely out of hand but the tingle of excitement remained and there was a promise in his eyes that was very likely mirrored in her own.

'They can stuff the job,' he said, gently pushing her away. 'I don't want it. I don't want the job. I've had it with local government. I'm going to take it but I'm giving in my notice in a couple of months when all the paperwork on the villa comes through. Now, this is a secret, Josie, but I'm buying this villa in Spain.'

'Are you? A second home?'

'The only home. Our home.'

She laughed. 'You are joking? I'm not coming with you to Spain. Are you daft?'

'You'll love it, Josie. All that sunshine and views of the sea. The garden slopes down in terraces. We can relax and take a swim in the pool whenever we feel it. Starkers if you like. There's nobody to see.'

'Kenny — ' She flashed an agitated glance at him. 'What about Dorothy?'

'It's kaput,' he said. 'As near as. It's run its course. I should never have married her. I think it was rebound stuff on both our parts.'

Josie frowned. It hadn't looked rebound stuff when she had seen Dorothy with him.

'And another thing, I'm fed up with work, with this rotten weather, with England. I need sunshine,' he went on. 'You need it too. I'm learning the lingo so we'll get by, you and me.'

'How can you afford a villa in Spain?' she asked, although she had a very good idea how. Dorothy was propping up the expensive lifestyle he led, a lifestyle a mere local government clerk could only dream of. They all suspected it, although Josie was reluctant to go with the general view that Kenny had married her purely for the money, Dorothy being a very attractive older woman. She was prepared to give him the benefit of the doubt. 'Don't tell me you've come into money?' she teased.

'Got it. I've won on the pools,' he said.

'Really? How much? You kept that pretty quiet,' she said, knowing he was lying.

'Look, I've got the money. Does it matter how I've got it? You don't need to know how.'

'My God — ' she looked at him as an awful suspicion gripped her. Surely he wouldn't stoop so low? 'How have you got the money?' she asked. 'You can tell me, Kenny.'

He caught on at once. 'How do you think? Does it matter, darling?'

'Of course it matters and don't call me that,' she gasped, hearing somebody coming past the door. 'I hope you haven't been doing anything underhand, Kenny.'

He laughed. 'I can't believe you. You think I've been fiddling the books?'

'I don't know what the hell you've been doing. It's nothing to do with me.'

'Josie.' He pulled her towards him again suddenly, tilting her chin so that she was forced to look at him. Even features. Devastating smile. He had a nice aftershave and, up close, he felt strong and, even now, despite everything, against all her instincts, she could feel her body betraying her, softening. 'Come with me,' he murmured against her hair. 'Don't you crave a bit of excitement in your life? We were made for each other. That bloke of yours is a dead loss. You've said so yourself.'

'When have I said that?' she said hotly, managing to break free and sorting herself out. 'I'm not coming anywhere with you. You can't leave Dorothy.'

He shrugged. 'She'll be relieved. She'll still have the house here. I'm letting her keep that.'

'Is it your house then?'

'Oh yes. I inherited some money way back, before I married Dorothy.'

'Who from?'

'Family, darling. And that's all I'm saying.'

She did not believe him. The impossible tumbled round in her mind and turned itself into a highly probable.

'Tell me you haven't been . . . doing some imaginative accounting?' she looked round anxiously. 'Oh God, Kenny, you could end up in prison.'

He laughed. 'I bet your old man wouldn't have the nerve to do it.'

'No, he would not,' she said, horrified at

the excitement she felt. 'Be careful, won't you?'

'Of course,' he said with confidence. 'Just leave it with me.'

'How?' Against her better judgement, the excitement soared. 'How the hell have you done it? And how do you know I won't go straight to Mr Walsh and tell him?'

'Tell him what? What are you talking about?' He grinned. 'Your word against mine, sweetheart. Oh come on, Josie, you won't shop me. After all, you love me. Don't you?'

The door rattled and the junior walked in, apologizing and walking out again.

'We'd better go,' he said, his hand finding its way once more to her waist and slipping to her bottom, giving it a squeeze. 'Give it some thought, darling. I've done it all for you, you know. You'll have a life of Riley out there. And by God, when I get my hands properly on you, I promise you one thing. You'll wonder why on earth we've waited so long.'

★　★　★

It was horrible twilight of the year weather. Grey and dark and dismal all day long and the town hall was hardly what you would call an airy light place to work in. Even though her in-tray was crammed with papers, she had done nothing all day. Oh, she had fussed round, looked busy, but how could she work with that whirling round in her head?

Kenny Balfour was out of his mind.

Ray was not in when she got back. She flung her bag on the chair and went to get a cup of tea. What she really needed was a stiff drink but she couldn't bring herself to drink alcohol at half past five in the afternoon. She was on flexitime and had left early simply because she couldn't stand the knowing looks Kenny kept shooting at her. She had no idea how he had done it and perhaps that was just as well. He was respected in the office despite his cockiness and she knew that Mr Walsh had been treading water for the last couple of years and was more than happy to palm a lot of work his way. Money flew in and out. Here and there, everywhere. It was like cooking an enormous hotpot, she supposed. You could take out a few onions and carrots and the end result would look much the same. It would take a very good chef to notice or, in the case of accounts, a very astute auditor. The accounts were audited internally and that probably explained it. Somehow or other, he had discovered a way of bucking the system.

My God, what should she do? She could shop him twice over now. Once for sexual harassment and also for being an embezzler.

Embezzlement. She let the word roll off her tongue. It didn't feel like stealing, not properly; half of this wretched council didn't really know what the other half was up to and filtering money from a very full pot could be done. The council was always denying it, saying they were barely making ends meet these days, forced to make cuts, puffing the blame squarely on Mrs T., but they had money, quite a lot of it from various sources, and, in her opinion, they wasted it left right and centre, and she wasn't referring to the controversial statues either. They wasted it on damned fool ideas, frittered away thousands on seminars about meetings, on management training and courses when, if folk were left to their own devices, they could manage very well thanks.

Even so. She knew the difference between right and wrong. Hadn't she had that drummed into her as a child?

She was shocked into stillness and sat a while, thinking about it. Kenny was a bit free and easy with his hands and not to be trusted in that department but this was a completely different game.

She shivered, switching the fire fully on and warming her hands. Something like this, a shock like this, chilled you to the bone and she wanted to talk about it, tell somebody. She did not have much time. If she did not walk into Mr Walsh's office tomorrow morning at nine prompt and tell him, then it would be too late. Had the junior stood at the door and listened in before he came in? If he had heard anything, he might try to blackmail her and then Kenny might have to silence him . . .

She laughed. Alone in the house, she laughed, aware that she was in danger of becoming hysterical. The ringing of the phone startled her and she went to answer it, switching on the hall light and pausing a moment with her hand on the receiver before she picked it up.

This might be the junior blackmailing her. Calm down.

To her relief, it was Margaret ringing from the nursing home. 'Now, you're not to get yourself into a state, Josie,' she said. 'But mum's had a mild stroke. A turn they call it. They sent for me this afternoon and I'm with her now.'

'A stroke?' She felt her heart pound, imagined the worst. 'They're serious, aren't they? Is she going to die?'

'She's all right now, but at her age . . . ' Margaret hesitated. 'It's the next forty-eight hours, love. That's what matters. If she does have another, it could see her off. And that's the truth.'

Josie felt her heart miss a beat, had to sit down abruptly on the chair by the phone table. What with Christmas and Kenny and now this . . . it was all getting to be too much to take in.

'I'm coming over. Do you want me to bring anything? Is she wearing her new nightdress?'

'Don't worry about nighties,' Margaret said. 'Don't you worry about anything, Josie. It will be all right, you'll see.'

Josie was not fooled. Margaret was using her big sister, mothering voice and that could only mean she was very worried herself.

She left a hastily scribbled note for Ray and left the house, not even bothering to apply a fresh coat of lipstick.

18

The speech was slightly slurred, the face just a little twisted, the eyes strange and empty.

Her mother didn't know what had hit her.

Margaret half-rose and smiled as Josie bustled in. She had come straight here, not even stopping off for some flowers. They had moved Hetty to another room, a simply furnished room nearest the nursing office, where they could keep an eye on her. Josie knew that, once here, the residents rarely made it back to their own rooms. They either ended up in hospital proper, or dead.

'Here's Josie now. Mum was waiting for you to get here. She's going to have a little sleep now that you've arrived,' Margaret said, speaking in a gentle motherly voice, holding their mother's hand, trying to tell Josie with her eyes that she must pull herself together and not look so shocked at what she saw. 'Take your coat off, pull out a chair and sit down,' she instructed, taking over as she was sometimes, rather surprisingly, apt to do.

Without a word, Josie did as she was told and they sat there, either side of the bed, and, just for a moment Josie was surprised at how emotional she felt. She could not, just then, trust herself to speak. She had felt pent-up on the way, feeling a sort of sob building up and it was taking a lot of effort to keep it at bay. The last thing she wanted was to start crying.

She did not want to feel like this about her mother.

This woman who had ruined her life.

★ ★ ★

'I don't know what you see in that Jack,' Lynn said with a sniff. 'He's too short for one.'

'He's not too short for me.' Josie gave her a look. She could take an awkward turn, could Lynn, if the mood was on her. Well, to heck with her. She wouldn't bother drawing her attention to the fact that she'd not smoothed her rouge in properly on one cheek. Lynn was hopeless with make-up. She was tall, always the tallest in the class, and she had tried to compensate by slouching. Now it seemed she could not straighten up, not fully. And she always wore flatties, which did nothing for her legs.

Glancing at her, Josie straightened herself up as tall as *she* could get, sticking out her bosom as she did so. Well you couldn't do one without the other. She noticed a boy on the other side of the arcade glancing her way appreciatively but she turned her back on him, not interested.

They were standing waiting for the boys to arrive and Josie was having kittens hoping to goodness they weren't going to be stood up. The trouble was that this arcade of shops where they had agreed to meet was the favourite spot for meeting — everybody eyeing everybody else up — and she didn't like to wait more than ten minutes at most or it looked bad. It was an elegant glass-roofed arcade with some fancy shops and more than a few jewellers. She kept her eyes on the rings and things. She fancied a diamond solitaire and her nails were ready for such an event; they were perfect tonight, painted a silvery pearl. It did no harm to dream.

'Is your watch fast?' she asked accusingly. It would be just like Lynn to have put them in this embarrassing position.

'Only five minutes and I allowed for that,' Lynn told her. 'Why don't you put your watch on?'

Because it was an old one, her school watch, dead plain with a black leather strap, and she liked to wear a few jangly silver bracelets instead. She had been on the bus the other day, moved her arm and the whole lot had slipped off on to the floor. Somebody had whipped them up, handed them back but she felt hot even now at the memory.

Nobody she knew of her age had a car, not yet, but Jack was having driving lessons and his father had promised to buy him a nearly new Mini if he passed. That brought it home more than anything how different they were. Her dad had bought an old car recently, splashing out over a hundred pounds, but he only used it for special occasions and on Sunday afternoons when he took her mum out for a drive. The buses were good anyway, less than ten minutes into the middle of town and that included all the stopping and starting. She had got away with half-fare until last year but, after she left school and was no longer wearing school uniform, she had to pay full. She wanted to pay full in any case. She didn't like being thought of as a child as much as her mother tried to make her out to be one.

'Five more minutes,' she told Lynn. 'And then we're off. Who do they think we are? Standing here like spare dinners.'

'It'll be Mick's fault,' Lynn said with a smile. 'You know what he's like.'

She did. He might be a mountain of a man, easily tall enough for Lynn, but he did not have a brain to match. Josie sighed. Lynn might be mystified about her interest in Jack but how Lynn and Mick had become almost inseparable was a complete mystery to her. Lynn for all her faults was a very bright girl and would have gone to university but there was a money problem and her parents just couldn't run to it. Lynn's mother needed her to be earning a wage, chipping in like the rest of the family.

Lynn was already muttering about getting engaged and Josie, at nearly eighteen, was getting fed up with it. If Lynn appeared first with a ring on her finger, she would go spare. Jack had made no move in that direction. No mention. And even if he did, she would be hard pressed to say yes because it would give her parents a heart attack. How she had managed to keep it a secret these last few months, she had no idea. Margaret knew and Margaret was getting herself into a state about it. And her mother was always on at her about Ray Bailey and what a good catch he would be.

'Here they are,' Lynn said triumphantly and, smile at the ready, Josie turned to face them, accepting Jack's profuse apologies with a murmured. 'That's OK'. He was here now and that's all that mattered. He kissed her once on each cheek as he always did, but Lynn and Mick just grinned daftly at each other as *they* always did.

West Side Story was showing at the new

cinema in town and they took their turn in the queue. They ended up in the stalls, middle of the row, limited therefore to just holding hands instead of having a snog in the back row. Jack squeezed her hand at the important moments in the film, particularly when Tony sang about his Maria. It didn't escape her notice that it was a Romeo and Juliet type thing, lovers from the wrong families and it occurred to her that their story was a bit like that too. At least on the part of *her* family who would go bananas if they knew where she was and who she was with at this very minute.

He chatted about his family, that Sazzoni mob as her dad called them, but she never talked to him about her family because she knew, deep down, that her mother was right.

It would never come to anything.

But she just wanted to hang on to it, this lovely warm feeling, for just a little bit longer.

★　　★　　★

'I want no ministers coming here to see me.'

They were both startled by the words for they had been sitting quietly, not speaking, smiling gently at each other from time to time across the bed. The counterpane was a very pale orange, a terrible sickly colour, doing no favours for mother's apricot nightdress.

'I want no ministers sitting there, spouting God words. Do you hear, you two?'

How she knew they were there was a mystery because she had only opened her eyes a few times and not seemed to be aware of them. For the last twenty minutes or so, she had been asleep, breathing quite calmly although Josie was watching every breath with some alarm, almost ready for the one that would never come. Hetty had lost weight recently and she was surprised that she hadn't noticed until now.

'No ministers,' Josie repeated, squeezing her mum's hand, suddenly aware of her own bright nail polish. Normally, she took off her nail polish before she visited because her mum just went on and on about it. She reckoned she was safe enough today.

'No ministers. After what happened to your dad, all that suffering, no ministers. I can't be doing with minsters. And no church service when I'm gone. No hymns. No nothing. Just pop me up the crem.'

'Mother, don't talk like that,' Margaret said, shaking her head at Josie.

'I'll talk how I want. If there is anybody up there waiting then I'll just have to explain that, with one thing and another, I've had enough.'

'Ssh,' Josie soothed, feeling their mother/daughter role beginning gently to reverse. She looked across at Margaret, who had tears in her eyes. 'It's all right, Mum.'

'I've never been one for babies,' she said. 'I'm not that maternal. And I can understand why you stopped at one, our Josie, after all you went through. One's enough if you ask me.'

Josie didn't bother to explain about Ray and his probable low sperm count. No point.

They watched as, seemingly exhausted by the effort of saying those few words, Hetty closed her eyes again.

After a moment, Margaret spoke, almost in a whisper, carefully watching their mother. 'When she told me she was expecting you, I was so happy.'

'*She* wasn't.'

'No. She'd had a bad time with me and she was frightened. She was right to be because she had another bad time with you. Wasn't that right, Mum?'

With her head against the pillows, Hetty sighed, opening her eyes briefly and then closing them again. Opposite her, Margaret mouthed the word 'careful'. Josie knew what she meant. Hetty was probably listening to all this.

'Dad should have supported her a bit

more,' Josie said. 'Getting rid of her like that. It wasn't right'

'Things were different just after the war,' Margaret said. 'Women got on with those things themselves. Men didn't like to be bothered and Dad was worse than most. He wanted nothing more to do with her when he heard. He was more than happy for her to go to Auntie Jenny's until it was all over. He had seen how bad she was when she was expecting me. She was really poorly from beginning to end. It wasn't unusual, Josie.'

'No wonder she was thrilled to bits when she found out she was expecting me.'

Margaret smiled, looking at Hetty who was now breathing quietly and easily. 'She wasn't back to normal for a while so she more or less passed you over to me. It was easier. I bottle fed you. Changed your nappies. All that. And I vowed then that he would never hurt you if I could help it. I'd have killed him, Josie, if he had hurt you when you were little. He didn't. For a while, he seemed all right with you. It was only when you got old enough to answer back that the trouble started.'

'He was a bully,' Josie said, glancing fearfully at their mother, but she was still sleeping. 'Why didn't we do something? Tell somebody?'

'Because she — ' She glanced down at their

sleeping mother. 'Because she didn't want it. You should never have let him do that, make you finish with Jack,' Margaret said and Josie could tell the words were hurting. 'Telling you that if you didn't finish with him, he'd take it out on me. I mean to say, that was blackmail. And you shouldn't have listened to him.'

'I couldn't risk it,' Josie said, feeling all the old emotions welling up. 'I'd known you all my life and I'd known him a few months. I didn't know for sure I loved him. I still don't know. That was all there was to it. You weren't well at the time and I was scared what would happen to you if he gave you one of his good hidings.'

'It wouldn't have mattered to me. I was used to it. I never felt that strap hitting me after a while. I just used to think of something else, something nice. Take my mind off it.'

Josie smiled. 'That's what you do when you're having a baby. It's called mind over matter. When I was having Matthew, they told me to think of a song, my song, and then sing it through the contractions. I chose 'Sweets for my Sweet' by The Searchers. Good song but it didn't work. It still hurt like buggery.'

'Ssh.' Margaret glanced anxiously at their

204

mother but she did not stir, her face relaxed now.

'Do you think they heard next door?' Josie asked. 'They must have heard. Why didn't they say something? Why didn't they report him to the NSPCC?'

'They would never have interfered. And I never made a sound. Making a sound meant he had succeeded in getting to me. I never gave him that satisfaction.'

Josie shivered. 'Bloody hell, Margaret,' she said.

'Ssh. Stop swearing.' Margaret looked warningly at their mother. 'It's over now, Josie.'

'Is it?'

They fell silent. Remembering.

★ ★ ★

She told Margaret first before, together, they told mum.

'How could you, Josie Pritchard?' her mum's eyes blazed. 'How did it happen? No, don't tell me. I don't want to know.'

Jack had passed his test and got his car and he had taken her for a drive out in the country and, afterwards, they had found a quiet spot in the afternoon sunshine where nobody could see them and they would not be disturbed and . . . that's how it happened. It had been sweet and beautiful, the sun hot, the grass fragrant. They had kept the bulk of their clothes on, she had insisted on that, and Jack had kept whispering how much he loved her, how she was so lovely, and she had thought it would be all right. She knew about this pill that had come out, wondered how you got hold of it, had been too embarrassed to ask the doctor, would not dare to ask Margaret who probably wouldn't know anyway. One of her friends was already on it, taking it every day. She had had a terrible time getting it prescribed with one doctor giving her a lecture and telling her to wait until she was married. In the end, she'd had to traipse all the way over to Blackpool where she had heard there was a sympathetic woman doctor who was dishing them out like nobody's business. Josie, whilst admiring her friend's tenacity and her new-found freedom, could not contemplate doing such a thing herself.

Anyway, it never happened the first time, did it?

But it had.

'Your dad will take it bad,' her mum said, stating the obvious. 'How far are you gone?'

'Only a few weeks,' Margaret said, standing half in front of her, protecting her. 'But she'll have it, Mum. We'll look after it. I'll look after it.'

'Oh no, you won't.' Her voice was icy. 'It'll be got rid off. There's no need to tell him. We'll keep it quiet. Just the three of us.'

'Get rid of it?' Josie peeped out from behind Margaret's broad comforting back. She hadn't thought of it as a baby, not yet, not properly, not a little baby but now . . . talking of getting rid of it, she felt something stirring deep inside. 'I will not,' she said, looking desperately at Margaret who was just standing there, in deep shock. 'It's mine. I won't kill it.'

Her mother dragged her then, away from Margaret, shook her and looked straight at her. 'Be told, madam,' she said in that quiet dangerous voice of hers. 'It's for the best. You'll have an abortion. There's nothing to it if it's done early enough. I know somebody who'll sort it out for you. Somebody who owes me a favour at that. There'll be no questions asked. It'll be all above board.'

'Who do you know?' Margaret was astonished, seemed to have recovered herself. 'Honestly, Mother, she's not going to go through that. I won't let you do it.'

'Will you shut up, our Margaret,' Hetty turned on her. 'This is nothing to do with you.'

'Yes it is,' Margaret said, eyes flashing. 'It's everything to do with me, Mum.'

'You shut up now or I'll clock you one,' Hetty said, making a threatening movement with her hand.

'Leave her alone,' Margaret said, standing firm. 'Just listen to yourself. There's no need for an abortion. It's not as bad as all that. It's not the dark ages anymore. It's the sixties. Lizzie Adams is expecting in Clarence Street and she's not married.'

'She's flaunting it,' Hetty said. 'Mrs Adams might be putting on a brave face but I shan't. Look at your father — a pillar of the community.'

Nobody knew.

Nobody knew what he was like behind closed doors.

Nobody knew that he, a great strapping man, had punched and kicked out at his own family for years. In between bouts, he was calm and quiet but, when he got mad, he lost control and lashed out. He was looked up to in this street, still walked tall and proud in that military gait of his. And just about everybody knew about the damned medal.

'It's not the end of the world,' Margaret repeated, casting Josie a reassuring glance.

'It would be for him,' Hetty said. 'The end of his world.' Her anger had gone, replaced by desperation and, her guard slipping, she looked at them both helplessly. 'You know what he's like. He'd likely kill her, Margaret.'

'He'd have to kill me first,' Margaret said, putting her arm round Josie. 'She's not having an abortion, Mum. I'm surprised at you for even suggesting it. We can brazen it out if we have to. And you never know, they might get married.'

'At her age?'

'Why not? Girls get married young. Some girls.'

'Has he asked you?' Her mother turned on her, spat out the question.

Josie shook her head. 'Not exactly.'

'Has he asked you or not?'

'No,' she mumbled. 'But he will when he knows.'

Her mother laughed then, a laugh without mirth, without warmth. 'That will be the last thing he'll do. And even if he did, your father wouldn't let you marry a foreigner and a Catholic at that. So you can forget that.'

In the event, Jack never did know about his baby and her dad never knew either. She lost it, naturally, a few days later and perhaps under the circumstances it was better like that. She had a few days off work, her mother phoning up to say she had a virus and would be back as soon as her temperature was down. There was no need to bother the doctor, her mother said, once she was over the worst of it. She would be fine now, so long as she kept her legs closed in future.

From then on, it remained a secret between just the three of them. But she knew one thing. For Margaret's sake, if not her own, she could not put them through another of their father's rages and when the news got back to him that she'd been seen out with Jack, he took her in the back room and gave her the ultimatum. She hardly dared look at his eyes for they were very nearly crazed with his anger. That night, she told Jack it was over and that was that. She did not love him any more and he was to forget her. He was bewildered but she was resolute. She took up with Ray Bailey because it was the easy thing to do, and had to call upon Ray eventually to hammer the point home when Jack was slow to take no for an answer.

★   ★   ★

They never talked of it these days, she and Margaret, but she knew Margaret was shocked when she broke the news about Alice being Jack's daughter.

'Oh Josie — ' she'd said, putting a hand to her mouth. 'Oh heck, Josie.'

The three of them had kept the secret, although lately Hetty's confused mind had threatened to blab, but soon it was to be just the two of them because, when they were both gone from her bedside, alone and without a comforting hand, their mother had another stroke, massive this time, and died next day.

19

Ray had a long drive out to one of the villages out in the country, where he was fitting a big bedroom carpet. It was a lovely shag pile that he had worked with before and it would present no problems. He might finish early and, if he did, he might catch Lynn in. It was Wednesday and it was her day off.

He was no good at all with this secret liaison stuff. He'd make a fine James Bond and no mistake. His face was a dead giveaway for a start. He would be a rotten poker player. He hated keeping things from Josie but he wanted to surprise her. Hadn't she accused him of being too damned predictable? Well, he was going to show her this time.

It had been a bit awkward at home since Christmas, what with Hetty going and dying shortly afterwards, and that to-do with Matthew and Alice. She was a nice girl and he'd taken it upon himself, knowing that Josie was iffy about it, to speak to Matthew on the phone to put him straight.

'What's wrong, Dad? Is Mum OK?' Matthew had sounded alarmed. Not surprising because Ray couldn't remember ever ringing him before, not off his own bat. Josie always did that, sometimes passing the phone over to him when she had finished. Whenever she did that, he and Matthew could never think of anything to say, so they resorted to talking about football or cricket, nice safe subjects like that, nothing personal, never anything personal.

'Nothing's wrong,' he said. 'Just thought I'd give you a call. I liked that girl of yours, Matthew. Make sure you look after her.'

Matthew laughed. 'Right. Thanks, Dad.'

'Take no notice of your mother,' he went on, needing to get this over with. 'You just do what you think fit. She'll come round. I'll see to that.'

And then, because there was nothing much else to say, he'd hung up pleading he was busy. He had not mentioned the phone call to Josie but he hoped that it would have cleared up any misgivings Matthew might have.

Hetty was gone now and he couldn't pretend it wasn't a relief, her being so frail and with nothing left to look forward to. He had never got on as well with Hetty — a ratty sort — as he had with old Jimmy. Jimmy had been a nice quiet man, could tell some tales about his time in the police, although he kept very quiet about that bit of bravery he had got the medal for. That's what proper heroes were like. Self-effacing. Ray was bloody proud of that medal but Josie, for some reason, would not display it, keeping it tucked away in a drawer. It was going to go to Matthew one day as Jimmy had stipulated in his will.

Josie and Margaret had taken their mother's death well, supporting each other and, although he was being careful with Josie, he worried that it hadn't sunk in properly yet and she might burst into tears at any given moment. Margaret had insisted on doing the worst bit — sorting out Hetty's things — and the will was going through, although neither of them was going to be left a fortune. Margaret would inherit the house she lived in which was only right and proper and there was just a bit of cash left over, nothing to write home about. Hetty, mindful of her age and condition, had left things in order and that was a relief because he'd heard of some right carry-ons when there was no will. It would get easier as the weeks went by, but he still felt he had to be very careful what he said in case it set Josie off.

As for the other business, he didn't know if Josie had been convinced by his pretending not to remember Jack Sazzoni, because he bloody well did. Right off. He remembered the feeling of wanting to ram his fist down that smug throat and how it had shaken him up having that feeling. He had made him feel inadequate with his fancy talk, breaking off into Italian sometimes. The girls liked that but he didn't. He could be calling him all the names under the sun and he wouldn't be any the wiser. Jack had known Ray was sweet on Josie — everybody knew — and, for a while, as he had watched from the sidelines, seeing the two of them laughing together, seeing the easy way Jack put his arm round her, the way she looked up at him, it had hurt. It had hurt so much that it was a genuine pain in his heart. He wasn't a violent man, never had been, but, when he told Jack to leave her alone, that was the nearest he had ever come to it. He had also felt it to be a hollow victory, because he knew full well where Josie's heart lay and it wasn't with him. His one hope had been that she would fall in love with him eventually, in her own time, and, after Matthew was born he had allowed himself to think that it had happened at last. Together they had produced this little lad, a belter of a little lad at that, and that surely had to count for something?

Would Jack remember that last time they met as he did? When they met again, what the hell would they say? They couldn't take up where they'd left off that was for sure. He

215

decided it would be best to say nothing, not refer to it in any way unless he did. Let bygones be bygones, which had been one of his mum's sayings.

He knew Josie was having problems at work and he could guess it would be something to do with that guy she worked with, that Kenny guy. He was a funny chap, cagey, and he wouldn't trust him with the council's money. He was married to this older fancy piece but he had the look of a man who played away, if he got half a chance. He had very nearly mentioned his concern to Matthew over Christmas, man to man, but he had let the moment pass and maybe it was just as well. He didn't want his son to get the feeling that he was jealous of this Kenny, worse that he didn't trust Josie.

He did trust her, but she was still pretty and she had a good figure, and she dressed in a way he liked and, he suspected, other men would like too. And she spent a lot of time with this guy at work and he'd read about things that went on in the work place. Nothing went on at Felston Carpet Centre because Eileen, the only woman in the office, was close to retiring age and as miserable as sin. But it might be a different matter at the town hall.

Stop it.

He pulled up outside the house, checked the number against his work sheet.

'Oh, you're here,' the woman said, opening the door at once, beaming. 'Lovely to see you. Everything's ready for you. Cup of tea before you start?'

Now that was more like it.

* * *

It was bizarre. Since the conversation in the kitchen just after Christmas, Kenny had not talked any more about that little matter. His appointment was now official and he would take up the job in due course when the changeover was complete. Sometimes she thought she must have imagined it or managed somehow to read too much into it, but Kenny had admitted his misdeeds, hadn't he? He had not denied them anyway. She could not work out why he had confessed because it would be so easy for her to shop him.

But she had not.

Their mother's funeral had been held at the crematorium as she had requested with the minimum of fuss. It was a cold clear January day and Josie kept it together, just about, tissues at the ready just in case. Margaret was composure itself, like stone, clear-eyed, level-voiced. They had both dressed in black because mother had not specified otherwise and Ray had worn his best grey suit and a black tie. It was a poor turn-out for eighty-five years of living in the same street, just a few old neighbours who were only after a nose around and a bite to eat afterwards. The funeral party — what there was of it — came back to Crook Terrace where Josie had got a caterer in to provide a few sandwiches, because she hadn't felt up to a trip to the supermarket, stocking up on sausage rolls and little pork pies and so on. The truth was it had knocked the stuffing out of her. At eighty-five you had to expect it any time but it was still a shock to see the coffin and realize that Hetty was inside it and yet not inside it, if you could fathom that one out. She was gone to wherever it is you went. For a moment, Josie hoped there was something other than a black hole. She sometimes regretted losing the religion as she had, but her dad had put her off it. People like him had no right to claim religion.

It was when the coffin went through those curtains that she nearly lost it. She felt Ray's big hand in hers at that point, felt the comforting pressure, nodded slightly as she caught his worried glance. And then they were outside, in the cold sunshine, being discreetly hurried along because another funeral party was already on its way. A conveyor belt, solemn or not, that's all it was. Wheeling them in one after the other. The man who had conducted the so-called service hadn't known Hetty from Adam, wouldn't know the next one either.

'I want more than this,' was all she said to Ray, hoping he understood.

The things they said about her mum when they got back to the house. It would have been laughable if it hadn't been so earnest. She had wondered for a minute if some of these folks were at the right funeral, if they weren't talking about some other poor soul. Hetty had been, amongst other wonderful things, kindness itself. She would give a stranger her last bite. A lovely woman, one of life's smilers.

That was a good one. Her mother had smiled as if they were on ration.

Matthew could not attend. But he was distraught and he would spend all day thinking about his grandma, he assured Josie, and as for Alice, well she was just pleased that she had met her the once at Christmas. He and Alice sent a nice wreath and she and Margaret clubbed together for a special one, her favourite white lilies.

'What shall we put on the card?' she asked Margaret.

'To Mum, who turned a blind eye,' Margaret said bitterly.

'Now, Margaret . . . ' Josie smiled a gentle smile, 'we can't put that. We shall have to put the usual stuff. We have to give her a good send-off. It's the least we can do.'

She waited until the funeral guests had departed, taking the opportunity whilst Ray was driving some of them home to tell Margaret, on pain of death, the whole story about Kenny. Margaret, recovering now and thawing out, told her exactly what she had expected her to say. She had to go to the boss and repeat word for word what Kenny had said. Well, not quite word for word.

'What's stopping you?' Margaret said, clearly agitated. 'You should have told him straightaway. Now you're going to have to think of a reason why you didn't do that. Oh Josie, you are daft. He's not worth protecting, that chap. He's a common thief, that's all he is. So don't start thinking you're doing him a favour by saying nothing. He's dug a grave for himself.'

They smiled ruefully at that, hardly an appropriate remark for today. Margaret had a point but Josie still hesitated because something did not seem quite right. Kenny didn't seriously expect her to move to Spain with him, did he? It had always been a bit of fun, a lark, and she regretted now that she had led him on, for that's what had happened. But never ever had anything been said about it being serious. No mention of divorce and she would have jumped a mile if there had been. No mention of her leaving Ray and his leaving Dorothy. No mention even of meeting outside work although, once or twice — and she felt hot and bothered now at the idea — that had crossed *her* mind. She had been cross with Ray at the time and would have done it, if Kenny had asked, simply because she wanted to give Ray a reason to be jealous. She wanted to see him fired up on her behalf again.

She had got herself into such a state that Mr Walsh offered her some time off, thinking she was fretting about her mother but she refused because she didn't want to sit at home and worry about it. She collared Kenny eventually just after work. They were both leaving early and exited together, quite naturally, pausing outside before they went their separate ways.

'Kenny?' She glanced nervously back at the building. 'Have you time for a quick coffee? We need to talk.'

'Stewing over it?' he asked with a grin. 'Thought you would.'

There was a snack bar nearby, a bit rough and ready, but it would suit their purposes. The place was packed, full of smokers, and Josie had to clear a table herself, piling used cups and plates and a mucky ashtray on to the one next to it and wiping it in a fashion with a tissue before Kenny appeared with two cups of brown liquid that passed for coffee.

'So you didn't bother to go scooting off to old Walsh then?' he asked, calm as you like, when he was settled. 'I knew you wouldn't.'

'I haven't been to see him because I can't believe what you told me,' she said. 'I think you were having me on. It was just a joke, wasn't it? You're trying to wind me up, that's all. We're not just colleagues, we're friends, Kenny, you and me.'

'A bit more than that.'

'No. Just friends,' she said firmly. 'I never meant it to be anything else. I'm sorry if you got the wrong end of the stick.'

'Oh come on, Josie — ' He glanced round but nobody was listening in to their conversation. 'You know it was no joke. I can always tell when a woman is interested. And you are. Like it or not. You're just confused. Wrestling with your conscience.'

'You have a big opinion of yourself,' she

222

said, annoyed because she half admired that peacock side of his nature. He was the exact opposite of Ray and maybe that was what attracted her to him in the first place. 'You're one of those men who think they are God's gift to women.'

He raised his eyebrows, grinned and, to her everlasting irritation, her heart gave a little excited leap. Damn him, he did have something, that elusive 'it' — whatever it was — that Ray, bless his heart, would never have even if he lived to be a hundred.

'I told you what I told you because I knew you wouldn't blab. And, even if I had misjudged you and you did go scuttling off to Walsh, I would claim complete ignorance. After all, it would be your word against mine, darling, and don't forget you're peeved as hell just now because I've got the promotion that, by rights, you think should be yours.'

'I am *not* peeved,' she said hotly, looking up as a waitress, a bit late in the day, appeared with a cloth. 'I've done it myself, thanks,' she said with a frown, waiting until the girl sloped off. 'All right, I admit I would have taken the job if it had been offered but I didn't honestly expect it. I know I've been there longer than you but that doesn't count for much and I'm only part qualified after all.'

'You *are* peeved and trying to make trouble for me,' he said. 'Right or wrong, you can say that the idea has something going for it. And when I point out that perhaps you've got yourself into a panic and are trying to cover up something that you have done your-self . . . ?'

'But I haven't done anything wrong. You can't pin that on me?'

'Can't I? Oh, Josie, you're such a little innocent and it's one of the things I like about you.'

'You bastard,' she said, an icy rage circling her. If she'd had a ready glass of wine, red wine, she would have thrown it at him, but they didn't do wine in this snack bar and there was nothing else handy, except the hot coffee and she couldn't do that for she might scald him and she wasn't into GBH. 'I don't know how you've the brass nerve. Why should I come with you?'

'Because you find me exciting and dangerous, darling.' he said. 'Because you can't quite work out what makes me tick and want to find out.'

'You . . . you — ' she tried to calm down because a woman at a nearby table was looking their way.

'You are beautiful when you're mad,' he whispered, moving slightly so that the words were for her alone. 'Eyes shining. Cheeks glowing. I bet Ray's never told you that.'

'How do you imagine for one minute that I — ' She looked round, lowered her voice as she felt it rising. 'That I would leave Ray for you. You can't love me, not if you'd drop me in it like that given half the chance.'

'Love?' He laughed in her face. 'Who said anything about love? Love is for kids. It's a teenage thing. It's not for the likes of us. Think about it. Sunshine. A gorgeous house. Plenty of free time. As many new clothes as you like. Pedicures. Manicures. It's not something you should dismiss out of hand.'

'I'm not coming with you to Spain, not even if you offered me a diamond ring the size of a marble,' she said firmly. 'You can go on your own. Or better still with Dorothy.'

'I'm leaving her. I don't need her any more, Josie. It'll be a new start.'

'The answer's no.'

He shrugged, not seeming too worried. 'OK. I had you down for somebody who was looking for excitement,' he said, pushing his cup away. 'Obviously I got it wrong but it's not too late, Josie. If you change your mind, the offer's still on.'

'Hah!'

'Your loss.'

In that moment all that she had felt for him

went up in a puff of smoke. What a fool. What a stupid fool. She rooted in her purse for some money, the money for *her* coffee, put it down on the table before standing up. Walking out, she caught a sympathetic glance from the woman at the next table, but did not give Kenny the satisfaction of looking back.

As she stormed out, nearly colliding with somebody coming in, she did not notice Margaret standing on the opposite pavement, trying to attract her attention. Having failed to do so, Margaret was still standing there a minute later when Kenny Balfour followed Josie out.

20

As February, a listless month, limped to a close, Valerie was spending a few days with Alice and Matthew. Officially, she was there in her capacity as gardener, giving her daughter some advice about planting and clearing. Alice had tried her best to sort out the little garden but had finally admitted she needed help. It was the right time of year for a good blitz and Valerie was relishing the challenge. She rather thought she should try her hand at garden design, had enquired about a course that would give her a diploma.

She had said nothing about it to Jack. For all his easy-going ways, he stood firm on her not working. Coming from a family where her mother had always worked, held an important job in fact, his attitude had been refreshing at first. Whatever her mother had done, she wanted to do the opposite and so she had been content to stay at home. Lorenzo, too, held the old-fashioned view that the woman looked after the home and she had not wanted to cross Lorenzo, a fat jovial man. She had liked him for all his faults, listened to him as he grumbled, in an amiable enough fashion, about what he endured in the war. What she did not like was the hold he had on the family, the iron grip, the way Jack never went against his father's wishes. When Lorenzo said something was right, it was right even if it was wrong. It was not a weakness, as Jack saw it, it was a strength. The solidarity of the family was all and, because it became her family as well, she had not wanted to do anything to upset things.

Lorenzo was gone and she wanted to do something else with her life before it was too late. She strongly suspected that Jack would not retire next year even though he was supposed to be considering it. He might hand over the business reins but he would not give up completely and all this talk of spending half the year in their villa was just talk. He would fret about what was happening back home. Home was not Italy any more, never had been for him.

If she got her diploma in garden design then she could start up a little business of her own. What fun that would be and Jack would fund it, get it going, and then it would be up to her to make a go of it. And she had no doubts that she could do it. She loved working in the garden and she thought she had a good eye, a natural talent for design.

Jack was away a few days on business and,

rather than stay home and listen to Mrs Parkinson's distressing tale of her trip to America and her sister's subsequent death, Valerie was taking the opportunity to spend time with Alice. Ostensibly, it was to attend to the garden but she knew there was more to it than that. Matthew was at work most of the time and, whenever they could, when Alice was free of her own job, they would have the opportunity to talk.

Now that Alice was engaged to be married, it was time they talked.

Alice was sporting her lovely engagement ring. For somebody who did not earn a huge salary, Matthew was remarkably generous with gifts, although that was worrying in that it might indicate a carefree attitude to money. She and Jack had always lived comfortably within their means and she wondered if Jack was still slipping Alice money on the sly. Once she married, that would have to stop although, remembering their own parents' generosity, that seemed unlikely. It did no harm. Jack was just a normal loving father in the way her own had not been. Her father had never been guilty of violence, heaven forbid, just indifference, and he and her mother had been wrapped up in each other to such an extent that she always felt an intruder. Coming late into their life as she had, unexpectedly at that, she had been treated almost like an unwanted gift except, in her case, they could not wrap her up and return her. They sometimes looked at her as if they were surprised she was there, scarcely acknowledging her before resuming their conversation. They talked endlessly, often about very serious matters.

Mother had died, not so much from the injuries received in the crash for they were not life threatening, but from a broken heart. The doctors did not say as much, certainly something so romantic and medically inconclusive could not be recorded on the death certificate, but Valerie was convinced it was true. On learning that father had died, she had given up. Smiled a sad smile and said 'That's it then.'

And those, so far as Valerie knew, were her last words.

★   ★   ★

On her knees in the border, scrabbling about giving it its winter tidy, Valerie felt at her happiest. It played havoc with the nails, of course, but she had finally discovered gardening gloves that were not only effective at keeping her hands clean but also not so bulky that she felt hampered by them. It was a good winter day, cool but not bitingly cold, with no wind and no frost. She recognized most of the plants and had discarded some of them already without asking Alice, but she knew best and she was firming up on ideas for what she might suggest Alice put in their place.

Now that Alice and Matthew were engaged, it was just a matter of time before they had to face the ordeal of meeting Josie and Ray Bailey. Try as she would, she could not bring Ray to mind at all. He must have been fairly nondescript then. There had been no happy family snaps taken at Christmas, but Alice had supplied a good description and it tallied exactly with what she might have supposed herself. Josie had not metamorphosed into an elegant, quietly restrained, well-dressed woman and, somewhat to her dismay, it would seem that Alice had taken to her. She had needed an ally in Alice and it did not look as if she was going to get it. Alice had hesitated when describing Josie's mode of dress, neatly sidestepping the word 'tarty', calling it colourful instead.

However, and she was forcing herself to be honest here, the more Valerie saw of Matthew, the more she liked him. Whatever she might think of Josie, it would seem she had made a decent job of bringing up her son. She and Alice had been to the theatre to see a comedy, best seats courtesy of Matthew, and they had met his boss, Helen, a charming if eccentric woman who reminded her a little of her own mother. Mother had not possessed a decent frock either and the suits she wore for school were sadly lacking in style. But it had not mattered an iota to her and Valerie wondered if she attached too much importance to appearance. It was such a superficial thing to mind what she looked like, to mind what other people looked like and who was she to judge anyway?

Sometimes she did not like herself very much.

'Mrs Sazzoni . . . are you there?'

Startled, she clambered to her feet and saw Alice's neighbour, Mrs Osborne, peering at her through a thinner portion of hedge.

'Hello.' Valerie smiled. 'I'm just having a potter.'

'You need a break,' the old lady said with authority. 'It's not good for your knees to be on them so long. You've been out there nearly an hour, Mrs Sazzoni. I've been timing you. Come and have a cup of tea and a scone.'

'That's very kind.' Valerie had not noticed the time slipping by and yes, she was ready for a break and how could she refuse such an offer from such a sweet lady? Amused that she had been 'timed', she said she would be around in a moment after she had washed her hands.

The cottage was identical to Alice's but there the resemblance ended. This was an old lady's home, full to bursting with memorabilia. A large ginger cat sat amongst the china ornaments on the window ledge, moving gracefully as they entered the room and, amazingly, not knocking any of them over.

Valerie surveyed it warily, trying not to make eye contact. She was not a cat person and sometimes the blessed things knew that and deliberately tormented her. It slipped out of the room and she breathed a sigh of relief, sitting down as directed on the little sofa.

'Excuse my appearance,' she said, noting that Mrs Osborne was dressed in a warm lavender-coloured dress with a scarf draped softly around her neck. Mrs Osborne came in the category of 'old lady, well preserved'. She had keen blue eyes and her hair, gently grey, was long, swept up and pinned back. A surprising number of expensive-looking rings adorned her aged hands and there was an air about her of a woman who had had an interesting life. Perhaps she was about to find out.

'Your husband is a charming man,' Mrs

Osborne said. She had not volunteered a Christian name and Valerie had not asked.

'Oh yes, I remember him saying that you and he had had a chat last time we were here,' Valerie said, moving some of the large embroidered cushions from behind her back. 'You are right. He is charming.'

'My husband was charming too,' she said, placing a tray on a circular coffee table. 'We were together forty years.'

'How lovely! We have a long way to go until we get to forty years.'

'But God willing, you shall,' Mrs Osborne said. 'You make a very nice couple if you don't mind me saying?'

'That's kind.' Valerie smiled, accepting a buttered scone, freshly made of course, and placing it on the small willow patterned plate. She did not normally eat between meals — a killer — but she would make an exception so as not to offend.

'I miss Norman.' The words were accompanied with a sigh. 'It's ten years ago now since he passed on but I miss him still. Not a day goes by without me thinking of him,' she added, walking across the room and picking up a framed photograph, which she held against her bosom a moment. 'What is it the Queen Mother says of widowhood? 'You don't get over it but you do get better at it.'

How true. And she should know. Isn't she wonderful? I do so admire her. She's six years my senior. I have a feeling she might make it to one hundred and then she'll get a telegram from her daughter. What a joy.'

Valerie did a rapid count. My goodness, Mrs Osborne *was* wearing well. However, she made no comment as it might seem a trite thing to say.

'There he is,' Mrs Osborne said proudly. 'This is Norman.'

Valerie took the photograph, studied it a moment before declaring him to be a handsome man.

'We were never blessed with children,' Mrs Osborne went on. 'You are so lucky to have Alice. She is a lovely girl. Very like you, Mrs Sazzoni.'

'Yes, she is. And we are lucky. We — ' She hesitated. 'We treasure her.'

'And the young man . . . ' There was a pause.

'Matthew is her fiancé,' Valerie said quickly. 'They are to be married in the autumn probably. They haven't fixed a date as yet. He works in the theatre. The Little Gem. Do you know it?'

'Oh yes. I go occasionally,' Mrs Osborne said with a smile. 'It's such a good thing in my opinion. This moving in together before you get married. I'm all for it. Aren't you? After all, how on earth do you know if you are suited to each other if you haven't lived together? Make or break I think they call it. I read it somewhere.' Her smile widened. 'I like to keep abreast of the news and the way the young are conducting themselves. I think it's very important that the old try to understand the young. After all, we were young once. All of us.'

'You've got a very modem outlook, Mrs Osborne,' Valerie said. 'A lot of people would be horrified by the idea of cohabitation. We never did. My husband's father would have put his foot down. He was a lovely man but he had very fixed ideas.'

'Stubborn?'

'You could say that.'

'I'm stubborn too,' Mrs Osborne said. 'I shall stay here until they carry me out. I will never go into a home because all those poor things do is talk about the past. They encourage it. I can't think why.'

'I think we all live in the past a little,' Valerie said thoughtfully. 'After all, your past is what makes you, isn't it? You live with your memories and unless you lose your memory, you're stuck with them. You can't shake them loose, even if you want to.'

'How true.' Mrs Osmond popped a piece

of scone into her mouth. 'I often wonder how our brains can keep track? They're so small but they hold on to such a vast amount of information. So many things, so many compartments and have you noticed that if you forget something — somebody's name for instance — your brain carries on thinking about it even when you're not aware of it doing so. Oh dear, it is confusing. And then, when you are least expecting it, the name will pop up, like bread out of a toaster. I'm forever doing it. I wake up in the middle of the night and think, 'Good heavens, that's it.'

Valerie laughed. 'That is annoying, isn't it? I'm afraid I do that too.'

'And you're half my age.'

'Just a little over half . . . '

The chat moved on to Christmas. Mrs Osborne seemed keen to explain that, although she had spent the time mostly alone, she had enjoyed it. Visitors had popped in throughout the day and her homemade Christmas cake had soon disappeared.

Valerie told her about their Christmas, about their house by the lake, their villa in Italy, about Jack and the business. And then . . .

'The strangest thing has happened. I didn't find out about it until New Year when Alice and Matthew came over to see us. You're not going to believe this but Matthew, Alice's fiancé, is the son of one of our friends from way back. We used to live down in Felston and they still do. We lost track over the years but we shall meet them again soon.' She added, 'Won't that be fascinating?'

'Will it?' Mrs Osborne sniffed, poured another cup of tea for herself as Valerie declined. 'You seem quite agitated about it, if you don't mind me saying?'

'Agitated?' She was about to deny it but, looking across at Mrs Osborne, at the knowing expression, she knew better. Good heavens, she hardly knew this woman yet she felt the waves of sympathy and she needed somebody to talk to about it. It was better to say these things to a stranger and she would do very well.

'The thing is — ' She took a deep breath, putting down her cup which rattled in its saucer. 'Josie, Matthew's mother, was Jack's girlfriend in those days. They haven't met in over twenty-five years and I just wonder what they will think when they do. It's making me rather nervous.'

To her relief, Mrs Osborne did not laugh. Instead, she fell silent, twisting one of her rings as if she, too, was agitated.

'I've lived here in Penington Bridge a long time, over ten years,' she said at last. 'But you're thought of as a newcomer unless you were born here. It suits me because nobody knows me properly. I prefer it that way. Once people know they can be difficult, wanting to contact their loved ones who have died, that sort of thing, and I wanted to be rid of it, all that. Yes' — she smiled at Valerie — 'I confess. I do have a gift. I find I can keep it at a distance generally and if I do have any thoughts about people, I keep them very much to myself. All I can say is that I am usually proved right. It's all about auras, you know. Bad and good. I have the gift and it won't go away and sometimes I'm glad of it but not always.'

'Oh, I see . . . I'm sorry but I really don't believe in that sort of thing,' Valerie said, impatient to leave now but not wanting to be rude by rushing out. Perhaps the old lady was losing it a little. 'I'm a Catholic. At least, I was brought up as a Catholic. I have lapsed recently but — '

'People are frightened by it, by my gift,' Mrs Osborne said. 'You must not be. You have nothing to fear. I feel positive vibes coming from you and I felt the same about your husband. You have a very strong marriage and it will survive.'

That was such a comfort. Balderdash it might well be but she chose to take comfort from it. She wanted to tell Mrs Osborne that she had always worried that Jack did not love her as much as she loved him, if there could be scales of love that is. But she could not bring herself to be quite so open on that matter.

The door had been left ajar and the cat strolled in, standing still a moment before leaping on to the arm of Mrs Osborne's chair. She stroked it and it settled down, purring.

'If it's any consolation, I understand your sadness. I know about the babies you lost, my dear.'

'Did my husband tell you?' she asked, puzzled that he had done that, because they did not generally discuss that with other people. It was their private grief and they had long decided that they preferred to keep it that way. Too much sympathy even now, so long after the event, could still bring it unbearably to mind.

'Oh no. He didn't say a word.'

Valerie shivered, even though there was a coal fire in the grate and the little room was cosy. 'Then how do you know?' she asked.

'They are with you,' Mrs Osborne said in a matter of fact tone. 'They came in with you. Four strapping sons.'

Valerie felt the room spin, her heart race.

Was this woman completely mad? Alice must have said something to her. That was it. That had to be it. 'Oh really,' she laughed, although Mrs Osborne was conspicuously not amused.

To her relief, she heard a car stopping in the lane, saw Alice getting out, opening the gate, walking up the path. This was the signal to leave. And it was not a moment too soon.

'Thank you very much for the tea, Mrs Osborne,' she said, tightly polite.

'Not at all.' The old lady rose to her feet in a single fluid movement, touching her arm as she passed. 'I'm sorry, my dear. I see I have upset you. I do apologize. I shouldn't have said anything. I try not to say anything these days. It just slipped out. They all looked very well. Three of them very like your husband and the other like you. I thought you ought to know that.'

Shaken, Valerie left her.

21

'Between you and me, Mum, she's a little overweight,' Alice was saying, helping her with preparations for their evening meal. 'But she's keen to learn and I'm in favour of her being allowed to do that. Obviously, I'll have to keep an eye on things, but the other children are very sweet and I don't think there will be a problem, not at her age. It's only a problem when they get older. It's a shame though, isn't it? She's a lovely child, gorgeous ginger hair, but fairy elephant springs to mind, although I'm only saying that to you.'

'Oh dear. I see what you mean.'

'I have been asked to provide the babes for another musical production at the theatre,' Alice went on chattily. 'Please don't think Matthew's pulling strings for me. Now that I've established I can be relied on to produce the goods, other directors will follow suit. It saves them time if they can be put in touch with a reliable contact. Each production has its own choreographer but, once the children know the steps, he or she are more than happy to leave me to get them up to speed.

We shall need two teams of course, red and blue.'

'Teams?' Valerie was chopping vegetables, her mind not on this.

'To alternate, Mother. They are only allowed to work so many hours at a time. And, if they are doing the matinee and evening performance, I have to find all-day chaperones for the under-sixteens. The mothers are very willing to help out with that.'

'Lovely' Valerie glanced at the clock. 'What time will Matthew be home?'

'He won't. Not until late,' Alice said. 'It's a nuisance not having proper hours. Nine to five would be fantastic. But it's not to be so we have to make the best of it.'

'So there will be just the two of us then?' Valerie slid the vegetables into the dish. 'Alice, could we talk a minute?'

'OK.' She looked surprised but stopped what she was doing. 'Let's go and sit down. If this is about me and Matthew and our getting married then — '

'No. It's not about that. Well, not directly.'

There were too many pieces of her mother's furniture in Alice's little sitting room and, as she had not long ago been discussing with Mrs Osborne, it was enough of a jolt to her memory bank to bring it all back. The desk used to sit in the drawing room of the big house in Felston where it was well used by her mother, who was fond of writing letters and drawing up lists. The bookcase had sat in her father's study, crammed with medical books that were never looked at but just sat there gathering dust. As for the rosewood fire screen, she was surprised to see that here, for she found it fussy and over decorative but she had to admit that it suited the room. Alice had achieved an interesting mix of old and new, and Valerie chose to sit nearest the fire on a comfortable chair. The heavy curtains were drawn across against the winter evening and she wished for a moment she was away from all this, in Italy at the villa, returning only in late spring when the daffodils were in bloom.

'What's the matter, Mum?'

'It's Mrs Osborne next door.' Valerie looked at her, shook her head. 'I must be mad to believe a word she says. Did you know she has a *gift*? A gift she calls it. I think your father might have another word for it.'

Alice laughed. 'Oh yes. Didn't I tell you? She thinks it's a secret but everybody knows. Mrs Winter at number four told me. 'Don't catch her eye, she said. And don't ask, never ask.'

'Ask what?'

'Ask her to tell your fortune.' Alice was still smiling. 'What's she been telling you? Oh mum, she's not got you worried, has she? Just ignore it. Don't let it get to you, whatever she's been saying.'

'It has got to me a bit.'

'You shouldn't let it. How old do you think she is?'

'I know exactly how old she is. She told me. She's eighty-three.'

'Is she? She's quite sprightly then.'

'Yes. Body and mind. If she was a touch dippy, that would make it easier. I could just dismiss it then.'

'Dismiss what?' Alice asked as a pause developed. 'Oh come on, Mum, you can't keep me in suspense now.'

'The thing is . . . after we had you — ' Valerie paused, stretching out her legs and realizing to her surprise she had not changed and was still wearing the gardening trousers. 'We hoped for more children but I lost them. Four babies in all.'

'I know.' Alice looked across at her, surprised, wondering what had brought on this unexpected revelation. It was not exactly a secret but just something they never talked about. She could only guess how her mother felt about it, Dad, too, and it had seemed insensitive of her to be curious about it.

'Granny told me about it once but she said I wasn't to mention it because it would only upset you.'

'It would have upset me but I should have talked to you about it as soon as you were old enough to understand,' Valerie said. 'I should have told you how I felt. I don't know why I didn't. I could never talk about it with your father because he was as upset as I was. Not talking seemed the best way to deal with it. After you, we had a baby boy who lived only a few hours. We called him John.'

Alice nodded. Granny had told her that much.

'Then there were three pregnancies which all failed. The last got to five months. That was hard.'

'Why did it happen?'

'There were medical reasons. I have a faulty gene which affects baby boys. You were a girl and so you were fine. You might need to be checked at some point yourself, darling. Just to see you're not carrying the wretched thing.'

There was a silence whilst Alice digested this.

'Now you see what I've done,' Valerie said. 'I've upset *you*.'

'No, you haven't. It's just a bit of a shock, but it's not your fault, Mum.'

'Oh, but it is. It is my fault. I carry the gene. And, if I've passed the problem on to you that makes me a very good mother, doesn't it?'

'Look, that's all for the future,' Alice said firmly. 'Let's leave that. I shall tell Matthew but I don't suppose it's going to matter to him. In fact, if it does matter to him then it's best I find out now.' She smiled, shook her head. 'He's not so shallow. I know that.'

'Do you know what Mrs Osborne said?'

'Do I want to know?'

'She said they were with me, that they came in the room with me. And, the question is, if Dad didn't tell her, if you didn't, then how on earth did she know? It's weird, isn't it? Weird and wonderful at the same time.'

'Oh, Mum.' Alice went over to her, squatted beside her. She looked shattered, hair ruffled, and, although she didn't want to tell her, there was a smudge on her cheek — a speck of garden earth that she had rubbed in. It made her human all of a sudden, that and the moisture in her eyes. She looked suddenly every one of her forty-eight years. And the thought of her mother suffering that, the loss of a baby, the loss of several babies, forced up a torrent of emotion for Alice too. 'Poor you,' she said, knowing it was inadequate, holding her hand a minute, half-expecting her mother to push her away.

But she did not.

'So your father never had his son. If he'd married Josie he would have. Don't you see?'

'No I don't see,' Alice said. 'What are you talking about? I know dad would have liked a boy. All men do. But I think you're wrong. You're making it out to be more important than it is. You've got me,' she added. 'Or is that why you've always resented me?'

'Resented you?' Valerie sat upright. 'I've never resented you, Alice. What a thing to say.'

'But you — '

'I'm sorry if you've felt that way. I don't find it easy to be demonstrative, that's all. My parents were never that way with me either and it must have rubbed off.' Valerie flushed, gently removing her hand. 'But you mustn't think that I don't love you. I do. And as for your dad . . . well, he thinks the world of you. And you don't need me to tell you that. Goodness me.' She made an effort, smiled. 'This is getting very serious. Now, I've been thinking about inviting Josie and Ray over at Easter. What do you think? I'll keep it informal for them. Just the four of us and you and Matthew, of course, if he can get some time off.'

'I doubt it.' Alice pulled a face. 'No chance at all in fact. He reckons he isn't due any more time off until 1994 at the very least.'

'Never mind. They will come I'm sure. We need to meet up with them before the wedding. It will give us the chance to get some things sorted out. Will I send a formal invitation? Or will you just ask them for me?'

'Why don't you phone them yourself? Speak to Josie. She won't bite your head off.'

'I'd rather not. I don't want to speak to her for the first time on the phone.'

Alice smiled. It was so unlike her mother to be hesitant about something like that. But then she had seen a side of her mother today that she had never really seen before. Why had she bottled this up? Something as important as this? Why, when Alice was old enough to understand, why had they not talked about it? She had known about the lost babies but had never thought about them as people, brothers even, but now, for the first time, she did.

'I'll just ask them, Mum, if that's what you want. Josie rings me now. We chat quite often. I'll mention it next time she calls. I just need to know when and for how long?'

That established, Alice recognized the importance of this meeting between the four of them, was beginning to dread it too. She could not believe it would change things greatly. The idea that her father and Matthew's mother would take up where they had left off was plainly, after all this time, completely mad.

And yet, that was clearly what was uppermost in her mother's mind.

22

Josie was summoned to Mr Walsh's office and, waiting for the red 'come on in' light to switch on over his door, it took her back to her schooldays when, on more than enough occasions, she had found herself waiting outside the headmistress's office. She had sailed through her eleven plus and gone on to Felston Girls' Grammar but she did not pay attention, could not concentrate, was sometimes disruptive and — let's face it — a real pain in the neck. She remembered being particularly unimpressed by her headmistress laying down the law, even though it was bound to get back to her dad and that meant one thing only to look forward to.

'I hear you've been cheeky again, our Josie. How many times do I have to tell you that you've got to learn respect for your elders and betters? Get yourself in that back room . . . now!'

Sitting outside Mr Walsh's office, Josie flinched, her father's angry voice coming from nowhere, from somewhere, from everywhere. He'd had a softer voice reserved for other people, for Matthew particularly.

251

There would be no physical punishment today but that did not help much as she waited, feeling her stomach churning with nerves. If Kenny had been found out, lumbered, then he would be wriggling on the hook like a man possessed and, because he'd only ever thought of her as a good laugh, he would have no qualms about landing her well and truly in the dirt. She could not believe she had got herself into this situation. It was all her own fault. She had nobody else to blame.

The light buzzed and she jumped. Well, this was it and she was as ready as she would ever be.

'Come on in and sit down, Josie,' Mr Walsh said, smiling at her. 'I was sorry to hear about your dear mother. Please accept my condolences.'

'Thank you for the card. She *was* eighty-five,' she murmured as if that made it all right.

'A good innings.' Mr Walsh, a keen cricket fan, leant back in his chair, folding his arms over his ample stomach. He was a waistcoat man; sometimes they matched the suit, sometimes, like now, they were rather snazzy in various shades of silk. 'Life goes on.'

She nodded, letting her hands lie loosely on her lap. Waiting. He was apt to go off at a tangent and this might take some time, particularly if he was working up to reprimanding her or even threatening to sack her for something she did not do. The trouble was how could she deny knowing nothing about it when she did? Oh God, Ray would go nuts. And as for Margaret ... she wouldn't put it past Margaret to come storming in here and shouting the odds. Normally a mild-mannered woman, when it came to protecting Josie, Margaret was like a tigress with her cubs.

'How long have you been with us, Josie?'

'Twenty-eight years with a year's break,' she said promptly. 'I started as a junior when I was seventeen.'

'I remember you as a junior,' he said with a smile. 'You've done well, haven't you? I can always count on you. I've always regarded you as one of our more reliable members of staff. Loyal. Someone I can trust to get a job done.'

'Thank you.' She was trying to read his mind, to see behind the vague smile. Maybe she was a bit of a favourite with him because, over the years, he had been good to her. She had given her notice in when she was expecting Matthew — it was before the days of all these maternity benefits — and never expected to be welcomed back a year later, almost with open arms. Ray had not wanted her to go back to work even though they needed the money and had only relented because she had arranged for Matthew to be looked after by one of her friends with a child the same age. There had never been any question of the baby being looked after by her mother and Margaret was working so that ruled her out too.

The arrangement with Heather suited them both for Heather was happy to stay home and happy to have some money coming her way from looking after Matthew. Having one more to look after was neither here nor there, according to Heather, whose maternal instincts were coming out of her ears. Josie in turn, although she loved the baby, was happier to be working, to be with adults, to be doing a job that, way back then, she found interesting and absorbing.

It had surprised Josie, coming back to work, because nothing had changed. *She* had changed. She was now the mother of a little boy, her priorities in life had drastically shifted but work here was just the same, as if time had stood still in her absence.

'There's got to be some continuity, in my opinion,' Mr Walsh said, ignoring the phone on his desk as it rang and rang. Josie knew very little about him, the man, for he kept his private life private. There was a Mrs Walsh, a quiet background lady, and several Walsh children, grown-up now. 'I see myself as captain of the team and it's important to me that it carries on smoothly when I'm gone,' he continued in the pompous tone they found so amusing. 'We in local government do a tremendous job for the community and the adverse publicity we sometimes get really pains me. We are given no credit for the things we do well but regrettably, we have to suffer in silence.'

Josie, tempted to answer the phone herself, remained silent as the ringing ceased. Let him get this off his chest. She had things to do out in the main office, things piling up and she could do without this. The junior had just brought her a cup of tea and it would be stone cold by the time she got back to it. It might take some considerable time to get to the point of all this, the point that she was dreading.

'I have some surprising news, Josie. Mr Balfour has tendered his resignation,' he said and she straightened up at that. If it had to come to it, she would defend herself and sod the outcome. 'We shall be very sorry to lose him but, sadly, these things happen.'

She nodded, as that seemed the appropriate response. What the hell was Kenny up to?

It looked very much as if he had been rumbled and, in order to keep it all under wraps, he had been asked to resign. It struck her as a typical local government reaction, willing to go to any lengths to avoid scandal. Sometimes, she liked the organization she worked for, admired it even and sometimes, like now, she despised it.

'Why has he resigned?' she asked.

'Personal reasons,' he said. 'His dear wife is very ill, I'm sorry to say but keep that under your hat. It's not for general consumption. Suffice to say, we wish him well. He and Dorothy. He will be leaving as of now. Obviously, an official period of notice was required but there are occasions when it can be waived. This is one of them. He needs to be with her.'

Josie said nothing. Best say nothing.

Mr Walsh smiled slightly. 'The point of calling you in, Josie, is that as we have only recently had an interview procedure for this particular position as my deputy clerk, we feel — and I have spoken to everyone involved — that we should simply offer the job to the applicant who came a very close second to Mr Balfour. And that . . . ' He beamed. 'That is you. I am, as they call it, sounding you out. If you do accept the position then we can waive all the usual advertisements and so on.

It will save us a lot of trouble and time and I am confident you will be an admirable choice.'

'Oh — ' She looked at his face, his trusting face, and a huge mix of emotions tumbled about inside. She could think about the flat once again, properly this time, and wasn't this opportunity what she had been working towards for so long? She could do the job standing on her head, take on the extra responsibility with no problem and it would indeed be something to get her teeth into and she could finally implement some of the changes she felt ought to be made to the department. Why then did she feel less than thrilled?

'Perhaps you need some time to think about it?' Mr Walsh said. 'I suppose I can be accused of springing it on you. There is no great rush because Peter is here for another couple of months but I am looking for a smooth change-over period.'

Kenny was going to get away with it, scot-free. What the hell was this about Dorothy being ill? It was the first she'd heard of it. Could he really be going to Spain, courtesy of his ill-gotten gains, leaving a possibly ailing wife, to enjoy a life in the sun? She wouldn't put it past him. He was just the sort of man who would plough on regardless.

Mr Walsh's words stopped her in her tracks.

She would do as he suggested and take some time to think about it.

* * *

Dorothy answered the phone but Josie was prepared for that.

'This is Josie Bailey from work,' she said brightly. 'I've only just heard about Kenny leaving, Mrs Balfour.'

'News travels,' Dorothy said, her voice flat and unemotional. 'Does everybody know?'

'Not yet. Mr Walsh has only told me.'

'I see.'

The silence was hard.

'I just wanted to say,' Josie struggled. What on earth *did* she want to say?

'And I want to say something, too, but I can't talk about this over the phone. Have you time to pop round? It won't take long.'

* * *

The house was detached, mock Tudor, set well back from the road. She had been here just once before, shortly after Kenny took up his appointment and they were invited to a house-warming party. The house was not to

258

Josie's taste, not the sort of thing she would go for but each to his own. It occurred to her that Kenny had a damned cheek laughing at Ray's Christmas decorations when he lived in a monstrosity like this. There were two large cars in the drive, importantly side by side. Kenny's BMW and a Jaguar. Somehow she was not surprised that Dorothy drove a Jag. She didn't look the sweet little car type.

Pulling up outside, Josie wondered for the moment what on earth she was doing here. She was asking for trouble. Nobody knew, apart from her and Kenny, what had gone on between them, although in effect nothing had gone on. It was all whispering and giggling and the occasional odd furtive kiss. Very teenage and silly. It had been going nowhere. It was never meant to go anywhere.

She had been a fool. She saw that now. She should have clocked him one the very first time he tried it on and put an end to it. And now, here she was, outside his door, feeling very guilty. And to top it all, the rain which had been at it all day had upped a gear and turned torrential. She would get wet through just getting up the path.

Here goes. She opened the car door and by the time she got her umbrella up, her hair was plastered to her head. It had grown a little and the colour was not quite so vibrant but it would take some considerable time to recover.

'Come in.' Dorothy opened the door and managed a smile. She had a stiff smile, little facial expression and Josie wondered if she'd had a face-lift. Good for her if she had. She wasn't entirely sure she wouldn't do the same thing when she got to Dorothy's age, if she could afford it that is. 'Leave the brolly in the porch and would you mind taking off your shoes? I'm sorry to be fussy but it's the carpet . . . '

Ah yes. Pale cream, no pattern, a bugger, according to Ray, to keep clean unless you paid extra for special carpet protection and then you could drop red wine on it and it would just mop up. Stopping herself just in time from saying what a lovely carpet it was — she was getting more and more like Ray every day — Josie handed Dorothy her coat. Feeling at a disadvantage, shoeless, she followed Dorothy into the sitting room.

'Kenny won't be joining us,' Dorothy said tightly. 'Do take a seat.'

'Awful weather,' Josie said, for something to say. Dorothy looked blooming — so much for her being ill. Mr Walsh had talked about it as if she was at death's door.

'Let's not beat about the bush, Mrs Bailey.' Dorothy did not offer her tea or coffee but sat opposite on a green striped settee. She was wearing house shoes, backless silver mules and beautifully cut pale green trousers with a toning over-printed sweater with extravagant shoulder pads. 'This is all rather delicate but I have been informed by someone who doesn't wish to be identified that you and Kenny have been carrying on, for want of a better expression.'

'That's not true,' Josie gasped, feeling herself colour up which was a dead giveaway.

Dorothy raised her carefully waxed eyebrows. 'I know what he's like, so don't pretend. If it's not you, it would be somebody else. Well, I've had enough. I've given him an ultimatum. Unless he wants me to walk out on him, unless he wants to give up the car and the lifestyle, then he comes to heel. There is no need for him to work as he has a more than adequate allowance from me.'

'Then why does he?'

'A little bit of independence, I suppose. He doesn't care to be thought of as a kept man. A toy boy perhaps. But I should think the most likely reason he works is to get away from me for a while. We really cannot stand the sight of each other for too long at a time. Kenny is wonderful in small doses but we can't live in each other's pockets. Although that is what we are just about to do.'

Josie, not sure if she was serious, shared a slight smile with her.

'He is totally useless. He wastes a tremendous amount of money gambling and I refuse to fund that so he has to find that from his own sources. Did you know about the gambling?'

'No.'

'Did he ask you to move with him to Spain? To the villa?'

She nodded, knowing it was pointless to pretend otherwise. 'I said no. I'm not leaving my husband.'

'I should hope not. I remember your husband very well. A nice man.'

Josie managed a nervous smile, thinking it odd that Ray should have made an impression on a woman like this, but then she did recall the two of them huddled a while in a corner at that housewarming party. She couldn't imagine what on earth Ray had found to talk about to a sophisticated woman like this, unless he had had a hand in getting her the carpet at a special discount.

'Can I tell you something about this wonderful man of mine?' Dorothy said, taking a cigarette from a packet that lay on the coffee table and offering one to Josie who declined. Dorothy took her time lighting up and seemed to relax a little as she inhaled.

'He lives in a complete fantasy world, Mrs Bailey. For a start, it's my villa not his. I am buying it with my money. And that's where we are heading. He's coming with me to Spain and I intend to keep an eye on him in future. There will be no more straying or I'll be suing for divorce. I told him to say I was desperately ill so that he could cut short the notice. I wanted him out of there as quickly as possible so that we can get on with things. I shall be renting out this property and we shall be flying out in a couple of weeks.'

There was a steely glint in her eyes and Josie knew she meant it. It was difficult to imagine Kenny kowtowing to any woman, let alone his own wife, and it bemused her. This was developing into a girly chat and Josie found herself relaxing a little. It was all out in the open and about time — after all nothing had happened and now, thank God, nothing would happen.

'Where is he?'

They exchanged a womanly look that ultimately acknowledged the daftness of the male species in general and Kenny in particular.

'He's suffering from a severe bout of sulkiness,' Dorothy said with a small smile. 'He's thought about the options available and he now realizes that he's not going to get rid of me as easily as that. I can't believe he asked you to go with him to Spain. It's my villa, in my name, so I could have put a stop to that little scheme very quickly. Did it not occur to him that I would follow him? Did he imagine for one moment I would tolerate a little threesome? And, just to set the record straight, he has not been embezzling funds. I believe he told you that too? As I say, he tells these silly tales and ends up believing them. He craves excitement. He likes to be thought of as the bad boy. The girls always crowd round the bad boy. Hadn't you noticed? He's like a child. It's happened before. I have great trouble keeping him under control.' She laughed. 'How ever a man like that came to be working in local government of all things never ceases to amaze me. He has the qualifications. They're not fakes. And I believe he has the expertise but it's not enough for him.'

'Why don't you leave him?'

'Or rather, why do I stay with him? It does seem extraordinary, doesn't it? But I suppose I enjoy having him around. It's lonely on your own and I'm not somebody who enjoys her own company. I need a man about the house and you have to admit he's dishy. And he is rather good at some things.' She raised her eyebrows. 'My first husband was as miserable as sin. The only good thing he did was die and leave me pots of money. When I met Kenny, I found his outlook so refreshing. He can be very amusing. I don't mind the little flings but when they start to get serious . . . then something has to be done.'

'It was never serious,' Josie said, picking up on that.

'No. Looking at you, I don't suppose it was.'

She never did get the tea or coffee. What she did get was a rundown on their peculiar marriage.

'Just as a matter of interest, who told you?' she asked as she was leaving and slipping her shoes back on.

'I did promise I wouldn't say.'

'It wasn't my husband?' she asked, suddenly horrified that he might somehow have got wind of it.

'No. It was your sister Margaret.'

'Margaret? But I swore her to secrecy,' Josie said, not surprised. She felt a fool now for jumping to that conclusion about embezzlement. Daft idea all round.

Dorothy laughed, seeming to understand. 'Embezzlement eh? Kenny hasn't got the guts to do something like that. I have. I could do it but not Kenny. You were very gullible, Josie, to believe him.' They were on first name terms now.

Gullible. You could say that again. 'I hope things work out for you,' she said, meaning it, standing awkwardly now on the doorstep. The rain had eased and she kept the umbrella down. 'I did like him, Dorothy. I wouldn't have egged him on otherwise. And I'm sorry I did that. It was a very childish thing to do.'

Dorothy smiled. 'He's an arrogant bastard. It's not your fault.'

As she drove home, a weight lifted off her shoulders, she saw that now there was no obstacle to her taking the job. She would see if that flat was still on the market, the one she fancied.

And then she would have to persuade Ray.

23

Margaret had a lot to answer for. She had no business doing that. How could she trust her when she did things like that? She stopped off at Percy Street on the way back to have it out with her. As usual, there was nowhere to park and she ended up shoe-horning the car into a space three houses away from Margaret's. By the time she did that, not easy when you had an audience of interested children, her anger had abated a little. But, as she approached the front door, seeing Margaret waving at her from the window, she felt her hackles rising again.

'You had no right, interfering like that,' she said, as she bustled in, almost shoving Margaret out of the way. 'And how did you know Dorothy Balfour anyway?'

'I do have a life of my own,' Margaret said, looking at her reproachfully. 'If you must know, I don't know her that well, she's not my sort, but I have met her and I knew where she lived. And don't you come barging in here laying down the law, getting yourself in a tizzy. I only did it for you.'

'Did you go round to her house?' Josie

clicked her tongue. 'Honestly, Margaret, you have a cheek. Why can't you mind your own business?'

'And watch you ruin your life? You forget I've known you for ever, Josie. Sometimes I wonder if you have any sense at all. You might keep landing on your feet but one of these days, mark my words, you'll come a cropper. Poor Ray. I feel sorry for him. He's a good man and here you are going the right way about losing him.'

'It was only a bit of fun.'

'I've heard that before. Sit yourself down.' Margaret picked up her knitting and calmly carried on. 'Has she put you in the picture then?'

'Yes.' Josie sank down in the chair, weary of it all. 'I could murder a cup of tea. She never even offered me a cup of tea.'

'You know where the kettle is. I'll have a cup too.'

Waiting for the kettle to boil, standing at the little window, Josie shivered. Her mum and dad were both gone now but their presence in this house was strong. They were everywhere, in every damned corner. Ray had put fresh wallpaper in the back sitting room but the old one was still there, underneath, the flowery one. She had studied that wallpaper closely. It had been applied the wrong way up so that the flowers were upside down. Her mother had only noticed the mistake when they had done one wall already, so they left it because the general effect had been all right.

Margaret should have moved away. She could have sold up and got another house close by. With a bit of luck, she might have managed to get out, shut the door quick, and leave the memories trapped behind.

'All right then. I forgive you,' she said magnanimously when she returned to the sitting room with the tea and a plate of digestives. 'You meant it for the best and, in the end, it's all worked out. Kenny's left, so I won't have to put up with him any more. I can't believe he'll just let her drag him off like that. He either loves her, deep down, or he really is all about money and his damned car and his nice suits and his gambling. Just as well he's off anyway, I have enough on my plate just now with Matthew getting married in the autumn. She's invited us over at Easter.'

'Who has?'

'Who do you think? Valerie. Starchy knickers. Alice's mother. She wants me and Ray to go for the weekend. Informal, she says. I haven't spoken to her but she asked Alice to ask us. It's a posh house by all accounts, right by the lake. Matthew says it's like a mansion. Ray will have kittens. I don't know if we should bother. You know what Ray's like. He won't know where to put himself, what knives to use and everything.'

'He's not as bad as that.' Margaret tutted and gave her a sharp glance. 'He manages fine these days. You make him out to be worse than he is, Josie. Stop doing it. You'll knock all his confidence.'

'What confidence?' Josie laughed at that.

'Get yourself over there. You never know you might just enjoy it.' Margaret finished the row, switched needles, clicked off again, fingers flying. 'There's no question of you not going and don't you worry about Jack Sazzoni. Forget all that. He never knew about that little matter.'

She didn't spell it out and neither did Josie.

'And you're not likely to tell him.' She paused in mid-stitch, gave Josie a hard stare. 'You've not got any daft thoughts of telling him, have you?'

'No. I have not. Why would I do that? Ray doesn't even know about that. Although I nearly told Alice . . . she's got a nice way with her and I felt she ought to know. Then I thought better of it. I can't think what came over me. It's not fair to lumber her with a secret like that.'

'Talking of secrets, I've got something to tell you,' Margaret said, coming to the end of the row, giving the knitting a satisfied tug and putting it down, needles sticking up. 'We've had an invitation, me and you.'

'To what?'

'Give me a chance.' Margaret rose to her feet, went across to the bureau and rummaged in the drawer. 'Here it is. Read it yourself.'

Josie took the sheet of paper, read it quickly.

'We can't go.' She looked at her sister. 'You weren't thinking of going, were you?'

'My first thought was no, but I think we have to,' Margaret said. 'We can do it, Josie.'

'For him?' Josie spat out the words. 'Why should we do anything for him, Margaret?'

'We're not doing it for him,' Margaret said. 'It's for the girl. Don't you see? Try to put yourself in her position. When somebody saves your life, you would put that person on a pedestal. Wouldn't you? And now that she's grown-up and has a child of her own, she still remembers him. As she says, if it wasn't for him, she wouldn't have had the baby, she wouldn't have been here to have the baby.'

'Fancy naming a baby after him,' Josie said. 'Poor little mite.'

'Don't you see? We can't destroy what she

271

feels about him. So, we're not attending this ceremony for Dad, we're doing it for her. We put on a brave face and just do it. You're coming with me, Josie, you *and* Ray and I shan't take no for an answer. In any case, I've already accepted so it's too late.'

★　★　★

A showdown with Dorothy, a good talking to from Margaret and then, to cap it all, when she rang the estate agents, the flat by the old docks was under offer and off the market.

'Who's buying it?' she asked the girl, knowing she had no claim on the blessed place but feeling hard done by to have missed the opportunity.

'I can't tell you his name,' the girl said. 'All I can say is that he's a doctor and he's paid cash, so there won't be any hitches. We'll keep you informed, Mrs Bailey, if any of the others come back on the market.'

Ray was out when she got back so she rang Alice for a chat, which would help her get over the disappointment. She had taken to doing this, ringing Alice in preference to Matthew. Matthew was not chatty on the phone, just like his dad, and always in a tearing hurry, so she liked to phone Alice who always sounded, rightly or wrongly, as though she had all the time in the world.

'I'm going to be in the local paper,' she told her. 'Margaret and I have been invited to this little do. It's a long story. Did Matthew tell you about his granddad saving this little girl from a fire years ago?'

'Oh yes. That's very impressive, isn't it? He was a policeman, wasn't he? Matthew's told me lots about him. How he used to spend a lot of time reading to him and telling him stories. They got on very well, didn't they?'

'Yes, well . . . that little girl is grown up now and she's had a baby boy and she wants to call the baby after Matthew's granddad. She moved away after the incident and was brought up in Southampton, I think, and now for some reason she wants to come back to Felston and make a little bit of a fuss. She's an artist.'

'Isn't that lovely of her? It's so nice of her to have remembered.'

'It certainly makes a story for the local paper,' Josie said, unable to stop a little sniff. 'Just the sort of thing they like, being a bit soppy and everything. Human interest they call it. So, as Dad's not around any more, they've asked me and Margaret to come along as his representatives. There'll be a photograph and a little report of the incident and so on. It made headline news at the time.'

'You must have been very proud of him?'

'Yes,' Josie said quietly.

'How exciting! What will you wear?' Alice asked, a smile in her voice.

She laughed. 'What do you think I should wear? Is there a dress code for it? I'm more concerned with what Margaret will wear. I don't want her looking too frumpish. She has her black suit and her best coat and that's it.'

'My mother says she's looking forward to meeting you again by the way,' Alice said, acting as go-between as usual between the two of them. 'She's got nothing planned as such. It depends on the weather. You know what Easter's like. So unpredictable.'

'Will you be there?' Josie asked, wanting some support, knowing she would get it from Alice.

'I don't think so. Matthew and I thought it would be best to leave you to it. You can have a nice time together, just the four of you.' She paused. 'Don't worry about it, Josie. You must not feel yourself under any pressure. You mustn't think that you have got to be friends.'

'Just so long as we're not daggers drawn, is that it?' Josie said. 'Your wedding will be fine. Don't *you* worry about that. I wouldn't dream of doing anything to spoil it for you.'

She felt a sudden urge to tell Alice that she was starting to think of her as a daughter, the one she had never had, but she felt a bit shy of saying such a thing. Maybe it was too soon. 'Has he said anything about me? Your father?'

'No. When I told them, he laughed. He thought it was funny. Mother wasn't so amused. In fact . . . she's been in a very funny mood recently. She came over for a few days and I don't want to go into it but my next door neighbour upset her. She brought it all back to mum. Did you know she lost four babies after me?'

'I didn't know that. I heard from somebody that things hadn't gone well. But I didn't know it was so many. Four, you say? Poor Valerie.'

'It's still raw,' Alice said. 'Can you believe that? After all this time?'

'Oh yes . . . I can believe it.'

★ ★ ★

Ray had sworn Lynn to secrecy. He didn't want Josie getting wind of it too soon, not before things were finalized. He kept having cold feet but it was time he took a stand, did something unexpected. She would like that. He had been thinking about doing it for years but he had needed somebody like Lynn to push him a bit, to give him some encouragement. Lynn had changed since Mick had left her. She hadn't folded, as they thought she might, but had got herself over it, over him, and he thought she looked a damned sight better at forty-five than she had at twenty.

They were invited to the Sazzoni residence at Easter. He was not looking forward to that one little bit but, with Matthew and Alice now engaged, it had to be faced. Josie was going mad, buying him new clothes like there was no tomorrow, because, as she said, she didn't want him showing her up in the stuff he had at present.

'I wasn't thinking of taking my work clothes,' he had told her, a bit peeved about it. 'And how do we know what we'll need if we don't know where they'll be taking us?'

'That's why we have to prepare for all eventualities,' Josie told him, attacking one of her lists with a vengeance. 'You never know at Easter. It could be cold, raining, sunny. It's a nightmare knowing what to take. Now, where was I? Oh yes, your list. Underwear — '

'Bloody hell, Josie, nobody's going to see that except you.'

'It doesn't matter. You need new underpants anyway. Are you fussed what I get?'

He shook his head. Underpants were

underpants. He had never bought a pair in his life. He left that to the women in his life, first his mum and now Josie.

'They will probably want to take us out to dinner in a fancy restaurant up there and, if the weather's nice — ' She chewed thoughtfully on her pen. 'We might have a barbeque in the garden and then they might take us on a boat trip across the lake or we might just be going sightseeing. I don't know what their interests are.'

For crying out loud . . . 'Matthew says they're into walking, so we'll have to take walking boots,' he told her. 'I've got some but you'll have to get yourself a pair. And some thick socks. And we'll need haversacks.'

'Walking boots?' She looked horrified. 'But I can't walk in flat shoes.'

'We'll definitely need them in case they take us mountaineering. Have you considered that possibility?'

She looked at him, shook her head as she caught his smile. 'Stop fooling around, Ray, I haven't time for this. It's just as well I don't take you seriously. Walking boots indeed.'

He had left her to it. In the end, it would be business as usual. She could fill the suitcases and he would carry them.

In the meantime, they had this little reception in honour of Jimmy to attend and he was only going to that because for some reason Josie wanted him there with her. They were making a fuss because the girl whom Jimmy had rescued all those years ago was now something of a celebrity. He had never heard of her but she was an artist making a name for herself down in London, one of those modern artists, whose work left him bewildered. He hadn't said anything to Josie because it might offend her, but he reckoned that it was all a publicity stunt and that really this girl didn't give a monkey's about Jimmy, but maybe that was him being cynical. He would have to give her the benefit of the doubt.

It was billed as a little reception held at an art gallery in town, cocktails and a buffet at her expense, with some of her paintings on show and then a few speeches. He had no idea who would be speaking and didn't particularly care so long as he wasn't expected to say something. Josie would have a go if she had to but Margaret would be struck dumb.

'You can try out your new suit,' Josie said, laying his clothes out for him on the bed. 'Wear the blue shirt and the blue and pink tie.'

'OK.' He glanced at her. She looked nervous which puzzled him because normally she would love a free do like this. She had already changed twice and he had an idea the dark suit she was wearing at present would not last the course. 'Are we picking Margaret up?'

She nodded and then sat down abruptly on the bed, smack bang on his new suit.

And burst into tears.

24

This living together business was not easy and Matthew's irregular work pattern was a nuisance but there it was. She would have to get used to it and it was worth all the hassle just to have him here with her under the same roof, sharing the same bed.

It just felt right and, even if she sensed the slightest disapproval coming from some quarters, surprisingly her father rather than her mother, she dismissed that. Dad was happy that there was a wedding planned and they were now homing in on several dates with a view to bringing all the arrangements together very soon.

As to her own job, her contract with the education authority had been renewed for a further year, so that was something, and she had started up a Saturday morning dance class in Kirkley for under-tens, which was already oversubscribed.

Alice had said nothing to Matthew about her mother and Mrs Osborne. The thing about the faulty gene was worrying, of course, and she would have to get round to doing something about it at some point.

But not yet.

There was the wedding in autumn to look forward to and they were not intending to have a baby right away. They needed to get themselves sorted out first and Matthew would probably have to move away to get the job he wanted. So, the gene thing could wait.

As to her neighbour, she should have left well alone. Her mother had once suffered from depression and it was therefore irresponsible of the old lady for saying something that might have started it all off again. Putting ideas like that into the head of someone who had gone through a vulnerable period as her mother had was just not on. It was just pure luck that it had seemed to have the opposite effect and done her mother a world of good.

It was March and getting warmer. The daffodils were just out and her little garden was proving to be a constant surprise. Over the hedge, Mrs Osborne had a man in once a week to tidy hers — a neat and rather prim garden with a little pond and fish; not very sensible when she had a cat. The cat sneaked through the hedge into her garden sometimes and she didn't mind that, although she did mind when it caught the little fledgling birds that were starting to appear.

She had been to a show at the theatre last

night, a show that had received good reviews, although she found herself disappointed by it for some reason. Matthew had come up with the idea of treating their parents to a Shakespeare play at Easter. He would arrange to get tickets for the four of them, but she was not sure of the wisdom of that. A musical or a comedy would have been fine but somehow, she didn't feel Ray would be exactly enthralled by a Shakespeare production and she did not want him to feel uncomfortable and out of his depth. She liked Ray. He was big and uncomplicated and, in many ways, so like Matthew.

'You've got to give him a chance,' Matthew said when she told him of her concerns. 'He's no fool, my dad.'

'I didn't say he was.'

'You implied it.'

'No I did not.'

'Yes you bloody did.'

'Don't swear at me, Matthew.'

'Is it any wonder? There you are suggesting my dad is only half there when he's as bright as the next man. And he's got a helluva lot more common sense than some.'

'All right. We'll take them to your Shakespeare play,' she said, annoyed because she could not understand why he was being unreasonable. 'I'm only thinking of him. I worry he will feel very awkward and uncomfortable but if that's what you want, then just do it. And, if you're not going to take any notice of my opinion, you needn't bother asking me what I think in future. Just go ahead and do your own thing.'

'For God's sake, there's no need to go all snotty on me, Alice.'

She rushed out at that point, slamming the door rather satisfactorily behind her.

He did not follow. Joy of joys. Their first row.

Matthew had booked the seats that very afternoon before he could change his mind, so that was that. Her mother was thrilled, loved the idea of a Shakespeare play, her dad was more interested in where they would go for dinner the previous evening and when she gave Josie the news, to her surprise Josie asked which play it was.

'*The Merchant of Venice*,' Alice told her. 'It's one of my favourites. It's quite easy to follow. It's about this man called Shylock and — '

'I know what it's about,' Josie said, voice cooling. 'We did it at school. I went to Felston Girls' Grammar, Alice, and we didn't shirk on our Shakespeare.'

'Sorry, I didn't mean — ' She stopped, feeling awful.

'No, of course you didn't. It's me. I'm a bit touchy about it. Tell Matthew thanks for that. We'll look forward to it. I'll give Ray a run-down on the plot.'

Alice put down the phone, feeling no better. Had she a touch of her mother in her? How dare she make assumptions about Ray, or Josie for that matter? It was a little warning and she would take note of it.

She and Matthew had quickly made up and he had somehow found the time to buy her some flowers as an apology. Sticking them in a vase, she reflected ruefully that, as a first row, it didn't rate very highly. Certainly nothing had been flung, apart from a few nasty words. It had been rather tame, in fact, and if that was the best they could manage then it would be fine. Mind you, like his mother, he could be a mite touchy about some subjects and, if she was to avoid friction in future, she would do well to remember it.

* * *

Josie had accepted the new job but not yet told Ray. She wouldn't be starting it until next month, so there was time enough for that.

A few days before the photo shoot for this medal thing, she had seen Lynn. It was

Lynn's birthday, circled in Josie's diary like all the family birthdays, and, daft as it might seem, they still bought each other a little present and a card. She always agonized over what to buy Lynn because, living on her own as she did and earning a good salary, she had pretty much everything she wanted. She had got smarter as she got older, grown into her shape and was more relaxed about her height, even to the extent of wearing high heels. Josie settled on a leather purse because purses wore out and a new one was always appreciated. Then she bought a card, a little girl's pink card with the number 4 on it, a 4 to which she added a 6 to make 46. Silly, but they always did this sort of thing with cards. On her last birthday, Lynn had sent her a card with a badge inside 'I am 5', scratching a 4 in front of it and daring her to wear it for the entire day. She had agreed to do that, even though it was a work day and had spent that day with the badge pinned to her knickers. It had been enough to send the pair of them into a fit of giggles.

They were like two big kids. She couldn't do that sort of thing with anybody else but Lynn. Margaret liked sugary sweet cards with 'To my dearest sister' written on them, big fancy verses, the cornier the better for Margaret. She kept them, too, Josie knew that, kept them in a box in her wardrobe, together with bits and pieces of goodness knows what. A box of secrets and, although she had sneaked a peep from time to time, there wasn't anything in it that interested her.

Lynn lived in Clarence Street, off Clarence Square, in the first-floor apartment of an enormous three-storey town house close to Felston Park. Five minutes walk to her office and the shops, it was in an ideal location and, like Josie, her fingers were not tinged remotely green, so having no garden was a bonus. After Mick had left her, she had got rid of all the furniture the two of them had shared and bought new pieces. Everything was spanking new but it lacked any sense of being a home, more a show place. All photographs of the formerly happy couple had disappeared but, after a shaky start, Lynn seemed to have settled into her new life without him, and had long since told Josie to stop trying to find her a man. She did not want one.

'A purse!' Lynn shrieked, seeming as thrilled as if she had been given a diamond ring. 'Just what I needed. You clever thing.'

Josie beamed. It was always gratifying to be told that, whether or not it was true.

'Sit down. I haven't seen you in ages. We need to catch up,' Lynn said, scrunching up the wrapping paper and placing it in a wastepaper bin. 'Oh Josie, I was sorry to hear about your mum. Just after Christmas at that.'

'Yes. Thanks for your card. She was eighty-five, Lynn. At that age, it's hardly a surprise.'

'Surprise or not, it's still hard.' Lynn said.

'What have you been up to then?' Josie asked, settling back on the sofa. It was a dark blue leather chesterfield — gorgeous — and she could not help but run her hand along the seat beside her, the surface warm and soft to her touch. 'This is new, isn't it?'

'It cost a fortune but I got a bonus,' Lynn told her. 'I've nothing to spend it on except me. Doesn't that sound awful? Really selfish. But I'm darned if I'm going to be the woman who leaves thousands to her godchildren. They never come to see me from one year to the next so they can lump it. I'm booked for a Caribbean cruise in June.'

'Good for you. You never know who you'll meet on a trip like that. Make sure you take some nice bikinis with you.'

'You must be joking,' Lynn said with a sniff. 'Good heavens, Josie, you should stop wearing bikinis when you reach forty. Thirty if I had my way. I've always preferred a swimsuit and I'm taking a few nice ones and some cover-ups.' She reached for a ginger snap, nibbled at it. 'And that's not the reason I'm going. I don't want to meet anybody. I'm happy on my own, thank you very much.'

'I wish I was coming with you,' Josie said. 'Ray wouldn't hear of us going anywhere like that. You know what he's like. Real stay at home.'

'You might be surprised at Ray. He was telling me about your Matthew by the way and that girl of his. I bet that was a shock.'

'When did you see Ray? He never mentioned it.'

'I bumped into him. Can't remember when,' Lynn said, looking shifty.

'You're right. It was a shock. A terrible shock. It spoilt my Christmas I don't mind telling you.'

'What are you going to do?'

'What can I do? Put a brave face on it, that's what. I don't suppose he'll remember me.'

'Do you remember him?'

'Yes.'

'Well then. It stands to reason,' Lynn said triumphantly. 'I wonder what he's thinking about it all?'

'No idea. Look, Lynn, I'm trying not to make too much of it. It's a long time ago. He married Valerie and I married Ray.'

'I've often wondered why you chucked him, Josie. You two seemed so good together. Everybody said that. I know you said it was the religion thing but was it? You could have turned like everybody else does. I mean to say, it wasn't as if you were that bothered, was it? And your mum and dad would have come round. They always do,' she added brightly. 'My mum and dad weren't keen on Mick but they went along with it. Mind you, I could always get round my dad. And so could you have, if you'd tried.'

'No, I couldn't Lynn,' Josie said flatly. 'You don't know the half of it. I was only eighteen and you do all sorts of daft things at that age. You think you know it all and you know nothing.' She accepted another cup of coffee, watching Lynn closely as she poured it. 'Anyway, why did you finish with that first boy of yours? I can't even remember his name now.'

'Neither can I,' Lynn said with a dash of a smile. 'And that's the whole point, isn't it? I can't for the life of me remember him but you have just admitted you remember Jack. It's not a good situation. You're quite right to be worried. I would be if it was me.'

'Well, thanks for that.' Josie set her cup on the side table. 'What do you think will happen? Do you expect me and Jack to go rushing into each other's arms, just like that? It won't happen, Lynn. And it's not as if we're intending to have much to do with them. Wedding. Christening when it happens, if it happens. Family occasions are the only time we'll have to meet up. It's not as if we'll be in each other's pockets. We have no intention of going with them to their villa in Italy even if they asked, and Matthew seems to think they will.'

'Villa in Italy? Very nice. Just think what you've missed.' She smiled but behind it there was just a hint of satisfaction for the way things had turned out. Sometimes Josie wondered why their friendship had remained solid when sometimes, like just now, Lynn could suddenly turn as sharp as a bitter lemon.

'I've missed nothing,' she said stoutly, tempted to turn the tables on her by mentioning Mick, who was doing very well thank you as a jobbing builder. 'You do yourself no favours by harping back to the past, Lynn.'

'Exactly.' Lynn pounced on that. 'But you're going to be put in that position, like it or not, aren't you?'

Josie ignored that. Time for a swift change of subject. 'You're not to tell Ray yet — ' She had not intended to say anything but she was bursting to tell somebody outside the office and she wanted to surprise Lynn, who didn't think much of her accounting abilities. 'I've been offered that promotion. The one I told you about. It will mean a big rise. Ray's not going to like it.'

Lynn did not offer congratulations. 'No, he won't,' she said quietly, almost to herself. 'Oh heavens, Josie, I said I wouldn't say anything but you've put me in an awkward position. He's planning to surprise you, you see.'

'Why? What the hell has he done?'

'He's going into business, business with me,' Lynn said.

'Ray's going into business?' Josie repeated, looking at her in amazement.

Lynn nodded. 'There, I've done it now. I've been looking for something for a while to sink some money into. So, we've joined forces, business partners, and the paperwork is almost through. Ray's bought a little shop, do it yourself leaning towards plumbing.'

'A shop?'

'It's a little gold mine. I've looked through the accounts and it's very impressive, as sound as a bell. It's been family run for years and they have a very solid customer base. Customers like the individual touch. And there's room for expansion so he's not going to be limited. They've never stretched themselves to their full. Ray's very excited about it.'

'I bet he is. Has he given up his carpet job then?' Josie asked, completely bewildered by this. Ray had never done anything unexpected in his life. He was Mr Safe, no two ways about it, and he wouldn't give up a good job like his carpet fitting to take a chance on something else.

'Yes, although they've asked if they can call on him if they get a rush job on. He's highly regarded, Josie.' She looked at her closely. 'Don't you get it? He needs to do this. He needs to show you what he's made of.'

'No, he doesn't,' Josie said. 'I know what he's made of. He doesn't have to impress me. I'm his wife, for God's sake.'

'I know but I don't think you appreciate him fully. You're always doing him down, Josie. It's no wonder he's lacking in confidence.'

'Margaret said the same thing.' Josie moved uncomfortably on the sofa and it squeaked softly. 'You're both doing your best to make me feel guilty. I've not been fair to him, Lynn, and that's the truth. There was this chap at work . . . no, nothing happened. It was all a bit of fun but it nearly got out of hand and it scared me to death. I don't want to lose Ray but . . .'

'His idea . . . now, listen to this . . . his idea is that you can help him out in the business, save him getting somebody else in and you help him with the paperwork. He wants you to work with him and give up your own job.'

Josie huffed. 'Well, he can stuff that idea for a start. I've just got promoted, Lynn, I'm deputy clerk now. I'd have given my eye teeth for that job when I first started there. I shall have my own office. Ray has a bloody cheek if he thinks I'll give that up for some cock-eyed little shop. I would be a glorified shop assistant.'

'He's got his heart set on it and it's too late to back out now. We're committed,' Lynn told her, eyes hardening. 'Think about it. Oh, and another thing . . . it's got a lovely flat above the shop and you are always complaining about the garden and — '

'Where on earth is it? This shop?'

'Bank Parade.'

'Oh.' She fell silent, digesting that. Bank Parade was quite nice, all right Bank Parade was *very* nice, close to being Mayfair on Felston's monopoly board. A widely curving, tree-lined, cutting through street, the quickest way from Market Street to Pilcher Lane, so there would be lots of customers and now she came to think of it, she knew where the shop was. It would have a nice view out at the back of the top end of the park.

'But what about our house? There's the small matter of selling that first.'

'He's already got a buyer lined up,' Lynn said. 'When he gets an idea, he wastes no time. He's thought of everything. He was laying this carpet and he got to talking with this woman whose son was looking for his first place and he's got his mortgage arranged and everything, and your house is just what he's been looking for.'

'I can't believe it. Why hasn't he said? I can't bear secrets.'

'Can't you? I thought you were good at secrets. You and all your family.'

Josie said nothing. She could never be one hundred per cent sure that Lynn didn't know about that other baby, Jack Sazzoni's baby. True girlfriends knew about things like that, practically knew when you were having your period before you did. Lynn had come round to visit after she lost it, her mother having rigged up some cock and bull story about a virus.

'What's wrong with your mum?' she had asked, coming into Josie's bedroom after a brief are-you-decent knock. 'She wasn't too keen on me coming up to see you. Are you feeling better?'

'Not much.'

'I've brought you a magazine,' Lynn said, handing her a copy of *Honey*.

'Thanks.' She turned her head away, looked at the wallpaper pattern, the intricate shapes of the pink and blue flowers. Every room in their house had floral wallpaper. Her mother did not go in for real flowers in vases except on very special occasions, but she made up for it with the wallpaper. In answer to Lynn's question, Josie didn't know how she felt to be honest. She felt completely washed out, her mother's favourite expression, and her legs had let her down when she had gone to the bathroom. She felt peculiarly empty, pleased at first when it had happened but not so pleased now. That little slip of a thing had saved the bother of having a forced rejection anyway . . . She swallowed down a sob, fighting back the tears. If she cried, she might just tell Lynn.

'You look terrible,' Lynn said, eyeing her cheerfully. 'You've no colour. I hope it's not catching. Do you want me to pour you a glass of Lucozade?'

That particular drink was her mother's cure for every damned thing and a new bottle in its orange cellophane wrapper sat beside her on her bedside table. Her mother, thrilled to bits at the way things had turned out, had come over all maternal and caring. Later, there would be chicken soup followed by a milk pudding, which she would have to eat to keep her strength up. Lynn, as bad in some ways as her mother, was already pouring her a glass, screwing the top back on and standing there, poised as Josie awkwardly shuffled up and against the pillow. 'Here.'

No, Lynn, you don't understand. I've just lost my baby. A glass of Lucozade is not going to help. She had felt like saying that but, biting her tongue in order to keep the words in, she said thanks instead and drank the fizzy liquid.

★ ★ ★

'Don't you dare hurt Ray,' Lynn said, bringing Josie sharply back to the present. 'I know you wanted that promotion, but ask yourself this. Is it worth risking losing your husband? He'll be devastated if you say no. He's so excited about it all. And, don't you forget, he's done it all for you.'

Josie glanced sharply at her.

'I'm not going to hurt him. You make me out to be some sort of monster. You've been underhand though. I'm not happy at you being caught up with us. It ties the three of us together, Lynn, and I'm not sure I want that. Ray should have discussed it with me, something as important as this.'

'You can buy me out eventually if it bothers you that much,' Lynn said with a tight smile. 'You wouldn't be jealous by any chance?'

'Why would I be jealous?'

'I don't know but you needn't be. I'm not after him if that's what you're thinking? Ray wouldn't look at another woman. Surely you know that?'

25

'I don't want to go,' Josie wailed, holding on to him tightly as he sat beside her on the bed, on the suit 'I can't do it, Ray.'

'I know, love,' he said gently, arm round her. 'It's going to upset you coming on top of your mother and everything. But it's got to be done for your dad's sake. I've got the medal out of the drawer. They'll want us to show it in the photo. Now come on, dry your eyes and put your lipstick on and we'll get going. If you'll get off my suit that is.'

'Oh God, it'll be all crushed.' She stood up promptly, fussing, drying her eyes, blowing her nose, fixing her hair. He did not like the new hairstyle but it had grown a bit since Christmas and the colour was fading back to her brown. Why red? She wasn't a redhead. He hadn't fallen in love with a redhead. Each to his own and Prince Andrew's Fergie was a corker but even so . . . not for him.

'You've got to help me through this, Ray,' Josie said as they went out. 'I can't tell you why, but this is going to be dreadful for me and Margaret. I want it to be over and done with as soon as possible. We're not hanging about. We'll be polite, look at her paintings and then we're off.'

'You don't think we'll be expected to buy one, do you?' he asked. He had flipped through a catalogue to get some idea what they were like and he didn't fancy having one of those on his wall, assuming he could afford the price.

'No.' Josie managed a laugh. 'If she has anything about her, she'll be giving us one for free. If she does, look pleased, for heaven's sake. And, remember, I want out of there as soon as possible.'

'Leave it with me,' he said.

The boy who wanted to buy the house was coming to see it again at the weekend so he would have to break the news to Josie before then. He had managed to arrange the first viewing when Josie was out, panicking that she would suddenly turn up and wonder who the hell this strange man was. In the event, it had gone smoothly and it was all going through. The completion of this and the shop and flat would all take place on the same day. And it was looming fast.

He wanted to see her face when he told her. He hoped she would be all right about Lynn's part in it, but he couldn't have done it without her help and it wasn't as if it was charity. It was a good investment and Lynn had a business head on her shoulders. They were on to a winner. Do-it-yourself was booming and he was pretty much an expert himself. He would be able to offer proper sensible advice and he had plans to expand, take over that other room at the back and start selling fancy kitchen gadgets and so on. As to the flat . . . well, it had been rented out for the last few years and was a bit of a mess but nothing that couldn't be sorted out. He was looking forward to getting stuck in up there. Living and working on the premises; he couldn't imagine anything nicer than that.

He drove round to Margaret's and then to the gallery. Now that it was going to happen, he was not sure it was a good idea. He hoped this woman was doing it because she wanted to honour Jimmy's name and not because she thought it would be, what they called, good PR.

She was called Alison Jameson and she rushed over to them directly they were in the room, kissing them on the cheek, an over-familiarity which didn't go down well with Ray and Margaret, although they suffered it well.

Alison was a tiny creature, like a doll, with huge waif-like eyes and far too much gingery hair that made her head look too big. She was wearing a beautifully embroidered silk caftan in a gorgeous turquoise shade and floated about the room as if she were on skates.

Josie did her best. She was annoyed at herself for getting upset before they had even started but it was one damned thing after another and it was getting to her. She had given Ray the chance to say something about the shop but he was keeping it quiet as yet and she needed time to think about it before he supposedly sprang it on her. And still, at the back of her mind, there was this meeting with Jack looming and getting closer as Easter approached. She was terrified she would somehow make a fool of herself, do something stupid, get Jack on his own and come right out with it. Tell him she had loved him back then and she still did.

The press contingent was here already or rather what passed for it. It consisted of one chap in a badly-fitting suit and a bored-looking photographer.

'Here they are,' Alison said, aiming them both at the photographer. 'These are Jimmy Pritchard's daughters. Isn't it just too wonderful of them to come along?'

The reporter, hardly eagle-eyed, came over then and asked if he could have a word. Well, that was the whole point, wasn't it?

'Where do you want us?' Josie asked, taking charge as Margaret seemed struck dumb by the occasion.

'We'll just take a seat over here,' the reporter said, taking them over to a table. On the way, a glass of champagne was pressed into their hands. The room was heaving. Who were these people?

'Now, just a few words, ladies.' The reporter took out his notebook. 'I take it you're the older sister?' he asked, looking at Margaret. 'Let me see, you were a young woman at the time of the incident?'

'That's right. Josie, here, was thirteen.'

'And what were your feelings, Margaret, when you heard the news that your father had done this wonderful thing? That he was a hero?'

'No comment. We've nothing to add to what's been said already,' Margaret said firmly. 'We're very proud. Aren't we, Josie?'

'Very proud,' she echoed, looking at Ray who was sitting right beside her giving encouraging little nods.

'We've brought the medal,' he said, taking it out of his pocket. 'It has pride of place at home,' he added, looking pointedly at Josie.

'Right. What we're going to do is run a copy of the original article showing your father holding little Alison and then we'll

302

bring it up to date showing Alison holding her little James.'

'James Jameson,' Margaret pondered, looking at Josie. 'That's a mouthful. Has she thought about that?'

'I think he's going to be called by his middle name, David,' the reporter said. 'Can I ask you ladies a bit about yourselves? What do you do now for example?'

Josie bottled down her irritation. What the hell did that have to do with anything? However, they had to get through this evening and they did. The photographs were taken; Alison in the middle of the two of them holding baby James, Alison alone looking pensive, Alison and baby James, the two sisters — try not to look so stiff, Margaret — a picture of the lot of them with Margaret holding up the medal and lastly, a picture of Josie holding the baby.

They had another glass of champagne and some nibbles and then strolled round the exhibition. They were big bold canvasses for such a little lady and they made agreeable noises, Josie not daring to catch Ray's eye because she knew just what he would think of them. Alison's pictures were mainly of naked men, the nude from a woman's angle, she said with a completely straight face, and they didn't leave a lot to the imagination. On a cringing factor, Josie reckoned they rated a ten but there were a lot of oohs and aahs from those present.

Alison, who had never stopped talking since they had arrived, wanted to say a few words. She deposited baby James with Josie, who had not bargained for that and took the child warily. This navy suit was one of the new ones she had bought for work, suitably expensive for a deputy clerk, and baby James, or David as she preferred to think of him, looked perfectly capable of sabotaging it.

'Ladies and gentlemen . . . ' Alison began but they could barely see her, so there was a bit of a kerfuffle whilst somebody searched for and found a box for her to stand on. 'Hello again,' she said, beaming at them. 'May I say how privileged I feel this evening to be hosting this little thank you event and how proud I feel that Jimmy's two wonderful daughters have come along to represent him. It is a deep regret for me that I never had the chance to thank him properly for what he did. I want to tell you what happened that day.' She paused, seemed for a moment to be overcome with emotion. 'At least, what I can remember of it, which is very little because I was only a toddler. The fire started in the living room. I think the paper my mother was using to draw a draught up the chimney caught hold and she dropped it and it set fire to the rug and the chair. Anyway, it was spreading fast and she panicked. She ran into the street screaming and by sheer chance Jimmy was coming by. One of the neighbours set off to call the fire brigade but Jimmy said there was no time to waste. My mother was trying to get back into the house, screaming that her baby — that was me of course — was inside. Jimmy pushed her aside and some neighbours restrained her and then he ran inside and I think I remember him calling my name. It comes back to me sometimes in a sort of nightmare.' She paused and there were a few gasps. 'And then I have this vague memory of strong arms lifting me up, a man saying that it was all right, that it would be all right.'

Josie swallowed the bile that was rising in her throat, found herself clutching the baby to her breast, forgetting about her suit.

'And then he was carrying me out, past the smoke and the flames, holding me, protecting me with his arms and then he passed me over to my mother. By the time the fire brigade arrived, the house was well and truly alight and there was no way I would have been got out alive. He saved my life. Their father,' she pointed dramatically at Josie and Margaret, 'their wonderful father saved my life. And I want to say thank you.'

Margaret was ashen. Ray was standing there with a silly proud grin on his face. Josie wondered what she looked like herself. She passed the baby back to Alison who did seem genuinely moved. Ray had moved over to her, was exchanging a few words with her. Good for Ray. She didn't feel that she could say another word to this woman. The need to tell her the truth, to smash the illusion was intense and, looking at her sister, she knew she felt precisely the same. Catching Margaret's gaze, she saw her shake her head slightly and that was enough.

Illusions.

Strong arms indeed, but in their case, especially in Margaret's case, strong arms used for the wrong purpose.

They were silent on the way home. Alison had wanted to keep in touch, had even asked Margaret to be godmother to the baby but Margaret had, politely but firmly, refused. They had been presented with one of Alison's smaller pen and ink drawings and Josie would find a home for it somewhere, although it would only serve to remind her of her father whenever she looked at the damned thing.

Duty done.

'That went very well,' Ray said when they had deposited Margaret at Percy Street and were on their way. 'I think we should put the medal in a frame or something. Show it off. It's not right, Josie, it being stuck in a drawer like that. It's as if you were ashamed of it.'

'Yes, we'll do that,' she told him, knowing she would not. She would stick it back in the drawer where it belonged. It was fresh in Ray's mind just now but he would soon forget. Perhaps she would give it to Matthew sooner rather than later, let him do with it what he would. Anything to get it off her hands.

She still despised her father. He could do that to a strange child, save her life, hold her and comfort her, but he couldn't do that to his own child. That fleeting memory of being lifted up high and whirled round, giggling, emerged. That was him. That was dad.

Something had happened to change him. And now he was dead, she would never be able to ask him what and why?

26

The forecast for the Easter weekend was good and getting better. Hoping to goodness that weather girl had got it right, Josie left her smart mackintosh and some of the heavier-weight clothes behind, still managing to fill two suitcases and a squashy bag.

The itinerary had firmed up to include a quiet at-home dinner, a restaurant meal, the theatre and a lake cruise. Josie had managed to get her hair done and, although it was still shorter than she would like, it was not quite so shorn and the red tone had almost disappeared. For the journey up there, she was wearing a lilac trouser suit, not sure now if the colour suited her. There were two new dresses, one for the restaurant and one for the theatre, some tops and trousers, and most of the shoes in her wardrobe.

She worried all the way up about what she would say when she first saw him. She was remembering the time — *that* time — and the way he had looked at her and, afterwards, the way he had looked when she had told him it was all over. She was remembering her own wedding to Ray and how she had almost expected Jack to come running in to whisk her away just at the critical moment. She would have left Ray standing there at the altar if he had and to heck with the consequences. She would have . . . wouldn't she?

They were on the final leg of the journey, on the lakeside road looking for the house now. The roads had been packed with holidaymakers and caravans which had slowed them up, but now they were as close as they could be and Josie, peering ahead, looking for the cream-coloured house with the big weeping willow by the gate told Ray to start signalling because they were here.

Ray pulled into the drive and immediately the front door opened and Valerie stepped out, smiling at them, directing them into a space like a traffic warden, her clothes bearing some resemblance in that her dress was black with gold piping but there the similarity ended. Never had there been a traffic warden so elegant and good-looking.

'Lovely to see you,' she said as they climbed out. She shook hands with them both, a firm no-nonsense handshake. 'You must be exhausted. Come on in and have a cup of tea. Jack's waiting.'

She set off at a fast lick, high heels clicking across a parquet floor, and they followed. Josie caught Ray's reassuring glance but she was too far gone by now to acknowledge it and it did not make her feel any better. She felt so awful, heart pounding, feet dragging, thinking that she couldn't have felt any worse if she had been heading for the gallows.

★ ★ ★

To Valerie's supreme irritation, Josie looked fantastic. Lilac suited her. Yes, of course she had aged, as she had aged herself, but she had accomplished it gracefully. She was slimmer than Valerie had imagined but her eyes were the same. Very striking. She was wearing less make-up than she had expected and Valerie wished she had gone easy on her own.

Mrs Parkinson had given the house a thorough going over and it was spotless with lots of fresh spring flowers artfully arranged in pots and glass vases. Valerie was putting the Baileys in the guest room at the front, its wide window overlooking the lake, but before she showed them up, she took them into the sitting-room where they were to have tea and cake.

Jack had been surprisingly unmoved by all this, acting for all the world as if Josie and Ray were just any old guests and Valerie kept trying to catch him out, searching for some sign that he was simply putting on an act and that in fact, he was as wound up as she was. She had dreamed last night of finding Josie — as she had been — and Jack — as *he* had been — locked in a passionate embrace. Waking up this morning, she had reached out for her husband and found him there beside her and, for a moment, thought of telling him about the dream.

'What a lovely room!' Josie said, looking round the sitting-room. 'And such views. You're very lucky, Valerie.'

'Do sit down,' she said, regretting the formality of her voice, trying her best to be as free and easy as Josie seemed to be. 'Well . . . what do you think of our children then? It was quite a surprise, wasn't it?'

'A shock more like,' Ray said looming large by the window as Josie took a seat on a button-backed chair upholstered in pale green silk. 'Josie nearly fainted on the spot when she found out. Didn't you, love?'

'Not quite,' Josie said tightly, giving him a quick glance. 'But then you never know who your children are going to throw at you; do you?'

Valerie found she was looking at Ray, a big solid man, dark and handsome. Why had she not remembered him? He was, she thought, rather striking. Admittedly, he spoke with a pronounced Lancashire accent, more so than Josie and much more so than their son. So, accents diluted too, just like Italian blood.

'It could have been worse,' she said, thinking about the children. 'Is that what you mean, Josie?'

'No, not at all. We're very pleased,' Josie told her, smiling now with determination. 'Alice is a lovely girl. She looks like you.'

'And Matthew is delightful too. We like him very much.'

That was that sorted then.

'I'll get the tea or would you prefer coffee?' Valerie wished Jack would show his face, although in other ways she did not because, looking at Josie who was sitting with her legs crossed, she saw that, from a distance, from the doorway say, she would look very much as she had looked all those years ago, give or take the hairdo.

She heard Jack's footsteps in the hall.

'They've arrived, darling,' she called, waiting for him to come through.

★   ★   ★

Ray and Jack gave each other a firm handshake, held each other's gaze an instant. He hadn't changed a lot, Ray thought. Jack had put on some weight but that happened

312

round the middle forties and he had lost some hair but it wasn't enough to change his appearance that much. He watched as Jack kissed Josie on both cheeks, saying that she had not changed. She bloody *had* changed. She was his wife now for one and, for two, she was the mother of his son.

Tea was a torture for him. Tiny fine plates. Napkins. Fiddly little pastry forks. And a very squidgy chocolate cake. Result. Crumbs. Why was it that everybody else seemed to accomplish the eating with minimum fuss and kept the crumbs where they belonged. On the plate. His had ended up everywhere, mostly down the side of the sofa which being off-white would not take kindly to chocolate crumbs.

'Ray's setting up in business,' Josie was saying, casting him a wifely glance. It reminded him of the way his mother had used to talk about him to her friends, as if he wasn't there. 'He's bought a shop in Felston.'

Ray smiled to himself. She'd been annoyed at first that he'd kept it from her but she had quickly come round. She liked a challenge, did his Josie, and he had always known that.

They talked round him a moment and he sat there, wanting to join in but feeling uncomfortable about it. All he could do was watch Jack and Josie together. Look at their faces. Try to guess what they were both thinking. Josie was looking fantastic today, eyes sparkling, her whole manner sparkling at that. It was her way, he supposed, of keeping the edginess at bay. A bit of play-acting.

He loved her like this though, the warmth, the vitality, the sheer prettiness and he knew why he had fallen in love with this woman. Catching Jack sitting there, with a carefully neutral expression on his face, he wondered if Jack was thinking the same thing.

If Sazzo tried anything this weekend . . .

★　★　★

She couldn't believe it. She had, in fact, been hard pressed to recognize him. He was older, fatter, losing his hair and she couldn't take her eyes off him trying, in vain, to bring back the old Jack, the old Jack who seemed to have disappeared.

She had looked him straight in the eye, testing him and seen a quiet amusement there, nothing else. There was no hidden meaning there, no secret signal, and, even though she could not quite believe it, he was acting as if he had indeed forgotten what had happened between them. The talk briefly veered back to the old days, old times, but they did not dwell on it, bringing themselves back to the present day, to reality, to the marriage of her son and his daughter.

Valerie was making preliminary plans. The wedding would be here, of course, and could they pencil a September date in their diaries now? They could and they did although, as Ray didn't have a diary of his own, she did the pencilling in for him. It didn't matter. He always referred to her commitments anyway and she always told him what was what. She wished he would contribute a bit more to the conversation. Sometimes Ray was hard work and particularly in situations like this when they were dealing with strangers, for that was what they were, strangers.

After the tea and cake, Valerie showed them to their room, leading the way up the stairs to a galleried area and then a landing and a heavy cream door. 'You're in here. I hope you'll be comfortable,' she said, opening the door on to a large, rather pink room. 'There's a bathroom,' she said, indicating another door within the room. 'Come back down when you've unpacked and we'll perhaps take a walk down by the lake.'

There was so much space, so much light. There was a pale pink cover on the bed but the room itself was not overly pink, the window framed by curtains the colour of the weak tea they had just had downstairs.

Ray was in the bathroom directly Valerie had gone, on his knees examining the layout and the plumbing fixtures, impressed by the clever way they had managed to get so much into such a small space, wondering how he could adapt the bathroom at the flat in Bank Parade in a similar vein.

Josie refused to be excited by it, unpacking silently, annoyed with him and not quite knowing why. She felt cautiously optimistic about the rest of the weekend. The worst was over. They had met and there had not been any thunderclaps when he had kissed her a welcome. He was the same Jack and yet not the same. She did not know what she had expected, what she had hoped for but, whatever it was, it had not happened.

It was one very big disappointment and yet, at the same time, a very big relief too.

'Try to relax,' she told Ray, once he had completed his assessment of the bathroom and its fittings. 'Don't look so frightened.'

'I'm not,' he said at once. 'I don't have a lot to say. You know me. I'm not frightened of them. Bloody hell, Josie, what do you want me to do?'

'Be a bit more yourself,' she told him. 'Act natural.'

'How?' She caught the exasperated look. 'By being the life and soul of the party?

That's not me, Josie my love, and if that's what you want me to be like then the honest truth is I can't. I can't do that. Anyway, I like to listen, take it in. I was interested in what they had to say. I can see Alice in him, can't you? She doesn't look like him but she's got some of his mannerisms.'

That had not passed her by. It had jolted her, in fact, pushing the memory she had of him a step back, as it mixed and mingled with the memory of his daughter.

They changed for the walk but not into walking shoes. Valerie, in charge of the evening meal, did not accompany them and Josie found herself in the middle of the two men as they strolled along, Jack pointing out things of interest on the way. She was not listening. She was too aware of him, of Ray, of both of them. Ray, thank heavens, had loosened up finally, out here in the open air, and was telling Jack about the business and Jack, in turn, was offering up some advice which Ray seemed happy to take.

Could the impossible be happening? Could it be that these two men were actually beginning to get on together? Had they really put the past out of their heads?

By the next evening when they were due at the theatre, the relationship between the four of them had settled into how it would be. It was never going to be over friendly because of the past but they were adult enough to know that and to react accordingly. It would be friendly in a careful way and, so long as they kept to that, then all would be well.

There seemed to be a conspiracy to make sure that she and Jack were never left alone. Josie was not sure who instigated that but it was certainly working. She caught Valerie's glances at her husband, saw the concern there, and knew why and she caught Ray's glances at her, saw the very same thing. As for Jack, he would not look at her, not directly, and nor would she look at him.

And so the weekend passed.

Alice was busy with her dancing class, some sort of special session, but they met up with Matthew at the theatre and he made the time to have a coffee with them before showing them, in usherette fashion, to their seats. Comically, it took a moment for them to organize themselves into who was sitting where. There were, it seemed, an amazing number of combinations of how the four of them might sit in the row of four adjoining seats. Jack, Valerie, Ray, Josie. Jack, Josie, Valerie, Ray. And so on. In the end, forced into making a decision as people jostled impatiently from behind,

Josie found herself with Jack on the one side and Ray on the other. Her two men.

★   ★   ★

'Nightcap anyone?' Valerie asked when they got home. 'And can I tempt you to a light supper? It seems ages since we ate.'

It was tempting to say no, to shoot off to bed before any more conversation could take place and Josie was very tired, the effort she was making finally taking its toll.

'A light supper sounds good.' Ray leapt to his feet, went with Valerie to get whatever it was she was offering and the moment, for good or evil, had arrived.

She and Jack were alone.

27

'Did you enjoy the play?' he asked from the safety of his seat, the armchair nearest the fire. There was no fire in the hearth this evening and, even though it had been a pleasant day, it felt just a touch chilly now and Josie was glad of her wrap, a cream fringed cotton wrap that she was now allowing to drape loosely round her shoulders. The dress was scarlet with a darker splodgy pattern and with it she was wearing glossy barely-black tights and high heeled black shoes. She had loved it when she bought it, this dress, thought it very glamorous and perfect for theatre going but besides Valerie's gloriously understated pale grey outfit which she had teamed with pearls, it had felt cheap and cheerful.

'Yes I did enjoy it,' she replied, giving him a smile. 'It was a good production. I like the way it was set in Nazi Germany. It was a different slant and I don't expect everybody would approve but I liked it.'

He nodded. 'It wasn't for me. I don't go for modern productions.'

'Ah well — ' She shrugged. Ray had liked

it. He had been thrilled, too, because he had got the gist of it, despite the complicated language. Of course she had filled him in beforehand on the story but even so, she was dead pleased that he had been pleased.

There was a short silence, awkward when each of them was taking care not to look at the other. Then, as often happened on these occasions, they both began to talk at once.

They stopped. Smiled.

'After you,' she said. 'No, please . . .'

'All right. I didn't expect to meet you again, Josie. Not ever.'

'No. Look Jack, let's get this clear. Lots of people do what we did when we were young,' she said, anxious to get it over with, to clear the air. 'Meet. Go out together for a while, sleep together even,' she added, looking at him with a wry smile. 'And then it all gets too much, too serious too soon, and they split up. It's just part of growing up. It's not at all unusual but it is unusual to meet up again like this. It's a bit awkward, don't you think, but we've got to make the best of it, Jack. I've put it all to the back of my mind. Have you?'

'Oh yes.' His return smile was reassuring. 'As you say, it's all in the past. You seem very happy with Ray?'

'I am,' she said firmly for there was nothing

else to say. 'He's very excited about the business.'

'He has a right to be. It sounds good. He's thought about it, not rushed into it and he has some sound financial backing. It can't go wrong. If ever he wants any advice, just give me a call. I've had a bit of experience in the field.'

Sitting there, wanting to kick off her shoes but refraining because that would make it far too cosy, Josie felt as if the two of them were on the stage at the Little Gem acting their hearts out, as they had just seen the actors do. It was as if this scene had been rehearsed. There was a script from which they must not stray. Lines they had learnt. Certain actions they must do and those they must not do. Sitting here, in this room, they were close but far apart. Just for a fleeting moment, she wondered mischievously what would happen if she were to go across the room, across the stage, and slide herself on to his lap, put her arms round his neck, lower her head to his and kiss him as she had so often kissed him and held him.

She had not heard him speak in Italian since they had arrived but she wondered if he still did. Perhaps he whispered words of love in that language to Valerie as he once had to her?

Did he *still* love her?

That was a question that could never be asked.

Did she still love him?

She knew the answer to that.

★　★　★

'Do you think it's sensible to leave those two alone?' Valerie asked with a smile, bringing out a plate of tiny sandwiches and some other bits and bobs from the fridge. She proceeded to dispense with the cling film, handing him the plates as she did so. 'Goodness knows what they might get up to.'

'It was a surprise all right, our Matthew and your Alice,' Ray said. 'I couldn't believe it at first. But these things happen.'

'Do they? I've never heard of it happening to anybody else. Do you think, Ray, there's still anything left between them? Or has it all fizzled out?'

'All fizzled out,' he told her, telling her what she wanted to know. 'Do you remember me at all from those days?'

She shook her head. 'Sorry. You can't have made much of an impact on me. Oh goodness, that sounds dreadful. I'm sure you must have made some impact a man like you . . . ' She blushed and he found himself warming to her.

'I wasn't on your level, Val,' he said. 'Oh sorry, can I call you Val?'

'Yes.' She laughed. 'Nobody does. But why not? And what on earth are you talking about? On your level? I must have been a terrible snob, Ray.'

'We were young,' he said with a shrug. 'You get these ideas fixed in your head when you're young.'

'I'm afraid I was very selfish. I had my sights set on Jack and I hoped that if I just bided my time ... Now, have we got everything?'

They took the things through. If Jack and Josie had been wrapped up in each other's arms, they had moved pretty damned quick, Ray thought with satisfaction, knowing that neither of them had moved a muscle. He caught Jack's glance as he put down the tray. He looked calm, controlled, and yet there was an undercurrent, a sizzling undercurrent, that he alone caught.

Watch it, Sazzo ...

Neither of them said a word.

★ ★ ★

'I want to go home,' Josie said, as they lay in each other's arms in the big bed in the guest room on their last night. They had not drawn

324

the curtains, preferring to watch the night sky and the pale half moon.

'I know.' He moved slightly so that he could stroke her hair, hair that felt wrong, too short, too straight. 'So what's the verdict then?'

'He's not the man I thought he was,' she said quietly. 'It's a big disappointment. I've made him out to be something very special all these years. And he's not. He's just an ordinary man. Like you.'

'I see. So I'm nothing special either.'

'Oh yes, you are, Ray. You are to me.'

He relaxed. For the first time in goodness knows how long, he relaxed. It was going to be OK. And maybe this had been a good thing, all this, because it had finally brought it all to a head. When push came to shove, she was still his girl and always would be.

'Ray, can I tell you something? It's something I should have told you a long time ago. I'm scared of telling you because I don't want you to take it the wrong way. I don't want you leaving me. I couldn't bear it if you left me.'

'Go on,' he said softly, willing her to say it.

'I was pregnant. Before we got married, I was pregnant with Jack's baby. I lost it at just a few weeks. He never knew. And he never will know.'

He continued to stroke her hair. 'Lynn told me that,' he said.

'When did she tell you that?'

'Ages ago. Before we got married anyway. I told her straight it wouldn't make a scrap of difference.'

'You mean you've known all these years and never said a word?'

'I knew you'd get round to telling me one of these days. In your own time that is.'

'Damn her for telling you. She had no right.'

'Let's not talk about her.'

'You seem very close.'

He laughed softly. 'Josie, when will you learn that secrets just aren't worth the trouble? I know all about you and Kenny as well.'

'Nothing happened there either,' she said. 'OK, so it might have at one point but that was when I was really fed up with you.'

He chuckled. He knew his Josie. And he supposed, looking back, he had been a pain in the neck sometimes. He was really going to make an effort, not be so caught up in the things he liked to do that he neglected her.

'Fed up or not, I'm stuck with you,' she said. 'For better or worse was never a truer saying, Ray Bailey.'

They snuggled together comfortably. He

would have liked to make love to her tonight but not here, not here in the guest room of Jack's home. He wondered whether to tell her about Margaret, but it wasn't up to him to do it. It would have to come from Margaret herself when she was ready. It amazed him that a family could have so many secrets. His hadn't. It had all been open and above board with his lot.

But Josie's family was something else.

★ ★ ★

They said their goodbyes, promising to keep in touch. The ladies would consult, nearer the time, about their choice of wedding outfits. After all, they didn't want to clash, did they?

Valerie smiled as Ray and Josie drove off, feeling Jack's arm around her shoulder. He didn't often do that these days, put his arm around her shoulder and, from habit, she leant slightly into him. Why on earth had she worried? There had been no reason to worry because it had gone very well. She was warming to Josie and she really liked Ray. As for Jack . . . well, he had behaved as if they were ordinary family guests and she had never once caught him looking at Josie with anything approaching tenderness. They had mentioned the past in passing but not dwelt

327

on it. They had, she thought, handled it remarkably well in a very civilized fashion. Everything, the meals, the lake cruise, the theatre — everything had gone much better than she had hoped.

She turned to go back indoors. There were things to do. There were always things to do when you'd had guests and she was delighted that she had Mrs Parkinson back with her, helping her. She had been most discreet this weekend, remaining largely in the annexe, for Valerie had not been keen for her to be thought of as a servant.

Standing in the porch, alone, Jack dawdled a moment, waiting until Ray's car had slipped out of the drive into the holiday traffic. With nobody looking, his face crumpled, his emotions rising to the fore at last. It had been hard keeping them in check these last few days. He had been under intense scrutiny, from Valerie, from Ray who had watched him like a hawk, and from Josie herself. She had teased him a little but he had chosen not to respond. She had always known how to tease him.

She was just the same.

His Josie.

It was just as well that Valerie could not see his face at that moment.

* * *

It was good to be home, Josie thought, as they passed the Felston boundary. The Lake District was lovely to visit but she wouldn't want to live there. This town for all its faults was home. They were getting the keys to the flat next month but already they were thinking about what they would do to it. She loved it. She loved it from the first moment she saw it. She loved being on the first floor and, from the room that would be their sitting room, they had great views over the town on one side and the park on the other.

The house in Crook Terrace, so long home, was beginning to feel less so as her thoughts shifted to the flat on Bank Parade. The more she saw of the shop, the more she thought they would make a go of it. It was a long thin shop, seemed to go on for ever once you were inside and Ray was giving her free rein, more or less, with choosing the stock for the new part. He was enthusiastic, a changed man because he was doing something he really wanted to do, something that gave him scope, something that would stretch his abilities.

That's all he had ever needed.

The chance.

'Drop me off at Margaret's, love,' she asked Ray. 'She'll want to know what happened this weekend.'

'What *did* happen then?' Ray's voice was full of fun.

'You know full well what happened,' she told him. 'I've got him out of my head, Ray. That's what happened.'

'Thought so,' he said triumphantly. 'Thank God for that. Now we can get on with things, you and me.'

He had to park halfway up Percy Street, nipping smartly into a vacant space. He switched off the engine as Josie fussed around, looking for her handbag. How you could lose a handbag in a car was beyond him but that was Josie?

'Are you coming in then? To see Margaret?' she asked, locating it at last.

'Best not. She might have things to say to you,' he said.

'What sort of things?' Josie paused, handbag on her lap. 'What have you two been up to? You're being very secretive. What's Margaret been saying?' She drew a breath sharply. 'She's never been telling you about Dad, has she?'

He glanced at her. This was a new one.

'What about him?'

'Oh, nothing. Nothing important.'

＊　＊　＊

Before they went to the Lakes, Margaret had come to see him on Saturday afternoon when she knew Josie was out shopping. He was freshening up the spare room because it was scuffed and he didn't want the new owners complaining; he had just started painting the door when he heard Margaret coming up the path.

Bloody hell. What did she want?

'Can I have a word, Ray? It's a bit private,' she said, taking her coat off and hanging it, unasked, on the peg in the hall.

'Course you can, love. Come on in. Make yourself at home while I clean up.'

'Oh sorry, Ray, you're busy.'

'It's OK. It'll keep.'

'It's about Josie,' she said when he was back and she was settled. 'It's all very delicate. There was only me and my mother knew about it. And Auntie Jenny of course.'

He nodded, resisting the urge to look at the clock.

'My boyfriend went off to war, Ray . . . I was only eighteen and he was twenty-five. He had his whole life before him. I said I'd wait for him. Well, that's what everyone said.'

'I know. Hard luck that,' he said. Josie thought the boyfriend was a figment of her imagination but he had never been sure. It wasn't something you asked about.

'He was called Harold,' she said. 'You'll have seen his picture.'

'Nice-looking lad,' he said. 'What happened, Margaret?'

'He died in Singapore,' she said. 'Or thereabouts. We would have been married I think if he had come back. But he didn't and his mum had to tell me that. She was his next of kin, you see, not me.'

'I'm sorry,' he said, worried that she might break down. They got a bit emotional, did the ladies, about things like this.

'And then I met Robert,' she said, folding her hands on her lap. 'It was 1943. You were only a little child at the time. Anyway, we'd gone through a lot during the war but we were starting to hope, to look forward. Robert was older than me, a married man, Ray, and he reminded me of Harold. I know it was wrong of us but he was a lovely man and I felt so alone with Harold gone.' Her face flushed and she didn't look at him. He hoped to God she wasn't going to give him the details. He didn't want them. He could guess what had happened. At least so far as Margaret was concerned. As to the man, a married man, well there must have been a good reason.

He had thought as much. He had always

thought that there was more to Margaret than met the eye. 'You don't have to go on,' he told her as she lapsed into silence. 'If it's too much for you . . . '

'No, no. I have to tell you. Josie's my baby. Robert was her father.'

'What?' That made him sit up. 'What are you saying, Margaret?'

'You heard,' she said sharply.

'But how? I don't get it. How did you keep that secret?'

'It wasn't easy,' she said with a very small smile. 'We had to keep it from dad. At all costs, we had to keep it from him. I didn't know for sure I was expecting until I was very nearly six months. I didn't show or anything.'

Ray shuffled uncomfortably.

'My mum had a bad time with me,' Margaret went on, her face still flushed, although she was looking at him now. 'She was ill for all the pregnancy and she had a terrible labour and she worked out how we would do it. She told dad she was expecting again and said she wanted to go up to be with Auntie Jenny in Carlisle and she wanted me to come with her. Dad didn't mind. In fact, I think he was pleased that he wouldn't have to see her getting bloated. That's what he called it. Getting bloated. He wasn't thrilled about the thought of a new baby and he hated pregnancy, all that stuff, and he wanted to be as far away as possible when it was born. The trouble was he got used to being on his own and it was a shock to his system when we came back, three of us, me, mum and the baby.' Her eyes were bright but there would be no tears. 'I know it's hard to believe and nowadays I don't suppose you would get away with it but nobody ever thought anything of it then. I was so plain. Nobody thought I could be attractive to a man.'

'That's not fair,' he said quickly. 'You should have seen my mum,' he added, trying to make light of it, to make her smile, to ease her pain at the telling.

'I knew your mum,' she reminded him. 'She was a lovely lady.'

'She was,' he said with a smile. 'Not in looks but in every other way.'

'When we came back, the three of us, it was just taken for granted that Josie was mum's baby and my sister. She told everybody she had had a rotten time again and she was glad I was around to help. If anybody guessed, had an inkling, they never said.'

'I'm surprised my mum didn't guess,' Ray said, for she had known everything that happened in the neighbourhood. 'So it was all down to Hetty then. All the conniving.'

'Don't call it that,' Margaret said uneasily. 'It wouldn't have been right for me to have a baby, Ray. Robert was a married man with a family of his own. It wouldn't have been right. And it was unheard of then to have a child out of wedlock.'

He smiled at the old-fashioned expression.

'Well I never,' he said. 'I don't know what to say. Did he ever know? This Robert?'

She nodded. 'He knew. Later. I took a bit of a risk, met him in the park once, took Josie along. She was only little and she didn't know who he was but he was very pleased.' She sniffed back sudden tears. 'He had children of his own and he loved them. And he loved her. He would have loved her. He picked her up and whirled her round and she laughed and laughed.'

'And then what?'

'He had to go back to his wife. There was no question of doing anything else and then, a year on, he went and died of a sudden heart attack and then she moved, went to live with her parents. Took the children with her.'

'Do you want *me* to tell her?'

She shook her head. 'No thanks. I should tell her. I'll pick the moment. I am doing the right thing in telling her, aren't I, Ray?'

'Yes. She should know.'

'I just wanted to be sure. I always knew I

would tell her one day when mother was dead. You don't blame me, Ray, do you? It matters to me what you think.'

'Blame you? Oh Margaret.'

He did something then he never thought he would do. He went over to her, pulled her out of the chair and gave her a hug, holding her close a minute. He could feel her shaking under his touch. Smell the medicated shampoo.

'It's all right, love,' he muttered, stopping short of dropping a kiss on top of her head. 'I'll put the kettle on, shall I?'

'I'll do it,' she said, recovering herself. 'Thanks, Ray.'

* * *

'I'll walk back,' Josie said, half out of the car. 'Just take the bags in and leave them in the hall. Don't start rummaging. I know what's what.'

'OK. See you later,' he said.

'Bye, love.'

He watched through the car mirror as she set off, hips swaying in that way of hers, heels clicking. His girl. He was smiling as he moved off.

* * *

'It's been a lovely weekend,' Josie said, pushing past Margaret. 'Terrible traffic all the way back. You'll be wanting to know what Jack was like? I've been dying to tell you.' Her eyes twinkled as she glanced at her reflection in Margaret's hall mirror. 'He was short — I'm sure he's shrunk — fat and balding. He talked too much. And we hadn't a thing in common. Tell you what, Margaret, he wasn't a patch on my Ray.'

Margaret smiled.

'I'm going to hand in my resignation,' Josie went on. 'It's my decision. Ray hasn't tried to persuade me one way or the other. So, what if it was deputy clerk, it was just a job and a pretty boring one at that. Ray and me have a business to run together and I want to be sure I'm around. Lynn doesn't fool me. She's always fancied him.'

'You've no need to worry there.'

'I know.' Josie was bubbling. 'You know what Margaret, I feel like a weight's lifted off my shoulders. I can cope now. Ray was great. He calls her Val and she loves it. She's really taken a shine to him. I shall enjoy the wedding and Valerie's all right when you get to know her. I won't be calling her starchy knickers in future. I feel sorry for her, losing all those babies. Only a mother understands such things,' she added gently.

337

'Have you time for a cup of tea?' Margaret asked.

'It will have to be a quick one,' Josie said. 'I've got the unpacking to do yet.'

'Sit yourself down,' Margaret said, moving her knitting to make room on a chair. 'This may take some time.'

Puzzled by the serious tone, Josie did just that, noticing that the shoebox was out on the coffee table, lid off, full of photos and stuff. She sat down, saw a few of her baby photographs, a tag with Baby Pritchard written on it which must have been round her baby wrist, some baby clothes, a little stuffed rabbit and some letters.

Margaret was taking a long time with the tea.

Josie looked at the photographs of herself, some of which she had never seen. A baby. One year old. A toddler. Three or four maybe. And always, in each photograph, Margaret was beside her. Not her mother but Margaret.

She looked up. Margaret was standing there calmly, smiling slightly.

'You've found the photographs?' she said. 'Well . . . have you worked it out yet?'

'Worked what out?'

'Oh, Josie. Has the penny not dropped? I kept your bits and pieces. Once we were back home, once we came back from Carlisle, as soon as we turned into the street with you, well . . . that was it really. You were Mum's from then on. Not mine. I had to pretend you weren't mine and I've been pretending ever since.'

The penny dropped with an almighty clang.

They stared at each other a minute, a long minute and then Margaret nodded. 'His picture's there,' she said. 'That one on top.'

'This one?' she picked up the photograph of a stranger, not the young man who had gone to war but somebody else. 'Did he ever see me?'

'Yes, that's him and yes, he did see you the once. He said you were a grand little girl. He picked you up and whirled you round and you laughed and laughed,' she said, a slight trembling of her lip giving her away.

'Oh, Margaret . . . ' Josie tried to smile but could not. 'I remember him,' she said. 'I think I remember him.'

'The tea will be brewed by now. Can you pour us a cup? There's extra sugar if you need it. For the shock.'

And then, without a word, she sat down, picked up her knitting and, with a quick check on the pattern, began to click away.

We do hope that you have enjoyed reading this large print book.

Did you know that all of our titles are available for purchase?

We publish a wide range of high quality large print books including:
Romances, Mysteries, Classics
General Fiction
Non Fiction and Westerns

Special interest titles available in large print are:
The Little Oxford Dictionary
Music Book
Song Book
Hymn Book
Service Book

Also available from us courtesy of Oxford University Press:
Young Readers' Dictionary
(large print edition)
Young Readers' Thesaurus
(large print edition)

For further information or a free brochure, please contact us at:
Ulverscroft Large Print Books Ltd.,
The Green, Bradgate Road, Anstey,
Leicester, LE7 7FU, England.
Tel: (00 44) **0116 236 4325**
Fax: (00 44) **0116 234 0205**

Other titles published by
The House of Ulverscroft:

EMILY'S WEDDING

Patricia Fawcett

With her wedding date fixed and her mother powering ahead with the preparations, Emily puts aside her niggling doubts about Simon and his refusal to talk about his past. Corinne is making the wedding dress, but she is a woman with problems of her own, not least her troubled relationship with her son Daniel, who hides a terrible secret . . . It is Emily in whom he eventually confides as the two find themselves drawn inexorably together. Pulled in all directions, she is faced with a dilemma — and her wedding day is fast approaching . . .

RETURN TO ROSEMOUNT

Patricia Fawcett

Together, Clementine and Anthony Scarr had co-founded the school known as Florey Park on the headland. Then, after Anthony's tragic death in a car accident, Clemmie's priorities changed to making sure his memory remained untarnished for their two daughters, Nina and Julia — Clemmie is delighted when her grown children return home — Nina due to a doomed love affair, whilst Julia's reason remains a secret — along with Julia's feisty daughter, Francesca. And then Nina meets Alex and the promise of a new relationship blossoms — But, outside the beautiful gardens of Rosemount, forces are shifting that will threaten their happiness.

THE CUCKOO'S NEST

Patricia Fawcett

Maddy and Ed buy their dream house in the country. Maddy and the children set up home whilst Ed, a wine trader, has a flat in Manchester and visits at weekends . . . But Maddy's new lifestyle falters when Jean, their previous neighbour, loses her home and Maddy invites her to stay. Jean proves to be the guest from hell. And Maddy's idyll is marred by feelings of suspicion when Jean makes incredible accusations against one of Maddy's new friends . . . And then Ed, living on his own and fighting off the advances of the beautiful Alexandra, drops the bomb-shell . . .

OLIVIA'S GARDEN

Patricia Fawcett

Olivia, Anna and Rosie form an unlikely schoolgirl friendship. Olivia is the beauty and the dreamer; plain Anna's future career as a doctor is already mapped out; whilst bubbly, flame-haired Rosie simply wants to marry a millionaire. Leaving school, they lose touch with each other until, years later, Olivia meets Rosie once more. Then Anna's brother Ben, himself a doctor, seeks Olivia's help with a family crisis. The happy result is that she and Ben are drawn together. However, she is shocked by Anna's stubbornness, dismayed by Rosie's refusal to speak to her again after a bitter row and rocked by a personal tragedy.

BETTER OFF DEAD

www.penguin.co.uk

For more information see www.jackreacher.com

BETTER OFF DEAD

Lee Child
and
Andrew Child

BANTAM PRESS

TRANSWORLD PUBLISHERS
Penguin Random House, One Embassy Gardens,
8 Viaduct Gardens, London SW11 7BW
www.penguin.co.uk

Transworld is part of the Penguin Random House group of companies
whose addresses can be found at global.penguinrandomhouse.com

Penguin
Random House
UK

First published in Great Britain in 2021 by Bantam Press
an imprint of Transworld Publishers

A CIP catalogue record for this book
is available from the British Library.

ISBNs 9781787633735 (cased)
9781787633742 (tpb)

Typeset in 11.25/15.75 pt Century Old Style by Jouve (UK), Milton Keynes
Printed and bound in Great Britain by Clays Ltd, Elcograf S.p.A.

The authorized representative in the EEA is Penguin Random House Ireland,
Morrison Chambers, 32 Nassau Street, Dublin D02 YH68.

Penguin Random House is committed to a sustainable
future for our business, our readers and our planet. This book
is made from Forest Stewardship Council® certified paper.

MIX
Paper from
responsible sources
FSC® C018179

For Jane and Tasha

ONE

The stranger got into position under the streetlight at eleven p.m., as agreed.

The light had been easy to find, just like he'd been told it would be. It was the only one in the compound that was still working, all the way at the far end, six feet shy of the jagged metal fence that separated the United States from Mexico.

He was alone. And unarmed.

As agreed.

The car showed up at 11:02. It kept to the centre of the space between the parallel rows of lock-up garages. They were made of metal, too. Roofs warped by the sun. Walls scoured by the sand. Five on the right. Four on the left. And the remains of one more lying torn and corroded ten feet to the side, like something had exploded inside it years ago.

The car's lights were on bright, making it hard to

recognize the make and model. And impossible to see inside. It continued until it was fifteen feet away then braked to a stop, rocking on its worn springs and settling into a low cloud of sandy dust. Then its front doors opened. Both of them. And two men climbed out.

Not as agreed.

Both the car's back doors opened. Two more men climbed out.

Definitely not as agreed.

The four men paused and sized the stranger up. They'd been told to expect someone big and this guy sure fit the bill. He was six feet five. Two hundred and fifty pounds. Chest like a gun safe and hands like backhoe buckets. And scruffy. His hair was coarse and unkempt. He hadn't shaved for days. His clothes looked cheap and ill-fitting, except for his shoes. Somewhere between a hobo and a Neanderthal. Not someone who was going to be missed.

The driver stepped forward. He was a couple of inches shorter than the stranger, and a good fifty pounds lighter. He was wearing black jeans and a black sleeveless T-shirt. He had on black combat-style boots. His head was shaved, but his face was hidden by a full beard. The other guys followed, lining up alongside him.

'The money?' the driver said.

The stranger patted the back pocket of his jeans.

'Good.' The driver nodded towards the car. 'Back seat. Get in.'

'Why?'

'So I can take you to Michael.'

'That wasn't the deal.'

'Sure it was.'

The stranger shook his head. 'The deal was, you tell me where Michael is.'

'Tell you. Show you. What's the difference?'

The stranger said nothing.

'Come on. What are you waiting for? Give me the money and get in the car.'

'I make a deal, I stick to it. You want the money, tell me where Michael is.'

The driver shrugged. 'The deal's changed. Take it or leave it.'

'I'll leave it.'

'Enough of this.' The driver reached behind his back and took a pistol from his waistband. 'Cut the crap. Get in the car.'

'You were never going to take me to Michael.'

'No shit, Sherlock.'

'You were going to take me to someone else. Someone who has questions for me.'

'No more talking. Get in the car.'

'Which means you can't shoot me.'

'Which means I can't kill you. Yet. I can still shoot you.'

The stranger said, 'Can you?'

A witness would have said the stranger hardly moved at all but somehow in a split second he had closed the gap between them and had his hand on the driver's wrist. Which he pulled up, like a proud fisherman hauling something from the sea. He forced the guy's arm way above his head. Hoisted it so high the guy was raised up on his tiptoes. Then he drove his left fist into the guy's side. Hard. The kind of punch that would normally knock a man down. And keep him down. Only the driver didn't fall. He couldn't. He was suspended by his arm. His feet slid back. The gun fell from his fingers. His shoulder dislocated. Tendons stretched. Ribs shattered. It was a grotesque cascade of injuries. Each one debilitating in its own right. But in the moment he hardly noticed any of them. Because his entire upper body was convulsing in agony. Searing bolts of pain shot through him, all stemming from one place. A spot just below his armpit where a dense tangle of nerves and lymph nodes nestled beneath the skin. The exact spot that had just been crushed by the stranger's massive knuckles.

The stranger retrieved the driver's fallen gun and carried him over to the hood of the car. He laid him back, squealing and gasping and writhing on the dull paintwork, then turned to the other three guys and said, 'You should walk away. Now. While you have the chance.'

The guy at the centre of the trio stepped forward. He was about the same height as the driver. Maybe a little broader. He had hair, cropped short. No beard. Three chunky silver chains around his neck. And a nasty sneer on his face. 'You got lucky once. That won't happen again. Now get in the car before we hurt you.'

The stranger said, 'Really? Again?'

But he didn't move. He saw the three guys swap furtive glances. He figured that if they were smart, they'd opt for a tactical retreat. Or if they were proficient, they'd attack together. But first they'd work one of them around to the rear. He could pretend to check on the injured driver. Or to give up and get in the car. Or even to run away. The other two could create a distraction. Then, when he was in place,

4

they'd all rush in at once. A simultaneous assault from three directions. One of the guys was certain to take some damage. Probably two. But the third might have a chance. An opening might present itself. If someone had the skill to exploit it.

They weren't smart. And they weren't proficient. They didn't withdraw. And no one tried to circle around. Instead, the centre guy took another step forward, alone. He dropped into some kind of generic martial arts stance. Let out a high-pitched wail. Feinted a jab to the stranger's face. Then launched a reverse punch to the solar plexus. The stranger brushed it aside with the back of his left hand and punched the guy's bicep with his right, his middle knuckle extended. The guy shrieked and jumped back, his axillary nerve over-loaded and his arm temporarily useless.

'You should walk away,' the stranger said. 'Before you hurt yourself.'

The guy sprang forward. He made no attempt at disguise this time. He just twisted into a wild roundhouse punch with his good arm. The stranger leaned back. The guy's fist sailed past. The stranger watched it go then drove his knuckle into the meat of the guy's tricep. Both his arms were now out of action.

'Walk away,' the stranger said. 'While you still can.'

The guy lunged. His right leg rose. His thigh first, then his foot, pivoting at the knee. Going for maximum power. Aiming for the stranger's groin. But not getting close. Because the stranger countered with a kick of his own. A sneaky one. Straight and low. Directly into the guy's shin. Just as it reached maximum speed. Bone against toecap. The stranger's shoes. The only thing about him that wasn't scruffy.

5

Bought in London years ago. Layer upon layer of leather and polish and glue. Seasoned by time. Hardened by the elements. And now as solid as steel.

The guy's ankle cracked. He screamed and shied away. He lost his balance and couldn't regain it without the use of his arms. His foot touched the ground. The fractured ends of the bone connected. They grated together. Pain ripped through his leg. It burned along every nerve. Way more than his system could handle. He remained upright for another half second, already unconscious. Then he toppled on to his back and lay there, as still as a fallen tree.

The remaining two guys turned and made for the car. They kept going past its front doors. Past its rear doors. All the way around the back. The trunk lid popped open. One of the guys dropped out of sight. The shorter one. Then he reappeared. He was holding something in each hand. Like a pair of baseball bats, only longer. And thicker and squarer at one end. Pickaxe handles. Effective tools, in the right hands. He passed one to the taller guy and the pair strode back, stopping about four feet away.

'Say we break your legs?' The taller guy licked his lips. 'You could still answer questions. But you'd never walk again. Not without a cane. So stop dicking us around. Get in the car. Let's go.'

The stranger saw no need to give them another warning. He'd been clear with them from the start. And they were the ones who'd chosen to up the ante.

The shorter guy made as if to swing, but checked. Then the taller guy took over. He did swing. He put all his weight into it. Which was bad technique. A serious mistake with that kind of weapon. All the stranger had to do was take a step

6

back. The heavy hunk of wood whistled past his midriff. It continued relentlessly through its arc. There was too much momentum for the guy to stop it. And both his hands were clinging to the handle. Which left his head exposed. And his torso. And his knees. A whole menu of tempting targets, all available, all totally unguarded. Any other day the stranger could have taken his pick. But on this occasion he had no time. The taller guy got off the hook. His buddy bailed him out. By jabbing at the stranger's gut, using the axe handle like a spear. He went short, aiming to get the stranger's attention. He jabbed a second time, hoping to back the stranger off. Then he lunged. It was the money shot. Or it would have been, if he hadn't paused a beat too long. Set his feet a fraction too firm. So that when he thrust, the stranger knew it was coming. He moved to the side. Grabbed the axe handle at its mid-point. And pulled. Hard. The guy was dragged forward a yard before he realized what was happening. He let go. But by then it was too late. His fate was sealed. The stranger whipped the captured axe handle over and around and brought it scything down, square on to the top of the guy's head. His eyes rolled back. His knees buckled and he wilted, slumping limp and lifeless at the stranger's feet. He wouldn't be getting up any time soon. That was for sure.

The taller guy glanced down. Saw the shape his buddy was in. And swung his axe handle back the opposite way. Aiming for the stranger's head. He swung harder than before. Wanting revenge. Hoping to survive. And he missed. Again. He left himself vulnerable. Again. But this time something else saved him. The fact that he was the last of his crew left standing. The only available source of information. He now had strategic value. Which gave him the chance to swing again.

He took it, and the stranger parried. The guy kept going, chopping left and right, left and right, like a crazed lumberjack. He managed a dozen more strokes at full speed, then he ran out of gas.

'Screw this.' The guy dropped the axe handle. Reached behind him. And pulled out his gun. 'Screw answering questions. Screw taking you alive.'

The guy took two steps back. He should have taken three. He hadn't accounted for the length of the stranger's arms.

'Let's not be hasty.' The stranger flicked out with his axe handle and sent the gun flying. Then he stepped closer and grabbed the guy by the neck. 'Maybe we will take that drive. Turns out I have some questions of my own. You can—'

'Stop.' It was a female voice. Confident. Commanding. Coming from the shadows near the right-hand row of garages. Someone new was on the scene. The stranger had arrived at eight p.m., three hours early, and searched every inch of the compound. He was certain no one had been hiding, then.

'Let him go.' A silhouette broke free from the darkness. A woman's. She was around five ten. Slim. Limping slightly. Her arms were out in front and there was the squat outline of a matte-black pistol in her hands. 'Step away.'

The stranger didn't move. He didn't relax his grip.

The woman hesitated. The other guy was between her and the stranger. Not an ideal position. But he was six inches shorter. And slightly to the side. That did leave her a target. An area on the stranger's chest. A rectangle. It was maybe six inches by ten. That was big enough, she figured. And it was more or less in the right position. She took a breath in. Exhaled gently. And pulled the trigger.

The stranger fell back. He landed with his arms spread wide, one knee raised, and his head turned so that he was facing the border fence. He was completely still. His shirt was ragged and torn. His entire chest was slick and slimy and red. But there was no arterial spray. No sign of a heartbeat.

No sign of life at all.

The tidy, manicured area people now called *The Plaza* had once been a sprawling grove of trees. Black walnuts. They'd grown, undisturbed, for centuries. Then in the 1870s a trader took to resting his mules in their shade on his treks back and forth to California. He liked the spot, so he built a shack there. And when he grew too old to rattle across the continent he sold his beasts and he stayed.

Other people followed suit. The shanty became a village. The village became a town. The town split in two like a cell, multiplying greedily. Both halves flourished. One to the south. One to the north. There were many more years of steady growth. Then stagnation. Then decline. Slow and grim and unstoppable. Until an unexpected shot in the arm was delivered, in the late 1930s. An army of surveyors showed up. Then labourers. Builders. Engineers. Even some artists and sculptors. All sent by the Works Progress Administration.

No one local knew why those two towns had been chosen. Some said it was a mistake. A bureaucrat misreading a file note and dispatching the resources to the wrong place. Others figured that someone in DC must have owed the mayor a favour. But whatever the reason, no one objected. Not with all the new roads that were being laid. New bridges being built. And all kinds of buildings rising up. The project went on for years. And it left a permanent mark. The towns' traditional

adobe arches became a little more square. The stucco exter-
iors a little more uniform. The layout of the streets a little more
regimented. And the amenities a lot more generous. The area
gained schools. Municipal offices. Fire houses. A police station. A courthouse. A museum. And a medical centre.

The population had dwindled again over the decades
since the government money dried up. Some of the facilities
became obsolete. Some were sold off. Others demolished.
But the medical centre was still the main source of health
care for miles around. It contained a doctor's office. A pharmacy. A clinic, with a couple of dozen beds. A paediatric
suite, with places for parents to stay with their sick kids.
And thanks to the largesse of those New Deal planners,
even a morgue. It was tucked away in the basement. And it
was where Dr Houllier was working, the next morning.

Dr Houllier was seventy-two years old. He had served the
town his whole life. Once, he was part of a team. Now, he
was the only physician left. He was responsible for everything from delivering babies to treating colds to diagnosing
cancer. And for dealing with the deceased. Which was the
reason for that day's early start. He'd been on duty since the
small hours. Since he'd received the call about a shooting
on the outskirts of town. It was the kind of thing that would
attract attention. He knew that from experience. He was
expecting a visit. Soon. And he needed to be ready.

There was a computer on the desk, but it was switched off.
Dr Houllier preferred to write his notes longhand. He remembered things better that way. And he had a format. One he'd
developed himself. It wasn't fancy, but it worked. It was better
than anything those Silicon Valley whizz-kids had ever tried
to foist on him. And more importantly in that particular

10

situation, it left no electronic trace for anyone to ever recover. Dr Houllier sat down, picked up the Mont Blanc his father had bought him when he graduated medical school, and started to record the results of his night's work.

There was no knock. No greeting. No courtesy at all. The door just opened and a man came in. The same one as usual. Early forties, tight curly hair, tan linen suit. *Perky*, Dr Houllier privately called him, because of the bouncy way the guy walked. He didn't know his real name. He didn't want to know.

The guy started at the far end of the room. The cold-storage area. The *meat locker*, as Dr Houllier thought of it, after decades of dealing with its contents. There was a line of five steel doors. The guy approached, examined each handle in turn, but didn't touch any of them. He never did. He moved on to the autopsy table in the centre. Crossed to the line of steel trolleys against the far wall, near the auto-clave. Then he approached the desk.

'Phone.' He held out his hand.

Dr Houllier passed the guy his cell. The guy checked to make sure it wasn't recording, slipped it into his pants pocket and turned to the door. 'Clear,' he said.

Another man walked in. *Mantis*, Dr Houllier called him, because whenever he looked at the guy, with his long skinny limbs, angular torso and bulging eyes, he couldn't help but think of the insect. The large triangular burn scar on the guy's cheek and the way his three missing fingers made his right hand look like a claw added to the effect. Although Dr Houllier did know this guy's real name. Waad Dendoncker. Everyone in town knew it, even if they'd never met him.

11

A third man followed Dendoncker in. He looked a little like *Perky*, but with straighter hair and a darker suit. And with such an anonymous face and bland way of moving that Dr Houllier had never been inspired to find him a nickname.

Dendoncker stopped in the centre of the room. His pale hair was almost invisible in the harsh light. He turned through 360 degrees, slowly, scanning the space around him. Then he turned to Dr Houllier.

'Show me,' he said.

Dr Houllier crossed the room. He checked his watch, then worked the lever that opened the centre door of the meat locker. He pulled out the sliding rack, revealing a body covered by a sheet. It was tall. Almost as long as the tray it lay on. And broad. The shoulders only just fit through the opening. Dr Houllier pulled the sheet, slowly, revealing the head. It was a man's. Its hair was messy. The face was craggy and pale, and the eyes were taped shut.

'Move.' Dendoncker shoved Dr Houllier aside. He pulled the sheet off and dropped it on the floor. The body was naked. If Michelangelo's *David* was made to embody masculine beauty, this guy could have been another in the series. But at the opposite end of the spectrum. There was nothing elegant. Nothing delicate. This one was all about power and brutality. Pure and simple.

'That's what killed him?' Dendoncker pointed to a wound on the guy's chest. It was slightly raised. Its edges were rough and ragged and they were turning brown.

'Well, he didn't die of sloth.' Dr Houllier glanced at his watch. 'I can guarantee that.'

'He'd been shot before.' Dendoncker pointed at a set of scars on the other side of the guy's chest. 'And there's *that*.'

12

'The scar on his abdomen?' Dr Houllier glanced down. 'Like some kind of sea creature. He must have been stabbed at some point.'

'That's no knife wound. That's something else altogether.'

'Like what?'

'Doesn't matter. What else do we know about him?'

'Not much.' Dr Houllier snatched up the sheet and spread it loosely over the body, including its head.

Dendoncker pulled the sheet off again and dropped it back on the floor. He wasn't done staring at the biggest of the dead guy's scars.

'I spoke to the sheriff.' Dr Houllier moved away, towards his desk. 'Sounds like the guy was a drifter. He had a room at the Border Inn. He'd paid through next weekend, in cash, but he had no belongings there. And he'd registered under a false address. One East 161st Street, the Bronx, New York.'

'How do you know that's false?'

'Because I've been there. It's another way of saying *Yankee Stadium*. And the guy used a false name, too. He signed the register as John Smith.'

'Smith? Could be his real name.'

Dr Houllier shook his head. He took a Ziploc bag from the top drawer of his desk and handed it to Dendoncker. 'See for yourself. This was in his pocket.'

Dendoncker popped the seal and fished out a passport. It was crumpled and worn. He turned to the second page. Personal information. 'This has expired.'

'Doesn't matter. The ID's still valid. And look at the photo. It's old, but it's a match.'

'OK. Let's see. Name: Reacher. Jack, none. Nationality:

United States of America. Place of birth: Berlin, West Germany. Interesting.' Dendoncker looked back at the body on the rack. At the scar on its abdomen. 'Maybe he wasn't looking for Michael. Maybe he was looking for me. It's a good job that crazy bitch killed him after all.' Dendoncker turned away and tossed the passport in the trash can next to Dr Houllier's desk. 'Observations?'

Dr Houllier held out one of his special forms. The one he'd just finished filling in. Dendoncker read each comment twice then crumpled the paper and dropped it into the trash on top of the passport.

'Burn those.' He turned to the two guys he arrived with. 'Get rid of the body. Dump it in the usual place.'

TWO

I first encountered the woman with the limp two days earlier. We met on a road outside the town with the dimly lit compound and the medical centre where Dr Houllier worked. The whole area was deserted. I was on foot. She was in a Jeep. It looked like it was ex-military. Old. Maybe Vietnam War era. Its stencilled markings were too faded to read. Its olive-drab paintwork was caked and crusted with pale dust. It had no roof. No doors. Its windshield was folded forward, but not latched. The racks and straps for holding fuel cans and tools were empty and slack. The tread on its tyres was worn way below the recommended minimum. Its motor wasn't running. Its spare wheel was missing. Not the kind of thing anyone would call a well-maintained vehicle.

The sun was high in the sky. I guess a thermometer would have said it was a little over eighty, but the lack of shade made it feel much hotter. Sweat was trickling down my back. The wind was picking up and grit was stinging my face. Walking hadn't been part of my plan when I woke up that morning. But plans change. And not always for the better. It looked like the woman's plans had taken an unwelcome turn as well. A fair chunk of the Jeep's remaining rubber was now streaked across the faded blacktop from where she'd skidded. She'd gone right off the road and ploughed into the trunk of a tree. A stunted, twisted, ugly thing with hardly any leaves. It wasn't going to win any prizes for appearance. That was for sure. But it was clearly resilient. It was the only thing growing taller than knee height for miles in either direction. If the driver had lost control at any other point she would have wound up in the rough scrub on either side of the road. Probably been able to reverse right back out. The landscape looked like a bunch of giants had shoved their hands under a coarse green blanket and stretched their fingers wide.

How the woman had hit that exact spot was a mystery. Maybe the sun had blinded her. Maybe an animal had run out, or a bird had swooped down. It was unlikely that another vehicle had been involved. Maybe she was depressed and had done it on purpose. But whatever had caused her accident, that was a problem for another time.

The woman was slumped over the steering wheel. Her left arm was stretched forward across the flattened windshield. Her hand was open like she was reaching out to the tree for help. Her right arm was folded into her abdomen. She was facing down, into the footwell. She was completely inert. There was no sign of bleeding. No sign of any other injuries, which was good. But there was also no sound of breathing. I figured I should check for a pulse or some other indication she was alive so I stepped in close to the side of

16

the Jeep. I reached for her neck, slowly and gently. I brushed her hair aside and homed in on her carotid. Then she sat up. Fast. She twisted around to face me. Used her left hand to bat my arm away. And her right to point a pistol at my gut.

She waited a beat, presumably to make sure I wasn't about to freak out. She wanted my full attention. That was clear. Then she said, 'Move back. One step only.' Her voice was firm but calm, with no hint of panic or doubt.

I moved back. One step. I made it a large one. And I realized why she'd been looking down through the steering wheel at the floor of the vehicle. There was a piece of mirror wedged between the gas pedal and the transmission tunnel. She must have cut it to the right size and positioned it to give an early warning of anyone who approached her.

'Where's your buddy?' She glanced left and right.

'There's no one else,' I said. 'Just me.'

Her eyes darted across to the rear-view mirror. It was angled so she could spot anyone sneaking up behind her. 'They only sent one guy? Really?'

She sounded half offended, half disappointed. I was starting to like her.

'No one sent me.'

'Don't lie.' She jabbed the gun forward for emphasis. 'Anyway, it doesn't matter. One of you or a whole squad? You get the same deal. Tell me where Michael is. Tell me now. And tell me the truth, or I'll shoot you in the stomach and leave you here to die.'

'I would love to tell you.' I held my hands up, palms out. 'But there's a problem. I can't. I don't know who Michael is.'

'Don't . . .' She paused and glanced around again. 'Wait. Where's your car?'

'I don't have a car.'

'Don't get smart. Your Jeep, then. Your motorcycle. What-ever mode of transport you used to get here.'

'I walked here.'

'Bullshit.'

'Did you hear an engine just now? Any kind of mechanical sound?'

'OK,' she said after a long moment. 'You walked. From where? And why?'

'Slow down.' I tried to make my voice sound friendly and unthreatening. 'Let's think this through. I could recount my day to you, minute by minute. In other circumstances, I'd be happy to. But right now, are my travel arrangements that important? Maybe a better question would be, am I the person you were waiting for? The person with information about Michael?'

She didn't answer.

'Because if I'm not, and the real guy shows up with me still here, your whole crashed car routine is never going to fly.'

She still didn't respond.

'Is there some law that says only people you want to ambush can use this road? Is it off limits to everyone else?'

I saw her glance at her watch.

'Look at me. I'm on my own. I'm on foot. I'm unarmed. Is that what you were expecting? Does it make sense to you?'

Her head moved an inch to the left and her eyes narrowed a fraction. A moment later I caught it, too. There was a sound. In the distance. A vehicle engine. Rough. Ragged. And moving closer.

'Decision time,' I said.

18

She stayed silent. The engine note grew louder.

'Think about Michael,' I said. 'I don't know where he is. But if whoever's coming does, and you keep me here, you'll lose your chance. You'll never find out.'

She didn't speak. The engine note grew louder still. Then she gestured towards the other side of the road. 'Over there. Quick. Ten yards up there's a ditch. At an angle. Like a stream bed. It's dried out. Get in it. Keep your head down. Stay still. Don't make a sound. Don't alert them. Don't do anything to screw this up. Because if you do . . .'

'Don't worry.' I was already moving. 'I get the picture.'

THREE

The ditch was right where she said it would be. I found it, no problem. I got there before the approaching vehicle was in sight. The stream bed was dry. I figured it could provide adequate cover. But the bigger issue was whether to hide at all. Or to leave.

I looked over at the Jeep. The woman was back in position, slumped across the steering wheel. Her head was turned away from me. I was out of range of her mirror. I was pretty sure she wouldn't be able to see me. But even if she did spot me I doubted she would risk taking a shot. She wouldn't want to alert whoever was coming for her.

Leaving was the sensible option. There was no doubt about that. But there was a problem. I had questions. A whole bunch of them. Like who was this woman? Who was Michael? Who was coming after her? And would she really shoot someone in the stomach and leave them to die?

I checked the road. Saw a speck in the distance, shrouded in dust. I figured I still had time so I picked up a rock from the floor of the ditch. It was about the size of a cinderblock. I positioned it on the lip, between me and the Jeep. I found another, a little narrower and flatter. Rested it at an angle against the first one so that there was a triangular gap between them. A small one. Just the right size for me to squint through with one eye. High school physics at work. The sight line opened up away from me like I was looking through an invisible cone. It gave me a clear view of the Jeep and the area around it. But the angle narrowed correspondingly in reverse so no one at that distance would be able to spot me watching them.

The approaching vehicle emerged from its cloud. It was another Jeep. Also ex-military. It was making steady progress. Slow and unhurried. Then, when it was close to the spot where I'd been when I noticed the skid marks, it slewed a little to the side and stopped. There were two men in it. A driver and a passenger. Both were wearing khaki T-shirts. They had khaki baseball caps and mirrored sunglasses. Some kind of an urgent conversation broke out between them. There was a whole lot of gesticulating and pointing towards the tree. That told me they hadn't expected anyone to be in place before them. Or that they hadn't expected anyone with a matching vehicle, which suggested they were from the same outfit. Or that they hadn't expected either thing. I thought maybe they'd call the new development in. Ask for updated orders. Or if they were smart, withdraw altogether. But they did neither. They started moving again, faster than before, then pulled in next to the driver's side of the woman's Jeep.

21

'Unbelievable.' The passenger jumped down and stood between the two vehicles. I could see the grip of a pistol protruding from the waistband of his cargo pants. It was knurled and worn. 'Her?'

The driver looped around and joined him. He put his hands on his hips. He also had a gun. 'Shit. Dendoncker's going to be pissed.'

'Not our problem.' The passenger took hold of his pistol. 'Come on. Let's do it.'

'Is she still alive?' The driver scratched his temple.

'I hope so.' The passenger stepped forward. 'We deserve a little fun.' He reached for the side of the woman's neck with his free hand. 'Ever done it with a gimp? I haven't. Always wondered what it would be like.'

The driver crowded in closer. 'I—'

The woman sat up. She twisted to the side. Raised her gun. And shot the passenger in the face. The top of his skull was obliterated. One moment it was there. The next it was a hint of pink mist drifting in the surrounding air. His empty cap fluttered to the ground. His body folded over backward. One arm was still stretched out and it swung around and slapped the driver on the thigh as he fell. His neck clattered into the open doorway of his Jeep.

The driver went for his gun. He grabbed it, right-handed. He started to pull it clear of his waistband. Got it about three quarters of the way out. Then he tried to bring it to bear. The move was premature. It was a sloppy mistake. The barrel was still trapped by his belt. His hand slipped off the grip. The weapon was left hanging loose and unbalanced. It pivoted around and fell. He tried to catch it. And missed. He leaned down, started to scratch around frantically in the

22

dirt, then saw the woman's gun. Its muzzle was moving. Zeroing in on his face. He stopped himself. Jumped back. Dived for cover behind the woman's Jeep. Crawled forward a couple of yards until he reached the road then scrambled to his feet. He started to run. The woman swivelled around in her seat. She took a breath. Aimed. Then she pulled the trigger. The bullet must have come within an inch of removing the guy's right ear. He flung himself down to the left and rolled over twice. The woman climbed out of the Jeep. She moved around to its rear. That was the first time I noticed she favoured her left leg. She waited for the guy to get back on his feet then fired again. This time the bullet almost took off his left ear. He threw himself down the opposite way and started to wriggle along on the ground like a snake.

'Stop.' The woman sounded like she was running short of patience.

The guy continued to crawl.

'The next bullet won't miss,' she said. 'But it won't kill you, either. It'll sever your spine.'

The guy rolled on to his back, as if that would protect him. He threw a couple of kicks like he was trying to swim. The effort was futile. It stirred up plenty of dust but only bought him a few more inches. His arms and legs went limp. His head flopped back against the ground. He closed his eyes. He lay there for a moment, breathing deeply. Then he sat up and held his hands out in front like he was warding off some kind of invisible demon.

'Let's talk about this.' His voice was shrill and shaky. 'It doesn't have to be this way. My partner. I'll pin it on him. I'll tell the boss he set the whole thing up. We got here, no one else showed, he pulled his gun on me – 'cause he was the

23

traitor all along – but I was faster. We've got the body. That's proof, right? What else do we need?'

'Get up.'

'It'll work. I can sell it. I promise. Just don't kill me. Please.'

'Get up.'

'You don't understand. I had—'

The woman raised her gun. 'Get up or I'll blow *your* leg off. See how *you* like being called *gimp*.'

'No, please!' The guy scrambled to his feet.

'Move back.'

The guy took a step. A small one.

'Further.'

He took another step. That left him out of range if he was dumb enough to try his luck with a punch or a kick. He stopped with his ankles pressed together and his arms clamped tight by his sides. It was a weird position. He reminded me of a dancer I saw busking on the street in Boston, years ago.

'Good. Now. You want me to let you live?'

'Oh yes.' His head bobbed up and down like a novelty doll's. 'I do.'

'All right. I'm prepared to do that. But you have to do one thing for me first.'

'Anything.' The guy kept on nodding. 'Whatever you want. Name it.'

'Tell me where Michael is.'

FOUR

The guy's head stopped moving. He didn't speak. His legs were still together. His arms were still by his sides. His posture still looked awkward.

'Tell me where I can find Michael. If you don't, I will kill you. But not quickly, like your friend. No. Not like that at all.'

The guy didn't respond.

'Have you ever seen anyone get shot in the stomach?' The woman made a show of taking aim at the guy's abdomen. 'How long they take to die? The agony they're in, the entire time?'

'No.' The guy shook his head. 'Don't do that. I'll tell you.'

Then I realized why the guy looked strange. It was his hands, still pressed against his sides. One was open. His left. But his right was clenched. His wrist was bent back. He was holding something and trying to conceal the fact. I wanted to shout a warning, but I couldn't. Breaking the

25

woman's concentration right at that moment wasn't going to help her.

'Well?' A sharp edge had crept into her voice.

'So, Michael's whereabouts. OK. It's kind of complicated, but he's—'

The guy's right arm snapped up. His fingers opened and a swirl of sandy grit flew right at the woman's face. She reacted fast. Her left hand came up in front of her eyes and she pivoted away on her good leg. She dodged the worst of the cloud. But not the guy himself. He launched himself forward, swatted her arm aside, and slammed his shoulder into her chest. He was only a couple of inches taller than her but must have been at least eighty pounds heavier. The impact sent her reeling. Her feet couldn't keep up and she tumbled over backward. She was still holding the gun. She tried to raise it but he followed in and stamped on her wrist. She clung on. He pressed his foot down harder. And harder still until she shrieked with frustration and let go of the weapon. He kicked it away then stepped across her body, one foot either side, and stood there looming over her.

'Well now, *gimp*. I'd say the boot's on the other foot, but that would be cruel, as you only have one.'

The woman lay still. I stood up. The guy had his back to me. He was less than fifteen yards away.

'My friend had a plan for you.' The guy started to fumble with the front of his pants. 'A kind of dying wish. I figure I should see it through. Once for him. Once for me. Maybe more, if I like it.'

I climbed out of the trench.

'Then I'll kill you.' The guy pulled his belt clear and tossed

26

it away to the side. 'Maybe I'll shoot *you* in the stomach. See how long it takes *you* to die.'

I started down the slope.

'It could take hours.' The guy started to unbutton his fly. 'All night, even. Dendoncker won't care. And he won't care what condition you wind up in. Just as long as you're dead when I hand you over.'

I forced myself to slow down. I didn't want to make a sound on the loose gravel.

The woman shifted her position a little then stretched her arms out on both sides. 'So you know about my foot. Gold star to you for observation. But do you know much about titanium?'

The guy's hands stopped moving.

I reached the blacktop on the far side of the road.

'It's a very interesting metal.' The woman braced her palms against the ground. 'It's very strong. Very light. And very hard.'

The woman whipped her right leg up, bent it at the knee, and drove her prosthetic foot towards the guy's groin. It connected. Front and centre. Full power. No mistake. Nothing held back. The guy screamed and gasped and pitched forward. He landed face down in the dirt. She rolled to the side and only just avoided getting crushed. She rolled a couple more times and retrieved her gun. Then she used both arms to lever herself up off the ground.

I stopped where I was, halfway across the blacktop, one foot either side of the faded yellow line.

The guy rolled on to his side and curled into a ball. He was whimpering like a whipped dog.

27

'One last chance.' The woman raised the gun. 'Michael. Where is he?'

'Michael's history, you idiot.' The guy was breathing hard. 'Forget about him.'

'He's history? What do you mean?'

'What do you think I mean? Dendoncker takes some poor schmuck in for interrogation, then ... Want me to draw a diagram?'

'No need for a diagram.' Her voice was suddenly flat. 'But I do need to be sure.'

'He was a dead man the moment he started swapping secret notes.' The guy raised his head. 'You know about Dendoncker. He's the most paranoid guy on the planet. He was bound to find out.'

'Who killed him? You?'

'No. I swear.'

'Then who?'

'I thought it was going to be us. Dendoncker told us to be ready as soon as he was done with his questions. We dropped everything. No one lasts very long when Dendoncker goes to work on them. You know that. So we were good to go. Then he told us we weren't needed after all.'

'Why not? What changed?'

'I don't know. I wasn't there. Maybe Michael was too slow with his answers. Or too smart with his mouth. Or just had a weak heart. Anyway, Dendoncker stood us down. Then this morning he sent us for you.'

The woman was quiet for a moment. Then she said, 'Michael's body. Where is it?'

'Usual place, I guess. If there was enough of it left.'

The woman's shoulders sagged a little. She lowered the

gun. The guy curled back up. He reached for his ankle. Slowly and smoothly. He slid something out of his boot. Rolled on to his front. A second later he was on his feet. The sun glinted off whatever he had in his right hand. A blade. It was short and broad. He launched himself forward. His arm was high. He was swinging, horizontally. Trying to slash the woman's forehead. He wanted her eyes to fill with blood. So she couldn't see. Couldn't aim. She leaned back, bending sharply at the waist. Just far enough. He missed. He switched the knife to his other hand. Shaped up for another try.

This time she didn't hesitate. She just pulled the trigger. The guy went over backward. He dropped the knife, screamed, and clutched his gut with both hands. A dark stain spread across the fabric. She'd hit him in the stomach. Exactly like she'd threatened to. She stepped in close. She stood and looked down at him. Thirty seconds crawled past. No doubt the longest half minute of the guy's life. He was writhing and moaning and trying to stem the stream of blood with his palms and his fingers. She took a step back. Then she raised the gun. Lined it up on his head. And pulled the trigger. Again.

Some of my questions had been answered, at least. But now I had another one on my mind. Something much more urgent. The woman had just killed two people. I had watched her do it. I was the only witness. I needed to know what she was going to do about that. Her actions could be classed as self-defence, for sure. She had a solid case. I wouldn't argue against it. But she had no way of knowing that. Relying on a stranger's support was a gamble. And any trial she faced would come with its own risks. The skill of the lawyers. The disposition of the jurors. And she would inevitably spend months in jail before seeing the inside of a courtroom. An unappealing prospect in itself. And a dangerous one. Jails don't generally boost the life expectancy of anyone who gets locked up in them.

I stepped forward. There was no point going back. A couple of extra yards between us wasn't going to make any difference. The gun she was holding was a Glock 17. One of the most reliable pistols in the world. It had a misfire rate of around one in ten thousand. Great odds from her side of the trigger. Not so good from mine. The magazine held seventeen rounds. She had fired five shots, to my knowledge. There was no reason to assume she hadn't started out with a full load. So she would have twelve bullets left. There was no way she would need even a quarter of that number. She was an excellent markswoman. She had demonstrated that. And she had shown no hesitation when a violent solution was called for. The two guys who were now on the ground had found that out the hard way.

I took another step. Then my new question was answered, too. And not in a way I expected. The woman nodded to me. She turned. Walked back to her Jeep. Leaned against its rear. Shrugged her shoulders. Sighed. Raised her gun. And pressed its muzzle against her temple.

'Stop.' I hurried towards her. 'You don't have to do that.'

She looked at me with wide, clear eyes. 'Oh yes. I do.'

'No. You did what–'

'Get back.' She held up her free hand, palm out. 'Unless you want to wind up covered in blood and brains. I'll give you three seconds. Then I'm going to pull the trigger.'

I believed her. I couldn't see any way to stop her. All I could think to do was ask, 'Why?'

She looked at me like the answer was so self-evident it was barely worth the energy it would take to respond. Then she said, 'Because I lost my job. I disgraced myself. I put innocent people in harm's way. And I got my brother killed. I have nothing left to live for. I'd be better off dead.'

FIVE

Losing a job can be a blow. I know. I've had the experience. But the feeling pales into nothing beside losing a brother. Into less than nothing. I know. I've lived through that experience, too. And if you think you're responsible for your brother's death, the burden must be even heavier. Maybe too heavy to bear. Maybe there isn't a path back. I wasn't sure. But I hoped there was a way to survive. In this case, at least. I didn't know what shape it should take, but I hoped something could help this woman. I liked the way she stood up for herself. I didn't want her story to end with a self-inflicted bullet at the side of some lonely road.

I stood my ground and counted to three in my head. Slowly. The woman didn't pull the trigger. I didn't get covered in her blood and brains. I took that as a good sign.

'I heard what that guy was saying.' I waited a couple more

seconds. My eyes didn't leave her trigger finger. 'Michael's your brother?'

'Was my brother.' The gun was still pressed to her head.

'You were looking for him?'

'That's what got him killed.'

'You were looking for him on your own is what I mean. You hadn't gone to the police.'

'Was he on the wrong side of the law? Was he a criminal? That's what you mean. And the answer's yes. He was.' She lowered the gun. 'Gold star to you for figuring that out.'

'And you?'

'No. Well, yes. Technically. By association. But only because I infiltrated Michael's group. I was trying to get him out. He wanted to leave. Straighten himself out. He got a message to me. You didn't know him. He was a good man. In his heart. That last tour changed him. What the army did was wrong. It derailed him. Left him vulnerable. Some other guys got their hooks into him. Took advantage. He made some bad choices. Clearly. Which is on him. I'm not making excuses. But it was a temporary thing. A blip. The real Michael was still in there somewhere. I know it. If I could have just gotten to him in time . . .'

'I'm not judging. I understand why you didn't go to the police before. But things have changed.'

The woman didn't reply.

I said, 'The guy who killed Michael? Get him arrested. Go to his trial. Give evidence. Put him away for the rest of his life.'

She shook her head. 'It wouldn't work. The guy who killed Michael is too careful. He won't have left any proof.

Even if they believe me the police could look for months and not find anything.'

'Maybe the police don't need to find anything. We could go visit the guy. I heard a name. Dendoncker?'

'That's the asshole.'

'We could chat. I'm sure he'd soon feel the urge to confess. With the correct kind of encouragement.'

A small, sad smile spread across the woman's face. 'I would love to go visit Dendoncker. Believe me. I'd be there in a heartbeat. But it's impossible.'

'No such thing as impossible. Just inadequate preparation.'

'Not in this case. Getting your hands on Dendoncker cannot be done.'

'How do you know?'

'I've tried.'

'What stopped you?'

'For a start, no one ever knows where he is.'

'So make him come to you.'

'Not possible. He only shows his face in one particular circumstance.'

'Then create that circumstance.'

'I'm about to. But it won't help.'

'I don't follow.'

'He only breaks cover when someone who was a threat to him is dead. Even if he only thought they were a threat. Even if he only imagined it or dreamed it. He has them killed. Then he has to see the body for himself. It's like a paranoid compulsion he has. He won't take anyone's word. He won't trust a photograph or a video or a death certificate or a coroner's report. He only believes his own eyes.'

I took a moment to think. Then I said, 'So, two people.'

34

'What?'

'If that's his MO it'll take two people to capture him. You and I could do it. If we worked together.'

'Bullshit. You don't know what you're talking about.'

'Actually, I do. I spent thirteen years catching people who didn't want to get caught. And I was good at it.'

'You're serious?'

'Absolutely.'

'You were a bounty hunter?'

'Guess again.'

'Not a cop?'

'A military cop.'

'Really? You don't look like one. What happened to you?'

I didn't respond to that.

The woman was silent for a moment, too. Then she said, 'What difference does a second person make? I don't see it.'

'All in good time. The question right now is: Capturing Dendoncker – is that worth living for?'

The woman blinked a couple of times then looked away towards the horizon. She gazed in silence for a whole minute. Then she looked me in the eye. 'Stopping . . . Capturing Dendoncker. That would be a start, I guess. But two people. Working together. You and me. Why would you do that?'

'Michael was a veteran. You're one, too. I can see it in you. Too many of us have been lost already. I'm not going to stand by and watch another life get wasted.'

'I can't ask you to help.'

'You're not asking. I'm offering.'

'It would be dangerous.'

'Crossing the street can be dangerous.'

35

She paused for a moment. 'OK. But can we actually do it?'

'Sure.'

'You promise?'

'Of course,' I said. 'Would I lie to a woman with a gun in her hand?'

SIX

My fingers weren't literally crossed, but they might as well have been. I had no idea how to capture Dendoncker. And no intention of finding a way. I had no desire to get tangled up with a crazy person. He hadn't done anything to me, as far as I knew.

I guess the overall scenario carried a certain amount of intrigue. It sounded like the guy had come up with his own take on catch-22. You could only get close enough to kill him by being in a condition that prevented you from killing him. It was ingenious. Almost a challenge in itself. I was sure it could be done, if I thought about it hard enough. Gathered enough intel. Maybe deployed the right kind of specialized equipment.

The truth was I had no interest in any of those things. But I wasn't about to tell the woman. I figured that the prospect of capturing her brother's killer was a lifeline I could use to pull her ashore. Probably the only thing I could use. It would be stupid to cut it before her feet were safely on dry land. Worse than stupid. Criminal. I may not have been serious about capturing some guy I'd never met. But I meant every word about helping her. Suicide has claimed far too many veterans. One would have been too many. So if I could prevent there being one more, that's what I was going to do.

I planned to take things slow. Give her time to see that the police were her best option. I was going to deceive her, yes. In the short term. But better deceived than dead.

The woman pushed herself away from the Jeep and stood still for a moment, staring at the ground. She seemed smaller than before. Stooped. Deflated. Finally, she looked up at me. She slid the gun into her waistband and held out her hand. 'I'm Michaela. Michaela Fenton. And before you say anything – yes. Michael and Michaela. We were twins. Our parents thought it was cute. We didn't.'

I shrugged. 'I'm Reacher.'

Her hand was long and narrow and a little cold. Her fingers curled around mine. She squeezed and I felt a tiny shiver flicker up my arm.

'Well, Reacher.' She pulled away, glanced to her left and right, and her shoulders seemed to sag even further. 'These bodies. Guess we should do something with them. Any ideas?'

That was a good question. If Dendoncker had sent his goons after me I would have left their remains someplace he couldn't miss them. Like on his front lawn. Or in his bed. So that he was clear about the message I was sending. I don't like to leave any room for misunderstanding. But

Dendoncker hadn't sent them after me. And if we were really out to capture him, a more subtle approach would be called for. Hiding the bodies would be the right move. Something that kept our cards close to our chests. But we were in the middle of the desert. The sun was high in the sky. Digging graves had not been part of my plans when I woke up that morning and I felt like I'd been flexible enough for one day.

I said, 'One of them must have a phone. We'll call 911. Let the police handle it.'

'Is that smart? These guys have obviously been . . . well, they didn't die of natural causes.'

'It'll be fine.'

'But won't the police send in a bunch of detectives? Forensic teams? The whole nine yards?' She paused for a moment. 'Look, if I have to pay a price for what I did, I'm fine with that. I'll take what I deserve. In due course. But I don't want to wind up in jail while Dendoncker is out here, free. And I don't want some huge investigation getting in our way and stopping us from catching him.'

My agenda was different. I hoped the police would send in a bunch of guys. As many as possible. I wanted them swarming around all over the place. It's not smart to try and snatch anyone with the law watching you. I was counting on Fenton to realize that. Just not yet.

'That's all part of the plan.' I pulled what I hoped was a reassuring smile. 'You said Dendoncker is paranoid. If he sees the police sniffing around, he'll panic. Make a mistake. Something we can use.'

'I guess.' She didn't sound convinced.

I moved across to the guy she'd shot second and searched his pockets. He had a bunch of keys on a ring with a square plastic fob. One was for a vehicle. A Ford. Two looked like house keys. One was a Yale. It was new and shiny. The other was for a mortice lock. It was old and scratched. I figured it was for a separate building. A garage, maybe. Or a storage shed. The guy also had a phone. And a wallet. It had no ID in it. No credit cards. But there were two hundred dollars in twenties, which I took. Spoils of war. Only fair.

The other dead guy's pockets yielded a similar haul. He had a key ring with the same kind of plastic fob. One of the keys was for a Dodge. Two were Yales. And one was a mortice, which was also old and scratched. He had a wallet with a hundred and twenty dollars in twenties. And a phone with a cracked case. I pressed the guy's thumb to its central button and held it there until the screen lit up.

'Where are we, exactly?' I asked Fenton.

She shrugged. 'Everyone in town just calls it *The Tree*. Hold on a sec. I'll see what I can find.' She pulled out her phone and prodded and swiped at the screen, then held it up for me to see. 'Here you go. Map reference.'

When the emergency operator came on the line I gave him the coordinates and told him I had seen two guys shoot each other during an argument. Then I wiped the phone clean of prints and tossed it away.

I asked Fenton, 'Is your Jeep wrecked?'

'No. I didn't touch the tree. See for yourself.'

I walked around to the front of her Jeep and looked. There was maybe room to slide a cigarette paper between the fender and the trunk, but no more. She must be one hell of a driver.

I said, 'Good. We'll take yours. Leave the other one here.'

'Why? An extra vehicle might be useful.'

40

'True.' The tainted Jeep certainly could be useful. As another juicy morsel for the forensic guys to get their teeth into. Not as transport. 'But it's too big a risk. Dendoncker is bound to freak out when he doesn't hear from his guys. He'll send a search party. If either of us is seen with their Jeep, that would screw things up big time.'

'I guess.'

I retrieved the guys' guns, plus a baseball cap and a pair of sunglasses. 'I doubt the cavalry will arrive anytime soon. But we should still get out of here.'

'Where to?'

'Somewhere private. We have a lot to talk about.'

'OK.' Fenton made her way around to the driver's side of her Jeep and flipped up the windshield. 'My hotel.' She fired up the engine and shifted into reverse, then sat with one foot on the brake and the other pressing down on the clutch. Both her hands were on the wheel. At the top. Pressed together at the twelve o'clock position. She was hanging on tight. Her knuckles were white. Veins and tendons began to bulge. She closed her eyes. Her chest heaved, like she was having trouble catching her breath. Then she regained control. Slowly. She relaxed her grip. She opened her eyes, which dislodged a couple of tears. 'Sorry.' She brushed her cheeks then switched her right foot to the gas pedal and raised the clutch. 'I was thinking of Michael. I can't believe he's gone.'

SEVEN

Fenton pushed the Jeep hard. The aged suspension creaked and squealed. The motor rattled. The transmission howled. Clouds of dark smoke spewed out of the tailpipe. She worked constantly at the wheel, sawing back and forth, but she still struggled to keep us going straight. I tried to focus on the road ahead but after ten minutes she caught me glancing down at her right foot.

'IED,' she said. 'Afghanistan.'

She meant *Improvised Explosive Device*. It was a term I objected to. It had become prevalent during the Second Gulf War. Probably coined by some government PR guy to make the insurgents' weapons sound low-tech. Unsophisticated. Like they were nothing to worry about. To conjure the image of them being cobbled together by unskilled rubes in caves and cellars. Whereas the truth was the opposite. I knew. I was in a compound in Beirut, years ago, when a dump truck

42

loaded with twelve thousand pounds of explosives burst through the barracks gates. Two hundred and forty-one US Marines and sailors died that day. Fifty-eight French paratroopers were killed in another attack nearby. And since then things had only gotten worse. The bomb makers now have access to complex electronics. Remote detonators. Infrared triggers. Proximity sensors. They've become experts in positioning. Concealment. And they've become even nastier. More ruthless. As well as nails and metal fragments designed to tear human flesh, they routinely load their devices with bacterial agents and anticoagulants. Then even if their victims survive the initial blast they're still likely to bleed out or die of some hideous disease.

I pushed those thoughts aside and asked her, 'Army?'

She nodded. 'Sixty-sixth Military Intelligence Group. Out of Wiesbaden, Germany. But this didn't happen while I was in uniform. There was no Purple Heart for me.'

'You joined a private contractor?'

She shook her head. 'Not me. I have no time for those guys. Call me crazy, but I don't think wars should be fought for profit.'

'What then? Not many civilians go to Afghanistan.'

'I did. It's a long story. I'll tell you some other time. Meanwhile, what about you? What brings you from the Military Police to this particular place? On foot? Of all the roads in all the towns . . .'

'Also a long story.'

'Touché. So I'm going to come straight out and ask you. Are you on the run? Are you some kind of fugitive?'

I thought about her question for a moment. About the last town I'd been to. It was in Texas. I'd left the previous morning.

In a hurry. I ran into a little trouble there. It had resulted in a fire. A destroyed building. And three dead bodies. But no major risk of blowback. Nothing she needed to know about.

I said, 'No. I'm not a fugitive.'

'Because if you are, no judgement. Not after what you saw me do today. But stopping Dendoncker is important to me. It's all I have right now. And if we're going to do it, there are going to be risks. We have to trust each other. So I have to know. Why are you here?'

'No special reason. I'm on my way out west. A guy was giving me a ride. He had to turn around and go back east, so I got out.'

'Got out? Or got kicked out?'

'Got out.'

'In such a hurry you forgot to grab your luggage? Come on. What really happened?'

'I don't have any luggage. And I could have carried on riding with the guy. He asked me to. But I don't like turning around. I like to keep moving forward. So I got out.'

'OK. First things first. No luggage? Really?'

'Why would I need luggage? What would I put in it?'

'I'm going to take a wild shot in the dark here and say, I don't know, you're on a cross-country road trip, so, clothes? Nightwear? Toiletries? Personal items?'

'I'm wearing my clothes. They have toiletries at hotels. And my personal items are in my pocket.'

'You have one set of clothes?'

'How many does a person need?'

'I don't know. More than one. What do you do when they need to be washed?'

'Throw them away and buy more.'

44

'Isn't that wasteful? And impractical?'

'No.'

'Why not take them home? Clean them?'

'Laundry's not my thing. Nor are laundry rooms. Or houses.'

'So you're homeless.'

'Call it what you like. The reality is I have no use for a home. Not at the moment. Maybe I'll get one, someday. Maybe I'll get a dog. Maybe I'll settle down. But not yet. Not for a long time.'

'So you do what? Just roam around the country?'

'That's the general idea.'

'How? Do you even have a car?'

'Never felt the need.'

'You prefer hitching rides?'

'I don't mind it. Sometimes I take the bus.'

'You take the bus? Really?'

I didn't reply.

'OK. Back to the guy who was driving you this morning. Why his sudden one-eighty?'

'He wanted to buy some old British sports car. He'd been to Texas to buy a different one. But he backed out. The seller tried to rip him off. Something about numbers that didn't match. I don't know why that's a big deal. I'm not much of a car guy. So he was driving home again. To someplace in western Arizona. He wanted to let off steam. So he wanted an audience. So he picked me up. Outside a motel near El Paso.'

'Wait a minute. We're nowhere near the regular route west from El Paso.'

'The radio said I-10 was snarled up. Some kind of multi-car accident. So he took a bunch of smaller roads. Cut across the

45

south-west corner of New Mexico. Made it all the way past the Arizona state line. Then his phone rang. It was his wife. She had a lead on another of these old cars. In Oklahoma this time.'

'But you wanted to keep heading west. Why? What's out there for you?'

'The Pacific Ocean.'

'I don't follow.'

'Call it a whim. I was in Nashville, Tennessee. There's a band I like. I caught them at a couple of clubs, then when I was on my way out of the city this weird bird flew by. For a moment I thought it was a pelican. It wasn't, but it made me think of Alcatraz. Which made me think of the ocean.'

'And you thought the ocean was somewhere up this road?'

'No. I got bored of waiting for another ride. I started to walk. And I saw a giant stone structure at the side of the highway with an arrow pointing this way. An obelisk. Or a monument. It was covered with carvings and fancy patterns. And it made me curious. I thought, if the sign's that elaborate, what will the town be like?'

'See for yourself,' she said. 'We're nearly there.'

EIGHT

We had been climbing gradually since we left The Tree and just at that moment we crested the hill and the town came into view. It was spread out below us, maybe half a mile away. I could see clusters of buildings with pale stucco walls and terracotta roofs. It was hard to make sense of the layout. It looked like the place was made up of two rough ovals. They partially overlapped, like a Venn diagram drawn by a kid with a shaky hand. The buildings in the segment to the left were lower. Mainly single-storey. Their walls looked a little rougher. They were scattered around a little more randomly. The ones in the other part were taller. Straighter. More evenly laid out. The section in the centre had buildings that were taller still. I could see arches and curves and courtyards. Maybe it was the municipal district. Maybe the bars and restaurants were around there too. If the place ran to that kind of thing.

On the far side of the town a row of tall metal ribs rose out of the ground and extended east and west as far as the eye could see. They looked solid. Permanent. Unwelcoming. They were set close together and their tips were pointed and sharp. I guessed the land beyond them belonged to Mexico. It looked pretty much the same as the land on the US side. The incline picked up again and there was a slope a few hundred yards long that was undeveloped, like a kind of no-man's-land. Then at the top of the rise the buildings began again. I could see another set of pale stucco walls and terracotta roofs stretching far into the distance.

'What do you think?' Fenton said.

'I think I'm missing something.'

Dendoncker had just ordered Fenton killed. He had at least three others on his payroll. Fenton had talked about him like he was the second coming of Al Capone, only with added craziness. That meant he must be based someplace that could sustain a decent level of crime. Protection. Drugs. Prostitution. The usual staples, most likely. But this town looked like nothing more than a sleepy backwater. The kind of place you would come to get over insomnia. I'd be surprised if they'd ever even had a shoplifting problem.

I asked, 'Was Dendoncker born here?'

Fenton didn't answer. She seemed lost in thought.

I asked her again, 'Was Dendoncker born in the town?'

'What?' she said. 'No. He was born in France.'

'So out of the entire United States, maybe the entire world, he chose to settle here. I'm wondering why. What else do you know about him?'

'Not as much as I'd like.' Fenton stared at the road ahead without speaking for a moment, then dragged her attention

48

back to my question. 'OK. His full name is Waad Ahmed Dendoncker. His father was German. His mother was Lebanese. He lived in Paris until he was eighteen, went to high school there, then was accepted by the University of Pennsylvania. He was a bright enough kid, by all accounts. He got through his Bachelor's and stayed on to do a Ph.D. in engineering, but dropped out after eighteen months. He went back to France, bounced around Europe and the Middle East for a couple of years, and then I lost his trail. I couldn't find any other trace of him until 2003, when he resurfaced in Iraq. He started working for the army as one of those general translator/fixer/facilitators. Then in 2007 the government started a programme to bring a bunch of those guys over to the States to save them from reprisals. Dendoncker applied in May '08. The vetting process is pretty thorough so he didn't get his visa until April '10. The government set him up in a town called Goose Neck, Georgia, and got him a job in a chicken processing plant. He kept his nose clean. His attendance record was perfect. He travelled a fair bit, but only in the lower forty-eight, and he spent a lot of time in the library. Then after a year he quit and moved here.'

Fenton took a left after the first couple of buildings on the outskirts of town and started to thread her way through a warren of meandering streets.

'I can understand him not wanting to chop up chickens for the rest of his life,' I said. 'But it doesn't explain why he picked this place.'

'I have a theory.' Fenton pulled through an archway and into a courtyard that had been converted into a parking lot. 'Right after he arrived here Dendoncker set up a business.

49

On the QT. He owns it through half a dozen shell corporations. That implies a strong desire for secrecy. So it follows that he wouldn't want his operation to attract a whole lot of attention. This place is perfect for that. It's on its own, tucked away at the ass-end of a single road, in or out. The population's been declining for years. The locals say it's turning into a ghost town. Plus, there's no border crossing for miles. Official or unofficial. The fence is secure. There have been no reported breaches in more than ten years. So there's nothing for any department or agency to take an interest in.'

'What kind of business did he set up?'

'Catering. A company called *Pie in the Sky, Inc.*' Fenton stayed to the right and continued to the far end of the row of spaces. She took the final spot. It lay between a dull white panel van and a blank wall, and she pulled all the way in so that the Jeep was pretty much hidden.

'So why would he need to stay out of the limelight? You think he's hiding from the health inspector?'

'It's not what he cooks. Or how. It's who for. It's a specialist company he owns. It makes in-flight meals, but not for mainstream airlines. For private jets only. Dendoncker has contracts with half a dozen operators. His people pack up the food. Put it in those special metal boxes or trolleys, depending on the quantity. Take it to the airport. Load it right on to the plane. And retrieve the containers afterwards. Sometimes he provides the flight attendants, too.'

The set-up could be totally innocent, of course. People who fly on private planes need food and drink just the same as if they were stuck in economy on a 737. Dendoncker could have hidden his involvement because he has a bunch

50

of ex-wives he owes money to. He could be shy about paying his taxes. Or the set-up could be something else
altogether. The kind of airports most private jets operate
out of aren't like JFK or LAX. Security is minimal. For the
passengers. And for the support services. I could see how
that kind of set-up could provide a guy like Dendoncker
with certain opportunities. And why he would want to keep
his comings and goings out of sight.

Fenton shut off the Jeep's motor. 'He could be moving
drugs. Diamonds. Weapons. Pretty much anything.'

I asked, 'Any proof?'

'Just suspicion at this point. But it's not unfounded. Take
my first day on Dendoncker's crew. I got sent to cover for
another woman. As a flight attendant. It was a last-minute
thing. She was out sick. Or she knew what was in store. The
whole experience was gross. There were two of us and four
passengers. Rich assholes. They were constantly trying to
grope us. Making suggestions about extra services we
could perform. One guy was obsessed with my leg. Kept
trying to touch it. I nearly took him to the bathroom and
beat him to death with it. Not even the food distracted him.
Or the drink. It was obscene. The most expensive stuff you
can imagine. Caviar – Kolikof albino. Ham – jamón Ibérico.
Cheese – Pule. Champagne – Boërl & Kroff. Brandy –
Lecompte Secret. There was a ton of it. A dozen containers.
Large ones. And here's the thing. We only used ten of them.
Two went untouched.'

'Maybe they over-ordered. Or Dendoncker was padding
the bill.'

'No. I was going to take a look inside the spare ones while
the other woman was in the bathroom, but they had seals

on them. Tiny things. Little blobs of lead on short skinny wires. Partly hidden by the latches. I almost didn't see them. So I checked the containers we did open. There were no broken seals on any of them.'

'What happened to the sealed ones?'

'They got offloaded at the destination airport. Two more got put on in their place. Same size. Same shape. Same seals.'

'What would have happened if you opened one *by mistake*?'

'I thought about trying that, but the plane flew back empty. No new passengers got on board, so there was no need to open any of the containers. And when I thought back to the outbound flight I realized something. It was the other woman who picked which container we should open. At the time it seemed reasonable. I was new, she had experience, she knew where things were. But later it felt different, like she had been steering me away from the sealed ones. And it was the same basic picture with all the other flights I worked on. Different passengers. Different destinations. But there were always containers that weren't accounted for.'

Fenton climbed out of the Jeep. She started towards a door at the centre of the long side of the courtyard. I followed. I saw that the buildings on all four sides had originally been separate. Now they were joined together. Some were sticking out. Some were set back. But they were all the same height. The roof that connected them was continuous and uniform. It must have been added later.

Each original section of the building had a sign mounted on its front wall. I guessed they stated the initial occupant. There were lots of names. Lots of different businesses and services. A blacksmith. A cooper. A hardware store. A place to buy provisions. A warehouse. One whole side had been a

saloon. Presumably the places had originally been inde-
pendent, but now their signs were all the same shape. They
used the same colours. The same font. The doors and windows were laid out in different configurations but they were
the same style. They used the same materials. They looked
the same age. And each one had a glass rectangle mounted
on the wall near the door, the size of a typical security keypad but with no buttons.

I said, 'What is this place?'

'My hotel. Where I'm staying. Where we're staying, I
guess.'

I looked around all four sides. 'Where's the office?'

'There isn't one. The place is unmanned. It's a new concept. Part of a new chain. They're in five cities. Maybe six,
now. I don't remember.'

'So how do you get a room?'

'You book online. You don't see anyone. You don't interact
with anyone. That's the beauty of it.'

'How do you get a key? They send it in the mail?'

Fenton shook her head. 'There isn't a physical key. They
email you a QR code.'

I said nothing.

'A QR code. You know. Like a two-dimensional barcode.
You display it on your phone and the scanners by the doors
read it. It's excellent.'

'It is?'

'It is. Particularly if you happen to book with a false ID.
And a false credit card. And a made-up email address. That
way, no one can ever trace you.'

'This isn't going to work for me. I don't have a false ID. I
don't have any kind of a credit card. Or a phone.'

'Oh.' She shrugged. 'Well, never mind. We'll figure that out later.'

'There are cameras.' I gestured to a pair of them. They were mounted on the wall near the Jeep's parking spot. A mesh cage protected them. 'Someone could trace you that way.'

'They could try. The cameras do appear to be working. But if anyone tries to access their files, they won't see any-thing. They'll just get snow. That's the beauty of the training they give you at Fort Huachuca. It's the gift that keeps on giving.'

NINE

Fenton fiddled with her phone then held its screen up to a scanner below a sign that read *Carlisle Smith, Wheelwright*. The door clicked open. I followed her inside. I couldn't picture any hard manual labour taking place in there now. The room was all pastel colours and throw cushions and nostalgic black-and-white photographs. Plus the standard hotel stuff. A bed. A couch. A work area. A closet. A bathroom. Everything you could need for a comfy night, except for a coffeemaker. There was no sign of one of those. But there was a suitcase, neatly squared away, sitting on its own by the door. Fenton saw me looking at it.

'Old habits.' She wheeled the case across to the bed. 'Always be ready to move.' She turned to look at me. 'I figured I would be moving again today. I hoped it would be with Michael. But really, I knew. There was no chance. I was always going to be leaving alone. I just had to be sure.

It wasn't a surprise. But still, back there, at The Tree, it hit me. Harder than I expected. Pushed me close to the edge for a second or two. I'm sorry you had to see that. It won't happen again. Now, let's focus. Come on. Make yourself at home.'

I figured it was a minute after three p.m. I was hungry. Breakfast was a long time ago. I'd made an early start, back in El Paso. I didn't know if Fenton had eaten at all that day. But she must have burned plenty of adrenaline. I figured food would help both of us. I suggested we order some. Fenton didn't argue. She just pulled out her phone. 'Pizza work for you?'

She took the chair from under the desk and tapped away at her phone. I sat on the couch. I waited until she was done summoning up our food, then said, 'I told you why I'm here. Now it's your turn.'

She paused, like she was marshalling her thoughts. 'It started with Michael's message, I guess. We were always close, like most twins are, but we lost touch. He wasn't the same. Not after he left the army. I guess I should explain that. He was in a thing called a TEU. A Technical Escort Unit. They're the guys who are experts in bomb disposal and chemical warfare.'

'I've heard of them. If another unit is clearing an area and they find chemical ordnance, they call in a TEU.'

'They're supposed to. But that doesn't always happen. A grunt doesn't always know what a chemical artillery round looks like. In Iraq the enemy didn't have any, remember. Not officially. So they're not marked properly. Or they're deliberately mismarked. Plus they look like other shells. Signal shells, especially, because they also have a separate chamber for the precursor material. And even if the guys

56

know chemicals are involved they sometimes try to handle it themselves. They don't want to wait. With the best will in the world it can take twelve hours for a TEU to respond. Sometimes twenty-four. That's up to an extra day of exposure to enemy snipers and booby traps. And an extra day they're not clearing other areas. That leaves other caches for insurgents to find and raid, or for civilians to stumble across, maybe getting hurt or killed. So quite often Michael's team would arrive at a scene and find it contaminated. Like the first one they ever responded to. It was a brick chamber, underground. Some infantry guys literally fell into it. They busted through the ceiling. They started poking around, then got cold feet. The shells in there were old. They were in bad shape. The guys must have cracked one without realizing. It contained mustard gas. One of Michael's friends got exposed. It was horrible.'

'Did he make it?'

'By the skin of his teeth. They medevac'd him. The hospital induced a coma before the worst symptoms set in. That saved him a lot of agony. And probably saved his life.'

'Did Michael get exposed?'

'Not on that occasion. But he did, later. You see, however they come by chemical shells, the TEU has to dispose of them. If the area they're found in is inhabited, they have to move the shells before they can blow them up. And if there's some unusual feature, they have to recover them so they can be studied. That's what happened to Michael. He was transporting a pair of shells that the pointy heads wanted taken back to the Aberdeen Proving Ground. He had them in the back of his Humvee, heading to an RV with a Black Hawk. One of them leaked. It made him sick. He managed

57

to get back to base but the medics wouldn't believe his symptoms were real. He had no burns. No blisters. No missing body parts. He was accused of malingering, or treated like a drug addict because his pupils had shrunk. Anything to put the blame on him, not the army. He had spasms. Chest pain. He couldn't stop vomiting. His whole GI system was messed up. They finally sent him to Germany. To a hospital there. It took him weeks to recover.'

'That's harsh.'

'It was. The way they treated him was bad enough. But the real kicker? Michael, and his friend with the mustard gas, and a whole bunch of others who got hurt – the army refused to recognize them. There was no Purple Heart for them, either. You know why? The poison didn't leak out during an active engagement, so their injuries weren't deemed to have been caused by enemy action. It was like the army was telling them they did these awful things to themselves. And you know what? In the exact same circumstances, the Marines decorate their guys. It just wasn't right. Michael was demoralized. He left the army at the end of his next tour. He drifted for a few years, and I guess he went off the rails. I kept trying to reach out to him. But then I had problems of my own.' She patted her leg. 'And I was busy with my work.'

'What do you do?'

'I'm a lab technician. In a place near Huntsville, Alabama.'

'That the job that sent you to Afghanistan?'

She nodded. 'I went to supervise some sample collection. Stuff we had to bring back and analyse. My boss knew I was ex-army. He thought I'd be OK. I was out of action for a while, afterwards. Surgery. Physical therapy. And then I was a bit down for a while. A bit self-absorbed. But when I got Michael's message it shook me up. It was something I just couldn't ignore.'

'What did it say?'

'*M – help! M*. It was handwritten on the back of a card from a place called the Red Roan. It's a café, here, in town.'

'So you dropped everything and came?'

'I dropped everything. But I didn't come here right away. Old habits die hard. First, I did some digging. I got in touch with his friends. Some contacts of my own. Tried to find out what he might have been into. Where he might have been. Everyone said they didn't know. A few promised to ask around. Then a buddy from the 66th told me about a guy, kind of like an agent. If you were a vet and you wanted work, and you weren't too particular if it was legal, he could hook you up. I got in touch. Leaned on him. He admitted introducing Michael to Dendoncker. Indirectly. I pressed him some more and he admitted to placing a few guys with Dendoncker over the years. Sometimes Dendoncker just wanted anyone ex-military. Sometimes he wanted people with specialized skills. The guy recalled placing an ex-sniper who was an expert in .50 rifles. Michael got hired because he knew about land mines.'

'Sounds like Dendoncker could be smuggling weapons.'

'That was my first thought, too. So I came down. Poked around. But I couldn't find any sign of Michael or smuggling rings or other kinds of criminals. I got desperate. So I got back in touch with the agent guy and asked him to hook me up with Dendoncker. I expected an argument, but he was super-cooperative. Said I was doing him a favour. Dendoncker was in the market for another recruit. No particular specialty. Just had to be a woman. I was worried about what that could mean. But I figured my brother's life was on the line. So I said, all right. Set it up.'

'And you got the job, just like that?'

'No. My background was already legit but I made up a few false references to embellish it a little. Then I had an "interview". With Dendoncker's sidekick. A huge, creepy guy. He took me out into the desert and had me prove I could shoot and strip down a gun and drive.'

'Didn't Dendoncker connect you with Michael? You have virtually the same name.'

'No. We have different surnames. His was Curtis. Mine was too, obviously. Then I got married. I took my husband's name. And I kept it after he was killed. In Iraq.'

'I'm sorry.'

'Don't be. It's not your fault.'

Fenton looked away. I waited until she turned back to me.

I said, 'Dendoncker wanted Michael because he knew about land mines?'

'That's what the guy told me.'

'How's that connected to the catering business?'

'I don't know. My best guess is Dendoncker's some kind of procurer. He smuggles in whatever his customers want and sells it to them. He probably needs experts from time to time to evaluate the merchandise.'

'But Michael stayed on?'

Fenton nodded.

'You didn't come in contact with him, even when you were on the inside?'

'No. I tried, but I had to be discreet. Then two days ago I saw a woman I recognized. Renée. She was working at

Dendoncker's catering business, like me. With a different partner. She had different shifts. And she'd been there longer. She knew the lie of the land better.'

'Where did you know her from?'

'I didn't know her. I'd seen her in photos. Ones Michael had of his old unit.'

'She was at the place where the containers get loaded for the planes?'

Fenton shook her head. 'No. At the Red Roan. The place Michael sent the card from. I followed her when she left. Cornered her at her hotel. She admitted Michael was in town and still working for Dendoncker. But on some special project. She swore she didn't know what it was. Just that it involved Michael doing tests in the desert from time to time.'

'Land mines?'

'Maybe.' Fenton shrugged. 'So I asked this Renée to set it up for Michael and me to meet. She refused. Said it was too dangerous. She seemed genuinely terrified. So I asked her to at least give Michael a note for me. She agreed to that.'

'What did you write?'

'I kept it simple. I said, "I'm here. Contact me. I'll do whatever you need." And I gave an email address. One I'd set up specially. No one else knew it.'

'This was two days ago?'

'Right. She said she might not be able to get the note to Michael right away. Then an email came this morning. I knew Michael was in trouble the moment I read it. I feared the worst. But I had to find out for certain.'

'How did you know?'

'From the way the message was addressed. I had signed my note *Mickey*. That's what people who knew me as a kid

61

call me. The email that came which set up the rendezvous at The Tree? It was written to Mickey.'

'So? Michael obviously knew you when you were a kid.'

'You don't understand. When we were growing up we were always playing soldiers and spies. We started doing that thing from the movies where you only use the other person's real name if you're in danger. This note used my real name. So either Michael was in danger, or my note got intercepted and whoever replied didn't know our routine.'

'What happened to the woman who took the note?'

'Renée? I don't know. I went to her room at the hotel this morning, as soon as I got the email. Some of her clothes had been taken from the closet. All her underwear was gone. So were her toiletries. I think something spooked her. After she gave Michael the note. I think she ran for her life.'

TEN

Fenton's phone pinged and a moment later there was a knock at the door. She whispered, 'Pizza.' I moved along the side of the bed, where I'd be out of sight. I heard Fenton open the door and thank the delivery guy. Then she grabbed a towel from the bathroom, spread it on the bed like a tablecloth, and set down the giant square box.

We ate in silence. When we were finished I asked, 'You said Dendoncker inspects the bodies. Where? At the scene? Or does he have them taken someplace?'

'He always does it at the morgue. He likes the bodies properly laid out and examined. The whole nine yards.'

'Is the ME on his payroll?'

'I don't know. Could be, I guess.'

'That means to pull this thing off we need to clear three hurdles. To convince Dendoncker that one of us is a threat to him. To make him believe that person was killed. And to persuade the ME to cooperate. That's a big ask.'

'I came to the same conclusion.' Fenton brushed a crumb from her chin. 'I was thinking about it while we were eating. It is a big ask. But it's not impossible. And I have a way we can do one and two, if you play the role of the dead guy.'

'How?'

'OK. First hurdle. Make Dendoncker believe you're a threat. That's easy. All you have to do is play the part of Mickey. Dendoncker's already sold. He sent two guys to ambush him. Those guys didn't come back so Dendoncker must be doubly convinced that Mickey's a problem by now.'

I said nothing.

'Second hurdle. Make Dendoncker believe you're dead. That's harder, but still achievable. We do it by setting up another rendezvous with Mickey, which I will attend on Dendoncker's behalf. Then—'

'How do we set it up?'

'The foundations are already in place. Dendoncker must have gotten his hands on my note because he used the email address on it. But he didn't know I sent it or there would have been no need for the first rendezvous. He would have sent his guys straight after me. So I'll write another note. The handwriting will be the same, which will seal the deal.'

'Another note saying what?'

'That no one showed up today, so let's try again.'

'He'll know that's not true. At the least, he thinks his guys are missing. And if he has ears inside the police department he'll know they're dead.'

'Of course he'll know. But that's not the point. He won't care if Mickey is lying to him. All he'll want to do is eliminate

64

the threat he represents as quickly and cleanly as possible. What's he going to do? Leave Mickey out there, free to come at him whenever he wants, because he didn't tell the truth? No. He'll jump at the chance to take him out. He'll agree to the rendezvous and pull a double-cross. Again.'

'Say you're right. Say he agrees. Then what? He sends another couple of guys? Maybe more?'

'No. In the note I'll say Mickey knows he's not communicating with Michael. But he's willing to pay ten thousand dollars for information about Michael's whereabouts. And he will only deal with me.'

'How will you get the note to Dendoncker?'

'I'll give it to his deputy. I'll ask to meet him. Tell him I was approached by a guy outside the Red Roan. I'll describe you. That'll be plausible because they must assume the last note was brought to Michael by Renée, since she's gone missing. And if they bite, they'll offer another rendezvous. We'll both show up. And I'll shoot you. At least, that's what I'll report to Dendoncker.'

I thought for a moment. 'There's a big risk for you if they don't buy it.'

'I don't think so.' Fenton counted off on her fingers. 'The scenario, with someone getting one of Dendoncker's crew to carry a note? A match. The handwriting on the note? A match. The email address for Dendoncker to reply to? A match. The note leading to a rendezvous? A match. The set-up is plausible. I can sell it. I've done this kind of thing before, remember. Many times.'

I didn't reply.

'OK,' Fenton said. 'Yes. There is a risk. But whether to accept it is my choice.'

'That's fair. And getting them to set up a rendezvous might work. But what if they send someone with you? Or they have someone hidden, watching? You can't just report a shooting. We need to stage one. And we need it to look real.'

'That's easy enough. I've done it before. In Kosovo, years ago. I was there on a mission. We needed leverage over a local gangster so we made him believe he'd killed a guy who we revealed was a US diplomat. All we had was fake blood in a special kind of bag, a detonator, a transmitter and some tape. The army provided the supplies, of course, but I know where they came from. A store in New York. I could have the stuff shipped here. The only other prop is blanks, and I already have some. I brought them with me. I didn't know what kind of things Dendoncker would have me doing and I thought I might need to avoid killing the wrong people.'

The trick with the blanks and the fake blood could work. I knew, from experience. Only not in Kosovo. And not with a diplomat.

I said, 'That leaves the ME. Could be a problem if he's loyal to Dendoncker. We'll have to tread carefully.'

'That's true. Although I'm sure he could be convinced to take a sickie. Given the proper encouragement.' Fenton winked at me. 'But that's maybe best left until last. We should see if Dendoncker bites, first.'

'We also need a wound that looks convincing. We need Dendoncker to believe it's real. Even if only for a minute.'

'No problem there, either. When operatives go under cover they often use a false wound to hide a handcuff key or a blade. That way, they have it even if they get captured and stripped. It works, even if they get searched. Psychology

101. Humans instinctively avoid contact with wounds. You can get the stuff from the place that sells the fake blood. I'll add some to the order.'

Fenton cleared away the empty pizza box and lifted her case on to the bed. She opened it and took a card and a pen from a pocket in the lid.

'This is the same kind I used before.' She started to write. 'I took a bunch, just in case.'

After a minute Fenton put her pen down and showed me the card. There was a picture of a horse on one side. A red roan, I guessed. She'd written her message on the reverse, next to the café's address. It looked OK to me. I nodded. She put the card down, grabbed her phone, and tapped out a text.

'I said I've just been contacted by an angry stranger who asked me to carry a note to someone called Michael. Keep everything crossed.'

The reply came within a minute. 'All right,' Fenton said. 'That was Dendoncker's right-hand man. He wants to meet. He wants me to give him the note. We could be in business.'

She stood up and unfolded a jacket from her case. To conceal her gun.

I said, 'Where are you meeting?'

'The Border Inn.' She turned to the door. 'My other hotel. It's a regular-type place. I'm booked under my real name, but it's just for show. I never stay there. Don't worry. I'll be back soon.'

The door closed behind her and the room was suddenly quiet. It felt empty, with just a hint of her perfume to remind me she'd been there. I went back to the couch and lay down.

I wanted to play some music in my head. That always helps to pass the time. I figured John Primer would fit the bill. He backed Muddy Waters until he died. Then he backed Magic Slim for fourteen years until he died. John's music is as good as it gets. But try as I might, it wouldn't come. Because I was worried. About Fenton. That she would be able to sell our scam to Dendoncker's guy. Or worse, that she wouldn't be able to sell it. Then they'd kill her. If she was lucky.

I told myself to snap out of it. Fenton was ex-Military Intelligence. She'd have had extensive training in all kinds of black arts. She could no doubt convince anyone of anything. Only that thought made me more worried. I really knew nothing about her. Only what she'd told me. Which was what she wanted me to know. I got up and started to search the room. I didn't enjoy it. Even though she had invited me in, the old feeling of being a trespasser came back to me. I always used to feel it when I searched a dead person's place. I hoped it wasn't a premonition.

I went through her case. Everything was neatly folded or rolled. She had clothes. Toiletries. Extra ammunition for her Glock. A spare prosthetic foot. A blond wig. Glasses, with plain lenses. A field-dressing kit. But nothing that said she'd lied to me. I checked under the mattress. Along the seams of the curtains. Under the couch. And still found nothing. I went to sit back down but stopped myself. The solution was obvious. I should leave. Walk out and never look back. That would leave the plan dead in the water. It needed two people. There was no way Fenton could do it alone.

I took a step towards the door. And stopped again. If Fenton couldn't get Dendoncker, what would she do? I pictured her with a gun to her head. Again. I didn't like that image. I didn't like it at all. So I went back to the couch and waited in silence.

There was no sound of a key in the lock. Just a subdued click, seventy-two minutes later. Then the door swung open and Fenton appeared.

'I think they bought it.' She checked her phone. 'No confirmation yet. But I made progress while I was waiting for the guy. I ordered the fake blood and the other stuff we'll need. I expedited the shipping. It'll be here in the morning. I just hope they don't want to meet tonight.'

I agreed. But that wasn't all I hoped. We still had two hurdles to clear. I wanted it to stay that way.

ELEVEN

Fenton changed into blue silk pyjamas and climbed into the bed. I kept my clothes on and stretched out on the couch. She pulled a mask over her eyes and lay still. But I don't think she went straight to sleep. Her breathing wasn't right. It was too fast. Too shallow. Too tense.

I kept my eyes open and stayed awake for hours as well. Something was bothering me. I couldn't put my finger on exactly what, but red warning lights were flashing away deep in my brain. They stopped me from settling. I guess I finally dozed off at around four a.m. I got woken up again at seven. By Fenton, calling my name. She was sitting up in bed. Her mask was pushed up on her forehead. Her hair was dishevelled. And she was holding her phone at arm's length.

'Eleven p.m.' Her voice was husky. 'Tonight. They want to meet you. We've done it.'

This was not the start to the day I was hoping for. I'd been awake for fifteen seconds and already we were down to only one hurdle.

I said, 'You better reply. Remind them – just you, unarmed, and the deal is cash for information.'

Fenton fiddled with her phone for a moment. A minute later it made a *ping* sound. 'All right. They've agreed.'

After another minute Fenton's phone made a different kind of noise. It was an incoming text. Fenton read it then held her phone out for me to see. 'Hook, line and sinker. It's Dendoncker's deputy. Telling me to stand by for a job tonight.'

Fenton lay back on her pile of pillows and went to work with her phone. 'OK. I searched for MEs in this area. Only one name comes up. A Dr Houllier. He seems to be the doctor for everything here. He's based at the medical centre. The big building in the middle of the town. We'll wait for our delivery then head down there. It's due before noon. Should give us plenty of time.'

'We can't both go.' I sat up. 'The delivery. Will it need a signature?'

Fenton nodded.

'You better do that. I'll go talk to the doctor.'

Fenton did whatever was necessary with her phone to order some breakfast. I took a shower. I heard a knock at the door when I was getting dressed and when I came out of the bathroom I could smell coffee. It was sublime. There's nothing like the first mug of the day. Fenton had also ordered burritos. We ate in silence. Then I gathered up the paper plates, grabbed the sunglasses I'd taken from the guy at The Tree and started towards the door.

'No gun?' Fenton looked worried.

'I'm going to an official building. There will be metal detectors.'

'In this town? I don't think so.'

'It's not worth the risk. And I don't need one. If the doctor's straight, I'll persuade him to help. If he's in Dendoncker's pocket, it'll take more than a gun to convince him.'

I stepped out of the room and left the courtyard via the archway Fenton had driven through. It was a beautiful morning. Perfect for walking. The sun was bright but the temperature was comfortable. The last of the chill from the desert night was still to be chased away. The sky was so clear and so blue that if you painted it people would say you'd exaggerated the colour. The streets were narrow and winding and the buildings that lined them seemed old and honest. Like they'd sprouted years ago along the paths that people had walked with their donkeys or mules, or whatever animals they used to pull their wagons. There was no planning. No artifice. I could picture the people inside getting on with their lives, looking after their families, doing their jobs. I looked up at the roofs. Some had TV antennas but I could see no cell masts. That just added to the impression of a place that progress had passed by. Probably nothing substantial had changed for decades. Nothing, except the arrival of Dendoncker.

I found the medical centre without any problems. It was a solid, muscular building made out of pale stone. Pride had gone into its construction. That was clear. Real craftspeople had been involved. You could tell from the attention to detail in the doorway and the windows and the lintels. Inside, an ornate rendering of the staff of Hermes was set into the polished white floor. A large lamp shaped like the globe hung directly above it. The ceiling was domed. It was painted with scenes showing the history of medicine all the way from caves to hospitals, ending sometime before the Second World War. From its style the building could have been a courthouse or a library. But if you closed your eyes you would have no doubt you were in a hospital. The smell was unmistakable.

The reception area was unattended. There was a free-standing desk made out of rich teak. Its surface shone with years of polish. A laptop computer sat to one side, closed, along with a leather binder and a message pad. There was a directory in a frame on the wall. It was the old-fashioned kind with separate white letters pressed into the gaps between rolls of plush burgundy fabric. It made no mention of the morgue. Probably not the kind of place medical people like to advertise.

I went through a doorway to the side of the desk. It led to a corridor that was lined with plain wooden doors. They had numbers, but no names. There was a staircase at the far end. I went down. Partly because the directory had listed all kinds of wards and clinics and examination rooms on the upper floors. And partly out of instinct. It seemed fitting that the dead would be kept below ground.

I came out on to another corridor. It was bright. There were triple fluorescent tubes hanging from the ceiling at close intervals. But only one pair of doors. They were labelled *Morgue*. As I approached I could hear a voice. A man's. At first I thought he must have company. I couldn't make out all the words but when I picked up on the stylized way of speaking I realized it was just one person. He was

73

dictating. Probably medical notes. Probably into a machine. I raised my hand to knock. But I stopped myself. It was time to face facts.

Nothing I could say to the doctor was going to make a difference.

I turned around and went back up the stairs and out into the street.

TWELVE

I found my way to the Red Roan and walked past it. Just out of curiosity. It had a racing theme. It seemed incongruous, given its neighbouring buildings. And unappealing, so I continued to a diner further down the street. It was smaller. More down to earth. I ordered two black coffees to go and carried them back to the hotel. Fenton snatched the door open the instant I knocked.

'Well?' She let the door swing shut. 'Tell me.'

I handed her one of the cups. The bags of fake blood and miniature detonators and material to make imitation wounds were laid out on the bed. Her gun was there, too. There was a glass full of bullets on the nightstand.

'You switched to blanks?'

She nodded. 'Yes. But the ME? How did it go?'

Blanks were better than live rounds in a situation like that. But they were still dangerous, close up. Pull the trigger when the muzzle is in contact with your head and the jet of gas it emits can be fatal. I know. I investigated two cases in the army. One turned out to be a jackass playing the fool one time too many. The other was something else altogether.

I put my coffee down on the desk. 'Michaela, there's something we need to talk about. This plan. It's not going to work. It's time we thought about a plan B.'

'The ME wouldn't cooperate?' Fenton slammed her cup down on the nightstand so sharply it sent coffee spurting out of the slot in the lid. 'Why not? What was the problem? How hard did you lean on him?'

'I'm not going to lie. I didn't speak to the guy. There was no point. There are too many other holes in the plan. It's DOA. We need to find an alternative.'

'You said yourself there are three hurdles. The threat, the death and the ME. I took care of one and two. I can't believe you chickened out of three. I knew I should have gone myself. Never send a man to do a woman's job. I'll go now. I'll take care of it.'

Fenton reached for her gun. I stepped in her way.

I said, 'It doesn't matter which of us talks to him. Or if neither of us does. The outcome will be the same. The guy's either on Dendoncker's payroll, or he's not. He's well disposed to us, or he's not. We may need to persuade him, or threaten him, or bribe him. In any case, there's no guarantee of a result. Even if he agrees to help, can we trust him? What if he changes his mind later? What if he gets cold feet? And say he does stay away, how will Dendoncker behave? Will he poke the body? *My body*. Prod it? Stab it? Chop part of it off? Shoot it?'

Fenton didn't reply.

'And Dendoncker's unlikely to come alone. How many guys will he bring? What weapons will they have? Who else will be in the building?'

Fenton shrugged.

'And if we do snatch him, what about afterwards? We'll need time to encourage him to confess. Where would we go? How long would it take? Where's the nearest police station, when we're done?'

'I get the point.' Fenton crossed her arms. 'But it could still work.'

'It could. Nothing's impossible. I'd give it a fifty–fifty chance of success. No more. With a high risk of collateral damage.'

'I'll take those odds.'

'I won't. Not when there are alternatives.'

'There's no alternative. We must go ahead. OK. We'll swap roles. I'll tell them I'm sick. I'll play the part of Mickey at the rendezvous. I'll pretend to get shot. Let them take me to the morgue. I'll deal with Dendoncker myself when he shows up.'

'That won't work. If you're sick they'll send others in your place. Who will kill you, for real, unless you kill them first. Neither of which would help.'

'OK. So you go to the rendezvous too. Lurk around in the dark until everyone shows up. Then shoot me with a blank before anyone else has the chance. They won't care who fired as long as I'm dead. Or they think I am.'

'What happens when they check your pulse?'

Fenton was silent.

'Or if they give you a tap to the head, to make sure you're dead?'

Fenton opened her mouth, then closed it again without speaking.

I said, 'Why not get Dendoncker thrown in jail? There's a federal agent I know. You can trust him. You could work with him. Stay under cover. Provide intel. Isn't that what you trained for?'

'That would take too long. We have to do it tonight. I'll find a way. With or without you.'

'Why is this so urgent? The best way to honour Michael is to take the time to do it right. What about the vetting guys, for example? Who cleared Dendoncker for entry to the States. They must have plenty of muscle. And if they made a mistake, they'll want to put it right. To avoid embarrassment, if nothing else.'

'This isn't just about Michael. It never was.'

'No? Then who else is it about?'

'I don't know names. Innocent people.'

'The vets in Dendoncker's crew?'

'No. Random strangers.'

'Who? What kind of strangers?'

Fenton took a breath. 'Reacher, there's something I didn't tell you. I know what Dendoncker's doing with those planes. What he's going to transport in them. Bombs.'

'How do you know?'

'I know because Michael was making them.'

THIRTEEN

Fenton pushed the bags of fake blood aside and sat on the bed. She put her head in her hands. She rested her elbows on her knees. She was completely still for over a minute. Then she straightened up.

'I didn't lie to you, Reacher. I just didn't tell the whole truth.'

'You better tell it now. If you want me to reconsider.'

'OK. Rewind to when I left the army. I went into law enforcement. I joined the FBI. Became a special agent. Evidence processing was my specialty. I worked out of a couple of field offices, did well, and got assigned to TEDAC as a result. Do you know anything about it?'

'Not much.'

'It's the Terrorist Explosive Device Analytical Center. Think of it as bringing forensics to the battlefield. It began during the Second Gulf War. Our troops were taking a hammering. Someone got the idea of collecting evidence and sending it to Quantico. A team was put together to analyse everything that was brought in. They came up with ways to spot IEDs. To defend against them. Defuse them. Eventually they were able to identify the bombmakers. Sometimes right down to an individual. Sometimes to a factory. The recovered components tell a story. So do the techniques that are used. Even the way a wire is twisted can be significant. The team was so successful it expanded and moved to a new base in Alabama. Its scope expanded, too. Now it has a whole-world mission, with no constraints on time. Information is shared with partners. Arrests have been made all over the globe with TEDAC's help. London. Berlin. Addis Ababa. All in the last few weeks. Evidence is being brought in from more places, and from further back in time. Material from Lockerbie, Scotland, is on its way, I heard. And Yemen. And some already arrived from Beirut, that big barracks bomb, all the way back in the '80s.'

There was another weird echo from the past. I'd thought plenty over the years about the guy whose jawbone wound up in my abdomen. And the other Marines who died that day. But I hadn't dwelled too much on the physical evidence. I know it was examined thoroughly at the time. Picked over and combed through by experts, with all the best tools and techniques available back then. I figured once all the clues and leads had been sniffed out anything left would have been disposed of. Cleaned up. Thrown away. Preferably set on fire. I never imagined it getting brought back to the States, so long after all the bodies.

She said, 'There's an initiative to facilitate this kind of work. It's called ICEP. The International Collection and

Engagement Program. I was part of it. Specialists are sent to partner countries to help with training. That includes Afghanistan. Because of my background, I got sent there. To a scene that hadn't been cleared properly. It plays into a classic AQ tactic. They hide a bunch of devices. Some obvious. Some, not so much. The rest is history. For my foot, anyway.'

'That's why you moved to work in a lab?'

'Right. But I didn't leave the Bureau. I couldn't work in the field any more so they let me retrain. I'm a bio recovery technician now. Or I was. I pulled prints, but mostly from older devices. I recovered hairs, and anything that could yield DNA. It was uneventful, dull, but sometimes very satisfying. Like a month ago. We had a case involving a guy who used to work for a Kuwait oil company. A lead came in claiming that he was an AQI sympathizer. Al Qaeda in Iraq. The Bureau set up a sting operation and they got him on tape boasting to an undercover agent about how he used to build bombs in a basement in Abu Ghraib. They cross-referenced dates and places, pulled a bunch of evidence that hadn't been processed yet, and guess what? I pulled his print from a fragment of a roadside bomb. Gold star for me. Life in prison for him. I was happy with that result. Unlike my last case. An unexploded bomb came in. That's the holy grail to us. Everything is intact. It's a feast of evidence. This was no different. There were a bunch of stand-out things. First, it was found within the United States, not brought here from somewhere else. Second, it had a GPS chip in it, which we figure was to let the terrorists know when their target was near so they could detonate. But as a back-up. Because the third thing was it also had a transponder.'

'I don't know what that is.'

'OK. It's like this. There are two parts. One sends out a radio signal. The other bounces back a reply. One was in the bomb. The other would be carried by the target. Presumably without his or her knowledge. I think it was supposed to be the primary trigger.'

'What if something else sent a signal and triggered it?'

'They don't work that way. Each pair has a code. If the code doesn't match, nothing happens. Which is why I think it didn't go off. The other part of the transponder must not have come within range before the bomb was found. Which is fortunate. Because of all the lives that were saved. And because of the fourth thing in there. A fingerprint. Right on the transponder itself. It came to me for identification.'

'Whose was it?'

'It was Michael's.'

'What did you do?'

Fenton was silent for a moment. She looked at the floor. Then she looked at me. 'I was shocked, obviously. I double-checked the print. I triple-checked it. But there was no mistake. It was Michael's.'

'Could—'

'There's something else. I was also given the card from the Red Roan to examine. There was no writing on it. I made that part up, because I left the bomb part out. There was a condom in there, too. Still in its wrapper. I have no idea why. To make it look like random stuff had fallen in by accident, if one of Dendoncker's guys saw it, maybe? Anyway, I figured Michael was repenting. He wanted to stop. He wanted to get out. He knew where I worked. He knew what I did.

He knew I'd find his print. It was so prominent. And that's rare. Current bombmakers wear gloves because they know the kind of things we can recover now. So, and I'm not proud of this, I panicked. I destroyed his print. And the transponder. And the card from the Red Roan. And I quit. The rest you know. Everything else I told you is true.'

'Did you find out anything more?'

She closed her eyes, then opened them and shook her head. 'No. I never got to Michael.'

I took a sip of coffee and weighed up what Fenton had told me. A bomb had been found with a transponder hooked up to it. A fingerprint. A business card. And a condom. But no note. Something wasn't adding up. I said, 'The bomb. Where was it recovered from?'

'A private airfield.'

'Was that the target?'

'Don't know.'

'What size was it?'

'Small enough to conceal. Big enough to do a lot of damage. Depending on where it was detonated, if there were fewer than fifty casualties it would be a miracle.'

'What if it exploded on a plane? If the plane was the target, not just the transport. If it blew up over a city. Or a shopping mall. Or a stadium.'

'That's possible, but unlikely. The bomb we found was packed with shrapnel. That's an anti-personnel configuration. If a plane was its target we'd expect it to have a shaped projectile to ensure it could breach the fuselage or at least cause major system damage.'

'That's something, I guess. What about the timescale, if they have other bombs?'

She shrugged. 'Tomorrow. Next week. Next year. Can we afford to wait?'

'How many bombs did Michael make?'

She shrugged again. 'Could be any number. Distributed anywhere in the country.'

We were looking at hundreds dead, potentially. Maybe thousands. Dendoncker had the means. The opportunity. And there were plenty of groups out there with the cash to make it worth his while. All of a sudden fifty–fifty with a chance of collateral damage didn't look so bad. I drained my cup. 'Wait here. I'm going for a word with the ME.'

FOURTEEN

I walked faster. The sun was hotter. The buildings seemed closer together. The empty sidewalks narrower. The atmosphere was almost oppressive. I reached the medical centre and went straight in. The lobby was just as it was before except that there was a woman at the reception desk. It was hard to say how old she was. Not far from being the wrong side of retirement age, I would guess. Her hair was silver and it was wound up in an elaborate series of braids. Her glasses were pointy at the temples like ones I'd seen in pictures from the '60s. She had a discreet string of pearls and a neat cream blouse. She glanced up when I approached but when she realized I was heading for the door that led to the basement she looked away. A benefit of Dendoncker's people doing business there, I guess. But I wasn't happy about being mistaken for one of his goons.

I paused in the lower corridor and listened at the door to

the morgue. I could hear music. It was classical. Mainly piano. Something by Beethoven, I thought. I knocked and went in without waiting for an answer. Instantly I was hit by the stench. It was like an invisible wall. Made up of things I'd smelled before. Blood. Bodily products. Disinfectant. Preservative chemicals. But it was so strong it stopped me in my tracks.

Ahead of me there was a guy in the centre of the room. He had white hair. A white lab coat. Metal-rimmed glasses on a chain. And a pronounced stoop. Behind him was a row of steel doors. Five of them. To the side, a desk. It held a computer, which was switched off. A stack of blank forms. And a fancy pen.

Right at the guy's side there was a metal table. It was made of stainless steel. It had raised sides and a body was lying on it. A man's. It was naked. The top of its skull had been sawn off. Its rib cage cracked apart. Its abdomen cut open. Blood was running along the channels on both sides of the table and trickling down a drain. There was a trolley covered with tools. They were sharp and bloody. There was another trolley covered with jars full of red and brown gelatinous things, and some weighing scales. With a brain in its pan.

The guy took his glasses off and glared at me. 'At least you knocked. That's something. Now who are you? What do you want?'

He seemed like a straightforward guy, so I decided to take a straightforward approach. 'My name's Reacher. You're Dr Houllier?'

The guy nodded.

'I'm here to ask for your help.'

'I see. With what? Is someone sick? Hurt?'

'I need you to stay away from work tomorrow.'

'Out of the question. I've worked here for more than forty years and I've never missed a day.'

'That's an admirable record.'

'Don't blow smoke.'

'OK. Let's try this. There's a guy in this town I believe you're acquainted with. Waad Dendoncker.'

Dr Houllier's eyes narrowed. 'What about him?'

'Just how well acquainted are you?'

Dr Houllier snatched up a scalpel, still slick with blood, and brandished it at me. 'Cast an aspersion like that again and to hell with my oath. I'll cut your heart out. I don't care how big you are.' He gestured to the body at his side. 'You can see I know how.'

'So you're not a fan.'

Dr Houllier dropped the scalpel back on the table. 'Let me tell you a little about my history with Waad Dendoncker. Our paths first crossed ten years ago. I was here, working. The door flew open. And two of his guys barged in. No knock. No *excuse me*. They didn't say a word. Not right away. They just handed me an envelope. Inside was a photograph. Of my brother. Outside his house. In Albuquerque. You see, I'm not married. My parents have passed. Donald was the only family I had. And the guy told me, if I ever wanted to see my brother alive again, I had to go with them.'

'So you went?'

'Of course. They put me in a crummy old army Jeep. Drove out into the desert. Maybe ten miles. It's hard to tell out there. They stopped when we reached a group of men. Dendoncker. A couple of his guys. And two others. No one told me explicitly, but I worked out they were customers. There to buy hand grenades. They must have asked for a demonstration. A pit had been dug. Two people were in it. Both women. They were naked.'

'Who were they?'

'No one I recognized. Later the guy who drove me said they worked for Dendoncker. He said they'd disobeyed his orders. This was the consequence. Dendoncker threw in a grenade. I heard screams when it landed. Then an explosion. The others all rushed forward. They wanted to see. I didn't, but Dendoncker forced me. Believe me, I've seen injuries before. I've seen surgeries. Every kind of butchery you can imagine. But this was worse. What happened to those women's bodies . . . It disgusted me. I was sick, right there on the spot. I was worried that Dendoncker would expect me to deal with the remains, somehow. But no. A guy used one of the Jeeps. It had a snowplough blade on the front. He just filled in the hole. Dendoncker and his customers stayed there to talk business. The two guys who'd brought me took me back to the medical centre. They told me that the next day, or maybe the day after, a body would find its way on to my slab. They said I was to process it thoroughly, but not keep any official record. And to be ready to answer questions.'

'From Dendoncker?'

'Right.'

'And if you didn't go along?'

'They said there'd be another pit. That they'd throw my brother in it. And make me watch when the grenade went off. They said they'd cut my eyelids off, to make sure I saw everything.'

'The body they mentioned. It showed up?'

'Three days later. I couldn't sleep, picturing what kind of shape it would be in. In the end it was only shot. Luckily. For me, anyway.'

'How many since then?'

'Twenty-seven. Mostly shot. Some stabbed. A couple with their skulls bashed in.'

'Did Dendoncker come and see all of them?'

Dr Houllier nodded. 'He shows up every time. Like clockwork. Although he has calmed down a little. Originally he wanted a detailed analysis. Stomach contents. Residue on the skin and under the fingernails. Any indication of foreign travel. Things like that. Now he's happy with a brief report on the body.'

'But he still wants to see them?'

'Correct.'

'Why?'

'It could be one of several disorders. I'm not about to analyse him. It's not my field. And he gives me the creeps. Whenever he shows up I just want him out of my office as fast as possible.'

I said nothing.

'Strike that. What I really want is for him to stop coming at all. But I can't make him. So I find a way to live with it.'

'I have a way to stop him. All I need is this room.'

'If you're going to stop Dendoncker, and you're going to do it in this room, someone's going to play dead. You?'

I nodded, then told him about the gunshot wound to my chest and the props we were going to use to make it look real.

'Where is this shooting going to take place?'

I told him the location Dendoncker's guy had texted to Fenton.

'I see. And how are you going to get your body from there to here?'

I hadn't figured that out yet. When you're stuck with a plan full of holes, more have a habit of appearing.

'You don't know, do you?'

I said nothing.

'What time are you supposed to get shot?'

'It'll be a little after eleven p.m.'

'OK. I'll bring you in myself.'

'No. You can't be involved. Think of your brother.'

'Donald died. Last year.'

'Did he have a wife? Kids?'

'No kids. I don't like his wife. And she's sick, anyway. Cancer. Metastasized. If Dendoncker looked for her she'd be dead before he found out which hospice she's in. So. I'll give you a number for your sidekick to call me on. It's a direct line. It bypasses 911, which will make things easier.'

'Are you sure?'

'Yes. Now, Dendoncker won't come until morning. That means you'll have to sleep here. He may have people watching the place and it wouldn't do for a dead man to be seen leaving and returning. I'll come in early and get you ready for the meat locker. You'll have a companion, I'm afraid, so I can't raise the temperature. But I can give you a mild sedative so you won't start shivering. I'll tape your eyes, too. Just in case. How long can you hold your breath for?'

I'd once gone for a little over a minute without breathing. But that was under water. Swimming hard. Fighting for my

90

life. This would be different. No exertion. Just the effort of keeping completely still.

'Ninety seconds,' I said. 'Two minutes, maximum.'

'All right. I'll keep an eye on the time. I'll distract Dendoncker if he drags things out for too long. He's usually quick so I'm not too worried. Now, tell me. And you can be honest. After you stop him, what are you going to do with him?'

'Hand him over to the police.'

A flash of disappointment crossed Houllier's face.

I said, 'Does Dendoncker usually come alone? Or does he bring bodyguards?'

'Apes, I'd call them. Two. One comes in first to check the room. Then Dendoncker and the second guy follow.'

'Weapons?'

'None visible.'

'That's good. But even with your brother out of the picture, there's still a risk. To you. You'd be much safer at home. Or out of town.'

Houllier shook his head. 'No. Dendoncker's had the upper hand for too long. I promised myself, if I ever could resist, I would. I only have myself to worry about, with Donald gone. It seems like now is the time.'

'Thank you, Doctor. I appreciate that. But if you change your mind . . .'

'I won't.'

'OK. Until this evening, then.'

'One last thing, Mr Reacher. I'm a doctor. I swore an oath to do no harm. You didn't. Specifically, where Dendoncker is concerned. I hope you take my meaning.'

FIFTEEN

I got into position under the streetlight at eleven p.m., as agreed.

The evening was chilly. I'd been in the compound for three hours to make sure I was alone. I wished I had a coat. I only had on a T-shirt. A yellow one. It was huge. It was baggy, even on me. But it needed to be. It needed room to conceal the bag of fake blood I had taped to my chest. I couldn't risk a coat hanging wrong and ending up with no bullet hole where there should be one.

The car showed up at 11:02. Its lights were on bright so I couldn't tell the make or model, but I could see enough to know it wasn't a Jeep. Not what I was expecting Fenton to be driving. If Fenton was driving. I couldn't see inside, either. A moment later the front doors opened. Both of them. Two men climbed out.

Not what we'd agreed.

Both the car's back doors opened. Two more men climbed out.

Definitely not what we'd agreed.

I sized the guys up. They were all between maybe six one and six three. Each around two hundred pounds. I didn't see anything to worry me. But I was mainly waiting to see if Fenton appeared from the back seat.

She didn't.

Either she'd been benched because Dendoncker had opted for more firepower after losing two guys the day before. Or she'd been taken out of the game for good, if Dendoncker had seen through our ploy. I doubted any of the guys in front of me would know. Paranoid bosses don't generally share insights with their wet boys. So I decided on a different approach. Whittle down the numbers and persuade the last man standing it was in his interests to escort me up the food chain.

The last man standing wasn't going to be the driver. That was for damn sure. He stepped forward and immediately launched into a dumb routine designed to get me into the car. That wasn't going to happen. Not then, anyway. The guy realized he couldn't bluff me so he changed tack. He tried to use force. He pulled a gun. That's always a mistake when you're within arm's length. Or near it. Maybe he mistook size for slow. Maybe he was just stupid. Or overconfident. Either way I closed in fast, grabbed his wrist and neutralized his weapon. Then I neutralized him with a quick, easy punch.

I retrieved the driver's fallen gun in case the other guys were smart enough to attack together. They weren't. The one in the centre of the remaining trio was the next to try. He screamed like he thought that would frighten me, feinted a jab, then tried to land a punch in my gut. I blocked it and drove my middle knuckle into his bicep. I gave him the option to walk away. I figured that was only fair. He didn't take it. He rushed back in with a wild, crazy punch aimed at my head. I let it flail past, then immobilized his other arm. I gave him another chance. He repaid me by trying to kick me in the balls. He didn't get close. I slammed my foot into his shin. Used his effort against him. The guy's ankle broke. At least one bone. Maybe more. He screamed and hopped around for a second, then fainted when the severed ends of his bone touched together. Now I was down to two.

These guys tried to raise their game. They fetched axe handles from their trunk. The taller of the pair led off with a monster swing. He missed by a mile. Then his buddy weighed in. He started jabbing. Two feints to begin with, then he went for my gut. But he telegraphed it. I grabbed the axe handle, wrenched it out of his hands, spun it around, and smashed it down on to the top of his head like I was chopping wood.

The final guy panicked. He took a couple of wild swings but there was no hope of him connecting. He must have figured that out because he went for his gun. But like the driver, he was too close. I knocked the gun out of his hand. I grabbed hold of his neck. I started to outline his options. Then I heard a voice ordering me to stop.

It was Fenton. She emerged from the cover of the row of garages to my right. Her arms were stretched out and she was holding her gun with both hands. She was trying to resurrect our plan. But the last guy was standing between

94

us. That wasn't ideal. He was a witness, now. He wouldn't believe I'd been shot if Fenton's bullet would have had to pass through him to hit me. I could throw him aside but that would have been suspicious, too. It would be more realistic to pull him closer. Use him as a shield.

I looked at Fenton. Glanced down at my chest. Figured she could see the right area. Or close enough, anyway. Taking the shot was the best bet in the circumstances. I willed her to do it. I saw her breathe and exhale. I braced myself for the sound. I felt a flick on my chest first, then cold dampness. I threw myself back. I've seen plenty of people get shot dead. Some crumple and end up like they're asleep. Some fly through the air and end up in a contorted heap. I aimed for somewhere in the middle. I pushed my arms out wide, kept one knee raised and snapped my head right back.

'Didn't need me, huh?' Fenton was coming closer. 'Don't worry. There's no rush. You can apologize in your own sweet time. Just make it good.'

'What the hell did you do?' The guy sounded mad. 'Dendoncker wanted him alive. He had questions.'

Fenton paused for a moment. 'Dendoncker wanted *him* alive? Huh. Well, if I hadn't shown up this guy would have been the only one who was alive. Those three idiots are down and you weren't far behind.'

I felt fingers on my neck. They were long. Slim. A little cold. I felt myself shiver.

'Anyway, he's dead. No point crying about it.' Fenton reached around and pretended to check my back pockets. 'Like I thought, no cash. It was a set-up from the start. What an asshole. OK, I'll call 911 and get the body picked up. You

95

can call it in to Dendoncker. Throw me under the bus if you want. On one condition. You load up your buddies. I have a long walk back to my car after the ambulance shows up.'

SIXTEEN

I've spent more nights than I can count in weird, uncomfortable places, but never until then in a morgue. It was actually less uncomfortable than I expected. Physically, anyway. Dr Houllier brought me a bed roll, a sleeping bag and an eye mask like you get on commercial flights. He left me to sleep, then came back in at six a.m. He brought me some coffee and while I drank it he got busy making the simulated gunshot wound for my chest out of the special clay. He made sure to get the size just right. The shape. The ragged edges. The colours, which were a mixture of angry red and congealed brown. When he was happy he stuck it on to me. Then he gave me my shots. One in each arm. Each leg. My chest. And my stomach. He cleared away my bedding and hid it behind the right-hand fridge door. Then he checked the clock on the wall.

'OK. It's time.'

He opened the centre door and pulled out the sliding rack. I took my clothes off. He hid them along with the bedding. I lay down. He threw a sheet over me and stuck my eyelids down with some kind of tape.

He said, 'Good luck. Try not to trash my morgue when Dendoncker gets here.'

He pulled the sheet up over my head and pushed the rack into the refrigerator. All the way. I heard the door shut. I could sense the light being shut out. I could feel the darkness. The skin between my shoulders began to prickle. I hate enclosed spaces. Always have. It's something primal. I forced myself to picture the void all around me. Behind the doors the refrigerator was a single unit. Not individual compartments. There was plenty of room. I began to feel better. Until I remembered the chopped-up body. I wondered which side it was on. Part of me wished I could see. Most of me was glad I couldn't.

I'd been inside for close to an hour when the refrigerator door opened. There was no notice. I suddenly sensed light. The rack rolled out. Smoothly and gently. The sheet was pulled back from my face. I heard a voice. It was nasal, and it gave hard edges to the word 'Move.' The sheet was whipped off the rest of the way. I heard it settle on the floor. Then the nasal voice spoke again. I guessed it was Dendoncker. He questioned what had killed me. Dr Houllier replied. There was talk of my older wounds. The scars they'd left. What might have caused them. What else they knew about me.

Sixty seconds without a breath. Uncomfortable. But manageable.

The sheet covered me again. My body. Then my face. But

before I could inhale it was torn back off. There was a debate about my pretend fake ID. My real ID. My real name. Questions and answers, back and forth. Then I felt Dendoncker come closer. I couldn't see him but I knew he was staring at me.

Ninety seconds without a breath. I needed air. Badly. My lungs were starting to burn. My body was desperate to move.

I heard Dendoncker make a comment about me looking for him, not Michael. So he was narcissistic as well as paranoid. A charming combination. No wonder he didn't play well with others. I heard papers rustle. More questions. Then talk about burning my passport. Dumping my body. Dendoncker's voice was louder and sharper, like he was giving orders. It sounded like he was wrapping things up.

Two minutes without a breath. My lungs were done. I took a huge gulp of air. Pulled the tape off my eyes. And sat up.

There were four people in the room. All men. All with their mouths open in shock. There was Dr Houllier, at his desk. Two guys in suits, maybe in their forties, near the door. And one in the centre, facing me. He looked like he was in his sixties. He had an angular face with a burn scar on his left cheek. It was triangle-shaped. He had bulging eyes. Abnormally long arms and legs. Three fingers were missing from his right hand. He was using his thumb and remaining finger to pinch the bezel of his watch. I said, 'Dendoncker?' He didn't react. I jumped off the tray. He fumbled in his jacket pocket. Produced a gun. A revolver. An NAA-22S. It was a tiny little thing. Less than four inches long. I took it from him, tossed it into the refrigerator, and shoved him towards the back corner of the room. I wanted him well away from the door. I wanted no chance of him sneaking out while I was dealing with his goons. Both were approaching me. A pale-suited, curly-haired one on my left. A dark-suited, straight-haired one on my right. There was two feet between them. They were reaching under their jackets. Going for their guns. But they never got the chance to draw. I moved towards them, fast. Pulled back both fists. And punched them both in their jaws simultaneously. Maybe not the hardest blows ever. I felt like the sedative shots had affected me a little. Taken a few per cent off the total. Not that it mattered. My forward motion combined with their movement towards me made it like they'd walked into the front of a truck. They landed together in a tight tangle of arms and legs. They weren't moving. I turned to check on Dendoncker and saw him standing in the corner. I had a momentary impression of a stick insect in a cage at the zoo.

I heard a sound. Behind me. From the door. It was flung open like a gas main had blown someplace nearby. A guy stepped through. I got the impression he had to turn sideways to fit, he was so broad. And he was tall. Six feet six, minimum. I would guess at least three hundred and fifty pounds. He had no hair. His head was like a bowling ball. His eyes and mouth and nose were small and pinched, and they were all crammed together at the front. He had tiny protruding ears. Shiny pink skin. A black suit with a white shirt and no tie. Which was a shame. Ties can be useful for strangling people.

The guy started moving forward. He had a weird,

stomping, staccato motion like a robot. As he came closer his steps turned into kicks and his arm swings turned into punches. He was steady and repetitive and relentless, like he was doing a martial arts demonstration. It was mesmerizing. No doubt devastating if one of his blows connected. And deadly, if more than one did.

I stepped back to buy a little time. Dendoncker tried to scuttle past. I grabbed him and threw him behind me. I didn't look to see where he landed. There was no way I could risk taking my eyes off the human bludgeoning machine that was closing in on me. Dendoncker tried to creep by on the opposite side. I shoved him back again. The huge guy was still coming. I figured he wanted to toy with me for a while, back me up against the wall or into the corner and then pummel the life out of me when I could retreat no further. He didn't seem worried about keeping out of range of anything I could throw at him.

I took another step away. Then I launched myself the opposite way off my back foot and darted around him. I jabbed him in the kidney on my way past. It was a decent blow. It would have floored a lot of people. This guy showed no sign of even noticing it. He took another step then went into some kind of elaborate turning routine. His arms crossed and recrossed and finally opened the opposite way. He pivoted on the balls of his feet. He pushed off the floor and threw another kick, but I was already moving. I had turned faster. Pushed off the floor harder. I charged, head down, before his next kick.

I slammed into his chest, hard enough to throw him back, despite the difference in weight. He staggered. I tried to line up a punch before he could recover. I was

101

thinking, his throat. This was no time for gentlemanly conduct. But before I could launch anything the guy's legs connected with the fridge rack. It was still extended. He toppled back on to it. The force was enough to release the latch and it started sliding. He had landed at an angle so he wouldn't fit through the door. His head slammed into the frame. Not hard enough to knock him out. But enough to stun him. For a moment. And a moment was all I needed.

I followed in and scythed my elbow down into the side of his head. I used all my strength. My full weight was behind it. It was a perfect connection. His arms and legs bounced up like a bug's then flopped down and dangled off either side of the rack. His tongue lolled out of his mouth. I waited a moment, to be sure. Then I turned to check on Dendoncker.

There was no sign of him. Aside from Dr Houllier and the three unconscious guys, the room was empty.

'She was so quick.' Dr Houllier's voice was flat. 'A woman. With a limp. She put a gun to Dendoncker's head. Dragged him out of here. She left this.'

Dr Houllier passed me a grocery store bag. Inside was the shirt I was wearing before swapping it for the baggy yellow one, which by then was ruined, and a single sheet of paper. I unfolded it. There was a handwritten message:

Reacher, I'm sorry. I was late to the rendezvous because Dendoncker sent me on a bullshit errand. And I didn't set out to use you. I hope you don't feel that way. But I have a feeling things could get very ugly, very soon, and there are lines I can't ask you to cross.

I'm glad we met, even briefly. I hope you make it to the ocean soon.

xoxo

PS You saved my life. I'm grateful, and I will never forget.

SEVENTEEN

I screwed the note into a ball and tossed it into the trash. Peeled the fake bullet wound off my chest. Pulled the shirt Fenton had brought over my head. Crossed to the right-hand refrigerator door. The one where Dr Houllier had stashed my clothes. Opened it and got dressed the rest of the way. And then retrieved my passport from his trash can.

'Where are you going?' Dr Houllier said. 'Wait a minute. What are you going to do about the woman? And Dendoncker?'

The way I saw it, I had two choices. I could let Fenton go. Or I could try to find her. And I couldn't see any point in finding her. I had no doubt she could handle herself when she was up against one old frail guy. Or numerous strong young guys, if that was how things shook out. I had no doubt she would do whatever she saw fit to stop Dendoncker's bombs.

She had the contacts. She just needed information. How she got it was up to her. Maybe she would cross a line. Maybe a whole bunch of lines. But that was her call. I wasn't her conscience, and I wasn't her priest. My nose was a little out of joint, the way she blindsided me. But at the same time I had to say, *nicely played.* The truth was, I liked her. I wished her the best.

'I'm not going to do anything about either of them,' I said. 'If Fenton wants to handle things from here, I'm happy to let her.'

'Oh.' Dr Houllier scratched the side of his head. 'Then what about these apes? You can't leave them on my floor. Especially not that big one. I treated him after one of his victims bit him and his arm got infected. He's called Mansour. He's a psychopath. What will he do when he wakes up and finds me? It's obvious I helped you.'

'Don't worry. I'll take the trash out when I leave. You won't see these guys again.'

I started with the guy Dr Houllier had called Mansour. I checked his pants pocket and found what I was looking for straight away. His keys. A big bunch on a plastic fob. With one kind in particular. A car key. The logo moulded into the plastic grip said *Lincoln.* I hoped it was for a Town Car. They're spacious vehicles. Plenty of room for passengers. Conscious or unconscious. Alive or dead. That fact was established almost immediately after the first model rolled off the production line. They'd been popular with people who appreciated that quality ever since. People like me, at that moment.

I figured I could tie the three guys up. Load them in. Dump the car. And call 911. I bet they all had pretty substantial records. Although I wasn't impressed with the way the police had responded to my report of the bodies by The Tree. I hadn't seen a single uniformed cop in the town. Or a detective. Or a crime scene truck. It made me think of a conversation I had recently with a guy in Texas. He had a theory. He said that in remote regions any officer sent to deal with something messy like a bunch of dead bodies must be on his boss's bad side. Which meant he wouldn't be looking to carry out a thorough investigation. He'd be looking to get the case closed, quickly and tidily. To get back in his boss's good graces. And to make sure someone else would get sent the next time there was a problem out in the sticks.

Maybe the guy had been right. Maybe I'd be better dumping the car somewhere further away. At the side of the highway. Or in a bigger town. Or a city. I didn't want to invite extra work. But I did want the right result. And on top of that, I was hungry. Making plans on an empty stomach is a bad idea. It can distort your priorities. I figured I should grab something to eat, then decide.

I said, 'It's been a busy morning. I could use some breakfast. Want to join me?'

Dr Houllier pulled a face like he'd smelled something vile. 'Eat? Now? No. No, thank you. I couldn't.'

I tried to slip Mansour's keys into my pocket but the bunch got all snagged up. It was big. And heavy. When I tried to streamline it one key in particular stood out. A mortice. It was similar to the ones the guys had been carrying yesterday.

I said, 'Which place around here has the best coffee?'

Dr Houllier blinked a few times. Then he shrugged. 'You could try the Prairie Rose. I've heard theirs is good. Turn

106

left out of the main exit. Walk a hundred yards. You can't miss it.'

'Thanks. I'll do that.' I glanced around the room. 'Have you got anything I could use to tie these guys up?'

Dr Houllier thought for a moment. 'Wait here. I have an idea.' Then he hurried out through the door.

I used the time to work my way through Mansour's other pockets. I found his wallet. He had cash, but no ID. Nothing with an address. I tried his phone. It asked for a Face ID. I had no idea what that was but on a whim I held it level with the guy's nose. After a second its screen unlocked. There was no record of any calls being received. Or made. There were no texts. And no contacts. Nothing to help me, so I took his gun and moved on to the guys in the suits. They had a similar range of stuff. Guns, wallets, phones and keys. Including plastic fobs. And a mortice key. The keys were scuffed and scratched. I held them up next to one another. The teeth lined up. They were a perfect match. I tried Mansour's. It matched just as well. I figured the keys must be connected to Dendoncker's operation in some way. I was curious, but the question didn't need to be answered. Dendoncker was at the wrong end of Fenton's Glock. His crew were heading to jail. And I would be on my way out of town as soon as I had eaten.

The door swung open. There was no knock, but it was pushed gently this time. Dr Houllier appeared in the gap. He was clutching a bunch of packages. They were identical. Wrapped in clear packaging. And they were slippery. He tried to pass one to me and the whole lot fell and went skittling across the floor. I helped him gather them up and saw they were crepe bandages. They each had a manufacturer's logo and a sticker indicating their size. Four inches wide by five feet long.

'They're elasticated,' Dr Houllier said. 'They'll stretch, but they shouldn't break. They're full of polyurethane fibres. They're added to the cotton. It makes them strong. In most places they're used to immobilize limbs. After a sprain, normally. Here we need them for snakebites. You have to bind the area around a wound really tight to stop the venom from spreading.'

I opened one of the packets and tried to break the material.

'If you double it up it'll be even stronger,' Dr Houllier said.

I used the first bandage to tie Mansour's ankles. I checked the knot and figured Dr Houllier was right. It should hold. I secured Mansour's hands behind his back. Then I did the same with the guys in the suits. Dr Houllier watched me work and when I was done he scooped up the pile of empty wrappers and dumped them in the trash. I dropped the guys' guns and wallets and other stuff in the clinical waste bucket.

I said, 'If I was a secretive person and wanted to get in and out of the building without being seen, how would I do it?'

'Through the ambulance bay. The way I brought you in last night.'

'I was in a body bag last night. You could have brought me down the chimney for all I could see.'

'Oh. Of course. Well, it's all the way at the rear of the building. It's on its own. It has a separate entrance from the street. There's a gate, but it's not locked and you can't see in from the outside. The doors are automatic and the corridor bifurcates before you get to the ER. One branch leads to an elevator which comes straight down to the basement. As long as a casualty isn't incoming at that moment no one would have a clue you'd been there.'

'Security cameras?'

Dr Houllier shook his head. 'It's been proposed a couple of times, but never acted on. Privacy issues. That's the official line. But there's also the question of budget. That's the real reason, if you ask me. Come on. I'll show you.'

I followed Dr Houllier out of the morgue and along to the far end of the corridor. He hit the call button for the elevator. We waited side by side, in silence. The doors jerked open after less than a minute. The elevator car was spacious. It was broad and deep and lined with stainless steel. We rode up one floor then stepped out and followed another corridor around to a pair of tall glass doors. They slid apart as we approached and dumped us out into a rectangular court-yard. A series of red lines was painted on the flaking asphalt. I figured they marked the route for ambulances. One arc to turn, and another to reverse into the unloading zone. There was ample space for two emergency vehicles. And tucked in next to the wall on the right side, facing away from the entrance, there was a lone sedan. A Lincoln Town Car.

I clicked a button on Mansour's key fob and the car's blinkers flashed. The locks in all the doors clunked open. It was the old style, square and severe. It was black. *Ubiqui-tous black*, the official name in the brochure should have been. And as a bonus it also had blacked-out windows. Maybe because of the climate. Maybe because of Dendon-cker's paranoia. Or maybe just because he thought it looked cool. I didn't know. And I didn't care. Because it meant no one would be able to see inside. The town seemed pretty quiet. It was unlikely the ER would be overrun by a spate of wounded citizens at that time of day. I figured I could safely leave the car where it was for a half hour or so.

I locked the Lincoln and Dr Houllier led the way back to the morgue. He helped me to wrestle Mansour on to a gurney. I hauled him along the corridor and into the elevator and around to the ambulance bay. I continued across to the back of the car. Popped the trunk and half lifted, half rolled the guy inside.

I made a second trip and returned with the curly-haired guy in the pale suit. He was easier to manoeuvre. I wheeled him up close to the side of the car and slid him on to the back seat like a plank. Then I fetched the straight-haired guy in the dark suit. I tried to lay him on top of his buddy but he slipped off and fell face down in the footwell. I left him there and returned the gurney to the morgue. I thanked Dr Houllier for his help. Said goodbye, and headed for the medical centre's main entrance.

EIGHTEEN

The Prairie Rose was as easy to find as Dr Houllier had promised. It was still in the central portion of the town, right on the edge, in a building with two floors. It was also built around a courtyard. That seemed to be the fashion in the area. The café was on the ground floor. There was some kind of office above it and a store on either side. The interior was simple and square. There were twelve tables. Three rows of four, evenly lined up, each with four chairs. The furniture was solid and durable. The silverware was plain and functional. Nothing stood out, either good or bad. There were no flowers. No ornaments. No knick-knacks. No other customers. I liked the place.

I took a seat at the table on the end of the right-hand row. After a couple of minutes a waitress pushed through the door from the kitchen. She was wearing a pink gingham dress with a frilly white apron and a pair of New Balance sneakers. They were also pink. She looked like she was in her sixties. She had no jewellery. Her hair was less elaborate and it was grey rather than silver, but something about her reminded me of the medical centre receptionist. A sister, maybe. Or a cousin. She flipped over a mug and filled it with coffee from a glass jug, then looked at me and raised an eyebrow. I ordered a full stack with extra bacon and an apple pie. She raised her eyebrow a little higher but she didn't pass any other kind of judgement.

There were four copies of the same local paper jammed into a rack on the wall near a payphone. I took one and leafed through it while I waited. It was light on news. Every other page had either a new poll or the result of a previous poll. I guess the publisher thought reader interaction was more important than reporting. Or maybe it was cheaper. One thing they didn't skimp on was the graphics. There were pie charts. Bar charts. Scattergrams. Other kinds of diagrams that hadn't even been invented when I was in high school. All in bright, vivid colours. Addressing all kinds of topics. Should there be an armadillo sanctuary nearby? Should the border fence be repainted? Were there enough recycling facilities in the town? Should the community try to attract wind and solar power? Or oppose it?

I was on the last page of the paper when my food arrived. The *Police Blotter*. A fancy name for an account of all the crimes committed in the area recently. I read it carefully. There was no mention of Dendoncker. Or smuggling. Or planes. Or bombs. Just a few minor misdemeanours. Most of them were pretty tame. And most resulted in an arrest for public intoxication.

I ate my last morsel. I drained my coffee. I was waiting for another refill when the door to the street opened. A man walked in. I recognized him. He was the fourth guy from the previous night. Under the street lamp. Who had tried to bludgeon me. And who had seen me get shot to death. He didn't seem very surprised by my resurrection. He just walked straight up to me. He was wearing the same clothes. He hadn't shaved. And he was holding a black trash bag.

There was something inside the bag. It was at least nine inches long, and heavy enough to keep the plastic sides taut. I gripped the edge of the table. I was ready to shove it into his legs at the first hint of a weapon. But the guy didn't draw. He stood and sneered. Raised the bag. Gripped the lower edge with one hand. Flipped it over. And sent an item crashing on to the table.

It was a single piece, but it had three distinct sections. A socket. Shaped with carbon fibre. The kind of size that would fit a residual limb. A shank. Shiny, made of titanium. And a boot. Just like the kind Fenton had been wearing the last time I saw her.

'Follow me, or the woman will be missing more than part of her leg.' The guy turned and headed for the door. 'You have thirty seconds.'

I stood and pulled a roll of bills out of my pocket. I peeled off a twenty and dropped it on the table. Ten seconds had passed. I picked up Fenton's leg. Walked to the door. Another ten seconds had gone. I waited nine more then stepped outside. The guy was still there. He was standing next to a car. A medium-size sedan. It was dusty. I figured it was the same one they'd used the previous night. In daylight I could see it was a Chevy Caprice. An ex-police vehicle. The search light on the driver's door was a dead giveaway.

Its paint was wavy and dull so I figured it had also spent time on taxi duty.

The guy grinned and opened the passenger door. He stepped back and gestured for me to climb in. I approached. Slowly. I switched Fenton's leg to my right hand. Stepped into the gap between the guy and the car door. Then I grabbed the back of his head and smashed his face into the car roof. His mouth hit the edge of the doorframe. Some of his teeth were knocked out. I couldn't see how many. There was too much blood. I took his gun from his waistband. Hauled him around. Jabbed him in the solar plexus, just hard enough to knock the wind out of him. I pushed him into the car. Folded him into the seat. Closed the door. Checked that no one was watching. Moved around to the other side. Racked the seat all the way back. Climbed in. Stretched across and grabbed the guy by the throat. And squeezed. I felt his larynx begin to collapse. His eyes bulged. His tongue flopped out of his mouth. But he couldn't make a sound.

I said, 'Here's how this is going to work. I'm going to ask a question. I'll give you a moment to think. Then I'll relax my grip just enough for you to speak. If you don't, I'll choke you to death. Same goes if I don't like your answer. Are we clear?'

I paused, then eased the pressure on his throat.

'Yes.' His voice was a scratchy gasp. 'Crystal.'

'The woman got taken. How?'

'Dendoncker has a GPS watch. With a transmitter in it. He triggered an emergency signal. We caught the woman before she got out of the building. We brought Dendoncker to safety. That's priority one. When the others didn't return, Dendoncker sent me after you.'

'Where's the woman now?'

'Don't know.'

'Is this really how you want to go? Here? Now?'

'I don't know. I swear.'

'Where's Dendoncker?'

'Don't know.'

'Then where were you supposed to take me?'

'To the house. That's all I was told to do.'

'Address?'

'I don't know the address. It's just "the house". That's what we call it.'

'So you get me to this house. Then what?'

'I send a text. Someone will come for you.'

'This house. Is it far?'

'No.'

'In the town?'

'Yes.'

'OK. You can show me. We'll go there together. Then you can send that text.'

NINETEEN

I heard a sound. From further up the street. A vehicle engine. I looked around and saw a car moving towards us. Not fast. Not slow. Just cruising around. Looking for trouble. It was a Dodge Charger. Its hood and fender were black. It had a bull bar on the front and a slimline lighting rig on the roof. Clearly the police. Probably local. Possibly state. Either way, their timing sucked.

I let go of the guy's neck, dropped my arm into my lap, and made my hand into a fist. 'Make any kind of a move . . .'

'Don't worry.' The guy pulled a road atlas out of the gap next to his seat. He opened it wide and held it up so that it covered his face. 'From frypan to fire? I'm not stupid.'

The police car drew closer. It slowed down. Came along-side us. And stopped. Two cops were inside it. They weren't looking at me. Or the guy with the bleeding mouth. Yet. They seemed more interested in the Chevy. They weren't young. They might have had a vehicle like it, once. Maybe even that actual one. Cops used to say the Caprice was the best patrol car ever. Maybe they were nostalgic. Maybe they were bored. I just hoped they weren't suspicious. They sat and stared for a minute. Two. Then the driver lit up their roof bar and sped away into the distance.

I reached for the guy's neck. He closed the atlas. Raised it. He had both his hands behind it. The cover was shiny. It was slippery. My hand slid off its surface. I wound up grabbing his shoulder. He jabbed at my eye with the corner of the map, then wriggled free. He scrabbled for the handle. Got the door open. Dived out. Rolled over on the sidewalk then scrambled up and started to run.

I jumped out and followed him. The guy was fast. He was well motivated. I'd made sure of that. The gap between us was growing. He reached a cluster of buildings. Another courtyard arrangement. The windows facing the street were all boarded up. The guy should have kept on running. I would never have caught him. And I couldn't have risked a shot. Not in a residential area. But he didn't keep going. The lure of potential cover was too strong. He bolted through the archway. And disappeared.

I covered the remaining ground as fast as possible and stopped just before the entrance. I didn't want to risk presenting a silhouette. He could have had a back-up weapon. I crouched and peered around the corner. I saw a bunch of disparate buildings like the ones that had been made into Fenton's hotel. Only these had two storeys. They were joined together and boarded up with solid wooden panels, like a fence. There was a scaffold tower in each corner, leading to the roof. The process of conversion was underway.

117

But there was no buzz of activity. No sound at all. The work had stalled. Maybe it had been abandoned altogether. Maybe the market had crashed. Maybe tastes had changed. I had no idea how the economics for that kind of development worked.

I craned my neck a little further and I spotted the guy. He was standing alone in the centre of the courtyard, just looking around. I guess the place was not what he had hoped for. There was no way out. And nowhere to hide. He moved a couple of feet to the left, then to the right, like he couldn't decide which way to go. I straightened up and stepped through the arch. He heard me and turned around. His face was pale and the blood from his mouth was flowing faster. The price of exertion, I guess.

'Do what I tell you and you won't get hurt.' I kept my voice calm and even.

The guy took one step towards me then stopped. His eyes were flicking from me to the arch, back and forth, over and over. He was figuring the distance. The angles. Weighing the odds of getting past me. Then he turned. He ran for the scaffold tower on the right. He started to climb. There was no way I was going to follow him up. He was lighter. Far more nimble. He would reach the top long before me. There was no doubt about that. So I would emerge with my head exposed and no way to defend myself. He could have a weapon already. He could find something to use as one. A scaffolding pole. A hunk of masonry. A roof tile. Or he could just keep things simple and kick me.

Following him up was definitely out of the question. But so was letting him get away.

I ran to the tower on the left. I started to climb. Quickly, but carefully. I had to keep an eye on the guy in case he turned and went back down. I saw him make it to the top. He scrambled off the tower and disappeared. I made myself go faster. I got to the roof. Stepped out on to it. And steadied myself. The surface was slippery. The terracotta tiles were old. They seemed brittle. I didn't know if they could take my weight. The guy was almost at the far side. He must have been hoping there was another tower with access to the street. I doubted there would be one. I went after him. I tried to move smoothly. And I tried to be quiet. I didn't want him to bolt back the way he came before I was in a position to block him. He made it to the edge of the roof and peered over. I drew level. He turned towards me. His face was paler still.

I said, 'Come on. You're out of options. It's time to go down. Take me to the house. Then I'll let you walk away.'

'Do you think I'm crazy?' The guy's voice was shaking and shrill. 'Do you have any idea what Dendoncker does to people who betray him?'

He seemed on the verge of panic. I figured I would have to knock him out and carry him down. I would have to calibrate the punch very carefully. That would be the critical part. I didn't want to wait too long for him to come around, afterwards. I moved a yard closer. He turned away. And stepped off the roof. He didn't hesitate. Just plunged straight off the edge.

I figured there must be a tower there after all. Or a ledge. Or a lower building. Then I heard a sound. It was like a wet hand slapping a table in a distant room. I got to the edge and looked over. The guy's body was lying on the ground, directly below. One leg was twisted. One arm was bent. And a deep red halo was spreading around the remains of his head.

I crossed to the tower and hustled down to the courtyard. I went through the archway. Worked my way around the perimeter of the site. And finally found a route through to the far side of the buildings. The guy was lying there on the sidewalk, completely still. There was no point checking for a pulse. So I went straight to his pockets.

I found nothing with an address or an ID. But he did have a phone. It had survived the fall. He said he was supposed to send a text when he got me to the house. Which gave me an idea. If I could come up with a good enough reason, I could change the location of the rendezvous. To somewhere that gave me an advantage. And to somewhere I could find. I used the guy's fingerprint to unlock the screen. But the phone was empty. There were no contacts. No saved numbers. No messages to reply to. Nothing I could use. And there was nothing else in his pockets. I was at a dead end. So I wiped the phone with my shirt. Dialled 911 through the material. Tapped the green phone icon. Dropped the phone on the guy's chest. And made my way back to his car.

I started with the glovebox. I found the insurance and registration right away. They were the only two pieces of paper in there. Both showed the name of a corporation. Moon Shadow Associates. It was based in Delaware. Presumably one of the shell companies Fenton had mentioned. But whether it was or not, it didn't help me.

I found the page the town was on in the atlas. Nothing was circled. There were no marks. No addresses scrawled in the margins. No phone numbers written down. I tried the door pockets. The floor, front and back. The trunk. Under the carpet and around the spare wheel. There was nothing. No receipts from drug stores or gas stations. No carry-out menus or to-go cups from a coffee shop. The car was completely sterile.

I climbed in behind the wheel, trying to figure out where to look next, and something hit my thigh. It was the guy's keys. They were hanging down from the ignition. One was a mortice. It was scratched and worn. I compared it with the one on Mansour's key ring. It was identical. I'd thought it might be for a garage, or a store. But now I had another theory as to what it would unlock. And, I realized, another person to worry about. Ever since the guy had dumped Fenton's foot on my table at the Prairie Rose, I'd been completely focused on finding her. But the guy had known where to find me. That was clear. And there was only one way he could have found that out.

TWENTY

I knocked on the morgue door and went straight in. Dr Houllier was there. Alone. He was on the floor, slumped against his autopsy table. His head was on his chest. Blood was dribbling out of one nostril and the corner of his mouth. His lab coat was hanging open. Its buttons had been ripped off. His tie was stretched and askew. He'd lost one shoe. His right wrist was fastened to the table leg with a cable tie. I stepped towards him and he raised his head, then turned away. Fear flashed across his face. Then he recognized me and turned back.

'Are you all right?' He sounded breathless. 'Did that ape find you? I'm so sorry. I had to tell him where you went.'

I said, 'You did the right thing. I'm fine. But what about you? Are you hurt?'

Dr Houllier dabbed at his face with his free hand. 'It's nothing serious. Yet. The ape said he was going to get you,

122

then come back for me.' He shivered. 'And take me to Dendoncker.'

'That guy won't be coming back.' I crossed to the autoclave and picked up a scalpel. Then I went back to the table, cut the cable tie, put the scalpel in my pocket, and helped Dr Houllier to his feet. 'But others might. Do you have a car?'

'Yes. Of course. Would you like to borrow it?'

'Where is it?'

'Here. In the staff parking lot.'

'Good. I want you to get in it. And drive out of town. Directly out. Don't go home. Don't stop to buy anything. Can you do that?'

Dr Houllier touched his face again. 'I've worked here for more than forty years . . .'

'I know. You told me. But you have to think about your patients. You can't help them if you're dead. These guys are serious.'

Dr Houllier was silent for moment. Then he said, 'How long would I have to stay away?'

'Not long. A day? Two? Give me your number. I'll call you when it's safe to come back.'

'I guess the world won't stop spinning if I go away for forty-eight hours.' He crossed to his desk and scrawled a number across the bottom of one of his forms. 'What are you going to do?'

'Things you're better off not knowing about. They'll conflict with your Hippocratic oath. That's pretty much guaranteed.'

Dr Houllier retrieved his shoe, dropped his ruined lab coat in the trash, straightened his tie and led the way to his parking spot. A Cadillac was sitting in it. It was white. Maybe from the 1980s. It was a giant barge. It looked like it should have been in a soap opera with cattle horns on its hood. Dr Houllier climbed in. I watched him drive away then found my way back to the ambulance bay. The Lincoln was still there, exactly where I left it. I was relieved. Ever since I'd found Dr Houllier on the morgue floor a worry had been nagging at the back of my mind. I figured there was a chance Dendoncker's guy had come across it when he was looking for me. I opened the back door. The guys in the suits were awake. Both of them. They started wriggling. Trying to get out. Or trying to get me. And also trying to speak. I couldn't understand what they wanted to say. I guess their jaws were messed up. I took the scalpel out of my pocket and held it up so they would be clear what it was. I tossed it behind the guy in the dark suit's back, on the floor, where he could reach it. I threw Mansour's keys in after it. Then I closed the door and went back inside. I hurried to the main entrance. Passed the woman with the pearls. Crossed under the globe and the dome and emerged on to the street. I looped around the outside of the building to the place where I'd left the Caprice. It was in a gap between two smaller, municipal-style buildings diagonally opposite the ambulance bay's gate. I pushed a dumpster in front of it. It wasn't great cover, but it obscured the car a little. It was better than nothing.

It took me four and a half minutes to get from the Lincoln to the Chevy. After another nine I saw the ambulance bay gates twitch. They began to slide open. I started the Chevy's motor. As soon as the gap between the two halves was wide enough the Lincoln burst out on to the street. It turned right, so it didn't pass in front of me. I waited two seconds. That wasn't nearly long enough, but it was as long as I could risk in the circumstances. I swung around the dumpster and turned to follow.

The conditions were terrible for tailing anyone. I was in a car that might well be recognized. There was no traffic to use as cover. I had no team members to rotate with. The streets were twisty and chaotically laid out so I had no option but to keep close. Which was easier said than done. Whoever was driving the Lincoln knew where he was going. He knew the route. He knew when to turn. When to accelerate. When to slow down. And when he didn't have to.

I was pushing the Chevy as hard as I could but the Lincoln was still pulling away from me. It took a turn, fast. I lost sight of it. I leaned harder on the gas. Harder than I was comfortable with. The car pitched on its worn springs and the tyres squealed as I barrelled around a bend. A cardinal error when you're trying to avoid drawing attention. I made it around another tight curve. The tyres squealed again. But the noise didn't give me away. Because there was no one to hear it.

There was no sign of the Lincoln. Just empty asphalt leading to a T-junction. I leaned on the gas harder still, then slammed on the brakes. The tyres squealed again and I stopped with the hood sticking out into the perpendicular street. There was a little store in front of me. It sold flowers. A woman was tending to the window display. She glared at me then retreated from sight. I looked right. I looked left. There was no trace of the Lincoln. There were no signs to suggest that one way led to a more popular destination. No marks on the pavement to indicate one way carried more traffic. No clue to tell me which way the other car had gone.

I knew I was facing west. So if I turned left, the road would

125

take me south. Towards the border. Which was another dead end. If I turned right, it would take me north. It would maybe loop back to the long road past The Tree. To the highway. Away from the town. Away from Dendoncker and his goons and his bombs. But also away from Fenton.

I turned left. The road opened out. Stores and businesses gave way to houses. They were low and curved and roughly rendered. They had flat roofs with the ends of wide, round beams protruding from the tops of their walls. Their windows were small and they were set back like sunken eyes in tired old faces. All the houses had some kind of porch or covered area so the owners could come outside and still be protected from the sun. But no one was outside, just then. No people were in sight. And no black Lincolns. No cars at all.

Soon a street branched off to the right. I slowed and took a good look. Nothing was moving. There was a gap, then a street branched off to the left. Nothing was moving any-where along it, either. There was a longer gap, and another street to the right. Something blinked red. All the way at the far end. A car's brake lights going out after the transmission was shifted into Park and the motor was shut off. I made the turn and crept closer. The car was the Lincoln. It was at the kerb outside the last house on the right. A truck was stopped halfway along the street, next to a telegraph pole. It was from the telephone company. No one was working nearby so I pulled in behind it. I saw the three guys climb out of the Lincoln. Mansour had been driving. They hurried up the path. His keys were still in his hand. He selected one. The mortice, I guessed. Unlocked the door. Opened it. And they all disappeared inside.

I pulled out, looped around the truck, and stopped behind

126

the Lincoln. The walls of the house it was by were bleached and cracked by the sun. They were painted a deeper shade of orange than its neighbour's. It had green window frames. A low roof. It was surrounded by trees. They were short and twisted. There were no buildings beyond it. And none opposite. Just a long stretch of scrubby sand with a scattering of cacti leading up to the border. I took out the gun I'd captured and made my way up the path. The door was made from plain wooden planks. They looked like flotsam washed up on a desert island. The surface was rough. It had been bleached almost white. I tried the handle. It was made out of iron, pitted with age and use. And it was locked. I stood to the side and knocked. The way I used to when I was an MP. When I wasn't asking to be let in. When I was demanding.

TWENTY-ONE

There was no response. I knocked again. Still nothing. I took out the keys I'd found in the Chevy after
the guy jumped off the roof at the construction site.
Selected the mortice. Stretched out and slid it into the lock.

The key turned easily. I worked the handle and pushed the
door. Its hinges were dry. They screeched in protest. No one
came running. No one shouted a challenge. No one fired into
the gap. I waited for ten seconds, just listening. There was
nothing but silence. No footsteps. No creaking floorboards.
No breathing. Not even a ticking clock. I straightened and
stepped through the doorway. My plan was to shoot Mansour on sight. I had no desire to repeat our death match. And
I would shoot either of the others if they went for a gun. Then
I'd make the final one talk. Or maybe write, if his speech was
unintelligible due to his injured jaw. And finally I'd shoot him
too, in the interest of evening the odds.

It was cool in the house. The temperature was maybe fifteen degrees lower than outside. Whoever built the place knew what they were doing. The walls were thick. Made out of some incredibly dense material. The structure could absorb an immense amount of heat. That would make it comfortable in the day. And it would release the heat during the night, making it comfortable then, too.

The place also smelled musty. Of old furniture and possessions. It must have been a weird residual effect because there was nothing in the house. No chairs. No tables. No couches. And there were no people visible, either. The room I had stepped into was large and square. The floor was wooden. It was shiny with age and polish. The walls were smooth and white. The ceiling was all exposed beams and boards. Ahead there was a door. The top half was glass. I could see it led out to a terrace. It was covered, for shade. There was a kitchen to the right. It was basic. A few cupboards, a simple stove, a plain countertop made of wood. There were two windows set into the long wall on the right. They were small. And square. But even so they reminded me of portholes on a ship. There were three doors in the wall to the left. They were all closed. And in the centre of the floor there was something strange. A hole.

The hole was more or less circular. Its diameter was probably about eight feet, on average. Its edges were rough and jagged like someone had smashed their way through with a sledgehammer. The top of a ladder was sticking out. About three feet was visible. It was an old-fashioned wooden thing, angled towards the door I'd just come through. I approached it, treading softly, trying to make no noise. I peered into the space below. The floor was covered with tiles. They were

129

about a yard square. The walls were roughly boarded. There was a boiler. A water tank. And a whole bunch of pipes and wires. The pipes were lead. The wires were covered with cloth insulation. Anyone who lived there would be lucky not to get poisoned or electrocuted. The heating equipment looked newer, though. And large. Maybe too large for the original trap door. Maybe that's why someone had busted through the floor.

I walked around the hole. The full 360 degrees. I wanted to get a good look into all four corners of the cellar. No one was there. There was no one in the kitchen. I tried the first door in the left-hand wall. I kicked it open and ducked to the side. The room was empty. I guessed it had been a bedroom, but I couldn't be sure. There was no furniture. And no people. The next door led to a bathroom. There was a tub. A toilet. A basin. A medicine cabinet with a mirrored front, set into the wall. A drip from a dull metal faucet landed on a stained patch on the porcelain before trickling down the drain. It was the only thing I'd seen move since I entered the house. But I still had one room left to check. It was the furthest from the entrance. The most natural place to take shelter. Ancient psychology at work. I kicked the door. I guessed I'd found another bedroom. It was larger. Further from the street. More desirable. But just as empty.

There was nowhere else three guys could hide. There was no second floor. There were no other rooms. No closets. But there was one place I hadn't checked as thoroughly as the rest. One place I hadn't actually set foot in. I crossed to the edge of the hole in the floor. Looked down again. Still saw no one. I reached for the top of the ladder. Felt beads of sweat start to prickle across my shoulders. I didn't like the thought of disappearing below ground. Of the ladder breaking. Leaving me trapped. I pictured the Chevy, sitting outside. Its tank was three quarters full. I could leave the place far behind. Never look back. Then I pictured Fenton. Dendoncker. And his bombs.

I took a breath. Swung my left foot on to one of the rungs. Gradually transferred my weight. The ladder creaked. But it held. I swung my right foot over, two rungs down. Made my way to the bottom. Slowly and smoothly. The ladder wobbled. It flexed. But it didn't collapse.

I moved so that my back was to the wall and scanned the space. I was wasting my time down there. That was clear. There was nowhere one guy could hide, let alone three. The only cover came from the boiler and the water tank and I'd already seen them from above. No one was lurking behind either of them. I gave each one a good shove. Neither gave way. Neither was concealing a secret entrance to any kind of subterranean lair. I checked the walls for hidden exits. Examined the floor for disguised trap doors. And found nothing.

I crept back up the ladder. And crossed to the exit to the left of the kitchen. The door was locked. I tried the key. It opened easily. Beyond it another path snaked away to the street on the other side of the house. There was no sign of the three guys. And no sign of a car. I slammed the door. I was mad at myself. The guys weren't meeting anyone there. And they weren't hiding. The place was a classic cut-out. Designed to throw off a tail. As old as time itself. You go in one side. You come out the other. The guys must have had a vehicle stashed somewhere. They were probably gone before I was even out of the Chevy. And gone with them, any immediate hope of finding Fenton.

TWENTY-TWO

Losing contact with Dendoncker's guys was a setback. A major one. That was a fact. There was no denying it. There was no disguising it. And there was no point dwelling on it. What had happened, happened. I could rake over the coals later, if I felt there was anything to gain from it. But just then, all that mattered was picking up the scent. I had no idea where they had gone. They had a whole town to hide in. A town they knew a lot better than I did. Or they could have gone further afield. Fenton said Dendoncker was paranoid. I had no idea what kind of precautions he might take. I needed to narrow my options. Which meant I needed intel. If any was available.

I drove fast all the way to the arch which led to the court-yard at Fenton's hotel. The spot directly outside her room – the old wheelwright's shop – was free. I dumped the Chevy and jumped out. The next problem was getting the door open.

There was no physical key. No lock to pick. Just some weird code that showed up on a phone. Her phone. Even if I had it, I wouldn't know what to do. So I went old school. I turned my back to the door. Scanned all four directions. Saw no one on foot. No one in any vehicles. No one at any windows. I hoped what Fenton had said about knocking out the security cameras was right. Then I lifted my right knee and smashed the sole of my foot into the door.

The door flew open. It banged against the internal wall and bounced back. I turned and nipped through the gap before it closed. Inside, I saw Fenton's bed was made. The cushions had been straightened on the couch. And her suitcase was again sitting on the floor next to the door. I crossed to the window and closed the curtains. I took the chair from the desk and used it to wedge the door. It wouldn't withstand a serious attempt to get in but should at least stop the door swinging open in the breeze. I carried her case to the bed. Then I picked up the room phone and dialled a number from memory.

My call was answered after two rings. The guy at the other end was on a cell. His voice was echoey and disembodied but I could make out his words well enough.

'Wallwork,' he said. 'Who's this?'

Jefferson Wallwork was a special agent with the FBI. Our paths had crossed a little while ago. I had helped him with a case. Things had worked out, from his point of view. He said he owed me. He said I should call if I was ever in a bind. I figured this counted.

I said, 'This is Reacher.'

The line went silent for a moment.

'Is this a social call, Major? Only I'm kind of busy.'

'It's not Major any more. Just Reacher. I've told you before. And no. This is not social. I need some information.'

'There's this thing now. It's called the internet.'

'I need specialized information. A woman's life is on the line.'

'Call 911.'

'She's a veteran. She also worked for you guys. She got her foot blown off for her trouble.'

I heard Wallwork sigh.

'What do you need to know?'

'She worked at a place called TEDAC. The Terrorist Explosive Device Analytical Center. Do you know it?'

'I know of it.'

'She got wind of a plot to distribute bombs, here in the United States. There's the potential for a lot of people to get killed. The guy behind it is named Dendoncker. Waad Ahmed Dendoncker.'

'What kind of bombs?'

'I don't know. Ones that explode.'

'How many?'

'Don't know. Too many.'

'Shit. OK. I'll get the right people on it.'

'That's not all. The woman's missing. I believe Dendoncker's holding her. I believe he's planning to kill her. So I need all the addresses associated with him, and his business. It's called Pie in the Sky, Inc. You'll need to dig deep. He owns it through a whole bunch of shell companies. One's probably called Moon Shadow Associates.'

'This woman. What's her name?'

'Michaela Fenton.'

'Last known whereabouts?'

134

'Los Gemelos, Arizona. It's a small town, right on the border.'

'She's out there under cover? From TEDAC? That's not SOP. The nearest field office should be handling it. What's going on? Where's her partner?'

'She doesn't have a partner. She left the Bureau. This is more of a personal initiative.'

Wallwork was silent for a moment. 'I don't like the sound of that. The last former agent I know who went down the *personal initiative* route is now in federal prison. His ex-partner tried to help. It got her killed.'

I said nothing.

'All right. I'll try. But no promises. TEDAC's not the kind of place you mess around with. It's locked down tighter than a bullfrog's ass. They deal with some seriously sensitive shit. Ask the wrong person the wrong thing, it's not just the end of your career. You don't just get fired. You can wind up in jail.'

'I get that. Don't do anything to jam yourself up. Here's another angle you could try. I suspect Dendoncker is using his business as a front for smuggling. I don't know what, or who for.'

'OK. That might help. I have a buddy in the DEA. Another at ATF. I'll tap them up. When do you need this by?'

'Yesterday.'

'Can I get you on this number?'

'You should be able to. For a while, at least.'

I hung up the phone, made sure the ringer was on, and turned to the bed. I unzipped Fenton's case and flipped it open. Everything was neatly folded and rolled, just like before. A hint of her perfume floated up. I felt even more

135

intrusive than I had done two nights ago. I pulled her stuff out. There was the same combination of clothes and toiletries and props for changing her appearance. I found nothing new. No notes. No files. No 'If you're reading this . . .' letters.

The guns I'd taken from the guys at The Tree were missing. And she'd taken a couple of other things. The extra ammunition for her Glock. And her field-dressing kit. That made sense, given what she'd been planning. Everything else in her case was familiar. Including a stack of cards from the Red Roan. Like the one she said she found in the dud bomb, along with her brother's fingerprint. And a condom. Something about that had sounded off key when she told me. It still didn't ring true. I couldn't place why. It was like a discordant hum at the back of my mind. Faint, but there.

I started to replace Fenton's belongings and I uncovered her spare leg wrapped in a shirt. A thought hit me when I saw it. I felt a sudden surge of optimism. I rushed out to the car and grabbed the limb Dendoncker's guy had dropped on the table at the Prairie Rose. I brought it inside the room. Compared it with the one from the suitcase. Both had sockets made of carbon fibre. I ran my fingers around inside them, tracing the shape. The contours felt identical. Both had titanium shafts. They were the same length. The only thing that was different was the shoe. One was a boot. The other a sneaker. Not enough to prove that Dendoncker's claim to be holding her was a bluff.

I shook off the disappointment and finished repacking Fenton's case. I did it as neatly as I could. Replaced it by the door, ready to take to the car. Then I searched the rest of the room again. I checked every hiding place I had ever come across. Every trick I had ever heard of anyone using

136

to conceal stuff. And I found nothing. I was left alone with Fenton's leg lying in the centre of the bed and a digital clock on the nightstand. Its cursor was flashing despondently. It was counting the seconds. Seconds that Fenton may not have to spare.

I got brought back to the present by a sound. The phone, chirping away on the desk. It was Wallwork.

He said, 'Mixed progress. The smuggling? I got nowhere. My DEA guy quit last week. And my ATF buddy is out sick. Long-term. He got shot. But I do have better news about TEDAC. An old supervisor of mine transferred there. He trusts me. He'll help if he can. I reached out. He hasn't gotten back to me yet. But he will.'

'Addresses?'

'I turned up a bunch. All with connections to this Dendoncker guy's business. Most seemed like shells. I think you were right about that. I did find one that seemed legitimate. It's in the town you mentioned.' He recited a unit number and a street name.

'Where is that in relation to the town centre?'

I heard Wallwork's computer keys rattle. 'A mile west. It's a straight shot. Only one road goes out that way. It looks like Dendoncker's is the only building on that road.'

'OK. Anything else?'

'Not within five hundred miles. And nothing that isn't a lawyer's office or a PO box.'

'How about Dendoncker personally?'

'That's where things get stranger. There's no record of him owning any property anywhere in the state. I checked with the IRS. He does pay taxes. His returns are handled by his accountant. I found the address on his file.'

137

'Tell me.'

'It won't do you any good. I looked on Google Earth. It's a vacant lot. I'm trying to trace the owner, but so far it's just another bunch of shell corporations.'

'Is Dendoncker married? Is there anything in a wife's name?'

'There's no record of a marriage. Nothing about this smells right, Reacher. My advice is to walk away. I know you won't, so at least be careful.'

'There's one more place you could check.' I gave him the address of the house I had followed the Lincoln to.

Wallwork paused while he jotted the details down. 'OK. Will do. I'll get back to you the moment I learn more.'

TWENTY-THREE

I thanked Wallwork before I hung up the phone, but I was just being polite. The truth was his information was no use to me at all. Not in the short term, anyway. I figured his contact within TEDAC could bear fruit, in due course. He might help get an angle on Dendoncker's bomb plot. But my immediate concern was Fenton. Wallwork had only turned up one solid address for Dendoncker's business and I could tell from the location that it was one Fenton already knew about. It wasn't the place I was looking for now. That was obvious. It was too public for Dendoncker. His other employees went there whenever they had a flight to service. Fenton had been there for the same reason. And that was while she was actively searching for her brother. She would surely have found him if he was there. Which meant Dendoncker must have another site he used for his wet work. Maybe more than one. It depended on the scale of his operation. And I had an idea how to tap into that. It wasn't a sure thing. Far from it, in fact. But it was better than sitting around waiting for the phone to ring.

The Red Roan was busier than it had been when I passed by the day before. The lunchtime rush was still in full swing. There were two couples sitting outside. They were at round tables, perching on spindly metal chairs with brightly coloured cushions and off-white parasols. Another pair of tables had been pushed together at the edge of the patio. Nine people were crowded around them. They were all different ages. Smartly dressed. I guessed they were colleagues. Probably worked locally. Probably celebrating something.

Not the people I was looking for. I was sure about that.

A pair of tall double doors was standing open at the centre of the bar's facade. There was a hostess station to the right, just inside. It was unattended so I crossed to a U-shaped booth on the far side and slid around until my back was against the wall. The room was a broad rectangle. The bar and the entrance to the kitchen were at one end. The space between the booths and the windows was filled with square tables. They were scattered around apparently at random. Each had a potted cactus on it. The walls were roughly rendered with some kind of pale sandy material. They were covered with oversized paintings of horses. Some were being ridden by cowboys out on the plains, rounding up longhorns. Some were racing. Some were standing around, looking disdainful. There were ten other people in the place. Two couples. And two groups of three.

Not the people I was looking for. I was fairly sure of that.

Fenton had an advantage when she saw Michael's friend in there. She recognized her from a photograph. I didn't know any of Michael's friends. But I figured I had an advantage of my own. Experience. I was used to spotting soldiers in bars. Particularly when they were up to things they shouldn't have been.

A waiter approached. He was a skinny kid in his mid-twenties. He had curly red hair tied up in a bun on top of his head. I ordered coffee and a cheeseburger. I wasn't particularly hungry but the golden rule is to eat when you can. And it gave me something to do aside from flicking through a copy of the same paper I'd read at breakfast while I waited for more customers to arrive.

I sat and watched for thirty minutes. Both couples paid their checks and sauntered out. One of the trios followed suit. Another couple arrived. It was the receptionist from the medical centre and a guy in baggy linen clothes. He had white hair, neatly combed, and a pair of open leather sandals. They took a square table at the end of the room furthest from the bar. They were followed in by a group of four guys. They were wearing shorts and pale T-shirts. They were thin and wiry and tanned. They had probably worked outside their whole lives. They were probably regular customers. They took the table nearest the bar. The waiter brought them a tray of beers in tall, frosted glasses without needing to be asked. He stood and chatted with them for a couple of minutes then turned and smiled at the next customers who came in. Two women. One was wearing a yellow sundress. The other had cargo shorts and a Yankees T-shirt. They would both be in their mid-thirties. Both had brown hair down to their shoulders. Both looked fit and strong.

141

They moved with easy confidence. And they had purses large enough to conceal a gun.

Maybe the people I was looking for.

The women took the booth two away from mine. The Yankees fan slid in first. She continued all the way around until her back was against the wall. Like mine. Her head and body were perfectly still but her eyes were constantly moving. Flitting from the entrance to each occupied table to the bar to the kitchen door. Then back to the entrance. Round and round without stopping. The woman in the sundress slid in after her. She glanced at the drinks menu then dropped it back on the table.

'White wine,' she said, when the waiter approached. 'Pinot Grigio, I think.'

'That'll work,' the Yankees fan said. 'Bring the bottle. Don't spare the horses.'

The women waited for their drinks to arrive and I watched them out of the corner of my eye. They leaned in close together. They were talking, but too softly for me to make out what they were saying. No one left the bar. No one else came in. The waiter dropped off their wine. There was a picture of an elephant on the label. The bottle was slick with condensation. He wiped it down with a towel. He tucked the towel into his apron pocket then poured two glasses. He tried to strike up a conversation. The women ignored him. He soldiered on for another couple of minutes then gave up and drifted back to the bar. The woman in the sundress sipped her wine. She looked at her friend and started talking again. She was gesticulating with her free hand. The Yankees fan drained her glass in two mouthfuls and poured herself another. She wasn't saying much but her eyes never stopped moving.

142

I slid out from my booth and approached theirs. I wound up standing where the waiter had been.

I said, 'Sorry for the interruption but I have a problem. I need your help.'

The woman in the sundress put her glass down. Her hands rested lightly on the table in front of her. The Yankees fan switched her glass to her left hand. Her right started hovering over her purse. I waited a beat. I needed to see if it disappeared inside. It didn't, so I sat down. I leaned in and lowered my voice. 'I'm looking for a friend. His name is Michael. Michael Curtis.'

Neither woman's expression changed. The Yankees fan's eyes didn't stop scanning the room.

I said, 'He's in trouble. I need to find him. Fast.'

'What's his name again?' the woman in the sundress asked.

'Michael Curtis.'

The woman shook her head. 'Sorry. We don't know him.'

'I'm not with the police,' I said. 'Or the FBI. I know why Michael's here. I know what he's doing. I'm not looking to cause him any trouble. I've come to save his life.'

The woman shrugged. 'I'm sorry. We can't help you with that.'

'Just give me an address. One place to look.'

'Have you got a hearing problem?' The Yankees fan's eyes were finally still. They locked on to mine and didn't move. 'We don't know this Michael guy. We can't help you find him. Now go back to your table and stop bothering us.'

'One location. Please. No one will ever know it came from you.'

The Yankees fan reached into her purse. She rummaged around for a moment. Then her hand reappeared. She was holding something. Not a gun. A phone. She glanced down and it came to life. She tapped it. Tapped it again three times. Then held it up for me to see. The digits 911 were glowing on its screen. 'Do I make the call? Or do you leave us alone?'

I held up my hands. 'Sorry to have bothered you. Enjoy the rest of your wine.'

I slid back into my booth and pretended to read some more of the paper. The Yankees fan put her phone away and drained the rest of her drink. She picked up the bottle and topped up her friend's glass. Then she took the rest for herself. The receptionist from the medical centre and her companion got up and left. The four guys ordered another round of beer. No one else new arrived. The waiter approached the women's table. They waved him away. The Yankees fan finished her wine. She slid out of their booth and followed the sign to the restrooms. The woman in the sundress stood up, too. She made her way in the opposite direction. Towards me. She stopped in front of my booth. She put her palms down on the table and leaned forward until her head was as close to mine as she could get without sitting. 'The Border Inn.' Her voice was so quiet I could barely hear the words. 'Do you know it?'

'I could find it.'

'OK. Room 212. Twenty minutes. Come alone. It's about Michael.' She straightened up and made it halfway to her seat. Then she doubled back and leaned towards me again. 'When my friend comes back, don't say a word. This is just between you and me.'

TWENTY-FOUR

The Border Inn was on the south-east edge of the town. It was a wide building. Two storeys high with a flat roof tucked away behind a balustrade. Its name was sketched out in faded neon letters. At first the facade looked very plain. Then I realized I was approaching from what was originally its rear. The entrance was on the far side, facing the border. That wall was covered with all kinds of fancy carvings and symbols. The outline of a row of letters and numbers was still visible near the top. They spelled out GRAND CENTRAL HOTEL 1890. That must have been the place's original name. Whoever designed it must have expected the town to spread south. Not north. Now it seemed like it had been built the wrong way round.

The entrance opened into a wide rectangular lobby. There were dark wood panels on the walls. Most had cracks and peeling varnish. There were terracotta tiles on the floor.

Some were plain. Some had intricate patterns in shades of orange and brown. A chandelier hung from the ceiling. It looked like real crystal. It was cut into elaborate shapes but the pieces were dull and cloudy with age. And dust. More than half the bulbs were out. Maybe they were broken. Or maybe that was some kind of economy measure.

The reception desk was directly opposite the main door. It was five yards wide and also made of dark polished wood. A guy was behind it. He had his boots up on the counter. They were long, pointy things made of snakeskin. There were holes in the soles. The guy had faded jeans. A blue paisley-pattern shirt. A black leather waistcoat. It was unfastened. His arms were folded across his chest. A wide-brimmed hat was pulled down over his face. He looked like he was fast asleep. I didn't disturb him. I didn't need to. I knew where I was going so I crossed to the corridor which led to the stairs.

Room 212 was at the end of the second-floor corridor on the south side of the building. Its door was standing open half an inch. A skinny paperback book was down at floor level, stopping it from closing all the way. I peered through the gap. Saw nothing unusual. Just coarse brown carpet. The end of a bed with a floral comforter cover. The edge of a window with matching curtains. No people. No weapons. But still obviously a trap. It would have been safer to walk away. But playing it safe wasn't going to help Fenton. I needed information, and the only source I knew of was behind that door.

I stood to the side and knocked.

'Come in.' It was the woman from the Red Roan. I recognized her voice.

So far, so good.

146

I pushed the door and stepped into the room. The woman was in the corner to my left. The room was large enough and the gap between the door and the frame was narrow enough that I hadn't seen her from the corridor. She was still wearing the yellow sundress. And now she had a gun in her hand. A Beretta M9. A weapon she would be very familiar with if I was correct about who she was. She was aiming it right at my chest.

She had planned the set-up well. She was too far away for me to grab the gun without giving her ample time to pull the trigger. My only move was to dive back through the door. But she would be expecting that. There was no guarantee I would be fast enough. Plus, I didn't know where her friend was. She could have the corridor covered by now. And I needed whatever information she could give me. Whether she was in a sharing mood or not.

I pushed the book aside with my foot. Let go of the door. And raised my hands to chest height.

'To the bed.' The woman gestured with the gun.

I moved across.

She said, 'See the pictures?'

There was a stack of photographs on the pillow. I picked it up. There were five of them. Four-by-sixes. Colour. Of five different men. All in hot-weather ACUs.

'Show me which one's Michael,' she said. 'Then we'll talk.'

I shuffled through the images. Slowly and carefully.

'Show me the wrong one and the vultures are going to be well fed tonight.' She still had the gun levelled at my chest.

Two of the men were African American. One was Hispanic. The other two were Caucasian. Like Fenton. That narrowed the odds. One out of two is better than one out of five. But still

147

not close enough for comfort. I pictured Fenton's face. She wasn't Michael's identical twin. That was obvious. And I'd never seen him. I had no idea how similar they looked. But I had nothing else to work with. I compared the two guys' eyes to what I remembered of Fenton's. Their noses. Mouths. Ears. Hair colour. The shape of their heads. Their height. Then I thought about what I'd do if I wanted to catch someone in a lie.

I tossed all five pictures back on to the bed.

'What kind of game are you playing?' I kept my eyes on her trigger finger. 'Michael's not in any of those pictures.'

The woman didn't lower the gun. 'Are you sure? Look again. Like your life depends on it. Because it does.'

'I don't need to. His picture's not there.'

'OK. Maybe it isn't. How do you know him?'

'Through his sister. Michaela.'

'His older sister?'

'His twin.'

'Who joined the *chair force*?'

'Army intelligence.'

The woman lowered the gun.

'All right. I'm sorry. I had to be sure. Please, sit.'

TWENTY-FIVE

I lowered myself down on to the bed. The woman came out of the corner and crossed to the other side of the room. She perched on the edge of an armchair that looked like it had been made in the '50s. And not cleaned since the '60s. The gun was still in her hand.

She said, 'I'm Sonia.'

'Reacher. How do you know Michael?'

'We met in the hospital. In Germany.'

'Army hospital?'

She nodded. 'Why do you think Michael's in trouble?'

'Why do you?'

'I never said I did.'

'Then why are we having this conversation?'

Sonia didn't reply.

'My guess is that you haven't heard from Michael in three days. Maybe four.'

She didn't answer.

'Add the fact that Renée is missing too and you're starting to panic. Rumours are starting to fly. That's why you met your friend for that liquid lunch. It's why we're here now.'

'All right. I am worried. I can't reach Michael. It's not like him to drop out of sight like this. If it was just Renée who was missing, that would be one thing. But both of them?'

'I need to know where Dendoncker could have taken him.'

'Dendoncker? Why would he have taken Michael anywhere?'

'Michael was done working for Dendoncker. He wanted out. Dendoncker got wind of that. He didn't take it very well.'

'That's not possible.'

'That's what happened. Michael got a message to his sister. He asked for her help.'

'No.' Sonia shook her head. 'You've got this ass backward. Michael isn't working for Dendoncker. Dendoncker is working for Michael.'

'Michael's running a smuggling operation?'

'No. That's entirely Dendoncker's action. Michael just needs access to some of his equipment. And some raw materials.'

'Why?'

'How's that relevant?'

'Do you want to help him or not?'

Sonia sighed and rolled her eyes. 'There's a certain item Michael needs to build, OK? And transport. Secretly. And securely. Dendoncker has the infrastructure. Michael arranged access to it.'

'OK. So, aside from the place west of town, what other premises does Dendoncker have?'

'I don't know. I don't work for him. I'm just a friend of Michael's.'

'Where does Dendoncker live?'

'Nobody knows. Mexico, maybe? Michael mentioned something like that once. But I have no real idea.'

'Where does Michael live?'

'He has a room here. But he doesn't use it much any more. I guess he mostly sleeps at his workshop.'

'Where's that?'

'I don't know. I never went there.'

'But it's where he makes the bombs?'

Sonia was immediately on her feet. 'How do you know about that?'

I stood as well. She still had a gun in her hand. 'It's why he sent an SOS to his sister. He was in over his head. He knew it was wrong. He wanted to stop before it was too late.'

'No.' Sonia shook her head. 'That makes no sense. Look, Michael was no angel. I'm not pretending otherwise. He started down a bad path. The operation is his shot at redemption. He believes in it one hundred per cent. There's no way he wanted to stop. No reason he would want to. It's perfect. And it needs to be done.'

'No reason? Maybe the penny dropped that killing innocent people is something that never needs to be done.'

'What are you talking about? No one is going to get killed. He's a veteran, for God's sake. Not a murderer.'

'He's plotting to detonate a whole bunch of bombs. You're looking at hundreds of casualties.'

'No.' Sonia almost laughed. 'You don't understand.'

'Then explain it to me.'

'I can't.'

'You can. You mean you won't. So I guess you don't want my help.' I took a step towards the door.

'Wait. All right. Look, Michael's made a few prototypes. Sure. But he's only building one final device. He's using adapted signal shells. They emit smoke. That's all. A few people might get sore eyes, but nothing worse than that.'

'He's aiding Dendoncker's smuggling ring. And helping to sell illegal weapons. Just so he can plant a single smoke bomb? I don't buy it.'

Sonia sighed and slumped back into her chair. 'Dendoncker is a bad man. I give you that. I wasn't happy when Michael went to work for him. Far from it. But Michael was in a dark place then. Look, if Michael wasn't helping him, Dendoncker would find someone else. And it's a small price to pay in the greater scheme of things.'

'To pay for what?'

'Success. For Operation Clarion. That's what Michael named it.' Sonia leaned forward. 'Picture this. It's Veterans' Day. There are services and ceremonies all across the country. And at one of the biggest venues, at eleven minutes past eleven, the whole place fills with smoke. Beautiful red, white and blue smoke. It'll be a sensation. Everyone who sees it in person will ask, *why?* Everyone who sees it on TV will ask. It'll be all over the internet. And Michael will be there to answer. I'll be by his side. The Pentagon won't be able to ignore us any more. And the government won't be able to lie any more.'

'Lie about what?'

'Chemical weapons. Everywhere we fight. But in Iraq in particular. The Pentagon put together a report when the war was declared over. They sent a stuffed shirt to the

152

Senate to answer questions about it. The official line was that only a very small quantity of chemical rounds were found and the risk they posed to our troops was minor. Which is bullshit. And we know it's bullshit not only because we were the ones getting poisoned and burned and sick. But because at the same time the data for the report was getting cooked the army issued new instructions. For treating troops exposed to chemical agents. Detailed instructions. Which stated there was a continuing and significant risk to our deployed forces.'

'So they knew?'

'Damn right they knew. But they lied. And why? Because of the shell cases. You need special ones. M110s are the most common. They look just like conventional M107s. More so when they're corroded or deliberately mislabelled. But inside they have two chambers. They hold two separate compounds. Each inert on its own. But lethal when they mix. And where did the Iraqis get the shells from? The United States and our allies. Powerful corporations. The government turned a blind eye to it. A classified report Michael saw said hundreds of thousands were sold. The politicians were in danger of getting embarrassed. So they threw us soldiers under the bus to save their own asses. And we're not going to stand for it. Not any more.'

'This kind of shell. Michael's using it for the smoke bomb?'

'Correct. Appropriate, don't you think? Kind of poetic?'

'Are you sure we're only talking about a smoke bomb? If the shells look the same, is there any way he could be making regular explosive ones on the sly?'

Sonia leaned further forward. 'I should slap you for that.

153

Or shoot you. Yes, I'm sure. You think I'm an idiot? The shells look similar to a layperson. But not to me. Michael's done three separate tests. Out in the desert. In different wind conditions. I witnessed all of them. Do you think I'd be here talking to you if I'd been ten feet from an artillery shell when it went up?'

'I guess not. So when you do it for real, how will he set the bomb off?'

'The primary will be a timer. The secondary will be cellular.'

'So Michael will be at the venue?'

'Correct. He'll drive out. I'll join him there.'

'Where?'

'That was a secret. Even from me.'

'When was Michael planning to leave?'

'Tomorrow. Which makes it even stranger that Michael's dropped off the radar now.'

'Where does Dendoncker keep the equipment Michael was using? The raw materials?'

'I have no idea. Why are you so obsessed with this? Dendoncker isn't holding Michael. That would make no sense.'

'You said Michael has a room here. Do you know the number?'

Sonia nodded to the wall behind me. 'It's next door.'

'We should take a look.'

'There's no need. I already did.'

'When?'

'A couple of days ago.' Sonia looked at the floor. 'I wasn't snooping. I'm not a bunny-boiler. Michael didn't call me when he said he would. I was worried.'

'What did you find?'

154

'Nothing out of the ordinary. His bed was made. His toiletries were in the bathroom. His clothes were hanging in the wardrobe. His duffel was there. So was his go-bag. Nothing was missing. Not as far as I could tell.'

'Does Michael have a car?'

'He has two. A personal vehicle. And an old Jeep issued by Dendoncker. They're both still outside. Both as clean as whistles.'

I said nothing.

'Now do you see why I'm worried? If Michael left under his own steam he must have felt some major heat coming down not to take any of his stuff or his car. In which case, why wouldn't he call me? Let me know he's OK. Or warn me if I was in danger too?'

'We should take another look in his room.'

'Why? I told you what's there.'

'A fresh pair of eyes never hurts. And we're not going to find Michael by sticking around here talking.'

TWENTY-SIX

Sonia sighed and rolled her eyes. She scooped up her purse from the floor and tucked the gun inside. 'Fine. Come on.'

She locked the door to her own room with a big solid key. It was on a heavy brass fob that was shaped like a teardrop. She dropped it into her purse, started down the corridor, and took out another key. This one was made of thin shiny metal, and it was on a flimsy plastic fob stamped with the name of a local drugstore. She used it to unlock the next door we came to. She pushed the door all the way open, took one step inside, and stopped in her tracks. She clamped her hand over her mouth, but she didn't make a sound. I moved up alongside her and stopped still too. The room was a mirror image of hers. It was an efficient use of space. The bathrooms were half depth so they fitted neatly next to one another and kept the plumbing sounds away from the beds.

But while Sonia's room was immaculate, this one looked like a tornado had ripped through it. The bed was on its side. The mattress was torn open in a dozen places and clumps of grey fibrous material were hanging out. The wardrobe was face down on the floor. Shredded clothes were heaped up next to it. The chair was on its side. Its cushion was ripped. The curtain pole had been wrenched off the wall. The curtains had been sliced and left in ribbons on the floor.

Sonia said, 'Who did this? What were they looking for? I don't understand.'

'Does Renée have a room here?' I asked.

'Yes. At the other end of the corridor. You don't think . . . ?'

'I don't know. But we should find out.'

Sonia closed Michael's door and led the way to room 201. She tried the handle and shook her head.

She said, 'It's locked. Wait here. I'll go down to reception. Borrow a pass key.'

I shook my head. 'No. I don't want to involve anyone else. Have you got a knife in your bag? Or tweezers?'

Sonia rummaged in her purse and pulled out a little knurled black case. She opened it and revealed a whole array of small shiny tools. I guessed they had something to do with nails, but I had no idea what most of them did. She held out the set. 'Take your pick.'

I selected a pair of needle-nosed tweezers and a thin wooden rod. It was like a lollipop stick with a chamfered end. I bent the bottom of one leg of the tweezers to ninety degrees then crouched down and went to work on the lock. It was old and plain. But solid. From the days when things were built to last. It probably rolled off the line in a big, dirty

157

factory in Birmingham, Alabama. One of thousands used all across America. Probably millions. Probably used all over the world. It was a quality item, but not overcomplicated.

I felt for the tumblers and found them right away. Easing them aside was another story. I figured the lock hadn't seen a great deal of maintenance over the course of its life. It was stiff. It took more than a minute to force it to turn. Then I stood, opened the door, and looked inside. The scene was almost identical to the one in Michael's room. But nothing like what Fenton said she had seen there.

The bed and the wardrobe and the chair and the curtains had been tipped over and ripped open. The only real difference was that the heap of ruined clothes on the floor were women's, not men's. The find was no big surprise. It wasn't conclusive. But it was consistent with the theory that Renée was suspected of smuggling Fenton's note to Michael. You could understand Dendoncker wanting to have both their rooms searched. He'd have wanted to see if there was any other illicit communication between them. Or anyone else.

There was nothing to suggest I needed to change tack. But nor was there anything to help figure out where Fenton was. Maybe if I had access to a forensic lab I could have found something. Some microscopic trace of rare dirt or sand. Some tell-tale fibres. DNA, even. But with the resources available, which basically meant my eyes and my nose, there was no point wasting effort sifting through the wreckage. It was frustrating, but those were the facts. Time was passing and I was running out of places to look.

I turned to leave and almost knocked Sonia down. She had crept up close behind me and was standing stock still. Her eyes were wide and her mouth was hanging open.

'I don't understand.' She stepped around me. 'It looks like the same people did this. But why? What are they looking for? And where are Michael and Renée?'

I said nothing.

'Are they involved in something together? Wait. Are they ...? No. They can't be. They better not be.' Sonia strode further into the room and kicked Renée's ransacked heap of clothes up into the air.

I said, 'You and Michael? Were you ... more than friends? Is that why you have a key to his room?'

Sonia turned to look at me. Her face was drained and raw. 'It's nothing official. We aren't married or engaged or anything like that. We haven't told many people. But yes. We found each other in that hospital. We saved each other. He's everything to me. I can't even think about someone stealing him away ...'

This was not the scenario I had expected to walk into. I imagined I'd be dealing with a bunch of worthless, conscience-free mercenaries. The kind of people I'd happily pump for information then leave to rot when their half-assed scheme crashed down around their heads. Instead I found myself feeling sorry for this woman. Maybe she was naïve. But that isn't a crime. I guess she'd been duped by a guy who came into her life at a vulnerable moment. He must have been pretty persuasive. Even when he was off the rails.

I figured in the circumstances I should level with Sonia. There was no way to avoid it. Not without being unnecessarily cruel. But there was a problem. My death message skills were universally considered to be subpar. They were so bad the army had sent me for special remedial training. Years

159

ago. It hadn't helped very much. Since then my preference had been to break bad news in public places. People are less likely to break down or freak out in front of an audience. I found bars and restaurants and cafés are the best. The whole process of ordering food and having it delivered and cleared away provides natural punctuation. It helps reality to sink in. I thought about the Red Roan. I thought about taking Sonia back there. It was very tempting. But I decided not to. It would take time to get there. Just then time was not my friend. And it certainly wasn't Fenton's.

I took hold of Sonia's elbow and eased her out into the corridor. 'Come on. We better go back to your room. There are some things I need to tell you.'

TWENTY-SEVEN

Sonia took the chair. She perched at the front of it. Her whole body was rigid. She was wound up tight. I could tell she was a hair's breadth away from fight or flight. I sat on the edge of the bed and faced her. I kept one foot on the floor near her purse. Her gun was still inside it. There's a reason the expression *don't shoot the messenger* is a thing.

I said, 'I want to start with good news. There was nothing between Michael and Renée. That's for certain.'

'*Was* nothing?'

'I'm getting to that. First we need to back the truck up a little.'

I talked her through the whole story. All the way from Fenton receiving Michael's message to her botched attempt at snatching Dendoncker. Including the part where Dendoncker's guy told Fenton Michael was dead. Sonia was silent for a moment when I got to the end. Her eyes flickered from side

161

to side as she joined the dots. Then she said, 'Michael got caught with the note from his sister? That's how everything turned to shit?'

'That's the way I see it.'

'So Dendoncker had Michael killed?'

I nodded.

'No. I don't believe it.'

I said nothing.

'And Renée?'

'I think she saw it coming. I think she got away.'

'But not Michael? Are you sure?' Sonia's voice was on the edge of cracking up. 'Like, totally beyond any doubt? No matter how tiny?'

'I didn't see his body. But I heard one of Dendoncker's goons swear that Dendoncker had killed Michael. And he had nothing to gain by lying.'

Sonia got up and crossed to the window. She turned her back and pulled the curtain around her. 'I don't know what to do with this. I can't believe he's gone. This must be a mistake.'

I didn't know what else I could say.

Sonia disentangled herself from the curtain and spun around to face me. 'If you knew Michael was dead, why didn't you tell me right away?' Her eyes were damp and red. 'Why string me along? Why all that bullshit about wanting help finding him?'

'I didn't know what your deal was then.' I held up my hands. 'I might not be able to help Michael. But I can still help his sister. Maybe. If I can find her.'

'You still bullshitted me.' Sonia shuffled back to the chair and slumped down. 'I just can't deal with this. What should I do now?'

'Leave town would be my advice. Now, I have to get going. But first I need to ask you a question. It's going to sound insensitive. The timing's awful. But it could be important.'

'What is it?'

'In the message Michael sent his sister, along with the card from the Red Roan there was something else. A condom. That seems weird to me. Does it mean anything to you?'

'No. Michael wouldn't have a condom. We didn't use them. And he would never send one to his sister. That's gross.'

'It got in there somehow.'

'Someone else must have put it in.'

'I don't think so.'

Sonia shrugged. 'Maybe Michael was trying to tell her something. Like, to be careful. To take precautions. He did love cryptic messages. He was always leaving them for me. I generally didn't understand them, to be honest. I had to ask him to explain.'

A condom as a warning to take precautions? It was possible. In the sense that it couldn't be positively ruled out. But it didn't seem likely. And as an explanation it didn't feel right. The voice at the back of my brain still wasn't satisfied.

TWENTY-EIGHT

I guess the guy with the worn-out boots wasn't as heavy a sleeper as he'd made himself out to be.

His feet were no longer up on the reception counter when I got to the lobby. He was no longer lounging back in his chair. There was no sign of him at all. But two other guys were hanging around. Two of the guys from the previous night. The only two still able to walk. *They* were waiting for *me*, this time. That was clear. They both puffed up a little when they saw me. Then they moved. The guy who'd been driving stepped in front of the double exit doors, which were closed. And locked, presumably. The guy I'd hit with the axe handle slunk around in the opposite direction. He wound up blocking the way back to the corridor. He needn't have bothered. I had no intention of going that way.

The men were wearing the same kind of clothes as before. Black T-shirts. Black jeans. Black combat boots. But now

164

the driver's left arm was in a sling. And they each had a small backpack slung over one shoulder. Both packs were made out of ballistic nylon. Desert-sand colour, scuffed and stained and well used. And weighed down with something bulky.

The driver said, 'Down on the floor. On your front. Hands behind you.'

'Again?' I said. 'Really?'

'Get down. Do it now.'

I didn't move. 'Were you dropped on your head when you were a baby? Was your boss? Because, honestly, I'm worried. Virtually every creature on the planet has the ability to learn from experience. But not you, apparently. What happened last time you tried this? When you had three buddies to help out? Not just one.'

'Oh, we learn.' The driver nodded. The other guy swung his pack off his shoulder. He pulled back its flap and took out its contents. A full-face respirator. It was black with a butyl rubber coating, drooping, doleful triangular eye pieces and a round filter case mounted on the left side. It looked like an M40 field protective mask. The kind that had been used by the US army and the Marine Corps since the '90s. Not the newest design in the world. Not the most comfortable. But effective. The guy pulled it over his head and tugged on one of the straps.

The driver held his pack between his knees, opened it and took out an identical mask. He fumbled to put it on with one hand then stood still for a moment. It made him look like a depressed insect. Then he took out another item. A silver canister. It was about the size of a can of baked beans, and it had a ring and a lever sticking out of the top.

165

'Ever heard of CS gas?' The guy's words sounded muffled and tinny through the voice emitter at the front of the mask.

I'd more than heard of CS gas. I'd experienced it. Years ago, on the final day of a training module. A dozen of us were locked in a room with an instructor. The instructor placed a CS canister on a metal table in the centre of the space. He pulled the pin and tossed it in the air. He was already wearing his mask. An older model. An M17, which was the standard in those days. We had to wait until the pin hit the ground. Then we had twenty seconds to get our masks on. We all made it. That part of the exercise was fine. The next part wasn't. We had to remove our mask and shout out our name, rank and number. One at a time. And we could only put our mask back on when the instructor nodded. That was bad. Really bad. But it was even worse if the instructor didn't like you. If he pretended he couldn't hear you. If he made you repeat your information. He made one guy repeat his three times. Between each attempt he left a pause. Each one felt like an hour. To us. They must have felt like a year to the poor guy. The front of his smock was soaked with tears and snot and drool by the time we staggered out into the fresh air. He quit the programme about ten minutes later.

'Well, we call this DS gas.' The guy held the canister up higher. 'Dendoncker Special. It's like CS on steroids. It burns your eyes so bad you go blind if you don't get saline in time. And your nose? Your throat? Your lungs? Pain like you will not believe. I promise you.'

I said nothing.

'Last chance,' he said. 'Get down on the floor. Do yourself a favour. Because if I have to use this, the game changes.

You're going to have to crawl across to me. Lie at my feet. Beg me to save your eyesight.'

I stayed still. 'That's never going to happen.'

'Come on, man.' The other guy's voice sounded like a robot's. 'This is science we're talking about. You can't fight it. You've got to respect the chemistry.'

'Chemistry's fine.' I still had the gun I'd taken from the guy outside the café. I was tempted to use it. That would solve the immediate problem. But a shot would be heard. And I had no desire to attract attention. Not just then. What I had in mind called for privacy. So I moved slowly to my left. Just until the driver was directly between me and the exit. 'But me? I always preferred physics.'

'I warned you.' The driver flicked away the little clip that held the pin against the curved handle. He switched the canister to his left hand. Curled his right index finger through the ring. And gave it a tug.

It didn't budge.

I guessed this was the guy's first time. Arming a grenade is harder than it looks in the movies. The locking pin is made of surgical steel. One leg is bent at a steep angle. It needs to be. No one wants to be on the wrong end of an accidental discharge. The guy adjusted his grip. He raised his right elbow. Maybe he thought that would give him improved leverage. I didn't wait to see if he was right. I just pushed off my back foot, hard, and started to run. As fast as I could. Straight ahead. Directly towards him. I covered half the distance. Three quarters. Then I threw myself forward.

My shoulder sank into the guy's midriff. It knocked him off his feet. We clattered together into the doors. A combined four hundred and fifty pounds. And the effect of my weight was multiplied by the speed I'd gained. The old lock was no match for that. Not even close. The doors burst open. One swung around and crashed into the wall. The other came right off its hinges and cartwheeled away. The two of us landed on the ground. Him underneath, on his back. Me on top. I was crushing his chest. I felt some of his ribs shatter on impact. Maybe a collar bone, too. Maybe both of them. But those injuries didn't matter. He would never feel the pain. Because his shoulders wound up level with the lip of the top step leading down to the street. My bulk pinned his torso in place. But his head continued to move. It swung around another five inches. Then the back of his skull hit the concrete. It split open like a watermelon. Something sticky sprayed up across my face. The guy twitched. Just once. And then he was still.

TWENTY-NINE

Half a second later I felt a weight on my back. A couple of hundred pounds. Then an arm snaked around my neck. It was the other guy. He must have followed us out. Seen his opportunity, with me practically on the ground. Dived on top of me. Sandwiching me between him and his buddy. He kept stretching until the angle of his elbow was wrapped around my throat. Grabbed hold of his wrist with his other hand. Pulled back. Jammed his knee into my spine for extra leverage. He was using all his strength. Straining like a fisherman fighting to land the catch of his life. I reached around behind me, scrabbling for his head, but he was leaning too far back. That was smart. He'd anticipated the danger and was staying out of harm's way.

He was going after me. I was going after him. Neither of us was giving an inch. Neither of us was close to a breakthrough. He must have sensed the deadlock. That suited

169

me fine. If he was looking for a battle of endurance, he'd picked the wrong opponent. That was for damn sure. He must have sensed that too, because he started rocking back and forth, trying to ratchet up the pressure. That certainly raised his game. I was suddenly finding it hard to breathe. I flexed the muscles in my neck but I could still feel my wind-pipe starting to give way. Pain ripped through my larynx. My lungs began to burn. I needed to tip the scale in my favour. Fast.

I dipped my right shoulder and pushed down towards the ground at the side of the body I was still straddling. Lifted my left shoulder. Felt the guy on my back adjust his bal-ance. He was trying not to slide off. Compensating by leaning the other way. The instant he moved I corkscrewed in the opposite direction. Jammed my left shoulder down. My right shoulder up. Twisted at the waist. Drove my right knee into the ground and heaved myself up. The pair of us pivoted to the left. We teetered for a moment as the guy realized what was happening and tried to fight the momen-tum. To reverse the motion. But he was too late. And he was still clinging to my neck.

We flipped over. Together. He was underneath this time. On his back. I was on top. Also on my back. He was pinned down. But he was still trying to strangle me. He hadn't given up. The opposite. He was trying to squeeze even harder. I guess desperation was setting in. He probably couldn't breathe very well himself with my weight on his chest. And he couldn't get his head clear. The ground was stopping him. I stretched around. Felt his mask. It was facing away from me. Towards the street. The angle was impossible. Then I realized he must have pushed it up on to the top of

170

his head. He must have wanted to see better, but to be ready if the canister of gas erupted. I tore the mask off. Dropped it. Slid my hand down his forehead. Found the bridge of his nose. Pressed my thumb into his right eye. Poked my index finger into his left. And started to press.

I didn't press too hard. Not at first. He kept trying to crush my throat. I increased the pressure. He whimpered. Thrashed his head from side to side. Trying to break contact. But he didn't let go. I pressed harder. Harder still. I figured I was no more than a fraction of an inch away from his eyeballs bursting or popping out. I would normally consider that a satisfactory result. But in the circumstances I had to be careful. His presence was a bonus. I didn't want to waste it. I needed him capable of answering questions. So I didn't increase the force any further. I kept my finger and thumb steady. I arched my back. Pushed my other hand between our bodies. Moved it down, towards his groin. Grabbed hold. Started to squeeze. And twist. Harder. Tighter. Until he screamed and let go of my neck.

I jumped straight to my feet before he could change his mind or try something else. I stamped on his abdomen. Not too hard. Just enough to immobilize him for a moment. Then I gathered up his gun and his mask and the gas canister. It had slipped out of the other guy's hand and rolled on to the top step. The pin was still in place. I picked up his backpack. Checked inside. He had a bottle of water. A coil of paracord. Some kind of tool. And a bundle of zip ties. The tool was in a tan leather case. It was like a folding penknife, with a whole bunch of extra blades and screwdrivers and scissors. The ties were heavy duty. There were half a dozen. I put the knife and the ties in my pocket. I put the gun in the backpack. Then I prodded the guy in the ear with the toe of my shoe.

'That your car?' I gestured to the far side of the street. A Lincoln Town Car was parked by the kerb. It was black. It looked like the one the three guys had driven away from the morgue.

He craned his neck around to see what I was pointing at, then nodded.

'Where's the key?'

He pointed at the body lying next to him.

'Get it.'

'No way.' All the colour drained out of the guy's face. 'He's dead. I'm not touching him.'

'If you won't get the key you're no use to me.' I jabbed him in the ear again, a little harder. 'Want to wind up like him?'

The guy didn't reply. He just rolled on to all fours, stretched across his buddy's body, pulled the keys out of his pants pocket and held them up for me to see.

'Good. Now pick up the body. Put it in the trunk.'

'No way. I'm not carrying him.'

'His body's going in the trunk. Either you put it in there, or you join it in there. Your choice.'

The guy shook his head, scrambled to his feet, and trudged down the steps. He grabbed his buddy's hands and pulled. He made it to the sidewalk and a gun rattled free. He tried to pounce on it. But he was too slow. I pinned the gun down with one foot. And kicked him in the head with the other. Not too hard. Just a warning. Which worked. He went back to dragging the body. It left a trail of dark, congealing blood across the street. I waited until he was halfway to the car then scooped up the gun and added it to the stuff in the backpack.

The guy popped the trunk. He struggled to lift the body. It was heavy. Its head and limbs were flopping around all over the place. Eventually the guy hauled it into a sitting position. Propped its shoulder against the fender. Moved in close behind it. Wrapped his arms around its chest. Heaved it up. And posted it in head first. He slammed the trunk immediately, as if that would prevent him being pushed in too, and spun around. His eyes were wide. He was breathing hard. His forearms were smudged with blood.

I said, 'Unlock the doors.'

The guy prodded a button on the remote. I heard four almost simultaneous clunks as the mechanisms responded.

'Put the keys on the trunk.'

The guy did as he was told.

'Get in. Driver's seat.'

I collected the keys, followed him, and moved in close so he couldn't close the door. I took a zip tie from my pocket and dropped it in his lap. 'Secure your right hand to the wheel.'

He hesitated, then looped the tie around the rim. Fed the tail through the tie's mouth. Pulled until the first of the teeth started to engage. Slid his wrist through the gap. And tightened the tie halfway.

I said, 'Tighter.'

He took up half the remaining slack.

I leaned across, took hold of the loose end and pulled it hard. The plastic bit into his wrist. He grunted.

I said, 'Left hand on the wheel.'

He rested it at the ten o'clock position. I took another tie

173

and fastened it. I grabbed his elbow and tugged. He grunted again. His hand wouldn't slip through. I figured it was secure enough. So I closed the door and climbed into the seat behind him.

I said, 'Where's Dendoncker?'

The guy didn't answer.

I pulled the guy's mask over my head and made a show of adjusting the straps. Then I placed the canister of gas on the armrest between the front seats.

'DS gas, your friend said. Before he died. Like CS gas on steroids. Am I getting that right?'

The guy nodded.

'I don't believe him. I think this is a dummy. A prop. I think you guys were trying to bluff me. I think I should pull the pin. See what happens.'

The guy started thrashing around in his seat, sticking his elbow out, trying to knock the canister out of my reach. 'No!' he said. 'Please. It's real. Don't set it off.'

'Then answer my question.'

'I can't. You don't get it. Dendoncker – you don't cross him. Nothing's worth doing that.'

THIRTY

I tapped the gas canister. 'This stuff makes you blind, right? Keeping your eyesight – that sounds worth it.'

The guy shook his head. 'I had a friend. We worked together for five years. For Dendoncker. My friend used to go to Walmart, once a month. The nearest one's, like, a hundred miles away. They have some special drink he liked. Chai, he called it. From India. Dendoncker thought that was suspicious. He had my friend tailed. The guy following him saw someone in the store at the same time who looked like he might have been a fed.'

'Looked like a fed how?'

'He wasn't definitely a fed. But he might have been one. That was enough for Dendoncker. And at the same time, he was looking to sell a bunch of .50 cal sniper rifles. To some drug lord. From Mexico. There's a big demand for those things down there. A lot of money to be made. The buyer wanted a demonstration before he would part with his cash. So Dendoncker got my friend. Had him tied to a pole a few hundred yards away in the desert. Naked. Made the rest of us watch. Through binoculars. The rifle worked fine. The drug guy – he was a terrible shot. He fired a dozen rounds. Hit my friend in the leg. In the shoulder. Clipped him in his side, by his gut. He wasn't dead. But Dendoncker left him there. Sent someone to collect his body a couple of days later. I saw it. It made me puke. His eyes had been pecked out. Snakes had bitten his feet. Something big had taken chunks out of his legs. I tell you, I swore right there and then there was no way I was ever going to let anything like that happen to me.'

I tapped the canister.

The guy tried to twist around and face me. 'Another time, Dendoncker was selling land mines. To another drug lord. He was building a giant new compound. Wanted to fortify it. He also asked to see the merchandise in action. To prove it worked. Dendoncker had a bunch planted in some remote spot. Then he made a guy, I can't even remember what he was supposed to have done, walk through it. He made it ten feet. And that was the end of him.'

'When I'm done with Dendoncker he'll be in no position to hurt anyone. That's for damn sure.' I tapped the canister again. 'But this stuff? In this enclosed space?'

The guy leaned forward and banged his forehead on the steering wheel. Once. Twice. Three times. 'I couldn't tell you even if I wanted to. I don't know where Dendoncker is. No one does.'

'What do you know?'

'We were ordered to take you to the house. Someone

176

would come and collect you from there. I have no idea where they would take you. That's way above my pay grade.'

'How would they know to come for me?'

'I'd send a text.'

'To what number?'

The guy reeled off a string of ten digits. It was an Alaska area code. Presumably a burner phone, used to disguise its current location.

'What message were you to send? The exact words.'

'There are no exact words. Just that we have you.'

'How long after you send the message would they arrive?'

The guy shrugged. 'I don't know. Sometimes they're waiting when we get there. Sometimes we have to wait five minutes. The longest was maybe ten.'

'Where do you wait?'

'In the house.'

'Where is the house?' The guy described the place I'd followed the Lincoln to earlier.

'Always there?' I said. 'Ever anywhere else?'

'No.' The guy shook his head. 'It has to be there. Whoever comes, wherever they go, it's always through there. There's no other way, as far as I know.'

'What's your deadline for delivering me?'

'No deadline. We have as long as it takes to catch you.'

'Put your foot on the brake.'

The guy didn't move.

I tapped the canister.

The guy sighed, stretched out his foot, and pressed down on the pedal.

I took off the mask and slipped it into the pack. Dropped the gas canister in after it. Leaned through the gap between

177

the front seats. Cupped the side of the guy's head with my left hand and pressed it into the window. Used my right hand to slide the key into the ignition. I turned it. The big motor coughed into life. Then I slid the lever into Drive and dropped back into my seat.

I said, 'Take me to the house. The sooner Dendoncker's guys arrive, the sooner I'll let you go. If you don't try anything stupid.'

The guy wrapped his fingers around the wheel. The zip ties made it awkward but I figured he could get a good enough grip. And it would give him something to think about other than trying to escape. He switched his foot from the brake to the gas and pulled away from the kerb. He steered straight along the front of the hotel. Turned left at the end of the building. Towards the town centre. Slow. Steady. Not trying anything stupid. He continued for fifty yards, until we drew level with the mouth of a road on our left.

'No. I can't do this.' The guy spun the wheel. He crossed his arms at the elbows and twisted his wrists as far as they would go. Held on until we were facing the opposite direction. Back towards the border. Then he straightened up. Leaned harder on the gas. Picked up speed.

I pulled my gun, leaned around the side of his seat, and held it to his temple.

'Go ahead,' he said. 'Shoot me. Please. I want you to.'

We were back level with the front of the hotel. The guy didn't turn. He kept going straight and bumped up the kerb on to the rough sandy scrub. A cloud of dust was thrown up behind us. We slowed a little. We were pitching and bouncing. The car was not ideal for that kind of terrain. It was too long. Too low. But we kept going. The guy showed no sign of stopping. We were heading directly towards the steel barrier. The needle was a hair above twenty. The car was heavy but there was no chance of it busting through at that speed. The spikes were solid metal. Thick. No doubt with deep foundations. Designed specifically not to get breached. It wasn't likely that either of us would get hurt. Not badly anyway.

I leaned back and worked the seat belt, just in case. I guessed the guy was aiming to disable the car. The radiator was sure to rupture on impact. Which would be a problem in that kind of climate. The engine would overheat in no time. It would never make it all the way to the house.

I considered knocking the guy out. Or crushing his windpipe until he lost consciousness. But whatever I did it was most likely we would still hit the fence. Which wouldn't be a major problem. Sonia said Michael had two cars at the hotel. That was only yards away. I could use one of them. With this guy in the trunk. He could still be useful. Just not as a driver.

Twenty yards from the border the guy pulled back with his left hand. Hard. The steering wheel twitched. Blood started to ooze from where his skin had been broken by the edge of the zip tie. Fifteen yards from the border he pushed his arm forward through the tie as far as it would go. Then he snatched it back again. Harder. With more determination. This time a flap of skin over his thumb joint tore loose. He cried out in pain. I could see bone. And tendons. Blood gushed from the wound. Maybe that helped to lubricate the plastic. Maybe it was just brute force. But somehow, he got his hand free.

Ten yards from the border he shoved his hand into his pocket. He pulled out a quarter. Held it between his thumb

179

and index finger. And rested it at the centre of the steering wheel.

Five yards from the border he leaned forward. Tilted his head up. Exposed his throat. And pressed harder on the gas.

We hit the barrier square on and instantly about a dozen airbags deployed. The sound they made was louder than the crash. One sprang out of the door next to me. It hit my arm. It was hot. It almost burned my skin. My view of the outside world was blocked out. It was like being inside a cloud. The bags started to subside. The air was thick with white powder, like talc. There was a smell like cordite. I released my seat belt. Opened my door. And climbed out.

The engine had stopped. There was a hissing sound. A cloud of steam was escaping from under the hood. I pulled the driver's door open. The guy had been thrown back in his seat. His face was blackened and burned. His eyes were wide and sightless. One side of his jaw was dislocated. It was hanging down at a drunken angle. The front of his shirt was soaked with blood. And there was a gaping hole in his throat. It was like he'd been shot. Which he had, in a way. He'd used the coin as a bullet. It had been propelled by the explosive in the airbag. Probably not what the NHTSA had in mind when they mandated the technology.

I reached in. Took the guy's phone from his pocket. Collected his backpack. And started to walk to the hotel.

THIRTY-ONE

I made it five yards, then stopped. Because of the guy's phone. I was going to need to use it. Which meant I would have to unlock it. Which could be a problem.

The phone was the kind with just a screen. There were no numbered keys. No button to press, to read a fingerprint. I raised it and its screen lit up. The whole thing buzzed angrily in my hand. A message appeared. It said, 'Face ID not recognized. Try again?' Heaven help any phone that recognized my face, I thought. Then I turned back to the car. Returned to the driver's door. Opened it and held the phone level with the guy's nose. It buzzed angrily. I lowered it and tried again.

No success.

I figured the problem must be the guy's jaw. It had been broken by the airbag. The phone must keep a record of the shape of its owner's face. That was different now. Its outline had changed. I tried pushing the guy's chin up with my fingers, then lined up the phone. No luck. I shifted his jaw a little to the side. Tried the phone again. It still wouldn't unlock. It buzzed again, more angrily than before. A new message appeared. 'Passcode required to enable Face ID.'

Six circles popped up below the text. They were small and hollow and bunched up together in a horizontal line. Below them there were ten circles with the numbers 0 to 9. They were arranged like a conventional keypad. I touched the zero. The first small circle turned grey. So, the phone had a six-digit PIN. Far too many combinations to have a reasonable chance of cracking it. Not without knowing something about the dead guy. Something to narrow the odds. I hit the zero five more times, just in case. The other small circles filled in. The phone buzzed angrily. 'Passcode incorrect. Try again?' I thought, *maybe*. But not there. Not standing in the sun next to a car with two dead bodies inside it. And not when there was another avenue I could try.

I walked around to the rear of the car and popped the trunk. The other guy's body was all the way forward, piled up against the seats. It must have slid there with the force of the collision. I reached in, grabbed its belt, and pulled it back. I checked its pockets. Found another phone. Another one with no keys. It also asked for a Face ID. I wrestled the guy on to his back. Shuffled him down so that his face wasn't in the shadows. Held the phone level with his nose. It buzzed, and unlocked itself.

Getting one of the phones unlocked was good. But not perfect. I had no idea how long it would be until it locked itself again. Thirty seconds? A minute? Ten? However long it took it was no problem while I was near the car. I could use the guy's face to reactivate it. The issue was I didn't

182

want to stay near the car. And I didn't want to use the phone near the car. I wanted to get into position at the house before sending the text and summoning more of Dendoncker's guys. I wanted to watch them arrive. To see how many there were. What kind of weapons they brought. It would take me a while to get there. Half an hour, probably. At least. The Chevy was at Fenton's hotel. I had walked to the Red Roan from there. And then on to the Border Inn. I would have to retrace my steps to collect it. Or get hold of the keys to one of Michael's cars. And there were a couple of other things I wanted to attend to on the way.

In the circumstances I could see no alternative. I had to send the message and let the chips fall how they may. If I arrived second to the house no real harm would be done. I could surveil the place. Make a plan. It might impact the details. But not the outcome. The way I was feeling, it didn't matter how many guys Dendoncker sent or what they brought with them. They were all going to be taking a trip to the hospital. Or the morgue.

I touched the icon for messages and entered the number the guy had given me when he outlined his orders. He said no exact wording was required so I tapped out, 'Prisoner secured. Heading to house.' Then I added, 'ETA 40 minutes.' I figured that might make a difference. Or it might not. But it was worth a try.

I didn't know if the phone would be usable for long so I dialled Wallwork's number as I walked to the hotel. He answered on the first ring.

'This is Reacher. The clock's ticking on a lead so I've got to be brief. I have an update. I interrogated someone connected to a member of Dendoncker's crew. She admitted there's a plot to plant a bomb at a Veterans' Day ceremony. She claimed the bomb only releases smoke. For some kind of publicity stunt.'

'Do you believe her?'

'We know Dendoncker's guy built a real bomb. Fenton's work at TEDAC proved that. So, either the woman I spoke to has been duped and the harmless bomb will be switched, or there's a second plot.'

'Where's the target?'

'The woman didn't know.'

'OK. Better play it safe. I'll put out a general alert.'

'Good. Anything for me?'

'The address you gave me? I traced the owner. It's a shell corporation. Another one. No connection to Dendoncker or any of his other companies. No other assets. And there's something else weird. It changed hands ten years ago. Right after Dendoncker showed up in the town. I found a report in the local press. It says the previous owner was a nice old guy. He lived there for years and pretty much got driven out. The house wasn't on the market. He hadn't wanted to sell. Then some unnamed newcomer – presumably Dendoncker – came after it. Aggressively. Like it had been targeted specifically.'

'Why? No one lives in it now. It's empty. Dendoncker's guys use it as a cut-out. There must be dozens of places they could have picked. The town feels like it's on life support. Why go after that house in particular?'

'Maybe Dendoncker planned to live there and changed his mind? Or had some other scheme for it that didn't pan out? There could be dozens of reasons.'

'Could be, I guess. But do me a favour. Check who owns

the neighbouring houses. Check the whole street. See if anything else jumps out.'

The call ended just as I reached the steps to the hotel's main entrance. The blood trail was still there. It was dry now. It had turned brown and crusty. The surviving door was closed. Someone had retrieved the other. They'd propped it up against the wall. I went in through the gap it left. Scanned the lobby. Saw that the cowboy boots were back, propped up on the reception counter. They were the same ones. Snakeskin. Holes in their soles. I was glad they were there. It meant ticking the next item off my list would be nice and easy.

The guy was lounging back in his chair. His waistcoat was still unbuttoned. His hat was pulled down over his face again. And he still wasn't really asleep. His whole body stiffened as I came close. He hadn't been expecting to see me again. That was clear. He probably thought the blood on the ground outside was mine.

I said, 'How much?'

The guy fumbled with his hat, pushed it back, and did his best to look like he was only flustered because he'd suddenly woken up. 'How much? For what?'

'Calling Dendoncker. Telling him I was here. What did he pay you?'

'Nothing. I mean, I don't know what you're talking about.'

I grabbed the guy's ankles and pulled. His ass slid off the chair. He crashed on to the floor and squealed as he hit the tile. I vaulted over the counter and landed straddling his legs. He reached up towards a little shelf that wasn't visible from the other side. A shotgun was balanced there. It was an ancient thing. An L.C. Smith. Its barrel had been sawn

185

down to about six inches. That would make it easy to wield. And it would still be plenty lethal at close quarters.

I said, 'Leave it.'

The guy kept on trying to grab it so I kicked him in the face. Not hard. It was more of a push. Just enough to knock him on to his back. Then I stamped on his hand. To discourage him. In case he felt the urge to go for the gun again.

I said, 'How much?'

The guy was rolling from side to side, clutching his crushed hand to his chest. 'Nothing extra. He pays me every month. Five hundred dollars, cash. I report anything unusual. Or anything weird any of his people staying here get up to. Sometimes he puts out an alert. Like this morning. I got a text with a description of you. I had to call when I saw you. I had no choice. Mr Dendoncker – he's a bad man.'

'You always have a choice. Right or wrong. It's clear-cut. You just thought you wouldn't get caught. You chose greed. You used poor judgement. So this is what's going to happen. When you wake up, you're going to leave town. Immediately. And you're never going to come back. I'm going to check. And if I find you here, I'm going to make Dendoncker look like the Easter Bunny. Are we clear?'

'When I wake up? What, like, in the morning?'

'In the morning. The afternoon. Whenever it happens to be.'

I grabbed him by the front of his shirt and hauled him into a sitting position. Then I kicked him in the face again. A little harder that time.

THIRTY-TWO

I tapped on the door to room 212. Gently. I was trying to
sound friendly. There was no reply, so I tried again.

'Go away.' It was Sonia's voice, but there was an edge to
it. I couldn't tell if she was angry. Or sad. Or scared. Then a
thought crossed my mind. An unwelcome one. Maybe one of
Dendoncker's guys was in there with her. Someone could
have sneaked up while I was dealing with the pair downstairs.
Who knew what the reception guy had reported. Sonia could
have a gun to her head. Which meant I couldn't risk breaking
the door down. Which severely limited my options. Until I
remembered what Fenton had said about the routine she
and Michael had with names. Sonia and Michael had been a
couple. Maybe they did the same thing.

I stood to the side and knocked again. 'Heather? You in
there? You OK?'

I waited. I heard footsteps from inside the room. They

were light, but slow. A moment later the door opened. It was Sonia. She was still in her yellow sundress. And there was no gun in sight. She leaned out into the corridor. Looked left and right, and spotted me. Her eyes were red. Her cheeks were damp.

'Reacher?' she said. 'Thanks for checking in. But I'm fine. I just want to be on my own. So please go, OK?'

'I'm not checking in. I need your help.'

'Oh. OK. With what?'

'Have you got a car?'

'Of course. Do you want to borrow it?'

'Where is it?'

'Parked, out back.'

'Good. I want you to drive me someplace.'

'Where?'

'Have you got a go-bag handy?'

'Of course. Why?'

'Grab it. And your keys. I'll explain in the car.'

Sonia's car was tiny. It was called a Mini, and with good reason. I barely fit inside even with the passenger seat cranked all the way back. It was red with white wheels, and decals of Old Glory on the roof and the curved front edges of the door mirrors. I wished she drove something more discreet, in the circumstances. But at least it fitted in the hotel parking lot. It was in another courtyard, this one contained within the building itself. It was a small, cramped space with a low arch leading to the street on the east side. I guess it was originally for receiving deliveries and allowing light into the rooms on the inner side of the corridors.

The street which ran from the arch led to the road the

guy in the Lincoln had taken before making his final U-turn. Sonia turned left, towards town, and I brought her up to speed with events since I left her in her room. She saw the opportunity right away.

'I'll watch the back of the house,' she said. 'That way no one can sneak out unnoticed. Or in. I just have one question. If I see anyone, how do I warn you?'

'Honk your horn.'

'Wouldn't it be better for me to call you? Or text? Otherwise, I'll be warning them, too.'

'I don't have a phone.' I pulled out the one I'd taken from the guy in the Lincoln's trunk. The screen had locked itself. 'Not one I can use.'

Sonia reached around, took her purse from the Mini's token back seat, and balanced it on her lap. She rummaged inside with one hand, took out a phone, and passed it to me. 'Here. You can use this.'

The phone was old school. I flipped it open. There was a keypad on one side. A real one. And a screen on the other. It was small. Black and white. And it didn't even ask for a PIN.

'It's the one Michael used to call me on.' Sonia closed her eyes for a moment. 'He had a matching one. I guess he was getting paranoid, too. He didn't like the idea of lots of calls between numbers Dendoncker could find out about.'

Sonia took me to Fenton's hotel. I switched to the Chevy and she followed me around the maze of streets until we reached the turn just north of the house. She peeled off and I continued to the street to the south. There were no cars parked at the far end. There were no cars anywhere in sight. That could mean Dendoncker's guys had fallen for my ETA

189

ruse. Or they hadn't arrived yet for some other reason. It also meant I would have to find somewhere else to dump the Chevy. It was too conspicuous to leave on the route Dendoncker's guys would take.

I turned around, drove back to the bigger road, and tried the residential street on the far side. There was an RV parked halfway down. It was an antique. It looked like it hadn't moved in years. Its tyres were flat. Its windows were opaque with grime. Its paintwork was a mess of beige and brown stripes, all crusted over with sand and dirt. The only thing going for it was its size. It was easily big enough to conceal a regular sedan. I tucked the Chevy in on the far side and made my way back to the house on foot.

There were still no vehicles nearby. I approached slowly and pushed through the tangle of twisted trees between it and its neighbour. I peered in through the first square window. Saw no one inside. Tried the other windows in turn. There was no sign of anybody. I crept around to the front and shimmied under the large window, past the door, to the far side of the building. Checked the smaller bedroom's window. There was no one. The bathroom window was frosted so I couldn't make anything out. I ducked below it and tried the larger bedroom. No one was there, either.

I figured that, according to the guys' plan, if they were already inside and somehow concealed they would be expecting the door to open so that their buddies could deliver me. So I went back around, making sure not to pass in front of any windows. Slid the key into the lock. Turned it. Crouched down, and pushed. I figured that if anyone was attracted by the movement they would expect whoever was coming in to be standing. They would be aiming at head height, if they were over-endowed with caution. But no one was there to stare in my direction. No one was there to point a gun. So I went in and checked the house from the inside. I looked in every room. Looked down through the hole in the floor. Made absolutely certain. The place was deserted.

I had no car to take cover in. There were no buildings or natural features to give me shelter. So I went outside and pushed my way back into the thicket of trees. I sat and leaned against the wall of the house. The leaves and branches were dense enough. As long as I didn't move and didn't make any sound a person could pass within a few feet and not know I was there. The clock in my head told me that if Dendoncker's guys were aiming to synchronize their arrival with my bogus ETA they should be there within five minutes.

Five minutes crawled past. No cars arrived. No one walked up the path. There was no word from Sonia. I stayed where I was. Didn't make a sound. Another five minutes ticked away. And another. The guy in the Lincoln said he'd never had to wait more than ten minutes. I waited another ten. And another. That was thirty minutes. Half an hour after the implied RV. The waiting didn't bother me. I'd be happy to wait for the rest of the afternoon if it brought the right result. I'd wait all night. But what I didn't want to do was waste time. There was no point sitting around the water hole if the big game had been scared off. I checked the windows again, just in case. There was no one inside. So I made my way to the parallel street. I spotted Sonia's flag-on-wheels right away. I walked across to it and folded myself into the passenger seat.

I said, 'It was a bust.'

'Shit.' Sonia frowned. 'What now?'

'Any chance they approached from this side and saw you?'

191

'No.' Sonia shook her head. 'Nothing's moved the whole time I've been here.'

I couldn't see what had gone wrong. The plan should have been sound. Maybe the text should have come from the other guy's phone. Maybe there had been special wording. Maybe the guy had been flat-out lying. Which was why I had wanted to bring him. But that hadn't been possible, so there was no point dwelling on it. If Dendoncker's guys wouldn't come out on their own terms, I figured it was time to make them come out on mine.

THIRTY-THREE

Sonia said, 'It won't work. You won't be able to get in. You need a transponder. I know because Michael had one. He left it behind one day. It got him into hot water. There's no lock. No keypad. The only alternative is the intercom. You have to ask someone to open the gate. You think they'll open it for you?'

'You think I'll wait for permission?'

I left Sonia to watch the back of the house and walked to the street where the giant RV was parked. Climbed into the Chevy. And headed west.

Dendoncker's company building was on its own at the end of a straight road, just as Wallwork had described. It was a simple square shape. Steel frame. Brick infill. Flat roof. Plain. Functional. Cheap to construct. And cheap to maintain. It was like the kind you see in business parks all over the country. There was a parking lot laid out in front. It had spaces for twenty cars. None were taken, and there was no movement behind any of the windows. There was nothing to suggest the place was owned by a murderer. That it was the hub of a smuggling operation. Or that it was about to be used to distribute bombs. There was just a sign on one side of the main door saying, WELCOME TO PIE IN THE SKY, INC. and a picture of a cartoon plane on the other. It had eyes in place of cockpit windows, a broad smile beneath its nose, and it was rubbing the underneath of its bulging fuselage with one wing.

I pulled up to the gate, which was just two sliding sections of the fence which surrounded the site. Chain link, twenty feet high. The wire was a decent gauge. The metal posts supporting it were stout. They weren't spaced too far apart. But it was only a single barrier. There was no inner layer. It would provide adequate security at best. Which was understandable. Health inspectors could show up. Clients. People could evidently look at images of it on the internet, like Wallwork had done. If Dendoncker wanted to avoid attracting attention, he couldn't afford for the place to look like Fort Knox.

I wound down my window. Next to me there was a metal pole, painted white. Four boxes were attached to it. Two were level with my face as I sat in the car. Two were higher. They would be for truck drivers to use. Each pair was identical. First, there was an intercom with a call button and a speaker behind a metal grille. Then a thing the size of a keypad, but with no buttons. Just a plain white rectangle. Presumably part of the transponder system. Nothing I needed to be concerned with.

I reached out and triggered the intercom. I didn't expect to be let in. I didn't expect an answer. And I didn't need one either. What I was hoping for happened right away. A camera mounted on its own pole on the other side of the fence panned around until it was pointing right at me. I stared into its lens and hit the call button an extra time.

I said, 'I'm here. Come and get me.'

I made a beckoning motion to the camera to make sure the message got through. Then I reversed for ten yards and turned the car around. I doubted anything incriminating would be left lying about inside the building. Or that there would be any clues as to Dendoncker's other locations. But over my years as an MP I learned never to rule out stupidity. And never to rule out luck. Guys who went AWOL turned up under the bed at their girlfriend's house. Stolen equipment was stashed in the trunks of personal vehicles. Plus, I was already there. I figured it wouldn't hurt to give Dendoncker something more to worry about.

I made sure the rear lined up with the centre of the entrance. Selected Reverse and pushed the gas pedal to the floor. The impact tore both gates clean off their runners, but the Chevy hardly felt a thing. I could see why they had been so popular with the police. I continued across the compound. Across the two rows of parking spaces. Slowed, to check I was on target. Then accelerated again and ploughed into the building's main doors.

The Chevy punched straight through. I hit the brakes and shifted into Drive. Pulled forward. Stopped. Left the car facing the exit. Got out. And listened. There was silence. It was unlikely a place like that would be wired to a police

195

station. But not impossible. I figured I'd better work fast and keep an ear open for sirens.

I started in the office. There were desks against three of the walls. Each held a computer. They were all switched off. Each had one pedestal with regular drawers and one with a deeper drawer for files. They were all locked so I took two paperclips from a pile of old letters in someone's filing tray. Straightened them. Slid one into the lock on the nearest desk. Raked it back and forth until I felt the pins engage. Used the other to put pressure on the cylinder. Turned it. And opened the drawer. There was a bunch of regular clerical stuff inside. Quotations. Invoices. Records of other innocuous transactions. I flicked through the papers and only one thing stood out. The dates. There was nothing less than three weeks old.

There was no sign of the police. No sign of Dendoncker's guys. Yet.

The front left corner of the building was a receiving area. It had a roll-up door. A raised platform for trucks to back up against. And metal counters around three sides. Presumably for checking whatever got delivered. They would need ingredients for any meals they made from scratch. And from what Fenton had seen, plenty of high-end delicacies and beverages. There were no goods there that day. The bay was completely empty.

No sign of the police. No sign of Dendoncker's guys.

A door led to a storage room. It was next in line on the left-hand side. It had floor-to-ceiling shelves against every wall. Some had labels with different product names. Others had bar codes. There were only a few things there. A box with tiny packets of sugar, like some people use with their coffee. Some potato chips. A bunch of little bags of peanuts. Nothing to make it feel like the hub of a vibrant business.

The kitchen was at the back left corner. It was small. Clean. Sterile. There was nothing on the counters. Nothing in the fridge. The room to its side was a preparation area. It was full of shelves and packaging materials and boxes. I guessed it was where the orders for the different flights were assembled before getting loaded into containers for transport. There was a line of whiteboards along one wall. They were all wiped clean. It didn't look like there were any jobs in the pipeline.

No sign of the police. No sign of Dendoncker's guys.

The whole place seemed well set up. The different areas were lined up logically. They would make for an efficient workflow. There was nothing suspicious. Nothing out of place. But there was no reason for anything to be. According to Fenton, the outgoing contraband was brought in from elsewhere by Dendoncker's guys and loaded straight on to the trucks. Any illicit incoming goods were collected and carted away immediately. The absence of anything incriminating didn't mean the place was innocent. Just that Dendoncker was smart.

The trucks were the only things I hadn't seen. I found the corridor that led to the garage and followed it into a large rectangular bay. There were six panel vans. Neatly lined up. Nose in. They were like the kind I'd seen parcel delivery companies use, only these were white with red and blue trim and a cartoon plane painted on each side. I picked one at random and checked the cargo area. It was immaculate. It looked like it had recently been hosed out. Like it belonged to a catering company with both eyes on hygiene.

197

Or someone who didn't want to leave any physical evidence.

The trucks' cargo areas were fitted out with racks. They ran all the way along both sides. The tallest space was at the bottom. It would be big enough for the wheeled trolleys with drawers I'd seen flight attendants use on commercial flights. Above there was plenty of room for containers which could hold the kinds of food and drink Fenton had described. Or sniper rifles. Or land mines. Or bombs. I wondered where the containers were kept. If they used standard sizes for that kind of cargo. Maybe they picked the closest fit and shoved a bunch of padding in any extra space. Or maybe they had custom ones made. Maybe with foam inserts to ensure nothing got damaged.

Another thought struck me. The kind of container would be irrelevant if there were no serviceable trucks to carry them. I was at a caterer's depot. There was a food store nearby. There was plenty of sugar. I could pour it in the gas tanks. Or grab a wrench and smash up the engines. Cut the cables and the wires. Slash the tyres. Then I thought, no. This was Dendoncker's operation. Dendoncker, who had sent guys after me with CS gas. It was time to turn up the heat. Literally.

THIRTY-FOUR

I retraced my steps to the kitchen. There was a paper-towel dispenser on the wall. The cylindrical kind, packed with a continuous roll so you can tear off whatever amount you need. I took six pieces. Each six feet long. I brought them back to the garage. Removed the cap from each truck's gas tank and fed the strips inside. Pushed them all the way into the necks and left the excess hanging down to the floor. Then I went to the office. I grabbed the chair from the desk nearest the door and used it to smash the window. Took the chair and broke the windows in all the other rooms. Went back to the office. Opened the file drawer I'd broken. Pulled out half a dozen sheets of paper. Took them to the kitchen. Lit one of the burners on the stove. Rolled the papers into a cylinder. Lit it on fire, like a torch. Carried it to the garage. Held it to the strip of paper towel sticking out of the nearest truck's tank. Waited for the flame to jump across, and double-timed it to the exit.

The first truck exploded as I was opening the Chevy's door. I heard the hiss of the sprinklers springing into life. A bunch of floodlights lit up. They were mounted on the fence poles facing the building. I jumped into the car and started the engine. A second truck exploded. I pulled away, drove across the compound, and stopped in the middle of the road on the far side of the fence. Daylight was fading fast and fat fingers of angry orange flame were stretching up into the sky. They sent shadows of the trees and cacti dancing wildly across the rough ground. I got out and walked back to the pole with the low camera attached. I grabbed hold and wrenched it around. I kept going until it was pointing at the building. I didn't know what kind of alarms Dendoncker had and I wanted to make sure he didn't miss the show.

I heard sirens after four minutes. I looked in the Chevy's rear-view mirror. The right-hand side of the structure was consumed by flames. There was no chance any of the trucks could be saved. I was confident about that. It was possible some things could be salvaged from other parts of the building. I wasn't too worried on that score so I turned my headlights on bright. Made a note how far the beams reached on either side of the road. Doubled the distance to give myself a margin of error. Then I set off slowly to my right and bounced and weaved diagonally across the scrubland, away from the road, until I figured I'd gone far enough to not be seen by any cop cars or fire trucks that went barrelling past on their way towards the inferno. I found a spot I was happy with and switched off the Chevy's lights. Then I felt a buzzing in my pocket. It was the phone Sonia had given me. I flipped it open and held it to my ear.

She said, 'Contact. A man just came out of the back door

of the house. He's huge. Bigger than you, even. He looked like he was in a hurry. He went to the next-door house, opened its garage, and drove away. In a Jeep. It was old, like the one Michael had. Guess he could be heading your way.'

I thanked her and hung up. Less than a minute later an emergency convoy rumbled by. A Dodge Charger was in the lead. It had black-and-white livery and the light bar on its roof was flashing and whooping. Then there were two fire trucks. They looked like museum pieces, but in good shape. They were all shiny red paint and brass dials and valves. They all drove through the gap I'd made in the fence, then the police car pulled away to the left. Two cops got out and stood together, watching the flames. The fire trucks turned so they were facing away from the building. Crews jumped down and started swarming around. They got busy with their hoses and nozzles and pumps. It looked like a well-practised routine.

I turned away and focused on the road from town. A couple of minutes later I spotted another pair of headlights. They were a pale yellow colour. Feeble. They drew closer and I confirmed they were on a Jeep. It was a similar age to Fenton's but cleaner and in better shape. As it drew level I could see jerry cans strapped to the front and back. A spade and an axe hanging from the side. Mansour was behind the wheel. I watched the Jeep enter the compound. It stopped between the fire trucks. Mansour climbed out and headed for the building. A firefighter tried to stop him. He shoved the guy aside and kept going. The cops ignored him. Then he pulled his shirt up over his face and disappeared through the hole in the wall where the main entrance had been.

He emerged after two minutes. He strode over to the fire

truck and grabbed the firefighter he'd just shoved. It looked like he was demanding information. The cops made their way towards him. Slowly. He let go of the firefighter and turned to face them. He barked out more questions. The cops shrugged and shook their heads. He moved across to the Jeep and climbed in. The cops trailed along in his wake. It was like they were thinking about detaining him. But it was a half-hearted move. Mansour paid them no further attention. And they made no serious attempt at stopping him.

The Jeep sped back out of the compound. It passed me and I saw Mansour was on the phone. Probably reporting what he had found. I waited until he was fifty yards clear of me then started the Chevy rolling forward. I made it to the road. Picked up speed. Followed the Jeep's tail lights. They were like faint red pinpricks. I kept the Chevy's lights off. The road was a straight line all the way into town. I'd be fine as long as no animals ran out.

Mansour took a left in the outskirts of the town, then two rights. I moved in closer to be sure not to lose him. A couple of minutes later I saw him turn into the street to the north of the house. I continued and took the next right. After a moment my phone buzzed. It was Sonia again.

'He's back. He pulled into the neighbouring garage. Now he's out. He's on foot. Heading for the house. Unlocking the back door. OK. He's inside.'

I hung up and pulled over to the side of the street. I stopped in a pool of shadow between two streetlights, ten yards from the house. There was a light on inside. But no other vehicles outside. He must have had one in another garage. I scanned the nearby houses. There was nothing to suggest which one it could be. I took the gun from my waistband and focused on the front door. Nothing happened for twenty seconds. Then the lights went out in the house. I wound down my window, ready to shoot if the guy ran. But he didn't appear. The door didn't open. Ten more seconds passed. Another ten. I opened the phone. Found the button to return the last call I received. Hit it. Sonia answered on the first ring.

I said, 'Anything?'

'The lights went off. Did he come out your side?'

'No. Did he come back out yours?'

'No.'

'Sure?'

'A hundred per cent.'

'OK. Keep your eyes open. If he approaches, shoot first. Questions afterwards.'

THIRTY-FIVE

I closed the phone, slipped it into my pocket, and got out of the car. Mansour must have seen me tailing him after all. Or maybe he spotted Sonia's car. But whatever it was, something had spooked him. That was clear. Because he was staying inside. I could wait him out. There were no creature comforts in the house. And he didn't strike me as a patient kind of guy. Not as patient as me. I was pretty sure of that. But appearances can be deceptive. I had no idea how long he would stay. Every minute he lay low was a minute Fenton might not have. And there was no guarantee he would come out my side. He could sneak out of the back. Make me get involved with chasing him. Or he could go after Sonia. I didn't want to end up with two hostages to rescue. So I decided on a different approach.

I cut across diagonally from the sidewalk to the front right-hand corner of the house. Ducked down. Crept beneath the window. Past the door. Around to the far side. Ducked below the first bedroom window. And stopped outside the next room. The bathroom. The best room to break in through. The place you're least likely to find anyone hanging around. And if someone does happen to be there, they'll be in the least favourable position to fight back.

I took the knife I'd captured from the guy at the Border Inn out of my pocket. Discarded its sheath. Found its largest blade. Unfolded it. Heard it click into place. It felt solid so I reached across and worked the blade up into the gap between the two sash panels. I found the lock. It was stiff. I increased the pressure until it rotated far enough to disengage. I put the knife away. Switched the gun to my other hand. Raised the lower pane. Just an inch. And peeked in. It was dark. The room seemed empty. There was no movement. No breathing. No running water. Just a regular drip, drip, drip, like I'd heard earlier.

I opened the window the rest of the way and climbed through. I stood and listened. I couldn't hear anyone. Couldn't sense anyone's presence. I didn't move for five minutes. I needed my eyes to adjust to the dark as fully as possible. Then I moved to the main room. No one was there. I tried the large bedroom. The small bedroom. The kitchen. No one was in any of those places. I tried the external doors. They were locked. I found a light switch. Flicked it on. Saw nothing that helped. Which just left one place to check.

I went back into the bathroom and pulled the front off the medicine cabinet. The whole thing was a mirror. It was old. Its silver was tarnished in places. But it was good enough for what I needed. I approached the hole in the main room's floor. Stopped three feet from the edge. Used the mirror to look down. Saw the boiler. The water tank. But not Mansour. I worked my way around the circle. Started to the left of the ladder. Moved clockwise. Examined the space below. Inspected it from every angle. All the way around to the right of the ladder. No one was there. The guy had disappeared. There was no trace of him at all.

He must have heard me breaking into the bathroom and used the opportunity to escape. I figured I'd better check in with Sonia in case he went out the back and found her. I put the mirror down and reached for my phone, and I noticed something on the floor. It was faint, but definitely there. A footprint. It was large. Size eighteen, at least. Maybe twenty. Pointing towards the front door. I scanned the path whoever left it should have followed. But I couldn't see any other prints. I crouched down and looked from every angle. And realized why. The trail stretched in the opposite direction. The guy had come in through the back door. He'd walked around the hole. Got to the top of the ladder. Turned around. And gone down. His feet must have gotten soaked at Dendoncker's building. By the sprinklers, or all the water the firefighters had hosed in. They must have still been damp when he climbed down. They must have dried out the rest of the way while he was in the cellar. Then when he came back up, they left no more prints.

The drying-out part was fine. But I couldn't understand why he'd gone into the cellar in the first place. There was just a boiler down there. And a water tank. Maybe, when he heard me breaking in, he decided to hide. It was possible. But the guy didn't strike me as the hiding kind. There must have been some other reason. I wasn't thrilled at the idea of going below ground but whatever drew the guy down there

206

was my only clue as to where he might have gone. I stood up, grabbed the ladder, and started to descend. I went faster this time. I figured that if the rungs could take his weight, they could sure as hell take mine.

I found a footprint at the bottom of the ladder. Another big one. I could see where the guy had turned. And walked over to the wall. To the section directly below the door to the bathroom. Then he'd stopped. And stood still. There was a pair of prints, side by side. But I couldn't see where he went next. I crouched down and checked the floor from every available angle. There was nothing. The trail had vanished.

I spun around, gun out in front. I had a sudden vision of the guy charging at me from behind the boiler or the water tank. I figured he could have made the footprints as a lure so he could attack me from behind. But there was no one racing towards me. No one was there at all. It was like the guy had just walked through the wall.

I turned back and rapped the wall with my knuckles. Maybe there was a hiding place behind it. Or a safe room. But the wall wasn't hollow. It was the opposite. It sounded dense. Solid. Far more so than I would have expected for such an old structure. I moved to the side until I was beneath the smaller bedroom. I rapped again. The note was different. It was lighter. Emptier. I tried beneath the larger bedroom. That also sounded thin and flimsy. I went back to the centre. Tried again there. I hadn't imagined it. It was like a castle wall in comparison. I took out the knife. Extended the biggest blade. Stabbed the surface. The wood was old. It looked desiccated and weak. The knife penetrated. But not far. Only three quarters of an inch. Then it hit something hard. Some kind of metal. I tried six inches to the right. The result was the same. I shifted another six inches. And another. I hit metal every time. The tenth spot I tried was different. The knife sank in all the way to the handle. Six inches beyond there, it sank in again.

I moved to a thin gap between the panels near the third and fourth places I'd hit metal. I jammed the blade in as far as it would go, then pushed to the side and tried to lever the wood forward. The surface layer separated. It came off in a jagged hunk, but a strip was left behind. I tried a foot lower and got the same result. It was the original wood. I was sure of that. But it was stuck to something with incredibly strong glue. Something metal. It must be a door. I couldn't see any other explanation. But I also couldn't see any handle. Or keyhole. Or any method of opening it at all.

I started at the top left and worked systematically across and down. I was pushing with my fingertips, checking every square inch. Looking for a concealed button. Or a secret flap. Or anything a lock could be hidden behind. I found nothing. I tried the sections of wall on either side. Had no luck there, either. I tried kicking the wall. There wasn't a hint of movement. Not even any noise. It was muffled by the wooden skin. I turned, raised my knee, and drove my heel back like I had done at Fenton's hotel. It didn't even make a dent.

I began to search the walls further to the side, then stopped. Putting the controls so far away didn't make sense. I had no experience with safe rooms but I assumed that if someone like Dendoncker had one, he would want to be able to get in it quickly. The whole point was to use them in an emergency. That implied a high degree of urgency. You

208

wouldn't want to go to the far corner of the cellar to operate some kind of elaborate mechanism. Even keying in a PIN could be too much of a delay. Plus, PINs can be guessed or discovered or betrayed. Some kind of remote control would be a better solution. Like cars have. Then another thought struck me. Sonia said the gate at Dendoncker's plant was operated by a transponder. And if that was a technology Dendoncker trusted in one key area of his operation, why not in another?

If a transponder was needed to open this hidden door, Mansour must have one. I didn't know what they looked like. I thought back to that morning, when I searched his pockets at the morgue. To his key ring. Transponders serve the same function as keys. That would be a reasonable place to keep one. And Mansour's had one thing that stood out. The square piece of plastic. I had dismissed it at the time as a fob. The guys at The Tree also had them. I pulled out the Chevy's keys. There was nothing similar on its ring. I guess the guy I took it from wasn't senior enough. Which left me with a self-defeating proposition. The only way to get a transponder was to take one from Mansour. But if I could get my hands on him to take his transponder, I wouldn't need it any more. I figured the best option was to wait for him to come back out. Or to trick him into coming out. Or to lure another of Dendoncker's stooges down there. And hope he had enough juice to warrant a transponder.

Juice. Aka power. Status. And in some places, slang for electricity. If the door lock was remotely triggered by a signal from a transponder, it must run on electricity. I crossed to the wall, by the water tank. Where the fuse box was mounted. It was a decrepit-looking thing. Dark wood.

Scuffed and battered. Like an electrocution waiting to happen. I opened its door. There was a row of insulators inside. Old school. Made of porcelain. Six of them. Each cradling an exposed section of fuse wire. They all looked intact. They all looked equally obsolete. There were no labels. No markings. Nothing to indicate which circuits they served. I figured I could pull them, one at a time, and see what happened. But it would be quicker to hit the switch at the top that controlled them all. I reached for it, then stopped. At the bottom, tucked away in the right-hand corner, there was a pack of matches. I was amazed how often people put matches and flashlights in their fuse box. It made no sense. It was the wrong way round. The fuse box is the destination in a power failure. Not a starting point.

I took the pack, struck a match, and flicked the switch. The bulb on the first floor blinked out. The cellar shrank until it felt no bigger than the flickering pool of light from the flame. I couldn't see much. I couldn't swear to it, but I thought I heard something. Behind me. From the wall below the bathroom. A click. Soft. But definitely mechanical.

I moved back to the section I'd been gouging with the knife. I took out my gun. Leaned against the wall. And pushed. It didn't move. I slammed my shoulder against it. And felt it give. Just an inch. I figured it wasn't only the lock that was electric. The door itself was motorized. The mechanism wasn't designed to operate without power. So I pushed harder. The panel swung back another inch. And another.

A crack appeared and light shone through. It wasn't bright. It had kind of an orange tone. But the other side was definitely illuminated. I dropped the match and crushed out the flame with my shoe. I stepped aside. Listened. I picked up no sound at all. No movement. No breathing. I waited a minute. Then I threw my full weight at the door. I kept shoving. The crack stretched to four inches. I dropped into a crouch. My gun was ready. I peered through the gap. I could see a wall of bricks to the right. They were slightly uneven sizes. They'd been whitewashed at some point and now the surface was flaking away. The mortar was crumbling. The floor was covered with the same tiles as the main part of the cellar. There was no sign of Mansour. I braced myself. I expected him to try to push the door back and knock me flying. Or pull it open and send me sprawling at his feet. But nothing happened. There was no movement. No sound. None of the subliminal vibrations emitted by another living creature. I was left with the feeling of being alone. I waited two minutes. Just to be sure. Then I pushed the door until the gap was big enough to squeeze through.

THIRTY-SIX

The room on the far side was empty. There were no people. No things. The other walls were also brick. They had the same peeling surface. But the one ahead of me, at the west side of the house, below the bathroom window, was mainly missing. There was a hole, six feet tall by five feet wide. The top was straight. A steel girder had been installed. Presumably to reinforce the structure. And to stop the whole thing from collapsing. The edges were like cartoon teeth where the bricks had been removed. They'd been knocked out neatly, one by one. On the far side there were more bricks. These ones were pale yellow. The wall they were part of was curved. It was like looking into a circular passage. Or a giant pipe. But dry. A cable ran down the centre of its ceiling. It connected a daisy chain of lightbulbs. They were naked, and threw a subdued golden glow. There was a track set into the floor, like the kind trolleys run on in mines. The passage continued on the level, to the left, for a hundred yards. Then it began to climb, gradually, until it disappeared from sight. It looked like it originally extended to the right, as well, but now that side was all bricked up.

I had to go back to the main part of the cellar for my phone to pick up any signal. As soon as it was happy, I called Wallwork.

I said to him, 'I need a map of the town's water system.'

Wallwork was silent for a moment. 'I might be able to find something online. What exactly do you need to know?'

'I'm in the basement of the house I told you about. The one owned by Dendoncker's shell company. I found a way into some kind of hidden passage. An old storm drain, maybe. Or a sewer. The guy I was chasing escaped down it. I want to know where it goes.'

'All right. This drain. Does it look old? Or new?'

'Not new. That's for sure. How old, I couldn't say. Maybe seventy-five, eighty years. Could be more. I'm no expert.'

'OK. That kind of age, it was probably built by the WPA. From what I read about the town the WPA did a whole bunch of work there. Back in the '30s. Buildings. Roads. Amenities. And particularly improvements to the sewers and drains. That's why they originally went. The town had two parts. There was a gap between them. Something weird about how it grew from a trading post, or whatever. Anyway, the southern half is higher. After a big storm the drains couldn't cope. They overflowed and the water ran downhill and flooded the northern half. It messed things up real bad. Sometimes the sewers overflowed, too. That was even less pleasant. The

213

southern half is part of Mexico, technically, but the problem impacted the US side. And the government was less parochial in those days. If the United States saw a problem, it fixed it. Wherever it was. And everybody was happy.'

'If the WPA did the work there should be records.'

'For sure. That's the government for you. Someone probably kept track of how many paperclips they used. The question is, where are the records? Did they survive? Only on paper? Or digitized and put online? I'm not sure anyone would invest the time and effort.'

'They must exist. Dendoncker had to have seen them. You said he made an effort to get this particular house. There has to be a reason for that. And it's not the view. Trust me. He must have realized it gave access to what's essentially a system of tunnels.'

'Seems likely. But there's no guarantee he found the information online. That's the problem. If it was on paper, in a book, he had a year to sniff it out. Your missing woman doesn't. He could have been poking around in libraries. Municipal archives. Do you have time for that? And wherever it was, how many copies were there? He could have stolen them. Or destroyed them to protect his secret.'

'You're saying it's hopeless?'

'No. I'm saying I'll try. Just don't hold your breath.'

I went back outside and crouched down at the side of Sonia's car. She rolled down her window and I saw that her eyes were red and swollen again.

She said, 'I'm sorry. I just had a crazy vision of you coming out and saying you'd found Michael. That he was OK, after all.'

I said nothing.

'You haven't. Have you?'

'No. I wish I had.'

'Did you find anything?'

'The entrance to a tunnel. I don't know where it goes. Yet.'

Sonia reached for the door release. 'I'll come with you.'

'No. It looks like the kind of place you go in, you might not come back out.'

'I don't care.'

'I do.'

'But you're going anyway?'

I nodded. 'I have to. Michael's sister could be at the other end.'

'Michaela?'

'Right.'

'I hope you find her. I hope she's OK.'

'Do you know her?'

'No. We never met. But I heard all about her. I hoped one day she'd be my sister-in-law.'

I waited until Sonia's tail lights had disappeared around the corner then went back into the house. I paused at the top of the ladder. Felt a prickle spread between my shoulder blades. Ignored it. Climbed down. Went through the concealed door. And looked into the tunnel. It seemed like the rails were pointing into the distance. It was an illusion, of course. A trick of perspective. But I still wanted to know where they went. And why they were there at all.

Dendoncker must have installed them. There was no place for them in a functioning sewer. Or drain. Plus, they looked new. Newer than the surrounding brickwork, anyway. There was no sign of rust. The steel was shiny. It had recently been used. Polished by metal wheels running along it. Probably some kind of truck. Probably carrying Dendoncker's smuggled contraband. In which case it must link to a storage facility. Another house he took over. Or an abandoned pumping station. Someplace like that.

Which didn't make sense. Why not just drive the stuff to and from the depot from there? Why move it around underground and load it up here? It called for extra effort. Extra resources. Extra time. I couldn't see how it reduced the risk. But whatever the reason, I wanted to know where the other place was. I would rather ambush Mansour there, where he felt safe. From a direction he wasn't expecting. I didn't want to stalk him through the tunnel. That option didn't appeal to me at all. But the only alternative was to wait for Wallwork. To see if he found a map. He wasn't confident. There was no guarantee it would be conclusive. And there was no way of knowing how long it would take him.

I checked that the pack of matches was in my pocket. Retrieved the tarnished mirror. Stepped through the hole in the wall. Into the tunnel. And started to walk.

THIRTY-SEVEN

The temperature in the tunnel was cool. It was surprisingly comfortable. But the air quality was a different story. It was foul. Stale. It felt thick and dusty as I breathed it in. I fought the urge to turn back. Or if I had to keep going, to cover the ground as fast as possible. I forced myself to move slowly. To make as little noise as possible. I finally got into a rhythm, stepping on every third sleeper and pausing in the relative shadow between each pool of light thrown by the bulbs on the ceiling. I kept going for a hundred yards. To the point where the gradient increased. Then the presence of the rail track suddenly made sense.

From the base of the incline I could see how far the tunnel continued. Another four hundred yards. At least. It climbed all the way. But it was dead straight. I pictured the position of the border in relation to the house. Calculated the distance to the buildings on the far side. The ones I'd seen when I first entered the town with Fenton. It all added up. I thought about the WPA guys arriving all those years ago. How they must have seen things. They faced two challenges. Too much water. And gravity. They couldn't make the water disappear. They couldn't make it run uphill. And they didn't want it to keep flowing down and flooding the northern part of the town. So they must have gone lateral. Recruited gravity as an ally. Turned it to their advantage. And joined up the drainage systems.

To guys in the '30s it must have seemed like a practical solution to a natural problem. They were engineers, not politicians. Not border guards. The world was different in those days. Before they had to worry about drugs. Cartels. Border walls. Back then they would have seen two halves of a town separated by an arbitrary line on a map. They would have thought their work was making life better for the people who lived there. Now it looked more like they were setting up a smuggler's dream. No wonder Dendoncker chose that town. And that house. He was no fool. That was becoming clearer all the time.

I kept going up the slope. At the same speed. With the same rhythm. The further I went, the more obvious it became that this underground supply route hadn't just fallen into Dendoncker's lap. As I gained height I passed a bunch of newer sections of brick. The patches were circular. And dished. They followed the contours of the wall. There must have once been lots of smaller channels that were now blocked off. Dendoncker must have done his homework. He must have come across the records of the work. Including a diagram. The system would have looked like a tree. A broad, straight trunk with thinner branches

218

sprouting off right and left. The branches would run beneath the southern part of the town. Collecting the excess water. And carrying it to the trunk. That was the key. None of it originated in that central section. So, when Dendoncker chopped off the branches, he was left with a dry tunnel. I don't know what other impact it would have had. Maybe the population had shrunk to the point there was no longer enough water to be a problem. Maybe it rained less these days. Maybe the floods had started happening again. But whatever the outcome, I doubted Dendoncker cared. Not as long as he could roam back and forth beneath the border, carrying anything he wanted in his little railroad between two parts of a sleepy town that no one paid any attention to.

The original tunnel ended after four hundred and twenty yards. Or maybe it began there, as that was its maximum height and water ran downhill. I came to a wall made of the same pale yellow bricks. It had the same flaky surface. But the tracks veered to the left. They turned ninety degrees and disappeared through another hole. There was another steel girder at the top. And more jagged edges down both sides where the bricks had been chipped away.

I moved in close to the wall and used the mirror to look around the corner. The track only continued for ten extra feet. A rail truck was parked at the end in front of a concrete wall. It was long enough for four people to sit, single file. Or for a decent amount of cargo to be carried. There was room for a variety of sizes of boxes and containers. Like the kind Dendoncker transferred to private planes under cover of his business. A cable snaked away from the side of the truck. It was thick. Heavy-duty. Plenty of amps could flow

219

down it. Plenty of power. It stretched all the way to a grey box on the far wall. I figured the truck was battery-powered. That was smart. It was much easier to press a button than push something that size up the gradient. Empty, let alone fully loaded.

I caught movement in the mirror. It was a man. He was familiar. But he wasn't Mansour. He was the second guy from last night. Under the streetlight, by the border fence. Whose ankle I had broken. He was sitting behind a desk. It reminded me of the kind teachers in grade school used to have. I could see his foot. It was in plaster, sticking out of the gap between the twin pedestals. A clipboard was lying flat on the surface in front of him. There was a chessboard next to it. The pieces were laid out for the start of a game. The guy was paying it no attention. His arms were crossed. His head was back. The tendons were tight in his neck. He was fidgeting. He looked tense. Nervous. I put the mirror down before he spotted it. Took my keys out of my pocket. Picked one at random. Used it to scratch the wall. I started with a short, quick movement. Then I scratched again. A longer motion. Then another short scratch. I couldn't hear any response from the guy. So I kept going. I scratched out the letters to four words in Morse code. RUN FOR YOUR LIFE. Maybe that was unfair in the circumstances. Maybe it was impractical. Maybe HOBBLE FOR YOUR LIFE would have been more appropriate.

In the end, whether he understood or not, he came to investigate. I heard him crossing the space between us. He was using crutches. I could tell from the sound he made. He came closer. His head appeared around the

220

corner. His chest. His face registered surprise. But only for a moment. Because as he stepped forward I took a handful of his shirt, just below his neck. I twisted for a better grip and slammed him back against the wall. The wind was knocked out of him. He slumped forward, gasping for breath. Dropped one crutch and cradled the back of his head with his hand.

'Let go.' He could barely manage a whisper.

I twisted the shirt harder, increasing the pressure on his throat.

'I'll yell.' He summoned a little more volume. 'Get help. Others'll be here in two seconds.'

I said, 'Really? How many? There were four of you, last night. How did that work out?'

The guy tried to suck in some breath.

'Go ahead. I hope your buddies do come. I hope Dendoncker comes. I wonder if he'll be impressed? Only, the way I understand it, when you're on sentry duty you're supposed to stop intruders. Not let them in and then start crying.'

The guy breathed out, slowly. He made a mean hissing sound, but he didn't shout.

'Smart move,' I said. 'Let's do this instead. I'll ask you a couple of questions. You answer. And Dendoncker never finds out how useless you are.'

'No way. I won't tell you anything.'

'OK.' I hooked my foot behind the guy's standing leg and swept it out from under him. He crashed down next to the track in the gap between the rail and the wall. I grabbed his right pants leg, just above the ankle, and hauled it up to waist height. Pulled out my knife. Found a blade with a serrated edge, like a little saw. And slid it between the

221

plaster of Paris and his skin. 'Time for a new plan. Get rid of the bandage. Remember how it felt yesterday? When the bones broke? You screamed pretty good. I bet it was louder than you can shout. That should bring Dendoncker and his boys running. Save me the trouble of hunting them down later.'

'You wouldn't.'

I went to work with the blade. It cut through the powdery material with no effort at all. The guy was mesmerized for a moment. He was staring at the cloud of white dust puffing out and floating down to the ground.

'Stop.' His voice had risen an octave or two. 'OK. What kind of questions?'

'The woman Dendoncker took. Michaela Fenton. Is she here?'

'I think so.'

'You think?'

'I haven't seen her. But I heard some other guys talking. It sounded like she was here.'

'Where, exactly?'

'Dendoncker's half of the building. I think.'

'What kind of building is this?'

'I guess it's a school, from the way it looks. Was a school. There are no kids here now. I don't know much else. This is my first time here. I was never allowed through the tunnel before.'

'What does Dendoncker use it for?'

'Like, a warehouse, I think. For his merchandise. The stuff he takes on the planes. I saw the containers. I think there's a workshop here, too. Maybe an office.'

'What gets made in the workshop?'

The guy looked away. He didn't answer. I started sawing the plaster again.

'Dendoncker had someone working there. That's all I know.'

I paused with the knife. 'Making bombs?'

'Maybe. Probably. Look, I made sure not to find out. Some things, it's better not to know.'

'OK. How many people are here?'

'There's Dendoncker. There are three guys with him. At least. A bunch of locals. Maybe half a dozen. I don't know them. Haven't seen them before. I don't think Dendoncker trusts them all the way. They just do the cooking and the fetching and carrying. Plus the three guys who went to the town. We're still waiting for them to get back.'

'No need to wait.' I folded the knife and put it back in my pocket. 'They won't be coming.'

I let go of the guy's leg. He managed to stop his ankle crashing into the ground, but only just. Then he rolled on to all fours and struggled up on to his good foot.

'What happened to them?' The guy hopped around for a minute while he retrieved his crutches.

I shrugged. 'Your friends are an accident-prone bunch.'

The guy made a move around the corner. He acted like he was heading back to the desk. Then he spun around. He raised the crutch in his right hand and lunged. He was trying to spear me in the gut. I moved six inches to the side. Grabbed hold midway between the rubber tip and the handle. Stepped forward. And punched him. An upper cut. It lifted the guy right off his feet. His remaining crutch clattered to the ground. His body followed, completely inert. He landed on his back, neatly between the rails. I flipped him over. Secured his wrists with a zip tie. Took his pistol

223

from his waistband. A 1911. It was old, but well maintained. I bent his good leg at the knee. Used another zip tie to fasten it to the belt loop at the back of his pants. Picked him up. Tossed him in the rail truck. And threw his crutches in after him.

THIRTY-EIGHT

The desk the guy had been using was at the side of a plant room. It was a giant place. There were four huge boilers in a line along one wall. Four huge water tanks opposite them. The ceiling was hidden by a tangle of massive pipes. Some were lagged. Some were painted. They snaked away in every direction. There was a door in the far corner. It was the only way out I could see, apart from the tunnel. I crossed the room and opened it.

The door led to a staircase. It was made of wood. It had originally been painted white but patches of bare timber were peeking out from the centre of each tread. I guess Dendoncker's operation generated more traffic than the architect originally anticipated. I climbed up. Slowly. I kept my feet near the sides to avoid creaking. There was another door at the top. I stopped. Listened. And heard nothing.

I tried the handle. It wasn't locked. It swung open easily

and let me out in the corner of a kitchen. It was a huge industrial-scale place, all stainless steel and white tile. There were stoves. Ovens. Microwaves. Preparation areas. A line of giant fridges along one side wall. A line of cupboards along the other. I picked one at random. It was full of cans of baked beans. There were hundreds of them. They were tiny. Single servings, maybe, for children with no appetite. It seemed like a weird choice, given the scale of the equipment.

The kitchen was separated from the dining hall by a serving counter. It was low. A suitable height for kids, I guess. It ran the full width of the room. A section at the left was hinged. It was folded back so I went through. The rest of the space was dim. It felt cavernous. The ceiling was high. Maybe twenty feet. Only one bulb was working, roughly in the centre. I could barely make out my surroundings. The floor was made of rectangular wooden blocks. They were fitted together like herring bones. There was just one table. It was round. Made of white plastic. There were six plastic chairs in a scruffy circle around it. They seemed lost. The place looked like it was designed for long, solid refectory tables, lined up in neat parallel rows. Not cheap garden furniture. There was a set of double doors to the right. They were closed. And they were solid, so I couldn't see where they led. The rest of the wall was glass. Narrow metal frames divided the panes. They stretched from floor to ceiling. Harsh white light was spilling out from somewhere nearby. I moved forward to see what was causing it. Then I stopped dead in my tracks.

It was the lack of light in the dining hall that saved my bacon. It prevented the two guys from spotting me. The guys in suits who had accompanied Dendoncker to the morgue. They were at the far end of the corridor that led away from the other side of the double doors. They were sitting on stools in front of another identical set of doors. The corridor was eight feet wide. It was twenty feet long. It had glass walls and a glass ceiling. Three raised vents, evenly spaced. And a double line of fluorescent tubes. They ran the whole length. They were powerful. And bright. The human eye can't see from a brightly lit area into a much dimmer one. Which was fortunate for me. Because the guys were each holding a gun. An Uzi. An interesting choice of weapon. Not the lightest. Not the fastest cyclic rate. Not the greatest amount of rifling inside the barrel. There are better options out there. Any of the Heckler & Koch MP5 derivatives, for example. That's what I'd have picked in their shoes. But in mine? Alone? Against two Uzis? I wouldn't have liked my chances.

It looked like the glass corridor led to a mirror image of the part of the building I was in. On the outside, anyway. Inside, it most likely had a different set-up. I couldn't see why a school would need two kitchens and two dining halls. Given the guards with the Uzis, it seemed like a safe bet it would be what the guy with the broken ankle had called Dendoncker's half. It would be suicide to approach it along the corridor. I needed to find another entrance. I would have to loop around the exterior. Which meant finding a way out.

Ahead, at the end of the dining hall furthest from the kitchen, there were two doors. The one on the right had a sign that said *el Maestro Principal*. The one on the left, *el Diputado Maestro Principal*. I checked them both. They were both empty. There was no furniture. Nothing on the

227

walls. No closets or storage areas. And neither had an external door.

There were three sets of doors in the wall opposite the windows. I tried the closest. It opened into another large space. It was equally badly lit. It was the same width, but longer because it had no kitchen. To the right, adjacent to the offices, there was a raised area like a stage. On the far side there was another expanse of floor-to-ceiling windows. There was a pair of doors in the centre, leading outside. The other two walls were covered with climbing bars. Three ropes were suspended from a central ceiling joist. They were coiled up, ten feet from the ground. I guessed the place was a combined assembly hall/performance space/gymnasium. Originally. Now it was a storage area. For Dendoncker's aluminium containers.

The containers came in all sorts of shapes and sizes. Some had wheels. Some had none. Most were jumbled up at the far end of the hall. A few were lined up in some taped-off sections of floor. There were four rectangles. Each was labelled with a word made out of white duct tape. The first said *Out*. Then there was *Prep*. Then *In*. Then *Onward*.

The *Out* area was empty. There was one container in *Prep*. *In* was empty. And there were two containers in *Onward*. I opened the container in *Prep*. It had wheels. It was six feet long by three deep and four high. And it was empty. I moved along to *Onward*. These containers were smaller. They were both four by three by one. And they were both sealed.

There were little metal tags attached to wires that looped through their catches. I broke open the nearer one. I lifted the lid. It was crammed full of cash. Bundles of twenty-dollar bills. They were used. They smelled sweet and sharp, which made me think they were real. The second container was lined with blue foam, shaped into protective peaks. It was also full. Of cardboard boxes. All the same size. All the same shape. They were plain beige. There were no markings of any kind. I picked a box at random and looked inside. It was full of plastic bottles. Thirty-two of them. White, with child-safe lids. I took one out. There was a label stuck to its side. Printed in black and purple ink. There were logos and symbols and barcodes. And some text: Dilaudid (Hydromorphone) Instant Release, 8mg, 100 tablets.

There was nothing I could use so I crossed to the doors in the glass wall and headed outside. Orange light was spilling around the side of the building. Ahead there was a parking lot. There were spaces for forty vehicles but only two were taken. By a pair of SUVs. Cadillac Escalades. They were black and dusty and kitted out with dark glass. They were sitting low on their suspension. But evenly, front to back, which probably meant they were armoured to some degree. Beyond them there was a fence. It was twenty feet high. Made of stout chain link. There was another one, running parallel, the same height, the same material, twenty-five feet further out. That meant twice the amount of cutting for anyone looking to break in. Twice the time. Twice the exposure.

I checked for cameras. There was one on every other fence post. They were all facing out. None were moving so I went to my left and followed around the building. When I was near the corner I heard a sound. Someone was running. More than one person. But not continuously. They were starting and stopping and sprinting and turning. And there was another noise. A hollow thumping. I crouched down and peered around. I saw where the weird light was coming from. There was a pair of floodlights, on tripods, like you see at construction sites. They were mainly illuminating a long rectangular patch of dirt. It stretched along the side of the building, all the way past the gap that was filled by the glass corridor. There were four guys on it. Playing soccer. They were probably in their mid-twenties. They had bare feet, baggy shorts and no shirts. I took out my gun, held it behind my thigh, and stepped into the light.

The guys stopped and looked at me. The nearest one beckoned for me to join them. I waved, *thanks, but no*. And started moving again. I skirted around the far side of the pitch. They started playing again. One guy tried an extravagant flick. It didn't work. The ball bounced away, off the dirt and between the two halves of the building. It rolled towards the glass wall of the corridor. He ran to fetch it. The guys inside with the Uzis didn't react. Maybe they didn't notice, because of the light imbalance. Or maybe they were used to it, and didn't care.

If you looked down on the school from above it would have looked like a capital H. The assembly hall and dining hall would be one of the uprights. The glass corridor would be the cross bar. And the other upright would be Dendoncker's half. I was hoping that half would have plenty of doors and windows. And it did. There was a door in both of the short sides. Four doors in the long side. As well as four windows. They were big. Six feet high by twenty wide. But none of them were any use to me. They were all boarded up. With steel plates. Half an inch thick. With tamper-proof bolts. The kind that are used to keep thieves and squatters out of high-value construction sites. There was no way to break

230

through them. No way to prise them off. And no way up to the roof. All the down pipes had been sawn off fifteen feet from the ground. There was no way to smash through the side of the building with a vehicle. Giant dollops of concrete had been dumped all the way around. They were four feet in diameter, on average. Reinforced with steel rebar. With a gap between them of no more than three feet. The only way to breach the place would be with a tank. Or explosives. I didn't have either. Which left the glass corridor as the only possible way in. I figured I'd have to rethink my approach. It was time to get a little more creative.

There was nothing interesting between the long side of the building and the fence. Just a big patch of ground covered with weird, rubbery asphalt. Maybe the site of a playground, back in the day. Now it was empty so I followed around the next corner. I came upon a kind of rough shed. It was built of cinderblock, painted white, with a corrugated metal roof. It had a wooden door, secured with a padlock. A new one. Hefty. There was one window. At head height. It was barred, but there was no glass. I struck a match. Stretched in. Took a look. And instantly blew out the flame. The interior was packed full of cylindrical objects, sitting on flat bases with sharp noses pointing up to the ceiling. Artillery shells. Twenty rows of fifteen. At least. They looked in bad shape. Their cases were rusty and corroded. Some were dented and scraped. Not the kind of things I was in any hurry to get involved with.

I found another structure ten feet further on. It was smaller. Cube-shaped. And slightly irregular. Each side was no more than three feet long. It was all metal, including the roof. Or the lid. There was a row of holes punched along the

231

top edge of the sides. Maybe an inch diameter. The front was hinged. It was standing open a little. I opened it wider. Risked another match. And looked in. It was empty. It had been used recently, though. For something. Maybe animal related, judging by the stench. Or maybe part of Dendoncker's interrogation set-up. It was the kind of place no one would want to be cooped up in. Especially not in the midday sun.

THIRTY-NINE

I completed my circuit of the building and went back inside. I made my way through the assembly hall. Across the dining hall. And crouched in front of the doors leading to the glass corridor. I knocked. MP-style. I figured one of three things would happen. The guys on the other side would ignore me. They would call for reinforcements. Or they would investigate.

The first option would be no help. The second could work out OK. But I was hoping for the third. I was hoping that one guy would stay back, and one would approach. He'd open the door. The one on my left, judging by the way they fitted together. He would pull it back into the corridor. Then either his gun would appear, or his head. I didn't care which. I would grab whatever I saw. Yank the guy through. Break his neck. And I'd do it quickly, before the door swung closed again. I'd take the guy's Uzi and fire it through the gap. When the clip was empty I would follow up with a pistol. If that was still necessary. If the guy who'd stayed back didn't resemble Swiss cheese. After that it would be a question of taking his key or his transponder or whatever was needed to open the other pair of doors. Then I could find out what the guys were guarding. Or who. Probably Dendoncker. And hopefully Fenton.

There was no response to my first knock so I tried again. After a moment I heard footsteps. They were heavy. Deliberate. The door opened. The left one, as I'd thought. Then Mansour appeared. Not as I'd thought. He didn't pause. He didn't peer out. He just came striding through.

I straightened up. The door was already closing, but that was the least of my worries. Mansour spun around to face me. He was grinning. His left cheek was blue and bruised and swollen. A souvenir from my elbow, that morning. I threw a swift jab, looking to add to the damage, but he read it. He dodged sideways and right away he came back at me. He was fast. Crazy fast, given his size. He raised his knee. High. Almost instantly his massive foot flicked out. He was going for my stomach. It would have been like getting hit by a bowling ball if he'd connected. My organs would have been mashed. I'd have been thrown against the door. Maybe through the door.

It would have been game over, right there. No way was I going to let that happen so I danced to the side. Slipped around his kick and launched myself forward. I grabbed his thigh. Pinned it to my side and drove the heel of my hand up and into his chin. His head rocked back. It was a solid hit. Not the best ever, but it would have knocked most guys on their ass. I had no doubt about that. I felt him begin to topple backward. I thought the job was halfway done. Loosened my grip on his leg. Shaped up to kick him as soon as he was down. Which was a mistake. The guy was falling. But deliberately. He threw both his arms around me. Locked his hands behind my back and pulled me over with him. There was no way I could resist. He had at least a hundred pounds on me. And momentum was on his side.

We landed in a tangle, face to face, with me on top. But the moment his back hit the ground the guy levered with his legs. He twisted at the waist. My arms were trapped. I had nothing to brace against. Just empty air. A moment later our positions were reversed. I was under him. I couldn't move. I couldn't breathe. I was in serious trouble. I knew it. He could sense it. All he had to do was hold on. Let his bulk do the work. But he was impatient. Or he wanted to show off. He pulled his arms out from beneath me. Slid his knees forward and raised his chest off mine. I sucked in air. He leaned forward. Grabbed my head, one hand either side. I felt his thumbs moving around. Homing in on my eyes. I didn't know if he was just aiming to blind me. Or if he had something else in mind, like trying to crush my skull or lift my head and slam it into the floor.

I didn't wait to find out. I gripped his wrists and whipped my arms down towards my waist. At the same time I pushed down into the floor with my feet, driving my hips up into the air. A normal opponent would have been catapulted right over my head. He'd have landed winded and surprised on his back. This guy barely rose at all. Six inches at the most. But that was enough.

I rolled out, got on to all fours, and sprang up on to my feet. Mansour was already halfway up so I kicked him in the gut. The kind of kick that would send a football out of a stadium and clear across the parking lot. It flipped him on to his back. He sat right up, so I kicked him again in the side of the head. He went over. Rolled away. I followed. He tried to get back on his feet. No way was he going to succeed. It was the first rule. When you get your opponent down, you finish him. No hesitation. No second chances. No mistakes. One more kick was all it would take. I pulled my foot back. Picked my spot. And heard the door open behind me.

'Stop.' It was a man's voice. Raspy. Whispery.

It was Dendoncker.

The voice came closer. 'Move, and she dies. Then you do.'

I glanced over my shoulder. Dendoncker was there, and he wasn't alone. The guy in the pale suit was at his side, with his Uzi. Fenton was on Dendoncker's other side. She was using an old-school wooden crutch to keep her balance. The cuff of her right pant leg was hanging loose and empty. She had a rope around her neck. The other end was in Dendoncker's right hand. He was pinching it with his remaining finger and thumb. And holding a knife in his left. It had a long, narrow blade. Like the kind British commandos used in the Second World War. Designed for one thing. Killing. With maximum efficiency. He was pressing its tip into Fenton's throat.

'Don't listen to him.' Fenton's voice was hoarse. 'Kill the bastard.'

'He won't.' Dendoncker's eyes were glistening. 'He went to a lot of trouble to find you. He wants you alive. And even if he changed his mind and decided you're not worth it, he's not a fool. He knows he's quick with his feet and his fists. But he knows he's not as quick as a nine-millimetre bullet. And anyway, there's no need for anyone to get killed. I have a proposition. Something very simple. Very straightforward. Agree, and we all get to walk away without a scratch. No one else will get hurt either. So what do you say, Mr Reacher? Would you like to hear my terms?'

FORTY

The truth was I had no interest in hearing Dendon-cker's terms. None at all. But I had negative interest in getting shot by his stooge. And I didn't like see-ing Fenton trussed up and held at knife point. I didn't like that at all.

'Lose the rope,' I said. 'Lose the knife. Then you can say your piece. Beyond that, I'm making no promises.'

Dendoncker wanted to talk in what he called his office. Getting there involved going through the double doors, along the glass corridor, and through the doors at the far end. The guy in the dark suit unlocked them. He held his keys up to a white square attached to the frame. I guess he had a transponder hooked on to his key ring. Probably like the one Mansour had when I searched him at the morgue, but I was too far away to be certain.

The guy didn't go through. He stood to the side and

Dendoncker stepped past him and pushed the right-hand door open. He went first. I followed, with the guy in the pale suit behind me. He was close, but not so close I could easily grab him. Or the Uzi. We stepped into another corridor. This one ran at ninety degrees. It stretched away, left and right, running the whole width of this half of the building. There was an exit door at each end. Their handles were missing. I guess they had to be. To allow for the steel plates that covered them on the exterior. One side of the corridor was floor-to-ceiling glass, facing the dining hall. There was a wall on the other side. It was plain white, with four doors. Two to the left of the junction with the glass corridor. And two to the right. Each door had a window. The glass was laced with steel wires and covered on the other side with newspaper. It was turning yellow with age. All the text I could see was in Spanish.

Dendoncker led the way to the right. Behind me I heard footsteps peeling off in the opposite direction. I looked over my shoulder and saw Mansour with his hand wrapped around Fenton's elbow, guiding her away. It made her arm look like a tiny stick. She was moving freely enough, though. There was no sign that they'd hurt her. Which was fortunate. For them.

Dendoncker ignored the first door he came to. He stopped outside the next one. The one at the end. He worked the lock with a regular key. Went in and hit the light switch. Six pairs of fluorescent tubes flickered into life on the ceiling. There was a walled-off section to the right. It was square. There were two doors, marked *Niños* and *Niñas*. There was a wide window and another door straight ahead. Both were boarded up on the outside. There was a chalkboard on the

239

left-hand wall. It had been wiped clean. The place had been a classroom. That was clear. I could trace where the kids' desks had been from the scuff marks on the floor. They had been arranged in a horseshoe, with the open end in front of the chalkboard. It looked like there had been five pairs on each of the other sides. The teacher's desk had survived. It was set at an angle in the far left corner. A dining chair was next to it, with metal legs and an orange plastic seat. There was another half dozen of the same kind of chairs in a circle in the centre of the room. A beaten-up leather couch by the wall on the right. A low bookcase at its side. It was full of textbooks. About physics. A couple of French novels were lying on top. On the other side there was an army cot. It had a metal frame, painted olive green. There was a pillow in a white cotton case. Just one. A white sheet, pulled tight. And a footlocker on the floor. There was no natural light. No fresh air. It wasn't much of a place to work or sleep.

Dendoncker headed to the right. 'Against the wall. Feet apart. I'm sure this won't be the first time you've done this.'

'One minute.' I made it through the door to the boys' bathroom before the guy in the pale suit could stop me.

Inside, there were two stalls. Two urinals. Two basins. And two hand-driers. Everything was small and chipped and worn, but it was clean. Nothing offered many options for concealing things. I had two guns and a knife. I wasn't too concerned if they got taken. I could easily replace them. I was more worried about the phone. I had called Wallwork from it. And Sonia. I didn't want Dendoncker trying those numbers.

I thought about breaking the phone and flushing it away but I didn't know if the water pressure would be up to the job. If it wasn't, I would just be drawing attention to the fact I had something to hide. So I reconsidered. All the phones I had taken from Dendoncker's guys were blank. He was used to that kind of discipline. So he wouldn't see anything unusual in it. I hoped. I made sure the phone was set to silent. Worked my way through the menu until I found the option to delete all call records. Put the phone away. Waved my hand under the drier to trigger its motor. Then went back out into the classroom.

Dendoncker was standing between the pair of doors. He was fidgeting like a five-year-old. I turned and rested my hands on the wall and stood still while he searched me. He did a competent job. A little slow, but thorough. When he was done he handed me back my passport and my cash, but he kept my toothbrush and the other things.

'Come.' Dendoncker headed to the ring of dining chairs. 'Sit.'

I strolled across and took the seat opposite him.

Dendoncker didn't speak. He just sat and stared at me. His knees were pressed together. His hands were resting on his thighs. His head was tipped to one side. He looked like an inmate at a senior centre, waiting for an encounter group to get started and curious to find out all about the new arrival. But if he thought his silence would fill me with the urge to share, he had picked the wrong guy.

Dendoncker gave up after two minutes. He ran the remaining finger and thumb on his right hand through his wispy hair and wet his lips with his tongue. 'So. To business. But first, a question. Who do you work for, Mr Reacher?'

'No one.'

'OK. So you're freelance. Who hired you?'

241

'No one.'

'Someone did. And I know who it was. You can say his name. You won't be breaking any confidences. Just confirming what I already know.'

'No one hired me.'

Dendoncker looked me straight in the eye. 'Nader Khalil. Yes? You can nod your head. You don't have to say a word.'

'Never heard of the guy.'

Dendoncker didn't respond for a moment. His face was blank. I couldn't tell if he was relieved or disappointed.

'All right.' Dendoncker shook his head. 'Let's get back on track. My proposition. It's very simple. Easy to carry out. No one gets hurt. You and your friend walk away scot-free the moment it's done. How does that sound?'

I said nothing.

'All the job involves is driving. And a little lifting. Easy for a guy your size. It'll only take three days. I'll give you the route to follow and pay for your meals and a hotel for both nights. Nice places. Then, when you reach the destination, you'll drop off an item. Just one. See? Nothing could be easier. I take it you agree.'

'I do not.'

'Maybe I wasn't clear about the alternative?' Dendoncker nodded towards the guy with the Uzi. 'There's a lot of desert around here. A lot of scavengers. They'd never find the bodies. Yours. Or your friend's.'

'My answer's still no. I'm not your delivery boy. And it's better for two lives to be lost than fifty.'

'I don't follow.' Dendoncker pretended to look confused. 'How would fifty lives be lost?'

'The item you want me to deliver. I know what it is.'

242

Wrinkles furrowed Dendoncker's forehead. 'The item is harmless. I give you my word.'

I said nothing.

'I don't know what you heard, but if you think the item is dangerous you've been given bad information.' Dendoncker stood up. 'Come. See for yourself.'

FORTY-ONE

Dendoncker led the way to the next room along the corridor. Another former classroom. It was the same shape as Dendoncker's office. The same size. The same layout. It had the same kids' bathrooms. The same broad rectangular window and exit door, sealed up tight with steel plates. The same harsh lighting. Another army cot, against the wall. This one had a green blanket over its sheet, and two pillows. And in place of the circle of chairs in the centre of the room it looked like the contents of a mobile workshop had been unloaded. There was a folding metal work bench with a pair of goggles hanging over the handle of its vice. It was next to a trolley with two gas cylinders attached with chains. One was larger than the other. Oxygen and acetylene, I guessed. They were connected by a flexible pipe with a nozzle at one end. There were four tool chests on wheels with all kinds of drawers

244

and doors and handles. They were made of metal. Painted olive green. They were all scuffed and dented. This wasn't their first tour of duty. That was obvious.

Dendoncker crossed the room and stood against the left-hand wall, next to the chalkboard. He was at the end of a row of artillery shells. There were nine altogether. Divided into three groups of three. One in the centre of each set was pointing straight up. One was angled to the right. One was angled to the left. Each of the trios was fixed to a metal base, like a tray. The sides were four inches high and there was a wheel at each corner.

'This is what we're talking about.' Dendoncker pointed at the shells. 'One of these. They generate smoke. That's all. Nothing harmful. Nothing dangerous.'

I stayed near the door.

Dendoncker blinked a couple of times then stared off into the distance as if he was struggling to complete a complex calculation in his head. 'OK. I see the problem. This is what we're going to do. Pick one.'

I didn't move.

'The original plan was to go with three, but we decided a single one would get the point across better. Less is more. Isn't that what people say? So, pick one. We'll take it outside and trigger it. You'll see for yourself that it's benign.'

I figured that if Dendoncker was prepared to sacrifice one of his bombs it would be crazy not to let him. That would be one fewer to deal with later. I made my way over to the line of devices. Examined them each in turn. Saw that the shells all had a series of holes drilled around their bodies just below the point where the nose cone was attached. Each hole was half an inch in diameter. Each shell had a

245

tube sticking out of one of the holes. The tubes were made of black rubber and they snaked down to a pump mounted at the centre of each tray. Each pump was wired to a battery. The kind that might be used in a small car, or a lawnmower. Each battery was also wired to a watch and a cellphone. The watches were digital. Just the bodies. No straps. Some ancient Casio model. I remember my brother Joe had one just like it in the early '90s. They were secured to the left-hand shell of each device. The phones were taped to the shells on the right. They had real keys and small screens. They looked basic. Old-fashioned. But solid. Reliable. And presumably redundant if the watches did their jobs.

I had thought I would maybe see something different in one of them. Something small and subtle that showed it had been set up specially for the demonstration. Or that Dendoncker would try to trick me like a hustler who needs their mark to pick a particular card. Either way, I would go for one of the others. But there was nothing. The devices were identical as far as I could tell. Dendoncker stood back. He stayed still. His body language was silent. His expression was neutral.

'What are you waiting for?' Dendoncker swept his hand along the line, but without emphasizing one device over another. 'They're all the same. Just pick one.'

When in doubt, I always let the numbers guide me. There were three devices. There are two prime numbers between one and three. So I pointed to the second device.

Dendoncker pulled out his phone and told whoever answered his call to report to the workshop right away. Two minutes later Mansour appeared in the doorway. Dendoncker pointed to the device I'd picked and said he wanted it

246

taken outside. Mansour loped across the room and studied it for a moment. Then he grabbed it by its central upright shell. He dragged it away from the wall and steered it back towards the door. The whole time he was dealing with it he was ignoring me. Actively, the way feuding cats pretend not to notice each other.

We must have made a strange-looking procession. First Mansour wheeling the bomb in front of him. Then Dendoncker. Then me. And finally the guy with the Uzi, further back, keeping what he probably thought was a safe distance. No one spoke as we went through the first set of double doors. Along the glass corridor. Through the second set of doors. Across the dining hall. Through the assembly hall. And out into the parking lot. Mansour continued until he was level with the pair of SUVs. It was almost fully dark by then. His outline started to fade as he reached the limit of the glow that was spilling out through the tall windows. The orange light was no longer visible from around the corner of the building. There was no sound, except for the device's wheels skittering across the asphalt. The soccer players must have called it a night.

Dendoncker made another call. He said he wanted the floodlights switched on. A moment later the whole perimeter of the building lit up. It was like a castle moat, only made of light rather than water. Ahead of us Mansour prodded the device's wheels with his toe. One at a time. Engaging their locks. Then he made his way over and stood at Dendoncker's side.

Dendoncker dialled another number and held the phone out to me. 'Want to do it?'

I shook my head.

'OK.' Dendoncker hit the green button, closed the phone, and slid it back into his pocket. 'Just watch.'

Nothing happened for ten seconds. Twenty. Then I heard three beeps. From the device. High-pitched. Electronic. The pump began to hum. It built up to a steady drone. Smoke appeared. Just a wisp at first. White. From the holes in the central shell. It grew into a steady stream. It was thick. Dense. Like steam from a kettle. Blue smoke began to pour from the right-hand shell. It mingled into a single plume but maintained the two distinct colours. Finally the left-hand shell got in on the act. Red smoke gushed out. It was at full force right away, billowing upward and quickly matching the other shades for volume.

'See? Smoke.' Dendoncker walked forward until he was a couple of feet away from the device. He flapped his left arm and made a show of wafting some of each colour into his mouth and nose. He kept it up for ten seconds then coughed and retreated to his previous spot. 'It burns the throat a little. I can't deny that. But it's not poisonous. There are no explosions. And there's no danger. So, are you satisfied?'

I waited another minute, until the last of the smoke had petered out. The blue lasted longest, but all three shells had produced a prodigious quantity. The space between the wall and the fence along the whole width of the building was filled with a swirling patriotic cloud. I was impressed. When Sonia first told me about Michael's plan I was dubious. I pictured a tiny spurt. Pale colours. A blink-and-you-miss-it kind of deal. Nothing to impress an audience. Live, or on TV. But if a thing like this went off in the middle of a ceremony there was no way the crowd could fail to notice.

'Satisfied?' Dendoncker glared at me. 'Good to go?'

248

I was starting to think I'd been wrong. Maybe I should have been more interested in Dendoncker's proposal after all.

I said, 'You want me to take one of these things, drive for three days, then leave it somewhere?'

'Precisely.' Dendoncker nodded. 'That's all you have to do.'

'Where do you want me to leave it?'

'You'll be given directions, one day at a time.'

Three days' drive. Enough time to get all the way up into Canada. Or down into Central America. But realistically, given that kind of distance, the target would be on the East Coast. DC, maybe. Or the White House. Or the Pentagon.

I said, 'OK. But why do you want me to leave it anywhere? What's the point?'

'I have my reasons. You don't need to know them. And they're not up for debate. The only question is who drives the truck. You can do it and walk away when the job's done. Or you can choose a different outcome and I'll find some-one else to do it.'

'And the woman?'

'Her fate is your fate. You choose to live, she lives. You choose not to . . .'

'OK. She can come with me. In the truck. Share the driv-ing. Help with the navigation.'

Dendoncker shook his head. 'She's going to remain our guest until you complete the mission.'

'In other words, you don't trust me.'

Dendoncker didn't reply.

'That's OK,' I said. 'I don't trust you either. How do I know you won't kill the woman the moment I'm out of sight?'

Dendoncker took a moment to think. 'Fair point. Before

you leave I'll return your phone. I'll give you a number. You can call it anytime. Talk to her. Confirm she's OK.'

'You let a captive sit around all day with a phone?'

'Of course not. One of my guys will bring her the phone when you call.'

I would have been happier if I was sure which of his guys would answer the phone. If I could guarantee it would be one guy in particular. But I had a good idea who it would be. What role he would play, anyway. And in the circumstances I figured that was good enough.

FORTY-TWO

My mother was French. I was born in Germany. I've lived on bases in dozens of countries. I've listened to people speak all kinds of languages. Some sound familiar. Some I can make sense of pretty easily. Others, not so much.

The words I heard come out of Dendoncker's mouth sounded just like they were English. Only I knew they meant something else altogether. Something I could understand with no trouble at all. He wanted me to do his dirty work. To plant the device for him. He would keep Fenton alive until it was in place. Then he would kill her. And me. Maybe the truck he'd supply was booby-trapped. Maybe he'd have someone lying in wait with a sniper rifle. But one way or another there was no scenario in which he could let Fenton or me survive.

I understood Dendoncker's words when he laid out his

plan. I was sure I did. But whether he understood mine when I agreed was a whole other question. One he wasn't going to like the answer to.

The demonstration was over. Terms were agreed. The wind was picking up. It was tugging at our clothes. The desert night was growing chilly. There was no reason to stay outside so we headed back into the building. We trooped along in the same order as before. But two things were different this time. The first was that Mansour wasn't wheeling a bomb in front of him. He just left its spent remains outside in the parking lot, still shrouded in the last traces of smoke. The second came when we reached the far end of the glass corridor. We passed through the double doors and Mansour turned left. Dendoncker went to the right and headed for his office. I stopped and stood still. The guy with the Uzi almost clattered into me.

'This way, asshole.' Mansour stopped outside the first door he reached and worked its lock.

I let a moment tick past then moved up alongside him. The guy with the Uzi trailed along behind.

'In.' Mansour pushed the door open.

I stepped through and he shoved me in the back. Hard. His fingers were spread. His hand landed square between my shoulder blades. He put his full weight into it, like he was trying to launch me through the back wall. A little payback for earlier, I guessed. Probably hoping I'd at least end up flat on my face and look stupid in front of the guy with the Uzi. In which case he must have been disappointed. Because I saw him move. He was reflected in the glass. So I planted my foot. Leaned back into the pressure. And barely broke my stride.

The room was just like Dendoncker's office and the workshop, only it was laid out the opposite way round. The bathrooms were on the left and the chalkboard was on the right. There was only one piece of furniture. An army cot. It was in the dead centre of the room. It was bolted to the floor. And Fenton was sitting on it. She grabbed her crutch, stood up, and took one step in my direction.

The door slammed behind me. Footsteps stomped away down the corridor. Thirty seconds later they stomped back again. The door opened and a mattress came sailing in through the gap. I stepped to the side to avoid it landing on me. It was thin with cream and olive-green stripes. And it had more than its share of marks and stains. It was probably the one from the bed in the workshop. Minus its sheets and blanket. And pillows.

'Sleep well, assholes.' Mansour slammed the door again. I heard the key turn. And this time two sets of footsteps clattered away into the distance.

Fenton hustled around the crumpled mattress, closed the gap between us, and threw her free arm around me. She pulled me close and pressed her head against my chest.

She said, 'I can't believe you're here.' Then she let go and took a step back. 'You shouldn't have come. You know that, right? What were you thinking?'

'I'm like the proverbial bad penny. You can't get rid of me.'

'This isn't funny. Now we're both in trouble. Deep trouble. Honestly, there might be no way out of this. For either of us.'

I shook my head. 'Don't worry. Everything's going to work out fine. Give it three days, and we'll be home and dry.'

Fenton held up her free hand, then pointed to her ear,

then made a circular gesture indicating the room in general. 'All I can say is thank you. And I'm sorry I got you involved in all this.'

'Don't mention it.' I picked up the mattress and set it on the floor about six feet away from the bed. 'And seriously, don't worry.' I copied her *someone might be listening* signal. 'I've made an arrangement with Dendoncker. I do something for him, and he lets us both go.'

'Oh.' Fenton rolled her eyes. 'Good. That's reassuring.'

I used the bathroom and when I came out I saw that Fenton had moved her mattress off her bed frame and laid it on the floor next to mine. She'd spread her sheet out so that it covered about half of each side and had given us one pillow each. 'Want to get the light?' she said.

I hit the switch and made my way slowly through the darkness until my foot found the side of my mattress. I laid down and put my head on the pillow but didn't take off my shoes. I wanted to be ready for whatever might be in store before morning. I didn't trust Dendoncker one inch. And I could easily imagine Mansour and his buddies hatching some dumb scheme with me in their cross hairs.

A moment later Fenton sat down. I heard her crutch rattle against the floor. I felt her stretch out. She was still for a moment, then she wriggled across on to my half of the makeshift bed. She snuggled in close. Her breath was warm on my neck. Then she was twisted like she was having some sort of convulsion. Something landed on my head. It was rough against my cheek. And it stank. Like a mixture of diesel fuel and mildew. It was her blanket. Judging by the weight, she'd folded it multiple times. To muffle the sound.

She whispered, 'Where are we?'

'You don't know?' I whispered back.

'They threw a hood over my head. Made me go down a ladder. Felt like maybe through a tunnel. There were stairs at the far end.'

'We're in Mexico. The tunnel is actually a drain. It goes right under the border.'

'How did you know?'

'I'm good at finding people, remember?'

'You said you were good at catching people. Seems to me we're the ones who've been caught.'

'Don't worry. It's a temporary situation.'

'Why did you come?'

'I heard you were in trouble. Figured you'd do the same for me.'

'You came to help?'

'And to deal with Dendoncker.'

Fenton sighed. 'It's just, I was hoping . . . No. Forget it. I'm being stupid.'

'About what?'

'I was hoping you were bringing news. About Michael. That he was alive.'

I said nothing.

'So,' Fenton said after a moment. 'What happens next?'

'Dendoncker lets me go in the morning. I come back for you.'

'Think he'll let me live long enough?'

'I guarantee he will.'

'Why would he?'

'He thinks he has to. In order to get what he wants.'

'Just what kind of deal did you make?'

'One that won't turn out the way he thinks it will.'

'Why not?'

'Because I'm going to cheat.'

Fenton didn't reply. She rested her head on my shoulder but I knew she wasn't about to sleep. I could feel the tension in her.

'Reacher?' She lifted her head. 'Will you really come back?'

'Count on it.'

'I have no right to ask, but when you do, will you help me with one more thing?'

'What?'

'Michael's body. Help me find it. I want to take him home. Give him a proper funeral.'

I didn't answer right away. It was an understandable request. I didn't see how I could say no. But the body could be anywhere. Buried in the sand. Burned beyond recognition. Blown to pieces. I didn't want to commit to a never-ending, hopeless quest.

'Don't worry.' It was like she'd read my mind. 'I know where it will be. The guy at The Tree said "the usual place". I know where that is.'

It was getting stuffy under the blanket. Fenton raised her arm to push it away, but I stopped her.

I whispered, 'Wait. I have a question for you. About Michael. Is it true that he liked puzzles? Cryptic clues?'

'I guess. I never paid much attention to that kind of thing. I'm too literal. Too analytical. It's the one thing we don't have in common. Take crosswords, for example. Michael loved them. I hate them. I'm too pedantic. I can always give you ten reasons why the answers don't make sense. They drive me crazy.'

256

Fenton didn't wait for me to ask her anything else. She just flung the blanket aside. We lay still, side by side, breathing the slightly fresher air. Then she put her head on my shoulder. Rolled on to her side. Stretched her left arm out across my chest. And she was still again, except for a little shiver that ran down her spine. I brought my arm up and cupped her shoulder in my hand. She snuggled her face into my neck. Her hair smelled of lavender. All of a sudden I didn't care about the lumpy pillow. Or the paper-thin mattress. Or the hard floor beneath it. Spending the night there with Fenton was an upgrade on the morgue and the dismembered guy. That was for sure. Though I would have been even happier if we were somewhere else altogether.

'Reacher?' Fenton's voice was even quieter than before. 'Will this really turn out all right?'

'Absolutely,' I said. 'For us.'

FORTY-THREE

I felt Fenton's body relax and her breathing grow slower and deeper. But when I tried to follow her off to sleep I had no luck. Not right away. My head was too full of questions. And doubts. About Dendoncker. About the whole charade we were playing out. I'd almost caused him to get kidnapped. And I had killed a bunch of his guys. Burned down his business. Broken into his hidden HQ. He should have been angry. Resentful. Outraged. But instead he'd laid out his proposal like he was interviewing me for a job in a candy store. I was missing part of the picture. There was no other explanation. I just didn't know how big a part.

Dendoncker could have had someone from his regular smuggling crew deliver the bomb. The long-standing team Fenton had been allocated to back-fill when she infiltrated his organization. That would have been the easy thing to do. The straightforward thing. But he hadn't gone down that path. He'd gone out of his way to avoid it. Twice. First when he tapped Michael to transport the bomb, even though that wasn't his specialty. And now with me. He was determined to compartmentalize. To insulate the rest of his operation from this one job. And he was desperate to see it through to completion. Both those things were clear. But neither was consistent with helping Michael make an innocent protest.

My guess was that there was an additional layer to the scheme. That someone else had approached Dendoncker. Someone with an agenda that involved wreaking havoc on Veterans' Day. And with deep enough pockets to convince Dendoncker to play ball. Or with a big enough stick to force him to. Dendoncker already had Michael on board. Fenton's contact said Dendoncker hired Michael to help with the land mines he was selling. Michael was on shaky ground, psychologically, at that time. I doubt it would have been too hard for Dendoncker to finesse him into believing the protest was his own idea. So Michael designed the devices. Built them. Tested them. Then something happened. He got cold feet. And sent an SOS to his sister.

I didn't know Michael. I never met him. But I couldn't imagine anyone in his position wanting to pull the plug on an operation he'd worked so hard to create. Not unless something about it had fundamentally changed. Or had been fundamentally misunderstood from the outset. Like the ingredients of the smoke. Maybe Dendoncker was planning to add something to the final mix. Or maybe his paymaster was. Dendoncker had a bunch of artillery shells crammed into the shed beyond the school building. Three hundred of them. At least. Some of them could contain chemicals. All of them could. Mustard gas. Sarin. All kinds of nasty things. That could be what Michael had discovered. What brought him to his senses. What ultimately got him killed.

If I was right, Dendoncker and his guys were in for a busy night. The device wouldn't just need to be moved through the tunnel and carried up to ground level. It would need to be doctored. Filled with poison or loaded with extra explosives or made lethal in some other way. All without their resident bomb-maker's help. But whatever Dendoncker had in mind, it wouldn't make any difference. Not any more. Not combined with the demonstration. Because he hadn't just agreed to prepare another bomb for transport. He'd also promised me the keys to its truck. That meant two thirds of his immediate arsenal would soon be neutralized. Which left only one device to deal with. And it would be. Just as soon as Fenton was out of harm's way.

I slept for five hours, in the end. My eyes opened again at seven. Half an hour later I heard the key turn in the lock. The door was thrown open. Fenton woke with a start. She rolled back on to her own mattress. The lights flickered into life. And the guy in the pale suit stepped into the room. He covered us with his Uzi. The guy in the dark suit moved in behind him. He was carrying a tray in each hand. He set them down on the floor between the bathroom doors. Each had a plate covered with some kind of orange mush, and a mug of coffee.

'Thirty minutes,' the guy in the pale suit said. His words were slurred. I guess his jaw still wasn't working quite right. 'Be ready. Don't keep us waiting.'

The two guys backed out into the corridor and locked the

door. I collected the trays while Fenton hauled her mattress up on to the bed frame and then we sat together and drank our coffee. It was weak and lukewarm, and someone had put milk in both mugs. Not a promising start. And things got worse with the food. The stuff on the plates turned out to be baked beans. They must have been microwaved to death, but now they were cold. They had started to congeal. Fenton baulked at hers so I ate both platefuls. It was the golden rule. Eat when you can.

The guys came back after twenty-eight minutes. I was lying on my mattress, pretending to doze. Fenton was in the bathroom.

'On your feet.' The guy in the pale suit held the door open. 'Let's go.'

I stretched and yawned and stood up and ambled towards him. 'See you in three days,' I called as I passed the bathrooms. Then I left the room. The guy in the dark suit led the way. I was the meat in the sandwich, with the other guy following with his Uzi. We went through the double doors. Along the glass corridor. Diagonally across the dining hall. And into the kitchen.

The guy pointed to the door in the far corner. 'You know the way.'

Mansour was waiting for me at the bottom of the stairs. He didn't say anything. Just set off into the tunnel and beckoned for me to follow.

We walked in silence, side by side, breathing the stale air. We followed the rails, in and out of the pools of yellow light, until we reached the hole in the wall which led into the house. Mansour went through first. It was darker in the

261

little anteroom. The motorized door was closed. There was a button on its frame. A small thing, like a bell push. Mansour pressed it. A motor rumbled and the door started to move. It cranked its way through ninety degrees. We went through into the cellar. Mansour waved his keys near a spot on the rough wooden wall and the door started to close again. Then he nodded towards the ladder. I climbed up first. He followed, pushed past me, and led the way through the door to the side of the kitchen.

A U-Haul truck was sitting out on the street. It had been left in the spot Sonia had parked in the day before. It was a regular size. Not shiny. Not filthy. It had pictures of National Park scenes on both sides. It was a good choice of vehicle. It was so ubiquitous as to be practically invisible. The guy walked over to it then reached into his pocket and pulled out Sonia's phone.

'Here.' He handed it to me. 'There's a number in the memory. Call it, and you can talk to the woman. Nothing will happen to her. Nothing bad. Not as long as you follow your instructions.'

FORTY-FOUR

I opened the phone Mansour had just returned to me and worked my way through the menu. I located the memory. There was one entry. I called it, and after a couple of rings a man answered. I hadn't heard his voice before.

'What's up?' the new voice said. 'Why are you calling so soon?'

I said, 'Put Fenton on.'

'Already? You've got to be kidding.'

'I was told, *anytime*. Do you have a different understanding of the word?'

'Fine. Give me a minute.'

I heard a sound like a chair being pushed back on a wooden floor. Then footsteps. Five. Not hurried. Probably an average-length stride. A door opened. There were more footsteps. Another eight. Some keys jangled. Another door opened. And the guy called out, 'Hey. Phone call. Make it quick, will you?'

The door didn't close. The guy didn't move. After ten seconds I heard a squeak and hop, squeak and hop, as Fenton crossed the floor with her crutch. After another ten seconds her voice came on the line. 'Yes?'

I said, 'Miss me yet?'

'I'm learning to live with the disappointment.'

'Outstanding. Hang in there. I'll call again soon.'

I ended the call and slid the phone into my pocket.

Mansour passed me a bundle of twenty-dollar bills. 'For food and gas. There's five hundred dollars. Should be plenty. The hotels are already paid for.'

I put the money in my pocket.

Next he gave me a piece of paper. There were some directions written on it. By hand. First giving the route to I-10, heading east. Then continuing to a motel near a place called Big Spring, Texas. 'There's a room booked in your name. A fax will be waiting when you check out in the morning. Tomorrow's instructions will be on it. Keep your head down. Stay out of trouble.' He handed me a key. 'One last thing. If I ever see you again . . .'

'You'll do what?' I walked around to the back of the truck and rolled up the tailgate. 'Hand me your ass so I can give it another kicking?'

There was one item in the load bay. An aluminium container. It was on wheels. It looked like one that had been in the area marked *Prep* in the school assembly hall the day before. It was the same size. Six feet long. Three feet wide. Four feet tall. The only difference was that it had stencilled words painted in black on its long sides. *PREMIER EVENT*

MANAGEMENT. I reached in and touched the letters. The paint was dry.

Above the words, in the top right-hand corner, there was a line of digits. They were in the same font, but the size was smaller. There were six of them, then a hyphen, then four more. Maybe a serial number. Or an inventory reference of some kind.

The container was large enough to hold a device with three artillery shells. I was sure of that. But I couldn't verify that anything was actually inside. The lid was fixed down. With padlocks. Eight of them. Heavy and shiny and new. A line of holes had been drilled in the sides, near the top. An inch and a half in diameter. And the whole thing was secured to anchor points on the floor of the truck with orange straps. Six. Heavy-duty. Cinched down tight. It looked like checking the contents was going to be someone else's problem.

'You need to get going.' Mansour was pacing up and down alongside the truck. 'And remember. If you stop, we'll know. You deviate from the route, we'll know. You mess with the device, we'll know. Do any of those things and there'll be a price to pay. Only you won't pay it. The woman will. I'll see to it. Personally. I'll make a video and send it to you.'

I couldn't help wondering how important this guy was to Dendoncker. How he would react if I took a minute to finish what I started the day before. I was tempted to find out. Very tempted. But I forced myself to leave the guy alone. For the time being. There was no sense in jeopardizing the mission. Not with Fenton still behind enemy lines. And anyway, good things come to those who wait.

I rolled down the tailgate and latched it in place. 'In that case there are two things you need to know. First, I stop for coffee. Frequently. That's not negotiable. And second, I'm taking a detour. A short one. Down the street on the other side of the house. I parked my car there, yesterday. There's something in it I want.'

'What?'

'Fenton's suitcase.'

'Why do you need that?'

'I don't. But she will. When I've delivered the package and Dendoncker lets her go, we're going to get together.'

Mansour thought for a moment. He must have realized he was in a bind. He couldn't admit that Dendoncker had no intention of releasing Fenton or he knew I wouldn't do what they wanted me to. He said, 'The street parallel to this one?'

'Correct.'

He started towards the passenger door. 'All right. I'll come with you.'

The driver's seat was already pushed all the way back. The mirrors were fine. The controls seemed straightforward. So I fired up the engine and pulled away from the kerb. I took it easy on that first street. Negotiated my way around the next couple of turns. Continued to the end. Lumbered back and forth across the fishtail until I got the truck turned around. Then I pulled in behind the Chevy and climbed down. I didn't have the keys so I couldn't unlock the trunk – Dendoncker had kept them after he searched me – so I opened the driver's door and found the release lever. Mansour lifted the lid. He reached in and already had Fenton's case unzipped by the time I got to the back of the car. He rummaged around, messing up her neat packing and spilling the odd item, but he seemed satisfied there was nothing in there he needed to worry about. Nothing I could use to defuse their bomb or derail their scheme. He ran his fingers around the outside of the case one last time then closed it up, lifted it out, and set it on the sidewalk.

He said, 'OK. You can take it. Better get moving.'

I stepped around the case and opened the car's back door. 'There's one other thing she's going to need.' I picked up the backpack I'd retrieved from the Lincoln after the crash outside the Border Inn.

'Wait.' Mansour scowled at me. 'What's in there?'

'Just this.' I pulled out Fenton's prosthetic leg and shoved it in his face. 'Hard for her to walk without it.'

The guy jumped back. 'Fine. Take that, too. Now get out of here.'

I guess Fenton was right when she said people were freaked out by anything to do with wounds or injuries. Mansour certainly was. Enough not to find out if anything else was in the bag.

I left Mansour to walk back to the house and started out following Dendoncker's directions. They led me through the final few mazy streets on the outskirts of the town and on to the long straight road that went past The Tree. The spot where I first met Fenton. No one was staging an ambush there that day. No one was there at all. Alive. Or dead.

I drove slowly and steadily, like an old geezer taking his antique car for its weekly outing. I was mindful of the cargo in the back of the truck. I didn't want it blowing up if I hit a pothole. And I didn't want to get pulled over with it on board. I figured it was unlikely there would be any police patrols around those parts. But it's the things you don't expect that bite you in the ass.

267

I kept an eye on my mirrors the whole time. I wanted to know if I was being followed. I couldn't see anyone. No black Lincolns. No worn-out Jeeps. So I also scanned the sky. For small planes. Or helicopters. Or drones. And again I came up blank. Which wasn't a surprise. I believed Mansour when he said they'd be monitoring me. But it was more likely they'd have put a GPS chip in the bomb. Or in the truck. Or both. Which would be fine. That wouldn't hurt me at all. In fact, I was relying on it.

FORTY-FIVE

The small roads led me through scrub and desert for forty minutes, then I merged on to the highway. Traffic was light. I let the truck settle down to a steady fifty-five. I checked the mirrors. I checked the sky. No one was following. Nothing was watching. After twenty minutes I came to a truck stop. I pulled in. Topped off the truck's tank. Then headed into the little store to pay. I filled a to-go cup with coffee. Hot, this time. With no milk. And I asked the clerk for change for the payphone. The guy looked like I'd asked for a date with his mother. He must have been in his early twenties. I guess it wasn't a request he heard very often. Maybe it was a request he'd never heard at all.

There were two payphones. Both were outside, attached to the end wall of the building. They were covered with matching curved canopies made out of translucent plastic. Maybe for protection from the weather. Maybe for privacy. Either way, I wasn't too concerned. It wasn't too hot. It wasn't raining. And there was no one around to overhear anything I said.

I ducked under the nearer canopy. The wall beneath it was plastered with business-card-sized pieces of paper and cardboard. Adverts for escort services, mainly. Some were subtle. But most, not so much. I ignored them, picked up the handset, and dialled Wallwork's number. Nothing happened. The phone was dead. So I tried the second one. I was in luck this time. It had a dial tone. I tapped the digits in again and Wallwork answered on the second ring.

'Sorry, Reacher,' he said. 'The map of the drainage system? I've tried, but there's nothing.'

'Don't worry about it,' I said. 'The research phase is over.'

I brought him up to speed with how I came to have the truck. Its cargo. And my destination for the night.

'My ETA is around 21:00, local,' I said. 'Can you meet me there?'

Wallwork was silent for a moment. 'It won't be easy. I'll have to pull some strings. But to secure the device? Sure. I'll find a way.'

'You'll fly out?'

'I'll have to. I'm in the middle of Tennessee. Too far to drive to Texas in time.'

'OK. When you land, make sure the chopper doesn't leave right away. And tell the pilot to refuel. Fill the tanks to the brim.'

'Why?'

'I'm going to need a ride someplace.'

'Can't do that, Reacher. You're a civilian. The Bureau's not a taxi service.'

'I don't need a taxi. I need to get to Fenton before Dendoncker kills her.'

Wallwork went silent again.

'And I need to get Dendoncker. I'm the only one who can. Unless you'd rather he walks?'

'There might be a way,' Wallwork said, after a long moment. 'On one condition. When you get Dendoncker, you hand him over to me. Alive.'

'Understood. Now, two other things. You can't move the truck until the morning. That's critical. Fenton's life depends on it. And there are some items I need you to bring for me. Five, altogether.'

Wallwork wrote down my list then hung up. I refilled my coffee, climbed into the truck, and got back on the road. The truck wasn't fast. It wasn't fancy. But it was surprisingly relaxing to drive. It just did what it was designed to do. Ate up the miles, hour after hour, no fuss, no drama. I rolled along, nice and steady. Arizona gave way to New Mexico. New Mexico gave way to Texas. The tarmac stretched away in front of me. It seemed to go on for ever. The sky above was vast. Mainly blue, with occasional smudges of wispy white clouds. An ocean of grey-green scrub extended all around. Sometimes flat. Sometimes rising up or falling away. Sometimes with jagged peaks on the horizon, never coming closer, never getting further away.

I stopped for gas whenever the needle dropped below halfway. I kept an eye open for anyone who might take too much interest in me. No one did. And I called Fenton at random intervals. The same guy answered every time. And he followed the same routine when he brought the phone to her. His chair scraped back. He took five footsteps. He opened a door. He took eight footsteps. Then he unlocked Fenton's door. I figured he had to be coming from the next room. The one at the end of the corridor. The only one I hadn't seen the inside of. Yet.

I arrived at the hotel at 21:05. It was the first in a line of four. It was identical to the others except for the sign announcing which chain it belonged to. The building was rectangular. It had two storeys. Small windows. A flat roof. The office was at one end. A bunch of air-conditioning machines was clustered at the other, half hidden behind a line of spindly bushes. There were parking spots all along one wall, with an overflow lot between the building and the next hotel. It was empty, so I took a space at the far end of the last row. I climbed out. Stretched. Made sure the truck was locked. And made my way back to reception.

A woman was sitting behind the counter. She didn't notice me for a moment. She was too engrossed in a book she was reading. Her concentration didn't break until the phone rang on the desk in front of her. It was a complicated-looking thing all covered with buttons and lights. She stretched out to pick up the receiver, then stopped when she realized I was standing there.

'They can call back.' She smiled at me. 'Or leave a message. Sorry to keep you waiting. Can I help?'

'I have a reservation. Name of Reacher.'

The woman woke her computer and tapped on some keys. 'Here we are. Already paid for. An online booking. Just the one night?'

I nodded.

'Could I see some ID, please?'

272

I handed her my passport.

She flicked through to the information page, then narrowed her eyes. 'This is expired, sir.'

'Correct. No good for international travel. But still valid for identification.'

'I'm not sure . . .'

I pointed to her computer. 'Go online if you don't believe me. Check with the federal government.'

She paused with one hand hovering above the keyboard. She didn't believe me. That was obvious. I guess she was weighing the consequences of proving me wrong. The paperwork involved with issuing a refund. Explaining to her bosses why she'd turned away a customer. The impact on occupancy statistics. 'No need, Mr Reacher. I'm sure you're right.' She passed the passport back to me. 'How many room keys will you be needing?'

'Just one.'

The woman opened a drawer and took out a piece of plastic the size of a credit card. She fed it into a machine on her desk and tapped some more computer keys. A little light turned from red to green. She retrieved the card and handed it to me. 'Room 222. Would you like me to write that down for you?'

'No need.'

'OK, then. The breakfast bar's in the lobby and it's open from six until eight. Any questions, dial zero on your room phone. I hope you enjoy your stay with us, and visit again soon.'

The woman went back to her book. I went back to the truck. I sat on the rear fender, leaned my head against the tailgate, closed my eyes, and felt the cool evening breeze on my face. Ten minutes ticked past. Fifteen. Then I heard a vehicle approaching. More than one. I looked up and saw a line of silver sedans. Five of them. All identical. Chrysler 300s. The lead car swooped into the parking lot. The others followed, then fanned out and stopped in a row in front of me. The guy who was driving the nearest car climbed out. It was Wallwork. He hurried across, passed me a white plastic sack, then shook my hand.

'Reacher. Good to see you.' He nodded towards the truck. 'The device. It's in there?'

'As promised.'

'Excellent work.' Wallwork gave a thumbs-up to the guys in the car next to his. 'Thank you. We'll take it from here.'

I unlocked the door, took out the backpack, and handed the key to Wallwork. 'I've left a suitcase in there. It's Fenton's. Look after it until tomorrow?'

'Sure.' Wallwork took me by the elbow and led me away from the other vehicles. 'Listen.' He lowered his voice. 'I think we trust each other, so I'm going to be totally honest with you. After we spoke I called my old supervisor. The one who's at TEDAC now. He's on his way out here. We're going to secure the area, and he's going to examine the device. In situ. I know I said we wouldn't move it until tomorrow. But unless he's certain there's no risk to the public, I'm going to have to break that promise.'

I said nothing.

'Think about it, Reacher. What if the device explodes? If it spews toxic gas into the atmosphere? If it's radioactive? We have those risks on one hand. And a woman who put herself in harm's way on the other. A woman you might not even be able to save, whenever we move the truck.'

FORTY-SIX

'Impossible.' The pilot looked at the place I was pointing to on the map and shook his head. 'No. I refuse. I can't do it. I cannot cross into Mexican airspace. Not without authorization. It's out of the question. It's not going to happen. Not under any circumstances. Do you understand?'

I was surprised. A little disappointed. But not in any way confused. So I didn't feel the need to reply.

A pair of mechanics was watching us. So was the agent who had driven me from the hotel to the airfield. They were hanging around, not so close that the pilot might feel inhibited about yelling at me. But not so far away they would miss anything he said. The mechanics were apparently studying something on a hand-held computer screen that didn't have a keyboard. The agent was fiddling with his phone. All of them were overcompensating. Pretending not to be aware of us. But clearly listening to every word. And enjoying the confrontation. The pilot was belligerent. Unnecessarily so, I thought. The three of them had picked up on that, too. They were waiting to see where things went from there. Whether the pilot would be satisfied with a verbal argument. Or whether an escalation was on the cards. To something physical. Something to spice up their evening.

'I'll take you as close to the border as you like,' the pilot said. 'Right up to it. But we will stay on the US side. I will not be party to an illegal border crossing. So do not ask me again. Are we clear?'

I said, 'Fine. Los Gemelos it is. The US side. Let's just get going.'

When I came up with this plan I figured I would have until at least eight a.m. to carry it out. Maybe nine a.m. at a stretch. That would be plenty of time. But if Wallwork's guy insisted on moving the truck before morning, Dendoncker would know. I was certain of that. So he would also know that I'd double-crossed him. Not a problem for me. But a death sentence for Fenton. There was no longer a second to spare.

The mechanics quit gazing at their computer and drifted away towards the only hangar with an open door. The agent put his phone away and jumped in behind the wheel of his silver Chrysler. The pilot climbed up into the cockpit of the helicopter. Its silhouette was familiar. It was a Sikorsky UH-60M. The civilian version of the Black Hawk that the army uses. This one had more antennae than I remembered. It had wheels rather than skids. And it wasn't dusty green. It was gloss black. Long and sleek and menacing. Like a predator rather than a workhorse. There was an index number on its tail but nothing to indicate which agency owned it. Just a discreet UNITED STATES in grey letters towards the rear of its fuselage. I lifted my backpack into the rear compartment, climbed in after it, slid the door closed, buckled myself into one of the rear-facing jump seats, and put on my headset.

The pilot went to work on his preflight procedures and once the rotors were whirling and the aircraft was starting to hop on its suspension, eager to get off the ground, I heard his voice through the intercom.

He said, 'Sorry about that little show. I needed to make sure those guys will remember me refusing to cross the border. Just in case.'

'In case of what?'

'You getting caught. Here's what's going to happen. I'll attempt a landing, right by the barrier, just like I said I would. But we'll be in the desert. The wind is unpredictable. At the last minute I'll get blown off course. To the south. Just a few yards. The thermals happen to be patchy right there so we'll drop. To about three feet off the ground. Then I'll recover. Hold position for a couple of seconds. My wheels will never touch Mexican soil. No harm, no foul. But if you, without my prior knowledge or consent, take advantage of the situation and spontaneously jump out of the aircraft, there'll be nothing I can do about it.'

'Will that work?'

'Of course. It's the way we always do it.'

Including the walk through the tunnel, it took a whisker over twelve hours to get from Dendoncker's school HQ to the hotel in Big Spring. Including the two-mile walk from

277

the illicit drop zone, it took a shade under five hours to get back. The time in the air was uneventful. The pilot knew what he was doing. He flew fast and smooth and straight. And I dozed as much as the rattling of the fixtures and fittings and the throbbing of the rotors and engines would allow.

I woke when we plunged down twenty feet. The pilot was something of a method actor, I guess. That gave me my cue to unstrap my harness, abandon my headset, and haul back the door. The cabin filled with noise. The downdraught almost pulled me out. I couldn't see the ground. Three feet, the guy had said. The prospect of leaping into the darkness didn't appeal. However far there was to drop. Then I felt the helicopter begin to rise again. There was no more time. I stepped out. My feet touched the ground. I ducked down. And stayed that way until the roaring and the noise and the wind were no long directly overhead.

The next thing I did was check my phone. There was nothing from Wallwork. They must not have moved the truck.

Not yet.

I took a black hoodie out of my backpack – the first of the things I'd asked Wallwork to get for me – and pulled it on. Partly for concealment. Partly to ward off the chill of the desert night. Then I started to move. Quickly. But carefully. The ground was all sand and grit and gravel. Hard to cross without making a lot of noise. It was dark. And the surface was uneven. It rose and fell at unpredictable intervals and it was studded with holes and channels and cracks. The whole place was a broken ankle waiting to happen. And I didn't know what kind of company might be out there. Snakes.

Scorpions. Spiders. Nothing I was interested in having a close encounter with.

I was coming from the west so the glow of the US half of the town was away to my left. I kept moving until I was as close to the school's outer fence as I could risk, due to the cameras. The building was dark. Both halves. So were its grounds. Everything was wrapped in shadow except the glass corridor. It was ablaze with light. There was no way to approach it that wasn't transparent. And no other way into Dendoncker's side of the building.

I checked my phone. Nothing from Wallwork.

Not yet.

It was five to two in the morning. Normally I would have preferred to find some shelter and lay up for a couple of hours. Launch my attack at four a.m. The time the KGB had always used to stage their raids. When people are at their most vulnerable, psychologically. That was their scientific conclusion. Based on a whole lot of data. But that night I didn't have the luxury of waiting. I couldn't hold out until every detail was ideal. Two hours was plenty of time for the TEDAC guy to insist on moving the bomb. Plenty of time for Fenton to run out of luck.

I pulled out my phone and called the number in its memory.

The usual guy answered. His voice was thick and heavy with sleep. He just said, 'No.'

I said, 'I haven't asked you to do anything yet.'

'You want to speak to the woman. Again.'

'Correct. Put her on.'

'No.'

'Put. Her. On.'

279

'Are you crazy? It's the middle of the damn night. Go to sleep. Call back in the morning.'

'*Anytime*, remember? Has the word been redefined in the last twenty-four hours? Do I need to wake Dendoncker and ask him?'

The guy grunted, then I heard a rustling sound. A bed sheet being flung aside, I guess. Then footsteps. Seven, this time. Not five. Then a door being opened.

I moved forward until I reached the fence. I stopped at the foot of one of the posts with a camera mounted on it and set my backpack down on the ground.

The guy continued down the corridor. Eight more steps. He opened Fenton's door and yelled for her to come and take the phone. Her voice came on the line after another minute.

'Reacher? Why aren't you asleep? What's wrong?'

'Nothing's wrong,' I said. 'I need you to do something. It's very important. In a second I'm going to put the phone down, but I'm not going to hang up. I need you to keep talking like we're having a regular conversation. I'll be back in a flash. Can you do that?'

'Sure. I guess. Why?'

'Don't worry. It'll be clear soon.'

FORTY-SEVEN

I put my phone down on my backpack and began to climb the post. It was easy to grip with my hands. I could just hang on to the fence where it was attached on either side. But it was another story for my feet. The diamond-shaped gaps in the wire were not big enough for my shoes. The toecaps were too wide. Just a fraction. But enough to be a problem. I started with my right and my foot slipped straight out and slapped down on to the ground. I tried again. Slipped again. Then I found that if I pushed my toe in extra hard and pulled my foot up to a steep angle I could just about make it stick. I repeated the process with my left. Raised my right. Kept going. I didn't fall. But progress was slow. Painfully slow. Precious seconds were slipping away. I had no idea how long Fenton would be able to keep up the ruse with the phone. But then if I was wrong about the guy who'd brought it to her, it would already be too late.

I kept climbing until my chest was level with the top of the fence. My calves were burning from supporting my weight at such a weird angle. I gripped the wire with my left hand and stretched up with my right. I took hold of the camera. I tried to rotate it. Counter-clockwise. But it wouldn't move. It was jammed solid. I twisted harder and my right foot slipped. My left foot followed. I wound up hanging by my left hand. I grabbed the fence with my right. Jammed both feet back into their gaps. Straightened up. Took a fresh hold of the camera. Twisted again. And felt it give. Just a little. But there was movement. I was sure of that.

I didn't let up on the pressure. The camera shifted an eighth of an inch. Another eighth. I kept going until it had crept through twenty degrees. Then I climbed down. Slowly. I made it to the bottom without falling. Retrieved my phone. Held it to my ear. And heard Fenton's voice. She was mid-anecdote. Something to do with her aunt, a jar of marmalade and a TSA agent. I moved to my left until I was halfway across the section of fence. Put the backpack and the phone on the ground. Continued to the next post. And began to climb again. It was as awkward as with the first one. My right foot slipped twice before I made it to the top. My left, once. I grabbed the camera. Twisted it. This one moved more easily. I rotated it twenty degrees, clockwise. Then climbed down. Moved to my right. Picked up my phone. And heard nothing. Not Fenton. Not the guy. Just silence.

I put the phone in my pocket and tried to pick up any sound coming from the building. Maybe the guy had seen through Fenton's act. Maybe he just got tired and snatched the phone so he could go back to bed. But the important question was *when?* How long ago did he get back to his room? If he'd made it before I was done with the cameras there would soon be footsteps. Guys getting into position with their Uzis. Then the floodlights would come on, silhouetting me against the desert like a target at a shooting range. I crouched down, legs tensed, ready to run.

Nothing happened.

I took my phone out and checked for messages. There was nothing from Wallwork.

Not yet.

If my estimate was accurate I should now be in a dead zone between the cameras I'd moved. Just as long as no one had been watching the monitors when they were turning. And if not, then they didn't pick up on the slightly different view of the desert they would now be getting. I stayed in a crouch and took Wallwork's second item out of my backpack. A pair of bolt cutters. I removed a section of wire. A square, just broader than my shoulders. But I didn't crawl through. Not right away. I lay down and looked along the surface of the ground between the inner and outer sections of fence. I wanted to see if it was flat. Or if there were any tell-tale humps. Dendoncker had been selling land mines. If he'd kept any for himself this would be an ideal place to use them.

The verdict was inconclusive. The land wasn't flat. It wasn't even close. But there was nothing to say that the undulations weren't natural. Or random. The work of the wind. Or the rain. Or the original construction crew. So I took out Wallwork's third item. A knife. It had a long, broad blade. Ten inches by two, at its widest point. I slid the tip into the sandy surface and pushed it out ahead of me. Slowly. Gently. I kept it as horizontal as possible so that no part of the blade was more than an inch or so underground. It didn't come into contact with anything so I pulled it out and repeated the process six inches to the left. Nothing obstructed it so I tried again. I kept going until I had defined a two-foot-wide section I could be sure was safe. I crawled forward, placed my knees on the line my test holes had made, and probed the area six inches further forward.

It was a time-consuming procedure. I was moving forward at around a foot a minute. Around fifteen thousand times slower than when I'd been in the helicopter. I was expecting a text from Wallwork at any second. And I was completely exposed in a fenced-in no-man's-land. Completely at the mercy of anyone who came out on patrol. The only upside was that I hadn't come across any land mines. I was beginning to think I was being overcautious. I made it ten feet. I had fifteen to go. Then the tip of my knife hit something. Something hard. Something metal. I froze. Didn't breathe. Pulled back on the handle. The first fraction of an inch was the most critical. When the contact was broken. If the thing was a mine.

Whatever the thing was, it didn't explode. But I wasn't out of the woods. The knife still had to be removed the rest of the way. Shock waves could still be transmitted through the dirt. The tiniest movement could still be fatal.

The thing did not explode.

I forced myself to take a breath then started again, a foot to the right. I moved even more slowly after that. Found three more potential mines. But made it to the inner fence in one piece. I cut a hole. Crawled through. And hurried to the long wall at the back of Dendoncker's side of the building. I moved to the boarded-up window belonging to Fenton's room. I doubted anyone would be inside with her, and she was hardly

284

likely to raise the alarm if she heard me. I took Wallwork's fourth item out of my backpack. A weighted hook. It had four claws, covered in rubber. And it was attached to twenty-five feet of rope. I stepped back, took hold of the rope three feet from the hook, twirled it around a half dozen times to gauge the way it would fly, then launched it up towards the roof. It cleared the top of the wall. Disappeared. And landed with a dull *clunk*. I pulled my end of the rope. Gently. I teased the hook back towards the wall. It kept moving. Coming closer to the edge. Then it caught on something. I pulled harder. The hook held. So I started to climb. Hands on the rope. Feet flat on the wall. Like rappelling, but in reverse. I made it to the top. Scrambled up on to the roof. Pulled the rope up behind me. And started towards the far side of the building. The side that the glass corridor joined on to.

FORTY-EIGHT

The guys in the suits with the Uzis were there. Both of them. I hoped that meant Dendoncker was in his office. I hoped they were like the Royal Standard the Queen of England flies above whichever palace she's at, announcing her presence. I like efficiency. Two birds with one stone would suit me fine.

I could see the tops of the guys' heads through the glass roof. They were sitting on their stools, each leaning against one of the double doors. They were very still. Maybe in some kind of exhausted trance. Or if I was very lucky, asleep at the wheel. There was a gun in my backpack. Two, in fact. The Berettas I had captured at the Border Inn. It would have been convenient to just shoot these guys. But that was a high-risk strategy. They were on the other side of a pane of structural-grade glass. It was thick. Strong. My first shot would most likely penetrate. But its trajectory was bound to be affected. It would almost certainly miss. And with it would go my element of surprise. All I would be doing was advertising my presence to two men with Uzis. I would probably still get one of them. But the other would probably get me. Not the kind of odds I liked. So I took out Wallwork's final item. A pair of wire cutters. I gripped the handle in my teeth and lowered myself down on to the glass roof. And stood completely still. I checked on the two guys. Neither of them stirred so I inched forward. Kept going until I reached the vent. Snipped around the edge of the mesh bug screen. Checked on the guys again. Took the mask from my backpack. Put it on. Took the canister of DS gas. And pulled the pin.

The spoon kicked back. The metal skin started to get hot. The device was real. Not a prop. Which was fortunate, in the circumstances. But I still hesitated. I didn't know how fast the guys would react. How quickly they would move. If they were able to get through the double doors I would be left with a major problem.

Five seconds ticked away. Then wisps of white gas started to appear. I dropped the canister through the vent. It clattered against the floor and started to roll. The guys jolted upright. Jumped to their feet. A moment later they started grabbing their throats and clawing at their eyes. One tried to run. He was disoriented and crashed into the glass wall. He fell backwards. The other guy started to writhe and scream. I switched the wire cutters for the bolt cutters. Severed the metal posts at each corner of the vent's roof. Pulled it off and flung it away. Then leaned in through the hole and shot each of the guys in the head. Twice. For insurance.

287

I tucked the gun into my waistband, lowered myself down, and dropped the last few inches into the corridor. Moved across to the nearer guy's body. Took his keys and his Uzi. Collected the second guy's Uzi. Slung it over my shoulder. And used the transponder to unlock the door. I pushed it open. Stepped through. And pushed the mask up on to the top of my head.

Eight seconds had passed since the first gun shot. Nine at the most. Not much time to react. And yet there was Mansour, in the next corridor. There was a chair outside Dendoncker's office door. One of the orange ones. Mansour must have been stationed there, like a guard. But now he was coming towards me. Charging. Head down. Arms wide. Moving fast. Already too close for me to bring the Uzi to bear. So I stepped forward. I figured I could grab some part of him, move to the side, pivot, and use his weight and speed against him. Launch him into the window. Or the wall. Or at least send him sprawling on the floor. But the space was too narrow. He was too broad. His shoulder caught me in the chest. It was like being hit by a cannon ball. I was knocked off my feet. I landed on my back, half propped up by the pack, and slid along the shiny floor. One of the Uzis clattered into the glass. I lost track of the other. All the breath was knocked out of me. I couldn't suck any more in. My ribs felt like a million volts had been run through them. All I knew was that I had to get up. Get off the ground before the guy closed in with his feet or his fists or his overwhelming bulk. I clawed my way upright. And saw Dendoncker. He was disappearing into the glass corridor. He was wearing a gas mask. I realized it was mine. It must have fallen off when I fell. Mansour was following him. With no mask. Dendoncker had a way of inspiring loyalty. I had to admit that.

I retrieved the Uzis and started to chase after them. I reached the double doors. Then I heard a sound behind me. A guy had come out of the room at the far side of Fenton's. Someone I hadn't seen before. Presumably the guy I'd spoken to on the phone. He had already reached Fenton's door. He must have tiptoed along while I was reeling from the impact with Mansour. The noise was his key working the lock. He opened the door. Stepped inside. With a gun in his hand. I turned and ran back. The door swung closed. I couldn't see into the room because of the newspaper over the glass. But I could hear sounds from inside. A scream. A crash. And a shot.

Then silence.

I kicked the door open and strode inside, ready to empty the Uzi's magazine into the guy who had just entered. And I came face to face with Fenton. She was standing near the bed, without her crutch. She was pointing the guy's gun at me. The guy himself was on the floor. He was slumped half on the mattress I'd used the night before and half on the wood. His right wrist was twisted around at a crazy angle. It was broken. That was clear. And the top of his skull was missing.

'Guess we'll need new accommodations tonight.' Fenton lowered the gun.

'Guess we will.' I came further into the room. 'You all right?'

She nodded and sat on the bed. 'More or less.'

I opened my backpack and handed her the prosthetic leg. The one that Dendoncker's guy had brought to the café. Then I turned and headed for the door.

'Thanks,' she said. Then, 'Where are you going?'

'To get Dendoncker. If he's still here.'

FORTY-NINE

I paused in front of the double doors. Took a couple of deep breaths. Then went through, raced to the far end of the glass corridor, and burst into the dining hall. There was a breeze blowing over the roof now. It was helping to suck the gas out through the gap left by the vent. But Dendoncker's formula was potent. My eyes were stinging and raw even after such a tiny exposure. I resisted the urge to rub them. Made myself stay still and wait until my view of the world was less blurred.

Then I started to search. I didn't bother with the kitchen or the offices. I figured Dendoncker wouldn't want to hide. He would want to get out of the place. There were two ways to do that. The tunnel. Or the SUVs. I crossed the assembly hall and looked through the window. The parking lot was empty. There was no sign of the Cadillacs. And no sign of Dendoncker or Mansour. I went outside and crossed to the

291

gates. Both were still and closed and solid. But on the rough road beyond them I could make out four red pinpricks. Two pairs. The same configuration. The Cadillacs' tail lights.

The leading vehicle looked like it was riding lower on its suspension. Like it was carrying something heavy. But that was just an impression. I couldn't be sure. Not at that distance. Not with the way they were bouncing through the gloom. It didn't matter anyway. They were heading for the horizon. And there was nothing I could do to stop them.

Fenton was in the corridor when I got back to the far side of the building. She was moving gingerly, as if her re-fitted leg was causing her pain. She had already passed the door to the next room and she stopped when she heard me catching up to her.

'Someone else is here.' Her voice dropped to a whisper. 'Another prisoner. I don't think he's in good shape.'

I said, 'How do you know?'

'When you called me the guy who brought the phone always stood in the doorway while we talked. With the door open. One time when we were done I was taking the phone back to him and I saw two people in the corridor. Walking together. Coming from the right. One was Dendoncker's sidekick. The enormous guy. The other was a stranger. He was carrying a bag. A black leather one, all beat up, like doctors use. He was speaking. In Spanish. He said something like, "You have to dial it down. He can't take much more. Leave him alone for a while. Forty-eight hours. At least."'

'Who was he talking about?'

'I don't know.'

'How did Dendoncker's guy react?'

'He sounded annoyed. Said Dendoncker would never go for a delay. That he needed to know where *it* was, and there wasn't much time.'

'*It?*'

Fenton shook her head. 'I don't know what they meant.'

'So where are they holding this other guy?'

'I thought he would be in the room next to mine. But I just looked. No one's there. Just a bed and a bunch of security monitors. Nowhere to keep a prisoner. So there must be somewhere else.'

Fenton started moving again. With some difficulty. I followed, keeping to her pace. It seemed futile. The corridor must be a dead end. Like beyond Dendoncker's office. The exit was boarded up tight. I'd seen it when I was searching for an alternative way in. But as we went further I realized there was a difference. The final classroom's wall didn't run straight. Not all the way to the perpendicular wall. There was a recess at the very end. An alcove of about a foot. To draw attention away from another door. A solid wooden one. With a sign attached. It said *el Conserje*. The Janitor.

The door was locked. But not in any serious way. It only took one kick to open it. Inside, a set of stairs led down to another basement. They were wooden. Painted white, but less worn than the ones running from the kitchen down to the tunnel. I turned on the light and started to descend. Fenton followed. The space at the bottom was divided into two areas. One third was for cleaning equipment and supplies. Two thirds were for maintenance and repair. Or they had been. Now the tool benches and equipment lockers had been pushed to one end. Another army cot had been set up in the space that had created. There was an intravenous drip stand next to it. A tube ran down from a bag of clear fluid. It was hooked up to the arm of a guy on the bed. His body was covered by a sheet. So were his legs and his other arm. But his head was visible. His face was swollen and cut and covered with scabs and bruises and burns. There was a huge lump on his forehead. Big chunks of his hair were missing. Fenton screamed. She pushed past me. Rushed to the bed. She looked like she was going to pull the guy into her arms. But she stopped herself. Took hold of his hand. And said one word. Softly. With a voice full of guilt and pain.

'Michael.'

FIFTY

I moved closer to the bed, too. I thought maybe the guy in it was dead. I was worried about how to get Fenton out of there if that was the case. But after a moment one of his eyes flickered open.

'Mickey.' His voice was dry and scratchy and barely audible. 'You got my warning. You came?' Then his eye closed and his head rolled to the side.

Fenton checked his pulse. 'It's OK. He's still with us. Help me get him up.'

It was a tough call. Michael didn't look in any kind of shape to be moved. I would rather have brought the medics to him. But Dendoncker was on my mind. He couldn't know that Fenton had found out about Michael. And evidently Michael had information that Dendoncker wanted. So Dendoncker would come back for him. Or he would send some guys.

Either way we were in no position to defend that cellar. Not for any significant length of time. Which made evacuation the lesser of two evils.

I picked Michael up and carried him to the stairs, still wrapped in the sheet. Fenton followed with the IV bag. We moved slowly and gently, trying not to shake or jostle him, and we paused when we reached the corridor. We detoured into the room she'd been kept in and I laid Michael down on the bed. Fenton stayed with him while I went back to the glass corridor. I used one of the Uzis to blast out the windows. Half a magazine on each side. To allow the gas to dissipate faster. Then I went back to the room and called Wallwork. He answered immediately. There was no hint of sleep in his voice. I guessed he was with the TEDAC crew and they were pulling an all-nighter. I told him Fenton was safe so they were clear to move the truck whenever they wanted. I told him we had recovered a casualty and asked him how long it would take to send some agents to the medical centre in Los Gemelos. When Dendoncker discovered Michael was missing he wouldn't take it lying down. He would send out a search party, and knowing the condition Michael was in the closest hospital was the obvious place to start.

Wallwork took a minute to figure the timing and distances. Then he said, 'I'll have to make some calls. But best guess? A couple of agents could be there inside four hours. If you're worried about the guy, can you babysit until then? Unofficially?'

'I don't see why not.' Maybe my luck would change, I thought. Maybe Dendoncker would show up in person to look for Michael. Mansour, too. I hated to think of them walking around free. 'How's it going at your end?'

'Good. Just got off the phone with Quantico. After what I told them they're putting a major effort together to bring Dendoncker in. A full court press. Worldwide, if necessary.'

'And the bomb?'

'My guy's done inspecting. Now he's getting it ready for transport. We're flying it out first thing.'

'Did you take any flak for dragging him out there?'

'No. The opposite, actually. He's in hog heaven. Keeps taking photos and videos and emailing them to his lab. Says it's one of the most interesting things he's seen in a long time.'

'Because of the gas?'

'No. He doesn't have a definitive on that yet. Says it's too dangerous to mess around with the shells while they're in the field.'

'He doesn't think they're harmless?'

'He knows they're not. Because of what they were coated with. VX.'

VX. The most deadly nerve agent ever invented. Developed in Britain in the '50s. I don't recall everything about the chemistry. But I remember what the V stands for. Venom. And the name's not misplaced. A few years back two women wiped a little on Kim Jong-nam's face while he waited for a flight at Kuala Lumpur airport. He was Kim Jong-un's half-brother. Maybe he was making moves behind the scenes. Maybe someone just said he was. But either way, he was dead before he reached the hospital.

I said, 'Does your guy think Dendoncker added VX to the smoke?'

'He'll find out for sure at the lab. But look. All the shells had signs of recent tampering. And VX isn't like sarin. It's not a gas. It's a liquid, like oil or honey, so it would be easy to pour inside. Then it needs a heat source to vaporize it. Like the reaction that would produce the coloured smoke. And the smoke would then help to dissipate the poison. You couldn't find a system better suited to dispersing VX if you spent the rest of your life searching. Is that a coincidence?'

'Seems unlikely. No wonder your guy is excited.'

'I can see the cogs going round in his head. He's thinking about the papers he's going to write. The law enforcement conferences he's going to speak at. But that's not all that got his bell ringing. He also found something hidden away in the electronics. A third way to detonate the bomb. On top of the timer and the cellular.'

'What kind of a third way?'

'A transponder. A common enough doodad, apparently. But not generally used this way. I know he's an asshole, but this Dendoncker must be a hell of a creative guy. And thorough. A defensive coating of VX and three systems to do one job? Talk about leaving nothing to chance.'

Wallwork hung up, leaving me feeling a little guilty for not telling him that Dendoncker didn't build the bomb. Michael did. He was the thorough, creative one. Ordinarily, the TEDAC guys would have figured that out when they fed the details into their database. Aside from the last-minute addition of the VX, the components and the construction techniques would match the ones from the first bomb Michael had made. Which also had a transponder. With his fingerprint on it. Only TEDAC wouldn't make the connection this time. Because Fenton had destroyed the older evidence. I guess keeping quiet made me an accessory to some kind of federal crime. I didn't think it mattered too much, though. Michael's bomb-making career was over. And if the FBI followed through, Dendoncker's soon would be, too.

Fenton was anxious to get moving but I convinced her to wait while I made one more call. To Dr Houllier. On his cell. I didn't know if the medical centre was staffed 24/7 and I didn't want to show up with Michael and find there were no doctors in the place. Dr Houllier said he would make sure someone was there. He sounded cagey so I pressed him and he admitted he would come and treat Michael himself. He confessed he was already back in town and offered to come for us in an ambulance. That was tempting. My only concern was the risk involved. Someone could see him and inform Dendoncker. Reprisals could follow, depending on how long he remained on the loose. But a more immediate problem was that we had no other transport. Only the Chevy that should still be parked outside the house. Which we had no keys for. So I told Dr Houllier about the place. Gave him the address. And said I'd call him when we were ready to be picked up.

Dr Houllier set us up on the paediatric floor. That was a thoughtful move. Instead of regular rooms they had a series of little suites. The kind of places that enable parents to stay with their sick kids. A couple of nurses helped Dr Houllier get Michael squared away in the hospital bed. They hung extra IV bags. Took his temperature. Blood pressure. Peered into his eyes and ears with special machines. Daubed him with creams and lotions. And prodded and poked him in all kinds of different places.

Eventually Dr Houllier said he was happy. He said it might

take a while but he was sure Michael would be OK. He warned us that someone would come by every hour to do some observations. Then he left us to get comfortable. Fenton took an armchair. She shoved it close in at Michael's side and curled up, knees to chest. I took the other bed. It was close to five a.m. I'd been up for twenty-two hours. I was exhausted. But I was feeling quietly satisfied. Fenton was safe. Michael wasn't dead. The bomb was defused and on its way to be studied by the experts. I figured that things were basically good in the world.

It's funny how wrong a person can be.

FIFTY-ONE

I got woken up at a minute to seven. By my phone. I was dead asleep one moment. Wide awake the next. Like a switch being thrown. Some kind of instinctive response to anything unnatural. Or threatening.

I figured the electronic howl qualified as both.

I answered the call. It was the FBI. One of the special agents who Wallwork had rounded up to guard Michael. Her team had reached the outskirts of town and she wanted to know where we should rendezvous. I gave her directions. Then lay back down and closed my eyes. An argument was brewing in my head. The thought of taking a shower on one side. The appeal of not moving on the other. Both were persuasive. But neither got the chance to carry the day. Because my phone rang again. It was Wallwork this time.

'News,' he said. 'Huge. The pictures and samples my guy sent in from Dendoncker's bomb? One already hit the jackpot. The transponder? There was a fingerprint on it. They have an ID. The TEDAC guys say it's solid. Good enough to survive any test in court.'

I said, 'Michael Curtis, right?' I figured the day was about to go downhill for Fenton and her brother. Fast. So I might as well get out ahead of it.

'Who? No. It was Nader Khalil.'

'I don't know who that is.' That was true. Although I had heard the name. Dendoncker had accused me of working for the guy.

'Khalil's a big fish. Very big. I'm told the system lit up like a Christmas tree when it came back with his name. He's a terrorist. Out of Beirut. One of a family of terrorists. His father was one. He got killed by the police. His brother was one. He got killed too. A more notorious death. He was driving the truck that carried the Marine barracks bomb. Nader himself has been linked to a dozen different atrocities. But there was never any evidence. Until now.'

It was a strange detail from the past. That Khalil's brother was driving the barracks truck bomb. He must have died yards away from me. But there was something about the present that didn't add up. If Michael made the bomb, I couldn't see how someone else's fingerprint wound up on part of it.

Wallwork wasn't done. 'A manhunt has started for him. Worldwide. Unlimited resources. The guy's toast. It's just a question of when.'

Maybe Khalil had supplied the parts Michael had used, I thought. That could be how his fingerprint got to be there.

Wallwork kept going. 'The manhunt is worldwide. But there's another concern. Closer to home. The TEDAC guys are worried that Khalil is still in the States.'

Or maybe Dendoncker had stolen the parts, I thought. Or refused to pay. Or ripped Khalil off in some other way. That could be why he was expecting a reprisal.

Wallwork continued. 'The TEDAC guys are scared that Khalil is ramping up a bombing campaign. Here. And they figure Dendoncker's helping him. His family was from Beirut, too, remember. His mother was, anyway.'

'They think this on the strength of one fingerprint and a vague connection to a foreign city?'

'No. On the strength of this being the second of Khalil's bombs that they found.'

'Where was the other one?'

'I'm not sure where it turned up. It was a dud. It was taken to TEDAC. A few weeks ago. It was analysed. And it had enough identical features for them to be certain it was made by the same person.'

'Did it have a transponder?'

'No. And it didn't emit gas. But the components came from the same source. The wiring techniques were the same. The architecture was the same. There are enough hallmarks for them to be convinced. More than enough.'

This is the problem when a lie gets too much oxygen. It grows. Even a lie of omission. The smoke bomb had been made by Michael. So if the TEDAC guys had connected it with another one made by the same person, it must be the last bomb Fenton had worked on. The one Michael made and sent to her as an SOS. Only the TEDAC guys didn't know there had been a transponder in that one, too. Or that Fenton destroyed it. Because of Michael's fingerprint. If they had known, they'd have reached a different conclusion. I had no doubt about that. I was about to tell Wallwork.

Ask him to bring the TEDAC guys up to speed. To correct their misconception. But something stopped me. The nagging at the back of my mind. It had started when Fenton told me about finding Michael's message. With the card and the condom. It had grown louder with Dendoncker's weird responses. Now, with all the talk about the Khalil guy, it was practically deafening.

Wallwork was silent for a moment, too. Then he said, 'So, they're worried about what Khalil's up to. They think Dendoncker is helping him. And you're the only person who's been in contact with Dendoncker. Reacher, I might as well just come out and say it. The bosses at TEDAC want to talk to you.'

I wasn't buying the cooperation angle. Not when Dendoncker seemed to think that Khalil could have sent me to kill him. But there was a connection between them. It was a recipe for nothing good. That was for sure. And I had seen Dendoncker. How he operated. Where he hung out. How much he needed to be taken off the street. So I said, 'All right. Have them call me.'

'They don't want to talk on the phone, Reacher. They want to talk face to face.'

I said nothing.

'Think about it. If this goes south there's the potential for major casualties. Major loss of life. If that happens, and you were in their shoes, could you live with yourself if you hadn't adequately interviewed the only guy with first-hand information?'

He had a point.

'They only want you for an hour. Two, tops. So, what do you say?'

'I don't know. When?'

'Today.'

'Where?'

'TEDAC. It's at the Redstone Arsenal. Near Huntsville, Alabama.'

'How am I supposed to get there in a day? It must be more than fifteen hundred miles away.'

'They'll send a plane. To be honest, they've already sent one. It's waiting for you. There's an airfield an hour's drive from Los Gemelos. Four agents are on their way to safeguard the guy you rescued. One of them will drive you.'

I wondered if it was one of the airfields Dendoncker's crew used to smuggle things through. 'And afterwards?'

'They'll take you wherever you like. Within the United States.'

'San Francisco?'

'Sure. If that's what you want.'

'It is.'

'OK. I'll arrange it. Oh. One other thing. This might make you smile. A fax came for you at the hotel. At 12:34 a.m. From Dendoncker. He said the operation was on hold. You were to stay where you were. And not let *the item* out of your sight.'

The conversation had woken Fenton up. She was still in the armchair at Michael's side so I went and sat on his bed and filled her in on developments.

'Well then,' Fenton said when I was finished. 'Looks like you'll make it to the ocean, after all. A private jet. Sent by the government. Guess you're taking hitchhiking to a whole new level.'

I said, 'I hope Michael pulls through. And I'll put in a good word for both of you.'

She shook her head. 'Just for Michael. I knew what I was doing. I'll take what's coming to me.'

'Can you remember a number?'

'You're keeping that phone?'

'No. The number's for someone else. A woman. Her name's Sonia. I met her when I was looking for you. She helped me. And she was close to Michael. You should call her. Let her know he's alive.'

'She was close to Michael? How close?'

I shrugged. 'Very, I guess. They met in the hospital in Germany. Seems like they've been together ever since.'

I could see Fenton doing the math. She hadn't heard about this woman before. That was clear. And her own relationship with her brother had started to wither right around the time the two must have hooked up.

She said, 'What's she like, this Sonia? Will I like her?'

'I hope so. Could be your future sister-in-law we're talking about.'

FIFTY-TWO

The plane was waiting when I reached the airport. It was sitting near the end of the runway, alone and aloof from the handful of crop dusters and two-seater trainers that were dotted around. It was some kind of Gulfstream. All sharp angles and gloss-black paint so that it looked like it was going fast even when it wasn't moving. It had a tail number, but like the Sikorsky I'd flown back from Texas in there was no agency designation. Just the words UNITED STATES.

The agent flashed her badge at the video camera on the intercom at the gate and then drove right up to the plane. Its engines were turning over and when we looped around its tail I saw that the steps were down. Thirty seconds later I was on board and strapped into a seat. A couple of minutes after that we were in the air. No safety briefings. No lining up to take off. And no other passengers.

The vibe inside was more mobile office than luxury club. There was plenty of blond wood with all kinds of plugs and ports and connectors for computers. There were twelve seats. They were finished in navy leather and could be swivelled around. Tables could be folded out from under the windows. There was a projector on the ceiling. A display screen. And a coffee machine. I helped myself to a mug and then settled down to doze. The flight was smooth and quiet. The pilot flew high and fast. We were in the air for less than three hours. I woke up when she began our final descent. The landing was gentle. The taxi was short. And a car was waiting for me when I climbed down the steps.

The army airfield is in the north-west corner of the Redstone Arsenal complex. The TEDAC buildings are at the south-east, more than a mile away. The Bureau driver who collected me didn't say a word as he zig-zagged through the warren of NASA laboratories and army facilities and other kinds of FBI operations. I guess getting sent to ferry scruffy civilians around wasn't the plum choice of duty around there. He finally pulled up alongside a line of shiny, knee-high security bollards and pointed towards a glass-fronted building on the far side.

He said, 'In there. Ask for Agent Lane.'

Inside there were three security guards, all in private contractor's uniform. The first was sitting behind a reception desk. She asked to see my ID. I handed her my passport. She didn't care that it had expired. She just laid it on a scanner and a minute later a machine to its side spat out a laminated pass with my photo, the date and a two-hour validity period. I clipped it to my shirt and the next guy held out a bin for my other possessions. I dropped in my cash and my phone and he fed them through an X-ray machine. He asked for my shoes. I slipped them off and dumped them on the conveyor belt. The third guy then directed me through an arch-shaped metal detector. It didn't buzz or beep, and by the time I had replaced my shoes and retrieved my things a fourth guy had shown up. He looked like he was in his early forties. He was wearing a dark grey suit with a tie and he had an ID badge on a chain around his neck.

He said, 'I'm Supervisory Special Agent James Lane.' He held out his hand. 'Quite a mouthful, I know. I'm heading up the team we're putting together in response to these new developments. I appreciate you taking the time to talk to me. I hope you'll be able to help. Come on. This way. I'll show you what's what.'

A stone path stretched away from the exit to the security building. It led up two sets of matching stone steps to a broad, flat area that was full of wooden picnic tables with grey umbrellas. There were two neighbouring buildings. Lane pointed to the one on the left. It was big, grey, rectangular and featureless.

He said, 'We call that one *The Building*. Never tell me G-Men have no imagination, eh? Anyway, ever seen that Indiana Jones movie about the Ark of the Covenant? The scene at the end where they hide its crate in a warehouse? That's what it's like inside. Shelves, floor to ceiling, end to end. More than a hundred thousand containers. Every piece of every device we've analysed over the last eighteen years. The place is almost full. We've already broken ground on another one. But that's not where we're going.'

Lane started walking towards the right-hand building. This one had two distinct sections. A single-storey part with a flat roof, stone walls and tall windows. And a part with a higher, angled roof, white walls and no windows. The way they were butted up together made it look like the second half was trying to swallow the first.

'This is where the magic happens.' Lane paused at the door. 'The labs are here. Plus, the less interesting things. Like admin. And the meeting rooms. That's where we're going. Sorry.'

Lane used his ID to unlock the door then led the way along the main corridor until we reached a room labelled *Conference One*. Inside there was a space about fifteen feet by twenty. There was a wooden-topped table in the centre. It was rectangular. Surrounded by eleven chairs. They were angled towards the far wall, which was plain white. I guess it doubled as a projection screen. There were three closets built into the wall on the right. Windows to the left. And a carpet that looked like a kind of muted textile version of a Jackson Pollock painting.

Lane took the chair at the head of the table, facing the wall. He said, 'I'm sorry to be treating you like a regular visitor. I've read your record. I know all about your service. I would like to give you a full tour. But, you know, regulations. There was no time to get clearance. And at the end of the day more than two hundred people work here. We have a lot of equipment that would be extremely hard to replace. And a trove of evidence from all over the world that's vital in the war on terror. This place might not be the most glamorous target. But it's near the top of the list, strategically. It's what I'd hit if I were on the other side. So we have to take precautions. And we can't make exceptions. I hope you understand.'

'Of course.'

'So, down to business. Khalil's fingerprint. Finding it is a two-sided coin. The good thing is he can be arrested now. If anyone can find him. But the bad thing is that if he's active here, currently, we must stop him. Fast. The problem is figuring out where to look. There are so many potential targets available to him. We need to narrow them down. The bomb you helped us secure will be arriving in the next thirty minutes or so. That may give us some pointers. Or it may not. We won't know until we try. Either way, it will take time. In the interim, we're looking for all the help we can get. The angle I'd like to start with is the delivery mechanism. Khalil could be working on a bomb to be carried in a car, for example. Or a truck. Or a plane. Or worn as a vest. Or even sent in the mail. Did anything you saw or heard give any kind of a clue?'

'Dendoncker was running a smuggling operation. He was piggybacking it on a catering service for private planes out of small airfields. But that's pretty much been shut down. He seemed unconcerned about it. Strangely so, like he had already planned to move on to something else. The question is, *what*? I'm not convinced Dendoncker's working with Khalil. I think he was terrified of him.'

'These guys – they're weird. Paranoid, most of them. They start out as introverts, then live their whole lives doubly desperate not to draw attention to themselves. Trying not to visit the same electronics store too often. Or to buy from the same websites over and over. They wind up running from shadows. It's probably nothing. But even if they have fallen out already, there could still be useful clues from when they did work together.'

311

'The flight thing is all I can think of.'

'OK. Then the second angle is materials. Is he using precursors, for example. Things like ammonium nitrate or fuel oil or nitromethane. Or specialist compounds like TATP, or ethylene glycol dinitrate. Or even military-grade explosives like C-4.' Lane paused for a moment and looked right at me. 'As an aside, the Beirut barracks bomb used precursors. You were there. Well, we recently recovered new evidence, after all these years. We should have good news on that soon.'

There was something strange about the way Lane spoke those words. How he said, *You were there*. It sounded half like a question. Half like a statement. It caused an echo at the back of my mind. I'd heard something similar recently, but I couldn't put my finger on what.

Lane said, 'Mr Reacher? Materials?'

'Artillery shells,' I said. 'Dendoncker had a bunch of them. At least three hundred. They were locked in a shed. At the abandoned school he was camped out in.'

'Any idea what was in them?'

'No.'

'You didn't see a code book? If they were recovered from an enemy, they're often deliberately mislabelled. The code book is needed to confirm the contents.'

I shook my head.

'OK. Let me have the location. I'll arrange collection. Now, the third angle is the method of detonation. We know Khalil used two kinds in his first device. A timer and cellular. Those are quite normal. And three kinds in the device that's incoming. A timer, cellular and a transponder. That's unusual. But whether he was looking for another level of back-up, or whether he's messing with us, I don't know. Not yet.'

I said nothing.

'Do you know how transponders work?'

I said, 'I have an idea what they do. Not so much how they do it.'

'A good example is a car's ignition. Try to start the engine and a chip in the car sends out a radio signal. A transponder in the key automatically bounces back a reply. If the reply is correct, the chip completes the circuit. That's why you can't hotwire modern cars. Even if you join the right wires there's no transponder to reply to the car's chip, so the circuit remains open.'

'And the same thing could happen with this bomb?'

'I assume so. I haven't seen it yet, obviously. I need to examine it to be sure. But if it's a technique Khalil has perfected it could be a massive problem. Imagine you have a target with an unpredictable schedule. You plant a bomb somewhere along his route. Sneak a transponder on to his keychain or into his pocket. Anyone else could go by without a problem. But when he approaches – boom.'

'OK. But you said the transponder's in the key. Not the car.'

'Correct. The chip in the car initiates the communication. The key responds.'

'So the chip in the bomb would be like the chip in the car?'

'Correct. I'll verify that once the bomb is here, but I don't see another way it could work.'

'What kind of range do these things have?'

'They vary. Depends on the application. Planes use them for automatic identification, in which case the signal can travel many kilometres. If you use one to unlock a door in

313

place of a key you'd want the signal to only go a few milli-metres. You put one in a bomb, you'd want it to be similar, I guess, or your target would be out of the blast zone when it detonated. Unless it was a giant bomb and you didn't care about collateral damage.'

Lane had done it again. The way he spoke, I couldn't tell if 'You put one in a bomb' was a question or a statement. And I suddenly realized who he reminded me of. Michael. When he briefly spoke to Fenton, right after we first found him. He either said, 'You came.' Or 'You came?' And that was right after something else weird. He said, 'You got my warning?' Fenton had described it as a cry for help. An SOS. That was nothing like the same thing. I thought about what she had found. What she had based her conclusion on. And stood up.

I said, 'Excuse me, I have to make a call.'

'Now?' Lane checked his watch. 'The bomb will be here any minute. I'll have to step out. Can't you do it then?'

'No.' I moved to the corner of the room and dialled Dr Houllier's number. 'This can't wait.'

Dr Houllier answered and I asked to speak to Michael.

He said, 'Not possible. Sorry. He's unconscious again.'

'Again?'

'Correct. He was awake for a while earlier, though he wasn't saying much. Nothing coherent, anyway. Just ram-bling about finding a goal or something like that.'

I thanked Dr Houllier and hung up. Then immediately called him back and asked for Fenton.

I said, 'Please hurry. This is important.'

Fenton came on the line after thirty seconds. 'What's up? Make it quick. I want to get back to Michael.'

I said, 'I need you to think very carefully about a question. Don't guess. Only answer if you are one hundred per cent sure. OK?'

'Sure. Fire away.'

'The condom you found in the message Michael sent. What brand was it?'

'Trojan.'

'You sure?'

'One hundred per cent.'

FIFTY-THREE

A condom. And a business card. A Trojan. And the Red Roan.

Michael had been trying to tell his sister that the device she was given to analyse at TEDAC was a Trojan Horse. But Fenton had misunderstood from the start. She had made two false assumptions: that the bomb containing Michael's message had been intended to explode. And that the transponder inside it was the trigger.

I was betting that neither thing was true. The bomb was just a vehicle. Its job was to deliver the transponder. To a place where only a bomb could go. And the transponder's job was not to trigger the bomb it was in. It was to trigger something else. Which hadn't happened. Because Fenton had fixated on Michael's fingerprint. She hadn't realized it was to ensure that the bomb reached her desk. Or that it doubled as a way to sign the warning. She hated puzzles, after all. She was too pedantic. She'd taken it at face value. As damning evidence. So she destroyed it.

Fenton destroyed the first transponder. But now another one was coming. In the smoke bomb. It was minutes away. Heading for the building I was in. Where two hundred people worked. Which was full of irreplaceable machines and priceless evidence. No wonder Dendoncker had been so desperate to push me into transporting the device for him. He had wanted it at TEDAC from the start.

Lane was scowling. 'You broke off this meeting to talk about condoms? What's wrong with you?'

Michael's original bomb arrived at TEDAC weeks ago, initially with its transponder intact. But the place didn't blow up. So the thing it was supposed to trigger wasn't here at that time. It must have come in later.

I said, 'The last three weeks. Have any new devices been brought in?'

Lane checked his watch again. 'Of course.'

'Anything particularly large?'

'I can't share that kind of information. It's too sensitive.'

'Come on, Lane. This is important.'

'Why?'

'It's a long story. A guy with a liking for cryptic messages sent a warning that the transponder in the device that's about to arrive is supposed to trigger something else. Not be triggered itself.'

Lane smiled and shook his head. 'No. That theory doesn't hold water. For it to be right, the device already here would need to have the corresponding transponder. And no such devices have been brought in. Fact.'

'Are you sure? You said some evidence waits a while before you get to it.'

'We prioritize. Some evidence does have to wait for full analysis. That's true. But we don't just throw it in a closet when it shows up. It doesn't slip down the back of the couch. Every piece that's waitlisted is examined on delivery. Photographs are taken. Components are listed. Transponders are highly unusual. If anything had arrived containing one, I would know.'

'These inspections. They're done without exception?'

'Priority cases go straight to analysis planning, who handle the documentation and record keeping. It's integrated into their process. Everything else gets an initial inspection. Without exception.' Lane paused for a second. 'Actually, there was one exception. A truck bomb. A city destroyer. It came in from overseas. The vehicle was too large to fit into a work bay here so the minute it arrived we sent it away again. To our old premises. At Quantico. A huge place. You could fit dozens of trucks in it.'

'What if something arrived while we were talking?'

'That's possible, I suppose.' Lane took out his phone and had a brief conversation. 'No. There was nothing new today.'

The prickling at the back of my neck was worse. 'When M— Khalil's bomb arrives you should stop it. Don't let it in.'

'Impossible.'

'Why? You didn't let the big truck bomb in.'

'No. But it came by road. It already had an escort. Khalil's is being flown in. It doesn't have an escort. It can't go on the public roads without one. What if there was an accident? And it's full of chemical weapons? And people die? Because we sent it away, against procedure, and with no good reason. Based entirely on your whim.'

318

'It's—'

There was a knock on the door and another agent stepped into the room. A much younger guy. He looked freshly pressed and eager. 'It's here, sir. The device from Texas.'

'Excellent.' Lane stood and made for the door. 'You stay here. Keep Mr Reacher company. I'll be back as soon as the device had been processed.'

I thought about the truck bomb. Lane had called it a city destroyer. That didn't sound good. Not good at all. I was happy it was no longer here. And I figured it must be the one Michael's bomb was supposed to trigger. It had to be. It was the only one that hadn't been inspected, and all the others had been free of transponders. Then I realized something else. The truck being sent away could explain Dendoncker's sudden change of heart. Why he told me to keep the smoke bomb at the hotel. If he had someone watching TEDAC he would know there was no point sending a second transponder.

I turned to the new agent. 'The city destroyer. The one that wouldn't fit in the workshop. When did it get refused? I need to know exactly. To the minute.'

'Let me find out for you, sir.' The agent called someone. There was a lot of nodding and gesticulating and changing of facial expressions before he hung up. 'The destroyer's still here, sir. It actually never left. One of its escort vehicles broke down and they still haven't sent a replacement.'

'Where is it, exactly?'

'Parked between this building and The Building.'

'When did it arrive?'

'Around midnight, last night. I believe.'

319

'OK. Call Agent Lane. Tell him not to let the new device on to the site. Not under any circumstances.'

'If you're worried about the destroyer being here, sir, then please don't be. It's been made safe. Emergency procedure. It had three detonation systems, and they've all been disconnected.'

'Was one a transponder?'

'No, sir. It had cellular. Magnetic. And photosensitive.'

'Call Lane. Right now. No time to explain.'

The agent dialled a number, held the phone to his ear, then shook his head. 'Line's busy.'

'Call the driver.'

'OK. What's his number?'

'No idea.'

'His name?'

I shrugged.

'No problem.' The agent started tapping and swiping at his phone's screen. 'I'll go on the intranet. See if I can find a roster.'

'No time. What kind of truck is the destroyer?'

'It's ex-military. An M35 deuce and a half, I think.'

'Which is further? The truck, or the gate?'

'The gate.'

'Then you take the gate. Go now. Run. Keep trying Lane's number. One way or the other, stop him.'

FIFTY-FOUR

I rushed into the corridor. Sprinted to the exit. Burst through. Ran to the space between the two buildings. And saw the truck. Tried not to think about its cargo. Ran to the driver's door. Tugged on the handle. And couldn't get it to move. Which was weird. That kind of truck doesn't have locking doors. Then I noticed the problem. A padlock had been added. The hasp went through a hole in the door skin. It must have been attached to the inner bodywork.

I looked around. There was a border running along the bottom of the wall of the building. Filled with rocks. Some white, decorative kind. I grabbed the biggest one I could see. Smashed it down on the padlock. Hit it again and the lock sprang open. I pulled it free. Tossed it aside. Dropped the rock. Climbed up. Jammed myself into the seat. Which wasn't easy because there's no adjustment. I pushed down on the clutch. Then tried to remember how to get the motor

321

started. It was years since I'd been in a truck like this one. I knew there was no key. There were three steps to follow instead. I scanned all the knobs and levers and gauges. Most had no markings. The few that had labels were in Arabic, which didn't help me. I spotted a lever near the centre of the dash that looked familiar. I turned it. About twenty degrees, counter-clockwise. Which was as far as it would go. I found a knob on the left, with a spade handle. It was sticking out. I pushed it in. Then hit a red button, low down on the right. The heavy old diesel cranked and coughed into life. I found first gear. Which is where second is on most vehicles. Released the parking brake. Lifted the clutch. And the truck shuddered forward.

Ahead there was a road that led to a roll-up door at the back of the laboratory building. There was no point taking it, or I'd wind up closer to the vehicle I was trying to avoid. So when I reached the end I swung left. Continued around The Building. Swung left again and drove back along the far side. I came to the picnic area. The place was full of tables and umbrellas. There was no way through. They were too close together. So I drove over a bunch of them. I saw a dirt road to the right. It ran along the rear of eight buildings adjacent to the TEDAC site. They were new. The road was probably left over from the construction phase. And there were no vehicles its whole length. It was on the far side of a fence so I smashed through, straightened up, and pressed harder on the gas.

I heard sirens. Behind me. I checked my door mirror. It was shaking horribly. All I could make out was a pair of black sedans with flashing light bars on their roofs. They were catching me. Easily. But catching me wouldn't do them any good. They needed to stop me. I didn't know how they were planning to do that. Whether they knew what the truck was carrying. How reckless they were prepared to be. Or how stupid. I figured I was about a thousand feet away from the laboratory at that point. Roughly the width of the whole TEDAC campus. Probably far enough from the smoke bomb's transponder. The sedans were almost behind me. One disappeared from view. Trying to sneak up the passenger side. Then two more sedans appeared. Directly ahead. I decided that would have to do. I took my foot off the gas. Shifted down a couple of gears. Hit the brake. And coasted to as gentle a stop as possible. I took my shirt off. Hung it out of my window. It wasn't white, but I hoped the guys got the message all the same.

I spent the next hour in *Conference One* with two guys with guns. Neither of them spoke, which suited me fine. I sat in the same chair as before. Leaned forward. Cushioned my head in my arms. Ran through some Magic Slim. And followed up with a little Shawn Holt.

I didn't sit up until Lane came into the room. He walked to the head of the table and set down a small box. It was black. Dusty. And a bunch of coloured wires were sticking out of one corner.

'Mr Reacher, I owe you thanks. And an apology. Today was a bad day for terrorists because of you.' He pointed to the box. 'This was found in the city destroyer. It transmits and receives, and it's coded to the transponder in the smoke bomb. If they'd come within range of each other there'd be no more Redstone Arsenal. No more us. And maybe thousands of other casualties.'

I said nothing.

'One question.' Lane sat down. 'How did you know?'

Michael's warning had been the key. Along with Dendoncker's desperate behaviour. But those were all things I didn't want to get into. They'd only raise more questions. Ones I didn't feel like answering. So I said, 'No biggie. Just a lucky guess.'

'And motive? Khalil trying to destroy some evidence that's stored here?'

'Trying to destroy evidence, yes. Khalil, no.' I had no proof of that. Only a hunch. Which meant the West Coast was going to have to wait after all.

FIFTY-FIVE

'He won't come,' Fenton said. Again.

She first said it when she met me at the small airfield an hour from Los Gemelos.

She said it right after she climbed in behind the wheel of Dr Houllier's Cadillac.

She said it three more times as the huge car wafted and wallowed along the long straight roads into town.

She said it as she parked outside the house.

She said it as we walked through the tunnel.

She said it as we checked that the money and the narcotics were still there.

She said it as we confirmed that the final smoke bomb had been removed from Michael's workshop.

She said it as we sat down against the back wall of the old school's assembly hall.

And every time she said it I gave the same reply. 'He will.'

'How can you be sure?'

'He has no choice. His plan failed. That means he can't stay in the United States. He can't return to Beirut. He'll be on watch lists everywhere. So he'll have to go to ground. For ever. So he'll need every penny he can put his hands on. And every valuable thing he can sell.'

'What if the FBI has already caught him? He tried to destroy TEDAC. They'll have a hard-on for him like you wouldn't believe.'

'The Bureau wants to find him. Sure. But they don't know where to look.'

'You didn't tell them?'

I said nothing.

'Outstanding. Gold star for you. But what if they found him on their own? Or if you're wrong about his plan? What if you misunderstood? If it didn't fail?'

'Then he won't come.'

Fenton elbowed me in the ribs and we settled in to wait.

It was pushing seven p.m. Twelve hours since I was woken up by the phone. Six hours since I broke into the city destroyer. The sun was low. Everything its dipping rays touched turned orange or pink. The view was magnificent. If it only happened once a century everyone would gather to watch. Then rave about what they saw. The colours changed by the minute. The shadows shifted and lengthened. The sky began its final fade to grey. Then two brighter points appeared. Low down. Unsteady. But growing bigger. Coming our way.

Headlights.

Fenton and I moved into the dining hall. We left the doors open, just a crack. We peered through. Five minutes passed.

Ten. Then the tall windows lit up like giant mirrors. They went dark again. The outer doors opened. And Mansour walked in. He was followed by Dendoncker. They went straight for the aluminium containers. The ones that were full of cash and pills.

Fenton went first. She was carrying one of the captured Uzis. She raised it and lined it up on Dendoncker's chest.

She said, 'You. Against the wall. Hands in the air.'

Dendoncker didn't hesitate. He was a smart man. He did exactly what she told him to.

I took a step towards Mansour. He grinned, held out his hand, and gestured for me to keep on coming.

I said, 'You don't have to do this. You know you're going to lose. You should go sit in the car. I'll send your boss out when we're done talking. Assuming he can still walk.'

Mansour stretched both arms straight up above his head then started to bring them down slowly, out to each side, in a broad circle. His fingers were arrowed. It looked like the start of some kind of martial arts ritual. Maybe it was supposed to symbolize something. Maybe it was supposed to impress. Or intimidate. But whatever the purpose, I saw no advantage in letting him finish so I darted forward and kicked him in the right knee. Viciously. Hard enough to shatter most people's patellas. He grunted and threw a wild roundhouse punch at my head. I ducked under it and jabbed him in the kidney. I brought my other fist up under his chin. I put all my strength into it. Pushed up on to my tiptoes at just the right moment. Timed it perfectly. Against a normal guy the fight would have been over there and then. It almost was with him. He rocked on to his heels. His neck snapped back. He started to fall. If he'd hit the ground he would have been toast. There was no way I would have let him get up

327

again. But the wall saved him. Or the climbing bars that were attached to it did. He slammed into the centre of a section of the frame. It was ten feet tall by six wide. There was plenty of spring to it. Which cushioned the impact. Allowed him to stay on his feet. He staggered forward. The bars swung after him. They were hinged at the right side. The force of the impact had unhooked their latch. They continued through ninety degrees then stopped, sticking straight out into the hall. I guess they all did that to form a series of obstacles for the kids to climb when they were doing circuit training.

The guy held up his hands in surrender. 'OK. You win. I'm done.'

He took a step towards me. His legs were unsteady. His breathing was ragged. He took another slow step. Then a fast one. He curled his fingers into fists. And launched a punch straight at my face with his right. I deflected it and danced away to the side. Which was just what he wanted. He was already swinging his left. I saw it late. Twisted and ducked and caught the brunt on my shoulder. It felt like I'd been hit by a train. I saw him lining up another shot with his right. I planted my foot. Twisted back in the opposite direction. Raised my arm. And drove my elbow into the side of his head. It was the kind of contact that would have split most guys' skulls. His mouth opened. His arms slumped down to his sides. I reversed direction again and smashed my fist into his other temple. He staggered to the side. His legs were turning to jelly. For real this time. It was my opportunity. I had no intention of wasting it. There was no one to intervene. I jabbed him in the face three times in quick succession with my left. He reeled back. I switched to my right and drove a huge reverse punch into his gut. He doubled over. I stood him up straight again with a knee to the face. He staggered back further. I followed in and crashed the heel of my right hand into his chin. The back of his head cannoned into the wall. His eyes rolled up. His knees buckled. He flopped down into a kneeling position. He balanced like that for a moment and before he could fall the rest of the way I kicked him in the side of the head with my left foot. He spun around and down and wound up with his chest on the floor. His arms out to the sides. And his face jammed into a gap near the base of the climbing bars. I was pretty sure he was down and out. But I never take that kind of thing for granted. I stepped in close. And stamped on the base of his skull. I felt his spine snap. I was sure about that.

FIFTY-SIX

Dendoncker was standing still, staring at the body. His face was pale and completely expressionless. Fenton was covering him with the Uzi. I moved in close and felt his jacket pocket. He had a tiny revolver. Another NAA-22S. I took it and slipped it into my waistband.

'I offered Mansour the chance to walk out of here,' I said. 'Now I'm going to offer you the same. With one condition.'

'Which is?'

'You tell me the truth.'

Dendoncker wetted his lips with his tongue. 'What do you want to know?'

'How did you get hold of a transponder with Nader Khalil's fingerprint on it?'

'I didn't. Michael and Khalil, they tricked me. They were working together, but I didn't know. I bought Michael's story about a protest with smoke. I had no idea there was anything more going on.'

Fenton raised the Uzi. 'Shall I shoot him?'

Dendoncker lifted his arms like they could shield him from her bullets. I grabbed his wrist and dragged him around to the other side of the climbing bars. I forced him on to his knees. Held the back of his head. And pushed his face to within an inch of Mansour's.

I said, 'Think carefully. Is this how you want to go?'

'I bought the fingerprint.' Dendoncker squirmed away from the body. 'It took years. And lots of money. But finally I found someone who was ready to betray Khalil.'

I let Dendoncker stand up. 'How did you get your hands on it?'

'I used one of the women who worked for my catering company. I sent her to Beirut with the money. She brought the fingerprint back. It was fixed in sticky tape. Lifted from a drinking glass. It was easy to transfer it on to the transponder.'

'When was this?'

'A few weeks ago.' Dendoncker pointed at Fenton. 'It's why I hired her. I actually had to send two women. One stayed behind in Beirut. She was part of the price.'

'Did she know in advance? The one who stayed.'

'Of course not. Neither did the one who returned. She thought there'd been an accident.'

'What happened to the other women? You had six on your crew, from what I heard. Five, excluding Fenton.'

'One was plotting with Michael. She ran away. Two are coming with me. The other two are going to . . . retire.'

I caught movement out of the corner of my eye. It was Fenton. Heading for the exit. As planned.

I said, 'You used the fingerprint to frame Khalil. He was never actually involved.'

Dendoncker nodded.

'He was trying to kill you. There was some kind of feud going on.'

Dendoncker nodded again.

'Which is why you always checked the bodies of anyone who came after you. You're not just paranoid.'

'He sent others to kill me many times. I hoped one day he'd try in person. And fail. Then I would be free.'

'What was the feud about?'

Dendoncker wetted his lips. 'Khalil's father blamed me for his other son's death. Khalil carried it on when his father died.'

'Khalil's brother was killed. He was driving a truck bomb.'

'His father and I, we were rivals. I was young. Ambitious. Looking for a shortcut to the top of our group. He stood in my way. I thought if he lost his son it would break his spirit. He would fade away. I could fill the void.' Dendoncker shrugged. 'I was wrong. It only made him stronger. Harder.'

'You made his son drive the bomb?'

'Not made. Led him to the decision.'

'Not a distinction his father was impressed by, I guess.'

Dendoncker shook his head.

'So you saw the opportunity to get Khalil off your back. That's what this is all about?'

'Correct. It was the only way I could buy my freedom.'

'The way I see it, you planned on three steps. First you had Michael make you a bomb. A dud. It was left where it would be found. It had a GPS chip so you could confirm it

332

wound up at TEDAC. It also had a transponder. You knew the components would be studied. The details recorded. The pieces stored.'

Dendoncker nodded.

'Step two involved the city destroyer. It was supposed to arrive at TEDAC and get triggered by the transponder from Michael's bomb.'

I felt my phone buzz in my pocket. That told me Fenton had found what she was looking for in Dendoncker's SUV.

Dendoncker nodded again.

'One question. How do you get your hands on a city destroyer?'

Dendoncker shrugged. 'Same way you get anything. Money.'

'So the city destroyer detonates. Takes TEDAC with it. Then step three. The smoke bomb is found. It has the same technology inside it. Plus Khalil's fingerprint.'

'That's the way it was supposed to happen.'

'But the first transponder didn't trigger the city destroyer.'

'No. It should have done. I have no idea why it failed.'

I smiled. I was tempted to tell him that the transponder didn't fail. That it didn't have the chance to. Because Fenton had destroyed it weeks ago. But I resisted. I needed to keep him focused. He had some big questions coming up. So instead I said, 'Then why try to stop the smoke bomb? Why not make sure it went to TEDAC so its transponder could finish the job?'

'The smoke bomb had the same transponder. It would have triggered the truck bomb. That's true. But I didn't want to risk wasting the fingerprint.'

'Wasting it?'

'Right. It was damn expensive. Two million dollars and a fair employee. It might have survived. But a blast that size? It could easily have been destroyed. And think of the scene. A hundred thousand pieces of evidence are already there. The fingerprint could have survived then got mixed up with the rest. And got lost.'

'OK. Tell me what you did after the demonstration I watched. What you added to the smoke bomb before you put it in the truck for me to drive.'

'I added nothing. Why would I?'

'Because you didn't want the fingerprint to be wasted. The "T" in TEDAC stands for Terrorist. Not protester. Not attention-seeker. Those agents are specialists. They don't get out of bed for a pretty puff of smoke. So unless you spiced the bomb up a little it would have gone to a local field office, at best. Maybe just the police department. Where it would have sat on the shelves in the evidence room gathering dust until long after you're dead.'

'I disagree. TEDAC would have taken it. Because of all the press coverage. I didn't add a thing.'

'You didn't smear the outside of the shells with VX?'

'Where would I get VX from?'

'You didn't pour VX into the shells?' Fenton came back inside. She stayed near the exit door. She peeled off a pair of latex surgeon's gloves and jammed them into her pocket.

Dendoncker said, 'VX is a weapon of mass destruction. I wouldn't touch it.'

'And the third smoke bomb. The last one left in your workshop. You didn't fill it with VX?'

'I don't even know where it is.' Dendoncker pointed at Mansour. 'He disposed of it. He didn't say where or how.'

334

'You didn't add anything to either bomb. You don't know where the third bomb is. That's the story you're going with?'

'It's not a story.'

I waited a moment to give him one last chance to come clean. He didn't take it. So I said, 'OK. I choose to believe you.'

'Then I can go?'

'In a minute. There's still one thing I don't understand. You want to blow someplace up and let Khalil take the fall. But why does that place have to be TEDAC? There are plenty of softer targets out there.'

Dendoncker was silent for a moment. 'I thought if I hit part of the FBI they'd take it personally. Leave no stone unturned. Make sure the fingerprint was found and—'

'No.' I shook my head. 'Here's what I think. You learned that there was some evidence against you at TEDAC. Something that hadn't come to light yet. But that would. Soon. Then you were offered Khalil's fingerprint. And you saw your chance. Two birds, one bomb.'

Dendoncker didn't reply.

'I know what that evidence is. I've joined the dots. But I need to hear you admit it. And I want you to apologize. Do those two things, then you can walk.'

Dendoncker stayed silent.

I pointed at Mansour's body. 'Do those two things, or that's how you'll leave this world. Your choice.'

Dendoncker took a deep breath. 'OK. The Beirut barracks bomb. I didn't build it. But I taught the guys who did. They used parts I touched.'

'You were an instructor? That's how you were in a position to pick the driver?'

'Correct. And it's why I recognized your name when we first met at the morgue. You won the Purple Heart that day. I read about it afterwards.'

'OK. And?'

'And I'm sorry. I apologize. To everyone who got hurt. For everyone who got killed.'

I looked at Fenton. She nodded.

'OK.' I stepped back. 'You're free to go.'

Dendoncker was frozen to the spot. His eyes were darting around wildly, looking for a trap. He stayed still for twenty seconds. Then he started towards the door. First walking, then scuttling as fast as he could go. He kept moving until he reached the Cadillac. He jumped in. Fired it up. And steered for the gate.

I pulled out my phone. There was a message saying I'd missed a call. I'd never seen the number before. But I knew exactly who it was from. Or rather, what it was from. Thanks to Fenton's fishing expedition.

I hit the button to call the number back.

Fenton said, 'Are you sure you want to do this?'

'Why wouldn't I? If Dendoncker's telling the truth, he'll be OK.'

'He lied about not knowing where the third bomb is. I doubt he's telling the truth about the VX.'

'Then that's his problem. I'm still giving him more of a chance than he gave two hundred and forty-one Marines in Beirut that day.'

Dendoncker's Cadillac stopped at the inner gate. My phone showed that my call had been answered. The gate started to crawl to the side. The gap grew wide enough to drive through. The Cadillac stayed still. The gate opened the rest of the way. The Cadillac didn't move. Then its brake lights went out. It rolled forward. Barely above walking pace. Its horn blared. It trundled on. Slewed slightly to the left. And ran into a fence post.

Its horn continued to blare.

Fenton said, 'Want to check? To be sure? Confirm he added VX to the smoke?'

I shook my head. 'No chance. That car's not airtight. Dendoncker's right where he deserves to be. And I have no intention of joining him.'

FIFTY-SEVEN

I last encountered Michaela Fenton half a day later. We met on the road outside the town. I was on foot. She was in her Jeep. She roared past me then swung hard to her left. She blocked my path. Her front fender was a hair's breadth away from the trunk of a tree. A stunted, twisted, ugly thing with hardly any leaves. But the only thing growing taller than knee height for miles in either direction.

Fenton said, 'You left without saying goodbye.'

I shrugged. 'Everyone was asleep.'

'I tried to call you.'

'I don't have that phone any more. I dropped it in the trash.'

'I figured. That's why I came to look for you. I thought I might find you on this road.'

'It's the only one leading out of town.'

'Still heading for the ocean?'

'Won't stop till I get there.'

'Any chance you'll change your mind?'

I shook my head.

'In that case I want to thank you. And so does Michael.'

'He's awake?'

'He is. He's weak, but he's talking.'

'Did he say what he had that Dendoncker was so desperate to get?'

'He called it his insurance. It was a code book. It showed what was inside all the shells Dendoncker had stockpiled. He needed it to make the maximum money when he sold them.'

'Where did he hide it?'

'He said he rolled it up and shoved it inside the crossbar of a soccer goal at the school.'

'Outstanding.'

'And there's something else. I called Sonia. She came back. And you know what? I do like her. Maybe she is my future sister-in-law. And if she is, that's fine by me.'

I said nothing.

Fenton tipped her head to the side. 'You won't stay even another day?'

'No point. You'd be sick of me in ten minutes. You'd be begging me to leave.'

'I doubt it.'

'That's right.' I turned and started walking again. 'You'd probably shoot me instead.'

ABOUT THE AUTHORS

Lee Child is one of the world's leading thriller writers. He was born in Coventry, raised in Birmingham, and now lives in New York. It is said one of his novels featuring his hero Jack Reacher is sold somewhere in the world every nine seconds. His books consistently achieve the number-one slot on bestseller lists around the world and have sold over one hundred million copies. Lee is the recipient of many awards, most recently Author of the Year at the 2019 British Book Awards. He was appointed CBE in the 2019 Queen's Birthday Honours.

Andrew Child is the author of nine thrillers written under the name Andrew Grant. He is the younger brother of Lee Child. Born in Birmingham, he lives in Wyoming with his wife, the novelist Tasha Alexander.

dead good

Looking for more gripping must-reads?

Head over to Dead Good –
the home of killer crime books,
TV and film.

Whether you're on the hunt for an intriguing
mystery, an action-packed thriller
or a creepy psychological drama,
we're here to keep you in the loop.

Get recommendations and reviews from
crime fans, grab discounted books at bargain
prices and enter exclusive giveaways
for the chance to read brand-new releases
before they hit the shelves.

Sign up for the free newsletter:
www.deadgoodbooks.co.uk/newsletter

Find out more about the Jack Reacher books at www.JackReacher.com

- Take the book selector quiz
- Enter competitions
- Read and listen to extracts
- Find out more about the authors
- Discover Reacher coffee, music and more . . .

PLUS sign up for the monthly Jack Reacher newsletter to get all the latest news delivered direct to your inbox.

For up-to-the-minute news about Lee & Andrew Child find us on Facebook

f /JackReacherOfficial

f /LeeChildOfficial

and discover Jack Reacher books on Twitter

🐦 /LeeChildReacher

'Just the Clothes on my Back'
Competition

Jack Reacher is well known for travelling light. Turn out his pockets and you'll only find a toothbrush, passport (expired), maybe a bit of cash, and nothing else. So when Reacher needs a new set of clothes, he doesn't want to spend hours trawling through the racks, he wants speedy choices and effortless style.

Easy-wear is the name of the game: the fabric needs to be **strong but breathable** (suitable for all the elements), **stretchy** (for ease of movement), **robust** (in case of a hostile environment) and **non-iron**, so Reacher can stay looking sharp even in the midst of action. His shoes are **smart yet durable** – ideal for delivering swift kicks in case of a sudden attack from the bad guys.

All these options and more can be found at **Charles Tyrwhitt** – the British menswear brand that makes it easy for men to look effortlessly good. For your chance to win a wardrobe suitable for Reacher's nomadic lifestyle (or your own hectic one), visit the Jack Reacher website and complete the entry form.
You might win £500 worth of Charles Tyrwhitt clothes.

In case you don't win, we'll throw in **20% off at charlestyrwhitt.com** when you apply the code **JACK20** to your shopping bag, so you can still stock up on action-ready tailoring.

To enter, visit **www.jackreacher.com/wardrobe**
Closing date 31/12/2021. T&Cs apply.

LAST
TIME
I LIED

Also by Riley Sager:

Final Girls

LAST TIME I LIED

RILEY SAGER

1 3 5 7 9 10 8 6 4 2

Ebury Press, an imprint of Ebury Publishing
20 Vauxhall Bridge Road,
London SW1V 2SA

Penguin
Random House
UK

Ebury Press is part of the Penguin Random House group of companies whose
addresses can be found at global.penguinrandomhouse.com

First published in the US in 2018 by Dutton, a division of Penguin Random House
First published in the UK in 2018 by Ebury Press

www.penguin.co.uk

A CIP catalogue record for this book is available from the British Library

Hardback ISBN 9781785038396
Trade Paperback ISBN 9781785038402

Typeset in 11.5/15.5 pt Bell MT Std
by Integra Software Services Pvt. Ltd, Pondicherry

Printed and bound in Great Britain by Clays Ltd, Elcograf S.p.A.

Penguin Random House is committed to a sustainable future for our business,
our readers and our planet. This book is made from Forest Stewardship
Council® certified paper.

To Mike, as always

This is how it begins.

You wake to sunlight whispering through the trees just outside the window. It's a faint light, weak and gray at the edges. Dawn still shedding the skin of night. Yet it's bright enough to make you roll over and face the wall, the mattress creaking beneath you. Within that roll is a moment of disorientation, a split second when you don't know where you are. It happens sometimes after a deep, dreamless slumber. A temporary amnesia. You see the fine grains of the pine-plank wall, smell the traces of campfire smoke in your hair, and know exactly where you are.

Camp Nightingale.

You close your eyes and try to drop back into sleep, doing your best to ignore the nature noise rising from outside. It's a jarring, discordant sound—creatures of the night clashing with those of the day. You catch the drumroll of insects, the chirp of birds, a solitary loon letting out one last ghostly call that skates across the lake.

The racket of the outdoors temporarily masks the silence inside. But then a woodpecker's rat-a-tat-tat subsides into echo, and in that brief lull, you realize how quiet it is. How the only sound you're aware of is the steady rise and fall of your own sleep-heavy breathing.

Your eyes dart open again as you strain to hear something else—anything else—coming from inside the cabin.

There's nothing.

The woodpecker starts up again, and its rapid jackhammering tugs you away from the wall to face the rest of the cabin. It's a small space. Just enough room for two sets of bunk beds, a night table topped by a lantern, and four hickory trunks near the door for storage. Certainly tiny enough for you to be able to tell when it's empty, which it is.

You fling your gaze to the bunks across from you. The top one is neatly made, the sheets pulled taut. The bottom is the opposite—a tangle of blankets, something lumpy buried beneath them.

You check your watch in the early half-light. It's a few minutes past 5:00 a.m. Almost an hour until reveille. The revelation brings an undercurrent of panic that hums just under your skin, itchy and irritating.

Emergency scenarios trot though your brain. A sudden illness. A frantic call from home. You even try to tell yourself it's possible the girls had to leave so quickly they couldn't be bothered to wake you. Or maybe they tried but you couldn't be roused. Or maybe they did and you can't remember.

You kneel before the hickory trunks by the door, each one carved with names of campers past, and fling open all of them but yours. The inside of each satin-lined box is stuffed to the brim with clothes and magazines and simple camp crafts. Two of them hold cell phones, turned off, unused for days.

Only one of them took her phone.

You have no idea what that could mean.

The first—and only—logical place you think they can be is the latrine, a cedar-walled rectangle just beyond the cabins, planted right at the threshold of the forest. Maybe one of them had to go the bathroom and the others went with her. It's happened before. You've taken part in similar treks. Huddled together, scurrying along a path lit by a single, shared flashlight.

Yet the perfectly made bed suggests a planned absence. An extended one. Or, worse, that no one had even slept in it the night before.

Still, you open the cabin door and take a nervous step outside. It's a gray, chilly morning, one that makes you hug yourself for warmth as you head to the latrine. Inside, you check every stall and shower. They're all empty. The shower walls are dry. So are the sinks.

Back outside, you pause halfway between the latrine and the cabins, your head cocked, straining to hear signs of the girls hidden among all the buzzing and chirping and water gently lapping the lakeshore fifty yards away.

There's nothing.

The camp itself is completely silent.

A sense of isolation drops onto your shoulders, and for a moment you wonder if the whole camp has cleared out, leaving only you behind. More horrible scenarios fill your thoughts. Cabins emptying in a frenzied, worried rush. You sleeping right through it.

You head back to the cabins, circling them quietly, listening for signs of life. There are twenty cabins in all, laid out in a tidy grid covering a patch of cleared forest. You wind your way around them, fully aware of how ridiculous you look. Dressed in nothing more than a tank top and a pair of boxer shorts, dead pine needles and pathway mulch sticking to your bare feet.

Each cabin is named after a tree. Yours is Dogwood. Next door is Maple. You check the names of each, trying to pick one the girls might have wandered into it. You picture an impromptu sleepover. You begin to squint into windows and crack open, unlocked doors, scanning the double-decker rows of sleeping girls for signs of additional campers. In one of the cabins—Blue Spruce—you startle a girl awake. She sits up in her bottom bunk, a gasp caught in her throat.

"Sorry," you whisper before closing the door. "Sorry, sorry."

You make your way to the other side of the camp, which normally bustles with activity from sunrise until twilight. Right now, though, sunrise is still just a promise, nothing but faint pinkness inching above the horizon. The only activity involves you marching toward the sturdy mess hall. In an hour or so, the scents of coffee and burnt bacon should be wafting from the building. At the moment, there's no smell of food, no noise.

You try the door. It's locked.

When you press your face to a window, all you see is a darkened dining room, chairs still stacked atop long rows of tables.

It's the same at the arts and crafts building next door.

Locked.

Dark.

This time, your window peek reveals a semicircle of easels bearing the half-painted canvases of yesterday's lesson. You had been working on a still life. A vase of wild flowers beside a bowl of oranges. Now you can't shake the feeling the lesson will never be completed, the flowers always half-painted, the bowls forever missing their fruit.

You back away from the building, rotating slowly, contemplating your next move. To your right is the gravel drive that leads out of camp, through the woods, to the main road. You head in the opposite direction, right into the center of camp, where a mammoth, log-frame building sits at the end of a circular drive.

The Lodge.

The place where you least expect to find the girls.

It's an unwieldy hybrid of a building. More mansion than cabin. A constant reminder to campers of their own, meager lodgings. Right now, it's silent. Also dark. The ever-brightening sunrise behind it casts the front of the building in shadow, and you can barely make out its beveled windows, its fieldstone foundation, its red door.

Part of you wants to run to that door and pound on it until Franny answers. She needs to know that three girls are gone. She's the camp director, after all. The girls are her responsibility.

You resist because there's a possibility you could be wrong. That you overlooked some important place where the girls might have stashed themselves, as if this were all a game of hide-and-seek. Then there's the fact that you're reluctant to tell Franny until you absolutely must.

You've already disappointed her once. You don't want to do it again.

You're about to return to deserted Dogwood when something behind the Lodge catches your eye. A strip of orange light just beyond its sloped back lawn.

Lake Midnight, reflecting sky.

Please be there, *you think*. Please be safe. Please let me find you.

The girls aren't there, of course. There's no rational reason they would be. It feels like a bad dream. The kind you dread the most when you close your eyes at night. Only this nightmare has come true.

Maybe that's why you don't stop walking once you reach the lake's edge. You keep going, into the lake itself, slick rocks beneath your feet. Soon the water is up to your ankles. When you start to shiver, you can't tell if it's from the coldness of the lake or the sense of fear that's gripped you since you first checked your watch.

You rotate in the water, examining your surroundings. Behind you is the Lodge, the side facing the lake brightened by the sunrise, its windows glowing pink. The lakeshore stretches away from you on both sides, a seemingly endless line of rocky coast and leaning trees. You cast your gaze outward, to the great expanse of lake. The water is mirror-smooth, its surface reflecting the slowly emerging clouds and a smattering of fading stars. It's also deep, even in the middle of a drought that's lowered the waterline, leaving a foot-long strip of sun-dried pebbles along the shore.

The brightening sky allows you to see the opposite shore, although it's just a dark streak faintly visible in the mist. All of it—the camp, the lake, the surrounding forest—is private property, owned by Franny's family, passed down through generations.

So much water. So much land.

So many places to disappear.

The girls could be anywhere. That's what you realize as you stand in the water, shivering harder. They're out there. Somewhere. And it could take days to find them. Or weeks. There's a chance they'll never be found.

The idea is too terrible to think about, even though it's the only thing you can think about. You imagine them stumbling through the thick woods, unmoored and directionless, wondering if the moss on the trees really does point north. You think of them hungry and scared and shivering. You picture them under the water, sinking into the muck, trying in vain to grasp their way to the surface.

You think of all these things and begin to scream.

PART ONE

TWO TRUTHS

One

I paint the girls in the same order.

Vivian first.

Then Natalie.

Allison is last, even though she was first to leave the cabin and therefore technically the first to disappear.

My paintings are typically large. Massive, really. As big as a barn door, Randall likes to say. Yet the girls are always small. Inconsequential marks on a canvas that's alarmingly wide.

Their arrival heralds the second stage of a painting, after I've laid down a background of earth and sky in hues with appropriately dark names. Spider black. Shadow gray. Blood red.

And midnight blue, of course. In my paintings, there's always a bit of midnight.

Then come the girls, sometimes clustered together, sometimes scattered to far-flung corners of the canvas. I put them in white dresses that flare at the hems, as if they're running from something. They're usually turned so all that can be seen of them is their hair trailing behind them as they flee. On the rare occasions when I do paint a glimpse of their faces, it's only the slimmest of profiles, nothing more than a single curved brushstroke.

I create the woods last, using a putty knife to slather paint onto the canvas in wide, unwieldy strokes. This process can take days, even weeks, me slightly dizzy from fumes as I glob on more paint, layer upon layer, keeping it thick.

I've heard Randall boast to potential buyers that my surfaces are like Van Gogh's, with paint cresting as high as an inch off the canvas. I prefer to think I paint like nature, where true smoothness is a myth, especially in the woods. The chipped ridges of tree bark. The speckle of moss on rock. Several autumns' worth of leaves coating the ground. That's the nature I try to capture with my scrapes and bumps and whorls of paint.

So I add more and more, each wall-size canvas slowly succumbing to the forest of my imagination. Thick. Forbidding. Crowded with danger. The trees loom, dark and menacing. Vines don't creep so much as coil, their loops tightening into choke holds. Underbrush covers the forest floor. Leaves blot out the sky.

I paint until there's not a bare patch left on the canvas and the girls have been consumed by the forest, buried among the trees and vines and leaves, rendered invisible. Only then do I know a painting is finished, using the tip of a brush handle to swirl my name into the lower right-hand corner.

Emma Davis.

That same name, in that same borderline-illegible script, now graces a wall of the gallery, greeting visitors as they pass through the hulking sliding doors of this former warehouse in the Meatpacking District. Every other wall is filled with paintings. *My* paintings. Twenty-seven of them.

My first gallery show.

Randall has gone all out for the opening party, turning the place into a sort of urban forest. There are rust-colored walls and birch trees cut from a forest in New Jersey arranged in tasteful clumps. Ethereal house music throbs discreetly in the background. The lighting suggests October even though it's a week until St. Patrick's Day and outside the streets are piled with dirty slush.

The gallery is packed, though. I'll give Randall that. Collectors, critics, and lookyloos elbow for space in front of the canvases, champagne glasses in hand, reaching every so often for the mushroom-and-goat-cheese croquettes that float by. Already I've been introduced to dozens of people whose names I've instantly forgotten. People of importance. Important enough for Randall to whisper who they are in my ear as I shake their hands.

"From the *Times*," he says of a woman dressed head to toe in shades of purple. Of a man in an impeccably tailored suit and bright red sneakers, he simply whispers, "Christie's."

"Very impressive work," Mr. Christie's says, giving me a crooked smile. "They're so bold."

There's surprise in his voice, as if women are somehow incapable of boldness. Or maybe his surprise stems from the fact that, in person, I'm anything but bold. Compared with other outsize personalities in the art world, I'm positively demure. No all-purple ensemble or flashy footwear for me. Tonight's little black dress and black pumps with a kitten heel are as fancy as I get. Most days I dress in the same combination of khakis and paint-specked T-shirts. My only jewelry is the silver charm bracelet always wrapped around my left wrist. Hanging from it are three charms—tiny birds made of brushed pewter.

I once told Randall I dress so plainly because I want my paintings to stand out and not the other way around. In truth, boldness in one's personality and appearance seems futile to me.

Vivian was bold in every way.

It didn't keep her from disappearing.

During these meet and greets, I smile as wide as instructed, accept compliments, coyly defer the inevitable questions about what I plan to do next.

Once Randall has exhausted his supply of strangers to introduce, I hang back from the crowd, willing myself not to check each painting for the telltale red sticker signaling it's been sold. Instead, I nurse a glass of champagne in a corner, the branch of a recently deforested birch tapping against my shoulder as I look around the room for people I actually know. There are many, which makes me grateful, even though it's strange seeing them together in the same place. High school friends mingling with coworkers from the ad agency, fellow painters standing next to relatives who took the train in from Connecticut.

All of them, save for a single cousin, are men.

That's not entirely an accident.

I perk up once Marc arrives fashionably late, sporting a proud grin as he surveys the scene. Although he claims to loathe the art world, Marc fits in perfectly. Bearded with adorably mussed hair. A plaid sport coat thrown over his worn Mickey Mouse T-shirt. Red sneakers that make Mr. Christie's do a disappointed double take. Passing through the crowd, Marc snags a glass of champagne and one of the croquettes, which he pops into his mouth and chews thoughtfully.

"The cheese saves it," he informs me. "But those watery mushrooms are a major infraction."

"I haven't tried one yet," I say. "Too nervous."

Marc puts a hand on my shoulder, steadying me. Just like he used to do when we lived together during art school. Every person, especially artists, needs a calming influence. For me, that person is Marc Stewart. My voice of reason. My best friend. My probable husband if not for the fact that we both like men.

I'm drawn to the romantically unattainable. Again, not a coincidence.

"You're allowed to enjoy this, you know," he says.

"I know."

"And you can be proud of yourself. There's no need to feel guilty. Artists are supposed to be inspired by life experiences. That's what creativity is all about."

Marc's talking about the girls, of course, buried inside every painting. Other than me, only he knows about their existence. The only thing I haven't told him is why, fifteen years later, I continue to make them vanish over and over.

That's one thing he's better off not knowing.

I never intended to paint this way. In art school, I was drawn to simplicity in both color and form. Andy Warhol's soup cans. Jasper Johns's flags. Piet Mondrian's bold squares and rigid black lines. Then came an assignment to paint a portrait of someone I knew who had died.

I chose the girls.

I painted Vivian first because she burned brightest in my memory. That blond hair right out of a shampoo ad. Those incongruously dark eyes that looked black in the right light. The pert nose sprayed with freckles brought out by the sun. I put her in a white dress with an elaborate Victorian collar fanning around her swanlike neck and gave her the same enigmatic smile she displayed on her way out of the cabin.

You're too young for this, Em.

Natalie came next. High forehead. Square chin. Hair pulled tight in a ponytail. Her white dress got a dainty lace collar that downplayed her thick neck and broad shoulders.

Finally, there was Allison, with her wholesome look. Apple cheeks and slender nose. Brows two shades darker than her flaxen hair, so thin and perfect they looked like they had been drawn on with brown pencil. I painted an Elizabethan ruff around her neck, frilly and regal.

Yet there was something wrong with the finished painting. Something that gnawed at me until the night before the project was due, when I awoke at 2:00 a.m. and saw the three of them staring at me from across the room.

Seeing them. That was the problem.

I crept out of bed and approached the canvas. I grabbed a brush, dabbed it in some brown paint, and smeared a line over their eyes. A tree branch, blinding them. More branches followed. Then plants and vines and whole trees, all of them gliding off the brush onto the canvas, as if sprouting there. By dawn, most of the canvas had been besieged by forest. All that remained of Vivian, Natalie, and Allison were shreds of their white dresses, patches of skin, locks of hair.

That became No. 1. The first in my forest series. The only one where even a fraction of the girls is visible. That piece, which got the highest grade in the class after I explained its meaning to my instructor, is absent from the gallery show. It hangs in my loft, not for sale.

Most of the others are here, though, with each painting taking up a full wall of the multi-chambered gallery. Seeing them together like this, with their gnarled branches and vibrant leaves, makes me realize how obsessive the whole endeavor is. Knowing I've spent years painting the same subject unnerves me.

"I *am* proud," I tell Marc before taking a sip of champagne.

He downs his glass in one gulp and grabs a fresh one. "Then what's up? You seem *vexed.*"

He says it with a reedy British accent, a dead-on impersonation of Vincent Price in that campy horror movie neither of us can remember the name of. All we know is that we were stoned when we watched it on TV one night, and the line made us howl with laughter. We say it to each other far too often.

"It's just weird. All of *this.*" I use my champagne flute to gesture at the paintings dominating the walls, the people lined up in front of them, Randall kissing both cheeks of a svelte European couple who just walked through the door. "I never expected any of this."

I'm not being humble. It's the truth. If I had expected a gallery show, I would have actually named my work. Instead, I simply numbered them in the order they were painted. No. 1 through No. 33.

Randall, the gallery, this surreal opening reception—all of it is a happy accident. The product of being in the right place at the right time. That right place, incidentally, was Marc's bistro in the West Village. At the time, I was in my fourth year of being the in-house artist at an ad agency. It was neither enjoyable nor fulfilling, but it paid the rent on a crumbling loft big enough to fit my forest canvases. After an overhead pipe leaked into the bistro, Marc needed something to temporarily mask a wall's worth of water damage. I loaned him No. 8 because it was the biggest and most able to cover the square footage.

That right time was a week later, when the owner of a small gallery a few blocks away popped into Marc's place for lunch. He saw the painting, was suitably intrigued, and asked Marc about the artist.

That led to one of my paintings—No. 7—being displayed in the gallery. It sold within a week. The owner asked for more. I gave him three. One of the paintings—lucky No. 13—caught the eye of a young art lover who posted a picture of it on Instagram. That picture was noticed by her employer, a television actress known for setting trends. She bought the painting and hung it in her dining room, showing it off during a dinner party for a small group of friends. One of those friends, an editor at *Vogue*, told his cousin, the owner of a larger, more prestigious gallery. That cousin is Randall, who currently roams the gallery, coiling his arms around every guest he sees.

What none of them knows—not Randall, not the actress, not even Marc—is that those thirty-three canvases are the only things I've painted outside my duties at the ad agency. There are no fresh ideas percolating in this artist's brain, no inspiration sparking me into productivity. I've attempted other things, of course, more from a nagging sense of responsibility than actual desire. But I'm never able to move beyond those initial, halfhearted efforts. I return to the girls every damn time.

I know I can't keep painting them, losing them in the woods again and again. To that end, I've vowed not to paint another. There won't be a No. 34 or a No. 46 or, God forbid, a No. 112.

That's why I don't answer when everyone asks me what I'm working on next. I have no answer to give. My future is quite literally a blank canvas, waiting for me to fill it. The only thing I've painted in the past six months is my studio, using a roller to convert it from daffodil yellow to robin's-egg blue.

If there's anything vexing me, it's that. I'm a one-hit wonder. A bold lady painter whose life's work is on these walls.

As a result, I feel helpless when Marc leaves my side to chat up a handsome cater waiter, giving Randall the perfect moment to clutch my wrist and drag me to a slender woman studying No. 30, my largest work to date. Although I can't see the woman's face, I know she's important. Everyone else I've met tonight has been guided to me instead of the other way around.

"Here she is, darling," Randall announces. "The artist herself."

The woman whirls around, fixing me with a friendly, green-eyed gaze I haven't seen in fifteen years. It's a look you easily remember. The kind of gaze that, when aimed at you, makes you feel like the most important person in the world.

"Hello, Emma," she says.

I freeze, not sure what else to do. I have no idea how she'll act. Or what she'll say. Or even why she's here. I had assumed Francesca Harris-White wanted nothing to do with me.

Yet she smiles warmly before pulling me close until our cheeks touch. A semi-embrace that Randall witnesses with palpable jealousy.

"You already know each other?"

"Yes," I say, still stunned by her presence.

"It was ages ago. Emma was a mere slip of a girl. And I couldn't be more proud of the woman she's become."

She gives me another look. *The* look. And although that sense of surprise hasn't left me, I realize how happy I am to see her. I didn't think such a thing was possible.

"Thank you, Mrs. Harris-White," I tell her. "That's very kind of you to say."

She mock frowns. "What's with this 'Mrs. Harris-White' nonsense? It's Franny. Always Franny."

I remember that, too. Her standing before us in her khaki shorts and blue polo shirt, her bulky hiking boots making her feet look comically large. *Call me Franny. I insist upon it. Here in the great outdoors, we're all equals.*

It didn't last. Afterward, when what happened was in newspapers across the country, it was her full, formal name that was used. Francesca Harris-White. Only daughter of real estate magnate Theodore Harris. Sole grandchild of lumber baron Buchanan Harris. Much-younger widow of tobacco heir Robert White. Net worth estimated to be almost a billion, most of it old money stretching back to the Gilded Age.

Now she stands before me, seemingly untouched by time, even though she now must be in her late seventies. She wears her age well. Her skin is tan and radiant. Her sleeveless blue dress emphasizes her trim figure. Her hair, a shade balanced between blond and gray, has been pulled back in a chignon, showing off a single strand of pearls around her neck.

She turns to the painting again, her gaze scanning its formidable width. It's one of my darker works—all blacks, deep blues, and mud browns. The canvas dwarfs her, making it look as though she's actually standing in a forest, the trees about to overtake her.

"It's really quite marvelous," she says. "All of them are."

There's a catch in her voice. Something tremulous and uncertain, as if she can somehow glimpse the girls in their white dresses beneath the painted thicket.

"I must confess that I came here under false pretenses," she says, still staring at the painting, seemingly unable to look away. "I'm here for the art, of course. But also for something else. I have what you might call an interesting proposition."

At last, she turns away from the painting, fixing those green eyes on me. "I'd love to discuss it with you, when you have the time."

I shoot a glance to Randall, who stands behind Franny at a discreet distance. He mouths the word every artist longs to hear: *commission.*

The idea prompts me to immediately say, "Of course." Under any other circumstance, I already would have declined.

"Then join me for lunch tomorrow. Let's say twelve thirty? At my place? It will give us a chance to catch up."

I find myself nodding, even though I'm not entirely sure what's happening. Franny's unexpected appearance. Her even more unexpected invitation to lunch. The scary-yet-tantalizing prospect of being commissioned to paint something for her. It's another surreal touch to an already strange evening.

"Of course," I say again, lacking the wherewithal to utter anything else.

Franny beams. "Wonderful."

She presses a card into my hand. Navy print on heavy white vellum. Simple but elegant. It bears her name, a phone number, and a Park Avenue address. Before leaving, she pulls me into another half hug. Then she turns to Randall and gestures toward No. 30.

"I'll take it," she says.

Two

Franny's building is easy to find. It's the one that bears her family's name.

The Harris.

Much like its residents, the Harris is steadfastly inconspicuous. No Dakota-like dormers and gables here. Just understated architecture rising high over Park Avenue. Above the doorway is the Harris family crest carved in marble. It depicts two tall pines crossed together to form an *X*, surrounded by an ivy laurel. Appropriate, considering the family's initial fortune came from the culling of such trees.

The inside of the Harris is as somber and hushed as a cathedral. And I'm the sinner tiptoeing inside. An imposter. Someone who doesn't belong. Yet the doorman smiles and greets me by name, as if I've lived here for years.

The warm welcome continues when I'm directed to the elevator. Standing inside is another familiar face from Camp Nightingale.

"Lottie?" I say.

Unlike Franny, she's changed quite a bit in the past fifteen years. Older, of course. More sophisticated. The shorts and plaid shirt I last saw her wearing have been replaced with a charcoal pantsuit over a crisp white blouse. Her hair, once long and the color of mahogany, is now jet-black and cut into a sleek bob that frames her pale face. But the smile is the same. It has a warm, friendly glow that's just as vibrant now as it was at Camp Nightingale.

"Emma," she says, pulling me into a hug. "My God, it's nice to see you again."

I hug her back. "You too, Lottie. I wondered if you still worked for Franny."

"She couldn't get rid of me if she tried. Not that she'd ever want to."

Indeed, the two of them were rarely seen apart. Franny the master of the camp and Lottie the devoted assistant. Together they ruled not with an iron fist but with a velvet glove, their benevolent patience never strained, even when surprised by a latecomer like myself. I can still picture the moment I met Lottie. The unhurried way she emerged from the Lodge after my parents and I arrived hours later than expected. She greeted us with a smile, a wave, and a sincere *Welcome to Camp Nightingale.*

Now she ushers me into the elevator and presses the top button. As we're whisked upward, she says, "You and Franny will be lunching in the greenhouse. Just wait until you see it."

I nod, feigning excitement. Lottie sees right through me. She eyes me from head to toe, taking in my stiff-backed posture, my tapping foot, the uncontrollable wavering of my plastered-on smile.

"Don't be nervous," she says. "Franny's forgiven you a hundred times over."

I wish I could believe that. Even though Franny was nothing but friendly to me at the gallery, a gnawing doubt persists. I can't shake the feeling that this is more than just a friendly visit.

The elevator doors open, and I find myself looking at the entrance foyer to Franny's penthouse. To my surprise, the wall directly facing the elevator already bears the painting she had purchased the night before. No little red sticker or weeks of waiting for Francesca Harris-White. Randall must have been up all night organizing its shipment from the gallery to here.

"It's a beautiful piece," Lottie says of No. 30. "I can see why Franny was taken with it."

I wonder if Franny would still be taken if she knew the girls were secreted within the painting, hiding there, waiting to be found. I then wonder how the girls themselves would feel about taking up residence in Franny's penthouse. Allison and Natalie likely wouldn't care. But Vivian? She'd fucking love it.

"I plan on taking an afternoon off to visit the gallery and see what else you've painted," Lottie says. "I'm so proud of you, Emma. We all are."

She leads me down a short hallway to the left, past a formal dining room and through a sunken sitting room. "Here we are. The greenhouse."

The word doesn't begin to do the room justice. It's a greenhouse in the same way Grand Central is a train station. Both are so ornate it defies easy description.

Franny's greenhouse is in reality a two-story conservatory built on what was once the penthouse terrace. Panes of heavy glass rise from floor to vaulted ceiling, some still bearing triangles of snow in their exterior corners. Contained within this fanciful structure is a miniature forest. There are squat pines, flowering cherry trees, and rosebushes aflame with red blooms. Slick moss and tendrils of ivy cover the ground. There's even a babbling brook, which flows over a creek bed stippled with rocks. In the center of this fairy-tale forest is a redbrick patio. That's where I find Franny, seated at a wrought-iron table already set for lunch.

"Here she is," Lottie announces. "And probably famished. Which means I better start serving."

Franny greet me with another semi-embrace. "How wonderful to see you again, Emma. And dressed so beautifully, too."

Since I had no idea what to wear, I put on the nicest thing I own—a printed Diane von Furstenberg wrap dress my parents gave me for Christmas. It turns out I shouldn't have worried about being underdressed. Next to Franny's outfit of black pants and white button-down, I feel the opposite. Stiff, formal, and agonizingly nervous about why I've been summoned here.

"What do you think of my little greenhouse?" Franny asks.

I take another look around, spying details previously missed. The statue of an angel half-consumed by ivy. The daffodils sprouting beside the creek. "It's marvelous," I say. "Too beautiful for words."

"It's my tiny oasis in the big city. I decided years ago that if I couldn't live outdoors, then I'd have to bring the outdoors inside to live with me."

"So that's why you bought my biggest painting," I say.

"Exactly. Looking at it feels like standing before a dark woods, and I must decide if I should venture forth into it. The answer, of course, is yes."

That would be my answer, too. But unlike Franny, I'd go only because I know the girls are waiting for me just beyond the tree line.

Lunch is trout almondine and arugula salad, washed down with a crisp Riesling. The first glass of wine calms my nerves. The second lets me lower my guard. By the third, when Franny asks me about my job, my personal life, my family, I answer honestly—hate it, still single, parents retired to Boca Raton.

"Everything was delicious," I say when we finish a dessert of lemon tart so tasty I'm tempted to lick the plate.

"I'm so pleased," Franny says. "The trout came from Lake Midnight, you know."

The mention of the lake startles me. Franny notices my surprise and says, "We can still think fondly of a place where bad things have occurred. At least, I can. And I do."

It's understandable that Franny feels this way in spite of everything that happened. It is, after all, her family's property. Four thousand acres of wilderness at the southern base of the Adirondacks, all preserved by her grandfather after he spent a lifetime deforesting land five times that size. I suppose Buchanan Harris thought saving those four thousand acres made up for it. Perhaps it did, even though that preservation also came at a cost to the environment. Disappointed he couldn't find a tract of land that contained a large body of water, Franny's grandfather decided to create one himself. He dammed the tributary of a nearby river, slamming the gates shut with the push of a button at the stroke of midnight on a rainy New Year's Eve in 1902. Within days, what was once a quiet valley became a lake.

The story of Lake Midnight. It was told to every new arrival at Camp Nightingale.

"It hasn't changed one bit," Franny continues. "The Lodge is still there, of course. My home away from home. I was just there this past weekend, which is how I happened upon the trout. I caught them myself. The boys hate that I go so often. Especially when it's just Lottie and myself. Theo worries that there's no one around to help if something terrible befalls us."

Hearing about Franny's sons gives me another uneasy jolt.

Theodore and Chester Harris-White. Such unbearably WASPish names. Like their mother, they prefer their nicknames—Theo and Chet. The youngest, Chet, is hazy in my memory. He was just a boy when I was at Camp Nightingale, no more than ten. The product of a surprise, late-in-life adoption. I can't recall ever speaking to him, although I must have at some point. I simply remember getting occasional glimpses of him running barefoot down the Lodge's sloped back lawn to the edge of the lake.

Theo was also adopted. Years before Chet.

I remember a lot about him. Maybe too much.

"How are they?" I ask, even though I have no right to know. I do it only because Franny gives me an expectant look, clearly waiting for me to inquire about them.

"They're both well. Theo is spending the year in Africa, working with Doctors Without Borders. Chet will be getting his master's from Yale in the spring. He's engaged to a lovely girl." She pauses, allowing the information to settle over me. The silence speaks volumes. It tells me that her family is thriving, in spite of what I did to them. "I thought you might already know all this. I've heard the Camp Nightingale grapevine is still fully intact."

"I'm not really in touch with anyone from there anymore," I admit.

Not that the girls I knew at camp didn't try. When Facebook became the rage, I received friend requests from several former campers. I ignored them all, seeing no point in staying in touch. We had nothing in common other than spending two weeks in the same place at the same unfortunate time. That didn't stop me from being included in a Facebook group of Camp Nightingale alumni. I muted all posts years ago.

"Perhaps we can change that," Franny says.

"How?"

"I suppose it's time I reveal why I've asked you here today," she says, adding a tactful "Although I do enjoy your company very much."

"I'll admit I'm curious," I say, which is the understatement of the year.

"I'm going to reopen Camp Nightingale," Franny announces.

"Are you sure that's a good idea?"

The words tumble forth, unplanned. They contain a derisive edge. Cold and almost cruel.

"I'm sorry," I say. "That came out wrong."

Franny reaches across the table, gives my hand a squeeze, and says, "Don't feel bad at all. You're not the first person to have that reaction. And even I can admit it's not the most logical idea. But I feel like it's the right time. The camp has been quiet long enough."

Fifteen years. That's how long it's been. It feels like a lifetime ago. It also feels like yesterday.

The camp closed early that summer, shutting down after only two weeks and throwing lots of families' schedules into chaos. It couldn't be helped. Not after what happened. My parents vacillated between sympathy and annoyance after they picked me up a day later than everyone else. Last to arrive, last to leave. I remember sitting in our Volvo, staring out the back window as the camp receded. Even at thirteen, I knew it would never reopen.

A different camp could have survived the scrutiny. But Camp Nightingale wasn't just any summer camp. It was *the* summer camp if you lived in Manhattan and had a bit of money. The place where generations of young women from well-to-do families spent their summers swimming, sailing, gossiping. My mother went there. So did my aunt. At my school, it was known as Camp Rich Bitch. We said it with scorn, trying to hide both our jealousy and our disappointment that our parents couldn't quite afford to send us there. Except, in my case, for one summer.

The same summer that shattered the camp's reputation.

The people involved were all notable enough to keep the story in the news for the rest of the summer and into the fall. Natalie, the daughter of the city's top orthopedic surgeon. Allison, the child of a prominent Broadway actress. And Vivian, the senator's daughter, whose name often appeared in the newspaper with the word *troubled* in close proximity.

The press mostly left me alone. Compared with the others, I was a nobody. Just the daughter of a neglectful investment banker father and a high-functioning alcoholic mother. A gangly thirteen-year-old whose grandmother had recently died, leaving her with enough money to spend six weeks at one of the nation's most exclusive summer camps.

It was Franny who ultimately received the bulk of the media's scorn. Francesca Harris-White, the rich girl who had always befuddled the society columns with her refusal to play the game. Marrying a contemporary of her father at twenty-one. Burying him before she turned thirty. Adopting a child at forty, then another at fifty.

The coverage was brutal. Articles about how Lake Midnight was an unsafe place for a summer camp, especially considering that her husband had drowned there the year before Camp Nightingale opened. Claims that the camp was understaffed and unsupervised. Think pieces blaming Franny for standing by her son when suspicion swirled around him. Some even insinuated there might be something sinister about Camp Nightingale, about Franny, about her family.

I probably had something to do with that.

Scratch that. I know I did.

Yet Franny shows no ill will as she sits in her faux forest, outlining her vision for the new Camp Nightingale.

"It won't be the same, of course," she says. "It can't be. Although fifteen years is a long enough time, what happened will always be like a shadow hanging over the camp. That's why I'm going to do things differently this time. I've set up a charitable trust. No one will have to pay a penny to stay there. The camp will be completely free and merit-based, serving girls from around the tri-state area."

"That's very generous," I say.

"I don't want anyone's money. I certainly don't need it. All I need is to see the place filled again with girls enjoying the outdoors. And I'd truly love it if you would join me."

I gulp. Me? Spend the summer at Camp Nightingale? This is far different than the commission offer I had expected to receive. It's so outlandish I start to think I've misheard her.

"It's not that strange of an idea," Franny says. "I want the camp to have a strong arts component. Yes, the girls there will swim and hike and do all the usual camp activities. But I also want them to learn about writing, photography, painting."

"You want me to teach them to paint?"

"Of course," Franny says. "But you'll also have plenty of time to work on your own. There's no better inspiration than nature."

I still don't get why Franny wants me, of all people, to be there. I should be the last person she wants around. She senses my hesitation, of course. It's impossible not to, considering how I sit stiff-backed in my chair, fiddling with the napkin in my lap, twisting it into a coiled knot.

"I understand your trepidation," she says. "I'd feel the same way if our roles were reversed. But I don't blame you for what happened, Emma. You were young and confused, and the situation was horrible for everyone. I firmly believe in letting bygones be bygones. And it's my great wish to have some former campers there. To show everyone that it's a safe, happy place again. Rebecca Schoenfeld has agreed to do it."

Becca Schoenfeld. Notable photojournalist. Her image of two young Syrian refugees holding hands while covered in blood made front pages around the world. But more important for Franny's purposes, Becca's also a veteran of Camp Nightingale's final summer.

She noticeably wasn't one of the girls who sought me out on Facebook. Not that I expected her to. Becca was a mystery to me. Not standoffish, necessarily. Aloof. She was quiet, often alone, content to view the world through the lens of the camera that always hung around her neck, even when she was waist-deep in the lake.

I imagine her sitting at this very table, that same camera dangling from its canvas strap as Franny convinces her to return to Camp Nightingale. Knowing that she's agreed changes things. It makes Franny's idea seem less like a folly and more like something that could actually happen. Although not with me.

"It's an awfully big commitment," I say.

"You'll be compensated financially, of course."

"It's not that," I say, still twisting the napkin so hard it's starting to look like rope. "I'm not sure I can go back there again. Not after what happened."

"Maybe that's precisely why you *should* go back," Franny says. "I was afraid to return, too. I avoided it for two years. I thought I'd find nothing there but darkness and bad memories. That wasn't the case. It was as beautiful as ever. Nature heals, Emma. I firmly believe that."

I say nothing. It's hard to speak when Fanny's green-eyed gaze is fixed on me, intense and compassionate and, yes, a little bit needy.

"Tell me you'll at least give it some thought," she says.

"I will," I tell her. "I'll think about it."

Three

I don't think about it.

I obsess.

Franny's offer dominates my thoughts for the rest of the day. But it's not the kind of thinking she was hoping for. Instead of pondering how wonderful it might be to go back to Camp Nightingale, I think of all the reasons I shouldn't return. Crushing guilt I haven't been able to shake in fifteen years. Plain old anxiety. All of them continue to flutter through my thoughts when I meet Marc for dinner at his bistro.

"I think you should go," he says as he pushes a plate of ratatouille in front of me. It's my favorite dish on the menu, steaming and ripe with the scent of tomatoes and *herbs de Provence*. Normally, I'd already be digging in. But Franny's proposal has sapped my appetite. Marc senses this and slides a large wineglass next to the plate, filled almost to the rim with pinot noir. "It might do you some good."

"My therapist would beg to differ."

"I doubt that. It's a textbook case of closure."

God knows, I haven't had much of that. There were memorial services for all three girls, staggered over a six-month period, depending on when their families gave up hope. Allison's was first. All song and drama. Then Natalie's, always in the middle, her service a quiet, family-only affair. Vivian's was the last, on a bitterly cold

January morning. Hers was the only one I attended. My parents told me I couldn't go, but I went anyway, ditching school to slide into the last pew of the packed church, far away from her weeping parents. There were so many senators and congressmen present that it felt like watching C-SPAN.

The service didn't help. Neither did reading about Allison's and Natalie's services online. Mostly because there was the chance, however slim, that they could still be alive. It doesn't matter that the state of New York declared all of them legally dead after three years. Until their bodies are found, there's no way of knowing.

"I'm not sure closure is the issue," I say.

"Then what *is* the issue, Em?"

"It's the place where three people vanished into thin air. *That's* the issue."

"Understood," Marc says. "But there's something else going on. Something you're not telling me."

"Fine." I sigh into my ratatouille, steam skirting across the table. "I haven't painted a thing in the past six months."

A stricken look crosses Marc's face, like he doesn't quite believe me. "Are you serious?"

"Deadly."

"So you're stuck," he says.

"It's more than that."

I admit everything. How I can't seem to paint anything but the girls. How I refuse to continue down that path of obliterating their white-frocked forms with trees and vines. How day after day I stare at the giant canvas in my loft, trying to summon the will to create something new.

"Okay, so you're obsessed."

"Bingo," I say, reaching for the wine and taking a hearty gulp.

"I don't want to seem insensitive," Marc says. "And I certainly don't want to belittle your emotions. You feel what you feel, and I get that. What I don't understand is why, after all this time, what happened at that camp still haunts you so much. Those girls were practically strangers."

My therapist has said the same thing. As if I don't know how weird it is to be so affected by something that happened fifteen years ago and fixated on girls I knew for only two weeks.

"They were *friends*," I say. "And I feel bad about what happened to them."

"Bad or guilty?"

"Both."

I was the last person to see them alive. I could have stopped them from doing whatever the hell it was they had planned to do. Or I could have told Franny or a counselor as soon as they left. Instead, I went back to sleep. Now I still sometimes hear Vivian's parting words in my dreams.

You're too young for this, Em.

"And you're afraid that being back there again will make you feel even worse," Marc says.

Rather than answer, I reach for the glass, the wine catching my wobbly reflection. I stare at myself, shocked by how strange I appear. Do I really look that sad? I must, because Marc's tone softens as he says, "It's natural to be afraid. Friends of yours died."

"Vanished," I say.

"But they *are* dead, Emma. You know that, right? The worst thing that could happen has already taken place."

"There's something worse than death."

"Such as?"

"Not knowing," I say. "Which is why I'm only able to paint those girls. And I can't keep doing that, Marc. I need to move on."

There's more to it than that. Although he knows the basics of what took place, there's still plenty I haven't told Marc. Things that happened at Camp Nightingale. Things that happened afterward. The real reason I always wear the charm bracelet, the birds clinking each time I move my left arm. To admit them out loud would mean that they're true. And I don't want to confront that truth.

Some would say I've been lying to Marc. To everyone, really. But after my time at Camp Nightingale, I vowed never to lie again.

Omission. That's my tactic. A different sin entirely.

"This is all the more reason for you to go." Marc reaches across the table and clasps my hands. His palms are callused, his fingers lined with scars. The hands of a lifelong cook. "Maybe being there again is all you need to start painting something different. You know the old saying—sometimes the only way out is through."

After dinner, I return to my loft and stand before a blank canvas. Its emptiness taunts me, as it's done for weeks. A wide expanse of nothing daring me to fill it.

I grab a palette, well-worn and rainbow-hued. I smear some paint onto it, dab it with the tip of a brush, and will myself to paint something. Anything but the girls. I touch the brush to the canvas, bristles gliding, trailing color.

But then I take a step back and stare at the brushstroke, studying it. It's yellow. Slightly curved. Like an *S* that's been squished. It is, I realize, a length of Vivian's hair, the blond streak doing a little flip as she retreats. There's nothing else it could be.

I grab a nearby rag that reeks of turpentine and swipe it over the yellow paint until it's just a faint smudge marring the canvas. Tears spring from my eyes as I realize the only thing I've painted in weeks is this indistinct smear.

It's pathetic. *I'm* pathetic.

I wipe my eyes, noticing something on the edge of my vision. Near the window. A movement. A flash.

Blond hair. Pale skin.

Vivian.

I yelp and drop the rag, the fingers of my right hand grasping at the bracelet around my left. I give it a twist, the birds taking flight as I whirl around to face her.

Only it's not Vivian I see.

It's me, reflected in the window. In the night-darkened glass, I look startled, weak, and, above all else, shaken.

Shaken that the girls are always in my thoughts and on my canvases, even though it makes no sense. That after fifteen long years, I know as much about what happened now as I did the night they left the cabin. That in the days following the disappearance, I only made things worse. For Franny. For her family. For myself.

I could finally change that. Just one small hint about what happened could make a difference. It won't erase my sins. But there is a chance it could make them more bearable.

I turn away from the window, grab my phone, and dial the number printed so elegantly on the calling card Franny gave me last night. The call goes straight to voicemail and a recording of Lottie suggesting I leave a message.

"This is Emma Davis. I've given more thought about Franny's offer to spend the summer at Camp Nightingale." I pause, not quite believing what I'm about to say next. "And my answer is yes. I'll do it."

I hang up before I can change my mind. Even so, I'm struck with the urge to call again and take it all back. My finger twitches against the phone's screen, itching to do just that. Instead, I call Marc.

"I'm going back to Camp Nightingale," I announce before he can say hello.

"I'm glad to hear my pep talk worked," Marc says. "Closure is a good thing, Em."

"I want to try to find them."

There's silence on Marc's end. I picture him blinking a few times while running a hand through his hair—his normal reaction to something he can't quite comprehend. Eventually, he says, "I know I encouraged you to go, Em, but this doesn't sound like the best idea."

"Bad idea or not, that's why I'm going."

"But try to think clearly here. What do you rationally expect to find?"

"I don't know," I say. "Probably nothing."

I certainly don't expect to uncover Vivian, Natalie, and Allison. They literally vanished without a trace, which makes it hard to know where to start looking for them. Then there's the sheer size of the place. While Camp Nightingale may be small, much more land surrounds it. More than six square miles of forest. If several hundred searchers couldn't find them fifteen years ago, I'm not going to find them now.

"But what if one of them left something behind?" I say. "Something hinting at where they were going or what they were up to."

"And what if there is?" Marc asks. "It still won't bring them back."

"I understand that."

"Which begs another question: Why do you need this so much?"

I pause, thinking of a way to explain the unexplainable. It's not easy, especially when Marc doesn't know the full story. I settle on saying, "Have you ever regretted something days, weeks, even years after you've done it?"

"Sure," Marc says. "I think everyone has at least one big regret."

"What happened at that camp is mine. For fifteen years, I've waited for a clue. Just some small thing hinting at what happened to them. Now I have a chance to go back there and look for myself. Likely the last chance I'll get to try to find some answers. If I turn that down, I worry it will just become another thing to regret."

Marc sighs, which means I've convinced him. "Just promise me you won't do something stupid," he says.

"Like what?"

"Like put yourself in danger."

"It's a summer camp," I say. "It's not like I'm infiltrating the mob. I'm simply going to go, look around, maybe ask a few questions. And when those six weeks are over, perhaps I'll have some idea of what happened to them. Even if I don't, maybe being there again is all I need to start painting something different. You said it yourself—sometimes the only way out is through."

"Fine," Marc says with another sigh. "Plan your camping trip. Try to get some answers. Come back ready to paint."

As we say our good-nights, I get a glimpse of my first painting of the girls. No. 1, offering its scant views of Vivian, Natalie, and Allison. I approach it, looking for flashes of hair, bits of dress.

Even though a branch covers their eyes, I know they're staring back at me. It's as if they've understood all along that I'd one day return to Camp Nightingale. Only I can't tell if they're urging me to go or begging me to stay away.

FIFTEEN YEARS AGO

"Wake up, sunshine."

It was just past eight when my mother crept into my bedroom, her eyes already glazed from her morning Bloody Mary. Her lips were curled into the same smile she always wore when she was about to do something momentous. I called it her Mother of the Year smile. Seeing it never failed to make me nervous, mostly because there was usually a gaping chasm between her intentions and the end result. On that morning, I tightened into a ball beneath the covers, bracing myself for hours of forced mother-daughter bonding.

"You all ready to go?" she said.

"Go where?"

My mother stared at me, her hand fumbling with the collar of her chiffon robe. "Camp, of course."

"What camp?"

"*Summer* camp," my mother said, stressing the first word, letting me know that wherever I was headed, it was going to be for more than just a day or two.

I sat up, flinging aside the covers. "You never told me about any camp."

"I did, Emma. I told you weeks ago. It's the same place me and your aunt Julie went. Jesus, don't tell me you forgot."

"I didn't forget."

Being told I was going to be ripped away from my friends for the entire summer was something I would have remembered. It was more likely my mother had only thought about telling me. In her world, thinking about something was close enough to doing it. Yet knowing that didn't lessen the feeling of being ambushed. It reminded me of those extreme interventions in which parents hired rehab centers to abduct their junkie children.

"Then I'm telling you now," my mother said. "Where's your suit-case? We need to be on the road in an hour."

"An *hour*?" My stomach clenched as I thought of all my summer plans being snatched away from me. No lazing around with Heather and Marissa. No secret, unchaperoned train ride to Coney Island like we had planned in study hall. No flirting with Nolan Cunningham from next door, who wasn't quite as cute as Justin Timberlake but still had the same swaggering confidence. Plus, he was finally starting to notice me, now that my braces had come off. "Where are we going?"

"Camp Nightingale."

Camp Rich Bitch. Talk about a surprise on top of a surprise.

That changed things.

For two years I had begged my parents to send me, only to be told no. Now, after having given up hope, I was suddenly going. In an hour. That totally explained the Mother of the Year smile. For once, it was justified.

Still, I refused to show my mother how pleased I was. Doing that would have only encouraged her, subjecting me to more attempts at making up for lost time. High tea at the Plaza. A shopping spree at Saks. Anything to make her feel better about having zero interest in me for the first twelve years of my life.

"I'm not going," I announced as I laid back down and pulled the covers over my head.

My mother ignored me as she started to root through my closet, her voice muffled. "You'll love it there. It'll be a summer you'll remem-ber for the rest of your life."

Under the covers, an anticipatory shiver ran through me. Camp Nightingale. Six weeks of swimming and reading and hiking. Six weeks away from this stuffy apartment and my mother's disinterest and my father's eye rolls when she poured herself a third glass of

Chardonnay. Heather and Marissa were going to be so jealous. After pretending to be pissed at me for abandoning them the whole summer, of course.

"Whatever," I say, following it up with an indignant huff. "I'll go, even though I don't want to."

It was a lie.

My first in a summer filled with them.

Four

The drive to Camp Nightingale takes up most of the afternoon. Almost five hours when counting in rest stops. Most of it a straight shot north along truck-clogged I-87.

The length of the trip is something I'd forgotten from my first visit, when I had spent the drive huddled in the back seat while my parents blamed each other for not telling me I was going to camp. This time, I'm once again in the back, although the driver of the private town car Franny hired for me hardly says a word. But my nervousness is the same. That butterfly-trapped-in-the-chest feeling. Back then, it was because I didn't quite know what the camp would be like.

Now I know exactly where I'm going.

And who I'll see while I'm there.

In the months leading to my departure, I didn't have time to be nervous. I was too consumed with applying for a temporary leave of absence from the ad agency and finding someone to sublet the loft while I'm gone. The leave was approved, and I eventually found an artist acquaintance to stay in the loft. She paints trippy starscapes with wax melted in scalding-hot aluminum pots. I've seen her at work, each colorful pot bubbling like a witch's cauldron. I hope she doesn't burn the place down.

While all that was taking place, I received weekly emails from Lottie that filled in various details of my stay. The debut summer of the new Camp Nightingale planned to have roughly fifty-five campers, five counselors, and five specialized instructors made up of camp alumni. Just like in the past, none of the cabins had electricity. The camp was monitoring the threats of Zika, West Nile, and other mosquito-borne illnesses. I should remember to pack accordingly.

I took that last note to heart. When I was thirteen, the sudden notice about going to camp delayed our departure for hours. First there was the matter of finding my suitcase, which ended up being in the back of the hall closet, behind the vacuum cleaner. Then came the arduous task of packing, with me not knowing what to bring and my lack of preparation necessitating a trip to Nordstrom's to pick up the things I lacked. This time around, I went overboard in the sporting goods store, snapping up items with the whirlwind intensity of a romantic comedy heroine in a shopping montage. Much of it was necessary. Several pairs of shorts. Heavy-duty socks and a sturdy pair of hiking boots. An LED flashlight with a wrist strap. Some of it was not, such as the waterproof case that fits over my iPhone like a condom.

Then there was the matter of my parents. Neglectful as they were when I was growing up, I knew they wouldn't like the idea of my returning to Camp Nightingale. So I didn't tell them. I simply called to say I'd be away for six weeks and that they should contact Marc in case of an emergency. My father half listened. My mother simply told me to have "such a wonderful time," her words slurred from cocktail hour.

Now there's nothing left for me to do but quell my growing anxiety by sorting through all the things I thought I'd need to help my search. There's a map of Lake Midnight and the surrounding area, a satellite view of the same thing, courtesy of Google Maps, and a stack of old newspaper articles about the disappearance collected from the library and printed off the internet. I even brought along a dog-eared Nancy Drew paperback—*The Bungalow Mystery*—for inspiration.

I examine the map and satellite view first. From above, the lake resembles a giant comma that's been tipped over. More than two miles from end to end, with a width ranging from a half mile to five hundred yards. The narrowest area is the eastern point, the location of the dam Buchanan Harris used to create the lake on that cold and rainy stroke of midnight. From there the lake flows west, skirting the edge of a mountain, following the path of the valley it replaced.

Camp Nightingale sits to the south, nestled in the middle of the lake's gentle exterior curve. On the map, it's just a tiny black square, unlabeled, as if fifteen years of disuse had left it unworthy of mention.

The satellite view offers more detail, all of it colored grainy shades of green by the library printer that spat it out. The camp itself is a rectangle of fern green, speckled with buildings in variations of brown. The Lodge is clearly visible, as are the cabins, latrine, and other buildings. I can even see the dock jutting out over the water, the white specks of two motorboats moored to its sides. A gray line of road leads out of camp to the south, eventually connecting with a county road two miles away.

One theory about the girls' disappearance is that they walked to the main road and hitched a ride. To Canada. To New England. To unmarked graves when they climbed into the cab of a deranged trucker.

Yet no one reported seeing three teenage girls on the highway's edge in the middle of the night, even after their disappearance became national news. No one anonymously confessed to giving them a ride. No traces of their DNA were ever found inside the rigs of drivers arrested for violent crimes. Plus, all their belongings were left behind, tucked safely inside their hickory trunks. Clothes. Cash. Brightly colored Nokia cell phones just like the ones my parents said I was too young and irresponsible to own.

I don't think they planned to be gone for very long. Certainly not forever.

I put away the map and tackle the newspaper clippings and internet articles, none of which offer anything new. The details of the disappearance are as vague now as they were fifteen years ago. Vivian, Natalie, and Allison vanished in the early-morning hours of July 5. They were reported missing by yours truly a little before 6:00 a.m. A camp-wide search that morning turned up nothing. By the afternoon, the camp's director, Francesca Harris-White, had contacted the New York State Police, and an official search began. Because of the girls' high-profile parents—Vivian's, especially—the Secret Service and the

FBI joined the fray. Search parties of federal agents, state troopers, and local volunteers scoured the woods. Helicopters skimmed the treetops. Bloodhounds primed with scents from clothes the girls had left behind sniffed a trail around camp and back again, their keen sense of smell leading them in frustrating circles. Little was found. No footprints leading into the forest. No wispy strands of hair snagged on low-hanging branches.

Another team of searchers headed to the water, even though they were stymied by the lake itself. It was too deep to dredge, too filled with downed trees and other underwater remnants of its days as a valley to dive safely. All they could do was crisscross Lake Midnight in police rescue boats, knowing there was nothing left to rescue. If the girls were in the lake, surely only corpses would be found. The boats returned empty-handed, as everyone suspected they would.

The only trace of the girls anyone ever found was a sweat shirt.

Vivian's sweat shirt, to be precise. White with *Princeton* spelled out in orange across the chest. I'd seen her wear it to the campfire a few nights before the disappearance, which is how I was able to identify it as belonging to her.

It was found the morning after the disappearance, sitting on the forest floor two miles away, almost directly across the lake from Camp Nightingale. The volunteer searcher who discovered the sweat shirt—a local retiree and grandfather of six with no earthly reason to lie—said it was neatly folded into a square, like the sweaters you see on display at the Gap. A lab analysis of the sweat shirt found skin cells that matched Vivian's DNA. What it didn't find were any rips, tears, or traces of blood suggesting she had been attacked. It was simply discarded, apparently by Vivian on her way to whatever fate befell her.

But here's the weird part.

Vivian wasn't wearing the sweat shirt when I saw her leave the cabin.

In the days after the disappearance, various investigators repeatedly asked me if I was sure it wasn't tied around her waist or thrown over her shoulders, sleeves knotted in true Princeton preppy fashion.

It wasn't.

I'm certain of it.

Still, authorities treated that sweat shirt like a beacon, following it into the hills. The search of the lake was called off as everyone took to the forest, searching it in vain. No one—least of all me—had an inkling as to why the girls would have marched miles away from camp. But nothing about the disappearance made sense. It was one of those rare instances that defied all known logic and reason.

The only person ever considered a suspect was Franny's oldest son, Theo Harris-White. Nothing came of it. No traces of him were discovered on Vivian's sweat shirt. Nothing incriminating was found in his possession. He even had an alibi—he spent the night with Chet, teaching his younger brother how to play chess into the wee hours of the morning. With no evidence that a crime had actually taken place, Theo wasn't charged. Which meant he also wasn't officially exonerated. Even now, a Google search of Theo's name brings up true crime websites that suggest he killed the girls and managed to get away with it.

The hunt for the girls didn't officially end so much as it lost steam. The search parties fruitlessly continued for another few weeks, their numbers dwindling day by day until they eventually dried up. News coverage of the disappearance also evaporated as reporters moved on to newer, flashier stories.

Filling that void were darker theories. Ones found in the deepest corners of Reddit and conspiracy websites. Rumors swirl that the girls had been murdered by a savage madman who lived in the woods. That they had been abducted—either by humans or aliens, depending on which website you read. That something even more mystically sinister happened to them. Witches. Werewolves. Spontaneous cellular disintegration.

Not even former campers are immune from the rumors, which I learn when I open Facebook on my phone and finally unmute the posts from Camp Nightingale alumni. The first thing I see is a photo posted an hour ago by Casey Anderson, a short, red-haired counselor I had met on my first morning at camp. She was also, incidentally, the first Camp Nightingale veteran to seek me out on Facebook. Although I genuinely liked her, that friend request went ignored with all the others. Now I stare at a photo she took of the cabins with Lake Midnight glistening in the background.

Back again, she wrote. *Feels like old times.*

The picture had already received fifty likes and several responses.

Erica Hammond: *Have a great summer!*

Lena Gallagher: *Awwww. Brings back memories.*

Felecia Wellington: *I can't believe you went back there. Franny could offer me a million dollars and I still wouldn't go.*

Casey Anderson: *Which is probably why Franny didn't ask you. I'm happy to be here.*

Maggie Collins: *Agreed! That place always freaked me out.*

Hope Levin Smith: *I'm with Felecia. This is a bad, bad idea.*

Casey Anderson: *Why?*

Hope Levin Smith: *Because that place and its lake are messed up! We've all heard the legend. We all know there's a ring of truth to it.*

Lena Gallagher: *OMG, that legend! Scared me so much back then.*

Hope Levin Smith: *You had every right to be scared.*

Casey Anderson: *You're all being ridiculous.*

Hope Levin Smith: *Casey, you're the one who talked about it the most! You can't call it bullshit now that you're back there.*

Felecia Wellington: *Don't forget we all know what happened to Viv, Ally and Natalie wasn't an accident. You said so yourself.*

Brooke Tiffany Sample: *Who else is going to be there this summer?*

Casey Anderson: *Of people you know, me, Becca Schoenfeld and Emma Davis.*

Brooke Tiffany Sample: *Emma?!? Holy fuck!*

Maggie Collins: *After all that shit she said about Theo?*

Hope Levin Smith: *Wow.*

Lena Gallagher: *That's, um, interesting.*

Felecia Wellington: *I'd love to know how that happened. Watch your back, Casey. LOL*

Casey Anderson: *Be nice. I'm excited to see her.*
Erica Hammond: *Who's Emma Davis?*

I close Facebook and turn off my phone, unable to stomach reading another word of gossip and crackpot theories. Other than Casey, I can't recall meeting any of those women while at camp. Nor have I heard the stories that the lake is cursed or haunted. It's bullshit. All of it.

Only one of the responses is the absolute truth. What happened to Vivian, Natalie, and Allison wasn't an accident.

I know because I'm the one who caused it.

Although their eventual fate remains a mystery, I'm certain that what happened to those girls is all my fault.

Five

I bolt from my slumped position in the back seat when the rounded peaks of the Adirondacks push over the horizon. The sight of them sets my heart racing ever-so-slightly—a soft hum in my chest that I try to ignore. It gets worse once the driver turns off the highway and announces, "Almost there, Miss Davis."

Immediately, the car starts to bump down a gravel road. Both sides of the road are lined with forest that seems to get thicker and darker the deeper we go. Gnarled limbs stretch overhead, reaching for one another, branches intertwined. Towering pines diffuse the sun. The underbrush is a tangle of leaves, stems, thorns. It is, I realize, like one of my paintings come to life.

Soon we're at the wrought-iron gate that serves as the only way into Camp Nightingale. It's wide-open—an invitation to enter. But the gate and its surroundings are anything but inviting. Flanking the road are four-foot-high stone walls that stretch into the woods. An ornate archway, also wrought iron, curves over the road, giving the impression that we're about to enter a cemetery.

The camp reveals itself in increments. Structures slide into view as if pushed there by stagehands. All of them are remnants from when the land was a private retreat for the Harris family, now repurposed for camp use. The arts and crafts building, low-slung and quaint, used to be a horse stable. All white paint and gingerbread trim. A flower bed sits in front of it, bright with crocuses and tiger lilies. Next is the mess hall. Less pretty. More utilitarian. A former hay barn turned into a cafeteria. A side door gapes open as workers haul in cases of food from an idling delivery truck.

In the distance to my right are the cabins, barely visible through the trees. Nothing but edges of moss-stippled roof and slivers of pine siding. I catch glimpses of girls settling in. Bare legs. Slender arms. Glistening hair.

At first glance, the camp looks the same as it did when I left it all those years ago. It's a weird sensation, like I've been shuttled back in time. One foot in the present, another planted in the past. Yet something about the place feels slightly off. A lingering sensation of neglect hangs over everything like cobwebs. And the longer I'm here, the more I become aware of what has changed in the past fifteen years. The tennis court and archery range both now sit in a startling state of disuse. Spiky weeds burst through the court's surface in jagged lines. The grass in the archery range is knee-high, dotted on the far end with rotting hay bales that had once held targets.

Atop the otherwise immaculate arts and crafts building, a handyman nails shingles to the roof. He stills his hammer as the town car passes, peering down at me, his face round and reddened. I stare back, suddenly recognizing him from my first visit. I remember seeing him quite a bit around camp, constantly tinkering and fixing. He was younger then, of course. Better looking. Possessed a brooding intensity that intimidated some, intrigued others.

I'd grab his tool any day, Vivian once said at lunch, prompting eye rolls from the rest of us.

I wave to him, wondering if he also recognizes the older me. He returns his gaze to a shingle, raises his hammer, pounds it into place.

By then the town car is whipping around the circular drive in front of the Lodge. Franny's home away from home, as she calls it, although it's more home than most people will ever lay claim to. But that's been its purpose ever since it was built by her grandfather on the shore of the lake he also created. A summer house for a family that chose nature over Newport. Like most old structures, there's a heaviness to the Lodge, a somberness. I think of all the years it's witnessed. All those seasons and storms and secrets.

"We've arrived," the driver says as he stops the car in front of the Lodge's red front door. "I'll get your bags from the trunk."

I exit the car, legs stiff and back aching, and I'm immediately engulfed by fresh air. It's a smell I'd forgotten. Clean and pine-scented. So different from the city's fumes. It sparks a hundred memories I'd also forgotten. Simple ones of walking through the woods behind Vivian or sitting alone with my toes in the lake, contemplating everything and nothing all at once. The scent beckons me, pulls me forward. I start walking, unsure of where I'm headed.

"I'll be right back," I tell the driver, who's busily unloading my suitcase and box of painting supplies. "I need to stretch my legs."

I keep walking, around the Lodge to the grassy slope behind it. There I see what the fresh air has led me to.

Lake Midnight.

It's larger than I remember. In my memory, it had become similar to the Central Park Reservoir. Something contained. Something that could be controlled. In reality, it's a vast, sparkling presence that dominates the landscape. The trees lining its bank lean slightly toward it, branches bending over the water.

I start down the sloping lawn, continuing until I reach the tidy dock that juts over the water. Two motorboats are moored to it. On the shore nearby are two racks upon which upside-down canoes have been stacked like firewood. I walk the length of the dock, my footfalls slipping through cracks in the planks and echoing off the water. At its edge, I stop to look across the lake to the far shore a half mile away. The forest there is thicker—a dense wall of foliage shimmering in the sunlight, at once inviting and forbidding.

Vivian, Natalie, and Allison, or what's left of them, out there. Somewhere.

I'm still staring at the far shore when someone approaches. I hear the swish of sneakers in grass, followed by their thunk against the planks of the dock. Before I can turn around, a voice rises behind me like a bird chirp catching the breeze.

"There you are!"

The voice belongs to a twentysomething woman who rushes down the dock. Behind her, still on land, is a man roughly the same age. Both are young and tan and fit. If it wasn't for their official Camp Nightingale polos, they could easily be mistaken for J.Crew models. They have that same outdoorsy, sun-kissed glow.

"Emma, right?" the woman says. "Hooray! You're here!"

I reach out to shake her hand but wind up getting pulled into an enthusiastically tight embrace. No Franny-like half hugs with this girl.

"It's so nice to meet you," she says, breaking the embrace, slightly out of breath from the exertion of it all. "I'm Mindy. Chet's fiancée."

She gestures to the man on shore, and it takes me a moment to realize she's referring to Chester, Franny's younger son. He's grown into a handsome man, lean and lithe and tall. So tall that he towers over both Mindy and me, stooping in a slightly self-conscious way. It's a far cry from the short, skinny kid I had seen flitting around camp. Yet hints of that boyishness remain. In the sandy hair that flops over his face, covering one eye. In the shy smile that flickers across his lips as he calls out, "Hey there."

"I was just getting reacquainted with the lake," I say, when I'm not really sure that's the case. I can't shake the sense it was the other way around and Lake Midnight was getting reacquainted with me.

"Of course you were," Mindy says, politely ignoring how unusual it was for me to immediately roam to the water's edge. "It's nice, right? Although the weather isn't doing it any favors. It hasn't rained in weeks, and the lake is looking a little ragged, if you ask me."

It's only after she's pointed it out that I notice the telltale signs of drought around the lake. The plants on its bank bear several inches of browned stem—areas that had once been submerged. There was a drought happening the first time I was here, too. It didn't rain once in two weeks. I remember climbing into a canoe, leaving sneaker prints in a strip of sunbaked earth between the bank of the lake and the water itself.

I'm eyeing a similar thirsty patch of land when Mindy grabs my hand and leads me off the dock.

"We're thrilled to have you back, Emma," she says. "Franny especially. This summer is going to be awesome. I just know it."

Back on shore, I go to Chet and shake his hand.

"Emma Davis," I say. "You probably don't remember me."

It's wishful thinking. A hope that he remembers nothing about me. But the brow over Chet's only visible eye lifts slightly. "Oh, I remember you well," he says, not elaborating.

"Before you get settled in, Franny needs to see you," Mindy says.

"About what?"

"There's a slight problem with the rooming situation. But don't worry. Franny's going to sort it all out."

Leaving Chet behind, she loops an arm through mine, guiding me up the slope and into the Lodge. It's the first time I've ever been inside, and I'm surprised to see it's not at all what I was expecting. As a girl on the outside looking in, I had pictured something from *Architectural Digest*. The kind of tastefully rustic retreat where movie stars spend Christmas in Aspen.

The Lodge isn't like that. It's musty and dim, the air inside tinged with a century's worth of wood-fed blazes in the fireplace. The entrance hall we stand in leads to a general living area stuffed with worn furniture. Covering the walls are antlers, animal skins, and, oddly, an assortment of antique weapons. Rifles. Bowie knives with thick blades. A spear.

"Everything's so old, right?" Mindy says. "I'm all for antiques, but some of this stuff is ancient. The first time Chet brought me here, it felt like sleeping in a museum. I'm still not used to it. But if it takes spending a summer working at a camp to impress my future mother-in-law, then so be it."

She's clearly a talker. Exhausting but also potentially useful. When we pass a small office on the left, I pause and ask, "What's in there?"

"The study."

I crane my neck to peek into the room. One wall is filled with framed photos. Another contains a bookshelf. As we pass, I glimpse the corner of a desk, a rotary telephone, a Tiffany lampshade.

"I use the electrical outlet in there to charge my phone," Mindy says. "You're welcome to do the same. Just don't let Franny catch you.

She wants all of us to disconnect and commune with nature or whatever."

"How's service up here?"

Mindy makes a dramatic gagging sound. "Horrible. Like, one bar most of the time. I honestly don't know how these girls are going to cope."

"The campers can't use their phones?"

"They can until their batteries run out. No electricity in the cabins, remember? Franny's orders."

To my right, a staircase rises to the second floor, the steps tiny and impossibly narrow. Under the stairs sits a door intended to blend into the wall. The only things giving it away are a brass doorknob and an old-fashioned keyhole.

"And what's that?" I ask.

"The basement," Mindy says. "I've never been down there. It's probably nothing but old furniture and cobwebs."

We move on, Mindy playing tour guide, giving a running commentary about various family heirlooms. A portrait of Buchanan Harris that, I swear, might have been painted by John Singer Sargent, elicits a solemn "That's worth a fortune."

Soon we're at the back deck, which spans the entire width of the Lodge. Wooden boxes crammed with flowers line the twig-work railing. Scattered around the deck are several small tables and the obligatory Adirondack chairs, all painted as red as the front door. Two of the chairs are occupied by Franny and Lottie.

Both are dressed in the same khakis shorts and camp polo ensemble as Chet and Mindy. Franny surveys Lake Midnight from the heightened view provided by the deck. Lottie, meanwhile, taps the screen of an iPad, looking up when Mindy and I step outside.

"Emma," she says, her face brightening as she pulls me into what feels like my fifth hug of the day. "You have no idea how nice it is to see you back here."

"It is," Franny agrees. "It's wonderful."

Unlike Lottie, she doesn't get up from her chair to greet me. I'm surprised, until I notice her wan and tired appearance. It's the first time I've seen her since our lunch meeting months ago, and the change is startling. I had assumed being back at her beloved Lake Midnight would make her robust and hearty. Instead, it's the opposite. She looks, for lack of a better word, old.

Franny catches me staring and says, "There's worry in your eyes, my dear. Don't think I can't see it. But fear not. I'm just tired from all this activity. I'd forgotten how exhausting the first day of camp can be. Not a moment to spare, it seems. I'll be right as rain tomorrow."

"You need to rest," Lottie says.

"And that's what I'm doing," Franny replies, somewhat testily.

I clear my throat. "You needed to see me about something?"

"Yes. I'm afraid there's a bit of a problem."

Franny frowns slightly. It's an echo of the half frown she gave me upon my first arrival at camp, when the family Volvo finally pulled up to the Lodge at the cusp of eleven. Franny greeted us with the same expression I see now. *I wasn't expecting you*, she said. *When you didn't arrive with the others, I thought you had canceled.*

"A problem?" I say, trepidation thickening my voice.

"That sounds so dramatic, doesn't it?" Franny says. "I suppose it's more of a complication."

"About what?"

"Where to put you."

"Oh," I say, which I'm sure is what I said when Franny told me something similar fifteen years ago.

Back then, my lateness was to blame. They had already gotten all the girls settled into their cabins, grouped together that morning by age. Since there was no more room available with girls my own age, I was forced to bunk with ones who were several years older. That's how I ended up with Vivian, Natalie, and Allison, intimidated by their additional years of life experience, their acne-free complexions, their fully formed bodies.

Now Franny tells me it's the opposite problem.

"My intention was to give the instructors some privacy. Let you have a nice cabin all to yourselves. But there was a bit of a mix-up with planning, and we find ourselves with more girls than we initially expected."

"Fifteen more," Lottie says, unprompted.

"Which means all our instructors will have to share lodgings with some of the campers."

"Why can't the instructors bunk together?"

"I asked her the same thing, Emma," Lottie says.

"That's a fine idea in theory," Franny tells us. "But there are five of you and only four bunks in each cabin. One person would have to bunk with the campers anyway. Which wouldn't be remotely fair to that single person."

"Couldn't we stay in the Lodge instead?"

"The Lodge is for family only," Mindy pipes up from the corner of railing where she's been watching our conversation. She gives her ring finger a wiggle, drawing attention to the fat engagement ring circling it. The message isn't subtle, but it's clear. She's one of them. I'm not.

"What Mindy means," Franny says, "is that although I'd be thrilled to have all of you stay here with us, there simply isn't enough room. This house can be deceiving. From the outside, it looks plenty big. But the reality is that there aren't enough bedrooms to spare. Especially for all five instructors. And you know I can't play favorites. I do apologize."

"It's fine," I say, when in fact it isn't. I'm a twenty-eight-year-old woman being forced to spend the next six weeks living with strangers half my age. Definitely not what I signed up for. But there appears to be no way around it.

"It's not fine," Franny says. "It's an awkward situation, and I'm so sorry to be putting you into it. I wouldn't blame you one bit if you decided to get back in the car and demand to be driven directly home."

I'd be tempted to do just that if I had a home to return to. But the artist subletting the loft is probably moving in at this very minute, everything booked and paid for until the middle of August. It is what it is, as Marc likes to say.

"Can I at least choose my cabin?"

"Most of the campers are settling in now, but I think we can accommodate your request. What did you have in mind?"

I touch my charm bracelet, giving it a quick twirl. "I want to stay in Dogwood."

The same cabin I stayed in fifteen years ago.

Although Franny says nothing, I know what she's thinking. Her expression shifts as quickly as the sunlight glinting off the lake, revealing confusion, then understanding, then, finally, pride.

"Are you certain you want to do that?"

I'm not even sure I want to be here at all. Yet I give a firm nod, trying to convince not only Franny but also myself. At least Franny buys it, because she turns to Lottie and says, "Please arrange it so that Emma can stay in Dogwood." To me, she says, "You're either very brave or very foolish, Emma. I can't decide which one it is."

I can't, either. I suppose that, just by being here, I'm a little bit of both.

FIFTEEN YEARS AGO

As the sound of my parents' Volvo faded into the creaking, chirping night, I learned two things—that Francesca Harris-White was rich beyond words and that she had the stare of a movie star.

The rich part was only mildly intimidating. Obscene wealth was on display everywhere in our Upper West Side neighborhood. But Franny's stare? That stopped me cold.

It was intense. Those green eyes of hers latched on to me like twin spotlights, illuminating me, studying me. Yet hers wasn't a cruel stare. There was warmth in her gaze. A gentle curiosity. I couldn't remember the last time my parents looked at me that way, and it made me all too happy to stand completely still and let her take me in.

"I must admit, dear, I have absolutely no idea where to put you," Franny said, breaking her stare to turn to Lottie, who stood directly behind her. "Is there any room left in a cabin reserved for our junior campers?"

"They're all full," Lottie replied. "Three campers and one counselor in each. The only open spot is in a senior cabin. We could move one of the counselors there, but that might not go over too well. It will also leave a junior cabin unsupervised."

"Which I'm reluctant to do," Franny said. "What's the open cabin?"

"Dogwood."

Franny turned that green-eyed gaze back to me, smiling. "Then Dogwood it shall be. Lottie, be a dear and fetch Theo to take Miss Davis's bags."

Lottie vanished into the massive house behind us. A minute later, a young man emerged. Dressed in baggy shorts and a tight T-shirt, he had sleepy eyes and tousled brown hair. On his feet were flip-flops that clapped against the ground as he approached.

"Theo, this is Emma Davis, our latecomer," Franny told him. "She's headed to Dogwood."

Now it was my turn to stare, for Theo was unlike any boy I had ever seen. Not cute, like Nolan Cunningham. Handsome. With wide brown eyes, a prominent nose, a slightly crooked smile that slanted when he said, "Hey, latecomer. Welcome to Camp Nightingale. Let's get you to your cabin."

Franny bid me good-night as I followed Theo deeper into the camp, my heart beating so hard I feared he could hear it. I knew part of it was apprehension about being in an unknown place with unknown people. But another reason for my madly thrumming heart was Theo himself. I couldn't take my eyes off him as he walked a few paces ahead of me. I studied him the same way Franny had studied me, my gaze locked on his tall frame, the long, steady stride of his legs, the spread of his back and shoulders under his threadbare shirt. His biceps bulged as he carried my suitcase. No boy I knew had arms like that.

It didn't hurt that he was friendly, calling over his shoulder to ask me where I was from, what music I liked, if I had been to camp before. My answers were weak, barely audible over my pounding heart. My nervousness clearly showed, for when we reached the cabin, Theo turned and said, "Don't be nervous. You'll love it here."

He rapped on the door, prompting a response from inside. "Who is it?"

"Theo. Are you awake and decent?"

"Awake, yes," the same voice replied. "Decent, never."

Theo handed me the suitcase and gave an encouraging nod. "Go on in. And remember, their bark is worse than their bite."

He walked away, flip-flops clopping, as I turned the doorknob and stepped inside. The cabin's interior was dim, lit only by a lantern placed beside a window opposite the door. In that golden half-light, I saw two sets of bunk beds and three girls occupying them.

"I'm Vivian," announced the one sprawled on the top bunk to my right. She gestured to the bunk directly across from her. "That's Allison. Below is Natalie."

"Hi," I said, clutching my suitcase just inside the cabin, too frightened to enter farther.

"Your trunk is by the door," said the girl identified as Natalie, all wide cheeks and formidable chin. "You can put your clothes there."

"Thanks."

I opened the hickory trunk and started transferring all my frantically purchased clothes into it. Everything except my nightgown, which I kept out before sliding the suitcase under the bed.

Vivian slipped from the top bunk in a cropped T-shirt and a pair of panties, her exposure making me even more self-conscious as I stripped off my clothes under the protection of the nightgown.

"You're a little young. Are you sure you're supposed to be here?" She turned to the others in the cabin, both still ensconced in their bunks. "Isn't there a cabin for babies we can send her to?"

"I'm thirteen," I said. "Clearly not a baby."

Vivian terrified and dazzled me in equal measure. All three of them did. They seemed like women. I was just a girl. A skinny, scabby-kneed twerp with a flat chest.

"Is this your first night away from home?" asked Allison. She was thin and pretty, with hair the color of honey.

"No," I said, when it was, other than a handful of sleepovers at the apartments of friends who lived mere blocks away, which wasn't quite the same thing.

"You're not going to cry, are you?" Vivian said. "All newbies cry their first night. It's so fucking predictable."

Her casual use of the F-word made me freeze. It was different from when Heather or Marissa used it during desperate attempts to sound grown-up and cool. The word easily rolled off Vivian's tongue, making it clear she said it quite a lot. It told me these girls were older, wiser, and tougher. In order to survive, I had to be just like them. There was no other choice.

I closed the lid of my trunk and faced Vivian head on. "If I cry, it's because I've been put in here with you bitches."

A moment passed in which no one said anything. It wasn't long, yet time seemed to slow, feeling like minutes as I wondered if they were amused or angry and if I truly would end up crying, which, quite honestly, is what I had felt like doing since the moment my parents sped away from camp in a cloud of gravel dust. Then I noticed Natalie and Allison with blankets pulled to their noses, trying to hide the fact that they were giggling. Vivian grinned and shook her head, as if I had just paid them the highest compliment.

"Well played, kid."

"Don't call me kid," I said, feigning toughness despite the fact that I still wanted to cry, only this time with relief. "My name is Emma."

Vivian reached out and tousled my hair. "Well, Em, welcome to Camp Nightingale. You ready to help us rule this place?"

"Sure," I said, not quite believing that someone so effortlessly cool was paying attention to me. At school, I spent my days blending in with Heather and Marissa, all but ignored by the older girls. But there was Vivian, staring me down, asking me to join her clique.

"Awesome," she replied. "Because tomorrow, we kick ass."

Six

From the outside, Dogwood looks exactly the way I left it. Same rough brown walls. Same green-shingled roof speckled with pinecones. Same tidy sign announcing its name. I had expected it to be different somehow. Older. Decrepit. A firm reminder that I'm fifteen years and worlds away from the weeping girl who last set eyes upon the place.

Instead, it feels like no time has passed between then and now. That the last decade and a half of my life was nothing but a dream. It's a disorienting feeling. And slightly scary. But I continue to stare at the cabin, gripped not by fear but by something else. Something sharper.

Curiosity.

I *want* to go inside, look around, see what memories it dredges up. That's why I'm here, after all. Yet when I twist the doorknob, I realize my hand is shaking. I don't know what I'm expecting. Ghosts, I suppose.

Instead I find three different girls, all of them very much alive as they lounge on their respective bunks. They look up at me, surprised by my sudden intrusion.

"Hi," I say.

My voice is meek, almost apologetic, as if I'm sorry to be invading their space, dragging my suitcase behind me. I haven't been alone with a group of teenage girls since, well, not long after my first time at Camp Nightingale. After what happened here, I gravitated to boys. Shy, nerdy ones. Math whizzes, sci-fi geeks, and drama club members quakingly emerging from the closet. They became my tribe. They still are. I'm comfortable in their presence.

Yes, boys can break your heart and betray you, but not in the same stinging way girls can.

I clear my throat. "I'm Emma."

"Hi, Emma. I'm Sasha."

This is spoken by the youngest, a girl of about thirteen who's perched on the top bunk to my left, her skinny legs dangling. She's got a friendly face—huge smile, rounded cheeks, bright eyes made even more prominent by a pair of red-framed glasses. I find myself relaxing in her presence. At least one of them seems nice.

"Nice to meet you, Sasha."

"I'm Krystal," says the girl sprawled on the bunk below her. "Spelled with a *K*."

A few years older and several pounds heavier than Sasha, she's practically hidden inside an oversize hoodie and baggie shorts. White socks with blue stripes circling the cuff have been pulled up to her knees. On the bed next to her is a ragged-looking teddy bear. In her lap sits a comic book. Captain America.

"Krystal with a *K*. Got it."

I turn to the other girl in the room, who lies on her side on the top bunk, elbow bent, head propped up. She appraises me in silence, her almond-shaped eyes flashing a combination of disdain and curiosity. A diamond stud adorns her nose. She looks to be about sixteen and, like most girls her age, thoroughly unimpressed with everything.

"Miranda," she says. "I took the top bunk. Hope you don't mind."

"Bottom bunk is fine," I say as I hoist my suitcase onto the bed, the mattress springs sighing under its weight.

Miranda climbs down from the bunk and stretches, her arms and legs enviably thin. She's knotted her camp-mandated polo shirt at her midriff, revealing her taut stomach. Another diamond stud rests in her navel. She keeps stretching, although it's more of a silent declaration. She's an alpha female. Marking her territory. Making it abundantly clear she's the hottest in the room. An old Vivian trick.

I feel exactly like I did the first time I set foot inside this cabin. Naïve. Tremulous. Unsure of what to do next as the girls stare at me expectantly. Well, Sasha and Krystal do. Miranda climbs back to her top bunk and spreads herself across the bed with a dramatic sigh.

"They did tell you I'd be staying here, right?" I say.

"They said someone else would be here," Krystal informs me. "But they didn't say who it was."

Miranda's voice floats from above. "Or how old you are."

"Sorry to disappoint you," I say.

"Are you our camp counselor?" Sasha asks.

"More like babysitter," Krystal adds.

Miranda does her one better. "More like warden."

"I'm an artist," I tell them. "I'm here to teach you how to paint."

"What if we don't want to paint?" Sasha says.

"You don't have to, if you don't want to."

"I like to draw." This comes from Krystal, already leaning off the bed to reach beneath it, where several tattered notebooks sit. She pulls one from the pile and opens it up. "See?"

On the page is a sketch of a superhero. A woman with fiery eyes and the bulging muscles of a weight lifter. Her uniform is dark blue and skintight, with a green skull emblazoned across the chest. The skull's eyes glow red.

"You did this?" I say, sincerely impressed. "It's really good."

And it is. The hero's face is perfect. She's been given a square jaw, a sharp nose, eyes that blaze with defiance. Her hair flows off her head in dark tendrils. With a few strokes of her pencil, Krystal had conveyed this woman's strength, courage, and determination.

"Her name is Skull Crusher. She can kill a man with her bare hands."

"I wouldn't want it any other way," I say. "Since you're already an artist, I'll let you draw while the others paint."

Krystal accepts the deal with a smile. "Cool."

She and Sasha continue to stare as I unpack, waiting for me to say more. Feeling extremely awkward, I ask, "So why did you want to come to camp?"

"My guidance counselor at school suggested it," Sasha says. "She said it would be a good learning experience for me, seeing how I'm inquisitive."

"Oh?" I say. "About what?"

"Um, everything."

"I see."

"My dad wanted me to come," Krystal says. "It was either this or get a job flipping burgers somewhere."

"I think you made the right choice."

"I didn't want to come," Miranda says. "My grandmother forced me to. She said I'd only get in trouble if I stayed home this summer."

I look up at her. "And would you?"

Miranda shrugs. "Probably."

"Listen," I say, "whether you want to be here or not, I need to be clear about something. I'm not here to be your den mother. Or babysitter." I flick my gaze up at Miranda. "Or warden. I don't want to cramp your style."

All of them groan.

"What, don't kids say that anymore?"

"No," Krystal says emphatically.

"Definitely not," Sasha adds.

"Well, whatever the current equivalent of that is, it's not why I'm here. I'm here to help you learn, if you want. Or, if you'd like, we can just talk. Basically, think of me as your big sister for the summer. I just want you to enjoy yourselves."

"I have a question," Sasha says. "Are there bears here?"

"I guess so," I reply. "But they're more afraid of us than we are of them."

"I did some research before I left home and read that that's not true."

"It's probably not," I say. "But it's nice to imagine, don't you think?"

"What about snakes?"

"What about them?"

"How many do you think are in the woods? And how many of those are venomous?"

I look at Sasha, intimidated by her curiosity. What a delightfully strange girl, with her thick-framed glasses perched on her tiny nose, her eyes wide behind their immaculate lenses.

"I honestly don't know," I say. "But I don't think we need to worry too much about snakes."

Sasha pushes her glasses higher up the bridge of her nose. "So, we should be more worried about sinkholes? I read that hundreds of thousands of years ago, this whole area was covered by glaciers that left ice deep inside the earth. And that ice eventually melted and ate away at the sandstone, forming deep caves. And sometimes those caves collapse, leaving giant craters. And if you're standing above one when it collapses, you'll fall so deep into the earth that no one will ever find you."

She finally stops, slightly out of breath.

"I think we'll be okay," I say. "Honestly, the only thing you need to worry about is poison ivy."

"And getting lost in the woods," Sasha says. "According to Wikipedia, it's very common. People disappear all the time."

I nod. Finally, a fact I can confirm.

And one that I can't forget.

Seven

When it's time for dinner, I stay behind, using the excuse that I have to unpack and change into my shorts and camp polo. The truth is that I want to be alone with Dogwood, just for a moment.

I stand in the middle of the cabin, rotating slowly, taking it all in. It feels different from fifteen years ago. Smaller and tighter. Like the cramped sleeping car where Marc and I once spent a red-eye train ride from Paris to Nice. But the cabin's differences are outweighed by its similarities. It has the same smell. Pine and musty earth and the faintest trace of woodsmoke. The third floorboard from the door still creaks. The trim around the only window still bears its faded-blue paint job. A touch of whimsy I noticed even during my first stay here.

Memories of the girls' voices return to me, like an echo of an echo. Random snippets I had completely forgotten until now. Allison mock-singing "I Feel Pretty" while flouncing around in her too-big polo shirt. Natalie sitting on the edge of the bottom bunk, her legs spackled with calamine lotion.

These mosquitoes are, like, obsessed with me, she said. *There's something about my blood that attracts them.*

I don't think that's how it works, I said.

Then why are they biting me and not the rest of you?

It's your sweat, Vivian announced. *Bugs love it. So slather on that Teen Spirit, girls.*

My phone squawks deep inside my pocket, snapping me out of my self-indulgent, admittedly morbid reverie. I dig out the phone and see

LAST TIME I LIED

that Marc's attempting to FaceTime. With only one bar of signal, I have doubts it's going to work.

"Hey, Veronica Mars," he says once I answer. "How's the sleuthing going?"

"I'm just starting." I sit on the edge of my bed, holding out my arm so my entire face fits into the frame. "I can't talk very long. The signal here is terrible."

Marc gives me his dramatic pouting face in return. He's in the kitchen of his bistro, the glossy, stainless-steel door of the walk-in freezer behind him.

"How's Camp Crystal Lake?"

"Devoid of masked killers," I say.

"That's a plus, I suppose."

"But I'm rooming with three teenage girls."

"Definitely not in your wheelhouse," Marc says. "What are they like?"

"I would describe them as sassy, but that term is probably out of date."

"'Sassy' never goes out of style. It's like blue jeans. Or vodka. Is that a bunk bed?"

"It is indeed," I say. "It's about as comfortable as it looks."

Marc's expression changes from pouting to horrified. "Oh dear. I apologize for convincing you to go back there."

"You didn't convince me," I say. "You just nudged me a little closer."

"I wouldn't have nudged if I'd known bunk beds would be involved." His image sputters a moment. When he moves his head, an afterimage follows in a stream of pixels.

"You're breaking up," I say, when in reality it's me. The signal has dropped from one bar to none. On the screen, Marc's face is frozen, nothing but an abstract blur. Yet I can still hear him. His voice cuts in and out, letting me catch only every other word.

"You . . . out . . . bored . . . okay?"

The phone gives up the ghost, and the call dies. My screen goes blank. Replacing Marc's face is my own reflection. I stare at it, shocked at how tired I look. Worse than tired. Haggard. No wonder Miranda made that crack about my age. I look positively ancient compared with them.

It makes me wonder what the other girls of Dogwood would look like today. Allison would probably still be cute and petite like her mother, who I saw a few years ago in a revival of *Sweeney Todd*. I spent the whole show wondering how much she thought of her daughter, if there's a picture of Allison in her dressing room, if seeing it made her sad.

I suspect Natalie would have remained physically formidable, thanks to sports in college.

And Vivian? I'm certain she'd be the same. Slim. Stylish. A beauty that bordered on haughtiness. I imagine her taking one look at present-day me and saying, *We need to talk about your hair. And your wardrobe.*

I shove the phone back in my pocket and open my suitcase. Quickly, I change into a pair of shorts and one of the official camp polos that arrived in the mail two weeks ago. The rest go into my assigned trunk by the door. It's the same trunk from my previous stay here. I can tell from the grayish stain that mars the satin lining.

I close the trunk and run my hands across the lid, feeling the bumps and grooves of all the names that have been carved into the hickory. Another memory prods my thoughts. Me on my first morning at camp, kneeling before this very trunk with a dull pocketknife in my hand.

Carve your name, Allison urged.

Every girl does it, Natalie added. *It's tradition.*

I followed that tradition and carved my name. Two letters in all caps white against the dark wood.

EM

Vivian stood behind me as I did it, her voice soft and encouraging in my ear. *Make your mark. Let future generations know you were here. That you existed.*

I look to the other side of the cabin, at the two trunks resting by the door. Natalie's and Allison's. Their names have faded with time, barely distinguishable from all the others carved around them. I then move to the trunk next to mine. Vivian's. She had carved her name in the center of the lid, larger than all the others.

VIV

I crack open her trunk, even though I know it's Miranda's now and that inside aren't Vivian's clothes and crafts and bottle of Obsession she swore covered the scent of bug spray. In their place are Miranda's clothes—an assortment of too-tight shorts and lacy bras and panties utterly inappropriate for camp. In a corner sits a surprisingly high stack of paperbacks. *Gone Girl*, *Rosemary's Baby*, a few Agatha Christie mysteries.

But the lining inside the lid is the same. Burgundy satin. Just like mine. The only difference, other than the gray stain, is a six-inch tear in the fabric. It sits on the left side of the lid, running vertically, the edges feathery.

Vivian's hiding place, used to store the pendant necklace she took off only when she slept. A heart-shaped locket hung from it. Gold with a small emerald inlaid in its center.

I know of the hiding place only because I saw Vivian use it on the first full day of camp. I was at my own trunk, searching for my toothbrush, when she knelt in front of hers. She unclasped the necklace and held it for a moment in her cupped hands.

That's pretty, I said. *An heirloom?*

It belonged to my sister.

Belonged?

She died.

Sorry. Apprehension fluttered in my chest. I'd never met someone with a dead sibling before and didn't know how to act. *I didn't mean to bring it up.*

You didn't, Vivian said. *I did. And it's healthy to talk about it. That's what my therapist says.*

I felt another flutter. A dead sister *and* therapy? At that moment, Vivian was the most exotic creature I had ever met.

How'd she die?

She drowned.

Oh, I said, too surprised to say more.

Vivian didn't say anything else, either. She simply poked her fingers through the tear in the lining and let the necklace slither out of view behind it.

Now I stare at the slash in the fabric, fingering my own piece of jewelry. Unlike Vivian's necklace, I never remove the charm bracelet. Not to sleep. Not to shower. Not even when painting. The wear and tear shows. Each tiny bird has scratches in the pewter that stand out like scars. Dots of dried paint mar their beaks.

I pry my right hand away from the bracelet and plunge it through the tear in the lining. Fabric tickles my wrist as I stretch my fingers and feel around the inside of the lid. I'm not expecting to find anything. Certainly not the necklace, which Vivian had been wearing when she left the cabin for the very last time. I do it because once I check, I'll know there's no trace of Vivian left there.

Only there is.

Something is inside the lid, sitting at the bottom, wedged between wood and fabric. A piece of paper, folded in half. I run a finger along the crease, feeling its length. Then I pinch the edge between my thumb and forefinger and slide it from the lining.

Age has given the paper a yellowish tint—a sickly shade that reminds me of dried egg yolk. The page crackles when I unfold it, revealing an even older-looking photograph nestled in its crease.

I study the photo first. It's surprisingly old. Something more likely to be found in a museum than in a camp cabin. Sepia-toned and worn along the edges, it depicts a young woman in a plain dress. She sits before a bare wall, turned at an angle that shows off long, dark hair cascading down her back and out of frame.

Clutched in the woman's hands is a large silver hairbrush, which she holds to her chest like a prized possession. I find the gesture oddly endearing, although one could also assume it's vanity that makes her grip the brush so tightly. That she spends her days running it through that absurdly long hair, breaking up the tangles, smoothing the strands. But the woman's expression makes me assume that's not the case. Although she looks to be in repose, her face is anything but peaceful. Her lips are pressed together, forming a flat line. Her face is pinched. Her eyes, wild and dark, convey sadness, loneliness, and something else. An emotion I know well.

Distress.

I stare into those eyes, finding them disturbingly familiar. I've seen that same expression in my own eyes. Not long after I left Camp Nightingale for what I had thought was the last time.

I flip over the photo and see a name scrawled on its back in faded ink.

Eleanor Auburn.

Several questions settle uneasily onto my shoulders. Who is this woman? When was this picture taken? And, above all else, where did Vivian get it, and why was it hidden in her trunk?

The contents of the unfolded page don't provide any answers. Instead, I see a drawing crudely scratched onto a ruled piece of paper torn from some sort of notebook. The focal point of the drawing is a blob that resembles a paisley, strange and formless. Surrounding it are hundreds of dark slashes, each dashed off in strokes so quick and forceful my painting hand aches just from looking at them. Beneath the paisley, tucked among the slashes, are several shapes. Messy ones. Not quite circles, not quite squares. Off to their left is another circle-square. Bigger than the others.

I realize what it is and gasp.

For reasons I can't begin to understand, Vivian drew Camp Nightingale.

The paisley is Lake Midnight, dominating the landscape, demanding attention. The slashes are an abstract version of the woods surrounding it. The series of shapes are the cabins. I count twenty of them, just like in real life. The big splotch, of course, is the Lodge, commanding the southern shore of the lake.

On the other side of the lake, almost directly across from camp, Vivian had drawn another cabin-size shape. It sits next to the water, all alone. Only there aren't any structures on the other side of the lake. At least, none that I'm aware of.

Just like the photo, the sketch defies explanation. I try to think of a logical reason why Vivian drew it but come up empty. She had gone here three summers in a row. Surely there was no need for her to draw a map of the camp to find her way around.

Because that is indeed what it looks like. A map. Not just of camp but of the entire lake. It reminds me of the satellite view I studied on the ride here. All of Lake Midnight in one handy image.

I bring the page closer to my face, zeroing in not on the camp but on the area on the other side of the lake. A short distance behind the mystery structure is something barely distinguishable from the slashes that surround it.

An X.

Small but noticeable, it sits near a cluster of ragged triangles that resemble tiny mountains drawn by a kindergartener. Vivian had used extra force when drawing it. The lines push into the paper, creating two crisscrossed indentations.

That means it was important to her.

That something of interest was located there.

I fold the photograph inside the map and secure them both inside my own hickory trunk. It strikes me that if Vivian had taken such great care to hide them, then I should do the same thing.

It was, after all, her secret.

And I've become very good at keeping them.

FIFTEEN YEARS AGO

"There's one thing you need to know about this place," Vivian said. "Never arrive to anything on time. Either be there first or get there last."

"Even meals?" I asked.

"*Especially* meals. You won't believe how crazy some of these bitches get around food."

It was my first morning at camp, and Vivian and I had just left the latrine on the way to the mess hall. Although the mealtime bell rang fifteen minutes earlier, Vivian showed no sign of hurry. Her pace bordered on lackadaisical as she looped her arm through mine, forcing me to slow as well.

When we eventually did reach the mess hall, I noticed a girl with frizzy hair standing outside the arts and crafts building with a camera around her neck. She noticed us, too, because something flickered in her eyes. Recognition, maybe. Or worry. It lasted only a second before she raised her camera and aimed it our way, the blue-black lens following us as we entered the mess hall.

"Who was that taking our picture?" I asked.

"Becca?" Vivian said. "Don't mind her. She's a nobody."

Taking my hand, she pulled me toward the front of the room, where a handful of kitchen workers in hairnets stood before steaming trays of food. Because we were among the last to arrive, there was no wait. Vivian was right, not that I ever doubted her.

The only person later than us was a smiling redheaded counselor with the name *Casey* stitched onto her camp polo. She was short—

practically my height—and had a pear-shaped frame made more pronounced by the large pockets of her cargo shorts.

"Well, if it isn't Vivian Hawthorne," she said. "You told me last summer that you were done with this place. Couldn't stay away?"

"And miss out on a chance to torment you for another summer?" Vivian said as she grabbed two bananas, placing one of them on my tray. "No way."

"And here I thought I was going to have it easy this year." The counselor gave me an appraising look. She seemed surprised—not to mention a little confused—to see me by Vivian's side. "You're new, right?"

Vivian ordered two bowls of clumpy oatmeal, again giving one to me. "Emma, this is Casey. Former camper, current counselor, forever bane of my existence. Casey, meet Emma."

I lifted my tray up and down in a weak approximation of a wave. "Nice to meet you."

"She's my protégé," Vivian said.

"That's a scary thought." Casey turned to me again and put a hand on my shoulder. "Come see me if she starts to corrupt you too much. I'm in Birch."

She passed us on her way to a decanter of coffee and the platter of doughnuts next to it. Before leaving the food line, I also ordered what I really wanted for breakfast—toast and a plate of bacon. Vivian eyed the extra side dishes but said nothing.

We then made our way through the clanging, slurping girls huddled at tables in configurations familiar from my school's cafeteria. Younger girls on one side. Older ones on the other. And at that moment, I wasn't adhering to my socially acceptable pack. A few girls my age took notice and watched with envy as Vivian led me to the side of the mess hall populated by older girls. She waved to some and ignored others before sitting me down with Allison and Natalie.

I had been awake when the two of them left the cabin to head to the latrine. Although they invited me to join them, I stayed behind, waiting for Vivian to rise. She was the only one I wanted showing me the ropes. While Allison and Natalie seemed nice, they reminded me too much of girls I knew at school. Slightly older versions of Heather and Marissa.

Vivian was different. I'd never met anyone so unfiltered. To a shy girl like me, her attention was as warm and welcome as the sun.

"Morning, bitches," she said to the others. "Sleep well?"

"The usual," Allison said as she picked at a bowl of fruit salad. "You, Emma?"

"Great," I said.

It was a lie. The cabin was too stuffy, too quiet. I missed air conditioning and the sounds of Manhattan—all those irritated car horns and wailing sirens in the distance. At Camp Nightingale, there was nothing but bug noise and the lake lapping against the shore. I assumed I'd get used to it.

"Thank God you don't snore, Em," Vivian said. "We had a snorer last year. Sounded like a dying cow."

"It wasn't that bad," said Natalie. On her tray sat two servings of bacon and the syrupy remains of flapjacks. She bit into a bacon slice, chewing and talking at the same time. "You're just being mean because you don't like her anymore."

Already, I had noticed the weird dynamic between the three of them. Vivian was the ringleader. Obviously. Natalie, athletic and a little bit gruff, was the resistance. Pretty, subdued Allison was the peacekeeper, a role she assumed that very morning.

"Tell us about yourself, Emma," she said. "You don't go to our school, right?"

"Of course she doesn't," Vivian replied. "We'd know if she did. Half our school goes here."

"I go to Douglas Academy," I said.

Allison stabbed a chunk of melon, lifted it to her lips, put it back down. "Do you like it there?"

"It's nice, I guess. For an all-girls schools."

"Ours is, too," Vivian said. "And I'd honestly kill to spend a summer away from some of these sluts."

"Why?" Natalie asked. "You pretend half of them don't exist when we're here."

"Just like I'm pretending right now that you're not stuffing your face with bacon," Vivian shot back. "Keep eating like that and next year it'll be fat camp for you."

Natalie sighed and dropped the half-eaten bacon onto her plate. "You want any, Allison?"

Allison shook her head and pushed away her barely touched bowl of fruit. "I'm stuffed."

"I was just joking," Vivian said, looking genuinely remorseful. "I'm sorry, Nat. Really. You look . . . fine."

She smiled then, the word lingering like the insult it really was.

I spent the rest of the meal eyeing Vivian's plate, taking a bite of oatmeal only when she did, trying to make the portions match up exactly. I didn't touch the banana until she did. When she left half of it on her tray, I did the same. The bacon and toast remained untouched.

I told myself it would be worth it.

Vivian, Natalie, and Allison left the mess hall before me, preparing for an advanced archery lesson. Senior campers only. I was scheduled to take part in an activity with girls my own age. I assumed I'd find them boring. That's what one night in Dogwood had already done to me.

On my way there, I passed the girl with the camera. She veered into my path, halting me.

"What are you doing?"

"Warning you," she said. "About Vivian."

"What do you mean?"

"Don't be fooled. She'll turn on you eventually."

I took a step toward her, trying to match the same toughness I had summoned the previous night. "How so?"

Although the girl with the camera smiled, there was no humor there. It was a bitter grin. On the cusp of curdling into a sneer.

"You'll find out," she said.

Eight

Arriving at the mess hall for dinner, I find Franny standing at the head of the room, already halfway through her welcome speech. She appears more robust than before. It's clear she's in her element, dressed for the great outdoors before a packed room of girls while extolling the virtues of camp life. She sweeps her gaze across the room as she speaks, making momentary eye contact with each and every girl, silently welcoming them. When she spots me by the door, her eyes crinkle ever so slightly. An almost-wink.

The speech sounds just like the one I heard fifteen years ago. For all I know, it could be exactly the same, summoned from Franny's memory after all these years. She's already recited the part about how the lake was formed by her grandfather on that long-ago New Year's Eve and is now delving into the history of the camp itself.

"For years, this land served as a private retreat for my family. As a child, I spent every summer—and quite a few winters, springs, and falls—exploring the thousands of acres my family was fortunate enough to own. When my parents passed away, it was left to me. So, in 1973, I decided to turn the Harris family retreat into a camp for girls. Camp Nightingale opened a year later, where it welcomed generations of young women."

She pauses. Just long enough for her to take a breath. But contained in that brief silence are years of omitted history. About my friends, the camp's shame, its subsequent closure.

"Today, the camp welcomes all of you," Franny says. "Camp Night-ingale isn't about cliques or popularity contests or feeling superior. It's about you. All of you. Giving each and every one of you an experience to cherish long after the summer is over. So if you need anything at all, don't hesitate to ask Lottie, my sons, or Mindy, the newest member of our family."

She gestures to her left, where Chet stands against the wall, pre-tending not to notice the adoring gazes of half the girls in the room. Next to him, Mindy smiles and gives a beauty-pageant wave. I scan the room, looking for Theo. There's no sign of him, which is both a disappointment and a relief.

Franny clasps her hands together and bows her head, signaling that the speech is over. But I know it's not. There's still one part left, completely scripted but performed with the polish of a career politi-cian.

"Oh, one last thing," Franny says, pretending to think of it just now. "I don't want to hear a single one of you call me Mrs. Har-ris-White. Call me Franny. I insist upon it. Here in the great outdoors, we're all equals."

From her spot along the wall, Mindy starts clapping. Chet does, too, albeit with more reluctance. Soon the whole room is applauding as Franny, their benefactor, takes another quick bow. Then she's off, skirting out of the mess hall via a side door opened by Lottie.

I make my way to the food stations, where a small crew of white-uniformed cooks dish out greasy hamburgers, fries, and cole-slaw so runny that milky liquid sloshes around the bottom of the plate.

Rather than join Sasha, Krystal, and Miranda, who are sur-rounded on all sides by other campers, I head to a table near the door where eight women are seated. Five of them are young, definitely college age. The camp counselors. The other three range in age from midthirties to pushing sixty. My fellow instructors. Minus Rebecca Schoenfeld.

I recognize only one—Casey Anderson. Little about her has changed between then and now. She's still got that pear-shaped frame and red hair that grazes her shoulder when she tilts her head in sympathy upon seeing me again. She even gives me a hug and says, "It's good to see you back here, Emma."

The other instructors nod hello. The counselors merely stare. All of them, I realize, know not only who I am but also what happened while I was here.

Casey introduces me to the other instructors. Teaching creative writing is Roberta Wright-Smith, who attended Camp Nightingale for three summers, beginning with its inaugural season. She's plump and jolly and peers at me through a pair of glasses perched on her nose. Paige McAdams, who went here in the late eighties, is gray-haired and willowy, with bony fingers that clasp my hand too hard when she shakes it. She's here to teach pottery, which explains her grip.

Casey informs me she's been assigned to that catchall camp staple of arts and crafts. She's an eighth-grade English teacher during the school year, available to help out here because her two kids are away at their own camp and it's her first summer alone since she divorced her husband.

Divorce, it turns out, is a dominant theme among the other instructors. Casey wanted to escape six weeks alone in an empty house. Paige needed a place to go until her soon-to-be ex-husband moves out of their Brooklyn apartment. And Roberta, a creative-writing professor at Syracuse, wanted to go somewhere quiet after recently parting ways with her poet girlfriend. I'm the only one, it seems, who doesn't have a former spouse or partner to blame for being here. I'm not sure it that's liberating or merely pathetic.

I suppose I have more in common with the counselors, those college juniors who've yet to be touched by life's disappointments. They're all pretty and bland and basically interchangeable. Hair pulled into ponytails. Pink lip gloss. Their exfoliated faces glisten. They are, I realize, exactly the kind of girls who would have attended Camp Nightingale had it been open during their adolescence.

"Who else is psyched about the summer?" one of them says. I think her name is Kim. Or maybe it's Danica. Each of their names left my memory five seconds after I was introduced to them. "I definitely am."

"But don't you think it's weird?" Casey says. "I mean, I'm happy to help out for the summer, but I don't understand Franny's decision to open the camp again after all these years."

"I don't think it's necessarily weird," I say. "Surprising, maybe."

"I vote for weird," Paige says. "I mean, why now?"

"Why not now?"

This comes from Mindy, who's swooped up to the table without notice. I find her standing behind me, arms crossed. Although it's unclear how much she's heard, it was enough to make the edges of her plastered-on smile twitch.

"Does Franny need a reason for doing a good deed?" she says, directing the comment to Roberta, Paige, Casey, and me. "I didn't know it was wrong to try to give a new generation of girls the same experiences the four of you had."

If this is an attempt to sound like Franny, she's failing miserably. Franny's speeches might be scripted, but the emotion behind them is real. You believe every word she says. Mindy's tone is different. It comes off so sweetly sanctimonious that I can't help but say, "I wouldn't wish my experience here on anyone."

Mindy gives a sad shake of her head. Clearly, I've let her down. Holding her hand to her heart, she says, "I expected more from you, Emma. Franny showed a great deal of courage inviting you back here."

"And Emma showed courage by agreeing to come," Casey says, leaping to my defense.

"She did," Mindy replies. "Which is why I thought she'd show a little bit more Camp Nightingale spirit."

I roll my eyes so hard the sockets hurt. "Really?"

"Fine." Mindy plops into an empty chair and lets out a sigh that reminds me of air hissing from a punctured tire. "I've been told by Lottie that we need to make a cabin check schedule for the summer."

Ah, cabin check. The nightly examination of all the cabins by counselors to make sure everyone is present, accounted for, and staying out of trouble. Naturally, it was the highlight of Vivian's day.

"Each night, we need two people to check on the cabins that don't have counselors or instructors staying in them," Mindy says. "Who wants to volunteer first? And where's Rebecca?"

"Sleeping, I think," Casey says. "I saw her earlier, and she said she needed a nap or the jet lag was going to kill her. She was on assignment in London and came straight here from the airport."

"I guess we'll have to pencil her in later," Mindy says. "Who wants to do it tonight?"

As the others wrangle over the schedule, I see the mess hall's double doors open and watch as Rebecca Schoenfeld steps inside. Unlike Casey, she's changed quite a bit. Gone are the braces and the adolescent pudge. She's become harder, compact, with a worldly style. Her hair, once a frizzy mass kept in place with a scrunchie, is now sleek and short. She's accented her shorts-and-polo ensemble with a brightly colored scarf. Beneath it hangs her camera, which sways as she walks. Her movements are another change. Instead of the shuffling teenager I remember, she walks with swift precision—a woman on a mission. She crosses the mess hall to the food station and grabs an apple. She takes a bite on her way out, stopping only when she spots me on the other side of the room.

The look she gives me is unreadable. I can't tell if she's surprised, happy, or confused by my presence. After another sharp bite of apple, she turns and exits the mess hall.

"I need to go," I say.

Mindy emits another deflated-tire sigh. "What about cabin check?"

"Sign me up for whenever."

I leave the table, abandoning my tray, the food barely touched. Outside the mess hall, I search in every direction for signs of Becca. But she's nowhere to be found. The areas in front of both the mess hall and the arts and crafts building next door are empty. In the distance, I see Franny slowly making her way to the Lodge with Lottie by her side. Beyond the Lodge, on the patch of grass that leads down to the lake, I spot the maintenance man who was fixing the roof when I arrived. He pushes a wheelbarrow toward a rickety toolshed situated on the edge of the lawn. Lots of activity. None of it from Becca.

I start to head back to the cabins when someone says my name.

"Emma?"

I freeze, knowing exactly who the voice belongs to.

Theo Harris-White.

He calls to me from the open door of the arts and crafts building. Like Franny's speech, nothing about his voice has changed. Hearing it sends more memories shooting into me. They hurt. Like a quiver of arrows to the gut.

Seeing Theo for the very first time, shyly shaking his hand, trying not to notice how his T-shirt swelled across his chest, confused about why the sight made me feel so warm inside.

Theo waist-deep in the lake, skin sun-kissed and blazing, me cradled in his arms, practically trembling from his touch as he lowers me in the water until I'm floating.

Vivian nudging me toward the extra-wide crack in the latrine's exterior wall. Through the gap escaped the sound of a running shower and Theo absently humming a Green Day song. *Go on*, Vivian whispered. *Take a look. He'll never know.*

"Emma," he says again, this time without the questioning inflection. He knows it's me.

I turn around slowly, unsure what to expect. Part of me wants him to be ruddy and balding, the march toward middle age leaving him thick around the waist. Another part of me wants him to look exactly the same.

The reality is somewhere in between. He's aged, of course. No longer the strapping nineteen-year-old I remember him being. That youthful glow has dimmed into something darker, more intense. Yet he wears the years well. Too well, to be honest. There's more bulk than before, but it's all muscle. The flecks of gray in his dark hair and five o'clock shadow suit him. So does the slight weathering of his face. When he smiles at me, a few faint wrinkles crepe the skin around his mouth and eyes. I hate that it only makes him look more attractive.

"Hi."

It's not much of a greeting, but it's the best I can manage. Especially while I'm being blindsided by another memory. One that eclipses the others.

Theo, standing in front of the lodge, looking exhausted and di-sheveled after a day spent searching the woods. Me rushing at him, crying as I pound his chest and scream, *Where are they? What did you do to them?*

Until today, it was the last thing I ever said to him.

Now that he's right here in front of me again, I expect him to be angry or bitter about what I'd accused him of doing all those years ago. It makes me want to flee the same way Becca had left the mess hall, only faster. But I stay completely still as Theo steps forward and, shockingly, gives me a hug. I pull away after only a second, afraid touching him for too long will prompt even more memories.

Theo takes a step back, looks at me, shakes his head. "I can't be-lieve you're really here. My mother told me you were coming, but I just didn't think it would happen."

"Here I am."

"And it looks like life is treating you well. You look great."

He's being kind. I saw my reflection in the blank screen of my phone. I know how I look.

"So do you," I say.

"I hear you're a painter now. Mom told me she bought one of your works. I haven't had a chance to see it yet. I just got back from Africa two days ago."

"Franny mentioned that. You're a doctor?"

Theo gives a little shrug, scratches his beard. "Yeah. A pediatri-cian. I've spent the past year working with Doctors Without Borders. But for the next six weeks, I've been demoted to camp nurse."

"I guess that makes me the camp painter," I say.

"Speaking of which, I was just working on your studio for the summer." Theo jerks his head toward the arts and crafts building. "Care to take a peek?"

"Now?" I say, surprised by his casual willingness to remain alone with me.

"No time like the present," Theo says, head cocked, his face poised somewhere between curiosity and confusion. It is, I realize, the same look Franny gave me earlier on the Lodge's back deck.

"Sure," I say. "Lead the way."

I follow him inside, finding myself in the middle of an airy, open room. The walls have been painted a cheerful sky blue. The carpet and baseboard are as green as grass. The three support columns that rise from the floor to the ceiling in equal intervals have been painted to resemble trees. The areas where they meet on the ceiling contain fake branches that drip with paper leaves. It's like stepping into a picture book—happy and bright.

To our left is a little photo studio for Becca, complete with brand-new digital cameras, charging stations, and a handful of sleek computers used for processing pictures. The center of the room is an elaborate crafts station, full of circular tables, cubbyholes, and cabinets filled with string, beads, leather bands the color of saddles. I spot several dozen laptops for Roberta's writing classes and a pair of pottery wheels for Paige.

"I'm impressed," I say. "Franny did a great job fixing this place up."

"This is all Mindy's handiwork, actually," Theo tells me. "She's really thrown herself into reopening the camp."

"I'm not surprised. She's certainly—"

"Enthusiastic?"

"I was going to say 'overwhelming,' but that works, too."

Theo leads me to the far end of the room, where a semicircle of easels has been set up. Along one wall is a shelf holding tubes of oil paints and brushes clustered in mason jars. Clean palettes hang next to windows that let in natural light.

I roam the area, fingers trailing over a blank canvas leaning on one of the easels. At the shelf of paints, I see a hundred different colors, all arranged by hue. Lavender and chartreuse, cherry red and royal blue.

"I put your supplies over there," Theo says, gesturing to the box I brought with me. "I figured you'd want to unpack them yourself."

Honestly, there's no need. Everything I could possibly want is already here. Yet I go to the box anyway and start pulling out my personal supplies. The well-worn brushes. The squished tubes of paint. The palette so thoroughly speckled with color that it resembles a Pollock painting.

Theo stands on the other side of the box, watching me unpack. Fading light from the window falls across his face, highlighting something that's definitely different from fifteen years ago. Something I didn't notice until just now.

A scar.

Located on his left cheek, it's an inch-long line that slants toward his mouth. It's a single shade lighter than the rest of his face, which is why I had missed it earlier. But now that I know it's there, I can't stop looking at it. I'm about to ask Theo how he got it when he checks his watch and says, "I need to go help Chet with the campfire. Will I see you there?"

"Of course," I say. "I never turn down an opportunity to have s'mores."

"Good. That you're coming, I mean." Theo's departure is hesitant. A slow amble to the door. When he reaches it, he turns around and says, "Hey, Emma."

I look up from my supplies, the suddenly serious tone of his voice worrying me. I suspect he's about to mention the last time we saw each other. He's certainly thinking about it. The tension between us is like a fraying rope, pulled taut, ready to snap.

Theo opens his mouth, reconsiders what he's about to say, closes it again. When he finally does speak, sincerity tinges his voice. "I'm glad you're here. I know it isn't easy. But it means a lot to my mother. It means a lot to me, too."

Then he's gone, leaving me alone to wonder what, exactly, he meant by that. Does it mean a lot to him because it pleases Franny? Or does it mean my presence reminds him of happier times before the camp shuttered in disgrace?

Ultimately, I decide it's neither of those things.

In truth, I think it means he forgives me.

Now all I need is to somehow find a way to forgive myself.

Nine

Apparently to Mindy, *whenever* meant *tonight*, because after the camp-fire I find myself on cabin check duty. While not thrilled, I'm at least pleased to have Casey as my co-checker. Together we go from cabin to cabin, peeking inside to do a head count and ask if any of the campers need anything.

It's strange being on the other side of things. Especially with Casey in tow. When I was a camper here, she'd give a single rap on the door before throwing it open, trying to catch us in the act of some imagined misbehavior. We greeted her with wide-eyed innocence, lashes fluttering. Now I'm the one getting those looks—a surreal turn of events that makes me feel partly jealous of their mischievous youth, partly annoyed by it.

In two of the cabins, I find girls balled up in their bunks, crying from homesickness. While Vivian was wrong about all newbies crying their first night, a small few truly do. I spend a few minutes with each one, telling them that while camp may seem scary now, they'll soon grow to love it and will never want to go back home.

I hope it's the truth.

I never got the chance to find out.

After the cabins have all been checked, Casey and I walk to the patch of grass behind the latrine. It's dark back here, made even more oppressive by the forest that begins a yard or so away. Shadows crowd the trees, broken only by fireflies dancing among the leaves. The utility light affixed to the latrine's corner swarms with bugs.

Casey pulls a cigarette from a battered pack hidden in her cargo shorts and lights up. "I can't believe I'm sneaking cigarettes. I feel like I'm fourteen again."

"Better this than face the wrath of Mindy."

"Want to know a secret?" Casey says. "Her real name is Melinda. She goes by Mindy to be more like Franny."

"I get the feeling Franny doesn't like her very much."

"I can see why. She's the kind of girl I went out of my way to avoid in high school." Casey blows out a stream of smoke and watches it languidly float in the night air. "Honestly, though, it's probably for the best that she's here. Without her, it would be open season on poor Chet. These girls would eat him alive."

"But they're all so young."

"I'm a teacher," Casey says. "Trust me, girls that age are just as full of raging hormones as boys. Remember how you were back then. I saw the way you fawned over Theo. Not that I blamed you. He was a fine-looking young man."

"Have you seen him now?"

Casey gives a slow, knowing nod. "Why is it that men only look better with age? It's completely unfair."

"But he's still just as friendly," I say. "I didn't expect that."

"Because of what you said last time you were here?"

"And because of what people are saying now. I saw some of the responses to your Facebook book. They were pretty brutal."

"Ignore them." Casey gives her hand a casual flip, as if brushing away the smoke still spouting from her cigarette. "Most of those women are just adult versions of the bitchy teenagers they were when they went here."

"A few of them mentioned that this place gave them the creeps," I say. "Something about a legend."

"It's just a silly campfire tale."

"So you've heard it?"

"I've *told* it," Casey says. "That doesn't mean I think the story is true. I can't believe you never heard it."

"I guess I wasn't here long enough."

Casey looks at me, the cigarette held between her lips, its trail of smoke making her squint.

"The story is that there was a village here," she says. "Before the lake was made. Some will say it was full of deaf people. I heard it was a leper colony."

"A leper colony? Was an ancient Indian burial ground too much of a cliché?"

"I didn't make up the story," Casey snaps. "Now, do you want to hear it or not?"

I do, no matter how ridiculous it seems. So I nod for her to continue.

"Deaf village and leper colony aside, the rest of the story is the same," Casey says. "It's that Franny's grandfather saw this valley and decided on the spot it was where he was going to create his lake. But there was one problem. The village sat right in the middle of it. When Buchanan Harris approached the villagers and offered to buy their land, they refused. They were a small, tight-knit community, ostracized by the rest of the world. This was their home, and they weren't going to sell it. This made Mr. Harris angry. He was a man accustomed to getting what he wanted. So when he increased his offer and the villagers again refused, he bought all the land surrounding them instead. Then he built his dam and flooded the valley at the stroke of midnight, knowing the water would wash away the village and that everyone who lived there would drown."

She lowers her voice, speaking slowly. Full storyteller mode.

"The village is still there, deep below Lake Midnight. And the people who drowned now haunt the woods and the lake. They appear at midnight, rising from the water and roaming the forest. Anyone unlucky enough to encounter them gets dragged into the lake and pulled to the bottom, where they quickly drown. Then they become one of the ghosts, cursed to search the woods for all eternity looking for more victims."

I give her an incredulous look. "And that's what people think happened to Vivian, Natalie, and Allison?"

"No one truly believes that," Casey says. "But bad things have happened here, with no explanation. Franny's husband, for example. He was a champion swimmer. Almost made it to the Olympics. Yet he drowned. I heard that Franny's grandmother—the first wife of Buchanan Harris—also drowned here. So when Vivian and the others disappeared, some people said it was the ghosts of Lake Midnight. Or else the survivors."

"Survivors?"

"It's been said that a handful of villagers escaped the rising waters and fled into the hills. There they stayed, living off the land, rebuilding the village in a remote section of the woods where no one could find them. The whole time, they held a grudge against the Harris family, passing it on to their ancestors. Those ancestors are still there, hidden somewhere in the woods. And on nights when the moon is full, they sneak down to the land that used to belong to them and exact their revenge. Vivian, Natalie, and Allison were just three of their victims."

It turns out that Casey's an expert tale-spinner, for as she finishes, I feel a chill in the air. A light frisson that makes me look to the woods behind her, half expecting to see either a ghostly figure or mutant forest dweller emerging from the tree line.

"What do you really think happened to them?" I say.

"I think they got lost in the woods. Vivian was always wandering off." Casey drops her cigarette and grinds it out with the toe of her sneaker. "Which is why I've always felt partly responsible for what happened. I was a camp counselor. It was my job to make sure all of you were safe. And I regret not paying more attention to you and what was going on in that cabin."

I stare at her, surprised. "Were there things going on I didn't know about?"

"I don't know," Casey says as she fumbles in her pocket for another cigarette. "Maybe."

"Like what? You were friends with Vivian. Surely you noticed something."

"I wouldn't say the two of us were friends. I was a senior camper her first summer and then came back to work as a counselor the two years after that. She was always a troublemaker, but charming enough to get away with it."

Oh, I know that all too well. Vivian excelled at charm. That and lying were her two greatest skills.

"But something about her seemed off that last summer," Casey continues. "Not majorly different. Nothing that someone who only knew her casually would notice. But she wasn't the same. She seemed distracted."

I think of the strange map Vivian had drawn and the even stranger photo of the woman with long hair.

"By what?"

Casey shrugs and looks away again as she irritably puffs out more smoke. "I don't know, Emma. Like I said, we weren't that close."

"But you noticed things."

"*Little* things," Casey says. "I noticed her walking alone around camp a few times. Which never happened the previous summers. Vivian was always surrounded by people. And maybe she just wanted to be left alone. Or maybe..."

Her voice trails off as she takes one last draw of her cigarette.

"Maybe what?"

"She was up to no good," Casey says. "On the second day of camp, I caught her trying to sneak into the Lodge. She was hanging around the steps on the back deck, ready to run inside. She said she was looking for Franny, but I didn't buy it."

"Why would she want to break into the Lodge?"

Casey shrugs again. The gesture contains a note of annoyance, almost as if she wishes she'd never brought up the topic of Vivian. "Your guess is as good as mine," she says.

My final stop on cabin check is Dogwood, where I find all three girls on their beds, phones in hand, faces awash in the ice-blue light of their screens. Sasha is already under the covers, her glasses perched on the tip of her nose as she plays Candy Crush or some similarly frustrating time-waste of a game. A cacophony of chirps and beeps erupt from her phone.

In the bunk below her, Krystal has changed into baggy sweats. The matted teddy bear sits in the crook of her arm as she watches a Marvel movie on her phone, the soundtrack leaking out of her earbuds, tinny and shrill. I can hear blips of gunfire and the telltale crunch of fist hitting skull.

On the other side of the cabin, Miranda reclines on the top bunk, now dressed in a tight tank top and black shorts so small they barely qualify to be called that. She holds her phone close to her face, doing a faux-pout as she takes several pictures.

"You shouldn't be using your phones," I say, even though I was guilty of doing the same thing earlier. "Save your batteries."

Krystal tugs off her earbuds. "What else are we going to do?"

"We could, you know, talk," I suggest. "You may find it hard to believe, but people actually did that before everyone spent all their time squinting at screens."

"I saw you talking to Theo after dinner," Miranda says, her voice wavering between innocence and accusation. "Is he, like, your boy-friend?"

"No. He's a—"

I truly don't know what to call Theo. Several different labels apply.

My friend? Not necessarily.

One of my first crushes? Probably.

The person I accused of doing something horrible to Vivian, Natalie, and Allison?

Definitely.

"He's an acquaintance," I say.

"Do you have a boyfriend?" Sasha asks.

"Not at the moment."

I have plenty of friends who are boys, most of them gay or too so-cially awkward to consider a romantic relationship. When I do date someone, it's not for very long. A lot of men like the idea of being in a relationship with an artist, but few actually get used to the reality of the situation. The odd hours, the self-doubt and stained hands that stink of oil paint more often than not. The last guy I dated—a dorky-cute accountant at a rival ad agency—managed to put up with it for four months before breaking things off.

Lately, my romantic life has consisted of occasional dalliances with a French sculptor when he happens to be in the city on business. We meet for drinks, conversation, sex made more passionate by how infrequent it is.

"Then how do you know Theo?" Krystal says.

"From when I was a camper here."

Miranda latches on to this news like a shark biting into a baby seal. A wicked grin widens across her face, and her eyes light up. It reminds me so much of Vivian that it causes a strange ache in my heart.

"So you were at Camp Nightingale before?" she says. "Must have been a long time ago."

Rather than be offended, I smile, impressed by the stealthiness of her insult. She's a sly one. Vivian would have loved her.

"It was," I say.

"Did you like it here?" Sasha says as bombastic music rises from her phone and exploding candy pieces reflect off the lenses of her glasses.

"At first. Then not so much."

"Why did you come back?" Krystal asks.

"To make sure you girls have a better time than I did."

"What happened?" Miranda says. "Something horrible?"

She leans forward, her phone temporarily discarded as she waits for my answer. It gives me an idea.

"Phones off," I say. "I mean it."

All three of them groan. Miranda's is the most dramatic as she, like the others, switches off her phone. I sit cross-legged on the floor, my back pressed against the edge of my bunk. I pat the spaces on either side of me until the girls do the same.

"What are we doing?" Sasha asks.

"Playing a game. It's called Two Truths and a Lie. You say three things about yourself. Two of them must be true. One is false. The rest of us have to guess the lie."

We played it a lot during my brief time in Dogwood, including the night of my arrival. The four of us were laying on our bunks in the darkness of the cabin, listening to nature's chorus of crickets and bullfrogs outside the window, when Vivian suddenly said, *Two Truths and a Lie, ladies. I'll start.*

She began to utter three statements, either assuming we already knew how the game was played or just not caring if we didn't.

One: I once met the president. His palm was sweaty. Two: My parents were going to get a divorce but then decided not to when my dad got elected. Three: Once, on vacation in Australia, I got pooped on by a koala.

Three, Natalie said. *You used it last year.*

No, I didn't.

You totally did, Allison said. *You told us the koala peed on you.*

That's how it went every night. The four of us in the dark. Sharing things we'd never reveal in the light of day. Constructing our lies so they'd sound real. It's how I learned that Natalie once kissed a field hockey teammate and that Allison tried to sabotage a matinee of *Les Misérables* by spilling grape juice on her mother's costume five minutes before curtain.

The game was Vivian's favorite. She said you could learn more about a person from their lies than their truths. At the time, I didn't believe her. I do now.

"I'll start," Miranda says. "Number one: I once made out with an altar boy in the confessional during Christmas mass. Number two: I read a hundred books a year, mostly mysteries. Number three: I once threw up after riding the Cyclone at Coney Island."

"The second one," Krystal says.

"Definitely," Sasha adds.

Miranda pretends to be annoyed, even though I can tell she's secretly pleased with herself. "Just because I'm smoking hot doesn't make me illiterate. Hot girls read."

"Then what's the lie?" Sasha says.

"I'm not telling." Miranda gives us an impish grin. "Let's just say I've never been to Coney Island, but I go to mass all the time."

Krystal goes next, telling us that her favorite superhero is Spider-Man; that her middle name is also Crystal, although spelled with a *C*; and that she, too, threw up after riding the Cyclone.

"Second one," we all say in unison.

"Was it that obvious?"

"I'm sorry," Miranda says, "but Krystal Crystal? No parent would be that cruel."

When it's time for her turn, Sasha nervously pushes her glasses higher onto her nose and wrinkles her brow in concentration. Clearly, she's not used to lying.

"Um, my favorite food is pizza," she says. "That's number one. Number two: My favorite animal is the pygmy hippopotamus. Three: I don't think I can do this. Lying's wrong, you guys."

"It's okay," I tell her. "Your honesty is noble."

"She's lying," Miranda says. "Right, Sasha? The third one is the lie?"

Sasha shrugs broadly, feigning innocence. "I don't know. You'll have to wait and see."

"Your turn, Emma," Krystal says. "Two truths and one lie."

I take a deep breath, stalling. Even though I knew this was coming, I can't think of suitable things to say. There's so much I could reveal about myself. So little I actually want to have exposed.

"One: My favorite color is periwinkle blue," I announce. "Two: I have been to the Louvre. Twice."

"You still need to give us a third one," Miranda says.

I stall some more, mulling the possibilities in my head, ultimately settling on something perched between fiction and fact.

"During the summer of my thirteenth year, I did something terrible."

"Totally the last one," Miranda says to nods of agreement from the others. "I mean, if you truly had done something terrible, you're not going to admit it during a game."

I smile, pretending that they're right. What none of them understand is that the point of the game isn't to fool others with a lie.

The goal is to trick them by telling the truth.

FIFTEEN YEARS AGO

My second night at Camp Nightingale was as sleepless as the first. Possibly worse. No electricity in the cabin meant no air conditioning, no fan, nothing to act as a shield against the late June heat. I awoke before dawn, sweaty and uncomfortable, a patch of warm moisture between my legs. When I dipped an index finger into my underwear to investigate, it came back stained with blood.

I was seized with panic, unsure what to do. I knew about menstruation, of course. The girls in my class had been given "the talk" the year before, much to the relief of my mother, who was spared such awkwardness. We were told why it would happen. We were told how it would happen. But my gym teacher—kindly, clueless Miss Baxter— had neglected to tell us what to do *when* it happened.

Ignorant and fearful, I crawled out of bed and awkwardly climbed the ladder to the bunk above mine, afraid to part my legs too much. Rather than ascend one foot at a time, I gripped the ladder's sides and lifted both feet up each rung in quick, bunk-shaking hops. By the time I reached the top, Vivian was already half-awake. Her eyes fluttered beneath a swath of blond hair that covered her face like a veil.

"What the hell are you doing?"

"I'm bleeding," I whispered.

"What?"

"I'm *bleeding*," I said again, stressing the second word as much as I could.

"Then go get a Band-Aid."

"It's between my legs."

Vivian's eyes opened fully as she swiped the hair from her face. "You mean—"

I nodded.

"Is this your first time?"

"Yes."

"Fuck." She sighed, partly out of annoyance and partly out of pity. "Come on. There are tampons in the latrine."

I followed Vivian outside, waddling like a duck down the mulch-covered path. At one point, she glanced back at me and said, "Quit walking like that. You look like an idiot."

Inside the latrine, Vivian hit the light switch by the door and led me to the nearest stall. Along the way, she grabbed a tampon from the dispenser attached to the wall. I sequestered myself inside the stall, Vivian whispering instructions from the other side of the door.

"I think I did it right," I whispered back. "I'm not sure."

"You'd know if you did it wrong."

I remained in the stall, humiliated, humbled, and not sure how to feel. Womanhood had officially arrived. The thought filled me with sadness. And fear. I began to cry all the tears I had managed to hold back the night before. I couldn't help it.

Vivian, of course, heard me and said, "Are you crying?"

"No."

"You totally are. I'm coming in."

Before I could protest, she was in the stall, closing the door behind her and nudging me aside with her hips so she could join me on the toilet seat.

"Come on," she said. "It's not that bad."

"How would you know? You're only, like, three years older than me."

"Which is a lifetime. Trust me. Just ask your older sister."

"I'm an only child."

"That's a shame," Vivian said. "Big sisters are awesome. At least mine was."

"I always wanted a sister," I said. "One who could teach me things."

"Like how to shove cotton up your twat each month?"

I laughed then, in spite of my fear and discomfort. In fact, I laughed so hard I momentarily forgot about both.

"That's better," Vivian said. "No more crying. I forbid it. And since I've already gone above and beyond the call of duty here, I am offering up my services as surrogate big sister. For the next six weeks, you can talk to me about any damn thing you want."

"Like boys?"

"Oh, I happen to have lots of experience in that area." She let out a rueful chuckle. "Trust me, Em, they're more trouble than they're worth."

"How much experience?"

"If you're asking if I've had sex, the answer's yes."

I shrank away from her, suddenly intimidated. I'd never met a girl who'd done *it* before.

"You look scandalized," Vivian said.

"But you're only sixteen."

"Which is old enough."

"Did you like it?"

Vivian flashed a wicked grin. "Loved it."

"And did you love him?"

"Sometimes it's not about love," she said. "Sometimes it's just about seeing someone and wanting him."

I thought of Theo just then. How handsome he was, with muscles in all the right places. How looking at him made me feel deliciously unbalanced. Only in that cramped stall with Vivian did I understand that I had experienced the first flush of desire.

The realization almost made me start to cry again. The only thing that stopped me was the sound of the latrine door squeaking open, followed by the slap of flip-flops on the tile floor. Vivian peeked through the crack in the stall door. She turned back to me with wide eyes and mouthed two words: *Holy shit.*

Who is it? I mouthed back.

Vivian answered in an excited whisper, "Theo!"

Water began to blast inside a shower stall. The one in the far corner of the latrine. I started to feel dizzy as my brain filled with the same stew of emotions I had felt the night before. Warmth.

Happiness. Shame. I was in the same room with a boy who was show-ering!

No, not a boy. A man.

And not just any man. Theo Harris-White.

"What do we do?" I whispered to Vivian.

She didn't answer. Instead, she moved. Out of the stall. Toward the door. Dragging me with her, the two of us incapable of making a silent retreat. Vivian giggled madly. I tripped and slammed a shoulder into the paper towel dispenser.

"Halt!" Theo called from the shower stall. "Who goes there?"

Vivian and I exchanged looks. I'm certain mine was deer-in-head-lights panicked. Hers was delighted.

"It's *Vivian*," she said coyly, drawing out the end of her name into an extra syllable.

"Hey, Viv."

Theo said it so casually that jealousy bloomed in my chest. How lucky Vivian was. To be known by Theo. To be greeted with such easy familiar-ity. Vivian noticed the envy in my eyes and added, "Emma's here, too."

"Emma who?"

"Emma Davis. She's new."

"Oh, that Emma. Cool, fashionably late Emma."

I let out a squeak, shocked and elated that Theo knew who I was. That he remembered leading me to Dogwood at the cusp of midnight. That he had noticed me.

Vivian elbowed me in the ribs, prompting me to meekly reply, "Hi, Theo."

"Why are you two up so early?" he asked.

I froze, one hand latched on to Vivian's wrist, silently begging her not to tell him the truth. I wasn't sure if a thirteen-year-old girl could die of embarrassment, but I certainly didn't want to find out.

"Um, going to the bathroom," she replied. "The real question is why you're here. Isn't there a shower in the Lodge?"

"The water pressure there sucks," Theo said. "Those pipes are an-cient. Which is why I haul ass out of bed extra early and shower here before any of you girls can stumble in."

"We were here first," Vivian said.

"And I'd be grateful if you'd finally leave so I can shower in peace."

Vivian looked down at me, smirking, and whispered, "He means jerk off."

It was so dirty and inappropriate that a laugh burst out of me. Theo heard it, of course, and said, "I mean it, guys. I can't stay in here all day."

"Fine," Vivian called back. "We're gone."

We departed in a torrent of giggles, me still clutching Vivian's wrist, the two of us twirling each other in the predawn. We spun until I grew dizzy and everything—the camp, the latrine, Vivian's face— became a glorious, happy blur.

Ten

It takes me hours to fall asleep. The silence is once again too oppressive for my Manhattanite ears. When I finally do manage to drift off, my sleep is stormy with bad dreams. In one of them—the most vivid—I see the long-haired woman from the photo found in Vivian's trunk. I stare into those distressed eyes until it dawns on me that it's not a picture I'm looking at but a mirror.

I'm the woman in the photograph. It's *my* absurdly long hair trailing to the floor, *my* dark-cloud eyes staring back at me.

The realization jolts me from sleep. I sit up, my breath heavy and my skin coated in a thin sheen of sweat. I'm also struck by the need to pee, which tugs me reluctantly from bed. Careful not to wake the others, I fumble in the darkness for my flashlight and those newly purchased boots, which I stuff my bare feet into once I'm outside. The flashlight remains off as I indulge myself with a view of the darkened sky above. I'd forgotten how different night is here. Clearer than in the city. Unmarred by light pollution and constant air traffic, the sky spreads out like a vast canvas painted midnight blue and studded with stars. The moon sits low on the horizon, already dipping into the forest to the west. It's such a beautiful sight that I get the urge to paint it. Which, I suppose, is progress.

Inside the latrine, I hit the light switch by the door. Fluorescent bulbs overhead hum to life as I head to the nearest stall. The same stall, coincidently, where Vivian led me on that fraught, frightening night.

To this day, it amazes me how I entered the latrine that night feeling one thing and left feeling the complete opposite. Going in, I was terrified by the ways my body could betray me. I departed riding a wave of laughter, still clutching Vivian. I remember how happy I was in that moment. How *alive* I had felt.

The memory of that time makes me sigh as I prepare to leave the stall. I'm stopped by the sound of the latrine door being opened. At first, I think it might again be Theo. A sad, silly thought, when you get right down to it. But it's not entirely out of the realm of possibility, seeing how we're both back here after all this time.

Instead, when I peek through the crack in the stall door, I see a girl. Long, bare limbs. A flash of blond hair. She stands at the row of sinks along the wall, checking her features in the mirror. I check them, too, shifting slightly in the stall to get a better view of her reflection. I spot dark eyes, a perky nose, a chin that tapers to a point.

A gasp leaps from my throat as I push out of the stall, calling her name.

"Vivian?"

I know I'm wrong even before the girl at the sink spins around, startled. Her hair's not as blond as I had thought. Her skin is more tanned. When she fully faces me, I see the diamond stud in her nose, winking at me.

"Who the hell is Vivian?" Miranda asks.

"No one," I start to say, stopping myself mid-lie. "A camper I knew."

"Well you scared the shit out of me."

I have no doubt. I scared myself as well. When I look down at my hands, I see I'm clutching the charm bracelet, the birds rattling. I force myself to let go.

"I'm sorry," I tell Miranda. "I'm confused. And tired."

"Can't sleep?"

I shake my head. "You?"

"Same."

She says it with forced casualness, which instantly tips me off that it's a lie. I'm good at that kind of thing. I was trained by the best.

"Is everything okay?"

Miranda gives me a nod that soon veers into a slow shake of her head. The movement highlights the redness of her eyes and the faint shimmering lines that run down her cheeks. Tears, recently dried.

"What happened?"

"I was just dumped," she says. "Which is a first, by the way. I do the dumping. Always."

I go to the sink next to her and turn on the tap. The water rushing from the faucet is blessedly cold. I run a paper towel under the stream and press it to my cheeks and neck. The feeling is delicious—crisp water against my skin evaporating in the heat, the vanished droplets leaving pinpricks in their wake.

Miranda watches me, silently seeking comfort. It occurs to me that's also part of my job. One I'm woefully unprepared for. Yet I know about heartbreak. All too well.

"You want to talk about it?"

"No," Miranda says, but then adds, "It's not like we were serious. We'd only dated for, like, a month. And I get it. I'm gone for six weeks. He wants to have fun this summer."

"But . . ."

"But he dumped me by text. What kind of jackass does that?"

"One who clearly doesn't deserve you," I say.

"But I really liked him." More tears glisten at the edges of her eyes. Yet she refuses to let them fall, instead using a fist to wipe them away. "It's usually the other way around. Normally I couldn't care less about guys who really like me. But he was different. You must think I'm, like, such a baby."

"I think you're hurt," I tell her. "But you'll feel better sooner than you think. By the time you get back from camp, he'll be with some—"

"Skank," Miranda says.

"Exactly. He'll be with some skank, and you'll wonder why you even liked him in the first place."

"And he'll regret dumping me." Miranda checks her reflection in the mirror, smiling at what she sees. "Because I'm going to look so hot with my camp tan."

"That's the spirit," I say. "Now, go back to the cabin. I'll be there in a minute."

Miranda heads to the door, giving me a wiggle-finger wave as she goes. Once she's gone, I stay behind to splash more cold water on my face and compose myself. I can't believe I'd momentarily thought she was Vivian. Not a road I want to go down again. Those days are over. No thanks to this place and all these memories that keep returning like a bad habit.

When I step outside, even the sky is familiar—a shade of grayish blue that I've used often in my paintings. Muted and melancholy and just the tiniest bit hopeful. It was that same color when Vivian and I bolted from the latrine in the wee hours of the morning, laughing with abandon, the rest of camp sleepy and silent. It had felt like we were the only people on earth.

But there had been a third person also awake, as Vivian soon reminded me.

Come here, she whispered, standing by the latrine, her elbow bent against its cedar wall. *There's something I* know *you'll want to see.*

With a grin, she gestured to two planks in the latrine's exterior wall. One was slightly crooked, leaving a crack big enough for light to trickle through it. Occasionally, the light would blink out a moment, blocked by someone on the other side of the wall.

That someone was Theo. Still in the shower. I heard the rush of water and his faint humming of a Green Day tune.

How do you know about this? I asked.

Vivian grinned from ear to ear. *Found it last year. No one knows about it but me.*

And you want me to spy on Theo?

No, Vivian replied. *I* dare *you to spy on him.*

But it's wrong.

Go on. Take a look. He'll never know.

I swallowed hard, my throat suddenly parched. I edged closer to the wall, wanting to get a better look, ashamed by that want. Even more shameful was my need to please Vivian.

It's fine, Vivian whispered. *When you get an opportunity to look, you're a fool not to take it.*

So I looked. Even though I knew it was wrong. I leaned in and placed an eye to the crack in the wall, at first seeing nothing but steam and the water-specked shower wall. Then Theo appeared. Skin slick. Body smooth in some places, matted with dark hair in others. It was the most beautiful, frightening thing I had ever seen.

I didn't watch him for very long. After a few seconds, the wrongness of the situation crashed over me and I turned away, red-faced and dizzy. Vivian stood behind me, shaking her head in such a way that I couldn't tell if she thought I had looked too much or not enough.

Well, how was it? she asked as we headed back to the cabin.

Gross, I said.

Right. She bumped my hip with hers. *Totally gross.*

I'm halfway to the cabins when a strange, sudden noise gets my attention. It's a rustling sound. Like someone walking through the grass to my left.

My thoughts turn instantly to Casey's story about the victims of Lake Midnight. When something appears on the edge of my vision, I think for a split second it's one of the ghosts, ready to drag me to a watery grave. Or one of the rumored survivors' grandson wielding an axe. I switch on the flashlight and swing it toward the noise.

It turns out to be a fox slinking toward the forest. Something is in its mouth—an unknown creature, now dead. All I can make out is blood-slicked fur. The fox pauses in the flashlight's glare, its body coiled, eyes glowing greenish white as it stares at me, deciding if I'm a threat. I'm not. Even the fox can see that. It trots on, unconcerned, a dead limb of whatever's in its mouth flopping as it vanishes into the forest.

I, too, resume walking, feeling a little bit frightened and a lot foolish. The mood persists as I reach Dogwood. Because that's when I notice something out of the ordinary as I reach for the doorknob.

A light. Tiny and red. Flaring like the tip of a cigarette.

It glows from the back wall of the cabin in front of ours. Red Oak, I think. Or maybe Sycamore. I aim the flashlight at it and see a black rectangle tucked into the nook where the two sides of the roof connect. A slim cord drips down the wall to the ground.

A surveillance camera. The kind you see in the corners of conve-
nience stores.

I turn off the flashlight and stare at the camera's lens, which shim-
mers slightly in the darkness. I don't move a muscle.

The red light snaps off.

I wait five seconds before waving the flashlight over my head.

The red light flicks on again, triggered by the motion. I assume it
does this every time someone enters or exits the cabin.

I have no idea how long the camera's been doing this. Or why it's
there. Or if there are others scattered throughout camp. All I know is
that Franny or Theo or someone involved with Camp Nightingale
decided it was a good idea to keep an eye on the cabin.

The irony of the situation unsettles me.

Fifteen years later, I'm the one being watched.

Eleven

Inside, I'm unable to go back to sleep. I change into my bathing suit and a brightly patterned silk robe bought during a long-ago trip to Cozumel. I then grab a towel from my trunk and slip quietly out of the cabin. On my way out the door, I will myself not to look at the camera. I don't want to see its red light switch on. Nor do I want to face the lens' prying eye. I walk past it quickly, face averted, pretending I don't know it's there, just in case someone is watching.

As I make my way to the lake, I sneak glances at the other cabins, checking for cameras on those as well. I don't see any. Nor do I see any on the handful of light poles that dully illuminate the pathway into the heart of the camp. Or in the trees.

I try not to let that worry me.

At the edge of Lake Midnight, I place the towel on the cracked dirt of the shore, drop the robe, and step gingerly into the water. The lake is cold, bracing. Not at all like the heated pool at the local Y where I swim each morning. Lake Midnight is murkier. Although the water's only up to my knees, my bare feet look blurred and slightly greenish. When I scoop some into my cupped hands, I see swirling specks of feathery algae.

Steeling myself with a deep breath, I dive under, kicking hard, arms extended in front of me. I emerge only when my chest starts to tighten, lungs swelling. I then start to cut my way across the lake. Strands of mist hover just above the surface, breaking apart when I burst through them. In the water, yellow perch flee my path, startled.

I stop once I reach the middle of the lake—probably a quarter mile from shore. I have no idea how deep the water is there. Maybe ten feet. Maybe a hundred. I think about how everything below me used to be dry land. A valley filled with trees and rocks and animals. All of it is still down there. The trees rotted by water. The stones fuzzy with algae. The animals stripped of their flesh by fish, now nothing but bones.

Not a comforting thought.

I think of the story Casey told me. The village still at the bottom of the lake, its skeletal inhabitants tucked in their beds.

That's even less comforting.

Paddling in place, I turn back toward camp. At this hour, it's quiet and still, bathed in pinkish light from the rising sun that peeks above the mountains to the east. The only activity I see is a solitary figure standing at the dock's edge, watching me.

Even from this distance, I know the figure is Becca Schoenfeld. I see the splash of color from the scarf circling her neck and can make out the shape of her camera as she lifts it to her face.

Becca remains on the dock as I swim back to shore, her camera poised. I try not to feel self-conscious as the staccato clicks of the shutter echo across the water. Instead, I swim harder, increasing my strokes. If Becca's going to watch, then I'll give her something worth watching.

That's another, different lesson I learned in this lake.

I get to my feet a few yards from shore and wade the rest of the way. Becca has left the dock and is now directly in front of me, gesturing for me to stop. I indulge her, standing shin-deep in the water as she clicks off a few more shots.

"Sorry," she says once she's finished. "The light was so perfect, I couldn't resist. Such a beautiful sunrise."

She holds the camera in front of me as I dry off, scrolling through the photos. Of the last one, she says, "This one's the keeper."

In the picture, I've risen from the lake, water streaming down my body, backlit by the sunrise. I think Becca was going for something fierce and empowering. A woman emerging victorious from the surf, now determined to conquer land. But instead of fierce, I simply look lost. As if I've just woken up in the water, confused by how I'd gotten there. It makes me feel so self-conscious that I quickly reach for my robe and wrap it tight around me.

"Please delete that."

"But it looks great."

"Fine," I say. "Just promise me it won't end up on the cover of *National Geographic*."

We settle onto the grass and stare out at the water, which reflects the pinkish-orange sky so perfectly it's hard to tell which is which. At least Becca was right about that. The sunrise is indeed beautiful.

"So you're an artist," she says. "I read about your gallery show."

"And I've seen your photographs."

Having stated the obvious, we settle into an awkward silence. I pretend to adjust the sleeves of my robe. Becca fiddles with her camera strap. We both keep an eye on the sunrise, which has now gained a few streaks of gold.

"I can't believe I'm back here," Becca eventually says. "I can't believe *you're* back here."

"You and me both."

"Listen, I'm sorry for acting weird yesterday. I saw you in the mess hall and momentarily freaked out. I don't know why."

"I do," I say. "Seeing me brought back a hundred different memories. Some of which you weren't prepared to face."

"Exactly."

"It happens all the time to me," I admit. "Almost nonstop. Everywhere I look, a memory seems to be lurking."

"I'm assuming Franny lured you back," Becca says.

I nod, even though it's not entirely the truth.

"I volunteered," Becca says. "I mean, I already knew Franny was going to ask. She somehow managed to track me down during one of my rare returns to New York and invited me to lunch. As soon as she started talking about Camp Nightingale, I knew what she had planned. So I jumped at the chance."

"I took a little more convincing."

"Not me. For the past three years, I've been living out of a suitcase. Staying in one place for six weeks definitely had its appeal." Becca stretches out on the grass, as if to prove how relaxed she truly is. "I don't even mind that I'm bunking with three teenagers. It's worth it if I can get a camera into their hands and possibly inspire them. Plus, this feels like a vacation after some of the horrible shit I've seen."

She lifts her chin to the sunrise and closes her eyes. In that light clenching of her eyelids, I can see that she, too, is haunted by the unknown. The only difference between us is that she's returned to Camp Nightingale to forget. I'm here to remember.

"Yesterday, when I saw you in the mess hall, I wanted to ask you something."

"Let me guess," Becca says. "It's about that summer."

I give a curt nod. "Do you remember much?"

"About the summer or the... ?"

She doesn't finish her sentence. It's almost like she's afraid to utter that final word. I'm not.

"The disappearance," I say. "Did you notice anything strange the night before it happened? Or maybe the morning I realized they were gone?"

A memory arrives. A bad one. Me at the lake, telling Franny that the girls were missing as other campers gathered around. Becca stood in the crowd, watching it all unfold through her camera, the shutter clicking away.

"I remember you," she says. "How frantic and scared you were."

"Other than that, you don't recall anything out of the ordinary?"

"Nope." The word comes out too fast and pitched too high. Like a chirp. "Nothing."

"And how well did you know the girls in my cabin?"

"Allison, Natalie, and Vivian?"

"Yeah," I say. "You had all spent the previous summer here. I thought you might have known them."

"I didn't. Not really."

"Not even Vivian?" I think of Becca's warning my first morning at camp. *Don't be fooled. She'll turn on you eventually.* "I thought the two of you might have been friends."

"I mean, I knew her," Becca says. "Everyone here knew Vivian. And everyone had an opinion."

"What was the general consensus?"

"Honestly? That she was kind of a bitch."

I flinch at her tone. It's so surprisingly harsh that no other reaction is appropriate. Becca sees it happen and says, "I'm sorry. That was cruel."

"It was," I say, my voice quiet.

I expect Becca to backtrack a bit or maybe offer a better apology. Instead, she doubles down. Squaring her shoulders, she flashes me a hard look and says, "Come on, Emma. You don't need to pretend around me. Vivian doesn't automatically become a good person just because of what happened to her. I mean, you of all people should know that."

She stands and brushes dirt from her shorts. Then she walks away, slowly, silently, not looking back. I remain where I am, contemplating the two truths Becca just revealed to me.

The first is that she's right. Vivian wasn't a good person. Vanishing into thin air doesn't change that.

The second is that Becca remembers much more than she'd like to admit.

FIFTEEN YEARS AGO

The beach at Camp Nightingale—a combination of sand and pebbles strewn along a patch of Lake Midnight decades earlier—felt as uncomfortable as it looked. Not even spreading two towels on top of each other could completely dull the prodding of the stones below. Still, I grinned and tried to bear it as I watched waves of campers tiptoe into the water.

Although all four of us had changed into our bathing suits, only Natalie and Allison joined the others in the lake. Natalie swam like the natural athlete she was, using hard, long strokes to easily make it to the string of foam buoys marking the area no one was allowed to swim past. Allison was more of a show-off, somersaulting in the water like a synchronized swimmer.

I remained on shore, nervous in my modest one-piece swimsuit. Vivian sat behind me, coating my shoulders with Coppertone, its coconut scent sickeningly sweet.

"It's criminal how pretty you are," she said.

"I don't feel pretty."

"But you are," Vivian said. "Hasn't your mother ever told you that?"

"My mother gives me as little attention as possible. Same thing with my dad."

Vivian clucked with sympathy. "That sounds just like my parents. I'm surprised I didn't die of neglect as a newborn. But my sister and I learned how to fend for ourselves. She's the one who made me realize how pretty I was. Now I'll do the same for you."

"I'm far from pretty."

"You *are*," Vivian insisted. "And in a year or two, you'll be gorgeous. I can tell. Do you have a boyfriend back home?"

I shook my head, knowing how I was all but invisible to the boys in my neighborhood. I was among the last of the late bloomers. Flat as cardboard. No one paid attention to cardboard.

"That'll change," Vivian said. "You'll snag yourself a hottie like Theo."

She gestured to the lifeguard stand a few feet away, where Theo sat in red swim trunks, the whistle roped around his neck nestled in his chest hair. Every time I looked at him, which was often, I tried not to think about that morning at the latrine. Watching him. Wanting him. Instead, it was all I could think about.

"Why aren't you in the water?" he called down to us.

"No reason," Vivian said.

"I don't know how to swim," I said.

A grin spread across Theo's face. "That's quite a coincidence. One of my goals today is to teach someone."

He hopped down from the lifeguard stand and, before I could protest, took my hand and led me to the water. I paused when my feet touched the mossy rocks at the lake's edge. They were slick, which made me worry that I'd slip and plunge under. The dirty look of the water only heightened my anxiety. Bits of brown stuff floated just below the surface. When some touched my ankle, I recoiled.

Theo tightened his grip around my hand. "Relax. A little algae never hurt anyone."

He guided me deeper into the lake, the water rising against me in increments. To my knees. Then to my thighs. Soon I was up to my waist, the chill of the water leaving me momentarily breathless. Or maybe it wasn't the water. Maybe it was the way Theo's broad shoulders glowed in the late June sun. Or the way his crooked smile widened when I took another, unprompted step deeper into the water.

"Awesome, Em," he said. "You're doing great. But you need to relax more. The water is your friend. Let it hold you up."

Without warning, he slid behind me and scooped me up in his arms. One wrapped around my back. The other slid behind my knees. The areas where his skin touched mine became instantly hot, as if electricity coursed through them.

"Close your eyes," he said.

I closed them as he lowered me into the lake until I couldn't tell the difference between his arms and the water. When I opened my eyes, I saw him standing next to me, arms crossed. I was on my own, letting the water hold me up.

Theo grinned, his eyes sparkling. "You, my dear, are floating."

Just then, noise rippled across the lakes. Splashing. Urgent and panicked. A couple of girls in the deep end began to shriek, their arms flapping against the water like ducks unable to take flight. Beyond them, I saw a pair of hands rising and falling from the lake's surface, waving frantically, water flinging off the fingertips. A face poked out of the drink, gasped, slipped back under.

Vivian.

Theo left my side and surged toward her. Without him near me, I sank into the water, dropping until I hit the lake bed. I began to paddle, guided by instinct more than anything else, clawing at the water until my nose and mouth broke the surface. I continued to paddle and kick until, lo and behold, I was swimming.

I kept at it, looking across the water first to Vivian, still flailing, and then to Natalie and Allison, who bobbed in place, frozen with fear, their faces suddenly pale. I watched them watch Theo as he reached Vivian and clamped an arm around her waist. He swam to shore that way, not stopping until both of their backs were on the pebble-specked beach.

Vivian coughed once, and a bubble of lake water spurted from her throat. Tears streamed down her crimson cheeks.

"I-I don't know what happened," she said, gasping. "I went under and couldn't come up. I thought I was going to die."

"You would have if I hadn't been here," Theo said, anger peeking through his exhaustion. "Jesus, Viv, I thought you could swim."

Vivian sat up and shook her head, still crying. "I thought I'd try after watching you teach Emma. You made it look so easy."

Standing a few yards away from them was Becca. Her camera hung from her neck even though she was wearing a bathing suit. She clicked off a picture of Vivian sprawled on shore. Then she turned to the lake, picking me out of the crowd of still-stunned campers paddling in the water. She smiled and mouthed four words, each of them silent but unmistakable.

I told you so.

Twelve

I remain on the beach until reveille blasts from the ancient speaker atop the mess hall. The music rushes past me and across the lake, its sound skimming the water on its way to the far shore. The first full day of camp has begun.

Again.

Rather than battle a horde of teenage girls for space in the latrine, I shuffle to the mess hall, shy in my damp robe and clacking flip-flops. It's mostly empty, thank God. Nobody but me and the kitchen workers. One of them—a guy with dark hair and a patchy goatee—checks me out for half a second before turning away.

I ignore him and grab a doughnut, a banana, and a cup of coffee. The banana is consumed quickly. The doughnut not so much. Each bite brings a flash of Vivian squinting, her lips pursed. Her disapproving look. I set down the doughnut, sigh, pick it up, and shove what's left into my mouth. I wash it down with the coffee, pleased with my fifteen-years-too-late defiance.

My walk back to Dogwood is spent swimming against the tide of campers making their way to the mess hall. All of them are freshly scrubbed, trailing scents behind them. Baby powder. Noxzema. Shampoo that smells like strawberries.

One scent cuts through the others. Something thick and flowery. Perfume.

But not just any old perfume.

Obsession.

Vivian wore it, spritzing it on her neck and wrists twice a day. Once in the morning. Once in the afternoon. The scent used to fill the cabin, lingering there long after she had departed.

Now I get that same feeling. Like she's just been here, leaving only her scent behind. I spin among the stream of girls, searching for her in the departing crowd, knowing she's not there but looking anyway. I reach for my bracelet and tap a pewter beak. Just in case.

The girls surge forward, taking the perfume scent with them. Left behind is a clammy sensation on the back of my neck. It makes me shiver as I stop into Dogwood to grab my clothes for the day. I sniff the air for traces of perfume, detecting nothing but the tang of someone's deodorant.

In the latrine, I spot Miranda, Krystal, and Sasha amid the morning stragglers at the sinks. Miranda stares in the mirror, fussing with her hair. Beside her, Sasha says, "Can we go now? I'm *starving.*"

"Just a second." Miranda gives her hair one last flip. "There. Now we may go."

I give them a wave on my way to the shower stalls, all but one of which are in use. The empty stall is the last one in the row. Like the others, it's a cubicle of cedar walls and a door of smoked glass. A pinpoint of white light glows in the center of that door. Behind me, a similar light peeks through a crack in the cedar wall.

Alarm flares in my chest, calming a second later once I understand what's happening. The white glow is sunlight. Its source is a minuscule crack in the shower wall. The same crack I peered through to spy on Theo fifteen years ago.

I let out a breath, feeling both foolish for not realizing it sooner and relieved that it's not something worse, like another camera. One is enough to make me seriously paranoid. So much so that I consider waiting for another stall to open up. I decide against it for the simple reason that I'm already inside this one with the water running. And thanks to a morning of heavy use, it isn't getting any warmer.

Besides, Vivian was the only person who knew about that crack. She told me so herself.

So I stay where I am, showering as fast as possible. I give my hair a quick shampoo and an even quicker rinse, closing my eyes as the soapy water cascades down my face. I enjoy that moment of temporary blindness. It allows me to pretend, just for a moment, that I'm thirteen again and experiencing Camp Nightingale for the very first time. That Vivian, Natalie, and Allison are safe within the confines of Dogwood. That the events of fifteen years ago never happened.

It's a nice feeling. One that makes me want to linger under the shower's spray. But the water keeps getting colder, turning from luke-warm to the wrong side of chilly. In a minute or two, it'll be as cold as Lake Midnight.

I finish rinsing my hair and open my eyes.

The point of light on the door is gone.

I spin around, frantically checking the shower wall behind me. No light peeks through the crack. It's gone, eclipsed by something outside.

No, not something.

Someone.

Right on the other side the wall.

Watching me.

I yelp and rush to the door, fumbling for my towel and robe in the process. By the time I'm pushing my way out of the stall, the light has reappeared, both through the wall and onto the door as it swings open. Whoever was there is now gone.

That doesn't stop me from yanking on my robe and clutching it tight around me. I rush through the now-empty latrine, bursting through the door with the hope of catching whoever had been watching me.

No one is outside. The entire vicinity is deserted. The closest people I see are two campers more than a hundred yards away. Late for breakfast, they hurry to the mess hall, ponytails bobbing.

I'm the only one here.

Just to be safe, I do a quick, awkward circle around the building, seeing nothing. By the time I'm back at the latrine door, I start to wonder if I'm mistaken and that what I saw was merely someone lean-ing against the building, obliviously covering the crack in the wall.

Yet that explanation doesn't quite make sense. If it had been un-intentional, then the person responsible wouldn't have left the moment I realized they were there. They would be here still, no doubt wondering why I've rushed outside dripping wet, soap remnants sticky on my skin.

So I think of other possibilities. A low-flying bird swooping past the latrine. Or maybe those late-for-breakfast campers rushing by. There's even a chance it might not have been anything at all. I try to estimate how long the light through the crack was blocked. Not long. A fraction of a second at most. My eyes had been closed a lot longer than that. When I opened them again, it would have taken a second or two for them to adjust to the dimness of the shower stall. Maybe that's all it was—my vision catching up to reality.

By the time I'm back at Dogwood, I've concluded that's what it was. A trick of the light. A brief optical illusion.

At least that's what I force myself to believe.

Lying to myself.

It's the only falsehood I allow.

The first painting lesson of the summer is held outside, away from the arts and crafts building and its crowd of campers. Despite reassuring myself that it never happened, I remain shaken by my experience in the shower. Paranoia clings to me like cold sweat, making me hyper-alert to even the briefest of glances.

When Sasha suggests we paint the lake, I embrace the idea. It temporary soothes my anxiety while giving the dozen girls who arrived for the lesson something better to paint than the still life I had planned.

Now they stand at their easels, which have been carried to the lawn behind the Lodge, facing the lake. Palettes in hand, all of them contemplate their blank canvases, slightly nervous, fingers absently fiddling with the brushes poking from their cargo shorts. I'm nervous, too, and not just from the stress of the morning. The way the girls stare at me, seeking guidance, is intimidating. Marc was right. This is definitely not in my wheelhouse.

It helps slightly that the girls from Dogwood are here, including Krystal with her promised sketchpad and a set of charcoal pencils. They're familiar enough to give me a boost of confidence before I begin.

"The assignment this morning is to paint what you see," I announce. "Just look out at the lake and paint it as only you see it. Use whatever colors you want. Use any techniques you want. This isn't school. You won't be graded. The only person you need to please is you."

As the girls paint, I walk behind them, checking their progress. Watching them paint calms me. Some—such as Sasha and her meticulously clean lines—even show promise. Others, like Miranda's defiantly blue brushstrokes, do not. But at least they're painting, which is more than I've done for the past six months.

When I reach Krystal, I see that she's sketched a superhero in tight spandex and a flowing cape standing before an easel. The hero's face is my own. Her muscular body most definitely is not.

"I think I'm going to name her Monet," Krystal says. "Painter by day, crime fighter by night."

"What's her superpower?"

"I haven't decided yet."

"I'm sure you'll think of something."

Class ends when a bell clangs from the mess hall, signaling lunchtime. The girls put down their brushes and scurry off, leaving me alone to gather up their canvases and easels. I move the canvases first, carrying them back to the arts and crafts building two by two so as not to smudge the still-wet paint. Then I return for the easels, finding them already in the process of being collected.

The gatherer is the maintenance man I saw fixing the roof of the arts and crafts building when I arrived. He's come from the toolshed on the edge of the lawn. Its door sits open, offering a glimpse of lawn mower, a handsaw, chains hanging on the wall.

"I figured you could use some help," he says.

His voice is gruff, thickened by a trace of Maine accent.

"Thanks." I hold out my hand. "I'm Emma, by the way."

Instead of shaking my hand, the man nods and says, "I know."

He doesn't tell me how he knows this. He doesn't need to. He was here fifteen years ago. He knows the score.

"You were here before, right?" I say. "I recognized you when I arrived."

The man folds another easel, drops it onto a growing pile of them. "Yep."

"What did you do in the time the camp was closed?"

"I don't work for the camp. I work for the family. Doesn't matter if the camp is open or closed, I'm still here."

"I see."

Not wanting to feel useless, I collapse the last remaining easel and hand it to him. He adds it to the stack and scoops up all of them at once, carrying six under each arm. Impressive, considering I could have only managed one or two.

"Can I help carry some of those?" I say.

"I got 'em."

I step out of his way, revealing several splotches of paint that mar the grass. White and cerulean and a few dots of crimson that unnervingly resemble drops of blood. The maintenance man sees them and grunts his disapproval.

"Your girls made a mess," he says.

"It happens when you're painting. You should see my studio,"

I give him a smile, hoping it will appease him. When it doesn't, I remove the rag hanging from my back pocket and dab at the grass. "This should do the trick," I say, even though it does the opposite, spreading the paint in widening smears.

The man grunts again and says, "Mrs. Harris-White doesn't like messes."

Then he's off, carting away the easels as if they weigh nothing at all. I remain where I am, attempting a few more futile dabs at the grass. When that doesn't work, I simply pluck the blades from the parched earth and toss them into the air. They catch the dull breeze and scatter, rolling on the wind and out over the lake.

Thirteen

Before heading to lunch, I return to the arts and crafts building to root through Casey's supplies. I don't find what I'm looking for among the bins of wood glue and colored markers, so I head to Paige's pottery station. A dime-size chunk of wet clay sits on one of the pottery wheels. Perfect for what I have planned.

"Shouldn't you be at lunch?"

I whirl around to see Mindy in the doorway, her arms crossed, head tilted. She gives me a too-big smile as she steps inside. Pretend friendliness.

I smile, too. Pretending right back. "I had some things to finish up in here."

"You do pottery as well?"

"I was just admiring what you've done to the place," I say, curling my fingers around the bit of clay to hide it from her. I'd rather not explain to Mindy what I intend to do with it. She's suspicious enough as it is. "It looks incredible."

Mindy nods her thanks. "It was a lot of work and a lot of money."

"It really shows."

The extra compliment works. Mindy's gritted-teeth smile melts into something that almost resembles a human expression. "Thanks," she says. "And I'm sorry for acting so suspicious. I'm just on high alert now that camp's in full swing."

"No worries. I get it."

"Everything needs to go as smooth as possible," Mindy adds. "Which is why you should probably get to the mess hall now. If campers don't see you there, they'll think they can start skipping lunch, too. We lead by example, Emma."

First, I got a warning from the grounds keeper. Now here's one from Mindy. And it definitely is a warning. I'm supposed to tread lightly and not make any messes. In short, do the opposite of what I did last time I was here.

"Sure," I say. "Going there now."

It's a lie. But a justifiable one.

Instead of heading to the mess hall, I make my way to the latrine. A few stragglers mill about the front door, waiting for friends to accompany them to lunch. After they're all gone, I head to the side of the building, seeking out the crack on the exterior wall. Once I find it, I stuff a bit of clay between the two planks, covering the crack.

The irony of the act isn't lost on me. Fifteen years ago, I'd peered through this very crack, watching Theo without his knowledge or consent. While I'd like to blame that on youth and naiveté, I can't. I was thirteen. Old enough to know that spying on Theo was wrong. Yet I did it anyway.

Now no one can look inside. One act of atonement down. Many more to go.

When I finally do reach the mess hall, I find Theo waiting for me outside, a wicker basket at his feet. It's an unexpected sight. One that makes me irrationally think the mere memory of my long-ago transgression summoned his appearance. That after all these years, he somehow found out I had watched him. I stop a few steps short of him, bracing for confrontation. Instead, Theo announces, "I'm going on a picnic. And I thought you might like to come along."

"What's the occasion?"

He nods toward the mess hall doors. "Does one need a special occasion to skip the horror of whatever's being served in there?"

He says it with his brows arched, aiming for levity. But the same tension from last night is still present. Theo feels it, too. I can see it in the apprehensive twitch at the corners of his smile. A knot of guilt twists in my chest. Now there's no doubt he's forgiven me. What I don't understand is why.

Still, a picnic lunch does sound appealing. Especially because Mindy wouldn't like the idea one bit.

"Count me in," I say. "My taste buds thank you."

Theo lifts the basket and leads me away from the mess hall. Rather than go to the sloped lawn behind the Lodge, where I assumed we'd head, he instead guides me past the cabins and latrine and into the woods.

"Where are you taking me?"

Theo grins back at me before entering the forest. "Someplace special."

Although there's no path for us to follow, he walks with purpose, as if he knows exactly where he's going. I trail behind him, stepping over downed branches and crunching through fallen leaves. The idea of being led into the woods by Theo would have made my thirteen-year-old heart sing. Even now my pulse quickens a bit as I ponder the strange possibility that Theo might be interested in me. Young Emma would certainly think he was. Cynical, adult me highly doubts it. He couldn't. Not after everything I've done. Yet here we are, whisking through the forest.

Eventually, we come to a small clearing so unexpected that I force myself to blink just to make sure it's real. The area is a small circle cleared of dead leaves and underbrush. In its place is a patch of soft grass punctuated in spots by clusters of wild flowers. A halo of sunlight pours through the gap in the trees, catching the pollen drifting in the air and making it look as though a light snow is falling. A round table sits in the middle of the clearing, similar to the one where Franny and I had lunch in her fantastical greenhouse. And just like at that months-ago meal, Franny is present, already seated at the table with a napkin across her lap.

"There you are," she says with a warm smile. "Just in time, too. I'm positively famished."

"Hi," I say, hoping I don't sound as surprised as I feel. More heat spreads across my cheeks—a combination of disappointment that this picnic isn't some romantic gesture on Theo's part and embarrassment that I ever thought it might be. I feel something else, too. Apprehension. Franny's surprise appearance tells me that this isn't an impromptu picnic. Something else is going on.

Not helping is the presence of six marble statues arranged on the outskirts of the space, almost tucked into the trees, like silent witnesses. Each statue is of a woman in artful stages of half-dress. They're frozen in unnatural poses, their arms raised, hands open, as if waiting for small birds to perch on their delicate fingers. Others carry baskets overflowing with grapes, ripe apples, sheaths of wheat.

"Welcome to the sculpture garden," Franny says. "One of my grandfather's more fanciful ideas."

"It's lovely," I say, even though the opposite is true. While beautiful from a distance, the clearing gives off a creepier vibe once I'm seated in its center. The statues bear the scars of years spent exposed to the elements. The folds of their togas are crusted with dirt. Some have cracks running up their sides and chips in their otherwise flawless skin. One statue's face is stained by moss. All have blank eyes. It's as if they've been blinded. Punished for seeing something they shouldn't have.

"You don't need to be polite," Theo says as he places the picnic basket on the table and starts to unpack it. "It's creepy as hell. At least, I think so. I hated coming here as a kid."

"I'll admit it's not to everyone's taste," Franny says. "But my grandfather was proud of it. And so it must remain."

She gives a helpless shrug, drawing my attention to the statue directly behind her. Its face is exquisite, with fine-boned features and a daintily elegant chin. Yet whoever sculpted it had added an extra layer of emotion to the statue's face. Its lifeless eyes are wider than they should be and sit beneath a pair of dramatically arched brows. Its rosebud lips are parted ever-so-slightly, either in ecstasy or in surprise. I suspect it's the latter. The statue looks, for lack of a better word, startled.

"Lunch is served," Theo announces, snapping my attention from the statue to the table. A plate bearing an open-faced sandwich of smoked salmon heaped with crème fraiche, capers, and dill now sits in front of me. Definitely not what the others are currently being served in the mess hall. When Theo pours me a glass of prosecco, I take an extra-long sip in an effort to calm my nerves.

"Now that we're all cozy," Franny says, "I think it's time to reveal why we've brought you here under such mysterious circumstances. I thought it might be a good idea to have our conversation in relatively privacy."

"Conversation?"

"Yes," Franny says. "There's an important matter Theo and I would like to discuss with you."

"Oh?" I say it while cutting into my sandwich, pretending to be calm when I'm anything but. Apprehension clings to my insides. "What is it?"

"The camera outside your cabin," Franny says.

I freeze, a forkful of smoked salmon poised halfway to my mouth.

"We know you've seen it," Theo says. "We watched the footage this morning."

"To be completely frank, we were hoping it wouldn't be noticed," Franny adds. "But now that it has, I do hope you'll give us the chance to explain why it's there."

I set my fork on my plate. Any appetite I might have had is gone. "I'd certainly appreciate one. I didn't see any others around the camp."

"That's because it's the only one, dear," Franny says.

"How long has it been there?"

"Since last evening," Theo says. "Ben installed it during the campfire."

At first, the name is unfamiliar to me. Then I remember the grounds keeper. No wonder he was acting so strangely when gathering up those easels.

"Why did he put it there?"

"To keep an eye on Dogwood, of course," Franny says.

Since we're on the topic of surveillance, I'm tempted to tell her that someone might have watched me take a shower this morning. I don't because I'm not entirely sure there was. It would also require me to reveal just how I know about the crack in the shower wall. That's a conversation I'd like to avoid at all costs.

Instead, I say, "That doesn't answer my question."

But it does, actually. Only the answer is an unspoken one, left for me to infer on my own. The camera is trained on Dogwood because I'm staying there. That's why it was installed last night. They didn't know it was the cabin I'd be occupying until after I'd arrived.

Franny looks at me from across the table, her head tilted, concern glowing in her green eyes. "You're upset. And probably offended. I can't say I blame you. We should have told you immediately."

The slight throb of a headache presses against my temples. I chalk it up to confusion and too much hastily swallowed prosecco on an empty stomach. But Franny is right. I *am* upset and offended.

"You still haven't told me why it's there," I say. "Are you spying on me?"

"That's putting it a bit harshly. *Spying.*" Franny smacks her lips in distaste, as if just saying the word has soured her tongue. She takes a tiny sip of prosecco to wash it away. "I like to think it's there for your own protection."

"From what?"

"Yourself."

It's Theo who answers. Hearing it from him forces a huff of surprise from my lungs.

"Back when I was getting ready to reopen the camp, we did background checks on everyone staying here for the summer," Franny says, exhibiting more gentleness than her son. "I didn't think it was necessary, but my lawyers insisted on it. Instructors. Kitchen staff. Even the campers. We found nothing to be concerned about. Except with you."

"I don't understand," I say, when really I do. I know what's coming next.

A pained expression crosses Franny's face. It strikes me as exaggerated and not entirely sincere. Like she wants me to know just how much it hurts to utter whatever she's about to say.

"We know, Emma," she tells me. "We know what happened to you after you left Camp Nightingale."

Fourteen

I don't talk about it.

Not even with Marc.

The only other people who know what happened are my parents, who are all too happy to avoid discussing those horrible six months when I was fourteen.

I was still in school when it began. A gangly freshman desperately trying to fit in with all the other prep school girls. It wasn't easy. Not after what had happened that summer. Everyone knew about the disappearance at Camp Nightingale, giving me the kind of notoriety no one wanted anything to do with. My friends started pulling away from me. Even Heather and Marissa. My life became a form of solitary confinement. Weekends spent in my room. Cafeteria lunches consumed alone.

Just when it seemed like things couldn't get any worse, I saw the girls and everything truly went to hell.

It was during a class trip to the Metropolitan Museum of Art. A hundred schoolgirls tittering through the halls in a parade of plaid skirts and haughty insecurity. I had broken off from the group in the wing of nineteenth-century European paintings, roaming the labyrinth of galleries, dazzled by all the Gauguins and Renoirs and Cézannes.

One of the galleries was empty, save for three girls standing in front of a work by Gustave Courbet. *Young Ladies of the Village*. A massive landscape painted mostly in greens and golds and populated by four women. Three of them appear to be in their late teens. The young ladies of the title, casually elegant with their afternoon dresses, bonnets, and parasols. The other girl is younger. A peasant. Barefoot, kerchief on her head, apron around her waist.

I stared, but not at the painting. I was more interested in the girls studying it. They wore white dresses. Plain and subdued. They stood straight-backed and completely still, as poised as the young women Courbet had created. It was almost as if they had just emerged from the painting itself and were now curious to see how it looked without them.

It's beautiful, one of the girls said. *Don't you think so, Em?*

She didn't turn around. She didn't need to. I knew in my bones that it was Vivian, just as I knew the other two were Natalie and Allison. I didn't care if it was actually them or their ghosts or figments of my imagination. Their presence was enough to terrify me.

You seem surprised, Vivian said. *Guess you never pegged us as art lovers.*

I couldn't summon the nerve to reply. Fear had silenced me. It took all the strength I could muster to take a step backward, trying to put some distance between us. Once I managed that first tiny step, others followed in quick succession. My legs propelled me out of the gallery, saddle shoes tapping loudly against the parquet floor. Once I was safely out, I risked a glance behind me.

Vivian, Natalie, and Allison were still there, only now they were facing me. Before I could run away completely, Vivian winked and said, *See you soon.*

And I did. A few days later during a matinee of *Jersey Boys* my mother dragged me to during one of her rare instances of attentiveness. When she ducked out a minute before intermission to secure a prime spot at the lobby bar, Vivian took her place. The house lights rose, and there she was, once again in the white dress.

This show sucks, she said.

I didn't dare look at her. I stayed frozen in my seat, eyes fixed to the distant stage in front of me. Vivian remained where she was, a white blur on the edge of my vision.

You're not real. My voice was a murmur, pitched low so that no one else could hear it. *You don't exist.*

Come on, Em. You and I both know you don't believe that.

Why are you doing this?

Doing what?

Haunting me.

You know exactly why.

Vivian didn't sound angry when she said it. There was no accusation in her voice. If anything, she sounded sad. So desperately sad that a sob rose in my throat. I croaked it out through trembling lips, tears stinging the corners of my eyes.

Spare me the tears, Vivian said. *We both know they're not real.*

Then she was gone. I waited a full five minutes before summoning the courage to leave my seat and go to the ladies' room. I spent the second act hiding in a stall. After the show, I told my mother I wasn't feeling well. She was too buzzed on overpriced vodka tonics to realize I was lying.

The girls appeared frequently after that. I saw Natalie standing on the opposite side of the street as I walked to school. Allison stared at me across the cafeteria one day at lunch. All three roamed the lingerie department at Macy's as I tried to pick out a bra to accommodate my suddenly blossoming frame. I never said a word about it to anyone. I feared that no one would believe me.

It could have gone on like that for months if I hadn't woken up one night to find Vivian sitting on the edge of my bed.

I'm curious, Em, she said. *Did you really think you could get away it?*

I woke my parents with my screaming. They burst into my room to find me cowering under the covers, completely alone. I spent the rest of the night explaining that I kept seeing the girls, that they were haunting me, that I feared they wanted to do me harm. I talked for hours, most of what I said incoherent even to myself. My parents dismissed it as a vividly bad dream. I knew otherwise.

After that, I refused to leave the apartment. I skipped school. Feigned illness. Spent three days locked in my room, unwilling to shower or let a toothbrush touch my filmed-over teeth. My parents had no choice but to take me to a psychiatrist, who declared that the sightings of the girls were in fact hallucinations.

I was officially diagnosed with schizophreniform disorder, a kissing cousin to schizophrenia itself. The doctor made it clear that what happened at Camp Nightingale didn't cause the disorder. That particular chemical imbalance had always been there, lightly percolating in the recesses of my brain. All the girls' disappearance did was set it free like lava bursting forth from a long-dormant volcano.

The doctor also stressed that schizophreniform disorder was mostly temporary. He said those who suffered from it usually got better with the right treatment. Which is how I came to spend six months in a mental-health facility that specialized in treating teenage girls.

The place was clean, comfortable, professional. There was no raving insanity on display. No *Girl, Interrupted*–style drama. It was just a bunch of girls my age trying their best to get better. And I did, thanks to a combination of therapy, medication, and old-fashioned patience.

That hospital was where I first started painting. Art therapy, it was called. They set me down in front of a blank canvas, stuck a brush in my hand, and told me to paint my feelings. I sliced the canvas with a streak of blue. The instructor, a spindly woman with gray hair and a gentle demeanor, took the canvas away, replaced it with a fresh one, and said, *Paint what you see, Emma.*

I painted the girls.

Vivian, Natalie, Allison.

In that order.

It was far different from my later efforts. Rough and childish and awful. The girls in the painting bore no resemblance to their real-life counterparts. They were black squiggles protruding from triangular dresses. But I knew who they were, which was enough to help me heal.

Six months later, I was released, although I still had to take an antipsychotic and go to therapy once a week. The meds lasted another five years. The therapy continues to this day. It helps, although not as much as the sessions at the mental hospital with the kind, infinitely patient Dr. Shively. On my last day there, she presented me with a charm bracelet. Dangling from it were three delicate birds.

Consider it a talisman, she said as she clasped it around my wrist. *Never underestimate the power of positive thinking. If you ever experience another hallucination, I want you to touch this bracelet and tell yourself that what you're seeing isn't real, that it has no power over you, that you're stronger than everyone realizes.*

Instead of returning to my old prep school, my parents sent me to the nearest public one. I made friends. I got serious about art. I started to thrive.

I never saw the girls again.

Except in my paintings.

I had thought that information was private. That it was my secret to bear. Yet somehow Franny was able to find out. I'm not surprised. I suppose her kind of money can open a lot of doors. Now she and Theo stare at me, curiosity dancing in their eyes, likely wondering if I'm capable of snapping at any moment.

"It was a long time ago," I say.

"Of course it was," Theo says.

Franny adds, "The last thing we want is for you to feel ostracized or punished in any way. Which is why we should have told you about the camera in the first place."

I have no idea what they want me to say. That all is forgiven? That it's perfectly acceptable to be spied on because of something I experienced when I was still in high school?

"I understand," I say, my voice clipped. "It's better to be safe than sorry. After all, we don't want another mess on our hands, do we?"

I excuse myself from the table and make my escape between two of the statues. Both seem to stare at me as I depart, their blank eyes seeing nothing but knowing everything.

Theo follows me into the woods. His footsteps shush through the underbrush behind me, faster than my own, more familiar with the terrain. I quicken my pace, despite already knowing he'll catch up to me.

I just want to make him work for it. I veer left without warning, trying to outmaneuver him. Cutting across untrampled forest floor. When Theo follows suit, I do it again, this time zigging farther to the left.

He calls out to me. "Emma, don't be mad."

I make another sharp veer, heading off in a new direction. This time, my right foot gets caught on a tree root curving out of the ground. I trip and take a series of increasingly faltering steps, trying to right myself before succumbing to the inevitable fall.

The only thing I end up hurting is my pride. I land on my hands and knees, the blow cushioned by the leaves coating the soft, mossy earth. Getting to my feet, I see I'm in another clearing. One not as neatly maintained as the sculpture garden. It's darker, wilder, on the cusp of again becoming one with the forest.

I rotate slowly, looking around, trying to get my bearings.

That's when I notice the sundial.

It sits in the center of the clearing—a copper circle atop a tilted column of marble. Time has turned the copper a light blue, which makes the Roman numerals and compass rose etched into the surface stand out even more. The center of the dial bears a motto, written in Latin.

Omnes vulnerant, ultima necat.

I remember the phrase from high school Latin class, although not because I excelled at the language. In fact, I was terrible at it. I remember only because it sent a chill through me when I first learned what it meant.

All hours wound; the last one kills.

I touch the sundial, running my fingers over the words as Theo finally catches up to me. He emerges through the trees, slightly out of breath, his hair mussed by the chase.

"I don't want to talk to you," I say.

"Listen, you have every right to be angry. We should have just told you what we were doing. We completely handled it the wrong way."

"That we can agree on."

"I just want to know that you're better," he says. "As your friend."

"I'm one hundred percent fine."

"Then I'm sorry, okay? So is my mother."

The apology, more forced than sincere, angers me all over again. "If you don't trust me, then why did you invite me back here?"

"Because my mother wanted you here," Theo says. "We just didn't know what to expect. Fifteen years have passed, Emma. People change. And we had no idea what you'd be like, especially considering what happened the last time you were here. It was a matter of safety, not trust."

"Safety? What do you think I'm going to do to these girls?"

"Maybe the same thing you said I did to Vivian, Allison, and Natalie."

I stumble backward, gripping the sundial for support, the copper cold and smooth beneath my fingers.

"It's because of that, isn't it?" I say. "The camera. Digging up my health records. It's because I accused you of hurting them all those years ago."

Theo runs a hand through his hair, exasperated. "That couldn't be further from the truth. But since you brought it up, I have to say it was a lousy thing you did back then."

"It was," I admit. "And I've spent years beating myself up over it. But I was young and confused and scared."

"You think I wasn't?" Theo shoots back. "You should have seen the way the police grilled me. We had cops, state troopers, the fucking FBI coming to the Lodge, demanding that I tell them the truth. They made me take a lie-detector test. They made Chet do it, too. A ten-year-old kid hooked up to a polygraph. He cried for an entire week after that. And all because of what you accused me of doing."

His face has gone red, making the pale slash of scar on his cheek stand out. He's mad now, piling it on to make it clear how much I had wronged him.

"I didn't know any better," I say.

"There's more to it than that," Theo says. "We were friends, Em. Why did you think I had anything to do with what happened to them?"

I stare at him, dumbfounded. The fact that he has to ask why I accused him makes my anger flare up once again. He might not have caused Vivian and the others to vanish, but he's certainly not completely innocent. Neither of us are.

"You know exactly why," I say.

Then I'm off again, leaving Theo alone in the clearing. After a few wrong turns and another stumble-inducing sneak attack by exposed tree roots, I find my way make to camp. I march to the cabins, seething all the way. I'm mad at Franny. Even more mad at Theo. Yet the bulk of my anger is reserved for myself for thinking that returning here was a good idea.

Back at Dogwood, I throw open the door. Inside, something springs from the floor, taking flight. I see dark shapes at the window, hear the flap of wings.

Birds.

Three of them.

Crows. I can tell by their jet-black feathers.

They fly in a frenzied group, smacking against the ceiling, squawking. One of them swoops toward me. Clawed feet skim my hair. Another heads straight for my face. Black eyes staring. Sharp beak gaping.

I drop to the floor and cover my head. The crows keep flapping. Keep squawking. Keep slamming themselves against the cabin walls. I stretch across the floor, reaching for the door, opening it wide. The movement sends the birds in the opposite direction. Toward the window, where they strike glass in a series of sickening thuds.

I crawl toward them, my right hand over my eyes, my left one slicing the air to shoo them the other way. The bracelet slides up and down my wrist. Three more birds in motion. It does the trick. One crow spies the open door and darts through it, followed immediately by another.

The third bird lets out one last squawk, its feathers brushing the ceiling. Then it, too, is gone, leaving the cabin suddenly silent.

I remain on the floor, catching my breath and calming down. I look around the cabin, making sure there's not another bird inside waiting to attack. Not that attacking was their goal. They were just trapped and scared. I assume they came in through the window, curious and hungry. Once inside, they didn't know how to get back out, so they panicked.

It makes sense. I've been there.

But then I remember the birds thudding against the glass. Such a dreadful sound. I sit up and look to the window.

It was closed the entire time.

Fifteen

It takes me ten minutes to gather all the feathers the crows have left behind. More than a dozen littered the floor, with more scattered along Miranda's and Sasha's bunks. At least there were no bird droppings to go along with the feathers. I consider that a win.

While cleaning, I try to think of ways the birds could have gotten inside even though the window was closed. Two possibilities come to mind. The first is that they came in through a hole in the roof, one tucked in a corner where it's hard to spot. The second, more logical reason is that one of the girls left the door open and the birds flew in. Someone else came along and shut the door, not realizing they were trapping birds inside Dogwood.

But as I carry the handful of feathers behind the cabin, a third possibility enters my head—that someone caught the birds and released them inside on purpose. There were three of them, after all, echoing the number of charms on my bracelet, which are themselves symbols.

I shake my head while scattering the feathers. No, that can't be the reason. Like the idea of being spied on in the shower, it's too sinister to think about. Besides, who would do such a thing? And why? Just like that shadow in the shower stall, I tell myself the most innocent explanation is also the most logical.

Yet once I'm back inside the cabin, I can't shake the idea that something's not quite right here. Between the camera, the shadow at the shower stall, and the birds, I've been on edge all day. So much so that

I feel the need to get out of the cabin for a little bit. Maybe go for a hike. A little exercise might be just the thing to sweep away the weird thoughts I'm having.

I throw open my hickory trunk, looking for my hiking boots. The first thing I see is the folded piece of paper Vivian had hidden in her own trunk. My hands tremble when I pick it up. I tell myself it's residual stress from everything else that's happened today. But I know the truth.

That page makes me nervous. As does the photograph that once again slides from its fold.

I stare at the woman in the picture, getting another shudder of familiarity when I look into her eyes. It makes me wonder what the woman—this Eleanor Auburn—was thinking when the photograph was taken. Did she fear that she was going insane? Was she seeing something that wasn't really there?

Setting the picture aside, I make another examination of the map Vivian had drawn. I scan the entire page. The camp. The lake. The crudely drawn forest on the far shore. Yet my gaze lingers on the small *X* that's left two deep grooves in the paper. Vivian did that for a reason. It means something is located there.

It could be nothing but another old box found at the water's edge and buried under a pile of leaves. Or it could be a clue about what happened to the girls.

There's no way to know for certain until I go there myself.

Which is exactly what I intend to do. Heading across the lake will both get me out of the cabin and let me start the search for more information in earnest. Like killing two birds with one stone, which I realize is a bad metaphor when I spot a stray feather peeking out from behind my trunk.

I begin to gather supplies and stuff them into my backpack. Sunblock and hand sanitizer. My phone. A water bottle. The map also goes into the backpack, which I zip shut as I leave the cabin. On my way out, I give the camera a defiant stare, hoping both Theo and Franny will see it later.

Before departing camp, I stop by the mess hall to fill up my water bottle and grab a banana and granola bar in case I get hungry.

Two women and a man are outside. Kitchen workers spending the lull between lunch and dinner smoking in the shade of the over-hanging roof. One of the women gives a disinterested wave. The man beside her is the same guy with the goatee who briefly checked me out this morning. The tag affixed to his apron strap says his name is Marvin.

Now Marvin stares past me to the lake in the distance. Afternoon swimming lessons are taking place, the shore and water dotted with young women in bathing suits of varying degrees of modesty. He catches me watching him and displays a grin so slimy it makes me want to reach for the hand sanitizer in my backpack.

"It's not illegal to look," he says.

With that, Marvin jumps to the top of my list of suspected peep-ing Toms. In truth, he's the only suspect. A weak one at that. Marvin was working in the mess hall before I left for my shower. While there's a chance he followed me there, I doubt he could have done it without anyone else noticing.

Besides, it's possible no one was watching me.

Maybe.

"It might not be illegal, *Marvin.*" I put extra emphasis on his name, making sure he understands that I know it. "But those girls are young enough to be your daughters."

Marvin drops his cigarette, stubs it out, goes back inside. The women begin to chuckle. One of them nods my way. A silent thank-you.

I continue toward the lake, my backpack slung over my shoulder. I spot Miranda lingering by the lifeguard station in a bikini designed to expose the maximum amount of skin while still being legal.

The lifeguard for the afternoon is Chet, which explains Miranda's presence there. He's undeniably handsome up there on his perch, with his Ray-Bans and whistle. Miranda stares up at him, laughing too loudly at something he's just said, a finger twirling in her hair while she uses her big toe to trace a circle in the sand. Apparently she's al-ready gotten over the texter who broke her heart. She just better hope Mindy doesn't see her. I suspect flirting with Chet if definitely not a display of Camp Nightingale spirit.

Nearby, Sasha and Krystal share a large beach blanket. They sprawl across it, still in shorts and camp polos, listlessly flipping through a stack of comic books. I walk over to them, my shadow falling across the blanket.

"Did one of you leave the cabin door open?"

"No," Sasha says. "It lets in bugs, which cause disease."

"Not even for a little bit?"

"We didn't," Krystal replies. "Why?"

Now that the cabin's been cleared of feathers, I see no reason to tell them about the birds. It would only make Sasha more worried. I opt for a change of subject. "Why aren't you swimming?"

"Don't want to," Krystal says.

"Don't know how," Sasha says.

"I can teach you sometime, if you want."

Sasha wrinkles her nose, her glasses rising and falling. "In that dirty water? No thank you."

"Where are you going?" Krystal asks, eyeing my backpack.

"Canoe trip."

"Alone?" Sasha says.

"That's the plan."

"Are you sure that's a good idea? Each year, an average of eighty-seven people die in canoe and kayak accidents. I looked it up."

"I'm a good swimmer. I think I'll be okay."

"It's probably safer if someone is with you."

Next to her, Krystal slaps her comic book shut and sighs. "What Miss Wikipedia here is trying to say is that we want to come along. We're bored, and we've never been canoeing."

"Yeah," Sasha says. "That's what I meant."

"That's not a good idea. It's a long trip. And there'll be hiking involved."

"I've never hiked, either," Krystal says. "Please, can we come?"

Sasha bats her eyes at me, the lashes fluttering behind her glasses. "Pretty please?"

My plan was to cross the lake, find the spot marked on Vivian's map, and proceed from there. Sasha and Krystal will only slow me down. Nevertheless, a sense of duty tugs at me. Franny told me the purpose of reopening Camp Nightingale was to give the campers new experiences. That remains true, even if I'm currently pissed at Franny.

"Fine," I tell them. "Put on life vests and help me with the canoe."

The girls do as they're told, grabbing dirty life vests that hang from the sides of the canoe racks. They slip them on and help me lift a canoe off one of the racks. It's heavier than it looks and so unwieldy that we come close to dropping it. We remain a sorry sight as we awkwardly carry the canoe to the lake's edge, Krystal holding up the front and me taking the rear. Sasha is in the middle, hidden beneath the overturned boat, just a pair of knobby legs shuffling toward the water.

Our struggle is enough to tear Miranda's attention away from Chet. She trots over to us and says, "Where are you going?"

"Canoeing," Sasha says.

"And hiking," I add, hoping they'll be dissuaded by the fact that there's more to this trip than just paddling across the lake.

Instead, Miranda frowns. "Without me?"

"Do you want to come along?"

"Not really, but…"

Her voice trails off, the sentence unfinished but its meaning perfectly clear. She doesn't want to be the only one left behind. I know the feeling.

"Go get changed," I tell her. "We'll wait for you."

Another person means another canoe. So while Miranda runs back to the cabin to fetch shorts and a pair of sneakers, Krystal, Sasha, and I wrangle a second canoe to the water's edge. When Miranda returns, we climb in, she and Krystal in one canoe, Sasha and me in the other. Using oars, we push off and start to drift out onto the lake.

The bulk of the rowing in my boat falls to me. I sit in the back, paddling on alternating sides of the canoe. Sasha sits up front, her own paddle across her lap, dipping it into the water whenever I need to straighten things out.

"How deep do you think it is here?" she says.

"Pretty deep in parts."

"A hundred feet?"

"Maybe."

Sasha's eyes widen behind her glasses as her free hand uncon-sciously clasps her life vest. "You're a good swimmer, though, right?"

"I am," I say. "Although not as good as some people I know."

It takes us a half hour to cross the lake. We slow when the water's surface is darkened by tall pines along the shoreline, their reflections jagged and unwelcoming. Just beneath the surface are the remnants of trees submerged when the valley was flooded. Stripped of leaves and whitewashed by time, their branches seem to be grasping for fresh air that's just beyond their reach. It's a discomfiting sight. All those blanched limbs tangled together as mud-brown fish slip between them. Because the lake's been lowered by drought, the farthest-reaching branches scrape the bottoms of the canoes, sounding like fingernails trying to scratch their way out of a coffin.

More trees jut out of the lake in front of us. Although to call them trees isn't entirely accurate. They're more like ghosts of trees. Bare and sun-bleached. Trapped in a limbo between water and land. Gone are their bark, their leaves, their limbs. They've been reduced to sad, brittle sticks.

After passing through the graveyard of trees, we come to the shore itself. Instead of the welcoming flatness Camp Nightingale was built upon, the landscape rises sharply—an ascent that eventually leads to the rounded peaks in the distance. The trees here tower over the water. Pines, mostly, their limbs connecting to form a pale green wall that undulates in the slight breeze coming off the lake.

To our right, a heap of boulders sits partway out of the water. They look out of place, like they had rolled down the mountain one by one, eventually accumulating there. Beyond them is a cliff where the land has been chipped away by the elements. Small, tenacious vines cling to the cliff wall, and mineral deposits stripe the exposed rock. Trees line the ridge atop the cliff, some leaning forward, as if they're about to jump.

"I see something," Miranda says, pointing to a ragged-looking structure sitting farther down the shore.

I see it, too. It's a gazebo. Rather, it used to be. Now it's a leaning structure of splintered wood slowly being overtaken by weeds. Its floorboards sag. Its roof sits slightly askew. While I'm not certain, I think it might be the cabin-like structure marked on Vivian's map.

I start to row toward it. Miranda follows suit. On shore, we step out of the canoes, paddles clattering, life vests discarded. Then we drag the boats farther onto land to reduce the potential of them drifting away without us. I grab my backpack and pull out the map.

"What's that?" Sasha asks.

"A map."

"What does it lead to?"

"I don't know yet."

I frown at the woods before us. It's dense, dark, all silence and shadows. Now that we're on the other side of the lake, I have no idea how to proceed. Vivian's map is short on details, and the accuracy of what she did draw is questionable at best.

I run my finger from the spot that probably-is-but-might-not-be the gazebo to the ragged triangles nearby. I assume those are rocks. Which means we need to make our way northeast until we reach them. After that, it looks to be a short walk north until I find the X.

Our route now set, I open the compass app downloaded to my phone the morning I left for camp, rotating until it points northeast. Then I snag a handful of wild flowers and, with Miranda, Sasha, and Krystal in tow, march into the forest.

FIFTEEN YEARS AGO

"Let's go," Vivian said.

"Go where?"

I was curled up in my bunk, reading the dog-eared copy of *The Lovely Bones* I had brought with me to camp. Looking up from the book, I saw Vivian standing by the cabin door. She had tied a red handkerchief around her neck. Allison's floppy straw hat sat atop her head.

"On an adventure," she said. "To search for buried treasure."

I closed my book and crawled out of bed. As if there was any doubt I wouldn't. In the short time that I'd been there, it was already clear that what Vivian wanted, she got.

"Allison's going to need her hat, though," I told her. "You know how she is about UV rays."

"Allison's not coming. Neither is Natalie. It's just you and me, kid."

She didn't bother to tell me where, exactly, we were going. I simply let her lead the way. First to the canoes near the dock, then across Lake Midnight itself, me struggling with my oar the entire way.

"I'm going to take a wild guess and say you've never been in a canoe before," Vivian said.

"I've been in a rowboat," I told her. "Does that count?"

"Depends. Was it on a lake?"

"The pond in Central Park. I went there once with Heather and Marissa."

I almost told her how we jostled the boat so much that Heather fell in, but then I remembered about Vivian's sister and how she had drowned. Vivian never told me where it happened. Or how. Or even when. But I didn't want to bring it up, even in an innocent, roundabout way. I stayed quiet until we came ashore alongside a grassy area aflame with tiger lilies.

Vivian picked enough lilies to make a bouquet. When we entered the woods, she began to pluck their petals and drop them to the ground.

"Always leave a trail of bread crumbs," she said. "So you know how to find your way back. Franny taught me that my first summer here. I think she was afraid I'd get lost."

"Why?"

"Because I wandered off too much."

That didn't surprise me. Vivian's personality was too big to fit inside the tidy confines of camp life. All those tennis lessons and crafting sessions. I'd started to notice how she greeted each one with a bored sigh.

She dropped another petal, and I turned around to look at the long line of them stretching away from us, marking our progress. It was a comforting sight. Like tiny, tangerine-colored footprints we had left behind that would eventually guide us home.

"Two Truths and a Lie," Vivian said as she plucked off another petal and let it flutter to the ground. "I'll go first. One: A guy once flashed me in the subway. Two: I have a flask of whiskey hidden under my mattress. Three: I don't know how to swim."

"The second one," I said. "I'd have noticed if you were secretly drinking."

I thought of my mother and how she smelled when she greeted me after school. The spearmint gum she chewed did little to hide her wine breath. Even if it had, I was already an expert at noticing the slight dimness in her eyes whenever she drank too much.

"Aren't you the observant one," Vivian said. "That's why I thought you'd like to see this."

We had come to a large oak tree, its sturdy branches spread wide to create a canopy over the surrounding ground. An *X* had been carved into the bark, as big and bold as the way Vivian marked the lid of her trunk back in Dogwood. At the base of the tree sat a pile of leaves that camouflaged something beneath it.

Vivian pushed the leaves out of the way, exposing an old and rotting wooden box. Time had stripped the veneer from the lid, which allowed water and sunlight to do their damage, staining the wood in some spots, bleaching it in others. As a result, the box had become a patchwork of colors.

"It's cool, right?" Vivian said. "It's, like, ancient."

I ran a finger over the lid, feeling a series of groves in the wood. At first I thought it was just another product of age and the elements. But when I looked closer, I noticed two faint letters etched into the wood. They were so worn by exposure that it was hard to make them out. Only when I leaned in close, the odor of mold and wood rot filling my nostrils, could I read them.

CC

"Where did you find it?"

"Washed up on the shore last summer."

"While you were wandering off?"

Vivian smirked, pleased with herself. "Of course. God knows how long it was there. I brought it here for safekeeping. Go ahead and open it."

I lifted the lid, the wood so soft and waterlogged I feared it might disintegrate in my hands. The inside of the box was lined with a fabric that might have once been green velvet. I couldn't quite tell because the fabric was in tatters—nothing but dark, leathery strips.

Inside the box lay several pairs of scissors. Antique ones with ornate circles for finger holes and thin blades tapered like stork legs. I suspected the scissors were made of silver, although they'd been tarnished the same color as motor oil. The screws that held them together were swirled with rust. When I picked up a pair and tried to pry them open, they wouldn't budge. Age and disrepair had rendered them useless.

"Who do you think they belonged to?"

"A hospital or something. There's a name on the bottom." Vivian took the box and shut the lid, holding it closed. When she flipped it over, the scissors inside rattled together. It sounded like broken glass. "See?"

Engraved on the bottom of the box, in tiny letters dulled by time, were four words: *Property of Peaceful Valley.*

"I wonder how it got here."

Vivian shrugged. "Tossed into the lake, probably. Decades ago."

"Have you asked Franny about it?"

"No way. I want to keep it a secret. No one else knows about it but me. And now you."

"Why are you showing me this?"

I looked down at the box, a lock of hair falling over my face. Vivian leaned forward and tucked it behind my ear.

"I'm your big sister for the summer, remember?" she said. "This is what big sisters do. We share things. Things no one else knows."

Sixteen

I take the lead in the woods, trying to walk in a straight line, my eyes constantly flicking to the wavering compass for guidance. When I'm not looking at the app, I'm studying our surroundings, seeking out places in the brush where someone could be hiding. Although we're far from camp, the feeling of being watched stays with me. Every thicket gets a second, suspicious glance. I mistrust each shadow that stretches across the forest floor. Whenever a bird screeches in the trees, I fight the urge to duck.

Get a grip, Em, I tell myself. *The four of you are all alone out here.*

I can't decide if that makes me feel better or worse.

If the girls notice my jumpiness, they don't say anything. Krystal and Sasha walk behind me. Every so often, Sasha calls out the names of trees she recognizes.

"Sugar maple. American beech. White pine. Birch."

Behind them is Miranda, who peels off petals from the flowers I'd picked and drops them to the ground at regular intervals.

"Why do I have to do this again?" she asks.

"Always leave a trail of bread crumbs," I tell her. "It'll help us find our way back."

"From *where?*" Krystal says.

"I'll know it when I find it."

The ground slants upward as we walk, slightly at first, the incline hidden under a sheet of amber leaves that fell the previous autumn. We're aware of the rising land only from the warm ache in our legs and the growing heaviness of our breath. But soon the landscape becomes more obviously steep. A sharp, steady rise that can't be avoided. We press on, shoulders hunched, legs bent. Along the way we pass whippet-thin saplings, grabbing them for support, hauling ourselves higher.

"I want to go back," Krystal says, huffing out the words.

"Me, too," Sasha says.

"I told you there would be hiking," I remind them. "Hey, let's play another game. Instead of Two Truths and a Lie, let's just do truth. Tell me, in all honesty, what you'd like to be doing twenty years from now."

I look over my shoulder to Sasha, who's quickly losing steam. "You start. Any ideas about what you want to be doing?"

"Plenty," she says with a nudge of her glasses. "A professor. A scientist. Maybe an astronaut, unless everyone's already colonizing on Mars. I like to have options."

"And what about you, Krystal?"

She doesn't need to think about it. The answer is obvious to all.

"Working for Marvel. Hopefully illustrating my own superhero series. Someone cool that I came up with."

"Why do you like comic books so much?" Sasha asks.

"I dunno. I guess because most of the superheroes start off as regular people just like us. Nerdy and awkward."

"Speak for yourself," Miranda chimes in.

"Just like everyone *but* you," Krystal says, placating her. "But something happens that makes these average people realize they're stronger than they thought. Then they believe they can do anything. And what they choose to do is help people."

"I prefer regular books," Miranda says. "You know, without pictures."

She's passed Krystal and Sasha on the way up the incline and now walks beside me, the only one of us not fazed by the climb.

"Ever think about becoming a writer?" I ask her. "Since you like to read so much."

"I'm going to be a police detective like my uncle," she says. "Why write about crimes when you can solve them in real life?"

"Um, that's called a superhero," Krystal says with no small amount of satisfaction.

Miranda forges ahead to where the incline finally levels off into less wearying terrain, waiting impatiently for the rest of us. Once there, we pause to catch our breath and take in the scenery. On our right, slivers of blue sky peek through the trees. I move instinctively toward them, following the light, emerging from the trees onto a thin strip of craggy ground. Beyond it, the land drops away, and for a dizzying, disoriented moment, I think I'm about to drop with it. I wrap an arm around the nearest tree, steadying myself, my eyes aimed at my feet to make sure I remain on solid ground.

When the girls reach my side, one of them—I think it's Miranda—whistles with appreciation.

"*Day-um,*" Krystal says, stretching the word into two syllables. She sounds beyond impressed. Awed.

I lift my eyes to the horizon, seeing what they see. I realize we're atop the ridge I'd spotted from the canoe, overlooking the stone-walled cliff. The view it affords us is stunning. Lake Midnight spreads out below us, the water dappled with sunlight. From this height, I can see the full shape of the shoreline curving inward, the spot in the distance where it narrows toward the dam.

Across from us, hazy in the distance, sits Camp Nightingale. It looks so small from here. A miniature. Something placed in the center of a model railroad.

I dig the map from my pocket and give it a quick peek. Vivian drew nothing to indicate the cliff where we now stand. From what I can gather from her crude markings, we're close to the raggedly triangular rocks. Sure enough, when I turn away from the water and point north, I get a glimpse of rocks through the thick forest.

I'm getting closer. To what, I still have no clue.

The rocks on Vivian's map differ greatly from the ones I see in person. These are boulders. Dozens of them. Massive ones that only get larger as we approach, their weight palpable, so heavy and unwieldy it's a wonder the earth can support them. They sit in a line running up a sharp rise similar to the one we've just climbed.

The girls spread out among them, scaling the boulders like kids in a playground.

"I bet these rocks used to be part of the mountain's peak," Sasha says as she clambers up a boulder twice her height. "They froze and broke apart, then glaciers took them down the hill. Now they're here."

Explanation aside, the boulders still unsettle me. They make me think of the rumored survivors of Lake Midnight's creation. I picture them when the moon is full, creeping around these very boulders at night, searching for new victims. To push away the unease, I check both the compass and the map, making sure this is where we should be. It is.

"Hey, girls," I call out. "We should keep moving."

I squeeze between two boulders and edge around another. That's when I get a view of another rock farther up the incline. One bigger than the others. A monolith.

Nearly two stories tall, it rises from the ground like an enormous tombstone. The side facing me is mostly flat. A sheer wall of rock. A large fissure runs diagonally through it, widening at the top. A tree grows inside the crack, its roots curling along the rock face, seeking soil. Standing beside the tree, looking up into its branches, is Sasha.

Krystal is up there, too. She takes a step toward the boulder's edge and peers down at me. "Hey," she says.

"What are you doing up there?"

"Exploring," Sasha says.

"I'd prefer it if you stayed on the ground," I say. "Where's Miranda?"

"Right here."

Miranda's voice emanates from the northwestern side of the giant rock. It sounds watery, akin to an echo. I follow it as Sasha and Krystal scramble down the boulder's opposite side. I work my way around it, seeing another large crack in the rock's side. This one runs in a straight line, widening at the bottom. It opens up completely about a foot from the ground, creating a hole large enough for a person to crawl into.

Or, in Miranda's case, crawl out of. She climbs to her feet, circles of mud dotting her knees and elbows. "I wanted to see what was in there."

"Bears or snakes, probably," Sasha says.

"Exactly," I say. "So no more exploring. Understood?"

"Yes, ma'am," Krystal says.

"We understand," Sasha adds.

Miranda stands with her hand on her hip, annoyed. "Isn't that why we're out here?"

I say nothing. I'm too busy looking past her, my head tilted, eyes narrowed in curiosity. In the distance behind her are what appear to be ruins. I can make out a crumbled stone wall and one jagged wooden beam pointing skyward.

I start to creep toward it, the girls behind me. When I get closer, I see that it's the remains of what might have been a barn or farmhouse. The walls are mostly now a pile of rocks, but enough are intact to be able to make out the building's rectangular foundation. Inside are several pines that have sprouted from what's left of the building's roof and floor.

In much better shape is a nearby root cellar built into the slope of the land. There's no roof—just a slightly rounded mound of earth. A fieldstone wall forms the front. In the center is a wooden door, shut tight, its rusted slide bolt firmly in place.

"Creepy," says Sasha.

"Cool," says Miranda.

"Both," says Krystal. "It looks like something from *Lord of the Rings.*"

But I'm thinking of another, more ominous tale. One about a flooded valley, a clan of survivors hiding in the woods, a thirst for revenge. Maybe a small seed of truth lies in the legend Casey told me. Because someone used to live in these hills. The foundation and root cellar make that abundantly clear. And although there's no evidence showing it was the same people from Casey's story, my skin nonetheless starts to tickle. Goose bumps, running up my arm.

"We should—"

Go. That's what I intended to say. But I'm stopped by the sight of a large oak sitting fifty yards away. The tree is large, its thick branches spread wide. In its trunk is a familiar letter.

X

Immediately, I know it's not the same tree Vivian led me to fifteen years ago. I would have remembered the crumbled foundation and creepy-cool root cellar. No, this is a different tree and a different X. Yet I get the feeling both letters were carved by the same hand.

"Stay here," I tell the girls. "I'll be right back."

"Can we look inside that hobbit house?" Miranda asks.

"No. Don't go anywhere."

They mill about the crumbled foundation while I dash to the tree and search around its trunk. I take a step, and the ground beneath me thumps. A muffled, hollow sound.

Something is down there.

I drop to my knees and start scraping away years' worth of weeds and dead leaves until I reach soil. I swipe my hands back and forth, clearing the dirt. Something brown and moist appears.

Wood. A pine plank dyed brown from more than a decade underground. I sweep away more dirt before burrowing my fingers into the soil underneath it, prying the plank loose. Its bottom is coated with mold, mud, a few bugs that scurry away. Beneath the plank someone has dug a hole the size of a shoe box. Inside the hole is a yellow grocery bag wrapped tightly around a rectangular object.

I unfurl the bag and reach into it, feeling more plastic. A freezer bag. The kind that can be zipped shut. Through the clear plastic, I see a splash of green, the stubble of leather, the edges of pages kept dry by the double layers of protection.

A book. Auspiciously fancy.

I peer inside the yellow grocery bag, checking for anything else that might be inside. There's just a second freezer bag, empty and crumpled, and a single strand of hair. I set it on the ground and carefully open the other bag, letting the book slip out of it. It's floppy in my hands, made pliant by fifteen seasons of being frozen and thawed and frozen again. Yet I'm able to peel back the cover to the first page, where I see the chaotic swirl of someone's handwriting.

Vivian's handwriting, to be exact.

"What are you doing over there?" Miranda calls.

I slam the book shut and shove it into my backpack, hoping my body shields the action from the prying eyes of the girls.

"Nothing," I reply. "It's not what I was looking for. Let's head back."

I place the now-empty bags back in the hole and cover it with the plank. I kick some dirt and leaves over the wood, more out of respect for Vivian than caution. I want to keep her secret safe. Because whatever's inside this book, Vivian thought it important enough to hide it here, on the other side of the lake, as far away from prying eyes and Camp Nightingale as possible.

FIFTEEN YEARS AGO

"Two Truths and a Lie," Vivian said as we rowed back to camp. "Your turn."

I dipped my paddle into the lake, arms straining to push it through the resistant water. Vivian wasn't only older than me; she was also stronger. Each stroke of her oar forced me to paddle even harder just to keep up. Which I couldn't. As a result, our canoe curved through the water instead of cutting straight across it.

"Do we have to do this right now?" I asked through labored breaths.

"We don't *have* to," Vivian said. "Just like I don't *have* to tell Allison and Natalie you were too chickenshit to play today, even though I probably will."

I believed her, which is why I opted to play. I didn't really care what Allison and Natalie thought of me. Vivian's opinion was the only one that mattered. And the last thing I wanted was for her to think I was chickenshit about anything.

"One: My mother once got so drunk that she passed out in our building's elevator," I said. "Two: I've never kissed a boy. Three: I think Theo is the most handsome man I've ever seen."

"You're *cheating*," Vivian said, her voice singsongy. "None of those are a lie."

She was almost right. My mother had passed out *waiting* for our building's elevator. I had found her facedown in the hallway, snoring lightly, a small puddle of her drool seeping into the carpet.

"But I'll allow it," Vivian said as she pulled her oar from the water and set it aside. "Just this once. Mostly because of your incorrect guess during my turn."

"I don't think so," I said. "I totally know you don't have a flask. Besides, I saw that you can't swim."

"Guess again."

Vivian stood suddenly, the canoe rocking as she shed her clothes. There was no bathing suit underneath. Just matching pearl-colored bra and panties, silky and shiny in the afternoon glare. Before I could utter a word of protest, she dove into the lake, making the canoe pitch so sharply I thought I was going to tumble in as well. I yelped, grabbed the sides of the boat, waited for it to stop rocking.

It was only then that I noticed Vivian slicing the water like a knife through butter. Her strokes were quick, powerful, elegant. Tanned back flattening as her arms swept out in front of her before arcing to her sides. Feet flicking in short, strong kicks. Hair billowing like cream in coffee behind her. A mermaid.

When she finally came up for air, she was ten feet from the canoe.

"Wait," I said. "You really can swim?"

She grinned. Her smile was slanted, sly, colored pink by her lip gloss.

"Duh," she said.

"But the other day—"

I stopped talking as Vivian ducked below the surface again, emerging with a mouthful of water that she squirted through pursed lips, like a fountain.

"You told Theo you didn't know how," I said.

"You can't believe everything I tell you, Em."

I thought about the drama of that day on the beach. The panic. The splashing. Vivian's wide-eyed terror as she flailed. I remembered Becca, her camera trained on the chaos, yet her attention aimed at me.

I told you so.

"I thought you were drowning," I said. "We all did. Why would you lie about something like that?"

"Why not?"

"Because it wasn't one of your stupid games!"

Vivian sighed and began the swim back to the canoe. "Everything is a game, Em. Whether you know it or not. Which means that sometimes a lie is more than just a lie. Sometimes it's the only way to win."

Seventeen

The dinner hour is torture, and not just because of the food, which is predictably awful. Runny sloppy joes and French fries. Despite having consumed next to nothing all day, I can only stomach the fries, which glisten with grease. Right now, my only concern is getting back to Dogwood and learning what's in the book Vivian had buried. And that requires privacy, which is in short supply.

Skipping dinner to read it would only make the girls more suspicious than they already are. On the canoe trip back across the lake, they bombarded me with questions about the map, the rocks, our purpose for roaming so far from camp. My vague, mumbled answers did little to appease them. So I force myself to suffer through dinner, delaying the reading of the book until the girls are at the campfire.

I take my tray to what's already become known as the adults table. It's a full house tonight, with every counselor and instructor present, including Becca. She sits at a slight remove from the others, her eyes glued to her phone. I get the feeling she thinks there's nothing left to say to me. I think otherwise.

I head to the opposite end of the table, where Casey is listening to the counselors play a game of Do, Dump, or Marry. I remember it well, having played it fifteen years ago with Vivian, Natalie, and Allison. Only Vivian had given it a more brutal name—Fuck, Marry, Kill.

As the counselors choose between the men at Camp Nightingale, I sneak a glance at Casey, as if to say, *Isn't this such a silly, sexist game?* Yet I suspect Casey is mulling the choices, just like I secretly am.

"I'd do Chet, dump the janitor, and marry Theo," the counselor named Kim or Danica announces.

"I think he's technically a maintenance man," another one says.

"Grounds keeper," Casey tells them. "He's worked for the family for years. He's kind of creepy but also kind of hot. He'd be my Do."

Both counselors look scandalized, their mouths forming twin ovals of shock. "Over Chet and Theo?"

"I'm being realistic here. There's no way Mindy's going to let Chet out of her sight." Casey nudges me with an elbow. "And Emma's already got her hooks into Theo."

"Definitely not," I say. "He's all yours, ladies."

"But the rumor is the two of you had a picnic lunch in the woods."

Across the table, Becca looks up, clearly surprised. She stares at me a second too long before returning her gaze to her phone.

"We were just catching up," I say. "It's been years since we last saw each other."

"Of course," Casey says before leaning closer and whispering, "You can tell me all the sordid details later tonight."

On the other side of the mess hall, I see Mindy enter and make a beeline for our table. She's smiling, which doesn't necessarily mean good news. I've come to realize Mindy's the kind of girl who wields a smile like a scythe.

"Hi, Emma," she says without a hint of friendliness. "Next time you decide to vanish for an entire afternoon, I'd appreciate it if you told someone. Franny would, too. She was distressed to hear that you left with a group of campers without telling anyone where you were going."

"I didn't know that was a requirement."

"It's not," Mindy says. "But it certainly would have been a courtesy."

"I went canoeing with the girls from my cabin. In case you're keeping a record of my whereabouts."

I assume Mindy knows about the camera. And everything else, for that matter. Especially when she says, "It's just very noticeable when a group of campers goes missing. As you well know."

She stands there, pleased with herself, her next move predicated on how I react. I know because it's right out of the Vivian playbook. I opt for a curveball.

"Sit with us," I say, my voice chirpy, so unlike my natural tone. "Have some fries. They're *so* good."

I hold out a fry, the end sagging, its tip dripping grease. Mindy stares at it with thinly veiled repulsion. I suspect she hasn't consumed a trans fat since junior high.

"No thanks. I have to get back to the Lodge."

"Not even one fry?" I say. "If it's calories you're worried about, don't be. You look . . . fine."

Later in the night, I wait until the girls leave for the campfire before reclining in my bunk with the meager collection of snacks from my backpack. Gnawing absently on the granola bar, I open the book Vivian had left behind.

On the first page, I see a date written in her hand.

The first day of camp. Fifteen years ago.

This is a diary.

Vivian's diary.

I suck in a breath, exhale it back out, and begin to read.

June 22,

Well, here I am, back at Camp Nightmare for another six weeks. I can't say I'm thrilled to be back, unlike The Senator and Mrs. Senator, who were ECSTATIC when I told them I wanted to spend the summer here and not slutting my way through Europe with Brittney, Patricia and Kelly. If they only knew that I would absolutely love to be in Amsterdam with those bitches, sucking face with some stubbled douchebag wannabe deejay just for the weed.

Everyone seems to think I adore this place. That couldn't be further from the truth. It creeps me out. It has ever since I first got here. There's something not right about it.

But here is where I need to be. Just for one more summer. As they say in those shitty movies The Senator likes to watch, I've got unfinished business. But will I finish it? That's the big question hanging over this whole summer. Before I left, I asked it to Katherine's stupid Magic 8 Ball that she loved so much. All signs pointed to yes.

In the meantime, tomorrow I'll get the pleasure of hearing F give that goddamn speech for the umpteenth time. It's so pathetic how she goes out of her way trying to sound folksy when the rest of us know she's worth a billion dollars. You are not fucking fooling us! At least, not for long.

Nat and Ali are here, of course. Fourth camper to be announced. I hope that bottom bunk stays empty. It'll make things easier for all of us, but mostly me. If not, I'll settle for Theodore. I'd sleep on top of him any damn day of the week. My God, he's looking fine. Don't get me wrong, he's always looked fine. But I'm talking FINE. Worthy even of a dozen lame exclamation points.

!!!!!!!!!!!!

Pull it together, Viv. Don't get distracted by all that fineness. You're on a mission. Theo isn't part of it. Unless he needs to be. Sweet Jesus Lord I hope he needs to be.

Update: It's after dinner. No fourth camper has arrived. Fingers crossed she never does.

Update #2: The fourth camper just came in. A new girl. Time to either terrorize her or befriend her. I haven't decided which one it'll be.

June 23,

Today I showed New Girl the ropes. Someone had to. This place is not for the faint of heart.

New Girl has a name, by the way. It's Emma. Cute, right? And she is. So young and innocent and shaky. Like a newborn kitten. She reminds of me when I was that age, mostly because, underneath that My Little Pony exterior, I think she might actually be a bitch in training. She stood up to me last night, which took major ovaries. I was duly impressed. No one has stood up to me since Katherine died.

I missed that feeling of being put in my place. It's tough being the only alpha female in the pack.

But, like Theo's divine handsomeness, I can't let New Girl distract me too much. Mission first. Friendship second. You-know-who learned that the hard way.

At least I got to roam a little bit after archery. I scoped out all the places I haven't looked yet, including the Big L. I almost made it inside before Casey caught me sniffing around the place. With any other counselor, I would have tried to sneak in anyway. But not her. She's weirdly devoted to this place. I mean, a former camper coming back as a counselor for two summers in a row? I can't think of anything more pathetic.

My guess is she's obsessed with Theo. It's obvious she's got the hots for him. She throws herself at him every chance she can get. Last year she caught me flirting with Theo and got all huffy, like she fucking owned him or something. Ever since, she's been dying to get me kicked out. Hence the extra attention I receive during cabin check.

Like I said—pathetic.

June 24,

On her second night at camp, poor Emma had her VERY. FIRST. PERIOD. She woke me up last night with blood on her fingers like Carrie White. I felt so bad for her. I remember my first period. It was awful. I swear, the only thing that kept me sane was Katherine, who'd been through it all by that point. And where was Mrs. Senator, you ask? Gone, of course. Oblivious. She didn't even know I was menstruating until the maid told her six months later.

So I did for Em what Kath did for me. Which means, in Carrie terms, I'm Sue Snell in this scenario. Wait, I guess that actually makes me the gym teacher. No, I refuse to be that bore. I'm sticking with Sue.

She survived.

June 26,

I almost drowned this afternoon.

Well, pretended to drown, which isn't quite the same thing. It wasn't planned. I just spontaneously decided to do it. Still, I deserve an Oscar for that performance. Or at least a Golden Globe. Best Performance of Drowning by a Regional Champion in the 100-Meter Butterfly. The gulping-down-lake-water part sucked, though. There's probably some creepy water-borne microbe swimming in my stomach as I write this. But it was worth it. I got the reaction I was looking for.

While I'm on the subject of drowning, let's talk about Franny's husband for a sec. Don't you think it's strange that a dude who almost made it to the Olympics drowned? I sure as fuck do.

June 28,

Holy shit holy shit holy shit.

I made it into the Big L. At last! I went during lunch when I knew all the campers and counselors would be in the mess hall and F and her entourage would be dining on the back deck. That gave me enough time to slip in through the front door without anyone noticing. And wow, was it worth the wait. I knew F was hiding something in there. And, sure enough, she was. Several somethings. I managed to steal one before Lottie caught me in the study. She acted all cool about it, but I think she was seriously pissed to find me there. And now I'm freaking out because she's going to tell F. I just know it.

Not fucking good, diary.

My reading is interrupted by a sudden, startling rap on the cabin door. I'd fallen so far down the rabbit hole of Vivian's thoughts that the real world melted away, unnoticed. Now it's back, making me look up from the page and call out in a trembling voice, "Who is it?"

"Emma, it's Chet. Is everything okay?"

I slam the diary shut, stuff it under my pillow, and take a quick, calming breath before saying, "Yeah, I'm fine."

The door opens a crack, and Chet peers inside, his hair a swoosh over his eyes. He pushes it away and says, "Can I come in?"

"Make yourself at home."

He steps inside and takes a seat on my hickory trunk, his long legs extended, arms crossed. Although he and Theo aren't biologically related, the two nevertheless share some traits. Both have the height and physique that makes everything they wear seem perfectly tailored. Both move with athletic grace. And both radiate that laid-back, carefree vibe that comes from being to the manor born. Or, in their case, adopted.

"I noticed you weren't at the campfire," Chet says. "I wondered if something was wrong. You know, after what happened at lunch."

"Which one of them sent you? Your mother or your brother?"

"Neither, actually. I came on my own. I wanted to clear up a few things. About the camera and why my mother invited you back here. Both were my idea."

I sit up in surprise. Yesterday, I had wondered if Chet even remembered who I was. Clearly, he did.

"I had assumed both were Franny's idea."

"Technically, they were. But I'm the one who instigated them." Chet gives me a grin. It's a great smile. Another thing he and his brother have in common. "The camera was just a precaution. Theo and my mother had nothing to do with it. I thought it would be a good idea to monitor your cabin. Not that I expect anything bad to happen. But it doesn't hurt to be prepared in case it does."

It's a polite way of saying that he, too, knows about my fragile mental state after my first stay here. At this rate, it'll be common knowledge among every camper and kitchen worker by the end of the week.

"Please don't be offended," Chet says. "I understand why you felt unfairly targeted, and I'm sorry. We all are. And if you want it taken down, I'll get Ben to do it first thing tomorrow morning."

I'm tempted to demand that it be dismantled right this instant. But, oddly, I also understand the need for caution. After what happened in the shower this morning—or, more accurately, what *might* have happened—it's not a bad idea to monitor the camp.

"It can stay," I tell him. "For now. And only if you tell me why it was your idea to invite me back here."

"Because of what you said back then," Chet says. "About Theo."

There's no need for him to elaborate. I know he's referring to how I told police Theo had something to do with the girls' disappearance and never took it back. Both are actions I've come to regret. The former because of why I blamed him. The latter because it would mean admitting to all that I'm a liar.

Two truths I'm not yet ready to face.

"I can't change what I did back then," I say. "All I can do is tell you that I regret it and that I'm sorry."

Chet raises a hand to stop me. "Getting an apology isn't why I told my mother she should invite you back here. I did it because your presence says more than any apology ever could."

So that's why Franny was so eager to have me return to Camp Nightingale. She had pitched it as a way to show that the camp was a safe, happy place again. In truth, my being here is a silent retraction of what I said about Theo fifteen years ago.

"Because I'm here again, it means I think Theo is innocent," I say.

"Exactly," Chet says. "But it's more than that. It's an opportunity for closure."

"That's why I decided to come."

"Actually, I was talking about Theo. I thought having you here would be a chance to make amends. That it would do him some good. God knows, he needs it."

"Why?" It's the only thing I can think to say. Theo is handsome, wealthy, and successful. What else could he possibly need?

"Theo's not as put together as he looks," Chet says. "He had a rough time after what happened here. Not that I can blame him. The police kept questioning him. Vivian's father said some awful stuff about him, as did the press. And Theo couldn't take it. Dropped out of school. Went heavy on the drugs and alcohol. Rock bottom came on the Fourth of July. A year after the disappearance. Theo went to a party in Newport, got lit, borrowed someone's Ferrari, and smashed it into a tree a mile down the road."

I shudder, recalling the scar on Theo's cheek.

"It's a miracle he survived," Chet continues. "Theo got lucky, I guess. But the thing is, I'm pretty sure he didn't plan to survive that crash. He's never come out and admitted he was trying to kill himself, but that's my theory. For months he had certainly acted like someone with a death wish. Things got better after that. My mother made sure of it. Theo spent six months in rehab, went back to Harvard, finally became a doctor, although two years later than he had planned. Because everything eventually went back to normal, none of us talk about that time. I guess my mother and Theo think I was too young to remember. But I do. It's hard to forget watching your only brother go through something like that."

He stops talking, takes a deep breath, lets out a long, sad sigh.

"I'm so sorry," I say, even though it's meaningless. It doesn't change what happened. It can't erase the pale line that now runs down Theo's cheek.

"I don't know why you accused him," Chet says. "I don't need to know. What matters is that you don't believe it now; otherwise you wouldn't be here. I don't want you to feel bad."

But I feel worse than bad. Truly villainous. I can't even will myself to look at Chet. Instead, I stare at the floor, mute and guilt-ridden.

"Don't beat yourself up over it," Chet says as he stands to leave. "That's the last thing any of us want. It's time to let go of the past. That's why you're here. It's why we're all here. And I hope it'll do everyone some good."

Eighteen

I wait a full five minutes after Chet leaves before diving back into Vivian's diary. It stays under my pillow as I count the seconds. I'm not worried about him returning to interrupt me once again. It's more of a moment to decompress after what he said about Theo. Even though he told me not to beat myself up, I can't help it.

Theo spent six months in rehab. Probably at the same time I was being treated for my own problems. Our first years after Camp Nightingale were almost identical. The only difference was the demons we faced.

Mine looked like Vivian.

Theo's looked like me.

Again, I know I can't repair the damage I've caused him. That opportunity passed fifteen years ago. But I can prevent further damage if I find out more about what happened to Vivian, Natalie, and Allison. He'll no longer have suspicion trailing after him like a shadow.

He'll be free.

And if it happens to him, it could also happen to me.

When the five minutes have elapsed, I remove Vivian's diary from under my pillow, flip to where I had left off, and dive in once more.

June 29,

It turns out I was right. Lottie told F, who pulled me aside after lunch and basically went apeshit on me. She threatened to call The Senator, as if he'd fucking care. She also said I needed to respect personal boundaries. I felt like telling her to shove those personal boundaries up her dusty twat. I didn't because I need to keep my head down. I can't rock that damn boat until it must be capsized.

So, to recap:

Bad news: She definitely suspects something.

Good news: I'm close to finding out her dirty little secret.

July 1,

I'm thinking about telling Emma.

Someone needs to know in case something happens to me.

July 2,

Well, that sucked.

I decided not to tell Em the whole truth about what I'm doing. It's safer for her that way. Instead, I opted to hint at it by taking her to my secret stash in the woods. You guessed it, THE BOX. The thing that started this whole investigation when I found it last summer.

I thought showing it to Emma would spark her interest, just in case the Magic 8 Ball lied and all signs actually point to getting my sorry ass booted from camp. That way she can continue what I started, if she's so inclined. And I was right. It DID spark her interest. I saw it in her eyes as soon as she opened that box.

But then the bad stuff had to take place. Yep, I showed her that I could swim. I thought she should know, for several reasons. One: If, God forbid, my body washes up on the beach one morning, she'll be able to tell police that I'm an expert swimmer. Two: She needs to learn not to trust everything everyone tells her. Two Truths and a Lie isn't just a game. For most people, it's a lifestyle. Three: I'll need to break her heart eventually. Might as well put a crack in it now.

So now she's pissed at me. Rightly so. She spent the rest of the day ignoring me. And it hurt like a motherfucker. There's so much I want to tell her. That life is hard. That you need to punch it before it punches you.

I know she's hurt. I know she thinks she's the only one whose parents ignore her. But she should try being left behind in New York while The Senator and Mrs. Senator go off to D.C. two months after her sister dies! Now that's abandonment.

As for the fake drowning, I had to do it. Hopefully Em will only pout a day. I'll give her flowers tomorrow and she'll love me again.

July 3,

Fun fact: In the 1800s, women could be sent to asylums for these reasons:

Hysteria

Egotism

Immoral life

Nymphomania

Jealousy

Bad company

Masturbation

Novel reading (!)

Kicked in the head by a horse

Other than the horse kicking, every single woman I've ever met could have been declared insane back then. Which is exactly how men wanted it. It's how they managed to keep women down. Don't like something they've said? Call them crazy and ship them off to the loony bin. Don't fuck their husbands enough? Commit them. Want to fuck them too much? Commit them. It's sick.

And don't you dare think things have changed much, diary. They haven't. The Senator was ready to have me locked up after Kath died. Like it was wrong of me to mourn her. Like grief was a mental illness.

Anyway, that's the lesson I learned today. Every woman is crazy. The ones who can't hide it well enough are shit out of luck.

150.97768 WEST

164

Update: And now I'm fucked. I forgot I left you out, dear diary. Came back from the campfire to find Natalie and Allison reading you. Which doesn't surprise me. They've been trying to get a peek at you all week. And now they have. I'm sure it was an eyeful. Thank God I didn't write that Natalie's gotten so thick in the thighs she looks like a lady wrestler or that Allison's so pasty she might as well be an albino. That would be AWFUL if they read that about themselves, right?

And while I'm tempted to leave you open to this page so they can do exactly that, I've decided it's best to hide you. You're no longer safe here, baby.

The less they know, the better.

Update #2: Welcome to your new home, little book. Hope you don't rot here. Drawing a map so I don't forget where you are.

July 4,

Can't write much. Rowing here already took half the morning. Rowing back will take even longer. F has probably noticed I'm gone. She's got spies everywhere. I'm certain she told Casey to double-check on me each night.

But that might not matter for much longer.

Because. I. Found. It.

That clichéd missing piece that ties everything together. Everything makes sense now. I know the truth. All I need to do is expose it.

But there's a hitch. After reading you, dear diary, Natalie and Allison want in on it. And I've decided I'm going to tell them everything. Because I can't do this without their help. I thought I could, but that's no longer an option.

Yes, I know I could just drop it, forget the whole thing, spend my summer, my year, the rest of my goddamned life pretending it never happened. A sane person would do that.

But here's the thing: some wrongs are so terrible that the people responsible must be held accountable. Call it justice. Call it revenge. Call it whatever. I don't give a fuck.

All I care about is this particular wrong. It can't be ignored. It must be righted.

And I'm the bitch that's going to do it.

I'm scared

Nineteen

That's it. The rest of the pages—more than two thirds of the diary—are blank. I flip through them anyway, just in case I've missed something. I haven't. There's nothing.

I close the diary and exhale. Reading it has left me feeling the same way I did after each of Vivian's hallucinatory visits. Confused and light-headed, spent and frightened.

Vivian was looking for something, that much is clear. What it was—and what she eventually found—remain frustratingly out of reach. Honestly, the only thing I'm certain about is that the paper on which Vivian drew her map was torn from the journal. There's a page missing between her entry about its new location and the one she made on the Fourth of July. I remove the map from my backpack and hold it against the ragged remnants of the missing page. It's a match.

I reread the entire diary, studying each page, parsing every word, trying to make sense of it. Little does, least of all why Vivian, a person who rarely failed to say exactly what she was thinking and feeling, needed to keep some things secret. So I give it yet another read, this time from back to front, starting with Vivian's unsettling final entry.

I'm scared.

That one confounds me the most. Of all the myriad emotions Vivian displayed in the short time I knew her, fear wasn't one of them.

I flip to the previous page. That entry was made the morning of July 4, prompting two new questions: When did she write that final entry, and what was she afraid of?

I clutch the book, frustrated, aching for answers that refuse to reveal themselves. "What did you learn, Viv?" I murmur, as if she could somehow answer me.

Judging by the entry dates, I assume she buried the book sometime during the night of July 3. My guess is that she snuck out while the rest of us were asleep. Not unusual for her. She had also done it the night before.

I remember because I was still mad that she had lied to be me about her swimming skills. I was especially livid about the reason she lied—because Theo had been paying too much attention to me. She saw me in his arms, whispering encouraging words as he taught me how to swim. And she couldn't stand it. So she faked drowning just to become the center of attention again.

I ignored her the rest of that canoe trip back to camp. And the rest of the afternoon. And at dinner, where I took her advice and showed up so late I was last in line. I sat alone and picked at the dinnertime dregs—lukewarm meatloaf and mashed potatoes dried to a crust. At the campfire, I sat with girls my own age, who showed little interest in me. Afterward, I went to bed early, pretending to be asleep while the others played Two Truths and a Lie without me.

Later that night, I woke to find Vivian tiptoeing into the cabin. She tried to be sneaky about it, but the creak of the third floorboard from the door gave her away.

I sat up, bleary-eyed. *Where did you go?*

I had to pee, Vivian said. *Or is taking a piss something else you disapprove of?*

She said nothing else as she climbed up to her bunk. But in the morning, a handful of tiny flowers were sitting on my pillow, right beside my head. Forget-me-nots. Their petals were a delicate blue. In the center of each was a yellow starburst.

I later stored them in my hickory trunk, pressed inside my copy of *The Lovely Bones*. Although she never admitted to putting them there, I knew they were from Vivian. She had indeed given me flowers. And just as she thought, I loved her again.

I flip back to the page where Vivian had made that prediction, reading it feverishly, wondering again if my feelings had been that transparent. It's only after I reread the passage about her own parents that I get an answer—Vivian simply knew. Because she was just like me. Neglected and lonely. Basking in whatever scraps of attention she received. It's how she was able to foresee that a hastily picked bunch of forget-me-nots would be enough to appease me. Because it would have been enough for her, too.

More flipping. More pages. More questions.

I turn to the page with Vivian's musings about insanity. Of all the things she had written, this one shakes me to my core. Reading it feels as though she's speaking directly to me, as if she foresaw my slide into madness a year before it would happen.

But why did she seek out that information? And where?

I vividly remember the day she made that entry. Riding to town in the camp's mint-green Ford, squeezed tight between Vivian and Theo at the wheel. He drove one-handed, his legs spread wide so that his thigh kept bumping against mine. Each touch made my heart feel like a tiny bird trapped in a cage, fluttering against the gilded bars. I didn't mind at all when Vivian said she was going shopping and slipped away from us, leaving me alone with Theo.

I flip to the next page, where she had jotted down that strange set of numbers.

150.97768 WEST
164

At first, I think they might be coordinates on a map. But when I grab my phone and check the compass app, I discover that 150 degrees points southeast. Which means it's something else. Only Vivian knows for sure. But I'm certain she wrote down the numbers for a reason. Like everything else, I get the sense that she's urging me forward, step by step, to find out what she learned all those years ago.

I'm in the process of taking a picture of the numbers with my phone when the door to Dogwood opens and Miranda, Krystal, and Sasha burst inside. Their sudden presence sends me once again scrambling to close the book and shove it under my pillow. I'm not as quick this time around, allowing them to catch me in the act.

"What are you doing?" Sasha asks, eyeing first the corner of the book poking from beneath my pillow and then my phone, which remains clutched in my hand.

"Nothing."

"Right," Miranda says. "You're totally not acting like someone just caught looking at porn."

"It's not porn." I pause, trying to see if the girls believe me. It's clear they don't, so I tell them the truth, minus any context that would make them ask more questions. "I'm trying to decipher something. A code."

Miranda's face lights up at the idea of solving a mystery. "What kind of code?"

I glance at the picture on my phone, reading off the number. "What does 150.97768 WEST mean to you?"

"Easy," Miranda says. "It's the Dewey Decimal System. Some book has that call number."

"You positive?"

She gives me a disbelieving look. "Um, yeah. I've spent, like, half my life at the library."

The library. Maybe that's where Vivian went when she claimed to be shopping. While there, she found a book important enough to note its call number in her diary. It's clear she was looking for something. I even think she might have found it.

I recall her entry about getting somewhere she wasn't supposed to be. The Big L is the Lodge. F is Franny. Simple enough. But Vivian frustratingly failed to mention exactly what she found there and what she managed to steal.

Still, she wrote enough to thoroughly unnerve me. Thinking about Franny's reaction to her snooping sends a chill flapping through me. It doesn't sound like Franny at all, which makes me wonder if Vivian was being paranoid. It certainly seems that way, especially Vivian's line about wanting to tell me what she was doing in case something happened to her.

I'm close to finding out her dirty little secret.

It turns out something bad did happen, only there's no proof it had anything to do with Franny or a deep, dark secret. Yet some events are too connected to be mere coincidence. This feels like one of them.

I know the truth.

The idea that I might be closer to learning what happened to the girls should excite me. Instead, a hard ball of pain forms in the pit of my stomach. Worry snowballing inside me. I assume Vivian experienced this exact feeling when she scribbled those last two words in her diary.

I'm scared.

So am I.

Because it's possible I've stumbled upon something sinister, even dangerous.

That after years of wondering, I'm on the cusp of getting actual answers.

Above all, I'm scared that if I keep digging, I might not like what I'll find.

Twenty

That night, my dreams are haunted by Vivian.

It's not like the hallucinations of my youth. Never do I think she's really there, returned from the ether. There's a cinematic quality to them—like I'm seeing one of the film noirs my father still watches on Sunday afternoons. Vivian in expressionistic black and white. First running through a forest as wild as one of my paintings. Then on a barren island, holding a pair of scissors. Finally in a canoe, rowing mightily into a rolling fog bank that whooshes over her, swirling and hungry, ultimately consuming her.

I wake clutching my charm bracelet as reveille blasts through camp. To my utter surprise, I have slept through the night. My eyelids flutter, tentatively facing the light of morning. Even before they're fully open, I can make out something at Dogwood's sole window.

A shape, dark as a shadow.

A gasp catches in my throat, lodging there, momentarily blocking all breath as whoever's at the window flees. I can't tell who it is. All I see is a dark figure streaking away.

Only when it's gone do I swallow hard, suppressing the gasp, forcing it back down. I don't want to wake the girls. Nor do I want to scare them. When I notice Sasha squinting down at me from her upper bunk, I can tell she didn't see whoever was at the window. All she sees is me sitting up in bed, my face as white as my cotton pillowcase.

"I had a nightmare," I tell her.

"I read that bad dreams can be caused by eating before bed."

"Good to know," I say, although I'm pretty sure my dreams of Vivian were caused by her diary and not what little I ate last night.

As for what I saw at the window, I'm certain it wasn't a dream. Nor was it my imagination or a play of the light, like I tried to convince myself is what happened at the latrine. This time, there's no talking myself out of it, no matter how much I'd like to.

Someone was *there*.

I still feel their presence. A ghostly hum right outside the window. My pulse races, humming in response. It tells me that I wasn't mistaken about yesterday.

Someone had watched me in that shower.

Just like someone trapped those crows inside the cabin.

And now someone was just watching me sleep.

I shudder, horrified, my skin crawling. If the girls weren't here, I'd let out a scream, just because it might make me feel better. Instead, I slide out of bed and head to the door.

"Where are you going?" Sasha whispers.

"Latrine."

Another lie. Tossed off to keep Sasha calm. Unlike me with my still-furious pulse and continuing shudder as I bolt outside to see if I can spot whoever was at the window. But already dozens of girls are spilling out of their cabins, roused by reveille and groggily starting the day. All of them stop when they see me. They also stare, some with their heads tilted in curiosity, others with outright surprise. A few more campers join the fray, doing the same thing. As does Casey when she passes by with two fingers pressed to her lips, already craving that first cigarette.

That's when it dawns on me. They're not staring at me. Their gazes are fixed on the cabin behind me.

I turn around slowly, not sure if I want to see what the others do. Their expressions—a little fearful, a little stunned—tell me it's nothing good. But curiosity keeps me spinning until I'm facing the front of Dogwood.

The door has been smeared with paint. Red. Still wet. Sliding down the wood in rivulets that resemble streaks of blood.

The paint forms a word spelled out in all caps, the letters large and bold and as piercing as a knife to the ribs.

LIAR

Franny again stands before a mess hall filled with campers, although this time it's to give a different kind of speech.

"To say I'm disappointed is an understatement," she says. "I'm devastated. Vandalism of any sort will not be tolerated at Camp Nightingale. Under normal circumstances, the culprit would be asked to leave immediately. But since you all have only been here a few days and may not yet understand the rules, whoever painted on the door of Dogwood will be allowed to stay if you come forward now. If you don't and are later caught, you'll be banned from this place for life. So, please, if any of you are responsible, speak up now, apologize, and we'll put the entire incident behind us."

Silence follows, broken by a few coughs and the occasional squeak of a cafeteria chair. No girls stand to confess. Not that I was expecting it. Most teenage girls would rather die than admit they did something wrong.

I should know.

I survey the crowd from my spot by the door. Most of the girls have their heads bowed in collective shame. The few who don't stare ahead with wide-eyed innocence, including Krystal and Sasha. Miranda is the only girl from Dogwood who seems pissed off by the incident. She sneaks glances at the girls around her, trying to find the guilty culprit.

Standing along the wall are Lottie, Theo, Chet, and Mindy. Mindy catches me looking and gives me a scowl. I have officially ruined her goal of things running smoothly.

"Well then," Franny says after a suitably unbearable length of time. "My disappointment only grows. After breakfast, all of you will return to your cabins. Morning classes are canceled while we sort everything out."

She makes her way out of the mess hall with the rest of the Lodge denizens in tow. When they pass, Lottie taps my shoulder and says, "Emma, please come with us."

I follow them to the arts and crafts building next door. Once everyone's inside, Lottie closes the door. I stand next to it, my body coiled, resisting the urge to sprint. Not just from the room but from the camp itself. My left hand started trembling the moment I saw the paint on the door, and it hasn't stopped since. The birds around my wrist rattle.

"Well, this is a fine mess," Franny says. "Emma, do you have any idea who could have done this?"

The obvious answer would be someone in this room. A major clue lies in the painted word currently being scrubbed off Dogwood's door. Other than Mindy, I've lied to all of them in the past. About Theo. About what I accused him of doing. And while none of them have called me a liar to my face, I wouldn't be surprised if they all felt that way in private. I wouldn't blame them, either.

Yet my gut tells me none of them are responsible. They're the ones who invited me back here, after all. And petty vandalism seems beneath a member of the Harris-White clan. If they wanted to be rid of me, they'd just say so.

"I don't know." I debate telling them about the person I saw at the window. Call it paranoia from Vivian's diary rubbing off on me, but I'm not sure I can trust anyone with the truth. Not until I get a better grasp on what's going on. There's a chance that, considering my history, no one will believe it's happening at all unless I have more proof. "I only knew about it once I left the cabin."

Franny turns to her younger son. "Chet, did you check the camera?"

"Yeah," he says while swiping the hair from over his eyes. "There's nothing. Which is a big red flag. The slightest motion triggers that camera."

"But someone had to be outside that cabin," I say. "That door didn't paint itself."

"Is the camera working now?" Franny asks, keeping her tone calm to counter my growing shrillness.

"Yes," Chet says. "Which means it either malfunctioned overnight or someone tampered with it. I imagine it wouldn't be too hard to climb up there on a ladder and put tape over the sensor."

"Wouldn't there be video of that?" Theo says.

Chet answers with a shake of his head. "Not necessarily. The camera is programmed to automatically turn on at nine p.m. and turn off at six in the morning. Someone could have tampered with it before nine and removed the tape right at six."

Franny then fixes her green-eyed gaze on me. Although current circumstances have dimmed it slightly, I still feel trapped by her stare.

"Emma, have you told anyone else about the camera?"

"No. But that doesn't mean people don't know about it. If I noticed it, then others probably did, too."

"Let's talk about the paint," Theo says. "If we can figure out where it came from, maybe it'll give us a better idea of who did it."

"Emma's the painter," Mindy pipes up. "She's the one with the most access to it."

"Oil paint," I say, shooting her an angry look. "And that's not what was on the door. It doesn't run like that. If I had to guess, I'd say it was acrylic paint."

"What's it used for?" Theo says.

I look to the center of the room, where Casey's workstation sits. All those cabinets and cubbyholes, filled with supplies.

"Crafts," I say.

I edge around one of the circular crafting tables and head to the cabinet against the wall behind it. Flinging it open, I see rows of plastic paint bottles. They're translucent, giving a glimpse of the colors contained within them. All the bottles are full, save for one.

Basic red.

Sitting nearby is a trash can. I go to it and spot a medium-size paintbrush at the bottom. Red paint clings to the bristles, still wet.

"See?" I say. "Not my paint. Not my brush."

"So someone snuck in here early this morning and used the paint," Theo says.

"The door is locked overnight," Lottie replies. "At least, it's supposed to be. Maybe whoever was last to leave yesterday forgot to lock it."

"Or has a key," Chet adds.

Lottie shakes her head. "The only people with keys are me, Franny, and Ben."

"Neither Lottie nor I would do such a thing," Franny says. "And Ben was only just arriving when the paint was discovered."

"So that means the door was left unlocked," Theo says.

"Maybe not," Mindy says. "Yesterday, while everyone was going to lunch, I caught Emma snooping around the other workstations."

All eyes turn to me, and I wilt in the heat of their stares. I take a step back, bump into a plastic chair, drop into it. Mindy looks at me with a sad, scrunched face, as if to show how much making the accusation has pained her.

"You honestly think I'm the one who did this?" I say. "Why would I vandalize my own door?"

"Why have you done a lot of things?"

Although Mindy says it, I assume that question has occurred to everyone in the room at some point. They might not have spoken it aloud like Mindy, but it's been asked all the same. It's in every look of Franny's green eyes. It's in the red light of the camera that blinks on when I enter Dogwood.

I have every reason to believe they'd forgiven me. It doesn't mean any of them trust me.

Except for maybe Theo, who says, "If Emma says she didn't do it, then I believe her. What we should be doing is asking why someone would do this to her."

I know the answer. But like that unspoken question, it's one I can't say aloud. It's there all the same, visible in my still-shaking hands.

Because someone at camp knows.

That's why I was watched in the shower. Why those three birds were released into the cabin. Why someone was at the window and smeared paint across the door.

It was their way of telling me that they know.

Not what I did to Theo.

What I did to the girls.

The realization keeps me pinned to the flimsy chair, even after everyone starts to leave. Before exiting, Theo looks at me with concern, his cheeks flushed enough to make his scar stand out.

"Are you okay?" he says.

"No."

I picture Vivian, Natalie, and Allison as paint marks on one of my canvases, waiting for me to cover them up. One of the reasons I came back here is because I couldn't keep doing that. Because I thought that if I learned more about what happened to them, my conscience would be clean.

But now I can't foresee spending an entire six weeks here. Whoever's been watching me will continue to do so, stepping up the reminders bit by bit. Trapped birds and paint on the door, I fear, are only the beginning. If there are answers to be found, I have to do it quickly.

"I need to get out of here. Just for a little bit."

"Where do you want to go?" Theo says.

I think of Vivian's diary and the call letters of a book.

"Town," I say.

FIFTEEN YEARS AGO

The radio, like the rest of the truck, had seen better days. The little music that did fizz from the speakers sounded tinny and pockmarked with static. Not that it mattered. The only radio station Vivian and I could find played nothing but country music, the steel guitar and fiddle twang accompanying our journey out of Camp Nightingale.

"So why are we doing this again?" Theo asked as the truck passed under the camp's entrance arch.

"Because I'm in need of some hygiene products," Vivian said. "Personal, lady ones."

"That's more than I need to know." Theo shook his head, amused in spite of himself. "What about you, Em?"

"I'm just along for the ride."

And I was. Quite unexpectedly. I had been waiting for the others outside the mess hall, the pollen from Vivian's forget-me-nots still dusting my fingertips, when Natalie and Allison arrived.

"Vivian needs you," Allison said.

"Why?"

"She didn't say."

"Where is she?"

Natalie jerked her head toward the arts and crafts building on her way inside. "Over there."

That's where I found Vivian, Theo, and the mint-green pickup. Vivian was already inside, drumming her fingers against the sill of the open window. Theo leaned against the driver's-side door, his arms crossed.

"Hey there, latecomer," he said. "Hop in."

I squeezed between the two of them, their bodies warm against me as the truck bucked along the pothole-riddled road. Theo's legs continually bumped mine, as did his arm whenever he turned the steering wheel. Downy hairs from his forearm tickled my skin. The sensation made my stomach flutter and heart ache, as if they were being filled beyond capacity, becoming too large for my scrawny frame.

It stayed that way the entire drive into town, which had no discernible name but could have been any small town anywhere in the country. There was a main drag, quaint storefronts, red, white, and blue bunting on porches. We passed a town green with its generic war memorial and a sign promising a parade the next morning and fireworks at night.

Theo parked the truck, and Vivian and I quickly hopped out, stretching our legs, pretending the journey was uncomfortable, a burden. Better that than to have let Theo think I enjoyed his accidental touches.

Properly stretched, Vivian started to cross the street, heading toward an old-timey drugstore on the corner. "I'll see you losers in an hour," she said.

"An *hour*?" Theo said.

Vivian kept walking. "I plan to enjoy my freedom by going shopping. Maybe I'll buy myself something pretty. You and Emma go get lunch or something."

She strode into the pharmacy without another word. Through the window, I watched her pause at a rack of cheap sunglasses by the door and try on a pair shaped like hearts.

"Well, I guess it's just us," Theo said, turning my way. "You hungry?"

We walked to a diner that was as sleek and shiny as a bullet and settled into a booth by the window. Theo ordered a cheeseburger, fries, and a vanilla milk shake. I did the same, minus the milk shake, which Vivian never would have approved of in a million years. While we waited for the food, I stared out the window and watched cars lazily cruise up and down the street, their lowered windows revealing kids, dogs, harried mothers behind the wheel.

Even though he was across the table from me, I didn't want to look at Theo too much. Each time I did glance his way, I pictured him in the latrine shower, glistening and beautiful and oblivious to my prying gaze. The image brought a shameful warmth to my face, my stomach, between my legs. I wondered if Vivian knew that was going to happen when she urged me to peek between those ill-spaced cedar planks. I hoped not. Otherwise, it just seemed cruel.

And Vivian wasn't cruel, despite sometimes appearing that way. She was my friend. My summer camp big sister. As I sat there with Theo, listening to oldies drift from a corner jukebox, I understood that the whole trip was Vivian's ruse to let me spend time alone with him. Another apology. One better than flowers.

"How are you liking Camp Nightingale?" Theo asked once the food had arrived.

"I love it," I said, taking a rabbitlike nibble on a French fry.

"My mother will be pleased to hear that."

"Do you like it there?"

Theo took a bite of burger, leaving a smudge of ketchup on the corner of his mouth. I resisted the urge to swipe it off with a flick of my finger. "I love it, too. Unfortunately, this looks like it'll be my last summer before internships take over my life. College certainly keeps you busy. Especially when you're premed."

"You're going to be a doctor?"

"That's the plan. A pediatrician."

"That's so noble," I said. "I think it's great you want to help people."

"And what do you want to be?"

"I think I want to be a painter."

I don't know why I said it. I certainly had no artistic ambitions I didn't quite know what to do with. It just sounded like the kind of profession Theo would want a woman to have. It was adult and sophisticated. Like something from a movie.

"Emma Davis, famous painter. That has a nice ring to it." Theo gave me a smile that made my legs quiver. "Maybe I'll come to one of your gallery openings."

Within seconds, I had my entire future mapped out. We'd keep in touch after the summer, exchanging letters that would become more meaningful as time passed. Love would eventually be declared. Plans would be made. We'd have sex for the first time on my eighteenth birthday, preferably in a candlelit room at some exotic locale. We'd stay devoted as I went to art school and he completed his residency. Then we'd marry and be the kind of couple other people envied.

As outlandish as it seemed, I told myself it could come true. I was mature for my age, or so I thought. Smart. Cool. Like Vivian. And I knew exactly what she would have done in that situation.

So when Theo attempted to take a sip of his milk shake, I beat him to it, leaning in and sucking from his straw. The move was bold, so utterly unlike me. I blushed, my face turning the same shade of peachy pink as the lip gloss I left behind on Theo's straw.

Yet there was more boldness in store. The kind of thing I never would have attempted had I spent even a fraction of a second thinking about it. But I didn't think. I simply acted, closing my eyes and tilting my mouth toward Theo's, the vanilla taste on my tongue spreading to my lips as I kissed him. His breath was hot. His lips were cold. The warmth and chill merged into a sweet, fluttery sensation that filled my body.

I pulled away quickly, my eyes still closed. I didn't want to look at Theo. I didn't want to see his reaction and bring an end to the magic spell I was under. He ended it anyway, softly saying, "I'm flattered, Emma. I really am. But—"

"I was just kidding," I blurted out, my eyes still squeezed shut as my heart twisted inside my chest. "It was a joke. That's all."

Theo said nothing, which is why I leaned back in the booth, turning to the window before opening my eyes.

Vivian was on the other side of the glass, her presence an unwelcome surprise. She stood on the sidewalk, wearing the drugstore sunglasses. Heart-shaped frames. Dark lenses reflecting diner chrome. Although I couldn't see her eyes, the smile that played across her lips made it clear she had witnessed everything.

I couldn't tell if she was happy about what she saw or amused by it. Maybe it was both. Just like during her games of Two Truths and a Lie, it was sometimes hard to tell the difference.

Twenty-One

My excuse for going into town was to fill a prescription for allergy medicine I'd forgotten to bring with me. Yet another lie. At this point, I've fallen off the truth wagon completely. But again, I consider it justified, especially because it gave me the chance to return to Dogwood and grab my backpack and Vivian's diary. By then the paint on the door had been completely wiped away. The only evidence it had been there at all was a swath of freshly cleaned wood and the nose-tickling smell of turpentine.

Now Theo and I ride in the same mint-green pickup that had whisked us out of camp fifteen years ago. Inside, all is silent, the radio apparently having died years ago. Theo drives with one hand on the steering wheel, his bent elbow jutting out the open window. My window is also rolled down. I stare at the woods as we leave Camp Nightingale, the trees a blur, light sparking through their branches.

I'm long past being mad at Theo about the camera outside Dogwood. My silence stems not from anger but from guilt. It's the first time we've been alone together since I learned about his breakdown, and I'm not sure how to act. There's so much I want to ask. If he felt as lonely during his six months of rehab as I did in the mental hospital. If he thinks about me every time he sees his scar in the mirror. With questions like that, silence seems to be the best choice.

The truck hits a whopper of a pothole, and both of us bounce toward the center of the bench seat. When our legs touch, I quickly pull away, edging as far as the passenger door will allow.

"Sorry," I say.

More silence follows. Tense and thick with things unspoken. It becomes too much for Theo, for he suddenly says, "Can we start over?"

I wrinkle my brow, confused. "You mean go back to camp?"

"I mean go back to the beginning. Let's start fresh. Pretend it's fifteen years ago and you're just arriving at camp." Theo flashes the same crooked smile he gave when we first met. "Hi, I'm Theo."

Once again, I'm amazed by his forgiveness. Maybe all bitterness and anger left him the instant that car smashed into a tree. Whatever the reason, Theo's a better person than me. My default reaction to being hurt is to hurt right back, as he well knows.

"Feel free to play along," he urges.

I'd love nothing more than to erase much of what's happened between then and now. To rewind back to a time when Vivian, Natalie and Allison still existed, Theo was still the dreamiest boy I'd ever seen, and I was a knock-kneed innocent nervous about camp. But the past clings to the present. All those mistakes and humiliations following us as we march inevitably forward. There's no ignoring them.

"Thank you for doing this," I say instead. "I know it's an inconvenience."

Theo keeps his eyes on the road, trying to hide how I've disappointed him yet again. "It's nothing. I needed to go into town anyway. Lottie gave me a list of things to pick up from the hardware store. And what Lottie demands, she gets. She's the one who really runs this place. Always has been."

When we reach town, I see it's more or less the same as I had left it, although some of the charm has been rubbed away. No patriotic bunting hangs from porch railings. A couple of empty storefronts mar the main drag, and the diner is gone, replaced by a Dunkin' Donuts. The drugstore remains, although it's now part of a chain, the name spelled out in red letters garishly placed against the building's original brick exterior.

"After this, I might make a quick stop at the library. I need a place with good Wi-Fi to catch up on work emails," I say, aiming for breeziness, as if the idea has just occurred to me."

I guess it works, because Theo doesn't question the idea. Instead, he says, "Sure, I'll meet you there in an hour."

He remains in the idling truck, watching. This gives me no choice but to keep up the ruse and hurry into the drugstore. Since I know it'll look suspicious on the return trip if I'm not carrying a bag from the place, I spend a few minutes browsing the shelves for something small to buy. I settle on a four-pack of disposable phone chargers. One for me and each girl in Dogwood. Franny will never know. Even if she does, I'm not sure I care.

At the cash register, I notice a rotating rack of sunglasses. The kind with a tilted mirror on top so customers can see how they look in the dime-store shades. I give it a spin, barely eyeing the knockoff Ray-Bans and cheap aviators when a familiar pair whirls by.

Red plastic.

Heart-shaped frames.

I snatch the sunglasses from the rack and turn them over in my hands, remembering the pair Vivian wore the entire ride back to camp that long-ago summer. I spent the whole drive wondering what she was thinking. Vivian said little during the return trip, preferring instead to stare out the open window as the breeze whipped her hair across her face.

I try on the sunglasses and lift my face to the rack's mirror, checking how they look. Vivian wore them better, that's for damn sure. On me, they're just silly. I look exactly like what I am—a woman approaching thirty in cheap shades made for someone half her age.

I toss the sunglasses onto the counter anyway. I pay with cash and stuff the disposable chargers into my backpack. The sunglasses are worn out of the store, slid high up my forehead to keep my hair in place. I think Vivian would approve.

Next, it's on to the library, which sits a block back from the main street. Inside, I pass the usual blond-wood tables and elderly patrons at desktop computers on my way to the reference desk. There a friendly librarian named Diana points me to the nonfiction section, and soon I'm scanning the stacks for 150.97768 WEST.

Astonishingly, it's still there, tucked tightly on a shelf of books about mental illness and its treatment. If the subject matter didn't already make me uneasy, the title certainly did.

Dark Ages: Women and Mental Illness in the 1800s by Amanda West.

The cover is stark. Black letters on a white background. Very seventies, which is when the book was printed. The publisher is a university press I've never heard of, which makes it even more baffling as to how or why Vivian learned of its existence.

I take the book to a secluded cubicle in the corner, pausing for a few steadying breaths before opening it. Vivian read this book. She held it in her hands. Mere days before she disappeared. Knowing this makes me want to put it back on the shelf, walk away, find Theo, and return to camp.

But I can't.

I need to open the book and see what Vivian saw.

So I fling it open, seeing on the first page a vintage photo of a young woman confined in a straitjacket. Her legs are nothing but skin covering bone, her cheeks are beyond gaunt, and her hair is wild. Yet her eyes blaze with defiance. As wide as half-dollars, they stare at the photographer as if willing him to look at her—really look—and understand her predicament.

It's a startling image. Like a kick in the stomach. A shocked huff of air lodges in my throat, making me cough.

Below the photo is a caption as sad as it is vague. *Unknown asylum patient, 1887.*

I turn the page, unable to gaze at the image any longer, just the latest person who could bear to look at this unnamed woman for only a brief amount of time. In my own way, I've also failed her.

Skimming through the book is an exercise in masochism. There are more photos, more infuriating captions. There are tales of women being committed because their husbands abused them, their families didn't want them, polite society didn't want to see them. There are accounts of beatings, of starvation, of cold baths and scrubbings with wire brushes on skin that hadn't seen daylight in months.

Each time I find myself gasping at a new horror, I realize how lucky I am. Had I been born a hundred years earlier, I would have become one of these women. Misunderstood and suffering. Hoping that someone would figure out why my mind betrayed me and thus be able to fix it. Most of these women never enjoyed such a fate. They suffered in sorrow and confusion until the end of their days, whereas my madness was temporary. It left me.

The shame is another story.

After a half hour of torturous skimming, I finally come to page 164. The one Vivian noted in her diary. It contains another photo, one that fills most of the page. Like the others in the book, it bears the same sepia-toned fuzziness of something taken a century ago. But unlike those images of anonymous girls imprisoned within asylum walls, this photograph shows a man standing in front of an ornate, Victorian structure.

The man is young, tall, thick of chest and stomach. He boasts an impeccably waxed mustache and a distinct darkness to his eyes. One hand grips the lapel of his morning coat. The other is slid into a vest pocket. Such a pompous pose.

The building behind him is three stories tall, made of brick, with dormer windows on the top floor and a chimneylike turret gracing the roof. The windows are tall and arched. A weathervane in the shape of a rooster rises from the turret's peaked roof. A less showy wing shoots off from the building's left side. It has only one floor, no windows, patchy grass instead of a lawn.

Even without that utilitarian wing, there's something off about the place. Brittle strands of dead ivy cling to a corner. Sunlight shining onto the windows have made them opaque. It reminds me of an Edward Hopper painting—*House by the Railroad*. The one that's rumored to have inspired the house from *Psycho*. All three structures project the same aura of homespun menace.

Beneath the photo is a caption—*Dr. Charles Cutler poses outside Peaceful Valley Asylum, circa 1898.*

The name summons a memory from fifteen years ago. Vivian and I alone in the woods, reading the tiny name engraved on the bottom of a rotting box.

Peaceful Valley.

I remember being curious about it. Clearly, Vivian was, too, for she came here looking for more information. And what she learned was that Peaceful Valley had been an insane asylum.

I wonder if that realization stunned her as much as it does me. I wonder if she also sat blinking in disbelief at the page in front of her, trying to wrap her head around how a box of scissors from an insane asylum ended up on the banks of Lake Midnight. I wonder if her heart raced as much as mine does. Or if her legs also suddenly started to twitch.

That sense of shock subsides when I look at the text on the page opposite the photo. Someone had drawn a pencil line beneath two paragraphs. Vivian, most likely. She was the kind of person who'd have no problem defacing a library book. Especially if she found something important.

By the end of the nineteenth century, a growing divide had formed regarding the treatment of mentally ill women. In the nation's cities, asylums remained crowded with the poor and indigent, who, despite a growing call for reform, still lived in deplorable conditions and were subjected to harsh treatment from undertrained and underpaid staff. It was quite a different story for the wealthy, who turned to enterprising physicians opening small, for-profit asylums that operated without government control or assistance. These retreats, as they were commonly known, usually existed on country estates in areas remote enough for family members to send troubled relatives without fear of gossip or scandal. As a result, they paid handsomely to have these black sheep whisked away and cared for.

A few progressive doctors, appalled by the extreme difference in care between the rich and the poor, attempted to bridge the gap by opening the doors of their bucolic retreats to those less fortunate. For a time, Dr. Charles Cutler was a common sight in the asylums of New York and Boston, where he sought out patients in the most unfortunate of situations, became their legal guardian, and whisked them away to Peaceful Valley Asylum, a small retreat in upstate

New York. According to the diary of a doctor at New York's noto-
rious Blackwell's Island Asylum, Dr. Cutler intended to prove that
a more genteel course of care could benefit all mentally ill women
and not just the wealthy.

While I'm almost positive this is what Vivian was pointing to in
her diary, I have no idea what it has to do with Franny. In all likeli-
hood, it doesn't. So why was Vivian so convinced that it did?

There seems to be only one way to find out—I need to search the
Lodge. Vivian discovered something in the study there before Lottie
came in and disrupted her. Whatever she found led her here, to this
same book in this same library.

Always leave a trail of bread crumbs. That's what Vivian told me. *So*
you know how to find your way back.

Only I can't help but think that the trail she left for me won't be
enough. I'll need a little help from a friend.

I grab my phone and immediately FaceTime Marc. He answers in
a rush, his voice almost drowned out by the cacophony in his bistro's
kitchen. Behind him, a line cook mans a skillet that sizzles and pops.

"It's a bad time, I know," I tell him.

"The lunch rush," Marc says. "I've got exactly one minute."

I dive right in. "Remember that reference librarian at the New
York Public Library you used to date?"

"Billy? Of course. He was like a nerdy Matt Damon."

"Are the two of you still friendly?"

"Define friendly."

"Would he try to get a restraining order if he saw you again?"

"He follows me on Twitter," Marc says. "That's not a restraining
order level of animosity."

"Do you think he'd help you do some research for your best friend
in the entire world?"

"Possibly. What will we be researching?"

"Peaceful Valley Asylum."

Marc blinks a few times, no doubt wondering if he's heard me cor-
rectly. "I guess camp's not going so well."

I quickly tell him about Vivian, her diary of cryptic clues, the fact that an insane asylum, of all things, might be involved. "I think Vivian might have found something before she disappeared, Marc. Something that someone else didn't want her to know."

"About an asylum?"

"Maybe," I say. "In order to be sure, I need to know more about that asylum."

Marc pulls his phone closer to his face until all I can see is one large, squinting eye. "Where are you?"

"The local library."

"Well, someone there is watching you." Marc moves the phone even closer. "A *hot* someone."

My eyes dart to the lower corner of my screen, where my own image rests in a tiny rectangle. A man stands roughly ten feet behind me, his arms folded across his chest.

Theo.

"I need to go," I tell Marc before ending the call. As his image cuts out, I get a one-second glimpse of his face, which is stony with concern. It's the opposite of Theo's expression. When I finally turn around to face him, his face is a placid surface, unreadable.

"Are you ready to go?" he says, his voice as blank as his features. "Or do you need more time?"

"Nope," I reply. "All done."

I gather my things, leaving the book where it is. Its contents are stamped on my memory.

On our way out of the library, I pull the sunglasses over my eyes, shielding them not only from the midafternoon glare but from Theo's inquisitive gaze. The expression on his face hasn't wavered once since he caught me talking to Marc. The least I can do is match him in opaqueness.

"Nice sunglasses," he says once we're in the truck.

"Thanks," I reply, even though it didn't sound like a compliment.

Then we're off, heading back to camp in a fresh cocoon of silence. I'm not sure what it means. Nothing good, I assume. Gregariousness is second nature to Theo. Or I could simply be projecting, letting

Vivian's diary entries seep into my psyche and make me paranoid. Then again, considering what happened to her, Natalie, and Allison, maybe a little paranoia isn't such a bad thing.

It's only when the camp's gate slides into view that Theo says, "I need to ask you something. About that summer."

I already know he's going to bring up my false accusation against him. It's like barbed wire that's been stretched between us—invisible yet keenly felt whenever one of us nudges against it. Rather than respond, I roll down the window and turn my face toward the breeze, letting it tangle my hair just like Vivian's.

"It's about that day we drove into town," he continues.

I exhale into the rush of warm air hitting my face, relieved to not have to talk about why I had accused him. At least for now.

"What about it?"

"Well, we had lunch at that diner and—"

"I kissed you."

Theo chuckles at the memory. I don't. It's hard to laugh at one of the most humiliating moments of your adolescence.

"Yes, that. Were you lying then? About it being a joke?"

Rather than continue the lie, dragging it into a second decade, I say, "Why?"

"Because, at the time, I didn't think it was." Theo pauses, rubbing the salt-and-pepper stubble on his chin until he can summon the right words. "But I was flattered. And I want you to know that, had you been older, I probably would have kissed you back."

The same boldness I had felt in that diner returns out of nowhere. I think it might be the sunglasses. I feel different with them on. More direct. Less afraid.

I feel, I realize, like Vivian.

"And now?" I say.

Theo steers the truck to its spot behind the arts and crafts building. As it shudders to a stop, he says, "What about now?"

"I'm older. If I kissed you now, would you kiss me back?"

A grin spreads across Theo's face, and for a split second it's like we've been shuttled back in time, all those intervening years yet to be experienced. He's nineteen and the most handsome man I'd ever seen in my life. I'm thirteen and smitten, and every glimpse of him makes my heart explode into a flock of butterflies.

"You'll have to try it again sometime and see for yourself," he says.

I want to. Especially when he glances my way, a flirty glint in his eyes, that grin spreading wider until his lips part, practically begging to be kissed. It's enough to make me lean across the pickup's bench seat and do just that. Instead, I step out of the car and say, "That's probably not the best idea."

Theo—and the prospect of kissing him—is a distraction. And now that I'm inching closer to learning what Vivian was looking for, I can't be distracted.

Not by Theo.

Not by what I did to him.

And especially not by the lies both of us have told but aren't yet brave enough to admit.

Twenty-Two

That evening, the girls and I eat dinner at a picnic table outside the mess hall. The whole camp is still buzzing about the paint on the door. Liargate is what they're calling it, giving the incident the proper ring of scandal. I assume Casey, Becca, and the other instructors are also talking about it, which is why I'm fine with dining outdoors. I'm in no mood for their gossip.

"Where did you go this afternoon?" Sasha asks me.

"Into town."

"Why?"

"Why do you think?" Miranda snaps. "She did it to get away from this place."

Sasha swats at a fly buzzing around her tray of gray meatloaf and lumpy mashed potatoes. "Do you think one of the campers did it?"

"It sure wasn't one of the counselors," Krystal says.

"Some of the girls are saying you did it," Sasha tells me.

"Well, they're wrong," I say.

Across the picnic table, Miranda's face hardens. For a second, I think she's going to storm into the mess hall and punch the offending camper. She certainly looks ready for a fight.

"Why would Emma paint *liar* across our door?"

"Why would anyone do it?" Sasha asks.

Miranda answers before I get the chance, giving an answer far more pointed than mine. "Because some girls," she says, "are just basic bitches."

After dinner, I present them with their disposable chargers. "For emergencies only," I say, even though I know all that extended battery life will be wasted on Snapchat, Candy Crush, and Krystal's beloved superhero movies. Still, it puts the girls in a good mood as we head off to the nightly campfire. They deserve it after what they've endured today.

The fire pit is located on the outskirts of camp, as far away from the cabins as the property will allow. It sits in a round meadow that looks carved from the forest like a crop circle. In its center is the fire pit itself—a circle within the circle ringed by rocks hauled out of the woods and arranged there almost a century ago. The fire is already burning when we arrive, the engulfed logs placed in an upright triangle, like a teepee.

The four of us sit together on one of the sagging benches placed near the blaze. We roast marshmallows on twigs whittled to sharpness by Chet's Swiss Army knife, the handles sticky, the tips crusted and charred.

"You went here when you were our age, right?" Sasha asks.

"I did."

"Did you have campfires?"

"Of course," I say, pulling a freshly roasted marshmallow off my stick and popping it into my mouth. Although the hot sugar burns my tongue, it's not an unwelcome sensation. It brings back memories, both good and bad.

During my first, tragedy-shortened time here, I loved the campfire. It was hot, powerful, just the right amount of intimidating. I loved feeling its heat on my skin and watching the way it glowed white in the center. The burning logs popped and sizzled, like something alive, fighting the flames until they finally collapsed in a pile of embers, sending tiny dots of fire swirling upward.

"Why didn't you like this place again?" Miranda says.

"It's not the place I didn't like," I tell her. "It's what happened while I was here."

"Someone vandalized the cabin back then, too?"

"No," I say.

"Did you see ghosts?" Sasha asks, her eyes shiny and wide behind her glasses. "Because Lake Midnight is haunted, you know."

"Bullshit," Krystal says with a sniff.

"It's not. People really believe it," Sasha says: "A lot of people. Especially once those girls vanished."

My body tenses. The girls. That's who she's referring to. Vivian and Natalie and Allison. I had hoped their disappearance would somehow elude this new group of campers.

"Disappeared from where?" Krystal says.

"Right here," Sasha replies. "It's why Camp Nightingale closed in the first place. Three campers snuck out of their cabin, got lost in the woods, and died or something. Now their spirits roam the forest. On nights when the moon is full, they can be seen walking among the trees, trying to find the way back to their cabin."

In truth, it was inevitable that the missing girls of Dogwood would pass into legend. They're now as much a part of Camp Nightingale lore as Buchanan Harris's flooded valley and the villagers caught in the water's path. I picture the current campers whispering about them at night, huddled under sleeping bags, nervous eyes flicking to the cabin window.

"That's not true," Krystal says. "It's just a dumb-ass story to frighten people from going into the woods. Like that stupid movie by the guy who made *The Sixth Sense.*"

Miranda, not to be outdone, pulls out her phone and holds it to her ear, pretending to answer it.

"It's the creepy ghost girls calling," she announces to Sasha. "They said you're a terrible liar."

Later in the night, after the girls have gone to sleep, I remain awake in my bottom bunk, irritated and restless. The heat is partly to blame. It's a stifling, stuffy night made worse by a lack of airflow inside the cabin. I insisted on keeping the window closed and the door locked. After this morning, it felt like a necessary precaution.

That's the other reason sleep eludes me. I'm worried that whoever is watching me will make a repeat appearance. And I worry more about what they plan to do next. So I keep my gaze trained on the window, staring out at heat lightning flashing in the distance. Each flash brightens the cabin in throbbing intervals—a strobe light painting the walls an incandescent white.

During one blinding burst, I see something at the window.

Perhaps.

Because the flash of lightning is so quick, I can't quite tell. All I get is the briefest of glimpses. Half a glimpse, really. Just enough to make me think once again that someone is there, standing completely still, peering into the cabin.

I want to be wrong. I want it to be just the jagged shadows of the trees outside. But when the lightning returns, arriving in a bright flash that lingers for seconds, I realize I'm right.

There *is* someone at the window.

A girl.

I can't see her face. The lightning backlights her, turning her into a silhouette. Yet there's something familiar about her. The slenderness of her neck and shoulders. The slick tumble of her hair. Her poise.

Vivian.

It's her. I'm sure of it.

Only it's not the Vivian who could exist today. It's the one I knew fifteen years ago, unchanged. The Vivian who haunted me in my youth, prompting me to bury her in my paintings time and time again. Same white dress. Same preternatural poise. Held in her fist is a bouquet of forget-me-nots, which she holds out formally, like a silent-film suitor.

My right hand flies first to my chest, feeling the frightened thrum of my heart. Then it drops to my left arm, seeking out the bracelet around my wrist. I give it a sharp tug.

"I know you're not real," I whisper.

I pull harder, the bracelet digging into my skin. The bird charms clatter together—a muted, clicking sound almost drowned out by my panicked whispers.

"You have no power over me."

More tugging. More clicking.

"I'm stronger than everyone realizes."

The bracelet breaks. I hear a snap of the clasp, followed by the sensation of the chain slithering off my wrist. I fumble for it, catching it in my palm, squeezing my fingers around it. At the window, lightning flashes again. A burst of blinding light that quickly fizzles into darkness. All I see outside are a smattering of trees and a sliver of lake in the distance. No one is at the window.

The sight should bring relief. But with the bracelet now a curl of chain in my fist, it brings only more fear.

That Vivian will come again. If not tonight, then soon.

I'm stronger than everyone realizes, I think, repeating it in my head like a mantra. *I'm strong than everyone realizes. I'm strong. I'm*—

By the time I fall asleep—my heart hammering, body rigid, hand tight around my abused bracelet—the chant has mutated into something else. Less reassuring. More panicked. The words pinging against my skull.

I'm not going crazy. I'm not going crazy. I'm not going crazy.

FIFTEEN YEARS AGO

In the morning, instead of reveille blaring from the speakers on the mess hall roof, I was yanked from sleep by "The Star-Spangled Banner," in honor of Independence Day. Vivian slept right through it. When I climbed to her bunk to wake her, she swatted my hand and said, "Go the fuck away."

I did, pretending not to feel hurt as I headed to the latrine to shower and brush my teeth. After that, it was on to the mess hall, where kitchen workers dished out a Fourth of July special: pancakes topped with stripes of blueberries, strawberries, and whipped cream. I was told they were called Freedom Flapjacks. I called them ridiculous.

Vivian didn't show up for breakfast, not even fashionably late. Her absence freed Natalie to get a second helping of pancakes, which she consumed with abandon, strawberry sauce staining the corner of her mouth like stage blood.

Allison, on the other hand, didn't budge from her routine. She put down her fork after taking three bites and said, "I'm so full. Why am I such a pig?"

"You can eat more," I urged. "I won't tell Viv."

She gave me a hard stare. "What makes you think Vivian has anything to do with what I eat?"

"I just thought—"

"That I'm like you and do everything she tells me to?"

I looked down at my plate, more ashamed than offended. I had downed two-thirds of the pancakes without a second thought. Yet I knew that if Vivian had been there, I would have consumed only as much as she did. One bite or one hundred, it didn't matter.

"Sorry," I said. "I don't do it on purpose. It's just that—"

Allison reached across the table and patted my hand. "It's okay. *I'm* sorry. Vivian's very persuasive."

"And a bitch," Natalie added as she slid one of Allison's untouched pancakes onto her own plate. "We get it."

"I mean, we're friends," Allison explained. "Best friends. The three of us. But there are times when she can be—"

"A *bitch*," Natalie said, more emphatically that time. "Viv knows that. Hell, she'd say it herself if she were here."

My mind flashed back to the previous day. Her witnessing my disastrous attempt to kiss Theo. The smirk playing across her lips afterward. She had yet to bring it up, which worried me. I had expected some mention during the campfire or right before bed. Instead, there had been nothing, and it made me think she was saving it for a later game of Two Truths and a Lie, when it could inflict the most emotional damage.

"Why do you put up with it?" I said.

Allison shrugged. "Why do you?"

"Because I like her."

But it was more than that. She was the older girl who took me under her wing and shared her secrets. Plus, she was cool. And tough. And smarter than I thought she let on. To me, that was something worth clinging to.

"We like her, too," Natalie said. "And Viv's been through a lot, you know."

"But she's sometimes so mean to the two of you."

"That's just her way. We're used to it. We've known her for years."

"All our lives," Natalie chimed in. "We knew who she was and what she was like even before we became friends. You know, same school, same neighborhood."

Allison nodded. "We know how to handle her."

"What she means," Natalie said, "is that when Vivian gets in a mood, it's best to stay out of her way until it passes."

I spent the rest of the morning separated from the others in Dogwood, thanks to another advanced archery lesson. I was relegated to the arts and crafts building, where the camp's other thirteen-year-olds and I used leather presses to decorate rawhide bracelets. I would have preferred to shoot arrows.

After that it was lunch. That time, Natalie and Allison also didn't bother to show. Rather than eat alone, I declined the ham and Swiss sandwich on the menu and headed to Dogwood to look for them. To my surprise, I found them before I even reached the cabin. The roar of voices inside told me all three of them were there.

"Don't lecture us about secrets!" I heard Natalie yell. "Especially when you refuse to tell us where you were this morning."

"It doesn't matter where I went!" Vivian shouted back. "What matters is that you lied."

"We're *sorry*," Allison said with all the drama she could muster. "We told you a hundred times."

"That's not fucking good enough!"

I opened the door to see Natalie sitting shoulder to shoulder with Allison on the edge of her bunk. Vivian stood before them, her face flushed, hair stringy and unwashed. Natalie had her chest thrust forward, as if in the process of blocking a field hockey rival. Allison shrank into herself, her hair over her face, trying to hide what looked like tears. All three of them swiveled my way when I entered. The cabin plunged into silence.

"What's going on?" I asked.

"Nothing," Allison replied.

"Just bullshitting," Natalie said.

Only Vivian admitted the obvious truth. "Emma, we're in the middle of something. Shit needs to be sorted out. Come back later, okay?"

I backed out of the cabin, closing the door behind me and shutting out the raging storm taking place inside. Vivian was apparently having one of those moods Natalie and Allison had warned me about.

This time, they couldn't stay out of its path.

Not sure where else to go, I turned to head back to the center of camp. There was Lottie, standing right behind me. She wore a plaid shirt over a white tee. Her long hair was pulled back in a braid that ran down her back. Like me, she was close enough to hear the commotion coming from Dogwood, and her expression was one of curious surprise.

"Locked out?" she said.

"Sort of."

"They'll let you back in soon enough." Her gaze flicked from me to the cabin door and back again. "First time living with a group of girls?"

I nodded.

"It takes some getting used to. I was an only child, too, so coming here was a rude awakening."

"You were a camper here?"

"Yes, in my own special way," Lottie said. "But what I learned is that each summer there's always a fight or two in these cabins. It comes from being shoved together in such close quarters."

"This one sounds pretty bad," I said, surprised by how shaken seeing them fighting had left me. I couldn't stop picturing Vivian's cheeks flaring red or the tears glistening behind Allison's hair.

"Well, I know of a friendlier place we can go."

Lottie put a hand on my shoulder, steering me away from the cabin and into the heart of camp. To my surprise, we headed to the Lodge, skirting the side of the building to the steps that led to the back deck. At the top stood Franny, leaning against the railing, her eyes aimed at the lake.

"Emma," she said. "What a pleasant surprise."

"There's some drama in Dogwood," Lottie explained.

Franny shook her head. "I'm not surprised."

"Do you want me to defuse it?"

"No," Franny said. "It'll pass. It always does."

She waved me to her side, and the two of us stared at the water, Lake Midnight spread before us in all its sun-dappled glory.

"Gorgeous view," she said. "Makes you feel a little bit better, doesn't it? This place makes everything better. That's what my father used to say. And he learned it from *his* father, so it must be true."

I looked across the lake, finding it hard to believe the entire body
of water hadn't existed a hundred years earlier. Everything surrounding it—trees, rocks, the opposite shore shimmering in the distance—
felt like it had always been there.

"Did your grandfather really make the lake?"

"He did indeed. He saw this land and knew what it needed—a lake.
Because God had failed to put one here, he made it himself. One of the
first people to do that, I might add." Franny inhaled deeply, as if trying
to consume every scent, sight, and sensation the lake provided. "And
now it's yours to enjoy any way you'd like. You do enjoy it here, don't
you, Emma?"

I thought I did. I loved it here two days ago, before Vivian took me
out in the canoe to her secret spot. Since then, my impression of the
place had been chipped away by things I didn't quite understand. Vivian and her moods. Natalie and Allison's blind acceptance. Why the
thought of Theo continued to make my knees weak even after I humiliated myself in front of him.

Unable to let Franny know any of this, I simply nodded.

"Wonderful," Franny said, beaming at my answer. "Now try to
forget about the unpleasantness in your cabin. Don't let anything spoil
this place for you. I certainly don't. I won't let it."

Twenty-Three

I wake with the dawn, my fingers still curled around the broken brace-let. Because I spent the night clenched with worry, my lower back and shoulders hurt, the pain there beating as steadily as a drum. I slide out of bed, shuffle to my trunk, and dig out my bathing suit, towel, trusty robe, and drugstore sunglasses. On my way out, I do a quick check of the door. Nothing new has been painted there. I'm grateful that, for now, seeing Vivian again is the worst of my worries.

After that, it's more shuffling to the latrine, where I change into the bathing suit, then to the lake and finally into the water, which is such a relief that I actually sigh once I'm fully submerged. My body seems to right itself. Muscles stretch. Limbs unfurl. The pain settles to a mild ache. Annoying but manageable.

Rather than full-out swim, I lean back in the water, floating the way Theo taught me. It's a hazy morning, the clouds as gray as my mood. I stare up at them, searching in vain for hints of sunrise. A blush of pink. A yellow glow. Anything to take my mind off Vivian.

I shouldn't have been surprised by her appearance. Honestly, I should have expected it after three days of nonstop thinking about her. Now that I've seen her, I know she'll return. Yet another person watch-ing me.

I take a deep breath and slip beneath the lake's surface. The color-less sky wobbles as water comes between us, rushing over my open eyes, distorting my vision. I sink deeper until I'm certain no one can see me. Not even Vivian.

I stay submerged for almost two full minutes. By then my lung burn like wildfire and my limbs involuntarily scramble for the surface. When I emerge, I'm hit once again with the sensation of being watched from a distance. My muscles tighten. Bracing for Vivian.

On shore, someone sits near the water's edge, watching me. It's not Vivian, thank God. It's not even Becca.

It's Franny, sitting in the same grassy area Becca and I had occupied two mornings ago. She still wears her nightgown, a Navajo blanket wrapped around her shoulders. She waves to me as I swim back to shore.

"You're up early," she calls out. "I thought I was the only early riser around here."

I say nothing as I dry myself with the towel, put on the robe, and slip on the sunglasses. Although Franny appears happy to see me, the feeling isn't quite mutual. With Vivian now fresh in my thoughts, so, too, is her diary.

I'm close to finding out her dirty little secret.

That line, the appearance of the camera, and Franny's noticeable lack of support after Mindy accused me of vandalizing my own damn door have left me in a state of deep mistrust. I'm debating whether to walk away when Franny says, "I know you're still upset about yesterday. With good reason, I suppose. But I hope that doesn't mean you can't sit with an old woman looking for a little company."

She pats the grass next to her—a gesture that squeezes my heart a little. It makes me think I can forgive the camera and her failure to rush to my defense. As for Vivian's diary, I tell myself that she could have been lying about Franny keeping secrets. Being dramatic for drama's sake. It was, after all, her forte. Perhaps the diary was just another lie.

I end up brokering a compromise between my suspicious mind and my squishy heart. I sit beside Franny but refuse to engage her in conversation. Right now, it's the best I can do.

Franny seems to intuit my unspoken rules and doesn't press me for details about why I'm up so early. She simply talks.

"I have to say, Emma, I'm envious of your swimming ability. I used to spend so much time in that lake. As a girl, you couldn't get me to leave the water. From sunrise to dusk, I'd be out there paddling away. Not anymore, though. Not after what happened to Robert."

She doesn't need to elaborate. It's clear she's referring to Robert White. Her much-older husband. The man who died years before she adopted Theo and Chet. Another piece of Vivian's diary snakes into my thoughts.

Don't you think it's strange that a dude who almost made it to the Olympics drowned?

I push it away as Franny keeps talking.

"Now that my swimming days are over, I observe," she says. "Instead of being in the lake, I watch everything going on around it. Gives you a new perspective on things. For instance, this morning I've been keeping an eye on that hawk."

Franny leans back, putting her weight on one arm. The other emerges from her blanket and points to a hawk lazily circling over the lake.

"Looks like an osprey," she says. "I suspect he sees something he likes in the water. Once, years ago, two peregrine falcons made their nest right outside our living room window at the Harris. Chet was just a boy at the time. My word, was he fascinated by those birds. He'd stare out that window for hours, just watching, waiting for them to hatch. Soon enough, they did. Three eyesses. That's what falcon chicks are called. They were so small. Like squawking, wriggling cotton balls. Chet was overjoyed. As proud as if they were his own. It didn't last long. Nature can disappoint as easily as it entrances. This was no exception."

The osprey overhead suddenly dives toward the lake and, wings spread wide, slices its feet through the water. When it rises again, there's a fish gripped in its talons, unable to escape no matter how much it wriggles and flops. The osprey swoops away, heading to the far side of the lake, where it can eat in peace.

"Why did you reopen the camp?"

I blurt it out, surprising even myself. But Franny was expecting it. Or at least a question similar to it. She pauses long enough to take a breath before replying, "Because it was time, Emma. Fifteen years is too long for a place to stay empty."

"Then why didn't you do it sooner?"

"I didn't think I was ready, even though the camp was right here waiting for me."

"What convinced you that you were?"

This time, there's no pat answer at the ready. Franny thinks it over, her eyes on the lake, jaw working. Eventually, she says, "I'm about to tell you something, Emma. Something personal that very few people know. You must promise not to tell another soul."

"I promise," I say. "I won't say a word."

"Emma, I'm dying."

My heart feels squeezed again. Harder this time. Like it, too, has been scooped up by that osprey.

"Ovarian cancer," Franny says. "Stage four. The doctors gave me eight months. That was four months ago. I'm sure you can do the math."

"But there must be something you can do to fight it."

The implication is clear. She's worth millions. Certainly someone with that much money can seek out the best treatment. Yet Franny gives a sad shake of her head and says, "It's too late for all that fuss now. The cancer's spread too far. Any treatment would only be a way of delaying the inevitable."

I'm stunned by her calmness, her serene acceptance. I'm the exact opposite. My breath comes in short bursts. Tears burn the corners of my eyes, and I hold back a sniffle. Like Vivian, I now know one of Franny's secret. Only it's not dirty. It's sad and makes me think of that sundial hidden away in the forest. That last hour truly does kill.

"I'm so sorry, Franny. Truly I am."

She pats my knee the way my grandmother used to. "Don't you dare feel sorry for me. I understand how fortunate I am. I've lived a long life, Emma. A good one. And that should be enough. It is, really. But there's one thing in my life that wasn't fortunate."

"What happened here," I say.

"It's troubled me more than I let Theo and Chet know," Franny says.

"What do you think happened to them? To Vivian and the others?"

"I don't know, Emma. I really don't."

"You must have some theory. Everyone else does."

"Theories don't matter," Franny says. "It's no good dwelling on what happened. What's done is done. Besides, I don't like being reminded of how much that disappearance cost me in so many ways."

That's a sentiment I can understand. Camp Nightingale was forced to close. Franny's reputation was sullied. The taint of suspicion never entirely left Theo. Then there was the matter of three separate law-suits filed by Vivian's, Natalie's, and Allison's parents, accusing the camp of negligence. All three were settled immediately, for an undis-closed sum.

"I wanted to have one last summer of things being the way they used to be," she says. "That's why I reopened the camp. I thought if I could do that successfully, with a new mission, then it might ease the pain of what happened fifteen years ago. One last glorious summer here. And then I could die a content woman."

"That's a nice reason," I say.

"I think so," Franny replied. "And it would certainly be a shame if something happened to spoil it."

The ache in my heart fades to numbness as yet another thing Viv-ian wrote in her diary commands my thoughts.

She definitely suspects something.

"I'm sure it won't." I try to sound chipper when I say it, hoping it hides the sudden unease overcoming me. "Everyone I've talked to is having a great time."

Franny tears her gaze away from the water and looks at me, her green eyes untouched by illness. They're watchful, probing, as if they can read my thoughts. "And what about you, Emma? Are you enjoying your time here?"

"I am," I say, unable to stare back. "Very much."

"Good," Franny says. "I'm so pleased."

Her voice contains not a hint of pleasure. It's as chilly as the slight breeze that gusts across the lake and ripples the water. I pull my robe tight around me, fending off the sudden cold, and look to the Lodge, where Lottie has emerged on the back deck.

"There you are," she calls down to Franny. "Is everything okay?"

"Everything's fine, Lottie. Emma and I are just chatting about camp."

"Don't be too long," Lottie says. "Your breakfast isn't getting any warmer."

"You should go," I tell Franny. "And I should probably wake the girls in Dogwood."

"But I haven't finished my story about Chet and the falcons," Franny says. "It ends not long after those birds emerged from their eggs. Chet was obsessed with them, as I've said. Spent all his free time watching them. I think he truly grew to love those birds. But then something happened that he wasn't prepared for. Those eyesses got hungry. So the mother falcon did what mother falcons are known to do. She fed them. Chet watched her leave her perch outside our window and fly into the sky, circling, until prey appeared. It was a pigeon. A poor, unsuspecting pigeon probably on its way to Central Park. That mama falcon swooped down and snatched it in midair. She brought it back to the nest by our window, and as Chet watched, she used that sharp, curved beak to tear that pigeon apart and feed it to her babies, piece by piece."

I shudder as she talks, picturing flapping wings and downy feathers floating in the air like snow.

"You can't blame that mother falcon," Franny says matter-of-factly. "She was simply doing what she needed to do. Taking care of her children. That was her job. But it broke Chet's heart. He watched those squawking little eyesses too closely, and they showed their true natures. Some of his innocence was taken away that day. Not much. Just the tiniest bit. But it was a part of him he would never be able to get back. And although we don't talk about those falcons, I'm certain that he'd say he regrets watching them closely. I think he'd say that he wished he hadn't looked so much."

Franny climbs to her feet, struggling slightly, the effort leaving her body quivering. The blanket slips, and I get a peek at her rail-thin arms. Pulling the blanket around herself, she says, "You have a good morning, Emma."

She shuffles away, leaving me alone to contemplate the story of Chet and the falcons. While it didn't sound like a lie, it also didn't quite have the ring of truth.

It might have been, I realize with another robe-tightening chill, a threat.

Twenty-Four

The morning painting class is spent in a state of distraction. The girls arrange their easels in a circle around the usual still-life fodder. Table. Vase. Flowers. I monitor their progress with disinterest, more concerned with the bracelet that's once again around my wrist. I'd managed to fix the clasp with some colored string from Casey's craft station—a stopgap measure I suspect won't last until the end of the day, let alone the rest of the summer. Not the way I'm constantly twisting it.

I'm made nervous by all the activity drifting through the building like a tide. Becca and her budding photographers marching in from the woods. Casey and her crafters stringing slim leather necklaces with beads. All these girls. All these prying eyes.

And one of them knows what I did fifteen years ago. A fact I'm sure I'll be reminded of sooner rather than later.

I give the bracelet another tug as I stand next to Miranda, examining her work in progress. When her gaze lingers on my wrist, I pull my hand away from the bracelet and look out the window.

From the arts and crafts building, I have an angled view of the Lodge, where various members of the Harris-White family come and go. I see Mindy and Chet bickering about something as they head to the mess hall, followed by Theo trotting past on a morning jog. A minute later I spot Lottie gingerly guiding Franny toward the lake.

Right now, the Lodge is empty.

Franny's story returns to me, whispering in my ear.

He watched them too closely, and they showed their true natures.

I know I should heed her warning. This won't end well. Even if I do get answers, there's no guarantee my conscience will rid itself of guilt. But I'll never know if I don't try. Not knowing is what brought me here. Not knowing is why I kept seeing Vivian all those years ago. It's why I saw her last night. This is my only chance.

"I need to take care of something," I tell the class. "I'll be right back. Keep painting."

Outside, I slip away to Dogwood and retrieve my phone and charger. I then make my way to the Lodge, moving at an awkward half run, torn between being inconspicuous and being speedy. In truth, I need to be both.

At the Lodge, I knock on the red front door, just in case someone returned during my jaunt to the cabin and back. When seconds tick by and no one answers, I give the doorknob a twist. It's unlocked. I check to see if anyone is nearby and possibly watching. No one is. Quickly, I tiptoe inside and close the door behind me. Then it's through the entrance hall and living room before veering left into the study.

The room is roughly the same size as Dogwood, with a desk in the center and floor-to-ceiling bookshelves where our bunk beds would be. The wall behind the desk is covered with framed photographs. There's an air of neglect about the place—like a museum that's not very good at upkeep. A thin layer of dust covers the Tiffany lampshade on the desk. There's a thicker coat of it on the rotary phone, which looks like it hasn't been touched in years.

I lower myself onto my hands and knees, searching the walls for an outlet. I find one behind the desk and plug in the phone charger. Then I stand in the middle of the study, wondering where to look first. It's hard to decide without Vivian's diary to guide me. I recall her writing about how she managed to sneak something out of the study, which means there are multiple possible clues here.

I head to the bookshelf on my left, which holds dozens of thick, musty volumes about nature. Darwin's *On the Origin of Species.* Audubon's *Birds of America. Walden* by Thoreau. I grab a thick purple book and examine its cover. *Poisonous Plants of North America.* A quick flip through its pages reveals pictures of lacy white flowers, red berries, mushrooms colored a sickly green. I doubt these books are what Vivian was referring to.

I turn next to the desk, giving its phone, lamp, and blotter calendar a cursory glance before reaching for the three drawers stacked from floor to desktop. The first drawer is the usual menagerie of pen caps and paper clips. I close it and move to the middle one. Inside is a stack of folders. They bulge with documents, their edges brittle with age. I flip through them. Most appear to be receipts, financial statements, invoices for long-ago work on the property. None contain a hint of scandal. At least nothing that Vivian could suss out during a brief bit of snooping.

In the bottom drawer, I find a wooden box. It's just like the one Vivian showed me during our outing to the other side of the lake, only better preserved. Same size. Same surprising heft. Even the initials carved into the lid are the same.

CC

Charles Cutler.

The name slips into my head without warning or effort. One look at those initials and it's right there, summoned at will. I lift the box from its hiding place and carefully turn it over. On the bottom are four familiar words.

Property of Peaceful Valley.

I turn the box back over and open it, revealing a green velvet interior. Nestled inside are photographs.

Old ones.

Of women in gray with long hair draped down their backs.

Each one assumes the same pose as Eleanor Auburn, minus the clutched hairbrush.

This is where Vivian got that picture. I'm certain of it. It's merely one of what appears to be two dozen. I sort through them, unnerved by their uniformity. Same clothes. Same bare-wall background. Same eyes made dark by despair and hopelessness.

Just like the one of Eleanor, the back of each photo has been marked with a name.

Henrietta Golden. Lucille Tawny. Anya Flaxen.

These women were patients at Peaceful Valley. The unfortunates whom Charles Cutler rescued from squalid, crowded asylums and brought to Peaceful Valley. Only I have a gnawing suspicion his intentions weren't so noble. A chill settles over me, increasing with every name I read until I'm practically numb.

Auburn. Golden. Tawny. Flaxen.

Those aren't last names.

They're hair colors.

I'm struck by a dozen different thoughts, all clashing together in my brain. Scissors in that crumbling box. The broken-glass sound they made when Vivian turned it over. Watching Allison's mother in that guilt-inducing production of *Sweeney Todd*. A character sent to bedlam, at the mercy of wardens who sold their hair to wigmakers.

That's what Charles Cutler was doing. It explains these women's long locks and why their last names went unwritten, as if the only important aspect of their identity was the color of their hair.

It makes me wonder if any of them knew the purpose they served. That they weren't patients but commodities, ones who surely saw none of the money Charles Cutler received from wigmakers. The idea is so distractingly sad that I don't realize someone has entered the Lodge until a voice rings out from the entrance hall.

"Hello?"

I drop the photos back into the box and quickly replace the lid. The motion sets the charms on my bracelet clicking. I press my wrist against my stomach to silence them.

"Is someone in here?" the voice calls.

"I am," I say, hoping it will cover the sound of me closing the desk drawer. "Emma Davis."

Springing to my feet behind the desk, I find Lottie in the doorway. She's surprised to see me. The feeling is mutual.

"I'm charging my phone. Mindy told me I could do it here if I needed to."

"You're lucky Franny's not here to see you. She's a stickler about such things." Lottie sneaks a glance behind her, making sure Franny is indeed elsewhere. Then she creeps into the room with a conspiratorial gleam in her eyes. "It's a silly rule if you ask me. I warned her that girls are different now than they were back then. Always glued to their phones. But she insisted. You know how stubborn she can be."

Lottie joins me at the desk, and for a heart-stopping second, I think she knows what I've been doing. I brace myself for questions, perhaps a thinly veiled threat similar to the one Franny offered this morning. Instead, she focuses on the framed photographs cramming the wall behind the desk. They seem to have been placed there in no discernible order. Color photos mingle with black-and-white ones, forming a wall-size collage of images. I spot a grainy picture of an imposing man in front of what I presume to be Lake Midnight. A date has been hastily scrawled in the picture's lower right corner: 1903.

"That's Franny's grandfather," Lottie says. "Buchanan Harris himself."

He has a hugeness so many important men of that age possessed. Big shoulders. Big belly. Big, ruddy cheeks. He looks like the kind of man who could make a fortune stripping the land of its trees and then spend that money creating a lake just for his personal enjoyment.

Lottie points to a birdlike woman also in the photo. She has big eyes and Kewpie doll lips and is dwarfed by her husband. "Franny's grandmother."

"I heard she drowned," I say.

"Childbirth," Lottie replies. "It was Franny's husband who drowned."

"How did it happen?"

"The drowning? That was before my time. What I heard is that Franny and Robert went for a late-night swim together like they did every day. Nothing strange about that. Only on that particular night, Franny came back alone. She was hysterical. Carrying on about how Robert went under and never came back up. That she searched and searched but couldn't find him. They all went out in boats to look for him. His body wasn't found until the next morning. Washed up on shore. The poor man. This place certainly has seen its fair share of tragedy."

Lottie moves on to another black-and-white one showing a young girl leaning against a tree, a pair of binoculars around her neck. Clearly Franny. Below it is another photo of her, also taken at the lake, rendered in the garish colors of Kodachrome. She's a few years older in this one, standing on the Lodge's deck, her back turned to the water. Another girl stands beside her, smiling.

"There she is," Lottie says. "My mother."

I take a step closer to the photo, noticing the similarities between the woman posing with Franny and the one standing at my side. Same pale skin. Same Bette Davis eyebrows. Same heart-shaped faced that tapers to a pointed chin.

"Your mother knew Franny?"

"Oh, yes," Lottie says. "They grew up together. My grandmother was the personal secretary to Franny's mother. Before that, my great-grandfather was Buchanan Harris's right-hand man. In fact, he helped create Lake Midnight. When Franny turned eighteen, my mother became her secretary. When she passed away, Franny offered the job to me."

"Is this what you wanted to do?"

I'm aware of how rude the question sounds. Like I'm judging Lottie. In truth, I'm judging Franny for continuing the Harris tradition of using generations of the same family to make their own lives easier.

"Not exactly," Lottie says with unyielding tact. "I was going to be an actress. Which meant I was a waitress. When my mother died and Franny offered me the job, I almost turned it down. But then I came to my senses. I was in my thirties, barely scraping by. And the Harris-Whites have been so kind to me. I even think of them as family. I grew up with them. I've spent more time here at Lake Midnight than Theo and Chet combined. So I accepted Franny's offer and have been with them ever since."

There's so much more I want to ask. If she's happy doing the same thing her mother did. If the family treats her well. And, most important, if she knows why Franny keeps photos of asylum patients in her desk.

"I think I see Casey in this one," Lottie says farther down the wall, at a spot of pictures of Camp Nightingale during its prime. Groups of girls posing on the tennis court and lined up at the archery range, bows pulled back. "Right here. With Theo."

She points to a photo of the two of them swimming in the lake. Theo stands waist-deep in the water, the telltale lifeguard whistle around his neck. Cradled in his arms—in the exact way he cradled me during my swimming lesson—is Casey. She's slimmer in the picture, with a happy, youthful glow. I suspect it was taken when she was still a camper here.

Just above that picture is one of two girls in polo shirts. The sun is in their eyes, making them squint. The photographer's shadow stretches into the bottom of the frame, like an unnoticed ghost swooping down on them.

One of the girls in the photograph is Vivian.

The other is Rebecca Schoenfeld.

The realization stops my heart cold. Just for a second or so. In that pulseless moment, I stare at the two of them and their easy familiarity. Wide, unforced smiles. Skinny arms tossed over shoulders. Keds touching.

This isn't a photo of two girls who barely know each other.

It's a picture of friends.

"I should go," I say as I quickly gather my phone and charger. "You won't tell Franny about this, will you?"

Lottie shakes her head. "Some things Franny's better off not knowing."

She also starts to leave, skirting around the desk and giving me roughly two seconds to lift my phone and snap a picture of Vivian and Becca's photo. I then hurry out of the room, exiting the Lodge the same the way I came. At the front door, I literally bump into Theo, Chet, and Mindy. I bounce between the brothers. First Theo, then Chet, who grabs my arm to steady me.

"Whoa there," he says.

"Sorry," I say, holding up my phone. "I needed a charge."

I push past them into the heart of camp. The morning lessons have ended, and girls drift among their cabins, the mess hall, and the arts and crafts building. When I reach Dogwood, I find the girls inside, indulging in some reading time. A comic book for Krystal and an Agatha Christie paperback for Miranda. Sasha flips through a battered copy of *National Geographic*.

"Where did you go?" Krystal says. "You never came back."

"Sorry. I got tied up with something."

I kneel in front of my hickory trunk and run my hands over the lid, feeling the ridges of all the names that had been carved before mine.

"What are you doing?" Miranda asks.

"Looking for something."

"What?" Sasha says.

I lean to my right, my fingers tripping down the side of the trunk. That's where I find it. Five tiny letters scratched into the hickory, a mere inch from the floor.

becca

"A liar," I say.

FIFTEEN YEARS AGO

Campfire. Fourth of July.

There was a charge in the air that night. A combination of heat, freedom, and the holiday. The campfire seemed higher, hotter. The girls surrounding it were louder and, I noticed, happier. Even my group of girls.

Whatever had caused the earlier drama in Dogwood was resolved by dinner. Vivian, Natalie, and Allison laughed and joked through the entire meal. Vivian said nothing when Natalie had an extra helping. Allison, astonishingly, cleaned her plate. I simply felt relieved that Franny was right. The storm had passed. Now they surrounded me beside the fire, basking in the orange warmth of the leaping flames.

"We're sorry about earlier," Vivian told me. "It was nothing."

"Nothing," echoed Allison.

"Nothing at all," added Natalie.

I nodded, not because I believed them but because I didn't care. All that mattered was that they were with me now, at the end of my lonely day.

"You're best friends," I said. "I understand."

The counselors handed out sparklers, which we lowered into the campfire until they ignited into starbursts. Sizzling. White-hot.

Allison climbed to her feet and sliced the sparkler through the air, forming letters, spelling her name. Vivian did the same, the letters massive, hovering there in streaks of sparks.

A distant boom drew our attention to the sky, where golden tendrils of fireworks trickled to nothingness. More replaced them, painting the night red then yellow then green. The fireworks promised in the nearby town, only we at Camp Nightingale could also see them. Allison stood on one of the benches to improve her view. I stayed on the ground, pleasantly surprised when Vivian embraced me from behind and whispered in my ear, "Awesome, right?"

Although it seemed as though she was talking about the fireworks, I knew she was actually referring to something else. Us. This place. This moment.

"I want you to always remember this," she said as another bloom of color streaked through the sky. "Promise me you will."

"Of course," I said.

"You've got to promise, Em. Promise me you'll never forget."

"I promise."

"That's my little sister."

She kissed the top of my head and let me go. I kept my eyes on the sky, enthralled by the colors, how they shimmered and blended before fading away. I tried counting the colors, losing track as explosion after explosion erupted in the distance. The big finish. All the colors commingling until the sky grew so bright I was forced to squint.

Then it was over. The colors vanished, replaced by black sky and pinpoint stars.

"So pretty," I said, turning around to see if Vivian agreed.

But there was no one behind me. Just a campfire slowly reducing itself to glowing embers.

Vivian was gone.

Twenty-Five

I skip the campfire again, using tiredness as an excuse. It's not entirely a lie. All this being watched and sneaking around have left me exhausted. So I slip into comfortable clothes—a T-shirt and a pair of plaid boxers worn as shorts—and sprawl out in my bottom bunk. I tell the girls to go have fun without me. When they leave Dogwood, I check my newly charged phone for an email from Marc regarding his research assignment. All I get is a text reading, Mr. Library is still adorbs! Why did I ever break up with him? xoxo

I text back, Stay focused.

A few minutes later, I'm back outside and heading to another cabin. Golden Oak. I wait by the door until a trio of campers scurry out, on their way to the campfire. Becca is the last to emerge. Her body goes rigid when she sees me. Already she knows something is amiss.

"Don't wait up. I'm right behind you," she tells her campers before turning to me and, in a far less friendly voice, says, "Need something, Emma?"

"The truth would be nice." I hold up my phone, revealing a photo of a photo. Her and Vivian, their arms entangled, inseparable. "You feel like sharing this time?"

Becca nods, her lips pursed, and retreats back into the cabin. When a minute passes and she doesn't emerge, I start to think that she simply intends to ignore me. But she comes out eventually with a leather satchel slung over her shoulder.

"Supplies," she says. "I think we're going to need them."

We cut through the cabins and head to the lake. It's the thick of twilight, the sky tilting ever closer from day to night. A few stars spark to life overhead, and the moon sits low in the sky on the other side of the lake, still on the rise.

Becca and I each take a seat on rocks near the water's edge, so close our knees practically touch. She opens the satchel, removing a bottle of whiskey and a large folder. She opens the bottle and takes a deep gulp before passing it to me. I do the same, wincing at the whiskey's sharp burn in the back of my throat. Becca takes the bottle from my hands and replaces it with the folder.

"What's this?"

"Memories," she says.

I open the folder, and a stack of photographs spills onto my lap. "You took these?"

"Fifteen years ago."

I sort through the photos, marveling at how talented she was even at such a young age. The pictures are in black and white. Stark. Each one a spontaneous moment caught on the sly and preserved forever. Two girls hugging in front of the campfire, silhouetted by the soft-focus flames. The bare legs of someone playing tennis, white skirt flaring, exposing pale thighs. A girl swimming in Lake Midnight, the water up to her freckled shoulders, her hair as slick as a sea lion. Allison, I realize with a jolt. She's turned away from the camera, focused on something or someone just out of frame. Beads of water cling to her eyelashes.

The last photograph is of Vivian, a lit sparkler in her blurred hand, spelling her name in large slashes. Becca had set the exposure so the letters could be seen. Thin white streaks hanging in midair.

VIV

Fourth of July. Fifteen years ago. The night they vanished.

"My God," I say. "This could be—"

"The last picture ever taken of her? I think it is."

The realization makes me reach for the whiskey. The long gulp that follows creates a soft, numbing sensation that helps me ask, "What happened between you and Vivian? I know you stayed with them in Dogwood the year before I came to camp."

"The four of us have a complicated history." Becca stops to correct herself. "*Had* a complicated history. Even outside of this place. We all went to school together. Which wasn't unusual. Sometimes it felt like half our class came here in the summer."

"Camp Rich Bitch," I say. "That's what it was called at my school."

"Mean," Becca says. "But accurate. Because most of them were indeed bitches. Vivian especially. She was the ruler. The queen bee. People loved her. People hated her. Vivian didn't care as long as she was the center of attention. But I got to see a different side of her."

"So you were friends."

"We were best friends. For a time, anyway. I like to think of Vivian as my rebellious phase. We were fourteen, pissed off at the world, sick of being girls and wanting so badly to be women. Viv especially. She was perfect at finding trouble. Rich boys who'd get her anything she wanted. Beer. Weed. Fake IDs she'd use to get us into all the clubs. Then it suddenly stopped."

"Why?"

"The short answer? Because Vivian wanted it to."

"And the long answer?"

"I'm not entirely sure," Becca says. "I think it was because she went through some fucked-up identity crisis after her sister died. She ever tell you about it?"

"Once," I say. "I got the sense she didn't like to talk about it."

"Probably because it was such a stupid death."

"She drowned, right?"

"She did." Becca takes another swig from the bottle before pressing it into my hands. "One night in the dead of winter, Katherine—that was her name, in case Viv never told you—decided to get shit-faced and go to Central Park. The reservoir was frozen over. Katherine walked out onto it. The ice broke, she fell in, never came back up."

I'm struck by the memory of Vivian pretending to be drowning. Her sister had to have crossed her mind as she flailed in the water and gurgled for help. All to get a boy's attention. What kind of person does that?

"Katherine's death absolutely crushed her," Becca says. "I remember running to her apartment right after it happened. She was crazed, Emma. Wailing, pounding the walls, shaking uncontrollably. I couldn't look away. It was ugly and beautiful at the same time. I wanted to take a picture of it, just so I'd never forget. Yeah, I know that's weird."

But it's not. At least not as weird as making the same three girls continually vanish beneath layers of paint.

"That was the beginning of the end of us," Becca continues. "I did the best-friend thing and went to the wake and the funeral and was by her side when she came back to school. But even then I knew she was pulling away from me and being drawn to them."

"Them?"

"Allison and Natalie. They were Katherine's best friends. All three were in the same class."

"I always thought they were the same age as Vivian," I say.

"She was a year younger. Although you couldn't tell from the way she acted."

Becca reaches over and takes the bottle from my lap. Choosing the particular poison she needs to get through the conversation. She takes a long gulp and swallows hard.

"They found comfort in one another. I assume that was the appeal. Honestly, before Katherine died, Viv wanted nothing to do with them. You should have heard the way she made fun of them whenever all five of us were at her apartment. We were like warring factions, even when playing something as innocuous as Truth or Dare."

"Two Truths and a Lie," I say. "That was Vivian's game of choice."

"Not when we were friends," Becca says. "I think she joined in because Katherine liked to play it. She idolized her sister. And when she died, I think she transferred those same feelings to Natalie and Allison. I wasn't surprised when I found out we'd all be bunking here together in the summer. I had already assumed it would happen. What I wasn't ready for was how much I'd be left out. Around them, Vivian acted like she hardly knew me. Natalie and Allison had consumed her attention. By the time camp was over, we were barely speaking to each other. It was the same way back at school. She had them, so there was no need for me. When summer came around again, I knew I wasn't going to be bunking with them. I'm sure Vivian saw to that. I was banished from Dogwood and shuffled to the cabin next door."

It's fully dark now. Night settles over us, as does a prolonged silence in which Becca and I simply pass the bottle back and forth. The whiskey's starting to hit me hard. When I look up at the stars, they're brighter than they should be. I hear the sound of girls coming back from the campfire. Footsteps, voices, a few peals of laughter echoing off the cabin walls.

"Why didn't you tell me all this the other morning?" I say. "Why lie?"

"Because I didn't want to go into it. And I was surprised *you* did. I mean, Vivian treated you the same way, right?"

I don't answer, choosing instead to take another gulp of whiskey.

"It wasn't that hard of a question," Becca says.

Oh, but it is. It doesn't take into account the way I had treated Vivian.

"No," I say. "It wasn't the same."

"I think we're past lying to each other, Em," Becca says. "I know what happened right before the three of them disappeared. I was in the cabin next to Dogwood, remember? The windows were open. I heard every word."

My heart falters in my chest, skipping like a scratched record.

"It was you, wasn't it? You painted the cabin door. And put the birds inside. And you've been watching me."

Becca jerks the bottle from my hands. I've been officially cut off.

"What the fuck are you talking about?"

"Someone's been toying with me ever since I got here," I say. "At first, I thought it was all in my head. But it's not. It's really happening. And you've been doing it."

"I didn't write on your door," Becca replies with a huff. "I have absolutely zero reason to mess with your head."

"Why should I believe you?"

"Because it's the truth. I'm not judging you for what you told Vivian that night. In fact, I wish I'd said some of it myself. She definitely had it coming."

I stand, feeling shockingly unbalanced. I look to the bottle still gripped in Becca's hand. Only a third of the whiskey is left. I have no idea how much of that is my doing.

"Just stay away from me for the rest of the summer." I start to walk away, trying hard to stay upright as I call over my shoulder, "And as for what I said to Vivian that night, it wasn't what it sounded like."

Only it was. Most of it. All that Becca's missing is context.

What she actually overheard that night.

Why it happened.

And how it was so much worse than she could ever imagine.

FIFTEEN YEARS AGO

"Where's Viv?" I asked Natalie, who merely shrugged in response.

Allison did the same. "I don't know."

"She was just here."

"And now she's not," Natalie said. "She probably went back to the cabin."

But Vivian wasn't in Dogwood, either, which we discovered when we returned a few minutes later.

"I'm going to look for her," I announced.

"Maybe she doesn't want to be found," Natalie said as she scratched at a new round of mosquito bites.

I went anyway, heading to the latrine, which was the only logical place I thought she could be. When I tried the door, I found it locked. Strange. Especially at that late hour. I took a walk around the side of the building, pulled along by curiosity. When I reached the gap in the planks, I heard the sound of running water coming from inside.

The shower.

Humming just beneath it was another noise.

Moaning.

I should have left. I knew it even then. I should have simply turned around and gone back to Dogwood. Yet I couldn't resist taking a peek. That was something else Vivian had taught me. When you get an opportunity to look, you're a fool not to take it.

I leaned toward the gap. I looked.

What I saw was Vivian. Facing the shower wall, her palms flat against it, breasts pressing into the wood. Theo stood behind her.

Hands over hers. Hips thrusting. Face buried against her neck and muffling his grunts.

The sight of the two of them, doing something I'd only heard whispered about, cleaved my heart in two. It hurt so much I could hear it breaking. A sick, cracking sound. Like wood shattered by an axe.

I wanted to run away, afraid that Vivian and Theo would be able to hear it, too. But when I turned around, there was Casey, a lit cigarette dangling from her lips.

"Emma?" Smoke pushed from her mouth with each syllable. "Is something wrong?"

I shook my head, even though tears had already started to leak from my eyes. The movement set them free, flinging them away from my face.

"You're upset," Casey said.

"I'm not," I lied. "I just—I need to be alone."

I slipped past her, running not to the cabin but to the lake, where I stood so close that water lapped at my sneakers. Then I cried. I had no idea for how long. I just wept and wept, the tears falling directly from my eyes into the water, mixing with Lake Midnight.

After crying so much that my tears ran dry, I returned to Dogwood, finding Vivian, Natalie, and Allison all there. They sat in a circle on the floor, smack in the middle of a game of Two Truths and a Lie. In Vivian's hand was the flask she had told me about. Its existence truly wasn't a lie. Now she took a slow drink from it, as if to prove how foolish I had been to doubt her.

"There you are," she said, holding out the flask. "Want a swig?"

I stared at her damp ponytail, her pinkened skin, her stupid locket. And at that moment I despised her more than I had despised anyone in my life. I could feel the hatred boiling under my skin. It burned.

"No," I said.

Allison continued with the turn I had interrupted. Her choices were, as usual, either self-aggrandizing or stupid. "One: I met Sir Andrew Lloyd Webber. Two: I haven't consumed bread in a year. Three:

I think Madonna's version of 'Don't Cry for Me Argentina' is better than Patti LuPone's."

"The second one," Vivian said, taking another hit of the flask. "Not that I care."

Allison flashed a chorus-girl smile, trying not to act hurt. "Correct. I had pancakes this morning, and my mother made me French toast the morning I left for camp."

"My turn," I announced. "One: My name is Emma Davis. Two: I am spending the summer at Camp Nightingale."

I paused, ready for the lie.

"Three: I didn't just see Vivian and Theo fucking in the latrine showers."

Natalie slapped a hand over her gaping mouth. Allison shrieked, "Oh my God, Viv! Is that true?"

Vivian remained calm, looking at me with a dark glint in her eyes. "Clearly that upsets you."

I turned away, unable to endure the hardness of her stare and said nothing.

Vivian kept talking. "I'm the one who should be upset by this situation. Knowing that you were spying on me. Watching me have sex like some pervert. Is that what you are, Emma? A pervert?"

Her calmness was what ultimately got under my skin. The slow way she spoke. So deliberate, accented with just the right amount of disdain. I was sure she did it on purpose, lighting the fuse that would eventually make me explode.

I gave her what she wanted.

"You knew I liked him!" I screamed, the words raging forth, unstoppable. "You knew and couldn't stand the thought of having someone pay more attention to me than to you. So you fucked him. Because you could."

"Theo?" Vivian laughed. A single short, disbelieving burst. It was the cruelest sound I'd ever heard. "You actually think Theo is interested in you? Jesus, Em, you're just a baby."

"That's still better than being a bitch like you."

"I'm a bitch, but you're delusional. Truly fucking delusional."

Had any tears been left in my body, I'm certain I would have started crying on the spot. But I'd used them all up. All I could do was push past her and crawl into bed. I laid on my side, my back turned to them, knees pulled to my chest. I closed my eyes and breathed deeply, trying to ignore the horrible hollow feeling in my chest.

The three of them didn't say anything else after that. They went to the latrine to do their gossiping, sparing me the humiliation of having to listen. I fell asleep not long after they left, my brain and body deciding together that unconsciousness was the best remedy for my misery.

When I woke, it was the middle of the night. The creak of the floorboard was what roused me. The sound jolted me awake and propelled me upright. Light from the full moon outside slanted through the window in a gray-white beam. Each girl passed through it, shimmering a moment on their way out the door.

First Allison.

Then Natalie.

And finally Vivian, who froze when she saw me awake and watching.

"Where are you going?" I asked.

Vivian smiled, although no amusement could be found in that slight upturn of her lips. Instead, I sensed sadness, regret, the hint of an apology.

"You're too young for this, Em," she said.

She raised an index finger and pressed it to her lips. Shushing me. Conspiring with me. Requesting my silence.

I refused. I needed to have the last word.

Only after it was uttered, its sour echo lingering in the air, did Vivian leave the cabin, closing the door behind her, vanishing forever.

Twenty-Six

I'm drunk by the time I'm again walking among the cabins. Or, more accurately, stumbling. With each step, the mulch path seems to shift under my feet. I overcompensate by stomping, trying to pin it into place, which makes me lose my balance more often than not. The end result is dizziness. Or maybe that's just from the whiskey.

I try to sober up as I stumble along. Years of observing my mother has taught me a few tricks, and I utilize them all. I slap my cheeks. I shake my arms and take deep breaths. I widen my eyes, pretending there are invisible toothpicks holding up the lids.

Rather than head straight to Dogwood, I keep walking, pulled subconsciously in another direction. Past the cabins. To the latrine. But I don't go inside. Instead I lean against it, momentarily lost. I close my eyes and wonder why I've come here in the first place.

I open them only when I feel a nearby presence, alarmingly close and getting closer. On the edge of my vision, I see someone round the corner of the latrine. A shape. Dark and swift. My body tenses. I almost scream, somehow managing to stop it when the shape comes into focus.

Casey.

Checking to see who's there while sneaking a cigarette like a high school sophomore.

"You startled me," she says between a deep drag and a languid puff. "I thought you were Mindy."

I say nothing.

Casey drops the cigarette, stubs it out. "Are you okay?"

"I'm fine," I say, stifling a giggle even though my talk with Becca has left me feeling unbearably sad. "Just fine."

"My God, are you drunk?

"I'm not," I say, sounding just like my mother, the words slurred into one. *Imnot.*

Casey shakes her head, part horrified, part amused. "You better not let Mindy see you like this. She'll totally freak out."

She leaves. I stay, roaming the perimeter of the building, an index finger sliding along the cedar shingles. Then I see the crack. That gap between planks now stuffed with clay. And I remember why I'm here—I'm retracing my steps. Going to the same spot I went after Vivian disappeared from the campfire. Fifteen years later, I can still see her and Theo together in the shower stall. I can still feel the heartache that caused. A muted memory pain.

I also feel something else. A shiver of awareness jumping along the skin of my arms, the back of my neck.

I look up, expecting to see Casey again. Or, worse, Mindy.

Instead, I see Vivian.

Not all of her. Just a glimpse as she rounds the corner of the latrine. A spray of blond hair. A slip of white dress scraping the cedar wall. Before disappearing completely, she turns and peers at me from around the edge of the building. I see her smooth forehead, her dark eyes, her tiny nose. It's the same Vivian I remember from camp. The same one who later haunted me.

I instinctively reach for my bracelet, finding instead only a patch of skin where it should have been wound around my wrist.

It's not there.

I check my left arm, just to be sure. It's bare. That bit of string keeping the bracelet together had given way. Now it's lying somewhere on the grounds of Camp Nightingale.

Which means it could be anywhere.

Which means it's gone.

I flick my gaze to the corner of the latrine. Vivian is still there, peering at me.

I'm not going crazy, I think. *I'm not.*

I rub the skin of my left wrist, as if that will somehow work the same magic as the bracelet. It doesn't help. Vivian remains where she's at. Staring. Not speaking. Yet I keep rubbing, the friction heating my flesh.

I'm not going crazy.

I want to tell her that she's not real, that she has no power over me, that I'm stronger than everyone realizes. But I can't. Not with my bracelet God knows where and Vivian right there and fear shooting like a bottle rocket up my spine.

So I run.

I'm not going crazy.

Away from the latrine.

I'm not going crazy.

Back to Dogwood.

I'm not.

My run is really an uneasy combination of swaying, tripping, and lurching that ultimately lands me at the cabin door. I fling it open, push inside, slam it shut. I collapse against the door, breathless and frightened and sad about the lost bracelet.

Sasha, Krystal, and Miranda sit on the floor, hunched over a book. My presence makes them look up in surprise. Miranda slams the book shut and tries to slide it under my bunk. But she's too slow, the gesture too obvious. I can clearly see what they were reading.

Vivian's diary.

"So all of you know," I say, still out of breath from my awkward trip.

It's not a question. The guilt burning in their eyes already tells me that they do.

"We Googled you," Sasha says, a finger pointed Miranda's way. "It was her idea."

"I'm sorry," Miranda says. "You were acting so weird the past two days that we had to find out why."

"It's okay. Really, it's fine. I'm glad you know. You deserve to be aware of what happened in this cabin."

Exhaustion, whiskey, and sadness get the best of me, and I find myself listing to the side. Like a sailor on a rocking ship. Or my mother on Christmas Eve. I try to right myself, fail, plop down onto the lid of my hickory trunk.

"You probably have questions," I say.

Sasha's the first to ask one. Of course. Insatiably curious Sasha.

"What were they like?"

"Like the three of you but also very, very different."

"Where did they go?" Krystal asks.

"I don't know," I say.

Yet I would have gone with them. It's one of the few things I'm certain of. That, despite Vivian's hurtful betrayal with Theo, I still wanted her approval. And had she asked, I would have willingly followed, marching behind them into the darkness.

"But that's not the whole story," I say. "There's more. Things no one but me knows."

Seeing Vivian again has messed with my emotions. I want to laugh. I want to cry. I want to confess. Instead, I say, "Two Truths and a Lie. Let's play."

I slip off the trunk, joining them. It's a sudden, ungainly slump that makes the three of them recoil when I hit the floor. Even Miranda, who I thought was the bravest of the group.

"One: I have been to the Louvre. Twice. Two: Fifteen years ago, three of my friends left this cabin. No one saw them again."

I pause, hesitant to speak aloud something I've avoided saying for fifteen years. But no matter how much I want to stay silent, guilt compels me to keep talking.

"Three: Right before they left, I said something. Something I regret. Something that's haunted me ever since."

I hope you never come back.

The memory of that moment arrives without warning. It feels like a sharpened sword swooping toward me, slicing me open, exposing my cold heart.

"I told them I hoped they'd never come back," I say. "Right to Vivian's face. It was the last thing I ever said to her."

Tears burn the corners of my eyes—grief and guilt bubbling out of me.

"That doesn't mean what happened to them is your fault," Miranda says. "Those were words, Emma. You didn't make them disappear."

Sasha nods. "It's not your fault they didn't come back."

I stare at the floor, avoiding their sympathy. I don't deserve it. Not when there's still more to confess. Still more I've kept hidden from everyone.

"But they *did* come back." A tear slips out, rolls down my cheek. "Later that night. Only they couldn't get back into the cabin."

"Why?" Miranda asks.

I know I should stop. I've already said too much. But there's no turning back now. I'm tired of omitting things, which is practically the same as lying. I want to speak the truth. Maybe that's what might finally heal me.

"Because I locked the door behind them."

Miranda sucks in air. A muted gasp. Trying to hide her shock.

"You locked them out?"

I nod, another tear falling. It traces the path of the first, deviating only when it reaches my mouth. I taste it on my lips. Salty. Bitter.

"And I refused to let them back in. Even after they knocked. And jiggled the doorknob. And pleaded with me to let them in."

I look to the cabin door, picturing it the way it appeared that night. Pale in the darkness, dusted with moonlight, doorknob rattling back and forth. I hear the sharp rapping on the wood and someone calling my name on the other side.

Emma.

It was Vivian.

Come on, Em. Let me in.

I shrank into my bottom bunk, squeezing myself into the corner. I pulled the covers to my chin and huddled beneath them, trying to will away the sound coming from the other side of the door.

Emma, please.

I slid under the covers, lost in the darkness within, staying there until the knocking, the rattling, Vivian herself faded away.

"I could have let them in," I say. "I should have. But I didn't. Because I was young and stupid and angry. But if I *had* let them in, all three would still be here. And I wouldn't be carrying around this aw-ful feeling that I killed them."

Two more tears follow the designated path. I wipe them away with the back of my hand.

"I paint them. All three of them. Every painting I've finished for years has included them. Only no one knows they're there. I cover them up. And I don't know why. I can't help myself. But I can't keep on painting them. It's crazy. *I'm* crazy. But now I think that if I can somehow find out what happened, then maybe I'll be able to stop painting them. Which means that maybe I've finally forgiven myself."

I stop talking and look up from the floor. Sasha, Krystal, and Mi-randa stare at me, silent and motionless. They look at me the same way children eye a stranger. Curious and skittish.

"I'm sorry," I say. "I'm not feeling well. I'll be fine in the morning."

I stand, woozy, swaying like a storm-battered tree. The girls slide out of my way and start to climb to their feet. I gesture for them to stay where they are.

"Don't let me spoil your night. Keep playing."

They do. Because they're nervous. Because they're scared. Because they don't know what else to do but to keep playing, appeasing me, waiting until I pass out, which likely will be any second now.

"One more round," Miranda says, her decisiveness not quite mask-ing her fear. "I'll go."

I close my eyes before crawling into bed. Rather, they close on their own, no matter how much I try to keep them open. I'm too tired. Too drunk. Too emotionally flattened by my confession. Temporarily blinded, I feel my way into bed, reaching for the mattress, my pillow, the wall. I curl into a ball, my knees to my chest, back turned to the girls. My standard humiliation position.

"One: I once got sick after riding the Cyclone at Coney Island." Miranda's voice slows, cautious, pausing to hear if I'm asleep yet. "Two: I read about a hundred books a year."

Sleep overwhelms me immediately. It's like a trapdoor, opening up beneath me. I willingly fall, plummeting into unconsciousness. As I tumble, I can still hear Miranda, her voice faint and fading fast.

"Three: I'm worried about Emma."

This is how it continues.

You scream again.

And again.

You do it even though you don't know why. Yet you also sort of do. Because no matter how much you try, you can't rid your mind of those too-terrible-to-think thoughts. Deep down, you know that one of them is true.

So you scream one more time, waking the rest of the camp. Even standing in the lake, ten feet from shore, you can sense a wave of energy pulsing toward you. It's a sudden jolt. A collective surprise. A heron on the shore senses it and spreads its long, elegant wings. It takes flight, rising high, riding the sound of your screams.

The first person you see is Franny. She bursts onto the back deck of the Lodge. The screams have already tipped her off that something is wrong. One quick glance at you in the water confirms it. She flies down the wooden steps, the hem of her white nightgown fluttering.

Chet is next, all sleepy eyes and bedhead. He stays on the deck, unnerved, his hands gripping the railing. After that comes Theo, not even pausing, racing down the steps. You see that he's clad only in a pair of boxer shorts, the sight of all that exposed skin obscene under the circumstances. You look away, queasy.

Others have gathered along the shore, campers and counselors alike, standing motionless in the mist. All of them scared and startled and curious. That above everything else. Their curiosity comes at you like a frigid wind. You hate them just then. You hate their eagerness to learn something you already know, no matter how terrible it may be.

Becca Schoenfeld stands among them. You hate her most of all because she actually has the gall to chronicle what's happening. She elbows her way to the front of the crowd, her camera raised. When she clicks off a few shots, the noise of the shutter skips across the lake like a flat stone.

But it's only Franny who comes forward. She stands at the edge of the lake, her bare toes this close from the water.

"Emma?" she says. "What are you doing out here? Are you hurt?"

You don't answer. You're unsure how.

"Em?" It's Theo, whom you still can't bear to look at. "Come out of the water."

"Go back to the Lodge," Franny snaps at him. "I can handle this."

She enters the lake. Not wading like you did. She marches. Knees lifting. Arms pumping. Nightgown darkening at the hem as it sucks up water. She stops a few feet from you, her head cocked in concern. Her voice is low, strained but calm.

"Emma, what's the matter?"

"They're gone," you say.

"Who's gone?"

"The other girls in the cabin."

Franny swallows, sending a ripple down the graceful curve of her throat. "All of them?"

When you nod, the light in her green eyes dims.

That's when you realize it's serious.

Things move quickly after that. Everyone spreads out across the camp, going to places you've already looked. The fire pit. The latrine. The cabin, where Theo opens each hickory trunk cautiously, as if the girls could be inside them, waiting to spring out like a jack-in-the-box.

The hunt turns up nothing, which is no surprise to you. You know what's going on. You knew it the moment you woke up in that empty and silent cabin.

A search party is organized. Just a small one—an attempt by all to pretend the situation isn't as dire as everyone fears it truly is. You insist on tagging along, even though you're in no condition to be roaming the woods, calling out the names of girls who may or may not be missing. You march behind Theo, trying hard to keep up, ignoring how the chill of the lake water lingers on your skin. It makes you shiver, despite the fact that the temperature has inched past ninety degrees and that your skin is coated with a thin sheen of sweat. You search the woods that flank the camp. First one side, then the other. While marching through the forest, you picture Buchanan Harris doing the very same thing a hundred years earlier. Blazing a trail, armed with just a machete and willful optimism. It's a strange thought. Silly, too. Yet it takes your mind off your tired feet and sore limbs and the fact that a trio of dead girls might be waiting for you just around the next bend.

No girls appear, alive or dead. There's no trace of them. It's as if they had never existed at all. Like they were a figment of the camp's imagination. A mass hallucination.

You return to Camp Nightingale during lunch, with all the remaining campers in the mess hall, picking at plates of sad, soggy pizza slices. Everyone looks up as you hobble inside. Various emotions swirl in their eyes. Hope. Fear. Blame. It's that last one you feel the most as you make your way to Franny's table. It heats the back of your neck like a sunburn.

"Anything?" Franny asks.

Theo shakes his head. A few of the campers begin to weep, their sobs breaking out all around you, disrupting the otherwise quiet of the mess hall. It makes you hate them all over again. Most of these crying girls barely knew the missing. You're the one who should be crying. But you look to Franny for guidance. She's not weeping. She's calm in the face of this unfathomable storm.

"I think it's time I call the police," she says.

A half hour later, you're still in the mess hall. It's been cleared of crying campers and their equally moist-eyed counselors. The kitchen staff has been shuffled outside. The whole place is empty except for you and a state police detective whose name you've already forgotten.

"Now then," he says, "how many girls seem to be missing?"

You notice his choice of words. Seem *to be missing. Like you're making the whole thing up. Like he doesn't believe you.*

"I thought Franny already told you everything."

"I'd like to hear it from you." He leans back in his chair, crosses his arms. "If you don't mind."

"Three," you say.

"All staying in the same cabin?"

"Yes."

"And you're sure you've looked everywhere for them?"

"Not the whole property," you say. "But the entire camp's been searched."

The detective sighs, reaches into his suit coat, and removes a pen and a notebook. "Let's start by telling me their names."

You hesitate, because to identify them is to make it real. Once you say their names, they'll be known to the world as missing persons. And you don't think you're ready for that. You bite the inside of your cheek, stalling. But the detective stares you down, getting peeved, his face pinkening ever so slightly.

"Miss Davis?"

"Right," you say. "Their names."

You take a deep breath. Your heart does several sad, little flips in your chest.

"Their names are Sasha, Krystal, and Miranda."

PART TWO

AND A LIE

Twenty-Seven

The detective writes their names in his notebook, thus making the situation official. My heart completes another sorrowful flip-flop in my chest.

"Let's go back to the beginning," he says. "Back to the moment you realized the girls were missing from the cabin."

An awkward moment passes in which I'm not sure who he's talking about. *Which ones?* I almost say.

I can't help but feel like that thirteen-year-old cowering in the presence of a different detective asking me about a different set of missing girls. Everything is so similar. The empty mess hall and the slightly impatient lawman and my simmering panic. Other than my age and the new cast of missing persons, the only major difference is the mug of coffee sitting on the table in front of me. The first time around it was orange juice.

This isn't happening.

That's what I tell myself as I sit rigid in my plastic cafeteria chair, waiting for the mess hall walls and floor to melt away. Like a dream. A painting splashed with turpentine. And when it all slides away, I'll be somewhere else. Back in my loft, maybe. Awakening in front of an empty canvas.

But the walls and floor remain. As does the detective, whose name suddenly comes to me. Flynn. Detective Nathan Flynn.

This isn't happening. Not again.

Three girls go missing from the very same cabin at the very same camp where three other girls disappeared fifteen years earlier? The odds of that happening are astronomical. I'm sure Sasha, that tiny well of knowledge, would have a percentage at the ready.

Still, I can't believe it. Even as the floor and walls stubbornly refuse to evaporate and Detective Flynn keeps sitting there and I examine my hands to make sure they're the hands of a woman and not a thirteen-year-old girl.

This isn't happening.

I'm not going crazy.

"Miss Davis, I need you to focus, okay?" Flynn's voice slices through my thoughts. "I understand your shock. I really do. But every minute you spend not answering these questions means another minute goes by that those girls are still out there."

It's enough to shake off my lingering disbelief. At least for the moment. I look at him, fighting back tears, and say, "What was the question again?"

"When did you realize the girls were missing?"

"When I woke up."

"What time was this?"

I think back to the moment I awoke in the cabin. It was only hours ago yet feels like a lifetime.

"A little past five."

"You always such an early riser?"

"Not usually," I say. "But I am here."

Flynn makes a note of this. I'm not sure why.

"So you woke up and saw they were gone," he says. "Then what?"

"I went to look for them."

"Where?"

"All over the camp." I take a sip of the coffee. It's lukewarm, slightly bitter. "Latrine. Mess hall. Arts and crafts building. Even other cabins."

"And there was no sign of them?"

"No," I say, my voice cracking. "Nothing."

Flynn flips to a new page in his notebook even though what I've told him amounts to only a few measly sentences.

"Why did you go to the lake?"

Confusion rolls over me again. Does he mean now? Fifteen years ago?

"I don't understand the question," I say.

"Mrs. Harris-White told me they found you standing in the lake this morning. After you realized the girls in your cabin were missing. Did you think they'd be there?"

I barely remember that moment. I recall seeing the sun rise over the lake. That first blush of daylight. It drew me to it.

Flynn persists. "Did you have some reason to think the girls had gone swimming?"

"They can't swim. At least, I don't think they can."

I remember one of them telling me that. Krystal? Or was it Sasha? Now that I think about it, I don't recall seeing any of them actually go into the water.

"I just thought they might be there," I say. "Standing in the lake."

"The way *you* were standing in the lake?"

"I don't know why I did that."

The sound of my voice makes me cringe. I sound so weak, so confused. Pain nudges my temples, making it hard to think.

"Mrs. Harris-White also said you were screaming."

That I remember. In fact, I can still her my cries streaking across the water. I can still see that heron startled into flight.

"I was."

"Why?"

"Because I was scared," I say.

"Scared?"

"Wouldn't you be? If you woke up and everyone else in your cabin was gone?"

"I'd be worried," Flynn says. "I don't think I'd scream."

"Well, I did."

Because I knew what was going on. I was stupid enough to come back here, and now it's happening again.

Detective Flynn flips to a fresh page. "Is there a chance you screamed for another reason?"

"Such as?"

"I don't know. Maybe out of guilt."

I shift in my seat, discomfited by Flynn's tone. I detect slight mistrust, a sliver of suspicion.

"Guilt?" I say.

"You know, for losing them when they were under your care."

"I didn't *lose* them."

"But they *were* under your care, right? You were their camp counselor."

"Instructor," I say. "I told them when I first arrived that I was here to be a friend and not some authority figure."

"And were you?" Flynn says. "Friends, I mean."

"Yes."

"So you liked them?"

"Yes."

"And you had no issues with them? No disagreements or fights?"

"*No,*" I say, stressing the word. "I told you, I liked them."

Impatience nudges my ribs and shimmies down my legs. Why is he wasting all this time asking me questions when the girls are still out there, maybe hurt, definitely lost? Why doesn't anyone seem to be searching? I glance out the mess hall window and see a couple of police cruisers and a smattering of state troopers milling about outside.

"Is someone looking for them?" I ask. "There's going to be a search party, right?"

"There will be. We just need some more information from you."

"How much more?"

"Well, for starters, is there anything about the girls you think I should know? Something about them that might aid in the search?"

"Um, Krystal is spelled with a *K,*" I say. "In case that helps."

"It certainly will."

Flynn doesn't elaborate, leaving me to picture each of them on the sides of milk cartons, a noble public service that's actually horrible when you think about it. Who wants to open their fridge and see the face of a missing child staring back at them?

"Anything else?" Flynn asks.

I close my eyes, rub my temples. My head is killing me.

"Let me think," I say. "Sasha. She's so smart. The downside is she knows so much it makes her a little scared. She's afraid of bears. And snakes."

It occurs to me that Sasha might be afraid right now, wherever she is. The others, too. It breaks my heart to think of them lost in the woods, terrified of their surroundings. I hope they're all together, so they can comfort one another. Please, God, let them be together.

I keep talking, overcome with the urge to tell the detective everything I know about the girls. "Miranda's the oldest. And the bravest. Her uncle is a cop, I think. Or maybe it was her dad. Although she lives with her grandmother. She never mentioned parents, come to think of it."

A realization pops into my head, coming at me like a thunderclap.

"She took her phone."

"Who did?"

"Miranda. I mean, I'm not certain she took it with her, but it wasn't among her things. Could that be used to find her?"

Flynn, who had been sagging in his chair while I prattled on, suddenly perks up. "Yes, it definitely could. All cell phones come with a GPS. Do you know the carrier?"

"I don't."

"I'll have someone contact her grandmother and ask," Flynn says. "Now let's talk about *why* you think the girls are gone."

"I don't know."

"There has to be a reason, don't you think? Like maybe they left because they were mad at you about something?"

"Nothing I can think of."

That's a lie. The latest in a long line of them. Because there is something that would make them want to leave Dogwood.

Me.

The way I acted.

Drunk and crying and still touching my bare wrist, which now has a red streak on its side where my thumb kept rubbing the skin. I wasn't in my right mind last night, and it scared them. I saw it in their eyes.

"You think they ran away?" I ask.

"I'm saying that's the most logical reason. On average, more than two million youth run away each year. The vast majority are quickly located and returned home."

It sounds like another one of those statistics Sasha would have at the ready. But I don't believe for a second the three of them ran away. They gave no indication of unhappiness in their home lives.

"What if they didn't?" I say. "What would be another reason?"

"Foul play."

Flynn says it so quickly it makes me gasp. "Like kidnapping?"

"Is it a possibility? Yes. Is it likely? No. Less than one percent of all missing children are abducted by strangers."

"What if the kidnapper isn't a stranger?"

Flynn quickly flips to another page of his notebook, pen poised over paper. "Do you know of such a person?"

I do. Maybe.

"Has anyone talked to the kitchen staff?" I say. "The other day, I caught one of them staring at the campers on the beach. Not a good stare, either. It was creepy."

"Creepy?"

"Like he didn't think it was wrong to ogle a sixteen-year-old girl."

"So it was a male?"

I give a firm nod. "The tag on his apron said his name was Marvin. Two other kitchen workers were there. Women. They saw the whole thing."

"I'll be sure to ask around," Flynn says, writing down everything.

Seeing his pen scurry over the paper pleases me. It means I'm helping. Energized, I grab the coffee and take another bitter gulp.

"Let's talk about fifteen years ago," Flynn says. "I've been informed you were here when three other girls went missing. Is that correct?"

I stare at him, slightly uneasy. "I assume you already know that it is."

"You were staying in the same cabin, were you not?"

I detect more suspicion in his voice. Less subtle this time around.

"Yes," I say, buzzing with defensiveness. "None of them, by the way, were among the vast majority you claim to have been located and returned home."

"I'm aware of that."

"Then why are you asking me about it?"

Flynn pretends not to hear the question and plows ahead. "Back then, a fellow camper said she heard you and one of the girls who vanished fighting earlier that night."

Becca. Of course she told the police about what she'd heard. But I can't be too mad at her for that. I would have done the same thing if the roles had been reversed.

"It was an argument," I say weakly. "Not a fight."

"What was this argument about?"

"I honestly can't remember," I say, when of course I can. Me screaming at Vivian about Theo. Just a stupid girl fighting over a stupid boy.

"As you mentioned, none of those girls were seen or heard from again," Flynn says. "Why do you think that is?"

"I'm not an expert on disappearances."

"Yet you're hesitant to think this current set of missing girls ran away."

"Because I know them," I say. "They wouldn't do something like that."

"And what about the girls who went missing fifteen years ago? You knew them, too."

"I did."

"You knew them well enough to get angry at them."

"*One* of them."

I reach for the coffee and take another gulp, this time to steel myself.

"Maybe even violently angry."

Flynn catches me mid-sip. The coffee stops halfway down my throat, choking me. I let out a series of short, rough coughs. Coffee and spittle fling from my mouth.

"What are you implying?" I say between coughs.

"I'm just being thorough, Miss Davis."

"Maybe you should start searching for Miranda, Krystal, and Sasha instead. Be thorough with that."

I take another look out the window. The troopers are still there, milling outside the mess hall. It's as if they're guarding the place. Trying to keep someone out.

Or someone in.

A grim understanding settles over me. I now know the reason no one seems to be searching for the girls. Why Detective Flynn keeps focusing on my relationships with all of them. I should have seen it coming. I should have realized it the moment I woke up and Miranda, Sasha, and Krystal were gone.

I'm a suspect.

The *only* suspect.

"I didn't touch those girls. Then or now."

"You have to admit, it's an awfully big coincidence," Flynn says. "Fifteen years ago, all the girls from your cabin vanished in the night. All of them but you. Now here we are, with all the girls from your cabin once again vanishing in the night. All of them but you."

"I was thirteen the first time it happened. What kind of violence do you think a thirteen-year-old girl is capable of?"

"I have a daughter that age," Flynn says. "You'd be surprised."

"And what about now?" I say, wincing at both the hysterical pitch of my voice and the headache that accompanies it. "I'm an artist. I'm here to teach girls how to paint. I have absolutely no reason to hurt anyone."

In my head, a much cooler voice speaks to me. *Keep calm, Emma. Think clearly. Go over what you know.*

"I'm not the only one who was here back then," I say. "There are plenty of others."

Casey, for example, although I doubt she could swat a mosquito let alone hurt two sets of girls for no apparent reason. Then there's Becca, who definitely had a reason to hate Vivian, Natalie, and Allison.

I think about Theo. About seeing him with Vivian in the shower. About me pounding his chest. *Where are they? What did you do to them?*

But Theo had a sound alibi fifteen years ago. Franny is a different story entirely. Vivian's diary slides into my thoughts.

I'm close to finding out her dirty little secret.

I know the truth.

I'm scared.

"I think you should talk to Franny," I say.

"Why?"

"Vivian—she's one of the girls who vanished fifteen years ago—was poking around camp. Investigating."

"Investigating what?" Flynn asks, his impatience more pronounced.

God, I wish I knew. Although Vivian had left behind plenty of clues, there's nothing to pinpoint what, exactly, Franny might be hiding.

"Something Franny might have wanted to keep secret."

"Wait, are you saying you think Mrs. Harris-White did something to the girls in your cabin? Not just now, but also fifteen years ago?"

It sounds ridiculous. It *is* ridiculous. But it's the only reason I can think of to explain a situation that defies easy explanation. Everything I've learned since coming back to camp points to such a conclusion. Vivian was looking for something, possibly related to Peaceful Valley Asylum. She found it and enlisted the help of Natalie and Allison. All three promptly vanished. That can't be a coincidence. Now I'm back, looking for what Vivian was after, and Miranda, Krystal, and Sasha also go missing. Again, too strange to be a coincidence.

It's possible Vivian stumbled upon something Franny was desperate to keep hidden. Perhaps something worth killing over. Now maybe I'm on the verge of finding it out, too, and this is another warning from Franny.

Her story about the falcons shoots into my brain, breaking through all my other cluttered thoughts. Is that why she told it? To make me frightened enough to stop searching? Did she tell Vivian the same story after she'd been caught in the Lodge?

"It makes more sense than thinking I did it," I say.

"This is a good person you're talking about." Flynn puts down his notebook, pulls out a handkerchief, mops his brow. "Hell, she's the biggest taxpayer in this county. All this land? That's a lot of property taxes she pays each year. Yet she's never complained. Never tried to pay less. In fact, she gives just as much to charity. The main hospital in the county? Guess whose name is on the damn building?"

"All I know is that it wasn't me," I say. "It was never me."

"So you say. But no one knows what happened. We only have your word, which, if you'll excuse me, seems kind of suspect."

"Something strange is going on here."

The detective shoves the handkerchief back in his pocket and gives me an expectant look. "Would you care to elaborate?"

I'd been hoping it wouldn't reach this point. That Detective Flynn would accept my word as fact and start trying to find out what really happened to Miranda, Krystal, and Sasha. But now there's no choice. I have to tell him everything. Because maybe everything that happened—the shower, the birds, the person at the window—wasn't directed at me. Maybe it was meant for one of the girls.

"Someone's been watching me all week," I say. "I was spied on in the shower. Someone put birds in the cabin."

"Birds?" Flynn says, once again reaching for his notebook.

"Crows. Three of them. One morning, I woke up and saw someone standing at the window. They'd vandalized the outside of the cabin."

"When was this?"

"Two days ago."

"What was the vandalism?"

"Someone had painted the door." I hesitate before saying the rest. "They wrote the word *liar.*"

Flynn's brows arch. Exactly the reaction I'm expecting. "Interesting word choice. Any reason behind it?"

"Yes," I say, annoyed. "Maybe to preemptively make sure no one believes me."

"Or maybe you did it to deflect suspicion from yourself."

"You think I *planned* to abduct those girls?"

"That makes about as much sense as anything you've told me," Flynn says.

My headache flares—a fire at my temples.

This isn't happening.

I'm not going crazy.

"Someone was watching us," I say. "Someone was *there.*"

"It's hard to believe you without any proof," Flynn says. "And right now, there's nothing to back up your story."

Another realization swerves into my head. One I was too upset to conjure until just now. One that will prove to Flynn he's wrong about me.

"There is," I say. "A camera. Pointed right at the cabin door."

Twenty-Eight

The cabin glows green on the monitor, thanks to its night vision feature. It's an ugly green. A queasy shade made worse by the camera's position. Instead of a straight shot from the back of one cabin to the front of Dogwood, it's been angled downward into a bird's-eye view that induces vertigo.

"The camera is motion sensitive," Chet explains. "It starts recording only when movement is detected. It stops when whatever it's recording also stops moving. Each time the camera records something, a digital file is automatically saved. For instance, this is a paused shot from the night it was installed."

On-screen, the cabin door is ajar. The motion that triggered the camera. In that sliver of darkness, I can make out a foot and a green-tinted glimpse of leg.

Chet moves to a second monitor—one of three that sit side by side in the Lodge's basement. While most of the space is filled with tidily stacked boxes and cobwebbed furniture, just as Mindy had predicted on my arrival-day tour, one corner has been outfitted with unpainted drywall and a floor of white linoleum. This is where the monitors reside, sitting on a metal desk with two PC towers slid together like books on a shelf.

Chet occupies a creaky office chair in front of the desk. The rest of us—Theo, Franny, Detective Flynn, and myself—stand behind him.

"This all seems pretty elaborate for one camera at one cabin," Flynn says.

"It's just a test camera," Chet replies. "We're going to install more throughout the camp. For security reasons. At least, that was the plan."

Behind him, Franny flinches. Like the rest of us, she knows there won't be a camp left unless Krystal, Sasha, and Miranda are found by the end of the day. This could very well end her dream of one last glorious summer.

"The camera can also be set to a constant live feed. That's what this is." Chet points to the third monitor, a daytime view of Dogwood. "Usually the live feed is turned off because there's no one to constantly monitor it. I turned it on while we're all down here, just in case the girls return."

I stare at the screen, hoping against hope I'll see Sasha, Krystal, or Miranda come into view, returning from an extended hike, oblivious to all the worry they've caused. Instead, I see Casey pass by, leading a group of crying girls to their cabins. Mindy appears next, bringing up the rear. She gives the camera a fleeting glance as she passes.

"The recordings are stored here," Chet says, using a mouse to open a file folder located on the center monitor. Inside are dozens of digital files identified only by a series of numbers. "The file names correspond to the day, hour, minute, and second each recording was made. So this file—0630044833—means it was recorded on June thirtieth, thirty-three seconds after four forty-eight a.m."

He clicks once, and the image frozen on the first monitor jerks to life. The door opens wider, and I see myself slip out of the cabin and walk awkwardly out of the camera's view. I recall that moment well. Heading to the latrine at the break of dawn armed with a full bladder and a swarm of memories.

"What were you doing up at that hour?" Flynn asks.

"I was going to the bathroom," I say, bristling. "I assume that's still legal."

"Are there files from last night?" Flynn asks Chet, who uses the mouse to scroll down and check the folders.

"Several."

Flynn turns to me. "You said you realized the girls were gone at about five, right?"

"Yes," I say. "And they were there when I went to sleep last night."

"What time was this?"

I shake my head, unable to remember. I was too dazed—by whiskey, by memories—to keep track of the time.

"There's one file from between midnight and four," Chet announces. "Then there are three between four thirty and five thirty this morning."

"Let's see them," Flynn says.

"This is from a little after one."

Chet clicks the first file, and Dogwood appears. At first, there's no movement at all, making me wonder what triggered the camera. But then something appears—a green-white blur just on the edge of the screen. A mother deer and two fawns step into frame, their eyes giving off a chartreuse glow as they carefully cross in front of Dogwood. Twenty seconds tick by as they make their way past the cabin. Once the second fawn exits the frame, its white tail flicking, the camera shuts off.

"That's it for those hours," Chet says. "This one is about five minutes before five."

He clicks, and the first monitor lights up again. It's the same view as before, minus the deer but with the addition of the cabin door slowly opening.

Miranda is the first to emerge. She pokes her head outside, looking in both directions, making sure the coast is clear. Then she tiptoes out of the cabin, wearing her camp polo and cargo shorts. A pale rectangle is clenched in her hand. Her phone.

She's soon followed by Sasha and Krystal, sticking close together. Krystal carries a flashlight and a rolled-up comic book stuffed into the back pocket of her cargo shorts. I can make out the edge of Captain America's shield emblazoned on the cover. Sasha carries a water bottle, which she drops when closing the cabin door. It rolls along the ground, out of frame. Sasha runs after it, disappearing for a second. When she returns, the three of them confer in front of the cabin door, oblivious to the camera's presence. Eventually they go right, heading toward the heart of camp, vanishing one by one.

First Miranda, then Krystal, and finally Sasha.

I make a note of the order in which they depart, just in case I'll need to paint them one day. I hate myself for thinking this way.

"This is five minutes later," Chet says once the screen goes dark and he opens the next file.

I don't need to look at the monitor to know what it shows. Me emerging from the cabin in bare feet and the T-shirt and boxer shorts I wore to bed the night before. I pause outside the door, rubbing my arms to ward off the chill. Then I walk away in the opposite direction of the girls, toward the latrine. Even though I know what to expect, the footage is a gut punch.

Five minutes. That's how little time had passed between the girls leaving the cabin and my realizing they were gone.

Five fucking minutes.

I question every thought I had and every move I made this morning. If only I had awakened earlier. If only I hadn't wasted so much time thinking of reasons for why they'd be gone. If only I had gone to the mess hall instead of the latrine.

In any of those scenarios, I might have spotted the girls retreating to wherever it was they went to. I might have been able to stop them.

Even worse is how guilty it makes me look. Stepping outside mere minutes after the girls departed. While it was a complete coincidence, it doesn't appear that way. It looks intentional, like I was waiting to follow them at a discreet distance. It doesn't matter that I went in the opposite direction. Because the next video—the final one from that highly trafficked predawn hour—shows me walking past Dogwood during my wander around the cabins. I stare at my image on the monitor, noticing the hard set of my jaw and the blankness in my eyes. I know it's worry, but to others it might look like anger as I unwittingly followed the same path the girls had taken.

"I was looking for them," I say, preempting any questions from the others. "It was right after I woke up and realized they were gone. I searched the latrine first, then looked around the cabins before heading to the other side of camp."

"You've already mentioned that," Detective Flynn says. "But, again, there's no way to prove that. All this video does is confirm that you left the cabin not long after the girls did. And now no one can find them."

"I didn't do anything to those girls!"

I look to Chet, to Theo, to Franny, silently begging them to back me up, even though there's no reason they should. I'm not surprised when, instead of coming to my defense, Franny says, "Normally, I wouldn't feel comfortable sharing this. Everyone has a right to privacy, especially regarding incidents in their past. But under these circumstances, I feel I must. Emma, please forgive me."

She offers a look that's half-apology, half-pity. I don't want either. So I look away as Franny says, "Years ago, Miss Davis was under psychiatric care for an undisclosed mental illness."

While she talks, I stare at the third monitor. The live feed from outside the cabin. Currently, the area is empty. No campers. No Mindy or Casey. Just the front door of Dogwood at that Hitchcockian angle.

"We discovered this during a background check," Franny continues. "Against the advice of our attorneys, we invited her here for the summer. We didn't think she was a threat to herself or the campers. Nonetheless, precautions were taken."

Flynn, proving himself to be nobody's fool, says, "Hence the camera."

"Yes," Franny says. "I just thought you should know. To show we're doing everything we can to help in your search. I don't mean to imply in any way whatsoever that I think Emma had something to go with this disappearance."

Yet that's exactly what she's doing. I keep my gaze fixed on the monitor, unwilling to look away because it would mean facing Franny again. And I'm not sure I can do that.

On the screen, a girl edges into view, her back straight, her steps precise. She knows the camera is there. At first, I think it's a camper, maybe sneaking out of a neighboring cabin to get another peek of the state troopers milling around the mess hall.

Then I see the blond hair, the white dress, the locket around her neck.

It's Vivian.

Right there on the monitor.

I gasp in shock—a ragged, watery sound.

Chet's the first to notice and says, "Emma? What's wrong?"

My hand trembles as I point to the monitor. Vivian is still there. She looks directly into the camera and gives a coy smile. As if she knows I'm watching. She even waves to me.

"You see that, right?"

"See what?" It's Theo this time, his brow creasing with doctor-like concern.

"Her," I say. "In front of Dogwood."

All of them turn to the monitor, crowding around it, blocking my view.

"There's nothing there," Theo says.

"Did you see one of the missing girls?" Flynn says.

"Vivian. I saw Vivian."

I push between them, regaining my view of the live feed. On the monitor, all I see is that same angled view of Dogwood. Vivian's no longer there. Nor is anyone else.

I tell myself, *This isn't happening.*

I tell myself, *I'm not going crazy.*

It's no use. Panic and fear have already overtaken me, turning my body numb. A fuzzy blackness encroaches on the edge of my vision, pulsing across my eyes until I see nothing at all. My arm jabs forward, reaching for something to grab on to. Someone catches it. Theo. Or maybe Detective Flynn.

But it's too late.

My arm slips from their grasp, and I fall, crashing onto the cellar floor and fainting dead away.

FIFTEEN YEARS AGO

The sweatshirt sat on a table in the arts and crafts building, sleeves spread wide. It was the same way my mother laid out clothes she wanted me to wear. The whole ensemble revealed, enticing me to put it on. Only this shirt was different. Rather than wear it, the police wanted me to identify it.

"Do you recognize it?" asked a female state trooper with a warm smile and a matronly bosom.

I stared at the sweatshirt—white with *Princeton* spelled across the front in proud Tiger Orange—and nodded. "It's Vivian's."

"Are you sure?"

"Yes."

She had worn it to one of the campfires. I remembered because I had joked that it made her look like a marshmallow. She said it kept the mosquitoes away, fashion be damned.

The trooper shot a glance at a colleague on the other side of the table. He nodded and quickly folded the sweatshirt. Latex gloves covered his hands. I had no idea why.

"Did you take that out of Dogwood?" I said.

The female trooper ignored the question. "Was Vivian wearing that sweatshirt when you saw her leave the cabin?"

"No."

"Give it some more thought. Take your time."

"I don't need more time. She wasn't wearing it."

If I seemed irritable, it was justified. The girls had been missing for more than a day, and everyone was running out of hope. I felt it all throughout camp. It was like a leak in a tub of water, the optimism draining away drop by precious drop. During that time, the arts and crafts building had been taken over by the police, who used it to organize search parties, sign in volunteers, and, in my case, informally interrogate thirteen-year-old girls.

I had spent an hour there the night before, being grilled by a pair of detectives who took turns asking me questions. An exhausting back-and-forth, my neck sore from swiveling between them. I answered most of their questions. When the girls had left. What they were wearing. What Vivian said before departing the cabin. As for what I'd told her as she slipped outside and how I prevented them from getting back in, well, that remained unspoken.

The shame was too great. The guilt was even worse.

Now I was being asked a new round of questions, although the female trooper displayed far more patience than the detectives. In fact, she looked like she wanted to hug me to her oversize chest and tell me that everything would be okay.

"I believe you," she said.

"Where did you find that sweatshirt?"

"I'm not at liberty to say."

I looked to the other side of the room, where the folded sweatshirt was being passed to yet another trooper. He also wore gloves. The skin of his hands shone white beneath the latex as he placed the sweatshirt into a cardboard evidence box. Dread flooded my heart.

"Did any of the girls have secrets they might have shared with you but not with others?" the trooper said.

"I don't know."

"But they did have secrets?"

"It's kind of hard to call something a secret if I don't know who else they told."

My teenage bitchiness was intentional. An attempt to wipe that pitying look off the trooper's face. I didn't deserve her pity. Instead, it only made her lean in closer, acting like the cool guidance counselor at school who was always telling us to think of her as a friend and not as an authority figure.

"Most times teenage girls run away, they do so because they're meeting someone," she said. "A boyfriend. Or a lover. It's usually someone others don't approve of. A forbidden romance. Did any of the girls mention anything like that?"

I wasn't sure how much I should say, mostly because I didn't know what was going on.

"The girls ran away? Is that what you think?"

"We don't know, honey. Maybe. That's why we need your help. Because sometimes girls run away to meet a boy who ends up hurting them. We don't want your friends to get hurt. We just want to find them. So if you know anything—anything at all—I'd really appreciate it if you told me."

I thought of *The Lovely Bones*. The teenager found dead in a field. The creepy neighbor who killed her.

"Vivian *was* seeing someone," I said.

The trooper's eyes momentarily brightened before she settled back down, forcing herself to keep playing it cool.

"Did she happen to tell you who it was?"

"Do you think he might have done something to her?"

"We won't know until we talk to him."

I took that as a yes. Which meant they thought Vivian, Natalie, and Allison were more than lost. They thought they were dead. Murdered. Just three sets of lovely bones on the forest floor.

"Emma," the trooper said. "If you know his name, you need to tell us."

I opened my mouth. My heart thundered so hard I felt it in my teeth.

"It's Theo," I said. "Theodore Harris-White."

I didn't believe it, not even as I said it. Yet I wanted to. I wanted to think Theo had something to do with the girls' disappearance, that he was capable of hurting them. Because he already *had* hurt someone.

Me.

He shattered my heart without even realizing it.

This was my chance to hurt him back.

"Are you sure?" the trooper said.

I tried to convince myself it wasn't bitter jealousy making me do this. That it made sense Theo would be involved. Once Vivian, Natalie, and Allison returned to the locked cabin, the first thing they would have done was find a counselor. They didn't because they had been out after hours, not to mention drinking. Both offenses would have gotten them kicked out of camp. So, they had gone to the one person of authority they could trust—Theo. Now they were missing, likely presumed dead. That couldn't be a coincidence.

At least that's the lie I told myself.

"I'm certain," I said.

A few minutes later, I was allowed to return to Dogwood. The area outside the arts and crafts building hummed with activity as I left. There were cops and reporters and the bray of bloodhounds in the distance. Troopers had already started searching the camp pickup. I spotted them as I passed, peering into the open cab doors and rifling through the glove compartment.

When I turned away, I saw a search party just returning from a trek through the woods. Most of them were townies, come to help any way they could. But I spotted a few familiar faces in the crowd. The kitchen worker who had piled my plate with pancakes on the Fourth of July, which suddenly felt like weeks ago. The handyman who always seemed to be fixing something around camp.

Then there was Theo, looking haggard in jeans and a T-shirt darkened by sweat. His hair was a shambles. A smudge of dirt stained his cheek.

I flung myself toward him, not quite knowing what I intended to do until I was right there in front of him. I was both mad at Vivian and terrified for her, furious at Theo and in love with him. So my hands curled into fists. I pounded his chest.

"Where are they?" I cried. "What did you do to them?"

Theo didn't move, didn't flinch.

Further proof in my confused mind that he had already steeled himself for a beating from my tiny hands.

That, deep down, he knew he deserved it.

Twenty-Nine

This isn't happening.

I'm not going crazy.

The words crash into my brain the moment I regain consciousness, making me sit up with a start. My head slams into something hard above me. Pain pulses along my hairline, joining another, previously unnoticed pain at the back of my head.

"Whoa," someone says. "Easy."

A moment of pure confusion passes before I realize where I am. Camp Nightingale. Dogwood. Ensconced in a bunk bed, the top of which I just introduced to my forehead. The person who spoke is Theo. He sits on my hickory trunk with Sasha's copy of *National Geographic*, passing the time until I wake up.

I rub my head, my palm alternating between the two points of pain. The one in the front is already fading. The one in the back is the opposite. It grows in intensity.

"You took quite a tumble in the cellar," Theo says. "I broke some of your fall, but you still banged your head pretty bad."

I slide out of bed and stand, gripping Miranda's bunk in case I need support. My legs are rubbery but strong enough to keep me upright. Small traces of the dark fuzziness that engulfed me in the Lodge remain. I blink until they're gone.

"You need to rest," Theo says.

That's impossible at the moment. Not with him here. Not when my limbs tingle with anxiety, aching and restless. I look around the cabin and see everything is the same as it was this morning. Sasha's bed is still meticulously made. Krystal's teddy bear remains a lump beneath the blankets.

"They're still missing, aren't they?"

Theo confirms it with a solemn nod. My legs start to quiver, begging me to lie down again. I tighten my grip on the edge of Miranda's bunk and remain standing.

"Detective Flynn broke the news to their families. He asked if any of them have been contacted by one of the girls. No one has. Miranda's grandmother didn't even know she had a cell phone, so there's still no word on what carrier she uses."

"Did Flynn talk to the kitchen staff?"

"He did. All of them live in the next town over. They're all cafeteria staff at the middle school there. Just happy to have a job for the summer. They carpool together every morning before breakfast and every evening after dinner. No one stayed behind last night, and no one came in early this morning. Not even Marvin."

All that information I had given Flynn—all my attempts to help—ended up being for nothing. Disappointment swells in my chest, tight against my rib cage.

Theo sets the magazine aside and says, "Do you want to talk about what happened back at the Lodge?"

"Not really."

"You said you saw Vivian."

My mouth goes dry, making it hard to speak. My tongue feels too sticky and heavy to form words. A bottle of water sits next to Theo. He gives it to me, and I swallow all but a few drops.

"I did," I say after clearing my throat. "On the live feed of the cabin."

"I looked, Emma. No one was there."

"Oh, I know. It was…"

I'm unable to adequately describe it. A hallucination? My imagination?

"Stress," Theo says. "You're under a tremendous amount."

"But I've seen her before. When I was much younger. It's why I was sent away. I thought she was gone. But she's not. I keep seeing her. Here. Now."

Theo cocks his head, looking at me the same way I'm sure he looks at his patients when he has to give them bad news.

"I had a conversation with my mother," he says. "We both agree it was wrong to invite you back here, even if it was with the best intentions. That doesn't mean we think any of this is your fault. It's ours. We underestimated the effect being here would have on you."

"Are you telling me to leave camp?"

"Yes," Theo says. "I think it's for the best."

"But what about the girls?"

"There's a search party looking for them right now. They've split into two groups. One is taking the woods to the right of camp and another doing the same thing on the left."

"I need to join it," I say, making a move toward the door on unsteady legs. "I want to help."

Theo blocks my path. "You're in no condition to go trampling through the woods."

"But I need to find them."

"They'll be found," Theo says as he grips my arms, holding me in place. "I promise. The plan is to add more searchers tomorrow, if necessary. Within twenty-four hours, every square foot of this property will have been thoroughly searched."

I don't remind him that a similar search did little good fifteen years ago. Every square foot of land was covered then, too. All it yielded was a sweat shirt.

"I'm staying," I insist. "I'm not leaving until they're found."

A rumble sounds in the distance—a deep thudding that echoes across the valley like thunder. A helicopter joining the search. The sound is familiar to me. I heard it a lot fifteen years ago. The cabin rattles as the chopper roars overhead, low in the sky, practically skimming the trees. Theo grimaces as it passes.

"My mother doesn't trust you, Em," he says, raising his voice so it can compete with the helicopter. "I'm not sure I do, either."

I get louder, too. "I swear to you, I didn't hurt those girls."

"How can you be so sure? You were so messed-up last night that I doubt you'd remember it if you did."

The helicopter retreats from the area, zooming out over the lake. Its departure leaves the cabin draped in silence. Lingering in the new-found quiet are Theo's words—and the accusation coiled within them.

"What are you talking about?"

"Flynn talked to the other instructors," Theo says. "All of them. Casey said she saw you by the latrine last night. She said you seemed drunk. When we talked to Becca, she admitted the two of you shared a bottle of whiskey while the rest of us were at the campfire."

"I'm sorry," I say, my voice so incredibly meek I'm surprised Theo can even hear it.

"So you were drinking last night?"

I nod.

"Jesus, Emma. One of the campers could have seen you."

"I'm sorry," I say again. "It was stupid and wrong and completely unlike me. But it doesn't mean I did something to those girls. You saw the camera footage. You saw I went looking for them."

"Or followed them. There's no way of knowing with any certainty."

"There is," I tell him. "Because you know me. And you know I wouldn't hurt those girls."

He has no good reason to believe me. Not after all the lies I've told. One word from Theo to the police could thrust me into the same situation I had put him in fifteen years earlier. The fact that our roles are reversed isn't lost on me.

I tilt my head and stare into his brown eyes, willing him to look back. I want him to see me. Truly see me. If he does, maybe he'll recognize the girl I used to be. Not the damaged twenty-eight-year-old who is very likely losing her grip on sanity but the thirteen-year-old who adored him.

"Please believe me," I whisper.

A moment passes. A quivering period of time that lasts only a second but feels like minutes. During it, I can almost feel my fate hanging in the balance. Then Theo whispers back.

"I do."

I nod, overwhelmingly grateful. I resist the urge to cry with relief. Then I kiss him.

It's a surprise to both of us. Just like the last time I kissed him, only more forceful. This time, it's not boldness that makes me do it. It's desperation. The girls' disappearance has me feeling so utterly helpless that I now crave the distraction I avoided the other day. I need something to momentarily take my mind off what's happening. I ache for it.

Theo stays completely still, not reacting as I continue to press my lips to his. But soon he's kissing me back, upping the intensity.

I press against him, my palms on his chest. Not hitting this time. Caressing. Theo's arms snake around me, holding me tight, pulling me even closer. I know the deal. I'm as much a distraction for him as he is for me. I don't care. Not when his lips are on my neck and his hand is sliding under my shirt.

More thudding sounds erupt from outside the window. Another helicopter approaching. Or maybe it's the same one, making another pass. It swoops directly over Dogwood, so loud I can't hear anything but the thrum of its rotors. The window rattles.

Caught in that noise, Theo lifts me, carries me to my bunk, lowering me into it. He takes off his shirt, revealing more scars. A dozen at least. They crisscross his skin from shoulder to navel, looking like claw marks. I think of his accident—twisted metal, shattered glass, shards breaking skin and glancing off bone.

I caused those scars.

Every single one.

Now Theo's on top of me, heavy and safe and warm. But I can't let this go any further, distraction be damned.

"Theo, stop."

He pulls away from me, confusion skidding through his eyes. "What's wrong?"

"I can't do this." I slide out from under him and move to the other side of the cabin, where I'm less likely to reach out and touch his scars, my fingers tracing the length of each one. "Not until I tell you something."

Although the helicopter has moved on, I can still hear it thudding over the lake. I wait until the sound subsides before saying, "I know, Theo. About you and Vivian."

"There was no me and Vivian."

"You don't need to lie about it. Not anymore."

"I'm not lying. What are you talking about?"

"I saw you, Theo. You and Vivian. In the shower. I saw, and it broke my heart."

"When was this?" Theo says.

"The night they vanished."

I don't need to say anything else. Theo understands the rest. Why I accused him. How that accusation has followed him since. He sits up and rubs his jaw, his fingers cutting through the salt-and-pepper stubble.

I had always thought having the truth exposed would make me feel better. That relief would flood my body from my head to the tips of my toes. Instead, I only feel guilty. And petty. And unbearably sad.

"I'm so, so sorry," I say. "I was young and stupid and worried about the girls and heartbroken because of you. So when that state trooper asked me if any of them had a boyfriend no one knew about, I told her that you were secretly seeing Vivian."

"But I wasn't," he replies.

"Theo, I *saw* you."

"You saw *someone*. Just not me. Yes, Vivian flirted and made it clear she'd be up for it. But I was never interested."

I replay that moment in my mind. Hearing the moans muffled by the rush of the shower. Peering through the space between the planks. Seeing Vivian shoved against the wall, her hair running down her neck in wet tendrils, twisting like snakes. Theo behind her. Pushing into her. Face buried against her neck.

His face.

I never actually saw it.

I had just assumed it was Theo because I had seen him in the shower before.

"It had to be you," I say. "There's no one else it could be. You were the only man in the entire camp."

Even as the words emerge, I know I'm wrong. There was someone else here close to Theo's age. Someone who went unnoticed, simply doing his job, hiding in plain sight.

"The grounds keeper," I say.

"Ben," Theo says with a huff of disgust. "And if he did something like that back then, who knows what he's been up to now."

Thirty

"Tell me about the girls," Detective Flynn says. "The ones who are missing. Did you have any interactions with them?"

"I might have seen them. Don't remember if I did or not, but probably."

"Did you have any interactions with *any* of the girls in camp?"

"Not on purpose. Maybe if I needed to get somewhere and they were in my way, I'd say excuse me. Other than that, I keep to myself."

He looks up at us from a chair built for someone half his age, his gaze resting a moment on each of our faces. First me. Then Theo. And finally Detective Flynn.

We're all in the arts and crafts building, the mess hall having been taken over by the remaining campers and instructors for dinner. I spotted them glumly filing inside as Theo and I headed next door. A few of the girls still wept. Most wore stunned, blank expressions that were occasionally punctuated by disbelief. I saw it in their eyes when they lifted their faces to the sky as the search helicopter made another deafening pass over camp.

So we ended up here, in a former horse stable painted to resemble a storybook forest, lit by fluorescent bulbs that buzz overhead. I stand next to Theo, keeping several feet of space between us. I still don't entirely trust him. I'm sure he feels the same way about me. But for now, we're uncomfortable allies, united in our suspicion of a man whose full name I've only recently learned.

Ben Schumacher.

The grounds keeper. The man who had sex with Vivian. The same man who might know where Miranda, Krystal, and Sasha are. I let Flynn do the talking, choosing to stay silent even though all I want is to pummel Ben Schumacher until he tells me where they are and what he's done to them.

He certainly appears capable of doing harm. He's got a hard look about him. He's spent much of his life working outdoors, and it shows in the calluses on his hands and the sunburned streak on the bridge of his nose. He's big, too. There's a noticeable bulk hidden beneath his flannel shirt and white tee.

"Where were you at five this morning?" Detective Flynn asks him.

"Probably in the kitchen. About to get ready for work."

Flynn nods toward the gold wedding band on Ben's left hand. "Can your wife confirm that?"

"I hope so, seeing how she was in the kitchen with me. Although she's awfully groggy before that first cup of coffee."

Ben chuckles. The rest of us don't. He leans back in his chair and says, "Why are you asking me this stuff?"

"What's your job here?" Flynn says, ignoring the question.

"Grounds keeper. I told you that already."

"I know, but what specifically do you do?"

"Whatever needs doing. Mowing the lawn. Working on the buildings."

"So, general maintenance?"

"Yeah." Ben gives a half smirk at the vaguely genteel job description. "General maintenance."

"And how long have you worked for Camp Nightingale?"

"I don't. I work for the family. Sometimes that means doing some things for the camp. Sometimes it doesn't."

"Then how long have you worked for the Harris-Whites?"

"About fifteen years."

"Which means the summer Camp Nightingale closed was your first summer here?"

"It was," Ben says.

Flynn makes a note of it in the same notebook he jotted down all my useless information. "How did you get the job?"

"I was a year out of high school, picking up the odd job here and there around town. Barely scraping by. So when I got wind that Mrs. Harris-White was looking for a grounds keeper, I jumped at the chance. Been here ever since."

For confirmation, Flynn turns to Theo, who says, "It's true."

"Fifteen years is a long time to be working the same job," Flynn tells Ben. "Do you like working for the Harris-Whites?"

"It's decent work. Pays well. Puts a roof over my family's head and food in their stomachs. I got no complaints."

"What about the family? Do you like them?"

Ben looks to Theo, his expression unreadable. "Like I said, no complaints."

"Back to your interactions with the girls in camp," Flynn says. "Are you certain there wasn't any contact with them? Maybe you had to do some work in their cabin."

"He installed the camera outside Dogwood," Theo says.

Flynn writes that down in his notebook. "As you know, Mr. Schumacher, that's the cabin where the missing girls were staying. Did you happen to see them when you were putting up the camera?"

"No."

"What about the oldest one? Miranda. I've been told other camp workers noticed her."

"Not me," Ben says. "I keep my head down. None of this camp stuff is my business."

"What about fifteen years ago? Were you the same way back then?"

"Yes."

Flynn makes a move to write down the answer in his notebook. But he pauses, his pen tip a millimeter from the page. "I'm giving you another shot at the answer. Just so I don't have to waste time writing down something that might be a lie."

"Why do you think I'm lying?"

"One of the girls who disappeared back then was named Vivian Hawthorne. You probably remember her."

"I remember that she was never found."

"I was told you might have had a relationship with Miss Hawthorne. Which would be the complete opposite of minding your own business. So is it true? Was there a relationship between the two of you?"

I expect a denial. Ben gives us all a defiant look as that half smirk lifts the corner of his lips. But then he says, "Yeah. Although it wasn't much of what you'd call a relationship."

"It was strictly sexual in nature?" Flynn says.

"That's right. A one-and-done kind of deal."

Ben's smirk grows, on the verge of a leer. Again, I resist the urge to punch him. But I can't stop myself from saying, "She was only sixteen. You know that, right?"

"And I was only nineteen," Ben says. "That age difference didn't seem like such a big deal. Besides, it wasn't illegal. I got three daughters of my own now. So I know damn well what the statutory rape laws are."

"But you knew it was a bad idea," Flynn tells him. "Otherwise you would have told someone about it after Miss Hawthorne and two other girls from her cabin went missing."

"Because I knew the cops would think I had something to do with it. That's what this is about, right? You're all standing there thinking I had something to do with what happened to those poor girls."

"Did you?"

Ben stands suddenly, sending the chair skidding across the floor behind him. Veins bulge at his temples, and his hands curl into fists, as though he's about to take a swing at Flynn. He definitely looks like he wants to.

"I'm a father now. I'd be going crazy if my girls were missing. Makes me sick to my stomach just thinking about it. You should be out there looking for them instead of asking me about some dumb shit I did fifteen years ago."

He stops, out of breath. His chest heaves, and his fists unclench. Resigned exhaustion settles over him as he retrieves his too-small chair and sits back down.

"Keep on asking your goddamn questions," he says. "I'll answer them. I've got nothing to hide."

"Then let's go back to Vivian Hawthorne," Flynn says. "How did it start?"

"I don't know. It just kind of happened."

"Did you instigate it?"

"Hell no," Ben says. "Like I said, I wasn't looking for trouble. I mean, I saw her around camp. It was hard not to notice her."

"Did you find her attractive?" Flynn asks.

"Sure. She was hot, and she knew it. But there was something else about her. A confidence. It made her stand out from the other girls. She was different."

"Different how?"

"Most of those girls were stuck-up. Snooty. They'd look right past me like I wasn't even there. Like I didn't exist. Vivian wasn't like that. The very first day of camp she came up to me and introduced herself. *I don't remember you from last year.* That's what she said. She asked me about my job, how long I'd been here. Just friendly. It felt nice having someone like her pay attention to me."

That sounds like the Vivian I knew. A master at seduction. It didn't matter if you were the camp grounds keeper or a thirteen-year-old girl. She knew exactly what kind of attention you needed before you even knew it yourself.

"We hung out a few times those first days of camp. During lunch, she'd come find me working and talk for a few minutes. By then, I knew what she wanted. She wasn't shy about it."

Flynn, who's been steadily writing all this down in his notebook, pauses long enough to say, "How many times did the two of you engage in intercourse?"

"Once."

"Do you remember the date?"

"Only because it was the Fourth of July," Ben says. "I was working late that day, trying to milk the overtime money Mrs. Harris-White was offering. All the girls were at the campfire, and I was getting ready to go home when Vivian showed up. She didn't say anything. She just came right up to me and kissed me. Then she walked away, looking over her shoulder to make sure I followed."

He gives no further details. Not that I need them. I already know the rest.

What I don't know is why.

"That Fourth of July was the night Miss Hawthorne and the others disappeared," Flynn says.

Ben nods. "I know. I don't need a reminder."

"What did you do after it was over?"

"Vivian left before me. I remember she was in a hurry to get out of there. She said people would start to realize she was gone. So she got dressed and left."

"And was that the last time you saw her?"

"Yes, sir, it was." Ben pauses to scratch the back of his neck, giving the question more thought. "Sort of."

"So you did see her again after that?"

"Not her," Ben clarified. "Something she left behind."

"I don't follow," Flynn says, speaking for all of us.

"I left the latrine not long after Vivian did. On the drive home, I realized my keys were missing. The ones I use for camp."

"What do they access?"

"Camp buildings," Ben says. "The Lodge. Mess hall. The toolshed and latrine."

"The cabins?" Flynn asks.

Ben offers us another partial smirk. "I bet you wish it was that easy, but no. Not the cabins."

Flynn again looks to Theo for confirmation. He gives a slight nod and says, "He's telling the truth."

"I thought they might have fallen out of my pocket in the latrine," Ben continues. "Or maybe somewhere else. When I got to work the next morning, Vivian and the two others had already disappeared. At the time, no one seemed too worried. They'd only been gone a couple of hours, and everyone assumed they'd come back eventually. So I went looking for the keys. I ended up finding them at the toolshed behind the Lodge. The door was open. The keys were still in the lock."

"And you think Miss Hawthorne left them there?"

"I do. I think she took them out of my pocket when we were in the latrine."

"What was kept in the toolshed?" Flynn says.

"Equipment, mostly. The lawn mower. Chains for tires in winter. That kind of thing."

"Why would she need to go to the toolshed?"

The question elicits a shrug from Ben. "Damned if I know."

But I do. Vivian went there to retrieve a shovel. The same one she used to dig a hole that would eventually conceal her diary.

"You should have told us," Theo says. "About all of it. But you didn't, and now my family can never trust you again."

Ben gives him a hard stare. In his eyes burns what can only be described as barely concealed disgust.

"Don't you dare judge me, *Theodore*," he says, spitting out the name like something that's left a bad taste in his mouth. "You think you're better than me? Just because some rich woman plucked you out of an orphanage? That just means you're lucky."

The color drains from Theo's face. I can't tell if it's because of shock or anger. He opens his mouth to reply but is cut off by a noise rising suddenly from outside. Someone shouting. The voice echoes off the water.

"I see something!"

Theo turns to me, panicked. "That's Chet."

We rush out of the arts and crafts building, Detective Flynn in the lead, surprisingly quick on his feet. At the mess hall, a bunch of girls are pushing out of the door, clutching one another. Several of them cry out in distress, even though no one knows what's going on. No one but Chet, who stands at the lake's edge, pointing to something in the water.

A canoe.

Unmoored. Adrift.

It bobs a hundred yards from shore at a sideways angle, making it clear no one is guiding it.

I race into the lake, marching high-kneed until the water reaches my thighs. I then fall forward, swimming now, taking quick, forceful strokes toward the errant canoe. Behind me, others do the same thing. Theo and Chet. Glimpses of them flash over my shoulder whenever I pause to take a breath.

I'm first to the canoe, followed soon after by Chet, then Theo. We each grip the edge of the boat with one hand and start the swim ashore with the other. It's an awkward, labored trip. My wet fingers keep slipping from the canoe's edge and our strokes are out of sync, making the boat jerk from side to side as we swim.

Once in shallow water, the three of us stand and drag the canoe to shore. A crowd has gathered by then. Detective Flynn and Ben Schumacher. Most of the campers, kept at bay by counselors. At the Lodge, Franny, Lottie, and Mindy watch from the back deck. I risk a glance inside the canoe, and my legs grow weak.

The boat is empty.

No oars. No life vests. Certainly no people.

The only thing inside is a pair of glasses, twisted like a wrung-out washcloth, one of the lenses spiderwebbed with cracks.

Flynn uses a handkerchief to lift it from the canoe. "Does anyone recognize these?"

I stare at the red frames, somehow still standing, even though the sight of them should have sent me tumbling again into unconsciousness. I even manage to nod.

"Sasha," I say, my voice weak. "They belong to Sasha."

Thirty-One

Back in Dogwood, I lay in the bottom bunk, trying to keep it together. So far, I'm doing a shitty job. After the canoe was found, I went to the latrine and threw up. I then spent a half hour crying in the shower before changing into dry clothes. Now I hold Krystal's matted-fur teddy bear as Detective Flynn graces me with another disbelieving stare.

"That's an interesting thing you did back there," he says. "Swimming out to the canoe like that."

"You would have preferred I let it float away?"

Flynn remains standing in the center of the room. Some kind of power play, I assume. Letting me know that he's fully in charge here.

"I would have preferred for you to leave it alone and let the police retrieve it. It's evidence. Now it's been tainted by three additional people."

"Sorry," I say, only because it's what he obviously wants to hear.

"Maybe you are, maybe you aren't. Or maybe you did it on purpose. Covering up fingerprints or trace evidence you'd previously left behind."

Flynn pauses, waiting for I don't know what. A confession? A vehement denial? Instead, I say, "That's ridiculous."

"Is it? Then please explain this."

He reaches into his pocket and pulls out a clear plastic bag. Inside is a curl of silver chain on which hang three pewter birds.

My charm bracelet.

"I know it's yours," Flynn says. "Three people confirmed they saw you wearing it."

"Where did you find it?"

"In the canoe."

I tighten my grip on Krystal's teddy bear to stave off a sudden onslaught of nausea. The cabin spins. I feel like I'm going to throw up again. I tell myself for the fiftieth time today that this isn't really happening.

But it is.

It has.

"Would you like to explain how it got there?" Flynn asks. "I know it wasn't on your wrist when you swam out to that canoe."

"I-I lost it." Shock makes it a struggle to utter even the simplest words. "Yesterday."

"Lost it," Flynn says. "That's convenient."

"The clasp broke." I pause, take a breath, try to think of a way to not sound insane. "I fixed it. With string. But it fell off at some point."

"You don't remember when?"

"I didn't notice. Not until later."

I stop talking. Nothing I say will make sense to him. It certainly doesn't make sense to me. The bracelet was there. Until it wasn't. I don't know when or where it went from being on my wrist to being lost.

"So how do you think it got into the canoe?" Flynn says.

"Maybe one of the girls found it and picked it up, intending to return it to me later."

It's a stretch. Even I can see that. But it's the most logical chain of events. Miranda saw me twisting the bracelet during yesterday's painting lesson. I can easily picture her spotting it on the ground, scooping it up, dropping it into her pocket. The only other possible explanation is that it was found by the same person responsible for the girls' disappearance.

"What if I'm being framed?"

It's less a fully formed thought than a desperate attempt to get Flynn on my side. Yet the more I think about it, the more it starts to make sense.

"That bracelet fell off yesterday, *before* the girls vanished. And now it's in the same canoe as Sasha's broken glasses. Talk about convenient. What if whoever took the girls put it there on purpose to make me look guilty?"

"I think you're doing a pretty good job of that all by yourself."

"I didn't touch those girls! How many times do I have to say it before you believe me?"

"I'd love to believe you," Detective Flynn says. "But it turns out you're a difficult woman to believe, Miss Davis. Not with all that talk about seeing people who weren't really there. Or your conspiracy theories. This morning, you told me Francesca Harris-White had something to with it. But less than an hour ago, you were certain it was the grounds keeper."

"Maybe it was."

Flynn shakes his head. "We talked to his wife. She confirmed he was in the kitchen at five a.m., right where he said he was. And then there's all those things you said fifteen years ago about Theo Harris-White. Didn't you accuse him of hurting your friends back then?"

A sharp heat burns my cheeks.

"Yes," I say.

"I'm assuming you don't believe it now."

I look at the floor. "No."

"It would be interesting to know when you stopped believing he was guilty and started thinking he was innocent," Flynn says. "Because you never retracted that accusation. Officially, Mr. Harris-White is still a suspect in that disappearance. I guess you two now have something in common."

My face gets hotter with anger. Some of it's directed at Detective Flynn. The rest is reserved for me and how horribly I acted back then. Either way, I know I can't listen to Flynn rehash my bad behavior for a minute longer.

"Are you going to charge with me something?"

"Not yet," Flynn replies. "The girls haven't been found, dead or alive. And a bracelet isn't enough to charge you. At least not unless a lab analysis finds some of their DNA on it."

"Then get the hell out of this cabin until you do."

I don't regret saying it, even though I know it makes me look even guiltier. It occurs to me that some cops would even take it as an admission of guilt. Flynn, however, merely raises his hands in a don't-blame-me gesture and moves to the door.

"We're done, for now," he says. "But I'll be watching you, Miss Davis."

He won't be the only one. Between the camera outside the cabin and Vivian at my window, I've gotten used to being watched.

When Detective Flynn leaves, the open door lets in the sound of police boats out on the lake. They arrived shortly after the discovery of the canoe. Meanwhile, the helicopter is still going, rattling the cabin with each pass.

I can't remember if the helicopter fifteen years ago showed up the first day or the second. The boats and volunteer search party were the first. That I definitely remember. All those people wearing flimsy orange vests and grim expressions as they marched into the woods. All those boats crisscrossing the lake, giving up once Vivian's sweatshirt was found in the forest. That's when the dogs were brought in, on the second day. Each allowed to sniff a piece of clothing plucked from the girls' trunks to absorb their scents. By then, Franny had already decided to close the camp. So as the dogs were barking their way around the lake, hysterical campers were hustled onto buses or pulled into SUVs with dazed parents behind the wheels.

I wasn't so lucky. I had to spend another day here, for investigative purposes, I was told. Another twenty-four hours spent huddled in this very bunk, feeling pretty much the same way I do now.

The helicopter has just passed once again when I hear a knock on the cabin door.

"Come in," I say, too spent with worry to open it myself.

A second later, Becca pokes her head into the cabin. A surprise, considering the tone of last night's conversation. At first, I think she's here to offer condolences. I turn away when she enters, just so I can avoid the half-pity, half-sorry look I'm certain she'll give me. My gaze drifts instead to the camera in her hands.

"If you're here to take more pictures, you can leave right now," I say.

"Listen, I know you're pissed I told that cop we got drunk last night. I'm sorry. I got freaked out by the whole situation and told the truth, not thinking it would make you look suspicious. If it's any consolation, it makes me look suspicious, too."

"As far as I know, all the girls in your cabin are present and accounted for."

"I'm trying to help you, Emma."

"I don't need your help."

"I think you do," Becca says. "You should hear what they're saying about you out there. Everyone thinks you did it. That you snapped and made those girls disappear the same way Viv, Natalie, and Allison vanished."

"Even you?"

Becca gives me a pointed nod. "Even me. No use lying at this point, right? But then I started examining some of the photos I took around camp this morning. Looking to see if I accidentally captured any clues about what might have happened."

"I don't need you playing detective for me," I say.

"It's better than the job you've been doing," she remarks. "Which, by the way, everyone also knows about. You haven't exactly been subtle with your sneaking around camp and asking questions. Casey even told me she saw you slip into the Lodge yesterday."

Of course Camp Nightingale is just as gossipy now as it was fifteen years ago. Maybe even more so. God knows what the counselors and campers have been saying about me. Probably that I'm obsessive and crazy and make bad choices. Guilty as charged.

"I wasn't sneaking," I say. "And I'm assuming you found something interesting or you wouldn't be here."

Becca sits on the floor next to my bunk and holds up the camera so I can see it. On the display screen is an image of me standing dumbly in Lake Midnight and Franny wading in after me. Once again, I'm reminded of how great a photographer Becca is. She captured the moment in all its awful clarity, right down to the water seeping into the hem of Franny's nightgown.

Theo's in the middle of the photo, standing in his boxers between the lake and the Lodge. The pale patchwork of scars on his chest pop in the morning light, visible to all. Yet I had missed them completely. I had other things on my mind.

Beyond Theo is the Lodge itself, its back deck occupied by Chet and Mindy. He's in track shorts and a T-shirt. She's in a surprisingly sensible cotton nightgown.

"Now here's one from the reverse angle," Becca says.

The next photo shows the full crowd of campers drawn to the water's edge by my screams. The girls clutch one another, fear still etching itself onto their sleep-pinkened faces.

"I counted them," Becca says. "Seventy-five campers, counselors, and instructors. Out of a potential eighty."

I do the math. Three of the five people absent from the photo are Sasha, Miranda, and Krystal, for obvious reasons. I'm another, because at that moment I was being led by Franny from the chilly waters of Lake Midnight. The fifth missing person is Becca, the person taking the photo.

"I'm not sure what you're getting at."

"Only one person in the entire camp didn't come to see what was going on," Becca replies. "Don't you think that's strange?"

I snatch the camera from her hands and bring the display screen closer to my face, trying to identify who might be missing. I recognize nearly all the girls, either from the painting lessons or just roaming around camp. I spot Roberta and Paige, caught in the middle of exchanging worried looks. I see Kim, Danica, and the other three counselors. Each of them huddle with the girls from their respective cabins. Behind them is Casey, identifiable by her red hair.

I click to the previous photo, seeing me and Franny in the lake, Theo on the grass, Chet and Mindy up at the Lodge.

The only person missing is Lottie.

"Now you see it?" Becca says.

"Are you sure she's not there?" I scan the photo again, looking in vain for any sign of Lottie behind Chet and Mindy. There isn't one.

"Positive. Which begs this question: Why?"

Nothing I can think of makes sense. My screams were loud enough to bring the entire camp to the lakeshore, which makes it impossible for Lottie not to have heard them. Yes, there's a chance her absence is completely innocuous. Maybe she's a heavy sleeper. Or she was in the shower, its spray drowning out the sound of my screams.

But then I think about my bracelet. It feels like it's still wrapped around my left wrist. A phantom sensation. The last time I remember being aware of its presence was when I was in the Lodge, searching the study.

With Lottie.

Maybe it fell off. Or maybe she took it while I was engrossed by all those old photographs of Camp Nightingale.

I consider Vivian's diary, which by this point has become a kind of Rosetta Stone for trying to decipher what was happening fifteen years ago. Vivian mentioned Lottie, but only in passing. Just that one sentence about how Lottie caught her in the Lodge study and then told Franny about it. I didn't give it much attention, mostly because I had Franny's dirty little secret distracting me.

But now I wonder if that brief mention has greater meaning, especially in light of my own encounter with Lottie in the study. She spoke at length about her family's decades of service with the Harris-White clan. That suggests an unusual amount of devotion, passed down through generations. Just how devoted of an employee could Lottie be?

Enough to take action if she knew Vivian was close to learning what Franny's dark secret could be? Then do it again after realizing I'm on the verge of doing the same thing, only this time as some twisted kind of warning?

"Maybe," I say, "Lottie wasn't there because she already knew what was happening."

FIFTEEN YEARS AGO

After lashing out at Theo, I spent the rest of the day weeping in my bottom bunk. I cried so hard that by the time night fell, my pillow was soaked with tears. The pillowcase, salty and damp, stuck to my cheek when I looked up as the cabin door opened. It was Lottie, solemnly bearing a tray of food from the mess hall. Pizza. Side salad. Bottle of Snapple.

"You need to eat something, honey," she said.

"I'm not hungry," I told her, when in truth I was famished. Pain gnawed at my gut, reminding me that I'd barely eaten since the girls left the cabin.

"Starving yourself won't help anyone," Lottie said as she placed the tray on my hickory trunk. "You need a good meal to be ready for when your friends return."

"Do you really think they're coming back?"

"Of course they will."

"Then I won't eat until they do."

Lottie gave me a patient smile. "I'll leave the tray here in case you change your mind."

Once she was gone, I approached the tray, sniffing at the food like a feral cat. Ignoring the salad, I went straight for the pizza. I managed two bites before the pain in my gut worsened. It was sharper than hunger, shooting from my stomach into my heart.

Guilt.

That I'd said that horrible thing to Vivian right before she left.

That I'd locked the door before they returned.

That all day I'd told myself I simply provided an answer to that state trooper's innocent question. But deep down I knew the score. By saying Theo's name, I had accused him of harming Vivian, Natalie, and Allison. All because he picked Vivian over me.

Not that such an outcome had ever really been in doubt. I was a scrawny, flat-chested nothing. Of course Theo chose her. And now I assumed he and everyone else in camp hated me. I couldn't blame them. I hated myself more.

Which is why I was surprised when Franny came to Dogwood later in the night.

She had spent the previous night there. Not wanting me to be alone, she crept in with a sleeping bag, some snacks, and a pile of board games. When it was time to sleep, Franny unrolled the sleeping bag on the floor next to my bunk. That's where she slept, lulling me to sleep by singing Beatles songs in a soft, gentle voice.

Now she was back, the bag of snacks and games in one hand and her rolled-up sleeping bag in the other.

"I just got off the phone with your parents," she announced. "They'll be here tomorrow morning to take you home. So let's make your last night here a restful one."

I stared at her from my tear-stained pillow, confused. "You're staying here tonight, too?"

"Of course, my dear. It's not good to be here all by yourself."

She dropped the sleeping bag onto the floor and began to unroll it.

"You don't have to sleep on the floor again."

"Oh, but I do," Franny said. "We must keep the beds free for when your friends return any minute now."

I imagined Vivian, Natalie, and Allison flinging open the door and tramping inside, dirty and exhausted but very much alive. *We got lost,* Vivian would say. *Because Allison here doesn't know how to read a compass.* It was such a comforting thought that I glanced at the door, expecting them to do just that. When they didn't, I started to cry again, adding a few more drops to the pillowcase.

"Hush now," Franny said, swooping to my side. "No more tears for today, Emma."

"They've been gone so long."

"I know, but we mustn't lose hope. Ever."

She rubbed my back until I settled down, her gliding palm tender and soothing. I tried to recall if my own mother had ever done such a thing when I was sick or upset. I couldn't think of a single instance, which made me savor Franny's gentle touch all the more.

"Emma, I need to know something," she said, her voice on the edge of a whisper. "You don't really think Theo hurt your friends, do you?"

I said nothing in return. Fear kept me silent. I couldn't take back what I'd told the police. Not then. Yes, Theo was in a lot of trouble. But I also knew I'd be in trouble, too, if I admitted my accusation was a lie.

And that I'd locked Vivian, Natalie, and Allison out of the cabin.

And that we'd fought right before they left.

So many lies. Each one felt like a rock on my chest, holding me down, so heavy I could barely breath. I could either admit them and set myself free or add another one and hope I'd eventually get accustomed to the weight.

"Emma?" Franny said, this time with more insistence. "Do you?"

I remained silent.

"I see."

Franny removed her hand from my back, but not before I felt a tremor stirring in her fingers. They drummed along my spine a moment, then were gone. A few seconds later, Franny was gone, too. She left without saying another word. I spent the rest of the night alone, wide awake in my lower bunk, wondering just what kind of monster I'd become.

In the morning, it was Lottie who knocked on Dogwood's door to tell me my parents had arrived to take me home. Since I couldn't sleep, I'd packed hours earlier, transferring the contents of my hickory trunk into my suitcase as dawn broke over the lake.

I carried the suitcase out of the cabin and into a camp that had become a ghost town. Silence hung over the empty cabins and darkened buildings—an eerie hush broken only by the sound of my parents' Volvo idling near the mess hall. My mother got out of the car and opened the trunk. She then flashed Lottie an embarrassed smile, as if I had been sent home from a sleepover after wetting my sleeping bag.

"Franny apologizes for not being able to say good-bye," Lottie told me, pretending that neither of us knew it was a lie. "She wishes you a safe trip home."

In the distance, the front door to the Lodge opened up and Theo stepped outside, flanked by two of the detectives who had quickly become a common sight around camp. The firm grip they kept on Theo's elbows made it clear this wasn't a voluntary exit. I stood dumbly by the car and watched as they walked him to the arts and crafts building, likely for another interrogation. Theo caught sight of me and gave me a pleading look, silently begging me to intervene.

It was my last chance to tell the truth.

Instead, I climbed into the Volvo's back seat and said, "Please, Dad. Just go."

As my father started to drive away, the Lodge door gaped open yet again. This time, Chet ran out, his face tear-stained, legs a blur. He sprinted to the arts and crafts building, calling out Theo's name. Lottie rushed to intercept him and dragged him back to the Lodge, waving to my father to leave before we saw anything else.

Yet I continued to watch, turning around in my seat so I could look out the back window. I kept on looking as Lottie, Chet, and the quiet remains of Camp Nightingale faded from view.

Thirty-Two

When Becca leaves, I remain curled up in my bunk, Krystal's bear in my arms, trying to think of what to do about Lottie. Tell someone else, obviously. But my options are few. Detective Flynn doesn't trust me. I don't trust Franny. And even Theo would have a hard time believing my word over the word of the woman who's been with his family for decades.

I stare out the window, weighing my options while watching the evening sky succumb to thick darkness. The search crew in the helicopter has started using a spotlight, sweeping it across the water. When it rumbles overhead every fifteen minutes or so, the light brightens the trees outside the cabin window.

I'm watching the play of the light in the leaves when there's another knock on the door. It opens a second later, revealing Mindy bearing a tray from the cafeteria.

"I brought dinner," she announces.

What sits on the tray definitely isn't cafeteria food. This is dinner straight from the Lodge. Filet mignon still swirling with steam and roasted potatoes seasoned with rosemary. Their scents fill the cabin, making it smell like Thanksgiving.

"I'm not hungry," I say, even though under normal circumstances, I'd already be devouring the steak. Especially considering how stress and shitty cafeteria food have conspired to keep me from consuming, well, almost anything since I arrived. But I can't even look at the food, let alone eat it. Anxiety has knotted my stomach so tight I worry it might never unravel.

"I also brought wine," Mindy says, holding up a bottle of pinot noir. "That I'll take."

"I get half," Mindy says. "I'm telling you, it's been a day. The campers are terrified, and the rest of us are at our wit's end trying to keep them calm and occupied."

She sets the tray on the hickory trunk that was once Allison's and is now Sasha's. Maybe. Or maybe it doesn't belong to anyone anymore. It's like Krystal's teddy bear—temporarily ownerless.

From the way Mindy simply plucks the cork from the wine, I can tell the bottle had been opened back in the Lodge. Probably to prevent me from having access to a corkscrew. On the tray, I see that the fork and knife are plastic. When Mindy pours the wine, it's into plastic cups. It brings back memories of the mental hospital, where no sharp objects were allowed.

"Cheers," Mindy says as she hands me a cup and taps it with her own. "Drink up."

That I do, draining the entire cup before coming up for air and asking, "Why the special treatment?"

Mindy sits on the edge of Krystal's bed, facing me. "It was Franny's idea. She said you deserved something nice, considering all the stress you've been under. It's been a hard day for all of us, but you especially."

"I'm assuming there's an ulterior motive."

"I think she also thought it might be a good idea for us to share this wine and get comfortable with each other, seeing how I've been ordered to spend the night here."

"Why?" I ask.

"To keep an eye on you, I guess."

There's no need for her to elaborate. No one trusts me. Not when Sasha, Krystal, and Miranda remain missing. I'm still under suspicion until they're found. If they're found. Hence the flimsy knife and plastic cup, into which I pour more wine. Mindy watches as I fill it to the brim.

"The way I see it, we have two choices here," I say. "We can either ignore each other and sit in silence. Or we could chat."

"The second one," Mindy says. "I hate too much quiet."

It's exactly the answer I expected. Which is the reason I gave her the choice—to make it feel like it was her idea to gossip.

"How's the mood in the Lodge?" I ask. "Is everyone handling it well?"

"Of course not. They're worried sick. Especially Franny."

"What about Lottie?" I say. "She always struck me as a cool customer. I bet that's good in a time of crisis."

"I don't know. She seems just as worried as the rest of us."

"That doesn't surprise me. I imagine she must be pretty devoted to Franny after working for her all these years."

"You'd think," Mindy says. "But I also get the sense that Lottie considers it just a job, you know? She gets to Franny's penthouse in the morning and leaves in the evening like any employee would do. She gets sick days. She has vacation time. I don't think she's too happy about having to spend the summer here. Neither am I, but here I am, doing my best to impress Franny."

"And how's that working out for you?"

Mindy pours herself some more wine, filling her cup as high as I did. After taking a hearty sip, she says, "You don't like me very much, do you?"

"You're keeping me here under house arrest. So that would be a definite no."

"Even before this. When you first got to camp. It's okay to admit it."

I say nothing. Which, in its own way, is an answer.

"I knew it. I could tell," Mindy says. "I knew girls like you in college. So artsy and open-minded but so quick to judge people like me. Let me guess: you probably took one look at me and thought I was some spoiled sorority girl who screwed her way into the Harris-White family."

"Aren't you?"

"A sorority girl? Yes. And proud of it. Just like I'm proud of the fact that I was pretty enough and charming enough to catch the attention of someone like Chet Harris-White."

"I'll agree that you're pretty," I say, shedding any pretense of civility. Maybe it's the wine. Or the spirit of Vivian lingering in the cabin, encouraging bitchiness.

"For the record, Chet pursued me. And it took a lot of convincing. I had no interest in dating the spoiled rich kid."

"But aren't you spoiled and rich?"

"Far from it," Mindy says. "I grew up on a farm. Bet you didn't see that coming."

I had assumed she was born privileged. The daughter of a Southern attorney, perhaps, or a prominent physician, like Natalie was.

"It was a dairy farm," she tells me. "In middle-of-nowhere Pennsylvania. Every morning from kindergarten to graduation I was up before dawn, feeding and milking the cows. I hated every minute of it. But I knew I was smart, and I knew I was pretty. Two things women need most to get ahead in this world. I studied hard and socialized and tried my best to pretend that my hands didn't always stink of raw milk and cow manure. And it paid off. Class president. Homecoming queen. Valedictorian. When I got to Yale, the pretending continued, even after I started dating Chet."

Mindy leans back on the bed, swirling the wine in her plastic cup. She crosses her legs, getting comfortable. I think she might already be drunk. I envy her.

"I was so nervous the first time Chet took me to meet Franny. I thought she'd see right through me. Especially when I got out of the car and saw their name on that building. And then the ride in the elevator, all the way up to the top floor. Franny was waiting for us in the greenhouse. Have you seen it?"

"I have. It's impressive."

"It's *insane*," Mindy says. "But the nerves went away when I learned the truth."

She takes a gulp of wine, leaving me hanging.

"About what?"

"That they're not nearly as rich as they look. At least, not anymore. Franny sold the Harris years ago. All she owns now is the penthouse and Lake Midnight.

"That still sounds pretty rich to me."

"Oh, it is," Mindy says. "But now it's only a few million and not, like, a billion."

"How'd Franny lose so much money?"

"Because of this place." Even though Mindy looks around Dogwood's tight confines, I know she's referring to what lies beyond it. The camp. The lake. The woods. The girls. "Restoring a bad reputation can get expensive. For Franny that meant settlements to the families of those missing girls. Chet told me it was at least ten million each. I guess Franny threw it at them like it was nothing. She did the same thing to a whole bunch of charities, trying to get back in people's good graces. And don't even get me started on Theo."

"The accident," I say. "Chet mentioned it."

"That car he wrecked was chump change compared to what Franny had to spend to get Harvard to take him back. They weren't too keen on inviting an accused killer onto campus. No offense."

I nod, grudgingly respecting Mindy for giving as good as she gets. "None taken."

"Chet told me Franny had to pay for a new lab building before they'd even consider letting Theo return. I think that's around the same time she sold the Harris. In my opinion, she should have sold this place instead. Chet said he tried talking to her about selling the land around Lake Midnight, but she wouldn't even consider it. So I guess the sale will have to wait—"

Mindy cuts herself off before she can let slip that Franny is dying. Even though I already know about the cancer, I admire her discretion. It's nice to see there are some family secrets she's not willing to spill.

"Anyway, that's their money situation," she says. "Between you and me, I'm relieved. The thought of all that money scared the hell out of me. Don't get me wrong, there's still plenty. More than my family ever had. But it's less intimidating. The more money there is, the more I feel the need to pretend. Which means I'll keep worrying that my hands still smell like a dairy farm."

Mindy looks down at her hands, turning them over to inspect them in the light of the nightstand lantern.

"I'm sorry for judging you," I say.

"I'm used to it. Just don't tell Chet or Franny and anyone else. Please."

"I won't."

"Thank you. And for the record, I don't think you did anything to those girls. I've seen the way you act around them. You all liked one another. I could tell."

The mention of Miranda, Sasha, and Krystal sends another wave of worry crashing over me. To combat it, I gulp down more wine.

"I hope they're okay," I say. "I need them to be."

"I do, too." Mindy drains her cup, sets it on the nightstand, and crawls under Krystal's lumpy covers. "Otherwise the Harris-White name is going to be dragged through the mud again. And I've got a feeling that this time it's going to stick."

Thirty-Three

After the bottle of wine has been emptied and the steak and potatoes have long gone cold, Mindy falls asleep.

I don't.

Worry, fear, and the prospect of another nighttime visit from Vivian keep me awake. Whenever I close my eyes, I see Sasha's mangled glasses and think of her alone somewhere, stumbling blindly, possibly bleeding. So I keep them open and clutch Krystal's teddy bear to my chest while listening to Mindy snore on the other side of the room. Every so often, the sound is drowned out by the helicopter taking another pass over the camp. Each time its spotlight sweeps past the cabin means another update on the status of the search.

The girls are still missing.

It's almost midnight when my phone springs to life in the darkness. Marc is calling, the ringtone loud and insistent in the quiet cabin.

Mindy's snoring abruptly stops. "Too loud," she says, still half-asleep.

I silence the phone and whisper, "Sorry. Go back to sleep."

The phone vibrates in my hand. Marc's sent a text.

Found something. CALL ME!

I wait until Mindy's snoring returns before sliding out of bed and tiptoeing to the door. I grab the doorknob, on the verge of twisting it open, when I realize that I can't go outside. Not with a camera aimed directly at the door and one of Detective Flynn's minions surely sitting in the Lodge's cellar, monitoring the live feed.

Rather than risk raising all kinds of red flags, I go to the window. Carefully, I take the lantern off the nightstand and place it on Miranda's bed, where I won't trip over it on my way back inside. I then reach across the nightstand and gingerly lift the window first, then its screen.

I shoot a glance Mindy's way, making sure she's still asleep before climbing atop the nightstand and swinging my legs out the window. I twist, the sill pressing into my stomach as I lower myself to the ground.

To avoid the camera outside Dogwood completely, I have to cut behind the other cabins on my way to the latrine. I move in a half crouch, trying not to be noticed by anyone inside the cabins or roaming about outside.

The only real threat of being spotted comes from the helicopter and its stupid spotlight, which pass overhead within a minute of my being outside. I throw myself against the wall of the nearest cabin, my back flattened against it, arms at my sides. The spotlight's beam sweeps past me, oblivious to my presence.

I don't move until the helicopter skims over the lake. Then I run, sprinting to the latrine, my phone sliding around in my pocket. Inside, I turn on the lights and check each bathroom stall and shower. Just like during my search for the girls this morning, it's empty. Unlike then, I'm relieved to be alone.

I make my way to one of the stalls, closing the door and locking it for extra privacy. Then I pull out my phone and call Marc. The connection is weak. When he answers, static stutters into his words.

"Billy and . . . found . . . thing."

I check the phone. There's one bar of signal. Not good at all. I stand atop the toilet seat, holding the phone toward the ceiling, hoping for a better signal. It now shows two bars, the second one wavering and unsteady. I stay on the toilet, my body tilted, bent elbow jutting toward the ceiling. It works. The static is gone.

"What did you find?"

"Not much," Marc tells me. "Billy says it's hard to research something like a private asylum. Especially one so small and remote. He ended up looking everywhere. Books. Newspapers. Historical records. He had a friend search the library's photo archives and made a few calls to the library at Syracuse. I'm going to email everything he found. Some of it couldn't be scanned because it was too old or in bad condition. But I wrote those down."

The sound of rustling paper bursts from the phone, high-pitched and screechy.

"Billy found a few mentions of a Mr. C. Cutler of Peaceful Valley in the ledger of Hardiman Brothers, a wig company on the Lower East Side. Do any of those names sound familiar?"

"Charles Cutler," I say. "He was the owner. He sold his patients' hair to wigmakers."

"That's Dickensian," Marc says. "And it would explain why the Hardiman brothers paid him fifty dollars on three different occasions."

"When was this?"

"Once in 1901. Twice in 1902."

"That lines up with what I saw in the book Vivian found at the library. There was a picture of the place from 1898."

"Did the book mention when it closed?" Marc asks.

"No. Why?"

"Because something strange happened after that." There's more rustling on Marc's end, followed by more static, which makes me worry the signal is again getting worse. "Billy found a newspaper article from 1904. It's about a man named Helmut Schmidt of Yonkers. Does that ring a bell?"

"Never heard of him."

"Well, Helmut was a German immigrant who spent ten years out west. When he returned to New York, he sought out his sister, Anya."

That name *is* familiar to me. There was a photograph of someone named Anya tucked into the box I found in the Lodge. I even remember her hair color. Flaxen.

"Helmut described her as 'often confused and prone to nervous exasperation,'" Marc says. "We both know what that means."

All too well. Anya suffered from a mental ailment that probably didn't even have a name at the time.

"It appears that while Helmut was gone, Anya's condition worsened until she was committed to Blackwell's Island. He looked for her there and was told she had been put into the care of Dr. Cutler and taken to"

"Peaceful Valley," I say.

"Bingo. Which is why Helmut Schmidt then traveled upstate to Peaceful Valley to retrieve his sister. Only he couldn't find it, which is why he spoke to the press about it."

"Are you saying it didn't exist?"

"No," Marc says. "I'm saying it vanished."

That word again. Vanished. I've grown to hate the sound of it.

"How does an insane asylum just disappear?"

"No one knew. Or, more likely, no one cared," Marc says. "Especially because the place was in the middle of nowhere. And those who lived even remotely nearby wanted nothing to do with it. All they knew was that it was run by a doctor and his wife and that the land had been sold a year earlier."

"And that's it?"

"I guess so. Billy couldn't find any follow-up articles about Helmut Schmidt and his sister." I hear the clatter of keys, followed by a single, sharp click. "I just emailed the files."

My phone vibrates in my hand. An email alert.

"Got them," I say.

"I hope it helps." Darkness creeps into Marc's voice. The telltale sound of concern. "I'm worried about you, Em. Promise me you'll be careful."

"I will."

"Pinkie swear?"

"Yes," I say, smiling in spite of all my fear, exhaustion, and worry. "Pinkie swear."

I end the call and check my email. The first item Marc sent is scans of two pages from the same book I found in the library. One contains the paragraphs mentioning Peaceful Valley, minus Vivian's pencil mark. The other is the photograph of Charles Cutler cockily standing in front of his asylum.

The next few files are all text—pages from psychology books, psychiatric journals, a master's thesis that makes a cursory mention of Peaceful Valley in a section about the history of asylums and progressive treatments. I assume they all served as sources for one another, because the information is almost identical.

The final file Marc sent holds an assortment of images scanned from various archives. The first picture is the now-familiar one of Charles Cutler outside his domain, although the caption accompanying the photo identifies it only as Peaceful Valley, as if it had been a spa and not an asylum. The second photo is a shot of just the asylum itself—that Gothic main building with turret and weathervane, the utilitarian wing jutting out from its side.

But it's the third picture that makes my heart thrum like I've just chugged a pot of black coffee. Identified merely as the entrance to Peaceful Valley, it shows a low stone wall broken by a wrought-iron gate and ornate archway.

They're the same gate and arch I passed through the other day in Theo's truck.

The very same ones that now grace Camp Nightingale.

The blood freezes in my veins.

Peaceful Valley Asylum was here. Right on this very piece of land. Which explains why Helmut Schmidt couldn't find it. By the time he came looking for his sister, Buchanan Harris had already turned the area into Lake Midnight.

That, I realize, is the information Vivian was looking for. It's why she snuck into the Lodge and went to the library. It's why she was so worried about her diary getting into the wrong hands that she rowed across the lake to hide it.

And it's why she was so scared.

Because she learned that there's a ring of truth to the stories surrounding Lake Midnight. Only it wasn't a deaf village or a leper colony that got buried beneath the water.

It was an insane asylum.

Thirty-Four

Despite the late hour, Camp Nightingale still crawls with cops. They linger in the arts and crafts building, visible through the lit windows. More stand outside, chatting as they sip coffee, smoke cigarettes, wait for bad news to arrive. One trooper has a sleepy bloodhound at his feet. Both man and dog lift their heads as I hurry to the Lodge.

"You need something, sweetheart?" the trooper asks.

"Not from you," I say, tacking on a sarcastic *"Sweetheart."*

At the Lodge, I pound on the red front door, not even trying to be discreet about my arrival. I want the whole fucking place to know I'm here. The pounding continues for a full minute before the door swings away from my fist, revealing Chet. A lock of hair droops over his blood-shot eyes. He pushes it away and says, "You shouldn't be out of your cabin, Emma."

"I don't care."

"Where's Mindy?"

"Asleep. Where's your mother?"

Franny's voice drifts to the door. "In here, dear. Do you need something?"

I push past Chet into the entrance hall and then the living room. Franny is there, cocooned in her Navajo blanket. The antique weapons on the wall behind her take on new, sinister meaning. The rifles, the knives, the lone spear.

"This is certainly a pleasant surprise," Franny says with faked hospitality. "I suppose you can't sleep, either. Not with all this unpleasantness."

"We need to talk," I say.

Chet joins us in the living room. He touches my shoulder, trying to steer me back to the door. Franny gestures for him to stop.

"About what?" she says.

"Peaceful Valley Asylum. I know it was on this land. Vivian knew it, too."

It's easy to see why she went looking for it. She'd heard the story about Lake Midnight, possibly from Casey. Like me, she probably considered it nothing more than a campfire tale. But then she found that old box by the water's edge, filled with scissors that rattled like glass. She did some digging. Searching the Lodge. Sneaking off to the library. Eventually she realized the campfire tale was partially true.

And she needed to expose it. I suspect she felt a kinship with those women from the asylum, all of them likely drowned, just like her sister.

Keeping that secret must have made Vivian so lonely and scared. She hinted at it in her diary when referring to Natalie and Allison.

The less they know the better.

Vivian wasn't able to save them. Just like her, they had learned too much after finding her diary. But she had managed to keep me safe. I understand that now. Her mistreatment of me wasn't an act of cruelty but one of mercy. It was her way of trying to protect me from any danger her discovery created. To save me, she forced me to hate her.

It worked.

"The only people she told were Natalie and Allison," I say. "Then all three of them disappeared. I doubt that was a coincidence."

A dainty china cup and saucer sit in front of Franny, the tea inside steaming. When she reaches for them, the cup rattles against the saucer so violently that she sets it down without taking a sip. "I don't know what you want me to say."

"You can tell me what happened to that asylum. Something bad, right? And all those poor girls there, they suffered, too."

Franny tries to pull the blanket tighter around her, the noticeable tremor still in her hands. Veins pulse under her paper-white skin. She loses her grip, and the blanket drifts to her sides. Chet rushes in and pulls it back over her shoulders.

"That's enough, Emma," he barks. "You need to go back to your cabin."

I ignore him. "I know those women existed. I saw their pictures."

I march to the study, heading straight for the desk and its bottom drawer. I yank it open and see the familiar wooden box right where I had left it. I carry it into the living room and slam it down on the coffee table.

"These girls right here." I open the box and grab a handful of photos, holding them up so Franny and Chet see their haunted faces. "Charles Cutler made them grow their hair. Then he chopped it off and sold it. And then they vanished."

Franny's expression softens, turning from fear to something that resembles pity. "Oh, Emma. You poor thing. Now I know why you've been so distressed."

"Just tell me what happened to them!"

"Nothing," Franny says. "Nothing at all."

I study her face, looking for hints that she's lying. I can't find any.

"I don't understand," I say.

"I think perhaps I should explain."

It's Lottie who says it. She emerges from the kitchen wearing a silk robe over a nightgown. A mug of coffee rests in her hands.

"I think that might be best," Franny says.

Lottie sits down next to her and reaches for the wooden box. "It just occurred to me, Emma, that you might not know my given name."

"It's not Lottie?"

"Dear me, no," Lottie says. "That's just a nickname Franny gave me when I was a little girl. My real name is Charlotte. I was named after my great-grandfather. Charles Cutler."

I falter a moment, buzzing with confusion.

"His mother was insane," Lottie says. "My great-great-grandmother. Charles saw what madness did to her and decided to devote his life to helping others who suffered the same way. First at an asylum in New York City. A terrible place. The women forced to endure horrible conditions. They didn't get better. They only suffered more. So he got the idea to create Peaceful Valley on a large parcel of land owned by my great-grandmother's family. A small private retreat for a dozen women. For his patients, Charles chose the worst cases he observed in that filthy, overcrowded asylum. Madwomen too poor to afford proper care. Alone. No friends. No families. He took them in."

Lottie rifles through the open box, smiling at the photographs as if they were pictures of old friends. She pulls out one and looks at it. On the back, I see the words *Juliet Irish Red*.

"From the very beginning, it was a struggle. Even though he and my great-grandmother were the only employees, the asylum required so much money. The patients needed food, clothing, medicine. To make ends meet, he came up with the idea to sell the patients' hair— with their permission, of course. That kept things afloat for another year or so, but Charles knew Peaceful Valley would eventually have to close. His noble experiment had failed."

She pulls out two more photos. *Lucille Tawny* and *Henrietta Golden*.

"But he was a smart man, Emma," Lottie says. "In that failure, he saw opportunity. He knew an old friend was looking to buy a large parcel of land for a private retreat. A wealthy lumber man named Buchanan Harris. My great-grandfather offered the land at a discounted price if he was given a position in Mr. Harris's company. That was the start of a relationship between our families that continues today."

"But what happened to Peaceful Valley?"

"It stayed open while my grandfather went about building the dam that would create Lake Midnight," Franny says.

"During that time, Charles Cutler found new situations for the women in his care," Lottie adds. "None of them returned to those brutal asylums in the city. My great-grandfather made sure of it. He was a good man, Emma. He cared deeply about those women. Which is why I still have their photographs. They're my family's most prized possession."

I sway slightly, shocked my legs are still able to support me. They've gone numb, just like the rest of me. I had been so focused on learning Franny's dark secret that I never stopped to consider that Vivian was wrong.

"So it had nothing to do with what happened to Vivian and the others?"

"Not a thing," Franny says.

"Then why did you keep it a secret?"

"We didn't," Lottie says. "It's no secret. Just ancient history, which has been warped over the years."

"We know the stories campers tell about Lake Midnight," Franny adds. "All that hokum about curses, drowned villagers, and ghosts. People always prefer drama over the truth. If Vivian had wanted to know more about it, all she needed to do was ask."

I nod, feeling suddenly humiliated. It's just as bad as when Vivian cut me down right before she disappeared. Almost worse. Once again, I've accused someone in the Harris-White of doing a terrible deed.

"I'm sorry," I say, knowing that a simple apology isn't nearly adequate. "I'm going to go now."

"Emma, wait," Franny says. "Please stay. Have some tea until you feel better."

I edge out of the room, unable to accept any more kindness from her. In the entrance hall, I break into a run, fleeing out the front door without closing it behind me. I keep running. Past the cops outside the arts and crafts building. Past the cluster of dark and quiet cabins. All the way to the latrine, where I plan to hop into a shower stall with my clothes still on and pretend I'm not crying tears of shame.

I stop when I notice a girl standing just outside the latrine. Her stillness catches my attention. That and her white dress aglow in the moonlight.

Vivian.

She stands in the woods that encroach upon the camp, just a few feet from the line where the trees end and the grass begins. She says nothing. She only stares.

I'm not surprised to see her. Not after the day I've had. In fact, I've been expecting it. I don't even reach for the bracelet that's no longer there.

This meeting was inevitable.

Rather than speak, Vivian merely turns and walks deeper into the forest, the hem of her white dress scraping the underbrush.

I start walking, too. Not away from the woods but toward it. Pulled along against my will by Vivian's reemergence. I cross the threshold separating camp from forest. The point of no return. Under my feet, leaves crunch and sticks snap. A twig from a nearby tree, as slim and gnarled as a witch's finger, grasps a lock of my hair and gives it a yank. Pain pricks my scalp. Yet I keep walking, telling myself it's what I need to do. That it's perfectly normal.

"I'm not going crazy," I whisper. "I'm not going crazy."

Oh, but I am.

Of course I am.

Thirty-Five

I follow Vivian to the sculpture garden, where she sits in the same chair Franny occupied days earlier. The statues around us watch with their blank eyes.

"Long time, no see, Em," Vivian says as I cautiously step between two of the statues. "Miss me?"

I find my voice. It's small and meek and skitters like a mouse across the clearing.

"You're not real. You have no power over me."

Vivian leans back in her chair and crosses her legs, her hands primly folded on her knee. Such a strangely ladylike gesture, especially coming from her. "Then why are you here? I didn't ask you to follow me. You're still trailing after me like a lost puppy."

"Why did you come back?" I say. "I was doing fine without you. For years."

"Oh, you mean painting us then covering us up? Is that the *fine* you're talking about? If so, I hate to break it to you, girlfriend, but that's not fine. I mean, honestly, vanishing once should have been enough for you. But, no, you had to make us do it over and over."

"I don't do that anymore. I've stopped."

"You've *paused*," Vivian says. "There's a difference."

"That's why you're here, isn't it? Because I stopped painting you."

It's how I have kept her at bay all these years. Painting her. Covering her up. Doing it again. Then again. Now that I've vowed not to do it anymore, she's returned, demanding my attention.

"This has nothing to do with me," Vivian says. "It's all you, sweet-heart."

"Then why am I only seeing you and not—"

"Natalie and Allison?" Vivian lets out a knowing chuckle. "Come on, Em. We both know you don't really care about them."

"That's not true."

"You barely knew them."

Vivian stands, and for a quick, heart-halting moment, I think she's going to reach out and grab me. Instead, she begins to wind her way around the statues, caressing them like lovers. Fingers trickling up arms. Palms gliding across throats.

"I knew them as well as I knew you," I tell her.

"Really? Did you ever have a conversation with either of them? One on one?"

I did. I know I did. But when I scan my memory, no such recollec-tions appear.

"Now that I think about it, I'm not sure you even talked to them when I wasn't around," Vivian says. "At least not about something other than me."

She's right. It's true.

"That's not my fault," I say. "You made sure it was that way."

Vivian never wasn't around. She ruled the cabin the same way a queen bee ruled the hive. The rest of us were just drones, buzzing around her, catering to her needs, her whims, her interests.

"That's why you're not seeing Natalie and Allison right now," Vivian says. "I'm the puzzle you're still trying to figure out."

"Will you go away if I do?"

Vivian pauses before a sculpture of a woman carrying a jug on her shoulder, her toga slanted across her chest. "That depends. Do you want me to go away?"

Yes. And I hope you never come back.

I don't say it. I can't. Not that. So I think it. A mental whisper that floats across the clearing, wispy as fog. But Vivian hears it. I know by the way her lips curl upward in cruel amusement.

"Now *that* brings back old times," she says. "You certainly got your wish, didn't you?"

I want to run away, but guilt holds me in place. It's a numbing sensation. A flash freeze. By now, I'm used to it. I've been feeling it on and off for the past fifteen years.

"I'm sorry for saying that."

Vivian shrugs. "Sure. Whatever. It still doesn't change things between us."

"I want to make it right."

"Oh, I know. That's why you came back here, right? Trying to find out what happened. Snooping around just like I did. As a result, look what happened to your new best friends."

Her mention of the new girls catches me off guard. I spend a millisecond wondering just how she knows about them. Then it dawns on me.

She's not real.

She has no power over me.

I'm stronger than everyone realizes.

Strong enough to understand that Vivian isn't a ghost haunting me. Nor is she a hallucination. She's *me*. A fragment of my distressed brain trying to help me figure out what's happening.

Which is why I stare her down and say, "You know where they are, don't you? You know where I can find them."

"I can't tell you that."

"Why not?"

"Because I'm not real," Vivian says. "That's your motto, right? I have no power over you?"

"Just tell me."

Vivian moves on to another statue, hugging it from behind, her chin resting on its delicate shoulder. "Let's play a game, Emma. Two Truths and a Lie. One: Everything you need to know is already in your possession."

"Just tell me where they are."

She shifts to the statue's other shoulder, her head coyly tilted. "Two: The question isn't where to find them but where to find *us*. As in me and Natalie and Allison."

"Vivian, please."

"Three," she says. "As for where we are, that's not my place to say. But I can tell you this: *If* you find us, maybe—just maybe—I'll go away and never come back."

She slips behind the statue, temporarily eclipsed. I wait for her to pop into view again on the other side. When a minute passes and she doesn't appear, I take a few weak steps toward the statue.

"Vivian?" I say. "Viv?"

There's no answer. Nor is there any sign of her presence.

I continue my approach, picking up speed on my way to the statue. When I reach it, I peer around its marble shoulder.

Nothing is there.

Vivian is gone.

Yet her parting words remain, hovering in the middle of the clearing like moonlight. Those three statements. Two true, one a lie.

I have no idea about the first two. Like much of what Vivian said while she was alive, it's hard to tell the difference between what's true and what's false.

As for her third statement, I hope it isn't a lie.

I want it to be the truth.

Every word of it.

Thirty-Six

I return to Dogwood the same way I left—zigzagging around the cabins to avoid being spotted. The helicopter seems to have packed it in for the night. So, too, have the search boats. When I get a glimpse of the lake, I see no activity on the water. It's just an empty black mirror reflecting starlight. But the camera is a different story. I know it remains, ever watchful, which is why I slip to the back of the cabin and hoist myself inside through the open window.

Mindy's snores tell me she's still asleep. Good. I get to avoid having to explain both where I've been and where I plan on going next.

To find the girls.

Both sets of them.

Vivian's words—my words—haunt me as I crawl down from the nightstand.

The question isn't where to find them but where to find us.

Something Miranda said comes back to me. I heard the words as I was free-falling into sleep.

I'm worried about Emma.

That worry might have led her to action. Brash, confident Miranda. Mystery lover and future detective. Like Vivian, leading another set of girls into the woods for answers.

Then there's Vivian's toying suggestion that I might finally be rid of her if I find out what happened to the three of them. Maybe she's right. Maybe the only way to free myself from the grip of guilt is to learn the truth.

I hope you never come back.

Christ, I hate myself for saying that, even though I had no way of knowing it would come true. Natalie and Allison were already outside when I uttered those words. Vivian was right in that regard—I really didn't talk to them very much. Something else I regret. I should have paid more attention to them. Treated them as individuals and not just part of Vivian's entourage. All the same, I'm grateful they never heard what I said to Vivian. That those weren't my parting words to all of them.

I tiptoe across the cabin, careful to avoid that one creaky floorboard, the memory of something else Vivian said fresh in my mind.

Everything you need to know is already in your possession.

I know what she's referring to.

The map.

It's why they came back to the cabin, only to discover the door locked. Vivian needed her hand-drawn map to help her find the spot where her diary was hidden. She still thought there was something sinister behind the lake's creation and Peaceful Valley's end. I suspect she was planning to use it to expose whatever she thought she had found out about Franny and the Harris family.

I quietly open my trunk and remove my flashlight. Then I reach inside and feel around, searching for the map.

It's not there.

The girls must have taken it with them, bolstering my theory that they set off to find their predecessors.

More hope. That I'm right. That I'm not too late.

As Mindy keeps on snoring, I take another trip out the window. Soon I'm rushing headlong through a patch of trees to the edge of the lake. At the water, I make a left, hurrying along the lakeshore to the dock and canoe racks. Atop the slope of lawn, the Lodge rises heavy and dark. Only one window is illuminated. Second floor. Overlooking Lake Midnight.

Five minutes later, I'm out on the lake in a canoe. I row in strong, fast strokes, hoping the helicopter and search boats don't return until I reach the other side. My phone sits in my lap, set to the compass app.

I glance at it every few seconds, keeping myself on track, making sure I'm cutting across the lake in a straight line.

I know I'm near the far shore when I start to hear eerie scraping along the bottom of the canoe. Underwater tree branches, making their presence known. Flicking on the flashlight, I'm greeted by dozens of dead trees rising from the lake. They're a ghostly gray in the flashlight's beam. The same color as bones.

I wedge the flashlight between my neck and shoulder, tilting my head to keep it in place. Then I resume rowing, using the oars to push myself away from the submerged trees or, when a collision is unavoidable, blunt the impact. Soon I'm past the trees and close to the other side of the lake. The flashlight's beam skims the shore, brightening the tall pines there. A pair of deer at the water's edge freeze in the light before stomping away. Gray specks flutter within the beam itself. Insects, drawn to the light.

I steer the boat to the left and row parallel to the shore, flashlight aimed to the land on my right. The beam catches more trees, more bugs, the flap of an owl's wings, blurred white. Finally, it illuminates a wooden structure rotted beyond repair.

The gazebo.

I guide the canoe onto shore and hop out while it's still running aground. I shove my phone back into my pocket and aim the flashlight toward the woods. I breathe deeply, trying to focus, rewinding to that earlier trip and how we got from here to the X marking Vivian's diary. I can't remember how deep into the woods we traveled or how, exactly, we found our way there.

I sweep the flashlight's beam back and forth over the ground, looking for any footprints we might have left behind. All I see is hard dirt, dead leaves, pine needles dried to splinters. But then the beam catches something that glows dull-white. But there are also splashes of color—vibrant yellows, blues, and reds.

I step closer and see that it's a page of a comic book. Captain America, in all his patriotic heroism, fighting his way through several panels of action. A small rock rests atop the page, keeping it in place.

The girls were here.

Just recently.

The page's placement is no accident. It's their trail of bread crumbs, marking the way back to the lake and their canoe.

I step over the paper, tighten my grip around the flashlight, and, like the girls before me, vanish into the woods.

Thirty-Seven

The forest at night isn't silent. Far from it. It's alive with noise as I move deeper through the woods. Crickets screech and frogs belch, competing with the calls of night birds rustling the pines. I fear that other sounds are being drowned out. The footfall in the underbrush. The cracking twig signaling someone is near. Although there's no reason to believe I was followed here, I can't dismiss the idea. I've been watched too much not to be on alert.

My flashlight remains aimed at the ground a few feet ahead of me. I sweep it back and forth, looking for another page ripped from Krystal's comic book. I spot one where the ground begins to slant upward. It, too, sits beneath a rock. As does another one placed fifty yards ahead.

I pass five more pages as the incline sharpens. Captain America, leading me higher. Another page waits where the land flattens out at the top of the incline. It shows Captain America deflecting bullets with his raised shield. The dialogue bubble by his head reads, *I refuse to give up.*

I pause long enough to swing the flashlight in a circle, studying my surroundings. The beam brightens the birches around me, making them glow white. To my right are patches of starlight. I'm now atop the ridge, mere yards from the cliff that drops away into the lake. I turn left, approaching the line of boulders that punctuate yet another steep rise.

Captain America is there as well, placed atop several boulders, held in place with small rocks. I scramble among them until I reach the massive rock. The monolith. I aim the flashlight up the hill, angling for a better view of the path ahead.

There's still no sign of the girls. Not even more Captain America. Just more boulders, more trees, more leaf-strewn earth pitched sharply upward.

The forest around me continues to hum. I close my eyes, trying to tune out the noise and really listen.

That's when I hear something—a dull thud that sounds once, twice.

"Girls?" I shout it, the echo of my voice booming back at me. "Is that you?"

The forest noise ceases, save for the frightened scatter of some spooked animal fleeing to my left. In that blessed moment of silence, I hear a muted reply.

"Emma?"

Miranda. I'm sure of it. And she sounds close. So wonderfully, tantalizingly close.

"It's me," I call back. "Where are you?"

"The hobbit house."

"We're trapped," someone else says. Krystal, I think.

Miranda adds one more desperate word: *"Hurry."*

I rush onward, my flashlight gripped in my hand. I leap over tree roots. I dodge boulders. In my haste, I trip over a downed branch and fly forward, landing on my hands and knees. I stay that way and crawl up the incline, my fingers clawing the earth, feet flicking to propel me higher.

I don't slow down, not even when the crumbling stone foundation comes into view. Instead, I go faster, climbing back to my feet and running toward the root cellar cut into the earth. At the door, someone has pushed the ancient slide bolt into place, locking the girls inside. A knee-high boulder has been rolled in front of it for good measure.

Another thump arrives from inside the root cellar. The door shimmies. "Are you here yet?" Miranda calls. "We need to get the fuck out of here."

"In a second!"

I rap on the door, announcing my presence, before giving the slide bolt a mighty shove. Its rasps past the door itself, allowing Miranda to open it a crack before being stopped by the boulder. A thick, sickly odor drifts out. A mix of damp earth, sweat, and urine that makes my stomach roil. Miranda presses her face to the crack. I see one blood-shot eye, a red-rimmed nostril, her parted lips sucking in fresh air.

"Help us," she says with a gasp, giving the door another desperate rattle. "Why aren't you opening it?"

"It's still blocked," I say. "I'm working on it. How are Krystal and Sasha?"

"Awful. We all are. Now *please* let us out."

"One more minute. I promise."

I crouch, place my palms flat on the boulder, and give it a push. It's so heavy I can barely move it. I try again, this time gritting my teeth and grunting with exertion. The boulder doesn't budge.

Using the flashlight, I scan the ground for anything that can help. I grab a rounded rock that had chipped off the crumbled wall nearby. Then I spot a fat branch on the ground that's almost as long as I am. It looks sturdy enough to be used as a lever. I hope.

I shove one end of the branch as far under the boulder as it can go and place the rock under it a few feet away before grasping the other end of the branch and pushing downward. It does the trick, setting the rock rolling the tiniest bit. I drop the branch and run to the boulder, pushing again, continuing the momentum until it's past the door.

"All clear!"

The door flies open, and the girls burst out. Sweaty and dirt-smeared, they suck in fresh air, stretch their limbs, give dazed looks to the sky. Without her glasses, Sasha is forced to squint. Her nose is swollen and colored a brutal shade of purple. Rust-colored flecks run from her nose all the way to her neck. Dried blood.

"Is it really night?" she says with almost clinical detachment. Shock, with a dash of hunger and dehydration thrown in for good measure.

Rather than hug her, I run my hands up and down her arms, checking for injuries. I feel stupid for not bringing food. Or water. Or a damn first aid kit. All I can do is use the hem of my T-shirt to wipe some of the blood from Sasha's face.

"How long were we in there?" Miranda says as she spreads out on the ground, her arms and legs akimbo, panting with relief. "My phone died before noon."

"Almost a full day."

Hearing that makes Krystal's legs buckle. She staggers a moment before plopping down next to Miranda. "Damn."

"Tell me what happened," I say. "From the moment you left the cabin."

"We came here to look for your friends," Krystal says. "It was Miranda's idea."

Miranda sits up, too spent to be ashamed. "I only wanted to help. You were so upset last night. I could tell you needed to know what happened. And since this is where you found that diary, I thought there might be more clues here."

"Why didn't you say anything?"

"Because we knew you wouldn't have let us row here by ourselves."

I finish wiping Sasha's face. The dried blood leaves a dark-red stain on my shirt. "You came here and then what?"

"Someone jumped us," Miranda says, fear peeking through her exhaustion. Tears cling to the corners of her eyes.

"Who?"

"None of us got a good look."

"Miranda and Krystal went inside," Sasha says, nodding toward the root cellar. "I didn't want to, so I stayed out here. But then someone came out of nowhere."

She croaks out a sob. It's followed by more words that tumble forth in a rush, that clinical tone now long gone. "They punched me and my glasses fell off and I couldn't see who it was and then they shoved me inside and slammed the door."

Someone followed them here, attacked, trapped them rather than outright killing them. It makes no sense.

Unless whoever did it wanted them alive.

Which means they might be coming back any minute now.

Fear zips through me. I yank my phone from my pocket to see if I can call the police. There's no signal. Which explains why Miranda couldn't do the same right after they were trapped.

"We need to go," I tell the girls. "Right now. I know you're tired, but do you think you can run?"

Miranda climbs to her feet and shoots me a worried look. "Why do we need to run?"

"Because you're still in danger. We all are."

A beam of light hits my face. A flashlight. Bright enough to both silence and blind me. I put my hand over my eyes, shielding them from the glare. Behind the flashlight, I can make out a silhouette. Tall. Masculine.

The glare falls away. My vision blurs, eyes adjusting. When they come back into focus, I see Theo, flashlight in hand, taking a step toward us.

"Emma?" he says. "What are you doing here?"

Thirty-Eight

Seeing Theo here feels like a minor earthquake. The ground under my feet trembles. Only it's me who's really trembling. A seismic shifting in my body I'm powerless to control.

Because his presence can't be an accident.

He's here for a reason.

"What's going on?" he says.

"I'd ask you the same thing," I say, a catch in my throat. "But I think I already know."

He's come back for the girls.

He attacked them, locked them away, waited until the dead of night to return. A chain of events I suspect happened fifteen years ago with a different trio.

My accusation, as misguided as it was, might have been correct. Truth disguised as a lie.

I hate thinking this way. Of everyone in camp, he's the only one I truly hoped was innocent. But the suspicion refuses to leave, as uncontrollable as my quaking, exhausted body.

I edge in front of the girls, shielding them from Theo and whatever he might try to do next. I slip a trembling hand through my flashlight's wrist strap, securing it. Although not much of a weapon, it'll do in a pinch. If it comes to that. I desperately hope it doesn't.

"Miranda," I say with as much calm as I can muster, "there's a canoe on shore in the same place we landed the other day. Take Sasha and Krystal there as fast you can. If Sasha has trouble, you might need to carry her. Do you think you can do that?"

"Why?" Miranda says. "What's going on?"

"Just answer the question. Yes or no?"

Miranda's reply is streaked with fear. "Yes."

"Good. When you get to the canoe, row across the lake. Don't wait for me. Not even a second. Just row as fast as you can back to camp."

Theo aims his flashlight at my face again. "Emma, maybe you should step away from the girls. Let me see if they're hurt."

I ignore him. "Miranda, do you understand?"

"Yes," she says again, more forceful this time, steeling herself for the sprint.

"Good. Now go. *Hurry!*"

That last word—and the desperate way I say it—gets the girls moving. Miranda bolts away, all but dragging Sasha behind her. Krystal follows, slower but just as determined.

Theo makes a move to stop them, but I lunge forward, flashlight raised, threatening to strike. He freezes when I'm two feet away and drops his flashlight. He raises his hands, palms open. I don't lower my flashlight. I need to keep him like this. Just long enough to give the girls a head start.

"Don't you dare go after them," I warn.

"Emma, I don't know what's going on."

"Stop lying!" I shout. "You know exactly what's happening. What did you plan to do with those girls?"

Theo's eyes go wide. "Me? What were *you* going to do with them? I followed you here, Em. I watched from the Lodge as you got into that canoe and rowed across the lake."

It's another lie. It has to be.

"If you thought I was guilty, why didn't you tell the police?"

"Because," Theo says, "I wanted to be wrong."

As did I. All that guilt I'd felt about accusing him. All that shame and remorse. It was for nothing.

"I need to know why you did it," I say. "Both now and back then."

"I didn't—"

I lift the flashlight higher. Theo flinches.

"Hey, let's talk about this," he says. "Without the flashlight."

"I think you had the hots for Vivian," I tell him. "You wanted her, and she rejected you. You got mad. You made her disappear. Natalie and Allison, too."

"You're wrong, Emma. About everything."

Theo takes a step toward me. I stay put, trying not to show my fear. Yet my hand trembles, the flashlight's beam quivering skyward.

"Since you got away with it once, I guess you thought you could do it again. Only this time you tried to make me look guilty. My bracelet in the canoe was insurance."

"You're troubled, Emma," he says, carefully choosing his words, making sure not to offend me. "You need help. So how about you drop the flashlight and come with me. I won't hurt you. I promise."

Theo risks another step closer. This time, I take a step back.

"I'm done being lied to by you," I say.

"It's not a lie. I want to help you."

We repeat our steps. Forward for him, backward for me.

"You could have helped me fifteen years ago by admitting what you did."

If Theo had turned himself in, then maybe I wouldn't have felt so guilty about what happened.

Maybe I wouldn't have hallucinated the girls.

Maybe I would have been normal.

"Instead, I spent fifteen years blaming myself for what happened to them," I say. "And I blamed myself for causing you pain."

Another step for Theo.

"I don't blame you, Emma," he says. "This isn't your fault. You're sick."

Another step for me.

"Stop saying that!"

"But it's true, Em. You know it is."

Instead of one step forward, Theo takes two. I move backward, first shuffling then turning around and running. Theo chases after me, catching up within seconds. He grabs my arm and jerks me toward him. I cry out, the sound streaking through the dark woods. I hear its echo as I raise the flashlight and swing it against Theo's skull.

It's a weak blow. Just enough to shock him into letting me go.

I give him a shove, knocking him off balance. Then I run again, this time in the opposite direction. Back the way I came. Toward to the lake.

"Emma!" Theo shouts at my back. "Don't!"

I keep running. Heart pounding. Pulse loud in my ears. Trees and rocks seem to lurch at me from all sides. I dodge some, slam into others. But I don't stop. I can't.

Because Theo's also up and running. His footfalls echo through the woods behind me, outpacing my own. He'll catch up sooner rather than later. Outrunning him isn't an option.

I need to hide.

Something suddenly looms before me in the darkness.

The monolith.

I run to it, swerving right until I'm at its northwestern edge. I shine my light over the rock wall, seeing the fissure that opens up a foot from the ground.

The cave Miranda had crawled into.

I drop to my hands and knees in front of it and shine the flashlight inside. I see rock walls, dirt floor, a dark recess that runs at least a few feet into the ground. A shimmer of cool air wafts out of it, and I let out an involuntary shiver.

Theo's voice rings out from somewhere close. *Too* close.

"Emma? I know you're here. Come on out."

I flick off my own light, drop to my stomach, and back into the cave, worried I might not even fit. I do. Barely. There's roughly six inches of space above me and slightly less on each side.

The sky outside the cave brightens. Theo's flashlight. He's reached the rock.

I will myself not to breathe as I slide back even more. The cave floor feels uneven, like I'm on a slant, edging downhill.

A flower of light blooms on the ground near the mouth of the cave. I hear the crunch of Theo's footsteps, the sound of his labored breaths.

"Emma?" he says. "Are you here?"

I move back even farther, wondering how deep the cave goes, hoping it's far enough to escape the beam of Theo's flashlight if he aims it inside.

"Emma, please come out."

Theo's right outside the cave now. I see his shoes, his toes pointed in the opposite direction.

I continue to slide backward, faster now, praying he can't hear me. I feel water dripping down the cave walls. Mud starts to squish beneath me, gurgling up between my fingers.

I'm still sliding, although now it's not by choice. It's because of the mud and the tunnel's slant, which turns sharply steeper. I dig my knees and the heels of my palms into the mud, hoping they'll act as brakes. It only sends me slipping even more.

Soon I'm sliding fast, out of control, my chin leaving a groove in the mud. When I flick on the flashlight still around my wrist, all I see are gray walls, brown mud, the shockingly long path I've just traveled.

Then the ground below me vanishes, and I'm suddenly in midair.

Dropping.

Helpless and flailing.

My screams swallowed by their echoes ringing through the cave as I plummet into nothingness.

Thirty-Nine

Water breaks my fall.

I drop right into it, caught by surprise, unable to close my mouth before plunging under. Liquid pours in, choking me as I keep falling, somersaulting in the depths, the flashlight's beam streaking through the water, revealing dirt, algae, a darting fish.

When I finally do touch bottom, it's a gentle bump and not the life-ending crash against hard stone I expected. Still, it's a shock to my nervous system. I push off from the bottom as water continues to tickle the back of my throat. I gag, coughing air that bubbles past my face. Then I'm at the surface, my head emerging and water unplugging from my nostrils. I cough a few times, spitting up water. Then I breathe. Long and slow inhalations of dank, subterranean air.

With the flashlight miraculously still dangling from my arm, I paddle in place, trying to get a sense of my surroundings. I'm in a cavern roughly the same size as Camp Nightingale's mess hall. The beam of the flashlight stretches over black water, damp rock, a strip of dryish land surrounding the pool in a crescent shape. The water itself takes up about half the cave, no larger than a backyard swimming pool. When I aim the flashlight upward, I see a dome of rock above me dripping with stalactites. The cavern's shape makes me think of a stomach. I've tumbled into the belly of a beast.

A dark hollow sits in a corner where rock wall meets cave ceiling. The spot from which I fell. I sweep the flashlight up and down, trying to gauge how far I dropped. It looks to be about ten feet.

I swim forward, heading to the land that partially rings the water. The ground there is studded with pebbles, painted pale by the flashlight. I pull myself onto it and collapse, exhausted and aching.

I reach into my pocket and optimistically search for my phone. It's still there. Even better, it still works. Thank you, waterproof case.

The phone doesn't have any signal. Not that I was expecting any this far below ground. Still, I try calling 911 in case, by some small miracle, it actually goes through. It doesn't. I'm not surprised.

I remember what Detective Flynn said about tracking someone's location using the GPS on their phones. I can't help but wonder if that still applies when the missing person is underground. I doubt it. Even if it's possible, such a thing could take hours, maybe even days to pinpoint my location.

If I want to get out of here, I'll have to do it myself.

I aim the flashlight to the stretch of cave wall rising to the hole above me. It's steep. Not quite a ninety-degree angle, but mighty close. Before trying to climb it, I scan the rest of the cavern, looking for another way out. I aim the flashlight into every corner and dark cranny I can find, seeing nothing but more water, more rock, more dead ends.

Scaling that wall is my only option.

In desperation, I run to it, not pausing to look for places to grip. Instead I leap onto the wall, clawing at rock, scrambling for outcroppings. I get about three feet before I lose my grip and fly backward, landing hard on the cave floor.

I try again, this time making it four feet off the ground before getting bucked off. This time I land directly on my tailbone. Sharp pain shoots up my back, momentarily paralyzing me.

Yet I make a third attempt, slowing down a bit, puzzling together the best places to grip and the right direction in which to climb. It works. I find myself rising higher. Six feet. Seven.

When I'm about a foot from the tunnel that leads back outside, I realize there's nothing left to grasp. I reach up with my right arm, my palm smacking smooth rock that's cold and slippery. My left arm and shoulder, bearing all that weight, start to give out.

My body droops.

For a second, I dangle against the cave wall. Then I plummet back to earth, landing feet first, my right ankle twisting beneath me before buckling. I think I hear something snap. Or maybe it's my imagination as I collapse into a pained heap.

I scream, hoping it will take the edge off. It doesn't. The pain continues. So does the screaming. I look at my ankle and my foot, bent in a way it shouldn't ever be. There'll be no more climbing for me.

That's when reality sets in.

I'm trapped here.

No one knows where I am.

I'm now as lost as Vivian, Natalie, and Allison.

Forty

The flashlight dies shortly after four a.m. I know the time because I check my phone as soon as the dying beam flickers into nothingness. I regret looking, even as I'm comforted by the blue-white glow of the screen. Time continues to pass at an agonizing pace. It's as if the minutes last longer down here, stretching themselves until a single hour feels like three.

Wanting to preserve as much battery as possible, I shut off the phone and return it to my pocket. Then I sit in darkness so complete it feels like death. Nothing but black emptiness.

I start to shiver, realizing how alarmingly cold it is down here. The pool of frigid water doesn't help. Ditto my wet clothes, which cling to my clammy skin. My body trembles. My teeth chatter.

Yet none of that keeps me from dozing off as I huddle against the side of the cave, my knees pulled to my chest. Each blink in the darkness somehow ends with me falling asleep only to bolt awake with a spasm of pain and a startled yelp.

I'm beyond exhausted, if such a thing exists. I can't remember the last time I slept. I guess it was this morning, when I woke up inside Dogwood. I turn on my phone and do another time check.

Four thirty.

Fuck.

I then look for a signal, once again finding none.

Double fuck.

I turn off the phone and count the passing seconds, saying them aloud in the echo chamber of the cavern.

"One. Two. Three."

When I blink, my eyes stay closed.

"Four. Five. Six."

I'm suddenly too tired to speak. But the counting continues, now in my thoughts.

Seven. Eight. Nine.

I sleep after that. For how long, I have no idea. When I awake, it's with another pain-filled jolt, me still counting, the number flying from my parched lips.

"Ten."

My eyes snap open, my sleep-blurred gaze landing on Vivian right in front of me. She reclines on the cave floor, her elbow bent, head propped up. It's how she liked to play Two Truths and a Lie. She claimed the relaxed position made it harder to tell when she was lying.

"You're awake," she says. "Finally."

"How long was I asleep?" I saw, now long past trying to cast her away through sheer force of will.

"An hour or so."

"Have you been here that whole time?"

"Off and on. I guess you thought you were rid of me."

"I certainly wanted to be."

There's no point in lying to her. She's not real.

"Well, you're not." Vivian spreads her arms wide in mock delight. "Surprise!"

"You must find this amusing," I say as I sit up and roll my neck until it cracks. "I'm a lost girl, too."

"You think you're going to die down here?"

"Probably."

"That sucks," Vivian says with a sigh. "Although I guess it makes us even, then."

"I wanted you to come back," I say. "I didn't mean it. And I'm sorry. Just like I'm sorry for locking the cabin door. It was a horrible thing to do, and I regret it every day. That's all truth. No lies."

"I probably would have done the same thing," Vivian admits. "That's why I liked you, Em. We were both bitches when we had to be."

"Does that mean we still would have been friends if you hadn't disappeared?"

Vivian twirls a lock of hair around her finger, giving it some thought. "Maybe. There would have been a lot of drama. Lots of driving each other crazy. But there would have been good times, too. You being a bridesmaid at my wedding. Drinking with me after my inevitable divorce."

She smiles at me. Her kind smile. The one from the Vivian I thought of as a potential big sister. I miss that Vivian. I mourn her.

"Viv, what happened to you guys that night? Was it Theo?"

"I can't believe you haven't figurde it out yet. I left you so many clues, Em."

"Why can't you just tell me?"

"Because this is something you have to figure out on your own," Vivian says. "Your problem is that you're blinded by the past. Everything you need to know is right there in front of you. All you need to do is look."

She points to the other side of the cavern, where a snake of light crawls along the rock wall. Several more surround it, undulating like waves, making the dome of the cavern feel like a disco.

Then it hits me. I can *see*.

The darkness is gone, replaced by a warm light radiating through the entire cave. It comes, quite improbably, from the pool in the middle of the cavern. The light is a rich gold tinged with pink that makes the water glow like a hotel swimming pool. I check my phone, seeing that it's now six. Sunrise.

The presence of light means one thing—there's another way out of the cave.

"Vivian, I think I can get out!"

She's no longer there. Not that she ever truly was. But this time there's no lingering presence, no sense she could return at any moment.

Vivian might be gone for good.

I stand and limp to the water's edge. The light seems brightest to my right. Its undiluted glow suggests a straight path from the cave to the outside world. Most likely an underwater tunnel connecting cave to lake.

I slide back into the pool and face the light. Through the water, I see a glowing circle roughly the same size as the tunnel I entered through. If it stays that same width across its entire length, I might be able to swim my way out the cavern.

I do a few laps around the pool, loosening up while testing out my injured ankle. It hurts, of course. It's also swollen, which limits movement. I need to fight through both. I have no choice.

Properly warmed up, I line my body up with the tunnel entrance. I start shivering again, this time more from nerves than the chill of the water. I'm scared as hell and long for another way out of here. There isn't one. The only way out is through.

I take a deep breath. I slip under the water. I stare at that gold-and-pink light and start to swim toward it.

Forty-One

Swim.

That's all I need to do.

Swim and try not to think about how much my ankle hurts.

Or that the tunnel may slowly be closing in on me.

Or that I'm not even a quarter of the way through it yet.

I need to do nothing else but swim. As hard and as fast as I can. Straight toward the light like the little girl in that movie that gave me nightmares when I was nine.

Swim.

Don't think about that movie and its creepy clown and fizzing TV or how the silt from the lake water clouds my vision and stings my eyes.

Just swim.

Don't think about how the tunnel really is getting smaller or how my shoulders skim the walls, scraping away mossy blooms of algae that make it even harder to see.

Just fucking swim.

Don't think about the algae or the shrinking tunnel or how each flick of my right foot sends pain screaming through my ankle or how the pressure is building in my chest like a balloon that's about to pop.

I swim straight into the light, blinded by it, the glare forcing my eyes shut. My lungs scream. My ankle screams. I'm on the verge of screaming myself. But then the tunnel falls away, slipping from my shoulders like an unzipped dress. My eyes open to the sight of water everywhere. No cave. No walls. Just blessed open lake glowing yellow in the ever-brightening dawn.

I shoot to the surface and gasp, gulping down precious air until the ache in my lungs subsides. My ankle still hurts. As do my exhausted, limp-rag arms. Yet I have enough strength to stay afloat and keep my head above water. I might even be able to swim back to camp after some rest.

Hopefully it won't come to that. Hopefully people are looking for me.

Sure enough, I hear the hum of a motorboat in the distance. I rotate in the water until I can see it—a white skiff, one of two normally moored to Camp Nightingale's dock. Chet sits by the outboard motor, steering the boat across the lake.

I swing an arm out of the water, waving to him. With what little air I have in my lungs, I scream his name.

"Chet!"

He spots me, his face bright with surprise to see me floundering in the lake. He cuts the motor, grabs a wooden oar, and paddles my way.

"Emma? My God, we've been looking everywhere for you."

I resume swimming. He keeps paddling. Together we finally meet, and I latch on to the side of the boat. With Chet's help, I climb aboard and collapse inside, panting, too tired to move.

"Did you find the girls?" I ask, panting out the words, still catching my breath.

"Early this morning. They're dehydrated, hungry, and in shock, but they'll be fine. Last I heard, Theo was going to take them to the hospital."

I sit up, buzzing with alarm.

"Theo's back at camp?"

"Yes," Chet says. "He said he found you with the girls and that you attacked him before vanishing in the woods."

"He's lying."

"That's crazy, Emma. You know that, right?"

I keep talking. Setting the crazy free. "He hurt those girls, Chet. He can't be near them. We have to call the police."

I reach for my phone, amazingly still in my pocket and in working order. There's even a sliver of battery left. I start to dial 911 but am halted by a shadow crossing the screen.

Chet's reflection, as warped as a funhouse mirror.

Gripped in his hand is the oar. I see that reflection, too. A faint glimpse of wood swiping across my screen right before Chet swings it into the back of my head.

For a slice of a second, everything stops. My heart. My brain. My lungs and ears and eyes. As if my body needs a moment to figure out how to react.

In that thin sliver of time, I assume that this is what death must feel like. Not a drift into deep slumber or a slow edge toward a warm light. Just a sudden halt.

But then the pain arrives. A screaming, nerve-jolting pain that floods every part of me, telling me I'm still alive.

The dead don't feel this kind of pain.

It hurts so much I envy them.

Anguish takes over, rendering me helpless. My vision blurs. My head rings. I belch out a grunt of surprise as the phone springs from my hands, and I collapse to the bottom of the boat.

Forty-Two

I come to on the floor of the boat. I feel the scruff of fiberglass against my cheek, smell the fish stench, hear the echo of the water below.

The boat is moving now. The outboard motor hums like white noise. Occasional sprays of lake water mist my face.

I've landed on my side, my left arm pinned beneath me, my right one twitching slightly. My left eye is closed, smushed as it is against the floor. The lid of my right eye keeps blinking, the sky and clouds above flickering like an old movie. Rather than breath, I hyperventilate—short, gasping breaths that huff out air as quickly as I take it in.

I'm still in pain, but it's no longer all-consuming. A steady drumbeat instead of a clash of cymbals. I'm surprised to learn that I can move, if I really put my mind to it. That twitching right arms bends. Both legs stretch. I wiggle my fingers, marveling at the accomplishment.

The clarity of my thoughts is another surprise. I know what's going on. I'm not struck dumb or deaf or blind. I assume Chet pulled back on the swing of that oar right before striking me. Or else I'm just very lucky. Either way, I'll take it.

When the sound of the motor ceases and the boat slows, I'm able to flip onto my back, pleased to learn that my left eye also works. I see Chet standing over me. The oar is back in his hands, although he switches between holding it too tightly and almost letting it fall from his grip.

"I can't believe you had the nerve to come back here, Emma," he says. "Even though it was my idea, it still surprised me. Don't get me wrong. I'm glad you came back. I just didn't think you'd be that stupid."

"Why…" I pause to take a dry-mouthed swallow, hoping it will help get the words out. Each syllable is a struggle. "Why ask me back?"

"Because I thought it would be fun," Chet says. "I knew you were crazy. Theo told me all about that. And I wanted to see just how crazy you'd get. You know, trap a few birds and put them in the cabin. A little paint on the door and an appearance at the window. A little peek in the shower."

Chet pauses to give me a wink that makes my stomach roil.

"I totally didn't expect you to run with it, though. I thought it would take a lot more work to make you look guilty. But all that talk about seeing Vivian? That alone made everyone think you'd snapped."

"But *why*?"

"Because of the real reason I wanted you back here. Girls from your cabin go missing, and to put you at the scene of the crime, I drop something of yours into an empty canoe with a broken pair of glasses and set it adrift. That bracelet of yours worked wonders, by the way. When I snapped it off your wrist outside the Lodge, I knew it would be perfect."

He flashes me a twisted smile. It's the grin of a madman. Someone far more insane than I ever was.

"After that, all I needed to do was delete any surveillance video of me near your cabin and change the file name of the one showing you leaving Dogwood yesterday morning. I'll let you in on a little secret, Em. The girls didn't sneak out five minutes before you woke up. They'd been gone at least an hour."

I sit up, using my elbows for support. I tremble a moment before locking my arms and steadying myself. That small movement wakes me up a bit, gives me some lift. I hear the newfound strength in my voice as I say, "All that effort. I don't understand."

"Because you almost ruined our lives," Chet says with a snarl. "Especially Theo's. So much that he tried to kill himself. That's how

much you fucked him up, Emma. When you destroyed his reputation, you destroyed ours as well. When I got to Yale, half the school
wouldn't even talk to me. They saw me as the kid whose brother got
away with murder because we're filthy rich. And we're not. Not anymore. All we have left is my mother's apartment and this godfor-
saken lake."

Even though my skull is stormy with pain, I finally understand.
This is his revenge.

An attempt to make me look as guilty as I had made Theo look. He
wants me to live under the same cloud of suspicion. To lose everything.

"I didn't want to kill you, Emma," he says. "I would have much
rather watched you suffer for the next fifteen years. But the plan has
changed. You made sure of that when you freed those girls. Now I have
no choice but to make you disappear."

Chet grabs me by the shirt collar and hoists me off the floor. I
don't struggle. I can't. All I can do is wobble precariously as he
plops me onto the edge of the boat. The motion jars still more energy into me.

Now that I'm off the floor, I can see we're in a part of the lake I
don't recognize. A cove of sorts. Trees crowd the shore, ringing the
water like walls of a fortress. Muted light seeps through them, doing
little to burn away the fog that rolls across the water.

Something sits in the mist, jutting out of the water a few feet from
the boat.

A rooster weathervane.

It's the same weathervane I've seen in pictures, perched atop
Peaceful Valley Asylum. Only now it's edged with rust and crusted
with barnacles. And the asylum it sits upon rests deep beneath Lake
Midnight. I peer into the water, getting shimmery glimpses of its
mud-caked roof.

It's still here. Right where it's always been. Only now covered by
the lake. That part of Casey's story is true.

"I had a feeling you'd recognize it," Chet says. "You knowing about
this place was another surprise. Little nosy Emma has really been
doing her homework."

Judging from the ring of dried mud along the shore, I suspect the lake is usually high enough to completely cover the weathervane. It can be seen now only because of the current drought.

"I found it when I was a teenager," Chet says. "No one else knows it's still here. Not my mom. Not Lottie. I guess they think old Buchanan Harris razed it when he bought the land. Instead, he just left it here and flooded the place. And now no one will know to look for you here."

My heart gallops. Blood pumps to my brain, making me more alert as well as more afraid. Rather than silence me, the fear sparks my voice. "Don't do this, Chet. It's not too late."

"I think it is, Em."

"The girls didn't see you. They told me so. If you want me to tell the cops I did it, I will."

Words are my only defense. I have no strength to fight him off. Even if I did, I'd be no match against another swing of the oar.

"No one will know you did it," I say. "Just you and me. And I'm not going to tell anyone. I'll take the blame. I'll plead guilty."

Chet transfers the oar from one hand to the other. I think I'm getting through to him.

"You want to see me suffer, right? Then imagine me in prison. Think how much I'll suffer then."

I'm hit by a flash of memory. Me leaving Camp Nightingale fifteen years ago. Chet was there, calling after his brother, his face tear-streaked. Maybe that was the moment he decided he needed to get revenge. If so, I need to remind him of the boy he was before that.

"You're not a killer," I tell him. "You're too good of a person for that. I'm the one who did something bad. Don't be like me. Don't become someone you're not."

Chet raises the oar, ready to bring it down once more. I lurch forward before he can do it, slamming myself into him. The strength comes out of nowhere. A coiled energy ignited by terror and desperation. It sends Chet stumbling against one of the boat's seats. His legs catch on it, and he tumbles backward. The oar leaves his hands, clatters to the floor. I reach for it, but Chet's faster. He grabs the oar with one hand and slaps me with the back of the other.

Spikes of pain sting my cheek. But the blow also zaps one last bit of adrenaline into me. Enough to let me scramble to the front of the boat and crawl onto the bow.

Behind me, Chet's on his feet, oar in hand.

He lifts it.

He swings.

I close my eyes, screaming, waiting for the blow to connect with my skull.

Instead, a shot rings out, the sound careening across the cove. My eyes fly open in time to see the oar explode into a thousand splinters. I shut them again as wood sprays my face. I duck, trying to avoid it.

The boat tips.

I tip with it, tumbling backward, over the side of the boat and into Lake Midnight.

Forty-Three

My fall through the water is brief. Just a quick, disorienting drop before I slam into something a few feet from the surface. Wood, I think. Slick with moss and algae and a hundred years of lake water rising and falling.

A roof.

As I'm realizing this, the wood beneath me buckles, giving way. Soon I'm falling again. Still underwater but now also surrounded by walls, encased within them.

Peaceful Valley Asylum.

I'm inside it, dropping from the ceiling to the floor below. I brace myself for another smash through it. It never comes. Instead, I bounce off the floor and drift upward.

Faint light trickles through an algae-streaked windows. It's enough brightness for me to see an empty room taken over by mud. Everything is tilted—walls, ceiling, doorframe. The door itself has come off its hinges and now sits askew, revealing a short hall, stairs, more light. I swim toward them, struggling to make it through the doorway, across the hall, down the steps.

At the bottom, the front door gapes open. The door itself sits on the floor, all but blending in with the lake bottom. To my left is a sitting room. There's a hole in the wall where bricks and floorboards and scraps of wallpaper have tumbled out. A striped bass circles the room. I swim out the open door, passing from inside to outside, even though it's all part of the same watery landscape.

Pain pulses through my body. My lungs burn. I need air. I need sleep. I start to swim upward, heading to the surface, when something catches my eye.

A skull.

Bleached white.

Jaw missing.

Eye sockets aimed at the sky.

Scattered around it are more bones. A dozen, at least. I glimpse the arch of ribs, the curl of fingers, a second skull a few yards from the first.

The girls.

I know because nestled among the bones, shining faintly in the muck, is a length of gold chain and a locket in the shape of a heart. A tiny emerald sits in its center.

Something enters the water behind me. I feel it more than see it—a shuddering of the lake. An arm reaches out and wraps around my waist. Then I'm tugged upward, away from the girls, toward the water's surface.

Soon we're breaking through Lake Midnight. I see sky, trees, the camp's other motorboat bobbing on the water a few yards away. Within it stands Detective Flynn, his gun trained on Chet, who drops the decimated oar.

And I see Theo. Swimming next to me. Arm still around my waist. Lake water sloshing against his chin.

"Are you okay?" he says.

I think of Vivian, Natalie, and Allison lying directly below us.

I think of all the years they spent down there, waiting for me to find them.

So when Theo asks again if I'm okay, I can only nod, choke back a sob, and let the tears flow.

Forty-Four

I sit in the front seat of Detective Flynn's police-issued sedan, the hospital a distant memory in the rearview mirror. I ended up being more bruised and battered than I initially thought. The doctor's diagnosis was startling. A concussion from the oar. A sprained ankle from the fall. Lacerations, dehydration, a persistent headache.

I ended up spending two days in the hospital. The girls were there for one of them. I shared a room with Miranda, and we spent that time complaining about our sorry states, giggling over the ridiculousness of it all and gossiping about the handsome male nurse who worked the morning shift.

Visitors streamed in and out. Sasha and Krystal from the room next door. Miranda's grandmother—a whirling dervish of Catholic guilt and smothering hugs. Becca dropped by with a book of Ansel Adams photographs, and Casey brought apologies for ever thinking I had tried to hurt the girls of Dogwood. Marc arrived with a stack of gossip mags and the news that he's back together with Billy the librarian. Even my parents flew in from Florida, a gesture that touched me more than I expected.

We plan to head back to Manhattan later this afternoon. Marc is going to tag along. It'll be an interesting drive for all parties involved.

For now, though, I have unfinished business to attend to, as Detective Flynn reminds me.

"Here's what probably happened," he says. "Based on what she wrote in her diary, Vivian, like you, assumed the worst about Peaceful

Valley, Charles Cutler, and Buchanan Harris. She found the location of
the asylum and took Allison and Natalie with her to get proof of its
existence. From the way you described it, it's probably very easy to get
disoriented down there. They went into the water, swam around the
wreckage, never came back up. Accidental drowning."

Just because I had assumed exactly that doesn't make dealing with
it any easier. Not when I now know that Vivian died the same way her
sister did. It's too tragic to comprehend.

"So there's nothing to suggest Chet killed them?" I say, knowing
it's impossible.

Flynn shakes his head. "He swears he didn't do it. I have no reason
to doubt him. He was only ten at the time. Besides, there's still quite a
few bones at the bottom of that lake. It'll take a while to find them all.
Until then, we won't know for certain it's your friends down there."

But I already know. It was Vivian, Natalie, and Allison I saw in the
depths of the lake. The locket was all the proof I need. Now just thinking about it causes grief to balloon in my chest. A common occurrence
over the past two days.

"As for the second group of girls from Dogwood, Chet said he had
no plans to hurt them," Flynn says. "Seems to me like he didn't know
what he was going to do. He was just running on anger, not thinking
about the consequences."

"Where is he now?"

"County jail for the time being. He plans to plead guilty to all
charges tomorrow. From there, he'll probably be transferred to a mental-health facility for an unknown amount of time."

I'm relieved to hear it. I want Chet to get the help he needs. Because I know a thing or two about seeking vengeance. Like Chet, I've
felt the desire for revenge burn inside me. It's singed both of us.

But I've healed. Not completely, but definitely getting there.

"And I guess I owe you an apology," Flynn says. "For not believing
you."

"You were only doing your job."

"But I should have listened to you more. I was so quick to think
you did it because it was the easiest explanation. For that, I'm sorry."

"Apology accepted."

We ride in silence until we reach the wrought-iron gate of Camp Nightingale. When I straighten in my seat, Flynn looks my way and says, "Nervous to be back?"

"Not as much as I thought I'd be," I tell him.

Seeing the outskirts of camp brings a tumble of emotions. Sadness and regret, love and disgust. And brutal relief. The kind you feel when you learn the whole truth about something. The cheating spouse exposed. An official diagnosis. Having the truth revealed means you can finally start to unburden yourself of it.

Flynn steers the car into the heart of camp. It feels as empty and silent as the morning I woke to find the girls missing from Dogwood. This time, with good reason. All the campers, counselors, and instructors have been sent home. Camp Nightingale has closed early. This time for good.

As sad as it is, I know it's for the best. There's too much tragedy associated with the place. Besides, Franny has enough to deal with.

Lottie is outside waiting for me when the sedan pulls up to the Lodge. Because I'm loopy from painkillers and my ankle is wrapped with a mile of ACE bandage, she needs to help me from the car. Before letting go of my hand, she gives it an extra squeeze. A signal that she has no hard feelings about what I've said. I'm grateful for her forgiveness.

Flynn honks the horn and gives me a wave. Then he's off, steering the sedan out of camp as Lottie guides me to the Lodge. Inside, there's no sign of Mindy. I'm not surprised. When visiting me in the hospital, Casey mentioned that she was returning to the family farm. She said it with relish, as if Mindy got exactly what she deserved. If that means something better than being with Chet, then I'm inclined to agree.

"I'm afraid there's not much time," Lottie says. "Franny only has a few minutes before we need to go. The people at the jail are sticklers about visiting hours."

"I understand."

I'm led to the back deck, where Franny rests in an Adirondack chair tilted to face the sun. She greets me warmly, clasping my hand

and smiling as if the years of accusations and misdeeds between us mean nothing. Maybe now they don't. Maybe now we're even.

"Dear Emma. How nice to see you up and about again." She gestures to the floor next to her chair, where my suitcase and box of painting supplies have been placed. "It's all there. I made sure Lottie packed everything. The only things missing are Vivian's diary, which the police took, and the photograph she removed from the Lodge. That deserves to stay with Lottie, don't you think?"

"I couldn't agree more."

"Are you sure you don't want to have one last look around Dogwood?" Franny asks. "In case we missed something?"

"No," I say. "I'm fine."

Dogwood is the last place I want to be. It's too full of memories, both good and bad. With all that's happened—and all I now know—I'm not ready to face them. The sight of those names carved into hickory and the sound of that creaking third floorboard would probably break me.

Franny gives me a knowing look, like she understands completely. "I'm sorry I didn't visit you in the hospital. Under the circumstances, I thought it best to stay away."

"You have nothing to feel sorry about," I tell her, meaning every word.

"But I do. What Chet did is inexcusable. I'm truly, deeply sorry for whatever pain he caused. To you and the other girls in Dogwood. And please believe me when I say that I didn't know what he had planned. If I had, I never would have asked you back."

"I believe you," I say. "And I forgive you. Not that you did anything wrong. You've been nothing but kind to me, Franny. It's me who should be begging for your forgiveness."

"I already gave it. Long, long ago."

"But I didn't deserve it."

"You did," Franny says. "Because I saw goodness in you, even if you never knew it was there yourself. And speaking of forgiveness, I think there's someone else who has a thing or two to say about that."

She stretches out her hand, seeking help in getting out of her chair. I oblige and gently lift her to her feet. We lean against each other, wobbling in tandem to the deck's railing. Below is Lake Midnight, as beautiful as always. And sitting on the lawn, staring out at the water, is Theo.

"Go on," Franny urges. "You two have a lot to talk about."

At first, I say nothing to Theo. I simply join him on the lawn, my eyes on the lake. Theo is silent in return, for obvious reasons. I've now accused him twice. If anyone deserves the silent treatment, it's me.

I glance at his profile, studying the scar on his cheek and a new mark on his forehead—a deep-purple bruise where I had struck him with the flashlight. I've caused him so much pain. Chet's actions aside, he has every right to hate me.

Yet Theo still made sure I made it out of the lake alive. Detective Flynn talked at length about how quick Theo was to dive into the water after me. Zero hesitation. That's how he described it. It's a debt I'll never be able to properly repay. I could sit here and thank Theo for hours, beg for his forgiveness, or apologize so many times I lose count. But I don't. Instead, I hold out my hand and say, "Hi, I'm Emma."

Theo at last acknowledges my presence with a turn of his head. Shaking my hand, he replies, "I'm Theo. Nice to meet you."

It's all he needs to say.

Theo shifts beside me and pulls something out of his pocket, which he drops into my hand. I don't need to look to know it's my charm bracelet. I can feel the chain curled against my palm, the weight of the three pewter birds.

"I thought you'd like it back," Theo says, adding with a grin, "even though we've only just met."

I cup the bracelet in my hand. I've had it for such a long time. It's been my devoted companion for more than half my life. But it's time to say good-bye. Now that I know the truth, I won't be needing it anymore.

"Thank you," I say. "But..."

"But what?"

"I think I've outgrown it. Besides, I know a better place for it."

Without a second thought, I toss the bracelet into the air, the three birds taking flight at last. I close my eyes before it lands. I don't want the memory of seeing it vanish from view. But I hear it, reaching for Theo's hand as the bracelet drops with a light splash into the depths of Lake Midnight.

This is how it ends.

Franny passes away on a muggy evening in late September. She dies not at the lake but in the bedroom of her penthouse at the Harris. Theo and Lottie are with her. According to Theo, her last words are, "I'm ready."

A week later, you attend her funeral on a Monday that's been kissed by Indian summer. You think Franny would have appreciated that. After the service, you and Theo go for a walk in Central Park. You haven't seen him since leaving Camp Nightingale. With everything that was going, both of you agreed that space and time were necessary.

Now a host of unspoken emotions hang over the reunion. There's grief, of course. And happiness at seeing each other. And another, stranger feeling—trepidation. You don't know what kind of relationship the two of you will have going forward. Especially when halfway into your walk, Theo says, "I'm going away next week."

You come to a sudden stop. "Where?"

"Africa," Theo says. "I signed on for another tour with Doctors Without Borders. One year. I think it'll be good for me to get away. I need time to sort things out."

You understand. You think it sounds like a fine idea. You wish him well.

"When I get back, I'd love to have dinner," Theo says.

"You mean like a date?"

"It could just be a casual meal between two friends who have a habit of accusing each other of doing terrible things," Theo replies. "But I kind of like the date idea better."

"I do, too," you say.

That night, you begin to paint again. It strikes you after hours spent lying awake thinking about changing seasons and the passing of time. You get out of bed, stand before a blank canvas, and realize what you need to do—paint not what you see but what you saw.

You paint the girls in the same order. Always.

Vivian first.

Then Natalie.

Then Allison.

You cover them with sinuous shapes in various shades of blue and green and brown. Moss and cobalt, pewter and pine. You fill the canvas with algae, pondweed, underwater trees with branches twisting toward the surface. You paint a weathervane-topped building submerged in the chilly depths, dark and empty, waiting for someone to find it.

When that canvas is complete, you paint another. Then another. And another. Bold paintings of walls and foundations hidden underwater, engulfed by plant life, lost to time. Each time you paint over the girls feels like a burial, a funeral. You paint nonstop for weeks. Your wrist aches. Your fingers don't uncurl even when there's not a brush in them. When you sleep, you dream of colors.

Your therapist tells you that what you're doing is healthy. You're sorting through your feelings, dealing with your grief.

By January, you have completed twenty-one paintings. Your underwater series.

You show them to Randall, who's ecstatic. He gasps at each canvas. Marvels at how you've outdone yourself.

A new gallery show is planned, hastily put together by Randall to capitalize on all the publicity surrounding Lake Midnight. It's set for March. Buzz steadily builds. You're profiled in The New Yorker. Your parents plan to attend.

The morning of the opening, you get a phone call from Detective Nathan Flynn. He tells you what you've known all along—the bones discovered in the water belong to Natalie and Allison.

"What about Vivian?" you ask.

"That's a very good question," Flynn says.

He tells you that none of the bones are a match.

He tells you that both Natalie's and Allison's skulls were fractured in a way that suggests they were struck in the head, possibly with a shovel found near the bones.

He tells you that chains and bricks had also been discovered, indicating both bodies might have been weighed down.

He tells you the strand of hair in the plastic baggie you found buried with Vivian's diary is actually processed polyester used mostly in the making of wigs.

He tells you that same baggie also contained traces of a laminate and adhesive that were once common in the production of fake IDs.

"What are you suggesting?" you ask.

"Exactly what you're thinking," he says.

What you're thinking about are Vivian's last words to you, when she knocked on Dogwood's locked door.

Come on, Em. Let me in.

Me.

That's what she had said.

Not us.

Meaning that she was alone.

You hang up the phone with a queasy feeling in your gut. The conversation leaves you so stunned that you almost opt out of attending that night's opening. Only Marc keeps you from backing out. He nudges you through the motions of getting ready. Shower. Slinky blue dress. Black heels with red soles.

At the gallery, you see that Randall has once again pulled out all the stops. You sip wine and watch shrimp canapés float by on silver trays as you talk to the guy from Christie's, the lady from the Times, *the television actress who helped set your career in motion. Sasha, Krystal and Miranda attend. Marc takes a picture of the four of you standing in front of your largest painting, No. 6, which seems as massive as Lake Midnight itself.*

Later that night, you're at that very same work when a woman comes up beside you.

"This is lovely," she says, her eyes on the painting. "So beautifully strange. Are you the artist?"

"I am."

You glance her way, getting a glimpse of red hair, a striking frame, regal bearing. Her clothes are effortlessly cool. Black dress. Black gloves. Floppy black hat and a Burberry trench. You think she might be a model.

Then you recognize her pert nose and cruel smile, and your legs buckle.

"Vivian?"

She continues to stare at the painting, speaking in a calm whisper only the two of you can hear.

"Two Truths and a Lie, Emma," she says. "You ready to play?"

You want to say no. You have to say yes.

"One: Allison and Natalie were with my sister the night she died," she says. "They dared her to go out on that ice. They saw her fall in and drown.

Yet they told no one. But I had my suspicions. I knew Katherine wouldn't do something so dangerous unless she'd been coerced. So I befriended them, earned their trust, pretended to trust them in return. It's how I learned the truth, teasing it out of them on the Fourth of July. They swore they tried to help Katherine. I knew they were lying. After all, I pretended to drown in front of everyone. As I flailed in that water, only Theo made a move to help me. Natalie and Allison did nothing. They simply watched, just as they had watched Katherine drown."

You think about the day you came back to the cabin and found the girls fighting. You realize now that you had walked into their confession. And contrary to how friendly they had seemed afterward, nothing between them was fine.

"Two: Since I already suspected what Natalie and Allison had done, I spent a year researching and planning. I learned about the history of Lake Midnight. I found a place no one knew about—a flooded insane asylum. I placed a sweatshirt in the woods to confuse searchers. I fucked the grounds keeper and stole the key to his toolshed. Then I led Allison and Natalie to that secret spot on the lake where no one would ever look. I did to them what they had done to my sister."

Now you understand that you misinterpreted her diary. She didn't look for Peaceful Valley to expose its existence. She sought it out because it was the best place to hide her crime.

You think about the shovel stolen from the toolshed. You think about fractured skulls resting on the lake bed. You think about the locket, which you now know Vivian dropped into the water because just like you and your bracelet, she no longer needed it.

"Three: Vivian is dead."

Your mouth is so dry with shock you're not sure you can speak. But you do, managing to croak out, "The third one."

"Wrong," she says. *"Vivian died fifteen years ago. Let her rest in peace, Em."*

She leaves the gallery quickly, her boots clicking against the floor. You follow her, much slower, your legs wobbly from shock. Out on the street, you see a town car streak away from the curb. Tinted windows deny you a good look. No one else is on the block. It's just you and your palpitating heart.

Back in the gallery, you murmur your good-byes to Marc, Randall, all the others. You say you're not feeling well. You blame it on the shrimp you haven't even touched.

At home in your studio, you paint all night and into the dawn. You paint until garbage trucks rumble by and the sun peeks over the buildings on the other side of the street. When you stop, you stand before the finished canvas.

It's a portrait of Vivian.

Not how she looked back then but how she looks now. Her nose. Her chin. Her eyes, which you've painted midnight blue. She stares back at you with a coy smile playing across her lips.

It's the last time you'll ever paint her. You know that with bone-deep certainty.

In a few hours, when the post office opens, you'll ship the painting to Detective Flynn. You'll include a note telling him that Vivian is alive and was last seen in Manhattan. You'll ask that the painting be released to the media, who can use it any way they want.

You will expose who she is, how she looks, what she's done.

You won't hide her beneath layers of paint.

You will refuse to cover her up.

The time for lies is over.

ACKNOWLEDGMENTS

I need to thank the many people who helped with the writing and publication of this book, starting with my fabulous U.S. editor, Maya Ziv, whose gentle encouragement helped me transform it from an ungainly caterpillar into something that resembles a butterfly. Thanks are also due to Madeline Newquist, for keeping things on track; Andrea Monagle, for her eagle eye; and the publicity and marketing dream team of Emily Canders, Abigail Endler and Elina Vaysbeyn.

In the U.K., I must thank my dream team across the pond: Gillian Green, Stephenie Naulls and Joanna Bennett. (With special well wishes to Emily Yau.)

Additional thanks go to everyone at Aevitas Creative Management, especially my agent, Michelle Brower, who has stuck with me all these years, and Chelsey Heller, who continues to do stellar work on the international front.

Other necessary thanks go to Stephen King, for his generosity; Taylor Swift, whose lyrics from *Sad Beautiful Tragic* I shamelessly cribbed; Joan Lindsay and Peter Weir, whose *Picnic at Hanging Rock* initially inspired this book; Sarah Dutton, for being a great reader and an even better friend; and the Ritter and Livio families, for being so proud of me.

Finally, I could thank Mike Livio until the end of time and it still wouldn't be enough. I truly couldn't do this without his patience, calmness and steady hand.

ABOUT THE AUTHOR

Riley Sager is the pseudonym of a former journalist, editor and graphic designer who previously published mysteries under his real name.

Now a full-time author, Riley's first thriller, *Final Girls*, was a national and international bestseller that has been sold in 25 languages. A film version is being developed by Universal Pictures and Anonymous Content.

A native of Pennsylvania, he now lives in Princeton, New Jersey.

Make sure you've read

FINAL GIRLS

Also by Riley Sager

Turn over for an exclusive preview

PINE COTTAGE
1 A.M.

The forest had claws and teeth.

All those rocks and thorns and branches bit at Quincy as she ran screaming through the woods. But she didn't stop. Not when rocks dug into the soles of her bare feet. Not when a whip-thin branch lashed her face and a line of blood streaked down her cheek.

Stopping wasn't an option. To stop was to die. So she kept running, even as a bramble wrapped around her ankle and gnawed at her flesh. The bramble stretched, quivering, before Quincy's momentum yanked her free. If it hurt, she couldn't tell. Her body already held more pain than it could handle.

It was instinct that made her run. An unconscious knowledge that she needed to keep going, no matter what. Already she had forgotten why. Memories of five, ten, fifteen minutes ago were gone. If her life depended on remembering what prompted her flight through the woods, she was certain she'd die right there on the forest floor.

So she ran. She screamed. She tried not to think about dying.

A white glow appeared in the distance, faint along the tree-choked horizon.

Headlights.

Was she near a road? Quincy hoped she was. Like her memories, all sense of direction was lost.

She ran faster, increased her screams, raced toward the light.

Another branch whacked her face. It was thicker than the first, like a rolling pin, and the impact both stunned and blinded her. Pain pulsed through her head as blue sparks throbbed across her blurred vision. When they cleared, she saw a silhouette standing out in the head-lights' glow.

A man.

Him.

No. Not Him.

Someone else.

Safety.

Quincy quickened her pace. Her blood-drenched arms reached out, as if that could somehow pull the stranger closer. The movement caused the pain in her shoulder to flare. And with the pain came not a memory but an understanding. One so brutally awful that it had to be real.

Only Quincy remained.

All the others were dead.

She was the last one left alive.

*To survive a killer, you need
a killer's instinct*

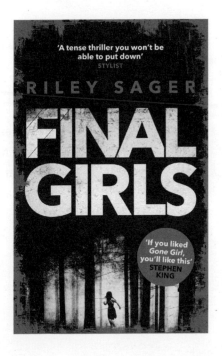

Three girls. Three tragedies. One unthinkable secret.

The media calls them the Final Girls – Quincy, Sam, Lisa – the infamous group that no one wants to be part of. The sole survivors of three separate killing sprees, they are linked by their shared trauma.

But when Lisa dies in mysterious circumstances and Sam shows up unannounced on her doorstep, Quincy must admit that she doesn't really know anything about the other Final Girls. *Can she trust them? Or can there only ever be one?*

All Quincy knows is one thing: she is next.

Available Now